ALASTOh

Tor books by Jack Vance

Araminta Station
Big Planet
Ecce and Old Earth
The Dragon Masters
The Gray Prince
Green Magic
The Languages of Pao
The Last Castle
Planet of Adventure
Showboat World
To Live Forever
Throy

JACK VANCE

ALASTOR

TRULLION: ALASTOR 2262

MARUNE: ALASTOR 933

WYST: ALASTOR 1716

ORB

A TOM DOHERTY ASSOCIATES BOOK / NEW YORK

ALASTOR

This book is an omnibus edition, consisting of the novels: *Trullion: Alastor 2262*, copyright © 1973 by Jack Vance, copyright renewed © 2001 by Jack Vance; *Marune: Alastor 933*, copyright © 1975 by Jack Vance; *Wyst: Alastor 1716*, copyright © 1978 by Jack Vance.

Book design by Lynn Newmark

An Orb Edition
Published by Tom Doherty Associates, LLC
175 Fifth Avenue
New York, NY 10010

www.tor.com

Library of Congress Cataloging-in-Publication Data

Vance, Jack.
    Alastor / Jack Vance.
        p. cm.
    "A Tom Doherty Associates book."
    Contents: Trullion: Alastor 2262—Marune: Alastor 933—
Wyst: Alastor 1716.
    ISBN 0-312-85966-X (hc)
    ISBN 0-312-86952-5 (pbk)
    1. Science fiction, American. I. Title.

PS3572.A424 A72 1995
813'.54—dc20   95-22691
                                                                   CIP

First Tor Hardcover Edition: October 1995
First Orb Trade Paperback Edition: July 2002

Printed in the United States of America

D 0 9 8 7 6 5

CONTENTS

TRULLION

ALASTOR 2262

Out toward the rim of the galaxy hangs Alastor Cluster, a whorl of thirty thousand live stars in an irregular volume twenty to thirty light-years in diameter. The surrounding region is dark and, except for a few hermit stars, unoccupied. To the exterior view, Alastor presents a flamboyant display of star-streams, luminous webs, sparkling nodes. Dust clouds hang across the brightness; the engulfed stars glow russet, rose, or smoky amber. Dark stars wander unseen among a million subplanetary oddments of iron, slag, and ice: the so-called "starments."

Scattered about the Cluster are three thousand inhabited planets with a human population of approximately five trillion persons. The worlds are diverse, the populations equally so; nevertheless they share a common language and all submit to the authority of the Connatic at Lusz, on the world Numenes.

The current Connatic is Oman Ursht, sixteenth in the Idite succession, a man of ordinary and undistinguished appearance. In portraits and on public occasions he wears a severe black uniform with a black casque, in order to project an image of inflexible authority, and this is how he is known to the folk of Alastor Cluster. In private Oman Ursht is a calm and reasonable man, who tends to under- rather than over-administrate. He ponders all aspects of his conduct, knowing well that his slightest act—a gesture, a word, a symbolic nuance—might start off an avalanche of unpredictable consequences. Hence his effort to create the image of a man rigid, terse, and unemotional.

To the casual observer, Alastor Cluster is a system placid and peaceful. The Connatic knows differently. He recognizes that wherever human beings strive for advantage, disequilibrium exists; lacking easement, the social fabric becomes taut and sometimes rips asunder. The Connatic conceives his function to be the identification and relief of social stresses.

Sometimes he ameliorates, sometimes he employs techniques of distraction. When harshness becomes unavoidable he deploys his military agency, the Whelm. Oman Ursht winces to see an insect injured; the Connatic without compunction orders a million persons to their doom. In many cases, believing that each condition generates its own counter-condition, he stands aloof, fearing to introduce a confusing third factor. *When in doubt, do nothing*: this is one of the Connatic's favorite credos.

After an ancient tradition he roams anonymously about the Cluster. Occasionally, in order to remedy an injustice, he represents himself as an important official; often he rewards kindness and self-sacrifice. He is fascinated by the ordinary life of his subjects and listens attentively to such dialogues as:

OLD MAN (*to a lazy youth*): If everybody had what they wanted, who would work? Nobody.

YOUTH: Not I, depend on it.

OLD MAN: And you'd be the first to cry out in anguish, for it's work what keeps the lights on. Get on with it now; put your shoulder into it. I can't bear sloth.

YOUTH (*grumbling*): If I were Connatic I'd arrange that everyone had their wishes. No toil! Free seats at the hussade game! A fine space-yacht! New clothes every day! Servants to lay forth delectable foods!

OLD MAN: The Connatic would have to be a genius to satisfy both you and the servants. They'd live only to box your ears. Now get on with your work.

Or again:

YOUNG MAN: Never go near Lusz, I beseech you! The Connatic would take you for his own!

GIRL (*mischievously*): Then what would you do?

YOUNG MAN: I'd rebel! I'd be the most magnificent starmenter* ever to terrify the skies! At last I'd conquer the power of Alastor—Whelm, Connatic, and all—and win you back for my very own.

GIRL: You're gallant, but never never never would the Connatic choose ordinary little me; already the most beautiful women of Alastor attend him at Lusz.

YOUNG MAN: What a merry life he must lead! To be Connatic: this is my dream!

*starmenters: pirates and marauders, whose occasional places of refuge are the so-called "starments."

GIRL *makes fretful sound and becomes cool.*
YOUNG MAN *is puzzled. Oman Ursht moves away.*

Lusz, the Connatic's palace, is indeed a remarkable structure, rising ten thousand feet above the sea on five great pylons. Visitors roam the lower promenades; from every world of Alastor Cluster they come, and from places beyond—the Darkling Regions, the Primarchic, the Erdic Sector, the Rubrimar Cluster, and all the other parts of the galaxy which men have made their own.

Above the public promenades are governmental offices, ceremonial halls, a communications complex, and somewhat higher, the famous Ring of the Worlds, with an informational chamber for each inhabited planet of the cluster. The highest pinnacles contain the Connatic's personal quarters. They penetrate the clouds and sometimes pierce through to the upper sky. When sunlight glistens on its iridescent surfaces, Lusz, the palace of the Connatic, is a wonderful sight and is often reckoned the most inspiring artifact of the human race.

CHAPTER *I*

C hamber 2262 along the Ring of the Worlds pertains to Trullion, the lone planet of a small white star, one spark in a spray curling out toward the Cluster's edge. Trullion is a small world, for the most part water, with a single narrow continent, Merlank,* at the equator. Great banks of cumulus drift in from the sea and break against the central mountains; hundreds of rivers return down broad valleys where fruit and cereals grow so plentifully as to command no value.

The original settlers upon Trullion brought with them those habits of thrift and zeal which had promoted survival in a previously harsh environment; the first era of Trill history produced a dozen wars, a thousand fortunes, a caste of hereditary aristocrats, and a waning of the initial dynamism. The Trill commonalty asked itself: Why toil, why carry weapons when a life of feasts, singing, revelry and ease is an equal option? In the space of three generations old Trullion became a memory. The ordinary Trill now worked as circumstances directed: to prepare for a feast, to indulge his taste for hussade, to earn a pulsor for his boat or a pot for his kitchen or a length of cloth for his *paray,* that easy shirtlike garment worn by man and woman alike. Occasionally he tilled his lush acres, fished the ocean, netted

---

*Merlank: a variety of lizard. The continent clasps the equator like a lizard clinging to a blue glass orb.

the river, harvested wild fruit, and when the mood was on him, dug emeralds and opals from the mountain slopes, or gathered *cauch*.* He worked perhaps an hour each day, or occasionally as much as two or three; he spent considerably more time musing on the verandah of his ramshackle house. He distrusted most technical devices, finding them unsympathetic, confusing, and—more important—expensive, though he gingerly used a telephone the better to order his social activities, and took the pulsor of his boat for granted.

As in most bucolic societies, the Trill knew his precise place in the hierarchy of classes. At the summit, almost a race apart, was the aristocracy; at the bottom were the nomad Trevanyi, a group equally distinct. The Trill disdained unfamiliar or exotic ideas. Ordinarily calm and gentle, he nonetheless, under sufficient provocation, demonstrated ferocious rages, and certain of his customs—particularly the macabre ritual at the *prutanshyr*—were almost barbaric.

The government of Trullion was rudimentary and a matter in which the average Trill took little interest. Merlank was divided into twenty prefectures, each administered by a few bureaus and a small group of officials, who constituted a caste superior to the ordinary Trill but considerably inferior to the aristocrats. Trade with the rest of the Cluster was unimportant; on all Trill only four space-ports existed; Port Gaw in the west of Merlank, Port Kerubian on the north coast, Port Maheul on the south coast, and Vayamenda in the east.

A hundred miles east of Port Maheul was the market town Welgen, famous for its fine hussade stadium. Beyond Welgen lay the Fens, a district of remarkable beauty. Thousands of waterways divided this area into a myriad islands, some tracts of good dimension, some so small as to support only a fisherman's cabin and a tree for the mooring of his boat.

Everywhere entrancing vistas merged one into another. Gray-green menas, silver-russet pomanders, black jerdine stood in stately rows along the waterways, giving each island its distinctive silhouette. Out upon their dilapidated verandahs sat the country folk, with jugs of homemade wine at hand. Sometimes they played music, using concertinas, small round-bellied guitars, mouth-calliopes that produced cheerful warbles and glissandes. The light of the Fens was pale and delicate, and shimmered with colors too transient and subtle for the eye to detect. In the morning a mist obscured the distances; the sunsets were subdued pageants of lime green and lavender. Skiffs and runabouts slid along the water; occasionally an aristocrat's yacht glided past, or the ferry that connected Welgen with the Fen villages.

---

*cauch: an aphrodisiac drug derived from the spore of a mountain mold and used by Trills to a greater or lesser extent. Some retreated so far into erotic fantasy as to become irresponsible, and thus the subject of mild ridicule. Irresponsibility, in the context of the Trill environment, could hardly be accounted a critical social problem.

In the dead center of the Fens, a few miles from the village of Saurkash, was Rabendary Island, where lived Jut Hulden, his wife Marucha, and their three sons. Rabendary Island comprised about a hundred acres, including a thirty-acre forest of mena, blackwood, candlenut, semprissima. To the south spread the wide expanse of Ambal Broad. Farwan Water bounded Rabendary on the west, Gilweg Water on the east, and along the north shore flowed the placid Saur River. At the western tip of the island the ramshackle old home of the Huldens stood between a pair of huge mimosa trees. Rosalia vine grew up the posts of the verandah and overhung the edge of the roof, producing a fragrant shade for the pleasure of those taking their ease in the old string chairs. To the south was a view of Ambal Broad and Ambal Isle, a property of three acres supporting a number of beautiful pomanders, russet-silver against a background of solemn menas, and three enormous fanzaneels, holding their great shaggy pompoms high in the air. Through the foliage gleamed the white façade of the manse where Lord Ambal long ago had maintained his mistresses. The property was now owned by Jut Hulden, but he had no inclination to dwell in the manor; his friends would think him absurd.

In his youth Jut Hulden had played hussade for the Saurkash Serpents. Marucha had been *sheirl** for the Welgen Warlocks; so they had met, and married, and brought into being three sons, Shira and the twins Glinnes and Glay, and a daughter, Sharue, who had been stolen by the merlings.†

CHAPTER 2

Glinnes Hulden entered the world crying and kicking; Glay followed an hour later, in watchful silence. From the first day of their lives the two differed—in appearance, in temperament, in all the circumstances of their lives. Glinnes, like Jut and Shira, was amiable, trusting, and easy-natured; he grew into a handsome lad with a clear complexion, dusty-blond hair, a wide, smiling mouth. Glinnes entirely enjoyed the pleasures of the Fens: feasts, amorous adventures, star-

*sheirl: an untranslatable term from the special vocabulary of hussade—a glorious nymph, radiant with ecstatic vitality, who impels the players of her team to impossible feats of strength and agility. The sheirl is a virgin who must be protected from the shame of defeat.

†merlings: amphibious half-intelligent indigenes of Trullion, living in tunnels burrowed into the riverbanks. Merlings and men lived on the edge of a most delicate truce; each hated and hunted the other, but under mutually tolerable conditions. The merlings prowled the land at night for carrion, small animals, and children. If they molested boats or entered a habitation, men retaliated by dropping explosives into the water. Should a man fall into the water or attempt to swim, he had intruded into the domain of the merlings and risked being dragged under. Similarly, a merling discovered on land was shown no mercy.

watching and sailing, hussade, nocturnal merling hunts, simple idleness.

Glay at first lacked sturdy good health; for his first six years he was fretful, captious and melancholy. Then he mended, and quickly overtaking Glinnes was thenceforth the taller of the two. His hair was black, his features taut and keen, his eyes intent. Glinnes accepted events and ideas without skepticism; Glay stood aloof and saturnine. Glinnes was instinctively skillful at hussade; Glay refused to set foot on the field. Though Jut was a fair man, he found it hard to conceal his preference for Glinnes. Marucha, herself tall, dark-haired, and inclined to romantic meditation, fancied Glay, in whom she thought to detect poetic sensibilities. She tried to interest Glay in music, and explained how through music he could express his emotions and make them intelligible to others. Glay was cold to the idea and produced only a few lackadaisical discords on her guitar.

Glay was a mystery even to himself. Introspection availed nothing; he found himself as confusing as did the rest of his family. As a youth his austere appearance and rather haughty self-sufficiency earned him the soubriquet "Lord Glay"; perhaps coincidentally, Glay was the only member of the household who wanted to move into the manor house on Ambal Isle. Even Marucha had put the idea away as a foolish if amusing daydream.

Glay's single confidant was Akadie the mentor, who lived in a remarkable house on Sarpassante Island, a few miles north of Rabendary. Akadie, a thin long-armed man with an ill-assorted set of features—a big nose, sparse curls of snuff-brown hair, glassy blue eyes, a mouth continually trembling at the verge of a smile—was, like Glay, something of a misfit. Unlike Glay, he had turned idiosyncrasy to advantage, and drew custom even from the aristocracy.

Akadie's profession included the offices of epigrammatist, poet, calligrapher, sage, arbiter of elegance, professional guest (hiring Akadie to grace a party was an act of conspicuous consumption), marriage broker, legal consultant, repository of local tradition, and source of scandalous gossip. Akadie's droll face, gentle voice, and subtle language rendered his gossip all the more mordant. Jut distrusted Akadie and had nothing to do with him, to the regret of Marucha, who had never relinquished her social ambitions, and who felt in her heart of hearts that she had married below herself. Hussade sheirls often married lords!

Akadie had traveled to other worlds. At night, during star-watchings,*

---

*star-watching: at night the stars of Alastor Cluster blaze in profusion. The atmosphere refracts their light; the sky quivers with beams, glitters, and errant flashes. The Trills go out into their gardens with jugs of wine; they name the stars and discuss localities. For the Trills, for almost anyone of Alastor, the night sky was no abstract empyrean but rather, a view across prodigious distances to known places—a vast luminous map. There was always talk of pirates—the so-called "starmenters"—and their grisly deeds. When Numenes Star shone in the sky, the conversation turned to the Connatic and glorious Lusz, and someone would always say, "Best to steady our tongues! Perhaps he sits here now, drinking our wine and marking the dissi-

he would mark the stars he had visited; then he would describe their splendor and the astounding habits of their peoples. Jut Hulden cared nothing for travel; his interest in the other worlds lay in the quality of their hussade teams and the location of the Cluster Champions.

When Glinnes was sixteen he saw a starmenter ship. It dropped from the sky above Ambal Broad and slid at reckless speed down toward Welgen. The radio provided a minute-by-minute report of the raid. The starmenters landed in the central square, and seething forth plundered the banks, the jewel factors, and the cauch warehouse, cauch being by far the most valuable commodity produced on Trullion. They also seized a number of important personages to be held for ransom. The raid was swift and well-executed; in ten minutes the starmenters had loaded their ship with loot and prisoners. Unluckily for them, a Whelm cruiser chanced to be putting into Port Maheul when the alarm was broadcast and merely altered course to arrive at Welgen instead. Glinnes ran out on the verandah to see the Whelm ship arrive—a beautiful stately craft enameled in beige, scarlet and black. The ship dropped like an eagle toward Welgen and passed beyond Glinnes' range of vision. The voice from the radio cried out in excitement: "—they rise into the air, but here comes the Whelm ship! By the Nine Glories, the Whelm ship is here! The starmenters can't go into whisk*; they'd burn up from the friction! They must fight!"

The announcer could no longer control his voice for excitement: "The Whelm ship strikes; the starmenter is disabled! Hurrah! it drops back into the square. No, no! Oh horror! What horror! It has fallen upon the market; a hundred persons are crushed! Attention! Bring in all ambulances, all medical men! Emergency at Welgen! I can hear the sad cries . . . The starmenter ship is broken; still it fights . . . a blue ray . . . Another . . . The Whelm ship answers. The starmenters are quiet. Their ship is broken." The announcer fell quiet a moment, then once more was prompted to excitement. "Now what a sight! The folk are crying with rage; they swarm in at the starmenters; they drag them forth . . ." He began to babble, then stopped short and spoke in a more subdued voice. "The constables have intervened. They have pushed back the crowds and the starmenters are now in custody, and this to their own rue, as well they know, for they desperately struggle. How they writhe and kick! It's the prutanshyr for them! They prefer the vengeance of the crowd! . . . What a dreadful deed they have done upon the hapless town Welgen . . ."

---

dents!"—creating a nervous titter, for the Connatic's habit of wandering quietly about the worlds was well known. Then someone always uttered the brave remark: "Here we are—ten (or twelve or sixteen or twenty, as the case might be) among five trillion! The Connatic among us? I'll take that chance!"

At such a star-watch, Sharue Hulden had wandered off into the darkness. Before her absence was noticed, the merlings had seized her and had taken her away underwater.

*whisk: star-drive.

Jut and Shira worked in the far orchard grafting scions to the apple trees. Glinnes ran to tell them the news. ". . . and at last the starmenters were captured and taken away!"

"So much the worse for them," Jut said gruffly, and continued with his work. For a Trill, he was a man unusually self-contained and taciturn, traits that had become intensified since the death of Sharue by the merlings.

Shira said, "They'll be sweeping off the prutanshyr. Perhaps we'd better learn the news."

Jut grunted. "One torturing is much like another. The fire burns, the wheels wrench, the rope strains. Some folk thrive on it. For my excitement I'll watch hussade."

Shira winked at Glinnes. "One game is much like another. The forwards spring, the water splashes, the sheirl loses her clothes, and one pretty girl's belly is much like another's."

"There speaks the voice of experience," said Glinnes, and Shira, the most notorious philanderer of the district, guffawed.

Shira did in fact attend the executions with his mother Marucha, though Jut kept Glinnes and Glay at home.

Shira and Marucha returned by the late ferry. Marucha was tired and went to bed; Shira, however, joined Jut, Glinnes and Glay on the verandah and rendered an account of what he had seen. "Thirty-three they caught, and had them all in cages out in the square. All the preparations were put up before their very eyes. A hard lot of men, I must say—I couldn't place their race. Some might have been Echalites and some might have been Satagones, and one tall white-skinned fellow was said to be a Blaweg. Unfortunates all, in retrospect. They were naked and painted for shame: heads green, one leg blue, the other red. All gelded, of course. Oh, the prutanshyr's a wicked place! And to hear the music! Sweet as flowers, strange and hoarse! It strikes through you as if your own nerves were being plucked for tones . . . Ah well, at any rate, a great pot of boiling oil was prepared, and a traveling-crane stood by. The music began—eight Trevanyi and all their horns and fiddles. How can such stern folk make such sweet music? It chills the bones and churns the bowels and puts the taste of blood in your mouth! Chief Constable Filidice was there, but First Agent Gerence was the executioner. One by one the starmenters were grappled by hooks, then lifted and dipped into the oil, then hung up on a great high frame; and I don't know which was more awful, the howls or the beautiful sad music. The people fell down on their knees; some fell into fits and cried out—for terror or joy I can't tell you. I don't know what to make of it . . . After about two hours all were dead."

"Hmmf," said Jut Hulden. "They won't be back in a hurry. So much, at least, can be said."

Glinnes had listened in horrified fascination. "It's a fearful punishment, even for a starmenter."

"Indeed, that's what it is," said Jut. "Can you guess the reason?"

Glinnes swallowed hard and could not choose between several theories. Jut asked, "Would you now want to be a starmenter and risk such an end?"

"Never," Glinnes declared, from the depths of his soul.

Jut turned to the brooding Glay. "And you?"

"I never planned to rob and kill in the first place."

Jut gave a hoarse chuckle. "One of the two, at least, has been dissuaded from crime."

Glinnes said, "I wouldn't like to hear music played to pain."

"And why not?" Shira demanded. "At hussade, when the sheirl is smirched, the music is sweet and wild. Music gives savor to the event, like salt with food."

Glay offered a comment: "Akadie claims that everybody needs catharsis, if it's only a nightmare."

"It may be so," said Jut. "I myself need no nightmares; I've got one before my eyes every moment." Jut referred, as all knew, to the taking of Sharue. Since that time, his nocturnal hunts for merling had become almost an obsession.

"Well, if you two twits aren't to be starmenters, what will you be?" asked Shira. "Assuming you don't care to stay in the household."

"I'm for hussade," said Glinnes. "I don't care to fish, nor to scrape cauch." He recalled the brave beige, scarlet, and black ship that had struck down the starmenters. "Or perhaps I'll join the Whelm and lead a life of adventure."

"I know nothing of the Whelm," said Jut ponderously, "but if it's hussade I can give you one or two useful hints. Run five miles every day to develop your stamina. Jump the practice pits until you can make sure landings blindfolded. Forbear with the girls, or there'll be no virgins left in the prefecture to be your sheirl."

"It's a chance I am willing to take," said Glinnes.

Jut squinted through his black eyebrows at Glay. "And what of you? Will you stay in the household?"

Glay gave a shrug. "If I could, I'd travel space and see the Cluster."

Jut raised his bushy eyebrows. "How will you travel, lacking money?"

"There are methods, according to Akadie. He visited twenty-two worlds, working from port to port."

"Hmmf. That may be. But never use Akadie for your model. He has derived nothing from his travels but useless erudition."

Glay thought a moment. "If this is true," he said, "as it must be, since you so assert, then Akadie learned his sympathy and breadth of intellect here on Trullion, which is all the more to his credit."

Jut, who never resented honest defeat, clapped Glay on the back. "In you he has a loyal friend."

"I am grateful to Akadie," said Glay. "He has explained many things to me."

Shira, who teemed with lewd ideas, gave Glay a sly nudge. "Follow Glinnes on his rounds, and you'll never need Akadie's explanations."

"I'm not talking about that sort of thing."

"Then what sort of thing are you talking about?"

"I don't care to explain. You'd only jeer at me, which is tiresome."

"No jeering!" declared Shira. "We'll give you a fair hearing! Say on."

"Very well. I don't really care whether you jeer or not. I've long felt a lack, or an emptiness. I want a weight to thrust my shoulder against; I want a challenge I can defy and conquer."

"Brave words," said Shira dubiously. "But—"

"But why should I so trouble myself? Because I have but one life, one existence. I want to make my mark, somewhere, somehow. When I think of it I grow almost frantic! My foe is the universe; it defies me to perform remarkable deeds so that ever after folk will remember me! Why should not the name 'Glay Hulden' ring as far and clear as 'Paro' and 'Slabar Velche'?* I will make it so; it is the least I owe myself!"

Jut said in a gloomy voice, "You had best become either a great hussade player or a great starmenter."

"I overspoke myself," said Glay. "In truth I want neither fame nor notoriety; I do not care whether I astonish a single person. I want only the chance to do my best."

There was silence on the verandah. From the reeds came the croak of nocturnal insects, and water lapped softly against the dock; a merling perhaps had risen to the surface, to listen for interesting sounds.

Jut said in a heavy voice, "The ambition does you no discredit. Still I wonder how it would be if everyone strove with such urgency. Where would peace abide?"

"It is a difficult problem," said Glinnes. "Indeed, I had never considered it before. Glay, you amaze me! You are unique!"

Glay gave a deprecatory grunt. "I'm not so sure of this. There must be many, many folk desperate to fulfill themselves."

"Perhaps this is why people become starmenters," suggested Glinnes. "They are bored at home, at hussade they're inept, the girls turn away from them—so off they go in their black hulls, for sheer revenge!"

---

*Paro: a hussade player, the darling of the cluster, celebrated for his aggressive and daring play.
Slabar Velche: a notorious starmenter.

"The theory is as good as any," agreed Jut Hulden. "But revenge cuts both ways, as thirty-three folk discovered today."

"There is something here I can't understand," said Glinnes. "The Connatic knows of their crimes. Why does he not deploy the Whelm and root them out once and for all?"

Shira laughed indulgently. "Do you think the Whelm sits idle? The ships are constantly on the prowl. But for every living world you'll find a hundred dead ones, not to mention moons, asteroids, hulks and starments. The hiding places are beyond enumeration. The Whelm can only do its best."

Glinnes turned to Glay. "There you are: join the Whelm and see the Cluster. Get paid while you travel!"

"It's a thought," said Glay.

CHAPTER 3

In the end it was Glinnes who went to Port Maheul and there enlisted in the Whelm. He was seventeen at the time. Glay neither enlisted in the Whelm, played hussade, nor became a starmenter. Shortly after Glinnes joined the Whelm, Glay also left home. He wandered the length and breadth of Merlank, from time to time working to gain a few ozols, as often living off of the land. On several occasions he attempted the ruses Akadie had recommended in order to travel to other worlds, but for one reason or another his efforts met no success, and he never accumulated sufficient funds to buy himself passage.

For a period he traveled with a band of Trevanyi,* finding their exactness and intensity an amusing contrast to the imprecision of the average Trill.

After eight years of wandering he returned to Rabendary Island, where everything went about as before, although Shira at last had given up hussade. Jut still waged his nocturnal war against the merlings; Marucha still hoped to win social acceptance among the local gentry, who had absolutely no intention of allowing her to succeed. Jut, at the behest of Marucha, now called himself Squire Hulden of Rabendary, but refused to move into Ambal Manse, which, despite its noble proportions, grand chambers and polished wainscoting, lacked a broad verandah overlooking the water.

*Trevanyi: nomadic folk of a distinctive racial stock, prone to thievery, sorcery, and other petty chicaneries; an excitable, passionate, vengeful people. They consider cauch a poison and guard the chastity of their women with fanatic zeal.

The family regularly received news from Glinnes, who had done well in the Whelm. At boot camp he had earned a recommendation to officer training school, after which he had been assigned to the Tactical Corps of the 191st Squadron and placed in command of Landing Craft No. 191–539 and its twenty-man complement.

Glinnes could now look forward to a rewarding career, with excellent retirement benefits. Still, he was not entirely happy. He had envisioned a life more romantically adventurous; he had seen himself prowling the Cluster in a patrol boat, searching out starmenter nests, then putting into remote and picturesque settlements for a few days' shore leave—a life far more dashing and haphazard than the perfectly organized routine in which he found himself. To relieve the monotony he played hussade; his team always placed high in fleet competition, and won two championships.

Glinnes at last requested transfer to a patrol craft, but his request was denied. He went before the squadron commander, who listened to Glinnes' protests and complaints with an attitude of easy unconcern. "The transfer was denied for a very good reason."

"What reason?" demanded Glinnes. "Certainly I am not considered indispensable to the survival of the squadron?"

"Not altogether. Still, we don't want to disrupt a smoothly functioning organization." He adjusted some papers on his desk, then leaned back in his chair. "In confidence, there's a rumor to the effect that we're going into action."

"Indeed? Against whom?"

"As to this, I can only guess. Have you ever heard of the Tamarchô?"

"Yes indeed. I read about them in a journal: a cult of fanatic warriors on a world whose name now escapes me. Apparently they destroy for the love of destruction, or something of the sort."

"Well then, you know as much as I," said the commander, "except that the world is Rhamnotis and the Tamarchô have laid waste an entire district. I would guess that we are going down on Rhamnotis."

"It's an explanation, at least," said Glinnes. "What about Rhamnotis? A gloomy desert of a place?"

"On the contrary." The commander swung about, fingered buttons; a screen burst into colors and a voice spoke: "Alastor 965, Rhamnotis. The physical characteristics are—" The annunciator read off a set of indices denoting mass, dimension, gravity, atmosphere, and climate, while the screen displayed a Mercator projection of the surface. The commander touched buttons to bypass historical and anthropological information, and brought in what was known as "informal briefing": "Rhamnotis is a world where every particular, every aspect, every institution, conduces to the health and pleasure of its inhabitants. The original settlers, arriving from the world Triskelion, resolved never to tolerate the ugliness which they had left behind them, and they pledged a covenant to this effect, which covenant is now the prime document of Rhamnotis, and the subject of great reverence.

"Today the usual detritus of civilization—discord, filth, waste, structural clutter—have been almost expelled from the consciousness of the population. Rhamnotis is now a world characterized by excellent management. Optimums have become the norms. Social evils are unknown; poverty is no more than a curious word. The work-week is ten hours, in which every member of the population participates; he then devotes his surplus energy to the carnivals and fantasies, which attract tourists from far worlds. The cuisine is considered equal to the best of the Cluster. Beaches, forests, lakes, and mountains provide unsurpassed scope for outdoor recreation. Hussade is a spectator sport, although local teams have never placed high in Cluster rankings."

The commander touched another button; the annunciator said: "In recent years the cult known as Tamarchô has attracted attention. The principles of Tamarchô are unclear, and seem to vary from individual to individual. In general, the Tamarchists engage in wanton violence, destruction, and defilement. They have burned thousands of acres of primeval forests; they pollute lakes, reservoirs, and fountains with corpses, filth and crude oil; they are known to have poisoned water holes in game preserves, and they set poison bait for birds and domestic animals. They fling excrement-bombs into the perfumed carnival crowds and urinate from high towers upon the throngs below. They worship ugliness and in fact call themselves the Ugly People."

The commander tapped a button to dull the screen. "So there you have it. The Tamarchô have seized a tract of land and won't disperse; apparently the Rhamnotes have called in the Whelm. Still, it's all speculation; we might be going down to Breakneck Island to disperse the prostitutes. Who knows?"

Standard strategy of the Whelm, validated across ten thousand campaigns, was to mass a tremendous force so extravagantly overpowering as to intimidate the enemy and impose upon him the certain conviction of defeat. In most cases the insurgence would evaporate and there would be no fighting whatever. To subdue Mad King Zag on Gray World, Alastor 1740, the Whelm poised a thousand Tyrant dreadnoughts over the Black capitol, almost blocking out the daylight. Squadrons of Vavarangi and Stingers drifted in concentric evolutions under the Tyrants, and at still lower levels combat-boats darted back and forth like wasps. On the fifth day twenty million heavy troops dropped down to confront King Zag's stupefied militia, who long before had given up all thought of resistance.

The same tactics were expected to prevail against the Tamarchists. Four fleets of Tyrants and Maulers converged from four directions to hover above the Silver Mountains, where the Ugly People had taken refuge. Intelligence from the surface reported no perceptible reaction from the Tamarchists.

The Tyrants descended lower, and all during the night netted the sky with ominous beams of crackling blue light. In the morning the Tamarchists had broken all their camps and were nowhere to be seen. Surface intelligence reported that they had taken cover in the forests.

Monitors flew to the area, and their voice-horns ordered the Ugly Folk to form orderly files and march down to a nearby resort town. The only response was a spatter of sniper fire.

With menacing deliberation the Tyrants began to descend. The Monitors issued a final ultimatum: Surrender or face attack. The Tamarchists failed to respond.

Sixteen Armadillo sky-forts dropped upon a high meadow, intending to secure the area for a troop-landing. They encountered not only the fire of small arms, but spasms of energy from a set of antique blue radiants. Rather than destroy an unknown number of maniacs, the Armadillos returned into the sky.

The Operation Commander, outraged and perplexed, decided to ring the Silver Mountain with troops, hoping to starve the Ugly Folk into submission.

Twenty-two hundred landing craft, among them No. 191–539, commanded by Glinnes Hulden, descended to the surface and sealed the Tamarchists into their mountain lair. Where expedient, the troops cautiously moved up the valleys, after sending Stinger combat-boats ahead to flush out snipers. Casualties occurred, and since the Tamarchô represented neither threat nor emergency, the Commander withdrew his troops from zones of Tamarchist fire.

For a month the siege persisted. Intelligence reported that the Tamarchists lacked provisions, that they were eating bark, insects, leaves, whatever came to hand.

The Commander once again sent Monitors over the area, demanding an orderly surrender. For answer the Tamarchists launched a series of breakout attempts, but were repulsed with considerable harm to themselves.

The Commander once more sent over his Monitors, threatening the use of pain-gas unless surrender was effected within six hours. The deadline came and went; Vavarangi descended to bombard shelter areas with cannisters of pain-gas. Choking, rolling on the ground, writhing and jerking, the Tamarchists broke into the open. The Commander ordered down a "living rain" of a hundred thousand troops, and after a few brisk fire-fights the area was secure. The Tamarchist captives numbered less than two thousand persons of both sexes. Glinnes was astounded to discover that some were little more than children, and very few older than himself. They lacked ammunition, energy, food and medical supplies. They grimaced and snarled at the Whelm troops—"Ugly Folk" they were indeed. Glinnes' astonishment increased. What had prompted these young people to battle so fanatically for a cause obviously lost? What, indeed, had impelled them to become Ugly Folk? Why had they defiled and defouled, destroyed and corrupted?

Glinnes attempted to question one of the prisoners who pretended not to understand his dialect. Shortly thereafter Glinnes was ordered back aloft with his ship.

Glinnes returned to base. Picking up his mail, he found a letter from Shira containing tragic news. Jut Hulden had gone out to hunt merling once too often; they had laid a cunning trap for him. Before Shira could come to his aid, Jut had been dragged into Farwan Water.

The news affected Glinnes with a rather irrational astonishment. He found it hard to imagine change in the timeless Fens, especially change so profound.

Shira was now Squire of Rabendary. Glinnes wondered what other changes might be in store. Probably none—Shira had no taste for innovation. He would bring in a wife and breed a family; so much at least could be expected—if not sooner, then later. Glinnes speculated as to who might marry bulky balding Shira with the red cheeks and lumpy nose. Even as a hussade player, Shira had found difficulty enticing girls into the shadows, for while Shira considered himself bluff, friendly and affable, others thought him coarse, lewd and boisterous.

Glinnes began to muse about his boyhood. He recalled the hazy mornings, the festive evenings, the star-watchings. He recalled his good friends and their quaint habits; he remembered the look of Rabendary Forest—the menas looming over russet pomanders, silver-green birches, dark-green pricklenuts. He thought of the shimmer that hung above the water and softened the outline of far shores; he thought of the ramshackle old family home, and discovered himself to be profoundly homesick.

Two months later, at the end of ten years' service, he resigned his commission and returned to Trullion.

G linnes had sent a letter announcing his arrival, but when he debarked at Port Maheul in Staveny Prefecture, none of his family was on hand to greet him, which he thought strange.

He loaded his baggage onto the ferry and took a seat on the top deck, to watch the scenery go by. How easy and gay were the country-folk in their parays of dull scarlet, blue, ocher! Glinnes' semi-military garments—black jacket, beige breeches tucked into black ankle-boots—felt stiff and constricted. He'd probably never wear them again!

The boat presently slid into the dock at Welgen. A delectable odor wafted past Glinnes' nose, which he traced to a nearby fried-fish booth. Glinnes went ashore and bought a packet of steamed reed-pods and a length of barbecued eel. He looked about for Shira or Glay or Marucha, though he hardly expected to find them here. A group of off-worlders attracted his attention: three young men, wearing what seemed to be a uniform—neat gray one-piece garments belted at the waist, highly polished tight black shoes—and three young women, in rather austere gowns of durable white duck. Both men and women wore their hair cropped short, in not-unbecoming style, and wore small medallions on their left shoulders. They passed close to Glinnes and he realized that they were not off-worlders after all, but Trills . . . Students at a doctrinaire academy? Members of a religious order? Either case was possible, for they carried books, calculators, and seemed to be engaged in earnest discussion. Glinnes gave the girls a second appraisal. There was, he thought, something unappealing about them, which at first he could not define. The ordinary Trill girl dressed herself in almost anything at hand, without over-anxiety that it might be rumpled or threadbare or soiled, and then made herself gay with flowers. These girls looked not only clean, but fastidious as well. Too clean, too fastidious . . . Glinnes shrugged and returned to the ferry.

The ferry moved on into the heart of the Fens, along waterways dank with the scent of still water, decaying reedstalks, and occasionally a hint of a rich fetor, suggesting the presence of merling. Ripil Broad appeared ahead, and a cluster of shacks that was Saurkash, the end of the line for Glinnes; here the ferry veered north for the villages along Great Vole Island. Glinnes unloaded his cases onto the dock, and for a moment stood looking around the village. The most prominent feature was the hussade field and its dilapidated old bleachers, once the home-field of the Saurkash Serpents. Almost adjacent was The Magic Tench, the most pleasant of Saurkash's three taverns. He walked down the dock to the office where ten years before Milo Harrad had rented boats and operated a water-taxi.

Harrad was nowhere to be seen. A young man whom Glinnes did not know sat dozing in the shade.

"Good day, friend," said Glinnes, and the young man, awaking, turned toward Glinnes a look of mild reproach. "Can you take me out to Rabendary Island?"

"Whenever you like." The young man looked Glinnes slowly up and down and lurched to his feet. "You'd be Glinnes Hulden, unless I'm mistaken."

"Quite right. But I don't remember you."

"You'd have no reason to do so. I'm old Harrad's nephew from Voulash. They call me Young Harrad, and I expect that's what I'll be the rest of my life. I mind when you played for the Serpents."

"That's some time ago. You've got an accurate memory."

"Not all that good. The Huldens have always been hussade types. Old Harrad talked much of Jut, the best rover Saurkash ever produced, or so said old Milo. Shira was a solid guard, right enough, but slow in the jumps. I doubt I ever saw him make a clean swing."

"That's a fair judgment." Glinnes looked along the waterway. "I expected him here to meet me, or my brother Glay. Evidently they had better things to do."

Young Harrad glanced at him sidewise, then shrugged and brought one of his neat green and white skiffs to the dock. Glinnes loaded his cases aboard and they set off eastward along Mellish Water.

Young Harrad cleared his throat. "You expected Shira to meet you?"

"I did indeed."

"You didn't hear about Shira then?"

"What happened to him?"

"He disappeared."

"Disappeared?" Glinnes looked around with a slack jaw. "Where?"

"No one knows. To the merling's dinner table, likely enough. That's where most folk disappear."

"Unless they go off to visit friends."*

"For two months? Shira was a great horn, so I've been told, but two months on cauch would be quite extraordinary."

Glinnes gave a despondent grunt and turned away, no longer in the mood for conversation. Just gone, Shira gone—his homecoming could only be a melancholy occasion. The scenery, ever more familiar, ever more rich with memories, now only served to increase his gloom. Islands he knew well

---

*going off to visit friends: a euphemism for cauch-crazy lovers going off to camp in the wilds.

slid by on each side: Jurzy Island, where the Jurzy Lightning-bolts, his first team, had practiced; Calceon Island, where lovely Loel Issam had resisted his most urgent blandishments. Later she became sheirl from the Gaspar Triptanes, and finally, after her shaming, had wed Lord Clois from Graven Table, north of the Fens . . . Memories thronged his mind; he wondered why he had ever departed the Fens. His ten years in the Whelm already seemed no more than a dream.

The boat moved out upon Seaward Broad. To the south, at the end of a mile's perspective, stood Near Island, and beyond, somewhat wider and higher, Middle Island, and yet beyond, still wider, still higher, Far Island: three silhouettes obscured by water-haze in three distinct degrees, Far Island showing only slightly more substance than the sky at the southern horizon.

The boat slid into narrow Athenry Water, with hushberry trees leaning together to form an arch over the still, dark water. Here the scent of merling was noticeable. Harrad and Glinnes both watched for water swirls. For reasons known best to themselves, merlings gathered in Athenry Water—perhaps for the hushberries, which were poisonous to men, perhaps for the shade, perhaps for the savor of hushberry roots in the water. The surface lay placid and cool; if merlings were nearby, they kept to their burrows. The boat passed out upon Fleharish Broad. On Five Islands, to the south, Thammas, Lord Gensifer maintained his ancient manse. Not far away a sailboat rode high across the Broad on hydrofoils; at the tiller sat Lord Gensifer himself: a hearty round-faced man ten years older than Glinnes, burly of shoulder and chest if rather thin in the legs. He tacked smartly and came foaming up on a reach beside Harrad's boat, then luffed his sail. The boat dropped from its foils and rode flat in the water. "If I'm not mistaken it's young Glinnes Hulden, back from starfaring!" Lord Gensifer called out. "Welcome back to the Fens!"

Glinnes and Harrad both rose to their feet and performed the salute due a lord of Gensifer's quality.

"Thank you," said Glinnes. "I'm glad to be back, no doubt about that."

"There's no place like the Fens! And what are your plans for the old place?"

Glinnes was puzzled. "Plans? None in particular . . . Should I have plans?"

"I would presume so. After all, you're now Squire of Rabendary."

Glinnes squinted across the water, off toward Rabendary Island. "I suppose I am, for a fact, if Shira is truly dead. I'm older than Glay by an hour."

"And a good job too, if you want my opinion . . . Ha, hmm. You'll see for yourself, no doubt." Lord Gensifer drew in the sheet. "What about hussade? Are you for the new club? We'd certainly like a Hulden on the team."

"I don't know anything about it, Lord Gensifer. I'm so bewildered by the turn of affairs I can't give any sensible answer."

"In due course, in due course." Lord Gensifer sheeted home the sail; the hull, surging forward, rose on its foils and skimmed across Fleharish Broad at great speed.

"There's sport for you," said Young Harrad enviously. "He had that contraption brought out from Illucante by Interworld. Think of the ozols it cost him!"

"It looks dangerous," said Glinnes. "If it goes over, he and the merlings are out there alone."

"Lord Gensifer is a daredevil sort of chap," said Harrad. "Still, they say the craft is safe enough. It can't sink, first of all, even if it did go over. He could always ride the hull until someone picked him up."

They continued across Fleharish Broad and out into Ilfish Water, with the Prefecture Free Commons on their left—an island of five hundred acres reserved for the use of casual wanderers, Trevanyi, Wrye, lovers "visiting friends." The boat entered Ambal Broad, and there ahead—the dear outline of Rabendary Island: home. Glinnes blinked at the moisture that came to his eyes. A sad homecoming, in truth. Ambal Island looked its loveliest. Looking toward the old manor, Glinnes thought to perceive a wisp of smoke rising from the chimneys. A startling theory came to him, which would account for Lord Gensifer's sniff. Had Glay taken up residence in the manor? Lord Gensifer would consider such an action ridiculous and discreditable—a vulgarian trying to ape his betters.

The boat pulled up to Rabendary dock; Glinnes unloaded his luggage, paid off Young Harrad. He stared toward the house. Had it always lurched and sagged? Had the weeds always grown so rank? There was a condition of comfortable shabbiness which the Trills considered endearing, but the old house had gone far past this state. As he mounted the steps to the verandah, they groaned and sagged under his weight.

Flecks of color caught his eye, across the field near Rabendary Forest. Glinnes squinted and focused his gaze. Three tents: red, black, dull orange. Trevanyi tents. Glinnes shook his head in angry disparagement. He had not returned too soon. He called out, "Hallo the house! Who's here but me?"

In the doorway appeared the tall figure of his mother. She looked at him incredulously, then ran forward a few steps. "Glinnes! How strange to see you!"

Glinnes hugged and kissed her, ignoring the overtones of the remark. "Yes I'm back, and it feels strange to me too. Where is Glay?"

"He's off with one of his comrades. But how well you look! You've grown into a very fine man!"

"You haven't changed by so much as a twitch; you're still my beautiful mother."

"Oh, Glinnes, such flattery, I feel old as the hills and I look it too, I'm sure . . . I suppose you've heard the sad news?"

"About Shira? Yes. It grieves me terribly. Doesn't anyone know what happened?"

"Nothing is known," said Marucha rather primly. "But sit down, Glinnes; take off those fine boots and rest your feet. Would you care for apple wine?"

"I would indeed, and a bite of whatever is handy. I'm ravenous."

Marucha served wine, bread, a cold mince of meat, fruit, and sea-jelly. She sat watching him eat. "It's so very nice to see you. What are your plans?"

Glinnes thought her voice almost imperceptibly cool. Still, Marucha had never been demonstrative. He answered, "I don't have any plans whatever, I've only just heard about Shira from Young Harrad. He never took a wife then?"

Marucha's mouth pursed into a disapproving line. "He could never quite make up his mind . . . He had friends here and there, naturally."

Again Glinnes sensed unspoken words, knowledge which his mother did not care to communicate. He began to feel a few small inklings of resentment, and carefully put them aside. It would not do to start out his new life on such a footing. Marucha asked in a bright, rather brittle voice, "But where is your uniform? I so wanted to see you as a captain in the Whelm."

"I resigned my commission. I decided to come home."

"Oh." Marucha's voice was flat. "Of course we're glad to have you home, but are you sure it's wise giving up your career?"

"I've already given it up." In spite of his resolve, Glinnes' voice had taken on an edge. "I'm needed here more than in the Whelm. The old place is falling apart. Doesn't Glay do anything whatever?"

"He's been most busy with—well, his activities. In his own way, he's quite an important person now."

"That shouldn't prevent him from fixing the steps. They're literally rotting away . . . Or—I saw smoke from Ambal Isle. Is Glay living over there?"

"No. We've sold Ambal Isle, to one of Glay's friends."

Glinnes started, thunderstruck. "You've sold Ambal Isle? What possible reason . . ." He gathered his thoughts. "Shira sold Ambal Isle?"

"No," said Marucha in a cool voice. "Glay and I decided to let it go."

"But . . ." Glinnes halted and chose his words deliberately. "I certainly don't want to part with Ambal Isle, nor any other part of our land."

"I'm afraid that the sale has been effected. We assumed that you were making a career in the Whelm and wouldn't be home. Naturally we would have considered your feelings had we known."

Glinnes spoke politely. "I most definitely feel that we should void the contract.* We certainly don't want to give up Ambal."

"But my dear Glinnes, it's already given up."

"Not after we return the money. Where is it?"

"You'll have to ask Glay."

Glinnes reflected upon the sardonic Glay of ten years before, who always had stayed aloof from the affairs of Rabendary. That Glay should make large decisions seemed altogether inappropriate and more, insulting to the memory of his father Jut, who loved each square inch of his land.

Glinnes asked, "How much did you take for Ambal?"

"Twelve thousand ozols."

Glinnes' voice cracked with angry astonishment. "That's giving it away! For a beauty spot like Ambal Isle, with a manor house in good condition? Someone's insane!"

Marucha's black eyes sparkled. "Surely it's not your place to protest. You weren't there when we needed you, and it isn't proper for you to cavil now."

"I'm doing more than cavil; I'm going to void the contract. If Shira is dead, I'm Squire of Rabendary, and no one else has authority to sell."

"But we don't know that Shira is dead," Marucha pointed out, sweetly reasonable. "He may only have gone off to visit friends."

Glinnes asked politely, "Do you know of any such 'friends'?"

Marucha gave her shoulder a disdainful jerk. "Not really. But you remember Shira. He has never changed."

"After two months he'd surely be home from his visit."

"Naturally we hope that he is alive. In fact we can't presume him dead for four years, which is the law."

"But by then the contract will be firm! Why should we part with any of our wonderful land?"

"We needed the money. Isn't that reason enough?"

"You needed money for what?"

"You'll have to ask that question of Glay."

"I'll do so. Where is he?"

"I really don't know. He'll probably be home before too long."

"Another matter: are those Trevanyi tents down by the forest?"

Marucha nodded. By now, neither was making any pretense of amiability. "Please don't criticize either me or Glay. Shira allowed them upon the property, and they have done no harm."

"Possibly not, but the year is young. You know our last experience with Trevanyi. They stole the kitchen cutlery."

---

*By Trill law, a contract for land sale is considered provisional for a period of a year, for the protection of both parties.

"The Drossets are not that sort," said Marucha. "For Trevanyi, they seem quite responsible. No doubt they're as honest as they find necessary."

Glinnes threw up his hands. "It's pointless to wrangle. But one last word about Ambal. Certainly Shira would never have wanted the Isle sold. If he's alive, you acted without his authorization. If he's dead, you acted without mine, and I insist that the contract be voided."

Marucha gave a cold shrug of her slender white shoulders. "This is a matter you must take up with Glay. I am really quite bored with the subject."

"Who bought Ambal Isle?"

"A person named Lute Casagave, very quiet and distinguished. I believe that he's an off-worlder; he's much too genteel to be a Trill."

Glinnes finished his meal, then went to his baggage. "I've brought a few oddments back with me." He gave his mother a parcel, which she took without comment. "Open it," said Glinnes. "It's for you."

She pulled the tab and drew forth a length of purple fabric embroidered with fantastic birds in thread of green, silver and gold. "How utterly wonderful!" She gasped. "Why Glinnes—what a delightful gift!"

"That's not all," said Glinnes. He brought forth other parcels, which Marucha opened in a rapture. Unlike the ordinary Trill, she delighted in precious possessions.

"These are star-crystals," said Glinnes. "They haven't any other name, but they're found just like this, facets and all, in the dust of dead stars. Nothing can scratch them, not even diamond, and they have very peculiar optical properties."

"My, how heavy they are!"

"This is an antique vase, no one knows how old. The writing on the bottom is said to be Erdish."

"It's charming!"

"Now this isn't very distinguished, just something that caught my fancy—a nutcracker in the shape of an Urtland crotchet. I picked it up in a junkshop, if the truth be known."

"But how cunning. It's for cracking nuts, you say?"

"Yes. You put the nuts between these mandibles and press down the tail . . . These were for Glay and Shira—knives forged from proteum. The cutting edges are single chains of interlocked molecules—absolutely indestructible. You can strike them into steel and they never dull."

"Glay will be delighted," said Marucha in a voice somewhat stiffer than before. "And Shira will be pleased."

Glinnes gave a skeptical snort, which Marucha took pains to ignore. "Thank you very much for the gifts. I think they're all wonderful." She looked out the door down across the verandah to the dock. "Here is Glay now."

Glinnes went out to stand on the verandah. Glay, coming up the path from the dock, halted, though he showed no surprise. Then he came forward slowly. Glinnes descended the steps and the brothers clapped each other's shoulders.

Glay was wearing, Glinnes noted, not the usual Trill paray, but gray trousers and dark jacket.

"Welcome home," said Glay. "I met Young Harrad; he told me you were here."

"I'm glad to be home," said Glinnes. "With just you and Marucha, it must have been gloomy. But now that I'm here I hope we can make the house the place it used to be."

Glay gave a noncommittal nod. "Yes. Life has been somewhat quiet. And things change, certainly, I hope for the better."

Glinnes was not sure he knew what Glay was talking about. "There's a great deal to discuss. But first, I'm glad to see you. You're looking remarkably wise and mature, and—what would be the word?—self-possessed."

Glay laughed. "When I look back, I see that I always pondered too much and tried to resolve too many paradoxes. I've given all that up. I've cut the Gordian knot, so to speak."

"How so?"

Glay made a deprecatory gesture. "It's too complicated to go into right now . . . You look well too. The Whelm has been good for you. When must you go back?"

"Into the Whelm? Never. I'm through, since I now seem to be Squire of Rabendary."

"Yes," said Glay in a colorless voice. "You've got an hour's edge on me."

"Come inside," said Glinnes. "I've brought you a gift. Also something for Shira. Do you think he's dead?"

Glay nodded gloomily. "There's no other explanation."

"That's my feeling. Mother feels he's 'visiting friends.' "

"For two months? Not a chance."

The two entered the house, and Glinnes brought out the knife he had bought at the Technical Laboratories in Boreal City on Maranian. "Be careful of the edge. You can't touch it without slicing yourself. But you can hack through a steel rod without damage."

Glay picked up the knife gingerly and squinted along the invisible edge. "It frightens me."

"Yes, it's almost weird. Now that Shira's dead, I'll keep the other one for myself."

Marucha spoke from across the room. "We're not sure that Shira is dead."

Neither Glay nor Glinnes made response. Glay put his knife on the mantelpiece of smoke-darkened old kaban. Glinnes took a seat. "We'd better clear the air about Ambal Isle."

Glay leaned back against the wall and inspected Glinnes with somber eyes. "There's nothing to say. For better or worse, I sold it to Lute Casagave."

"The sale was not only unwise, it was illegal. I intend to void the contract."

"Indeed. How will you proceed?"

"We'll return the money and ask Casagave to leave. The process is very simple."

"If you have twelve thousand ozols."

"I don't—but you do."

Glay slowly shook his head. "No longer."

"Where is the money?"

"I gave it away."

"To whom?"

"To a man called Junius Farfan. I gave it; he took it; I can't get it back."

"I think that we should go to see Junius Farfan—at this very moment."

Glay shook his head. "Please don't begrudge me this money. You have your share—you are Squire of Rabendary. Let me have Ambal Isle as my share."

"There's no question of shares, or who owns what," said Glinnes. "You and I both own Rabendary. It's our homeplace."

"That certainly is a valid point of view," said Glay. "But I choose to think differently. As I told you before, changes are coming over the land."

Glinnes sat back, unable to find words to convey his indignation.

"Let it rest there," said Glay wearily. "I took Ambal; you've got Rabendary. It's only fair, after all. I'll now move out and leave you in full enjoyment of your holding."

Glinnes tried to cry out a dissent, but the words clogged in his throat. He could only say, "The choice is yours. I hope you'll change your mind."

Glay's response was a cryptic smile, which Glinnes understood to mean no response at all. "Another matter," said Glinnes. "What of the Trevanyi yonder?"

"They are folk I traveled about with—the Drossets. Do you object to their presence?"

"They're your friends. If you insist upon changing your residence, why not take your friends with you?"

"I don't quite know where I'm going," said Glay. "If you want them gone, simply tell them so. You're Squire of Rabendary, not I."

Marucha spoke from her chair. "He's not squire until we know about Shira!"

"Shira is dead," said Glay.

"Still, Glinnes has no right to come home and instantly make difficulties. I vow, he's as obstinate as Shira and as hard as his father."

Glinnes said, "I've made no difficulties. You've made them. I've got to find twelve thousand ozols somewhere to save Ambal Isle, then evict a band of Trevanyi before they call in their whole clan. It's lucky I came home when I did, while we've still got a home."

Glay stonily poured himself a mug of apple wine. He seemed only bored . . . From across the field came a groaning, creaking sound, then a tremendous crash. Glinnes went to look from the end of the verandah. He turned back to Glay. "Your friends have just cut down one of our oldest barchnut trees."

"One of your trees," said Glay with a faint smile.

"You won't ask them to leave?"

"They wouldn't heed me. I owe them favors."

"Do they have names?"

"The het is Vang Drosset. His woman is Tingo. The sons are Ashmor and Harving. The daughter is Duissane. The crone is Immifalda."

Going to his luggage, Glinnes brought forth his service hand-gun, which he dropped into his pocket. Glay watched with a sardonic droop to his lips, then muttered something to Marucha.

Glinnes marched off across the meadow. The pleasant pale light of afternoon seemed to clarify all the close colors and invest the distances with a luminous shimmer. Glinnes' heart swelled with many emotions: grief, longing for the old sweet times, anger with Glay which surged past his attempts to subdue it.

He approached the camp. Six pairs of eyes watched his every step, appraised his every aspect. The camp was none too clean, although, on the other hand, it was not too dirty; Glinnes had seen worse. Two fires were burning. At one of these a boy turned a spit stuck full with plump young wood-hens. A caldron over the other fire emitted an acrid herbal stench: the Drossets were preparing a batch of Trevanyi beer, which eventually colored their eyeballs a startling golden yellow. The woman stirring the mess was stern and keen-featured. Her hair had been dyed bright red and hung in two plaits down her back. Glinnes moved to avoid the reek.

A man approached from the fallen tree, where he had been gathering barchnuts. Two hulking young men ambled behind him. All three wore black breeches tucked into sagging black boots, loose shirts of beige silk, colored neckerchiefs—typical Trevanyi costume. Vang Drosset wore a flat black hat from which his taffy-colored hair burst forth in exuberant curls. His skin was an odd biscuit-brown; his eyes glowed yellow, as if illuminated from behind. Altogether an impressive man, and not a person to be trifled with, thought Glinnes. He said, "You are Vang Drosset? I am Glinnes Hulden, Squire of Rabendary Island. I must ask you to move your camp."

Vang Drosset motioned to his sons, who brought forward a pair of wicker chairs. "Sit and take refreshment," said Vang Drosset. "We will discuss our leaving."

Glinnes smiled and shook his head. "I must stand." If he sat and drank their tea he became beholden, and they then could ask for favors. He glanced past Vang Drosset to the boy turning the spit, and now he saw that it was not a boy but a slender, shapely girl of seventeen or eighteen. Vang Drosset spoke a syllable over his shoulder; the girl rose to her feet and went to the dull red tent. As she entered, she turned a glance back over her shoulder. Glinnes glimpsed a pretty face, with eyes naturally golden, and golden-red curls that clung about her head and dangled past her ears to her neck.

Vang Drosset grinned, showing a set of gleaming white teeth. "As to moving camp, I beg that you give us leave to remain. We do no harm here."

"I'm not so sure. Trevanyi make uncomfortable neighbors. Beasts and fowl disappear, and other items as well."

"We have stolen neither beast nor fowl." Vang Drosset's voice was gentle.

"You have just destroyed a grand tree, and only to pick the nuts more easily."

"The forest is full of trees. We needed firewood. Surely it is no great matter."

"Not to you. Do you know I played in that tree when I was a boy? Look! See where I carved my mark! In that crotch I built an eyrie, where sometimes I slept at nights. That tree I loved!"

Vang Drosset gave a delicate grimace at the idea of a man loving a tree. His two sons laughed contemptuously, and turning away, began to throw knives at a target.

Glinnes continued. "Firewood? The forest is full of dead wood. You need only carry it here."

"A very long distance for folk with sore backs."

Glinnes pointed to the spit. "Those fowl—only half-grown; none have raised a brood. We hunt only the three-year birds, which no doubt you've already killed and eaten, and probably the two-year birds as well, and after you devour the yearlings none will be left. And there, on that platter—the ground fruit. You've pulled up entire clumps, roots and all; you've destroyed our future crop! You say you do no harm? You brutalize the land; it won't be the same for ten years. Strike your tents, load your wagons* and go."

Vang spoke in a subdued voice. "This is not gracious language, Squire Hulden."

*Trevanyi wagons are ponderous boats with wheels, capable on either land or water.

"How does one graciously order a man off his property?" asked Glinnes. "It can't be done. You require too much."

Vang Drosset swung away with a hiss of exasperation and stared off across the meadow. Ashmor and Harving were now engaged in a startling Trevanyi exercise that Glinnes had never before witnessed. They stood about thirty feet apart and each in turn threw a knife at the other's head. He toward whom the knife was aimed flicked up his own knife to catch the hurled knife in some miraculous manner and send it spinning into the air.

"Trevanyi make good friends but bad enemies," said Vang Drosset in a soft voice.

Glinnes replied, "Perhaps you have read the proverb: 'East of Zanzamar* live the friendly Trevanyi.' "

Vang Drosset spoke in a voice of spurious humility. "But we are not all that baneful! We add to the pleasures of Rabendary Island! We will play music at your feasts; we are adepts at the knife dances . . ." He twitched his fingers at his two sons, who hopped and jerked and swung their knives in shivering arcs.

By accident, by jocular or murderous design, a knife darted at Glinnes' head. Vang Drosset cawed, in either warning or exultation. Glinnes had been expecting some such demonstration. He ducked; the knife struck into a target behind him. Glinnes' gun jerked out and spat blue plasma. The end of the spit flared and the birds dropped into the coals.

From the tent darted the girl Duissane, her eyes projecting a dazzle as fierce as that of the gun. She snatched at the spit and burned her hand; she rolled the birds out on the ground with a stick, all the time crying out curses and invective: "Oh you wicked urush,† you've spoiled our meal! May your tongue grow a beard. And you with your vile paunch full of dog-guts, get away from the place before we name you a stiff-leg Fanscher. We know you, never fear! You're a worse spageen‡ than your horn of a brother; there were few like him . . ."

Vang Drosset held up his clenched hand. The girl closed her mouth and grimly began to clean the birds. Vang Drosset turned back to Glinnes, a hard smile on his face. "That was not a kind act," he said. "Did you not enjoy the knife games?"

"Not particularly," said Glinnes. He brought out his own new knife, and pulling the Trevanyi knife from the target, sliced off a shaving as if he were paring a withe. The Drossets stared in fascination. Glinnes sheathed the knife.

---

*Zanzamar: a town at the far eastern tip of Cape Sunrise.
†urush: derogatory Trevanyish cant for a Trill.
‡spag: state of rut; hence *spageen*: individual in such a condition.

"The common land is only a mile down Ilfish Water," said Glinnes. "You can camp there to no one's detriment."

"We came here from the common," cried Duissane. "The spageen Shira invited us; isn't that good enough for you?"

Glinnes could not comprehend the basis for Shira's generosity. "I thought it was Glay you traveled with."

Vang Drosset made another gesture. Duissane turned on her heel and took the birds to a serving table.

"Tomorrow we go our way," said Vang Drosset in a plangent, fateful voice. "*Forlostwenna** is on us, in any event: we are ready for departure."

Ashmor spat into the dirt. "It's Fanscherade which is on him. He's now too good for us."

"Too good for you as well," muttered Harving.

Fanscherade? The word meant nothing, but he would solicit no instruction from the Drossets. He spoke a word of farewell and turned away. As he crossed the field, six pairs of eyes stung his back. He was relieved to pass beyond the range of a thrown knife.

CHAPTER 5

A vness was the name of that pale hour immediately before sunset: a sad quiet time when all color seemed to have drained from the world, and the landscape revealed no dimensions other than those suggested by receding planes of ever paler haze. Avness, like dawn, was a time unsympathetic to the Trill temperament; the Trills had no taste for melancholy reverie.

Glinnes found the house empty upon his return: both Glay and Marucha had departed. Glinnes was plunged into a state of gloom. He went out on the verandah and looked toward the Drosset tents, half of a mind to call them over for a farewell feast—or more particularly Duissane, beyond dispute a fascinating creature, bad temper and all. Glinnes pictured her as she might look in a kindly mood . . . Duissane would enliven any occasion . . . An absurd idea. Vang Drosset would cut his heart out at the mere suspicion.

Glinnes went back into the house and poured himself a draught of wine. He opened the larder and considered the sparse contents. How different from the open-hearted bounty he remembered from the happy old times!

Forlostwenna: a word from the Trevanyi jargon—an urgent mood compelling departure; more immediate than the general term "wanderlust."

... He heard the gurgle and hiss of a prow cutting water. Going out onto the verandah, Glinnes watched the approaching boat. It contained not Marucha, whom he expected, but a thin long-armed man with narrow shoulders and sharp elbows, in a suit of dark brown and blue velvet cut after that fashion favored by the aristocrats. Wispy brown hair hung almost to his shoulders; his face was mild and gentle, with a hint of impish mischief in the cast of his eyes and the quirk of his mouth. Glinnes recognized Janno Akadie the mentor, whom he remembered as voluble, facetious, at times mordant or even malicious, and never at a loss for an epigram, an allusion, a profundity, which impressed many but irked Jut Hulden.

Glinnes walked down to the dock and, catching the mooring line, made the boat fast to the bollard. Jumping nimbly ashore, Akadie gave Glinnes an effusive greeting. "I heard you were home and couldn't rest till I saw you. A pleasure having you back among us!"

Glinnes gave polite acknowledgment to the compliments, and Akadie nodded more cordially than ever. "I fear we've had changes since your departure—perhaps not all of them to your liking."

"I really haven't had time to make up my mind," said Glinnes cautiously, but Akadie paid no attention and looked up at the dim house. "Your dear mother is away from home?"

"I don't know where she is, but come drink a pot or two of wine."

Akadie made an acquiescent gesture. The two walked up the dock toward the house. Akadie glanced toward Rabendary Forest, where the Drossets' fire showed as a flickering orange spark. "The Trevanyi are still on hand, I notice."

"They leave tomorrow."

Akadie nodded sagely. "The girl is charming but fey—that is to say, burdened with a weight of destiny. I wonder for whom she carries her message."

Glinnes lofted his eyebrows; he had not thought of Duissane in so dire a connection, and Akadie's remark struck reverberations within him. "As you say, she seems an extraordinary person."

Akadie settled into one of the old string chairs on the verandah. Glinnes brought out wine, cheese and nuts, and they sat back to watch the wan colors of the Trullion sunset.

"I take it you are home on leave?"

"No. I've left the Whelm. I now seem to be Squire of Rabendary—unless Shira returns, which no one considers likely."

"Two months is indeed an ominous period," said Akadie, somewhat sententiously.

"What do you think became of him?"

Akadie sipped his wine. "I know no more than you, in spite of my reputation."

"Quite bluntly, I find the situation incomprehensible," said Glinnes.

"Why did Glay sell Ambal? I can't understand it; he'll neither explain nor give back the money so that I can void the contract. I never expected to find so troublesome a situation. What is your opinion on all this?"

Akadie placed his mug delicately upon the table. "Are you consulting me professionally? It might well be money wasted, since, offhand, I see no remedy for your difficulties."

Glinnes heaved a patient sigh; here again: the Akadie with whom he never quite knew how to deal. He said, "If you can make yourself useful, I'll pay you." And he had the satisfaction of seeing Akadie purse his lips.

Akadie arranged his thoughts. "Hmmf. Naturally I can't charge you for casual gossip. I must make myself useful, as you put it. Sometimes the distinction between social grace and professional help is narrow. I suggest that we put this occasion on one basis or another."

"You can call it a consultation," said Glinnes, "since the matter has come to rest on these terms."

"Very well. What do you wish to consult about?"

"The general situation. I want to get a grip on affairs, but I'm working in the dark. First of all: Ambal Isle, which Glay had no right to sell."

"No problem here. Return the payment and void the contract."

"Glay won't give me the money, and I don't have twelve thousand ozols of my own."

"A difficult situation," agreed Akadie. "Shira, of course, refused to sell. The deal was made only after his disappearance."

"Hmmm. What are you suggesting?"

"Nothing whatever. I'm supplying facts from which you can draw whatever inferences you like."

"Who is Lute Casagave?"

"I don't know. Superficially he seems a gentleman of quiet tastes, who takes an amateur's interest in local genealogy. He's compiling a conspectus of the local nobility, or so he tells me. His motives might well be other than pure scholarship, it goes without saying. Might he be trying to establish a claim upon one or another of the local titles? If so, interesting events will be forthcoming . . . Hmm. What else do I know of the mysterious Lute Casagave? He claims to be a Bole from Ellent, which is Alastor 485, as you're no doubt aware. I have my doubts."

"How so?"

"I am an observant man, as you know. After my little lunch at his manor, I consulted my references. I found that, oddly enough, the great majority of Boles are left-handed. Casagave is right-handed. Most Boles are devoutly religious and their place of perdition is the Black Ocean at the South Pole of Ellent; submarine creatures house the souls of the damned. On Ellent, to eat wet food is to encompass within oneself a clutch of vile influences. No Bole eats fish. Yet Lute Casagave quite placidly enjoyed a stew of sea-spider, and afterward a fine grilled duck-fish, no less than I. Is Lute Casagave a Bole?" Akadie held out his hands. "I don't know."

"But why should he pretend to a false identity? Unless—"

"Exactly. Still, the explanation may be quite ordinary. Perhaps he is an emancipated Bole. Over-subtlety is an error as gross as innocence."

"No doubt. Well, this to the side. I still can't give him his money because Glay won't return it. Do you know where it is?"

"I do." Akadie darted a side glance toward Glinnes. "I must remark that this is Class Two information and I must calculate your fee accordingly."

"Quite all right," said Glinnes. "If it seems exorbitant, you can always recalculate. Where is the money?"

"Glay paid it to a man named Junius Farfan, who lives in Welgen."

Glinnes frowned off across Ambal Broad. "I've heard that name before."

"Quite likely. He is secretary of the local Fanschers."

"Oh? Why should Glay give him the money? Is Glay a Fanscher as well?"

"If not, he is on the brink. So far, he does not affect the mannerisms and idiosyncrasies."

Glinnes had a sudden insight. "The odd gray clothes? The shorn hair?"

"These are overt symbols. The movement has naturally provoked an angry reaction, and not unreasonably. The precepts of Fanscherade directly contradict conventional attitudes and must be considered anti-social."

"This means nothing to me," Glinnes grumbled. "I've never heard of Fanscherade till today."

Akadie spoke in his most didactic voice: "The name derives from old Glottisch: *Fan* is a corybantic celebration of glory. The thesis appears to be no more than an insipid truism: life is a commodity so precious that it must be used to best advantage. Who could argue otherwise? The Fanschers engender hostility when they try to implement the idea. They feel that each person must establish exalted goals, and fulfill them if he can. If he fails, he fails honorably and has satisfaction in his striving; he has used his life well. If he wins—" Akadie made a wry gesture. "Who in this life ever wins? Death wins. Still—Fanscherade is at its basis a glorious ideal."

Glinnes made a skeptical sound. "Five trillion folk of Alastor, all striving and straining? There'd be peace for no one."

Akadie gave a smiling nod. "Understand this: Fanscherade is not a policy for five trillion. Fanscherade is one single outcry of wild despair, the loneliness of a single man lost among an infinity of infinities. Through Fanscherade the one man defies and rejects anonymity; he insists upon his personal magnificence." Akadie paused, then made a wry grimace. "One might remark, parenthetically, that the only truly fulfilled Fanscher is the Connatic." He sipped his wine.

The sun had set. Overhead hung a high layer of frosty green cirrus; to south and north were wisps and tufts of rose, violet, and citron. For a period the two men sat in silence.

Akadie spoke in a soft voice. "So then—that is Fanscherade. Few Fanschers comprehend their new creed; after all, most are children distressed by the sloth, the erotic excesses, the irresponsibility, the slovenly appearance of their parents. They deplore the cauch, the wine, the gluttonous feasts, all of which are consumed in the name of immediacy and vivid experience. Perhaps their principal intent is to establish a new and distinctive image for themselves. They cultivate a neutral appearance, on the theory that a person should be known not by the symbols he elects to display but by his conduct."

"A group of strident and callow malcontents!" growled Glinnes. "Where do they find the insolence to challenge so many persons older and wiser than themselves?"

"Alas!" sighed Akadie. "You'll find no novelty there."

Glinnes poured more wine into the mugs. "It all seems foolish, unnecessary, and futile. What do people want from life? We Trills have all the good things: food, music, merriment. Is this mischievous? What else is there to live for? The Fanschers are gargoyles screaming at the sun."

"On the face of it, the business is absurd," said Akadie. "Still—" He shrugged. "—There is a certain grandeur in their point of view. Malcontents—but why? To wrench sense from archaic nonsense; to strike the sigil of human will upon elemental chaos; to affirm the shining brilliance of one soul alone but alive among five trillion placid gray corpuscles. Yes, it is wild and brave."

"You sound like a Fanscher yourself," snorted Glinnes.

Akadie shook his head. "There are worse attitudes, but no, not I. Fanscherade is a young man's game. I'm far too old."

"What do they think of hussade?"

"They consider it spurious activity, to distract folk from the true color and texture of life."

Glinnes shook his head in wonder. "And to think the Trevanyi girl called me a Fanscher!"

"What a singular notion!" said Akadie.

Glinnes turned Akadie a sharp glance but saw only an expression of limpid innocence. "How did Fanscherade start? I remember no such trend."

"The raw material has been long ready at hand, or so I would imagine. A certain spark of ideology was required, no more."

"And who then is the ideologue of Fanscherade?"

"Junius Farfan. He lives in Welgen."

"And Junius Farfan has my money!"

Akadie rose to his feet. "I hear a boat. It's Marucha at last." He went to the dock, followed by Glinnes. Along Ilfish Water came the boat behind its mustache of white water, across the edge of Ambal Broad and up to the dock. Glinnes took the line from Glay and made it fast to a bollard. Marucha stepped jauntily up to the dock. Glinnes looked in amazement at her clothes: a sheath of severe white linen, black ankle-boots, and a black cloche cap, which, in suppressing her hair, accentuated her resemblance to Glay.

Akadie came forward. "I'm sorry I missed you. Still, Glinnes and I have had a pleasant conversation. We've been discussing Fanscherade."

"How very nice!" said Marucha. "Have you brought him around?"

"I hardly think so," said Akadie with a grin. "The seed must lie before it germinates."

Glay, standing to the side, looked more sardonic than ever. Akadie continued. "I have certain articles for you. These"—he handed Marucha a small flask—"are sensitizers; they place your mind in its most receptive state, and conduce to learning. Be sure to take no more than a single capsule or you will become hyperesthesic." He handed Marucha a parcel of books. "Here we have a manual of mathematical logic, a discussion of minichronics, and a treatise on basic cosmology. All are important to your program."

"Very good," said Marucha somewhat stiffly. "I wonder what I would like to give you?"*

"Something on the order of fifteen ozols would be more than ample," said Akadie. "But no hurry, of course. And now I too must be on my way. The dusk is far along."

Still, Akadie lingered while Marucha counted out fifteen ozols and placed them in his limp-fingered hand. "Good night, my friend." She and Glay went to the house. Glinnes asked, "And what will I have the pleasure of forcing upon you for the consultation?"

"Ah indeed, let me consider. Twenty ozol would be more than generous, if my remarks have been of help."

Glinnes paid over the money, reflecting that Akadie set a rather high price on his expertise. Akadie departed up Farwan Water toward Saur River, thence by Tethryn Broad and Vernice Water to his eccentric old manse on Sarpassante Island.

Inside the house on Rabendary Island lights glowed. Glinnes slowly walked up to the verandah, where Glay stood watching him.

"I've learned what you did with the money," said Glinnes. "You've given away Ambal Isle for sheer absurdity."

---

*The question "How much do I owe you?" is considered crass on Trullion, where easy generosity is the way of life.

"We've discussed the situation as much as necessary. I'll be leaving your house in the morning. Marucha wants me to stay, but I think I'll be more comfortable elsewhere."

"Do your dirty little mess and run, eh?" The brothers glared at each other, then Glinnes swung off and into the house.

Marucha sat reading the manuals Akadie had brought. Glinnes opened his mouth, then shut it again and went out to sit brooding on the verandah. Inside the house Glay and Marucha spoke in low tones.

CHAPTER 6

In the morning Glay bundled up his belongings and Glinnes took him to Saurkash. Not a word was spoken during the trip. When he had stepped from the boat to Saurkash dock, Glay said, "I won't be far away, not for a while at any rate. Maybe I'll camp on the commons. Akadie will know where to find me in case I'm needed. Try to be kind to Marucha. She's had an unhappy life, and now if she wants to play at girlhood, where's the harm in it?"

"Bring back that twelve thousand ozols and I might pay you some heed," said Glinnes. "Right now, all I expect of you is nonsense."

"The more fool you," said Glay, and went off up the dock. Glinnes watched him go. Then, instead of returning to Rabendary, he continued west toward Welgen.

Less than an hour's skim across the placid waterways brought him into Blacklyn Broad, with the great Karbashe River entering from the north, and the sea a mile or so to the south.

Glinnes tied the boat to the public dock, almost in the shadow of the hussade stadium, a structure of gray-green mena poles joined with black iron straps and brackets. He noticed a great cream-colored placard printed in red and blue:

THE FLEHARISH BROAD HUSSADE CLUB
is now forming a team
to compete at tournament level.
Applicants of requisite skills
will please apply to
Jeral Estang, Secretary,
or to the honorable sponsor,
Thammas, Lord Gensifer.

Glinnes read the placard a second time, wondering where Lord Gensifer would assemble sufficient talent for a team of tournament quality. Ten years before, a dozen teams had played around the Fens: the Welgen Storm-devils, the Invincibles of the Altramar Hussade Club, the Voulash Gialospans* of Great Vole Island, the Gaspar Magnetics, the Saurkash Serpents—this last the somewhat disorganized and casual group for whom he and Jut and Shira had played—the Gorgets of the Loressamy Hussade Club, and various others of various quality and ever-shifting personnel. Competition had run keen; skilled players were sought after, cozened, subjected to a hundred inducements. Glinnes had no reason to doubt that a similar situation prevailed now.

Glinnes turned away from the stadium with a new thought itching at the back of his mind. A poor hussade team lost money, and unless subsidized, fell apart. A mediocre team might either win or lose, depending on whether it scheduled games below or above itself. But a successful aggressive team often earned substantial booty in the course of a year, which when divided might well yield twelve thousand ozols per man.

Glinnes walked thoughtfully to the central square. The structures seemed a trifle more weathered, the calepsis vines shading the arbor in front of the Aude de Lys Tavern were somewhat fuller and richer, and—now that Glinnes took the pains to notice—a surprising number of Fanscher uniforms and Fanscher-influenced garments were in evidence. Glinnes sneered in disgust for the faddishness of it all. At the center of the square, as before, stood the prutanshyr: a platform forty feet on a side, with a gantry above, and to the side a subsidiary platform or stand for the musicians who provided counterpoint to the rites of penitence.

Ten years had brought one or two new structures, most notable a new inn, The Noble Saint Gambrinus, raised on mena timbers above the ground-level beer-garden, where four Trevanyi musicians were playing for such folk who had elected to take early refreshment.

Today was market day. Costermongers had set up carts around the periphery of the square; they were uniformly of the Wrye race, a folk as separate and particular as the Trevanyi. Trills of Welgen and the countryside strolled at leisure past the barrows, examining and handling, haggling, occasionally buying. The country folk were distinguishable by their garments: the inevitable paray, with whatever other vestments fancy, convenience, whim, or aesthetic impulse dictated—oddments of this, trifles of that, gay scarves, embroidered vests, shirts emblazoned with odd designs, beads, necklaces, jangling bracelets, head-bands, cockades. Residents of the town wore clothes somewhat less idiosyncratic, and Glinnes noticed a sizable propor-

*gialospans: literally, girl-denuders, in reference to the anticipated plight of the enemy sheirl.

tion of Fanscher suits, of good gray material, smartly tailored, worn with polished black ankle-boots. Some wore bucket-caps of black felt pulled tight over the hair. Some of those wearing this costume were older folk, self-conscious in their stylish finery. Certainly, reflected Glinnes, not all of these could be Fanschers.

A thin long-armed man in dark gray approached Glinnes, who stared in shock and scornful amusement. "You too? Is it possible!"

Akadie showed no embarrassment. "Why not? Where is the harm in a fad? I enjoy pretending I'm young again."

"Must you pretend to Fanscherade at the same time?"

Akadie shrugged. "Again: why not? Perhaps they over-idealize themselves; perhaps they carp too earnestly at the superstition and sensuality of the rest of us. Still"—he made a deprecatory gesture—"I am as you see."

Glinnes shook his head in disapproval. "Suddenly these Fanschers control the wisdom of the world, and their parents, who gave them birth, are shiftless and squalid."

Akadie laughed. "Fads come, fads go. They relieve the tedium of routine; why not enjoy them?" Before Glinnes could answer, Akadie changed the subject. "I expected to find you here. You're naturally looking for Junius Farfan, and it just so happens that I can point him out to you. Look yonder, past that horrid instrument, to the parlor under The Noble Saint Gambrinus. In the deep shade to the left a Fanscher sits writing in a ledger. That man is Junius Farfan."

"I'll go talk to him now."

"Good luck," said Akadie.

Glinnes crossed the square and, stepping into the beer-parlor, approached the table Akadie had indicated. "You are Junius Farfan?"

The man looked up. Glinnes saw a face classically regular, if somewhat bloodless and cerebral. The gray suit hung with austere elegance on his spare frame, which seemed all nerve, bone, and sinew. A black cloth casque confined his hair and dramatized a square pale forehead and brooding gray eyes. His age was probably less than that of Glinnes himself. "I am Junius Farfan."

"My name is Glinnes Hulden. Glay Hulden is my brother. Recently he turned over to you a large sum, on the order of twelve thousand ozols."

Farfan signified assent. "True."

"I bring bad news. Glay derived this money illegally. He sold property that belonged not to him but to me. To cut to the bone of the matter, I must have this money back."

Farfan seemed neither surprised nor overly concerned. He gestured to a chair. "Sit down. Will you take refreshment?"

Glinnes, seating himself, accepted a mug of ale. "Thank you. And where is the money?"

Farfan gave him a dispassionate inspection. "Naturally you did not hope that I would hand over twelve thousand ozols in a bag."

"But I did hope so. I need the money to reclaim the property."

Farfan smiled in polite apology. "Your hopes cannot be realized, for I cannot return the money."

Glinnes put down the mug with a thump. "Why not?"

"The money has been invested; we have ordered the machinery to equip a factory. We intend to manufacture those goods which are now imported into Trullion."

Glinnes spoke in a voice hoarse with fury. "Then you had better get new money into your fund and pay me my twelve thousand ozols."

Farfan gave a grave assent. "If the money was indeed yours, I freely acknowledge the debt, and I will recommend that the money be repaid with interest from the first profits of our enterprises."

"And when will this be?"

"I don't know. We are hoping somehow to acquire a tract of land, by loan or donation or sequestration." Farfan grinned and his face became suddenly boyish. "Thereafter we must construct a plant, arrange for raw materials, learn appropriate techniques, produce and sell our goods, pay for the original stocks of raw materials, buy new stocks and supplies, and so forth."

Glinnes said, "This all takes an appreciable period of time."

Junius Farfan frowned up into the air. "Let us fix upon the interval of five years. If you will then be good enough to renew your claim, we can discuss the matter again, I hope to our mutual satisfaction. As an individual I sympathize with your plight," said Junius Farfan. "As secretary of an organization which desperately needs capital, I am only too happy to use your money; I conceive our need to be more urgent than yours." He closed the register and rose to his feet. "Good-day, Squire Hulden."

CHAPTER 7

Glinnes watched Junius Farfan cross the square, moving around and out of sight behind the prutanshyr. He had achieved about as much as he had expected—nothing. Nevertheless, his resentment now included the suave Junius Farfan as well as Glay. However, it now became time to forget the lost money and try to find new. He looked into his wallet, though he already knew its contents: three thousand-ozol certificates, four hundred-ozol certificates, another hundred ozols in smaller paper. He therefore needed nine thousand ozols. His retirement pension amounted to a hundred ozols a month, more than ample for a man in his circumstances. He left The Noble Saint Gambrinus and crossed the square to the Welgen Bank, where he introduced himself to the chief officer.

"To be brief," said Glinnes, "my problem is this: I need nine thousand ozols to repossess Ambal Isle, which my brother incorrectly sold to a certain Lute Casagave."

"Yes, Lute Casagave; I recall the transaction."

"I wish to take a loan of nine thousand ozols, which I can repay at a rate of a hundred ozols per month. This is the fixed and definite sum I receive from the Whelm. Your money is perfectly safe and you are assured of repayment."

"Unless you die. Then what?"

Glinnes had not reckoned upon such a possibility. "There is always Rabendary Island, which I can propose for security."

"Rabendary Island. You are the owner?"

"I am the current squire," said Glinnes with a sudden sense of defeat. "My brother Shira disappeared two months ago. He is almost certainly dead."

"Very likely true. Still, we cannot deal in 'almosts' and 'very likelys.' Shira Hulden cannot be presumed dead until four years have passed. Until then you lack legal control of Rabendary Island. Unless, of course, you can prove his death."

Glinnes shook his head in vexation. "By diving down to consult the merlings? The situation is absurd."

"I appreciate the difficulties, but we deal in many absurdities; this is no more than an ordinary example."

Glinnes threw up his hands in defeat. He left the bank and returned to his boat, pausing only to re-read the placard announcing the formation of the Fleharish Broad Hussade Club.

As the boat drove toward Rabendary, Glinnes performed a number of calculations, all with the same purport: nine thousand ozols was a great deal of money. He reckoned the utmost income he might derive from Rabendary Island: perhaps two thousand ozols a year and insufficient by a factor of five. Glinnes turned his mind to hussade. A member of an important team might well gain ten thousand or even twenty thousand ozols a year if his team played often and consistently won. Lord Gensifer apparently planned the formation of such a team. Well and good, except that all the other teams of the region strained and strove to the same end, scheming, intriguing, making large promises, propounding visions of wealth and glory—all in order to attract talented players, who were not plentiful. The aggressive man might be slow and clumsy; the quick man might have poor judgment or a bad memory or insufficient strength to tub his opponent. Each position made its specific demands. The ideal forward was fast, agile, daring, sufficiently strong to cope with the opponents' rovers and guards. A rover must also be quick and skillful; most urgently, he must be skillful with the buff— that padded implement used to thrust or trip the opponent from the ways or courses into the tanks. The rovers were the first line of defense against the thrusts of the forwards, and the guards were the last. The guards were massive powerful men, decisive with their buffs. Since they were not often required to trapeze, or leap the tanks, agility was not an essential attribute in a guard. The ideal hussade player comprised all these qualities; he was powerful, intelligent, cunning, nimble, and merciless. Such men were rare. How, then, did Lord Gensifer propose to recruit a tournament-quality team? At Fleharish Broad, Glinnes decided to find out and swung south toward the Five Islands.

Glinnes moored his boat beside Lord Gensifer's sleek offshore cruiser and leapt to the dock. A path led through a park to the manor. As he mounted the steps, the door slid aside. A footman in lavender and gray livery appraised him without warmth. A perfunctory bow expressed his opinion of Glinnes' status. "What is your wish, sir?"

"Be so good as to tell Lord Gensifer that Glinnes Hulden wants a few words with him."

"Will you come inside, sir?"

Glinnes stepped into a tall hexagonal foyer, which had a floor of gleaming gray and white stelt.* Overhead hung a chandelier of a hundred lightpoints and a thousand diamond prisms. In each wall a wainscot of white artica wood framed high narrow mirrors which cast back and forth the glitter of the chandelier.

The footman returned and conducted Glinnes to the library, where Thammas, Lord Gensifer, wearing a maroon lounge suit, sat at his ease before a screen, watching a hussade game.†

---

*stelt: a precious material quarried from volcanic necks upon certain types of dead stars; a composite of metal and natural glass, displaying infinite variations of pattern and color.

†The hussade field is a gridiron of "runs" (also called "ways") and "laterals" above a tank of water four feet deep. The runs are nine feet apart, the laterals twelve feet. Trapezes permit the players to swing sideways from run to run, but not from lateral to lateral. The central moat is eight feet wide and can be passed at either end, at the center, or jumped if the player is sufficiently agile. The "home" tanks at either end of the field flank the platform on which stands the sheirl.

Players buff or body-block opposing players into the tanks, but may not use their hands to push, pull, hold, or tackle.

The captain of each team carries the "hange"—a bulb on a three-foot pedestal. When the light glows the captain may not be attacked, nor may he attack. When he moves six feet from the hange, or when he lifts the hange to shift its position, the light goes dead; he may then attack and be attacked. An extremely strong captain may almost ignore his hange; a captain less able stations himself on a key junction, which he is then able to protect by virtue of his impregnability within the area of the live hange.

The sheirl stands on her platform at the end of the field between the home tanks. She wears a white gown with a gold ring at the front. The enemy players seek to lay hold of this gold ring; a single pull denudes the sheirl. The dignity of the sheirl may be ransomed by her captain for five hundred ozols, a thousand, two thousand, or higher, in accordance with a prearranged schedule.

"Sit down, Glinnes, sit down," said Lord Gensifer. "Will you take tea or perhaps a rum punch?"

"I'll have rum punch, please."

Lord Gensifer motioned to the screen. "Last year's finals at Cluster Stadium. The black and reds are the Hextar Zulans from Sigre. The greens are the Falifonics from Green Star. Marvelous play. I've watched the game four times now and each time I'm more amazed.."

"I saw the Falifonics two or three years ago," said Glinnes. "I thought them agile and deft, and swift as lightning."

"They're still the same. Not large, but they seem to be everywhere at once. They have no great defense, but they don't need any with the attack they mount."

The footman served rum punch in frosted silver goblets. For a period Lord Gensifer and Glinnes sat watching the play: charges and shifts, feints and ploys, apparently reckless feats of agility, timing so exact as to seem bizarre coincidence. Patterns formed to calls from the captain, aggressions were launched and repulsed. Gradually the combinations began to favor the Falifonics. The Falifonic middle forwards swung to fork a Zulan rover and Zulan guards charged to protect; the Falifonic right wing slid through the gap thus opened, gained the platform, seized the gold ring at the sheirl's waist, and play came to a halt for the paying of ransom. Lord Gensifer turned off the screen. "The Falifonics won handily, as no doubt you know. Booty shared out at four thousand ozols a man . . . But you didn't come to talk hussade. Or did you?"

"As a matter of fact, yes. I happened to be in Welgen today and noticed mention of the new Fleharish Broad Club."

Lord Gensifer made an expansive gesture. "I'm the sponsor. It's something I've wanted to do for a long time, and finally I took the plunge. Welgen Stadium is our home-field, and now all I've got to do is assemble a team. What about you? Are you still playing?"

"I played for my division," said Glinnes. "We took the sector championships."

"That sounds interesting. Why don't you try out with us?"

"I might just do so, but first I've got a problem you might help me work out."

Lord Gensifer blinked cautiously. "I'll be glad to, if I can. What's the problem?"

"As you probably know, my brother Glay sold Ambal Isle out from under me. He won't return the money; in fact, it's gone."

Lord Gensifer raised his eyebrows. "Fanscherade?"

"Exactly."

Lord Gensifer shook his head. "Silly young fool."

"My problem is this. I have three thousand ozols of my own. I need another nine thousand to pay off Lute Casagave and break the contract."

Lord Gensifer pursed his lips and fluttered his fingers. "If Glay had no right to sell, then Casagave had no right to buy. The matter would seem to be between Glay and Casagave, with you in legal possession."

"Unfortunately I have no legal possession unless I can prove Shira dead, which I can't. I need cold hard cash."

"It's a dilemma," Lord Gensifer agreed.

"Here is my proposal: suppose I were to play with you—could you advance me nine thousand ozols against booty?"

Lord Gensifer sat back in his chair. "That's a very chancy investment."

"Not if you can put together a good team. Though frankly I don't see where you'll get the personnel."

"They're on hand." Lord Gensifer sat up in his seat, his pink face alive with boyish excitement. "I've drawn up what I consider the strongest team that could be assembled from players of the region. Listen to this." He read from a paper. "Wings: Tyran Lucho, Lightning Latken. Strikes: Yalden Wirp, Gold Ring Gonniksen. Rovers: Nilo Basgard, Wild Man Wilmer Guff. Guards: Splasher Maveldip, Bughead Holub, Carbo Gilweg, Holbert Hanigatz." Lord Gensifer put down the paper and peered triumphantly at Glinnes. "What do you think of that team?"

"I've been away too long," said Glinnes. "I only know about half the names. I've played with Gonniksen and Carbo Gilweg, and against Guff and maybe one or two others. They were good ten years ago and they're probably better now. Are all these men on your team?"

"Well—not officially. My strategy is this. I'll talk to each man in turn. I'll show him the team and ask how he'd like to be a part of it. How can I lose? Everyone wants to earn some big booty for a change. No one is going to turn me down. As a matter of fact, I've already made contact with two or three of the fellows and they've all shown great interest."

"Where would I fit in? And what about the nine thousand ozols?"

Lord Gensifer said cautiously, "As to your first question, you must remember that I haven't seen you play recently. For all I know, you've gone slow and sour . . . Where are you going?"

"Thank you for the rum punch," said Glinnes.

"Just a minute. No need to get temperamental. After all, I spoke only the plain truth. I haven't seen you for ten years. Still, if you played with the sector champions, no doubt you're in good shape. What is your position?"

"Anything but sheirl. With the 93rd I played strike and rover."

Lord Gensifer poured Glinnes more punch. "No doubt something can be arranged. But you must understand my position. I'm going after the best.

If you're the best you'll play for the Gorgons. If you're not—well, we'll need substitutes. That's sheer common sense—nothing to get excited about."

"Well then, what about the nine thousand ozols?"

Lord Gensifer sipped his punch. "I should think that if all goes well, and if you are playing for the club, you should take nine thousand ozols in booty in a very short time."

"In other words—you won't advance me the money?"

Lord Gensifer held up his hands. "Do you imagine that ozols grow on trees? I need money as badly as anyone. In fact—well, I won't go into details."

"If you're all that short of money, how can you finance a treasure-box?"

Lord Gensifer airily flicked his fingers. "No difficulty there. Whatever funds are jointly available we'll use—your three thousand ozols as well. It's all for the common cause."

Glinnes could hardly believe his hears. "My three thousand ozols? You want me to advance the fund? While you take an owner's share of booty?"

Lord Gensifer, smiling, leaned back in his chair. "Why not? Each contributes his best and his most, and each of us profits. That's the only way to operate. There's no reason to be scandalized."

Glinnes replaced his goblet on the tray. "It's just not done. The players contribute their skills, the club funds the treasure-box. I wouldn't give you an ozol; I'd organize my own team first."

"Just a moment. Perhaps we can work out a procedure that will please us all. Frankly, I'm short of cash. You need twelve thousand ozols within the year; your three thousand is worthless without the other nine."

"Not exactly worthless. It represents ten years' service in the Whelm."

Lord Gensifer waved aside the remark. "Suppose that you advance three thousand ozols to the fund. The first three thousand ozols we earn will go to you; you'll have your money back, and then—"

"The other players wouldn't allow such an arrangement."

Lord Gensifer pulled at his lower lip. "Well, the money could come from the club's share of the booty—in other words, out of my personal purse."

"Suppose there isn't any purse; suppose we lose my three thousand ozols? Then what? Nothing!"

"We don't plan to lose. Think positive, Glinnes."

"I'm thinking positively about my money."

Lord Gensifer heaved a deep sigh. "As I say, my own financial status is at the moment up in the air . . . Suppose that we make this arrangement. You advance three thousand ozols to the club treasury. We will at first try for five-thousand-ozol teams, which we should handily demolish, and build up the treasury to ten thousand ozols. We then schedule ten-thousand ozol teams. At this point booty will be distributed and you will be repaid from the club's share—the work of a game or two. Thenceforth I will lend you half the club's share until you have your nine thousand ozols, which you can thereupon repay from your ordinary share."

Glinnes tried to calculate in his head. "I don't understand any of this. You've left me far behind."

"It's simple. If we win five ten-thousand-ozol games, you have your money."

"If we win. If we lose, I have nothing. Not even the three thousand that I have now."

Lord Gensifer flourished his list of names. "This team won't lose games, I assure you of that."

"You don't have that team! You don't have a fund. You don't even have a sheirl."

"No lack of applicants there, my boy. Not for the Fleharish Gorgons! I've already talked to a dozen beautiful creatures."

"All certified, no doubt."

"We'll certify them, never fear! But what a ridiculous business! A naked virgin looks like any other naked girl. Who's to know the difference?"

"The team. Irrational, I agree, but hussade is an irrational game."

"I'll drink to that," declared Lord Gensifer rather boisterously. "Who cares a fig for rationality? Only Fanschers and Trevanyi!"

Glinnes drained his goblet and rose to his feet. "I must be on my way home and see to my personal Trevanyi. Glay gave them the freedom of Rabendary and they plundered in all directions."

Lord Gensifer nodded sagely. "You can't give a Trevanyi anything but what he'll take double for contempt . . . Well, to revert to the three thousand ozols, what is your decision?"

"I'll want to consider the matter very carefully indeed. As for that list of players—how many have actually committed themselves?"

"Well—several."

"I'll talk to them all and learn if they're really serious."

Lord Gensifer frowned. "Hmm. Let's think this over a bit. In fact, will you stay for a bite of dinner? I'm quite alone tonight, and I detest dining in solitude."

"That's very kind of you, Lord Gensifer, but I'm hardly dressed for dinner at a manor."

Lord Gensifer made a deprecatory motion. "Tonight we'll dine informally—although I could lend you formal kit, if you insisted."

"Well, no. I'm not that meticulous, if you're not."

"Tonight we'll dine as we are. Perhaps you'd like to watch more of the championship game."

"As a matter of fact, I would."

"Good. Rallo! Fresh punch! This has lost its zest."

The great oval dinner table was set for two. Lord Gensifer and Glinnes faced each other across the expanse of white linen; silver and crystal glittered under the blaze of a chandelier.

"It may seem strange to you," said Lord Gensifer, "that I can live in what might seem extravagant style and still be strapped for cash. But it's simple enough. My income derives from invested capital, and I've had reverses. Starmenters looted a pair of warehouses and set my company back on its heels. Strictly temporary, of course, but for the moment my income just barely matches my outgo. Do you know of Bela Gazzardo?"

"I've heard the name. A starmenter?"

"The villain who cut my income in half. The Whelm can't seem to come to grips with him."

"Sooner or later he'll be taken. Only inconspicuous starmenters survive. When they attain reputation their number is up."

"Bela Gazzardo's been starmenting for many years," said Lord Gensifer. "The Whelm is always in a different sector."

"Sooner or later he'll be taken."

Dinner proceeded, a repast of a dozen excellent courses, each accompanied by flasks of fine wine. Glinnes reflected that life in a manor was not without its pleasant aspects, and his fancy roamed the future, when he had earned twenty or thirty thousand ozols, or a hundred thousand, and Lute Casagave had been expelled from Ambal Isle and the manse was empty. Then, what an adventure to renew, redecorate, refurnish! Glinnes saw himself in stately garments entertaining a throng of notables at a table like Lord Gensifer's . . . Glinnes laughed inwardly at the thought. Who would he invite to his dinner parties? Akadie? Young Harrad? Carbo Gilweg? The Drossets? Though for a fact Duissane would look extraordinarily lovely in such surroundings. Glinnes' imagination included the rest of the family and the picture burst.

Dusk had long since waned when Glinnes finally climbed into his boat. The night was clear; overhead hung a myriad stars, magnified to the size of lamps. Elevated by the wine, by the large prospects that Lord Gensifer had suggested, by the halcyon beauty of starlight on calm black water, Glinnes sent his boat scudding across Fleharish Broad and up Selma Water. Under the glorious Trullion night his problems dissolved into wisps of unreasonable petulance. Glay and Fanscherade? A fad, an antic, a trifle. Marucha and her foolishness? Let her be, let her be; what better occupation lay open to her? Lord Gensifer and his crafty proposals? They might just eventuate as Lord Gensifer hoped! But the absurdity of it all! Instead of borrowing nine thousand ozols, he had barely escaped with his own three thousand intact!

Lord Gensifer's schemes no doubt derived from a desperate need of money, thought Glinnes. No matter how affable and how ostensibly candid, Lord Gensifer was still a man to be dealt with most carefully.

Up narrow Selma Water drifted the boat, past hushberry brakes and bowers of soft white lanting, then out upon Ambal Broad, where a small breeze shivered the star-reflections into a tinkling twinkling carpet. To the right stood Ambal Isle, surmounted by fanzaneel frond-clusters; they lay on the sky like splashes of black ink. And there ahead—Rabendary Island, dear Rabendary, and his home dock. The house showed no light. Was no one at home? Where was Marucha? Visiting friends, most likely.

The boat coasted up to the dock. Glinnes climbed up on the groaning old boards, made fast the boat, walked up the path to the house.

A creak of leather, a shuffle of steps. Shadows moved; dark shapes occulted the stars. Heavy objects struck down upon his head and neck and shoulders, thudding and jarring, grinding his teeth, grating his vertebrae, filling his nose with an ammoniacal reek. He fell to the ground. Heavy blows struck into his ribs, his head; the impacts rumbled and groaned like thunder and filled the total space of the world. He tried to roll away, to curl into a knot, but his senses wandered away.

The kicking ceased; Glinnes floated on a cloud of enervation. From far far away he noticed hands exploring his person. A harsh whisper rang in his brain: "Get the knife, get the knife." Further touches, then another flurry of kicks. From a great distance Glinnes thought to hear a trill of reckless laughter. Consciousness fragmented like droplets of mercury; Glinnes lay in a torpor.

Time passed; the carpet of stars slid across the sky. Slowly, slowly, from many directions, the components of consciousness began to wander back together.

Something strong and cold seized Glinnes' ankle, drew him down the path toward the water. Glinnes groaned and spread out his fingers to clutch the sod, without effect. He kicked with all his strength and struck into something pulply. The grip on his ankle loosened. Glinnes painfully hunched up on hands and knees and crawled back up the path. The merling came after him and resumed its grip. Glinnes again kicked out and the merling croaked in annoyance.

Glinnes rolled weakly over. Under the Trullion starblaze man and merling confronted each other. Glinnes began to slide back on his haunches, a foot at a time. The merling hopped forward. Glinnes' back struck the steps leading up to the verandah. Underneath were fence-staves cut from prickle bush. Glinnes turned and groped; his fingers touched one of the staves. The merling snatched and once more dragged him toward the water. Glinnes thrashed like a grounded fish, and breaking free, struggled back to the verandah. The merling uttered a dismal croak and jumped forward, Glinnes grasped a stave and thrust it at the creature's groin; it sagged away. Glinnes hunched himself up on the stairs, stave ready; the merling dared approach no further. Glinnes crawled into the house, forced himself to stand erect. He tottered to the light-switch, and brought glow into the house. He stood swaying. His head throbbed, his eyes refused to focus. Breathing tore at his ribs; conceivably several were broken. His thighs ached where his attackers had sought to make pulp of his crotch, failing only for the poor illumination. A new and sharper pang struck him; he felt for his wallet. Nothing. He looked down at his boot scabbard; his marvelous proteum knife was gone.

Glinnes sighed in fury. Who had done this? He suspected the Drossets. Recalling the tinkle of merry laughter, he was certain.

CHAPTER 8

I n the morning Marucha had not yet arrived home; Glinnes presumed that she spent the night with a lover. Glinnes was happy that she was not on hand; she would have analyzed every aspect of his folly, for which he was not in the mood.

Glinnes lay on the couch, aching in every bone, sweating with hatred for the Drossets. He staggered into the bathroom, examined his purple face. In the cabinet he found a pain-relieving potion, with which he dosed himself, then limped back to the couch.

He dozed off and on throughout the morning. At noon the telephone chime sounded. Glinnes stumbled across the room and spoke into the mesh, without showing his face to the screen. "Who's calling?"

"This is Marucha," came his mother's clear voice. "Glinnes—are you there?"

"Yes, I'm here."

"Well then, show yourself; I detest speaking to persons I can't see."

Glinnes fumbled around with the vision-push. "The button seems to be stuck. Can you see me?"

"No, I cannot. Well, it doesn't matter. Glinnes, I've come to a decision. Akadie has long wanted me to share his home, and now that you are back and presently will be bringing a woman into the house, I have agreed to the arrangement."

Glinnes only half-restrained a mournful chuckle. How his father Jut would have roared in wrath! "My best wishes for your happiness, Mother, and please convey my respects to Akadie."

Marucha peered into the screen. "Glinnes, your voice sounds strange. Are you well?"

"Yes, indeed—just a bit hoarse. After you've settled yourself I'll come over for a visit."

"Very well, Glinnes. Do take care of yourself, and please don't be too stern with the Drossets. If they want to stay on Rabendary, where is the harm in it?"

"I'll certainly consider your advice, Mother."

"Good-bye, Glinnes." The screen faded.

Glinnes heaved a deep sigh and winced for the zig-zags of pain across his ribs. Were any broken? He explored with his fingers, prodding the most tender areas, and could come to no decision.

He took a bowl of porridge out on the verandah and ate a dreary meal. The Drossets, of course, had departed, leaving a litter of rubbish, a pile of dead foliage, a dispirited outhouse of branches and fronds to mark the site of their camp. Three thousand four hundred ozols they had earned by their night's work, as well as the pleasure of punishing their persecutor. The Drossets were well-pleased today.

Glinnes went to the telephone and called Egon Rimbold, the medical practitioner in Saurkash. He explained something of his difficulties and Rimbold agreed to pay him a visit.

Limping out to the verandah, Glinnes lowered himself into one of the old string chairs. The view as always was placid. Pearl-colored haze obscured the distance; Ambal seemed a floating fairy island. His mind drifted . . . Marucha, ostensibly disdainful of aristocratic ritual, had become a hussade princess, risking the poignant humiliation—or was it glory?—of public exposure in the hope that she might make an aristocratic marriage. She had settled for the Squire of Rabendary, Jut Hulden. Perhaps at the back of her mind had lurked the image of Ambal Manor, where nothing could have persuaded Jut to live . . . Jut was dead; Ambal had been sold and Marucha now found nothing on Rabendary to keep her . . . To regain Ambal Isle he could repay twelve thousand ozols to Casagave and tear up the contract. Or he could prove Shira's death, whereupon the transaction became illegal. Twelve thousand ozols were hard to come by, and a man taken down to the merling's dinner table left few traces . . . Glinnes hunched around to look along the path. There: where the Drossets had waited behind the prickle-berry hedge. There: where they had beaten him. There: the marks he had scratched into the sod. Not far beyond lay the placid surface of Farwan Water.

Egon Rimbold arrived in his narrow black runabout. "Instead of returning from wars," said Rimbold, "it appears that you've been through them."

Glinnes told him what had occurred: "I was beaten and robbed."

Rimbold looked across the meadow. "I notice that the Drossets are gone."

"Gone but not forgotten."

"Well, let's see what we can do for you."

Rimbold worked to good effect, using the advanced pharmacopoeia of Alastor and pads of adhesive constrict. Glinnes began to feel like a relatively sound man.

Packing his instruments, Rimbold asked, "I suppose you reported the attack to the constabulary?"

Glinnes blinked. "To tell the truth, the idea never occurred to me."

"It might be wise. The Drossets are a rough lot. The girl is as bad as the rest."

"I'll see to her as well as the others," said Glinnes. "I don't know how or when, but none will escape."

Rimbold made a gesture counseling moderation, or at least caution, and took his leave.

Glinnes reexamined himself in the mirror and took a glum satisfaction in his improved appearance. Returning to the verandah, and lowering himself gingerly into a chair, he considered how best to revenge himself on the Drossets. Threats and menaces might provide a temporary satisfaction, but when all was considered, they served no useful purpose.

Glinnes became restless. He limped here and there around the property and was dismayed by the neglect and dilapidation. Rabendary was disreputable even by Trill standards; Glinnes once again became angry at Glay and Marucha. Did they feel no friendliness whatever for the old home? No matter; he would set things straight, and Rabendary would be as he remembered it from his childhood.

Today he was too lame to work. With nothing better to do, he gingerly stepped into his boat and drove up Farwan Water to the Saur River, then over the top of Rabendary to Gilweg Island and the rambling old home of his friends the Gilwegs. The rest of the day was given to that typical Trill festivity which the Fanschers considered shiftless, untidy and dissolute. Glinnes became somewhat intoxicated; he sang old songs to the music of concertinas and guitars; he romped with the Gilweg girls and made himself so agreeable that the Gilwegs volunteered to come to Rabendary on the very next day to help clean up the Drosset camp.

The subject of hussade was broached. Glinnes mentioned Lord Gensifer and the Fleharish Gorgons. "So far the team is no more than a list of important names. Still, what if all became Gorgons? Stranger things have happened. He wants me at strike and I'm inclined to give it a try, if only for the sake of money."

"Bah," said Carbo Gilweg. "Lord Gensifer doesn't know wet from dry as far as hussade is concerned. And where will he find the ozols? Everyone knows that he lives from hand to mouth."

"Not so!" declared Glinnes. "I took a meal with him, and I can vouch that he stints himself very little."

"That may be, but operating an important team is another matter. He'll need uniforms, helmets, a respectable treasury—it amounts to five thousand ozols or more. I doubt if he can give substance to the idea. Who is to be his captain?"

Glinnes reflected. "I don't believe he specified a captain."

"There's a sticking point. If he recruits a reputable captain, he'll attract players more skeptical than yourself."

"Don't think me so innocent! I gave him nothing but an expression of interest."

"You'd be better off with our good old Saurkash Tanchinaros," declared Ao Gilweg.

"For a fact, we could use a pair of good forwards," said Carbo. "Our back line, if I say so myself, is as good as any, but we can't get our own men past the moat. Join the Tanchinaros! We'll sweep Jolany Prefecture clean."

"How much is your treasure?"

"We can't seem to push past a thousand ozols," Carbo admitted. "We win one, then lose one. Frankly, we've got uneven quality. Old Neronavy isn't the most inspiring captain; he never stirs from his hange, and he only knows three plays. I could go down the lineup, but it wouldn't mean much."

"You've just persuaded me to the Gorgons," said Glinnes. "I remember Neronavy from ten years ago. I'd rather have Akadie for captain."

"Apathy, torpor," said Ao Gilweg. "The group needs stirring up."

"We haven't had a pretty sheirl for two years," said Carbo. "Jenlis Wade—bland as a dead cavout. She just looked puzzled when she lost her gown. Barsilla Cloforeth—too tall and hungry. When they stripped her no one even bothered to look. Barsilla marched off in disgust."

"We have pretty sheirls here"—Ao Gilweg jerked his thumb at his daughters Rolanda and Berinda—"except that they prefer to play something other than hussade with the boys. Now they can't quite qualify."

Afternoon became avness, avness became dusk, dusk became dark, and Glinnes was persuaded to spend the night.

In the morning Glinnes returned to Rabendary and began to clear the site of the Drosset camp. A peculiar circumstance gave him pause. A hole had been dug two feet into the ground on the site of the fire. The hole was empty. Glinnes could form no sensible conjecture to account for such a hole, at the precise center of the old fire-site.

At noon the Gilwegs arrived, and two hours later every evidence of the Drosset presence had been expunged.

Meanwhile the Gilweg women prepared the best meal possible, disparaging Marucha's larder, which they considered austere. They had never cared much for Marucha to begin with; she gave herself too many airs.

The Gilwegs now knew every detail of Glinnes' troubles. They offered an amplitude of sympathy and as much conflicting advice. Ao Gilweg, the head of the family, had spoken to Lute Casagave on several occasions. "A canny character, seething with schemes! He's not out there on Ambal Isle for his health!"

"It's the usual way with off-world folk," his wife Clara declared. "I've seen many, all overwrought and anxious, fussy and fastidious. Not one knows how to live a normal life."

"Casagave is either bashful or blind," said Carbo. "If you pass his boat he never so much as lifts his head."

"He fancies himself a great noble," said Clara with a sniff. "He's far too good for us ordinary folk. We've never tasted a drop of his wine, that's for sure."

Clara's sister, Currance, asked, "Have you seen his servant? There's a sight for you! I believe he's half Polgonian ape, or some such mixture. That one will never set foot in my house, so much I swear."

"True," declared Clara. "He has the look of a villain. And never forget: birds of a feather flock together! Lute Casagave is undoubtedly as bad as his servant!"

Ao Gilweg held up his hands in remonstration. "Now, now! A moment for sensible thought! Nothing has been proved against either of these men; in fact, they're not even accused!"

"He sequestered Ambal Isle! Isn't that enough?"

"Perhaps he was misled, who knows? He might well be a just and innocent man."

"A just and innocent man would relinquish his illegal occupancy!"

"Exactly! Perhaps Lute Casagave is that man!" Ao turned to Glinnes. "Have you discussed the matter with Lute Casagave himself? I thought not."

Glinnes looked skeptically toward Ambal Isle. "I suppose I could speak to him. But one stark fact remains: Even a just man would want his twelve thousand ozols, which I am not prepared to supply."

"Refer him to Glay, to whom he paid the money," Carbo advised. "He should have assured a clear title before he closed the bargain."

"It's a strange circumstance, strange indeed . . . Unless he knew for a fact that Shira was indeed dead, which leads into a set of macabre speculations."

"Bah!" declared Ao Gilweg. "Take the bull by the horns; go speak to the man. Tell him to vacate your property and go for his money to Glay, the man to whom he paid it."

"By the Fifteen Devils, you're right!" exclaimed Glinnes. "It is absolutely clear and obvious—he hasn't a leg to stand on! I'll make this clear to him tomorrow."

"Remember Shira!" spoke Carbo Gilweg. "He may be a man without restraint!"

"Best to carry a weapon," Ao Gilweg advised. "Nothing to induce humility as well as an eight-bore blaster."

"At the moment I have no weapon," said Glinnes. "Those Trevanyi villains gleaned my belongings like a rumblesnout sucking bugs from a box. Still, I doubt if I'll need weapons; if Casagave, as I hope, is a reasonable man, we'll quickly reach an understanding."

Between Rabendary dock and Ambal Isle lay only a few hundred yards of still water, a trip that Glinnes had made uncounted times. Never had it seemed so long.

Ambal Isle showed no activity; only Casagave's gray runabout indicated his presence. Glinnes moored his boat, jumped up on the dock as jauntily as his still-aching ribs permitted. As etiquette demanded, he touched the bell-button before starting up the walk.

Ambal Manor was much like Gensifer Manor: a tall white structure of extravagant complexity. Bays projected from every wall; on fluted pilasters rested the roof: four milk-glass domes and a central golden spire. No smoke issued from the chimney; no sound could be heard from within. Glinnes touched the doorbell.

A minute passed. There was movement behind a bay window; then the door opened and Lute Casagave looked forth—a man considerably older than Glinnes, thin-legged, stoop-shouldered, in a loose off-worlder's suit of gray gabardine. Silver hair hung beside a sallow face, which included a long bony nose, long gaunt cheeks, eyes like chips of cold stone. Casagave's face expressed a stern and alert intelligence, but it did not seem the face of a man who might contribute twelve thousand ozols to the cause of abstract justice.

Casagave spoke neither greeting nor question but stared silently forth, waiting for Glinnes to define the reason for his presence.

Glinnes said politely, "I'm afraid I have some bad news for you, Lute Casagave."

"You may address me as Lord Ambal."

Glinnes' mouth went slack. "'Lord Ambal'?"

"This is how I choose to be known."

Glinnes shook his head dubiously. "That's all well and good; your blood may be the noblest of Trullion. Still, you can't be Lord Ambal, because Ambal Isle is not your property. That's the bad news to which I referred."

"Who are you?"

"I am Glinnes Hulden, Squire of Rabendary, and I own Ambal Isle. You gave my brother Glay money for property he neglected to own. It's an unpleasant situation. I certainly don't intend to charge you rent for your time here, but I'm afraid you'll have to find another residence."

Casagave's eyebrows contracted; his eyes became slits. "You talk nonsense. I am Lord Ambal, the sanguineal descendant to that Lord Ambal who illegally sought to dispose of the ancestral property. The original transaction was invalid; the Hulden title was never good to begin with. Be grateful for your twelve thousand ozols; I was not obliged to pay anything."

"Now then!" cried Glinnes. "The sale was made to my great-grandfather. It was recorded with the registrar at Welgen and cannot be invalidated!"

"I'm not so sure of that," said Lute Casagave. "You are Glinnes Hulden? This means nothing to me. Shira Hulden is the man from whom I bought the property, with your brother Glay acting as his agent."

"Shira is dead," said Glinnes. "The sale was fraudulent. I suggest that you make representations to Glay for your money."

"Shira is dead? How do you know?"

"He is dead, probably murdered and dragged off by the merlings."

" 'Probably'? Probably has no legal standing. My contract is sound unless you can prove otherwise, or unless you die, when the question becomes moot."

"I don't plan to die," said Glinnes.

"Who does? The event comes on us all willy-nilly."

"Do you threaten me now?"

Casagave merely gave a dry chuckle. "You are trespassing on Ambal Isle; you have ten seconds to remove yourself."

Glinnes's voice shook with rage. "The shoe is on the other foot. I provide you three days, and three days only, to get off my property."

"And then?" Lute Casagave's voice was sardonic.

"Never mind what then. Get off Ambal Isle or you'll learn."

Casagave gave a shrill whistle. Footsteps thudded; behind Glinnes appeared a man seven feet tall, weighing perhaps three hundred pounds. His skin was the color of teak; black hair clung to his head like fur. Casagave jerked his thumb toward the dock. "Either in your boat or into the water."

Glinnes, still sore from a previous beating, did not care to risk another. He turned on his heel and stalked down the path. Lord Ambal? What a travesty! So this had been the motivation for Casagave's researches.

The boat took Glinnes out upon the water. He slowly circled Ambal Isle; never had it seemed so lovely. What if Casagave ignored the three-day deadline—as he was sure to do? Glinnes gave his head a dreary shake. Force would bring him afoul of the constabulary—unless he could prove Shira's death.

CHAPTER 9

A kadie lived in a quaint old manse on a point of land known as Rorquin's Tooth overlooking Clinkhammer Broad, several miles northwest of Rabendary. Rorquin's Tooth was a jut of weathered black stone, perhaps the stump of an ancient volcano, now overgrown with jard, fire-blossom, and dwarf pomanders; at the back rose a copse of sentinellos. Akadie's manse, the folly of a long-forgotten lord, raised five towers to the sky, each of different height and architectural order. One was roofed with slate, another with tile, a third with green glass, the fourth with lead, the fifth with the artificial material spandex. Each supported at its summit a study, with special appurtenances and outlooks to suit one or another of Akadie's moods. Akadie recognized and enjoyed each of his own quirks and made a virtue of inconsistency.

In the early morning, while the haze still swirled in wisps, Glinnes drove his boat north up Farwan Water and the Saur, then west along narrow weed-choked Vernice Water into Clinkhammer Broad. Reflected double upon the smooth water stood Akadie's five-towered manse.

Akadie had only just arisen from his bed. His hair was rumpled into wisps; his eyes were barely half-open. Nevertheless he gave Glinnes an affable good-morning. "Please do not expound your business before breakfast; the world is not yet in focus."

"I came to see Marucha," said Glinnes. "I am not in need of your services."

"In that case, talk as you will."

Marucha, always an early riser, seemed taut and peevish, and greeted Glinnes without effusiveness. She served Akadie a breakfast of fruit, tea and buns, and poured Glinnes tea.

"Ah!" said Akadie, "the day begins, and once again I will concede that a world exists beyond the confines of this room." He sipped his tea. "And how go your affairs?"

"As well as could be expected. My troubles have not disappeared at a snap of the fingers."

"Sometimes," Akadie observed, "a person's troubles are only those which he creates for himself."

"This is absolutely true in my case," said Glinnes. "I strive to recover my property and protect what is left, and in so doing I stimulate my enemies."

Marucha, working in the kitchen, showed elaborate disdain for the conversation.

Glinnes went on. "The basic culprit is of course Glay. He worked a world of mischief, then walked away from the mess. I consider him a poor excuse for a Hulden, and for a brother."

Marucha could no longer contain her tongue. "I doubt if he cares whether he's a Hulden or not. As far as brotherhood is concerned the relationship extends in both directions. You are not helping him in his work, let me remind you."

"It costs too much," said Glinnes. "Glay can afford gifts of twelve thousand ozols because the money never belonged to him. I saved only thirty-four hundred ozols, which Glay's cronies the Drossets took from me. I now have nothing."

"You have Rabendary Island. That is a great deal."

"At last you acknowledge Shira's death."

Akadie held up his hand. "Now then! Let us take our tea up to the South Vantage. Come along up the stairs, but take care; the treads are narrow."

They mounted into the lowest and most spacious tower, which afforded a view over all of Clinkhammer Broad. Akadie had hung antique gonfalons about the dark paneling; a collection of eccentric red stoneware pots stood in a corner. Akadie put teapot and cups on the withe table and motioned Glinnes to pull up one of the fan-backed old withe chairs. "When I enticed Marucha into the house I did not expect a complement of family dissensions as well."

"Perhaps this morning I am a trifle out of sorts," Glinnes admitted. "The Drossets waylaid me in the dark, thrashed me soundly, and took all my money. For this reason I can't sleep of nights; my insides seethe and boil and twist with rage."

"An exasperation, to say the least. Are you planning counter-measures?"

Glinnes gave him an incredulous glare. "I plan nothing else! But nothing seems sensible. I could kill one or two Drossets, end up on the prutanshyr, and still lack my money. I could drug their wine and search their camp while they slept, but I have no such drug, and even if I had, how could I be sure that all had drunk the wine?"

"These feats are easier planned than accomplished," said Akadie. "But allow me a suggestion. Do you know the Glade of Xian?"

"I have never visited the place," said Glinnes. "It is the Trevanyi burial ground, so I understand."

"It is much more than that. The Bird of Death flies from the Vale of Xian, and the dying man hears its song. Trevanyi ghosts walk in the shade of the great ombrils, which grow nowhere else in Merlank. Now—and here is the point—if you located the Drosset crypt and secured one of the death urns, Vang Drosset would sacrifice his daughter's chastity to get it back."

"I am uninterested—or let us say, barely interested—in his daughter's chastity. I merely require my money. Your idea has merit."

Akadie made a deprecatory gesture. "You are very kind. But the proposal is as inept and hallucinatory as any of the others. The difficulties are
insuperable. For instance, how could you learn the location of the crypt
except from Vang Drosset? If he loved you well enough to confide this basic
secret of his existence, why would he deny you your ozols and the accommodation of his daughter as well? But assume you so beguiled Vang Drosset
that he told his secret and you went to the Vale of Xian. How would you
evade the Three Crones, not to mention the ghosts?"

· "I don't know," said Glinnes.

The two men sat in silence, sipping tea. After a moment Akadie asked,
"Have you made the acquaintance of Lute Casagave?"

"Yes. He refuses to leave Ambal Isle."

"Predictably. He would at least want his twelve thousand ozols back."

"He claims to be Lord Ambal."

Akadie sat up in his chair, eyes dancing with speculation. Here, for
Akadie, was a truly fascinating concept. Somewhat regretfully, he shook
his head and settled back into the chair. "Unlikely. Very unlikely. And
irrelevant in any case. I fear that you must resign yourself to the loss of
Ambal Isle."

"I can't resign myself to losing anything!" cried Glinnes in a passion.
"A hussade game, Ambal Isle: it's all the same. I'll never give up; I must
have what is due me!"

Akadie held up his hand. "Calm yourself. I will consider at leisure and
who knows what will occur? The fee is fifteen ozols."

"Fifteen ozols!" demanded Glinnes. "For what? All you did was tell me
to be calm."

Akadie made a suave gesture. "I gave you that negative advice which
often is as valuable as a positive program. For instance, suppose you asked
me: 'How can I leap from here to Welgen in a single bound?' I could utter
one word, 'Impossible!' to save you a great deal of useless exercise, and thus
justify a fee of twenty or thirty ozols."

Glinnes smiled grimly. "In the matter at hand, you save me no useless
exercise; you have told me nothing I don't know already. You must consider this a social call."

Akadie shrugged. "It is of no consequence."

The two men returned to the lower floor, where Marucha sat reading a
journal published in Port Maheul: *Interesting Activities of the Elite.*

"Good-bye, Mother," said Glinnes. "Thank you for the tea."

Marucha looked up from the journal. "You're more than welcome, of
course." She began to read once more.

As Glinnes drove back across Clinkhammer Broad, he wondered why
Marucha disliked him, though in his heart he knew the answer well
enough. Marucha did not dislike Glinnes; she disliked Jut and his "gross

behavior"—his carousing, bellowed songs, rude amorousness, and general lack of elegance. In short, she considered her husband a boor. Glinnes, though far more gracious and easy than his father, reminded her of Jut. There could never be real warmth between them. Good enough, thought Glinnes; he wasn't especially fond of Marucha either . . .

Glinnes turned the boat into Zeur Water, which bounded the Prefecture Commons on the northeast. On impulse he slowed and turned into the shore. Nosing his boat through the reeds, he made it fast to the crook of a casammon tree, and clambered up the bank to where he could look across the island.

Three hundred yards away, beside a copse of black candlenuts, the Drossets had pitched their three tents—the same rectangles of orange, dirty maroon, and black that had offended Glinnes' eyes on Rabendary. On a bench Vang Drosset sat hunched over a fruit of some kind—a melon, or perhaps a *cazaldo*. Tingo, wearing a lavender headkerchief, squatted beside the fire, chopping up tubers and throwing them into the caldron. The sons Ashmor and Harving were not in evidence, nor was Duissane.

Glinnes watched for five minutes. Vang Drosset finished the *cazaldo* and flung the husk at the fire. Then, hands on knees, he turned and spoke to Tingo, who continued her work.

Glinnes jumped down the bank to his boat and drove home at full speed.

An hour later he returned. During Glay's sojourning with the Trevanyi he had used their costume; these garments Glinnes now wore, as well as a Trevanyi turban. A young cavout lay on the floor of the boat, head muffled and legs tied. The boat also carried three empty cartons, several good iron pots, and a shovel.

Glinnes took the boat to where he had previously run it ashore. He climbed up the bank and observed the Drosset camp through binoculars. The caldron simmered over the fire. Tingo was nowhere to be seen. Vang Drosset sat on the bench carving a dako burl. Glinnes stared intently. Would Vang Drosset be using his knife? Chips and shavings effortlessly departed the dako, and Vang Drosset approvingly examined the knife from time to time.

Glinnes brought the cavout up from the boat and, removing the muffle, tethered the creature by one hind leg so that it might wander a few yards out upon the common.

Glinnes concealed himself behind a clump of hushberry, where he muffled the lower part of his face in the loose tail of the turban.

Vang Drosset carved the dako. He paused, stretched his arms, and noted the cavout. He watched it a moment, then, rising to his feet, scrutinized the entire common. No one in sight. He wiped the knife and tucked it into his boot. Tingo Drosset put her head from the tent; Vang Drosset had a word with her. She came forth and looked dubiously at the cavout. Vang Drosset set off across the common, walking with an air of furtive purpose. Ten yards from the cavout he seemed to see it for the first time, and halted as if in wonder. He noticed the tether and traced it to the casammon tree. He took four quiet steps forward, craning his neck. He saw the boat and stopped short, while his eyes performed an inventory of its contents. A shovel, several useful pots, and what might those cartons contain? He licked his lips, looked sharply right and left. Peculiar. Probably the work of a child. Still, why not take a look in the cartons? Certainly no harm in a look.

Vang Drosset walked cautiously down the bank, and he never knew what struck him. Glinnes, fury surging in his veins, leapt forth and almost tore Vang Drosset's head off with a pair of tremendous blows over each ear. Vang Drosset fell to the ground. Glinnes pushed his face into the mud, tied his hands behind his back, lashed his knees and ankles with a length of rope he had brought for the purpose. Then he gagged and blindfolded Vang Drosset, who was now uttering stertorous moans.

He brought the knife from Vang Drosset's black boot: his own. A delight to have the keen blade once more in his possession! He searched Vang Drosset's garments, slicing them with the knife to facilitate examination. Vang Drosset's purse held only twenty ozols, which Glinnes appropriated. He pulled off Vang Drosset's boots and sliced open the soles. He found nothing and threw the boots away.

Vang Drosset carried no large sum of money on his person. Glinnes gave him a kick in the ribs for disappointment. He looked across the commons to observe Tingo Drosset on her way to the outhouse. Glinnes hoisted the cavout to his shoulder, concealing his face, and marched across the commons. He reached the maroon tent just as Tingo Drosset had completed her errand. He looked into the maroon tent. Empty. He walked to the orange tent. Empty. He stepped inside. Tingo Drosset spoke to his back: "Looks to be a good beast. But don't take it inside! What's the matter with you? Slaughter it down by the water."

Glinnes put down the animal and waited. Tingo Drosset, expostulating over the strange behavior of her husband, entered the tent. Glinnes threw his turban over her head and bore her to the ground. Tingo Drosset squawked and cursed at this unexpected act of her husband's.

"Another sound from you," growled Glinnes, "I'll slit your throat ear to ear! Lie quiet if you know what's good for you!"

"Vang! Vang!" screeched Tingo Drosset. Glinnes thrust the tail of the turban into her mouth.

Tingo was squat and sturdy and caused Glinnes considerable exertion before she lay helplessly tied, blindfolded, and gagged. Glinnes' hand smarted from a bite. Tingo Drosset's head ached from the retaliatory blow. Not likely that Tingo Drosset would carry the family money, but stranger things had happened. Glinnes gingerly examined her garments while she groaned and grunted, thrashed and jerked in horrified outrage, expecting the worst.

He searched the black tent, then the orange tent, in a corner of which Duissane had ranged a few trinkets and keepsakes, and last the maroon tent. He found no money, nor had he expected to; the Trevanyi habit was to bury their valuables.

Glinnes seated himself on Vang Drosset's bench. Where would he bury money, were he Vang Drosset? The location must be convenient to hand and unmistakably identified by some sort of indicator: a post, a rock, a bush, a tree. The spot would be somewhere within the immediate field of vision; Vang Drosset would like to keep the hiding place under his benign surveillance. Glinnes looked here and there. Directly in front of him the caldron hung over the fire, with a rude table and a pair of benches to the side. Only a few feet away the ground had been seared by the heat of another fire. The old fire-site seemed a few steps more convenient than the spot where the caldron now hung. No explanation for the peculiar habits of the Trevanyi, thought Glinnes. At the camp on Rabendary . . . The thought trailed off as Glinnes recalled the camp on Rabendary Island, with the ground freshly dug on the site of the campfire.

Glinnes nodded sagely. Just so. He rose to his feet and walked to the fire. He moved tripod and caldron, and using an old broken-hafted spade, thrust the fire aside. The baked soil below yielded easily. Six inches below the surface the spade scraped on a black iron plate. Glinnes tipped up the iron to reveal a cake of dry clay, which he also removed. The cavity below held a pottery jar. Glinnes drew forth the jar. It contained a bundle of red and black hundred-ozol notes. Glinnes nodded complacently and tucked all in his pocket.

The cavout, now grazing, had defecated. Glinnes scraped the droppings into the pottery jar, replaced it in the cavity, and arranged all as before, with the fire burning under the caldron. To casual inspection, nothing had been disturbed.

Shouldering the cavout, Glinnes strode back across the common to where he had left his boat. Vang Drosset had been struggling to free himself, to no avail, and had only rolled himself down the slope into the mud at the water's edge. Glinnes smiled with indulgent amusement, and with all Vang Drosset's wealth in his pocket forbore kicking the contorted shape. He tethered the cavout in the stern of the boat and cast off. A hundred yards along the shore a giant casammon tree sprawled its twisted branches over the water. Glinnes drove the boat through the reeds to one of the crooked roots, made fast the painter, then climbed from the root into the branches. Through a gap in the foliage he could see the Drosset camp, which appeared quiet.

Glinnes made himself comfortable and counted the money. In the first bundle he reckoned three thousand-ozol certificates, four hundreds, and six tens. Glinnes chuckled in satisfaction. He removed the band from the second bundle, which was wound around a golden fob: fourteen hundred-ozol certificates. Glinnes paid them no heed, staring instead at the golden fob, eery chills tickling his back. The fob he remembered well; it had belonged to his father. There: ideograms for the name Jut Hulden. And below, a second set of ideograms: Shira Hulden.

There were two possibilities: the Drossets had either robbed Shira alive, or they had robbed him dead. And these were the boon comrades of his brother Glay! Glinnes spat toward the ground.

He sat now on the branch, his brain roiling with excitement and horrified disgust. Shira was dead. The Drossets could never have taken his money otherwise. This was now his conviction.

He sat watching and waiting. His euphoria waned and also his horror; he sat passively. An hour passed and part of another. Up from the dock on Ilfish Water came three persons: Ashmor, Harving, and Duissane. Ashmor and Harving went directly to the orange tent; Duissane stood still, apparently hearing a sound from Tingo. She ran into the maroon tent and instantly pushed her head out to call her brothers. She disappeared once more into the tent. Ashmor and Harving joined her. Five minutes later they slowly emerged in voluble conversation. Tingo, apparently none the worse for her experience, came forth. She pointed across the common. Ashmor and Harving set off, and in due course found and released Vang Drosset. The three returned across the common, the sons talking and gesticulating. Vang Drosset hobbling on bare feet, holding his tattered clothing close about himself. At the camp he looked all about, and especially he studied the fire. Apparently it had not been disturbed.

He went into the maroon tent. The sons stood arguing with Tingo, who was now making hysterical expostulations, pointing across the common. Vang Drosset came forth from the maroon tent, once more fully clad. He marched up to Tingo and cuffed her; she drew back bawling in anger. He came for her again; she seized a stout branch and stood her ground; Vang Drosset turned gloomily away. He went to look more closely at the campfire, bent his head sharply and saw embers and ashes where Glinnes had shifted the fire. He gave a hoarse call, audible to Glinnes in the tree. Jerking the tripod aside, he kicked the fire flying, and with his bare fingers tore up the iron plate. Then the clay block. Then the pottery jar. He looked within. He looked up at Ashmor and Harving, who stood by expectantly.

Vang Drosset raised his arms high in a magnificent gesture of despair. He dashed the pot to the ground; he jumped up and down on the shards; he kicked the fire and sent the brands flying; he held aloft his knotted arms and raved curses to all directions of the compass.

Now was the time to depart, thought Glinnes. He slipped down from the tree, stepped into his boat, and drove back to Rabendary Island. A highly satisfactory day. The Trevanyi garments had guarded his identity; the Drossets might suspect, but they could not know. At this moment all the Trevanyi of the region were suspect, and the Drossets would sleep little this night as they debated the culpability of each.

Glinnes prepared himself a meal and ate out on the verandah. Afternoon became avness, that melancholy dying-time of day, when all the sky and far spaces became suffused with the color of watered milk.

The chime of the telephone provided a sudden discord. Glinnes went within to find the face of Thammas, Lord Gensifer, looking forth from the screen. Glinnes touched the vision-push button. "Good afternoon, Lord Gensifer."

"A good afternoon to you, Glinnes Hulden! Are you ready to play hussade? I don't mean at this very instant, of course."

Glinnes responded with a cautious question of his own. "I take it your plans have matured?"

"Yes. The Fleharish Gorgons are now organized and ready to begin practice. I have your name penciled in at right strike."

"And who is left strike?"

Lord Gensifer looked down at his list. "A very promising young man by the name of Savat. You two should make a brilliant combination."

"Savat? I've never heard of him. Who are the wings?"

"Lucho and Helsing."

"Hmm. None of these names are familiar. Are these the players you originally had in mind?"

"Lucho, of course. As for the others—well, that list was always tentative, to be amended whenever something better could be arranged. As you well know, Glinnes, some of these established players are fairly inflexible. We're better off with people willing and anxious to learn. Enthusiasm, zest, dedication! These are the qualities that make for winning!"

"I see. Who else has signed up?"

"Iskelatz and Wilmer Guff are the rovers—how does that sound? You won't find two better rovers in the prefecture. The guards—Ramos is a crackerjack—and Pylan, who is also very good. Sinforetta and 'Bump' Candolf are not quite so mobile, but they are solid; no one will drive them aside. I'll play captain and—"

"Eh? What's this? Did I hear you correctly?"

Lord Gensifer frowned. "I'll play captain," he said in a measured voice. "And that more or less is the team, except for substitutes."

Glinnes was silent a moment or two. Then he asked, "What about the fund?"

"The fund will be three thousand ozols," said Lord Gensifer primly. "For the first few games we'll play a conservative fifteen hundred ozols, at least until the team jells."

"I see. When and where will you practice?"

"At Saurkash field, tomorrow morning. I take it then that you'll definitely play with the Gorgons?"

"I'll certainly come down tomorrow and we'll see how things go. But let me be candid, Lord Gensifer. A captain is the most important man on the team. He can make us or break us. We need an experienced captain. I doubt if you have that experience."

Lord Gensifer became haughty. "I have made a thorough study of the game. I've gone through Kalenshenko's *Hussade Tactics* three times; I've mastered the *Ordinary Hussade Manual*; I've explored all the latest theories, such as Counter-flow Principle, the Double Pyramid System, Overvallation—"

"All this may be true, Lord Gensifer. Many people can theorize about the game, but the reflexes are ultimately important, and unless you've played a great deal—"

Lord Gensifer said stiffly, "If you'll do your best, everyone else will do theirs. Is there anything more? . . . At the fourth gong, then." The screen went dead.

Glinnes growled in dismay. For half a broken ozol he'd tell Lord Gensifer to play captain, forward, rover, guard, and sheirl together. Lord Gensifer as captain indeed!

At least he had his money back, with compensation for the beating. Almost five thousand ozols; a tidy sum, which he ought to put in a safe place.

Glinnes sealed the money in a pottery jar like that the Drossets had used. He buried it in the backyard.

An hour later a boat issued from Ilfish Water and came across Ambal Broad. Within sat Vang Drosset and his two sons. As they passed the Rabendary dock, Vang Drosset rose to his feet and scrutinized the Hulden boat with eyes like needles. Glinnes had removed all the goods with which he had tempted Vang Drosset; the boat was undistinguishable from a hundred others. Glinnes sat on the verandah, feet on the rail. Vang Drosset and his sons looked from the boat to Glinnes, eyes full of suspicion; Glinnes returned the gaze impassively.

The Drosset boat continued up Farwan Water, the Drossets muttering among themselves and looking back toward Glinnes. There went the men who had killed his brother, thought Glinnes.

Lord Gensifer, wearing a new maroon and black uniform, stood on a bench and addressed his players. "This is an important day for all of us, and for the history of hussade in Jolany Prefecture! Today we start to mold the most efficient, adroit, and ruthless team ever to ravage the hussade fields of Merlank. Some of you are proficient already, with reputations; others are still unknown—"

Glinnes, considering the fifteen men around him, reflected that the proportion of these two sorts was on the order of one in eight.

"—but by dint of dedication, discipline, and sheer"—here Lord Gensifer used the word *kercha'an*: effort conducing to superhuman feats of strength and will—"we will sweep all before us! We'll expose the fundament of every virgin between here and Port Jaime! We'll carry booty home in buckets; we'll be rich and famous, one and all! . . .

"But first the toil and sweat of preparation. I have diligently researched the theory of hussade; I know Kalenshenko word for word. Everyone agrees: Defeat your opponent's strength and you've got the gold ring in your grasp. That means we must out-leap and out-swing the best forwards around; we've got to tub the sternest guards of Jolany; we've got to out-think the craftiest strategists of Trullion! . . .

"Now to work. I want the forwards to criss-cross the tanks, buffing* three procedures at each station. Establish a rhythm, you forwards! The rovers will go through standard drill, and the guards as well. We've got to master the fundamentals! I'd like to think that instead of two rovers and four guards, we have six agile powerful rovers all over the back stations, capable at any time of ramming home the piston." Lord Gensifer here alluded to the tactic of a strong team sweeping a weaker team ahead of it up the field. "All to work! Let's drill like men inspired!"

So the practice began, with Lord Gensifer running here and there, praising, criticizing, castigating, stimulating his team with shrill *ki-yik-yik-yiks*.

Twenty minutes later Glinnes had gauged the quality of the team. Left wing Lucho and right rover Wilmer Guff had been components of that hypothetical team Lord Gensifer had proposed to Glinnes, and were both excellent players—deft, sure, aggressive. Left rover Iskelatz also seemed a sound player, if of a self-contained, even surly, disposition. Iskelatz clearly

---

*buff: a three-foot padded club, used to thrust opponents into the tanks.

disliked strenuous practice and preferred to reserve his best energies for the game itself, a trait which almost immediately exasperated Lord Gensifer. Left strike Savat and right wing Helsing were young men, alert, active, but somewhat raw, and during buff-drill Glinnes continually feinted them off balance. Guards Ramos, Pylan, and Sinforetta were, respectively, slow, inept, and overweight; only left middle guard "Bump" Candolf combined sufficient mass, strength, cleverness and agility to qualify as an able athlete. A hussade truism asserted that a poor forward might defeat a poor guard but a good guard would restrain a good forward. A team lived by its forwards and died by its guards—so stated another aphorism of the game. Glinnes foresaw a number of long afternoons unless Lord Gensifer were able to strengthen his back-field.

The Gorgons, then, in their present phase, fielded a fair front line, a sound center, and a weak back-field. Lord Gensifer's capacity as captain was difficult to assess. The ideal captain, like the ideal rover, could play at any station of the field, though some captains, like old Neronavy of the Tanchinaros, never left the protection of their hanges.

In regard to Lord Gensifer, Glinnes reserved judgment. He seemed quick and strong enough, if somewhat overweight and sluggish on the swings . . .

Lord Gensifer uttered one of his *ki-yik-yik-yiks*. "You forwards there! Zest now, let's see those feet twinkle; are you a quartet of bears? Glinnes, must you caress Savat so lovingly with your buff? If he can't block you let him feel it! And you guards—let's see you prance! Knees bent, like angry animals! Remember, every time they take hold of that gold ring it costs us money . . . Better . . . Let's run through a few plays. First the Center Jet Series from the Lantoun System . . . "

The team drilled for two hours in an amiable spirit, then halted for lunch at The Magic Tench. After lunch Lord Gensifer diagrammed a group of formations he had conceived himself, variations on the difficult Diagonal Sequences. "If we can master these patterns, we thrust irresistibly against both wings and rovers; then when they collapse inward we plunge down either the right or left land."

"All very well," said Lucho, "but notice, you leave the wing lanes unprotected, and there's not a feather to prevent a counter-plunge down our own outside lanes."

Lord Gensifer frowned. "The rovers must swing to the side in such a case. Timing here is essential."

The team ran rather languidly through Lord Gensifer's deployments, for the warm time of day had arrived and all were tired after the morning's efforts. Finally Lord Gensifer, half-exasperated, half-rueful, dismissed the team. "Tomorrow, same time; but come expecting a workout. Today was a vacation. I know only one way to field a team, and that's drill!"

Three weeks the Gorgons practiced, with uneven results. Certain of the players became bored; certain others growled and muttered at Lord Gensifer's chivvying. Glinnes considered Lord Gensifer's repertory of plays far too complicated and chancy; he felt the back-field to be too weak to allow an effective attack. The rovers were forced to protect the guards, and the forwards were therefore limited in their range. Attrition took a toll. Left rover Iskelatz, who was competent but too casual to please Lord Gensifer, resigned from the team, as did right wing Helsing, in whom Glinnes discerned the potentials for excellence. The replacements were both weaker men. Lord Gensifer dropped Pylan and Sinforetta, the two most sluggish guards, and recruited a pair only slightly better, both of whom, so Glinnes learned from Carbo Gilweg, had been unable to win places with the Saurkash Tanchinaros.

Lord Gensifer entertained the team at Gensifer Manor and introduced the Gorgon sheirl, Zuranie Delcargo from the village Puzzlewater, so named for the nearby hot sulfur springs. Zuranie was pallidly pretty, if thin, and shy to the point of speechlessness. Her personality aroused Glinnes to wonder—what force or ambition could impel such a girl to risk public exposure? Whenever she was addressed, she jerked her head away so that long blond hair fell across her face, and she spoke only three words during the course of the evening. She displayed not an inkling of *sashei*, that wild and gallant élan which inspires a team to transcend its theoretical limitations.

Lord Gensifer took the occasion to announce the schedule of forthcoming games, the first of which would take place two weeks hence at Saurkash Stadium, against the Voulash Gannets.

A day or two later Zuranie came to watch the practice. Rain had fallen during the morning and a raw wind blew out of the south. The players were glum and peevish. Lord Gensifer ran up and down the field like a great bumbling insect, expostulating, wheedling, crying "*Ki-yik-yik-yik!*" to no effect. Huddling from the wind beside the pump-man's hut, Zuranie watched the sluggish maneuvers with foreboding and despondency. At last she made a timid motion to Lord Gensifer. He jogged across the field. "Yes, sheirl?"

Zuranie spoke in a petulant voice: "Don't call me sheirl; I don't know why I ever thought I'd want to do this. Really! I could never never stand on that place, with all those people watching me. I think I would absolutely die. Please, Lord Gensifer, don't be angry, but I simply can't."

Lord Gensifer raised his eyes to the scudding gray clouds, not far overhead. "My dear Zuranie! Of course you'll be with us! We play the Voulash Gannets in two days! You'll be famous and glorified!"

Zuranie made a helpless motion. "I don't want to be a famous sheirl; I don't want all my clothes pulled off—"

"That only happens to the losing sheirl," Lord Gensifer pointed out. "Do you think the Gannets can beat us, with Tyran Lucho and Glinnes Hulden and me and Bump Candolf ranging the stations? We'll sweep them back like chaff; we'll tank them so often they'll think they are fish!"

Zuranie was only partially reassured. She gave a tremulous sigh and said no more. Lord Gensifer, at last understanding that no useful purpose could be served by prolonging the practice, called a halt. "Same time tomorrow," he told the team. "We've got to put snap into our lateral movement, especially in the back court. You guards, you've got to range the field! This is hussade, not a tea party for you and your toy animals. Tomorrow at the fourth chime."

The Voulash Gannets were a young team lacking all reputation; the players seemed striplings. The Gannet captain was Denzel Warhound, a lanky tow-headed youth with the wise sly eyes of a mythical creature. The sheirl was a buxom round-faced girl with a flying mop of dark curls; in the pregame march about the field she conducted herself with full-blooded enthusiasm, strutting, bouncing, waving her arms, and the Gannets loped along beside her, barely able to contain their nervous activity. By contrast, the Gorgons seemed stately and dour, with Sheirl Zuranie a frail asthenic wraith. Her evident despair caused Lord Gensifer an exasperation he did not dare to express for fear of demoralizing her completely. "Brave girl; there's a brave girl!" he declared as if consoling a sick animal. "It won't be all that bad; you'll see I'm right!" But Zuranie's apprehensions were not dispelled.

Today the Gorgons wore their maroon and black uniforms for the first time. The helmets were especially dramatic, molded of a dull-rose metalloid, with black fleurettes for cheek-pieces. Black spikes bristled from the scalps; the eyeholes cunningly simulated the pupils of great staring eyes; the noses split to become black plush maws, from which hung lank red tongues. Some of the team thought the costume extravagant; a few disliked the flapping tongues; most were apathetic. The Gannets wore a brown uniform with an orange helmet, distinguished only by a crest of green feathers. Contrasting the mettlesome Gannets with the splendid but sluggish Gorgons, Glinnes felt impelled to discuss tactics with Lord Gensifer.

"Notice the Gannets if you will; they're like colt kevals, full of vigor and nonsense. I've seen such teams before, and we can expect aggressive, even rash, play. Our job is to make them beat themselves. We'll want to use our traps to cut off their forwards so that our guards and rovers can double on them. If we use our weight, we've got a chance to defeat them."

Lord Gensifer raised his eyebrows in displeasure. "A chance to defeat them? What nonsense is this? We'll sweep them up and down the field like a dog chasing chickens! We shouldn't even be playing them except that we need the practice."

"Still, I advise a careful game. Let them make the mistakes, or they might make capital of ours."

"Bah, Glinnes. I believe you're past your prime."

"To the extent that I'm not playing for fun. I want to earn money—nine thousand ozols, to be exact, and I want to win."

"Do you think your need is unique?" demanded Lord Gensifer in a voice thick with rage. "How do you think I financed the treasure-box? Bought the uniforms? Paid team expenses? I drained myself bloodless."

"Very well," said Glinnes. "You need money; I need money. So let's win, by playing the game we're best able to play."

"We'll win, never fear!" declared Lord Gensifer, once again bluff and hearty. "Do you think I'm a tyro? I know the game up one side and down the other. Now enough of this wailing; I declare, you're as timid as Zuranie. Notice the crowd—a good ten thousand people. That'll add ozols to the booty!"*

Glinnes nodded gloomily. "If we win." He noticed a man sitting alone in a box at the bottom of the Elite tier; Lute Casagave, with binoculars and camera. The gear was not unusual; many devotees of the game recorded the denuding of the sheirl in music and image. Notable collections of such events existed. Nonetheless Glinnes was surprised to find in Lute Casagave so lively an interest in hussade. He seemed not the type for frivolity.

The field judge went to the microphone; the music dwindled away; a hush came over the crowd. "Sportfolk of Saurkash and Jolany Prefecture! Today a match between the gallant Voulash Gannets, and their sheirl Baroba Felice, and the indomitable Gorgons of Thammas, Lord Gensifer, with the lovely sheirl Zuranie Delcargo! The teams pledge the inviolable dignity of their sheirls with all their valor and two treasures of fifteen hundred ozols. May the winners enjoy glory and the losers take pride in their fortitude and the tragic purity of their sheirl! Captains, approach!"

Lord Gensifer and Denzel Warhound came forward. A toss of the coin gave first call to the Gorgons; open transmission for the Gorgons would be signalized by the green light, with the red light for the Gannets.

"The penalties will be called with rigor," stated the field judge. "There must be neither kicking nor pulling. No verbal interchanges. I will not tolerate buff-clinging. A blow must fall cleanly. The team on defense must utter no distracting sounds. I am experienced in these matters, as are the monitors; we will be vigilant. A player in the foul tank must clasp the hand of his rescuer; a desultory wave or gesture will not be sufficient. Have you any questions? Very good, gentlemen. Dispose your forces and may the glory

---

*Half of the gate receipts were customarily divided between the competing teams in the proportion of three parts to the winning team, one part to the losers.

of your sheirls impel you both to noble feats. The green light to the Gorgons; the red light to the Gannets!"

The team deployed to their stations; the Trevanyi orchestra played traditional music as the captains conducted the sheirls to their respective pedestals.

The music stopped. The captains went out to their hanges and now came that electric moment before the first flash of light. The spectators were silent; the players strained with tension; the sheirls stood eager and palpitant, each willing with all her heart's intensity that the detested virgin at the other end of the field be the one to be bared and humiliated.

A gong! The signal lights flashed green. For twenty seconds the Gorgon captain might call plays, while the Gannets must act or react in silence. Lord Gensifer deployed the first phase of the Jet Stream Attack: a wedge-shaped driving tactic of strikes and wings up the middle, with rovers covering the side lanes. Lord Gensifer clearly had ignored Glinnes' advice. Cursing under his breath, Glinnes moved forward; unopposed, he jumped the moat, as did left strike Savat. The Gannet forwards had all slid aside; now they leapt the moat to attack Sarkado, the Gorgons' left rover. Glinnes met the Gannet left rover; the two feinted with buffs, prodded and pushed; the Gannet rover gave way. Glinnes' instincts told him exactly when to turn to meet the rush of the Gannet right rover. Glinnes struck him across the neck while he was still off balance and toppled him into the tank. He struck water with a most satisfactory splash.

Another splash: a Gannet guard had tanked Chust, the right wing.

Lord Gensifer's voice came sharp: "Ki-yik-yik-yik! Thirteen-thirty! Go then, Glinnes; Lucho, watch the rover! Yik-ki-yik!"

The green light changed to red; now Denzel Warhound called signals and brought his hange to the moat. The middle guards jumped forward, two against Glinnes; he engaged them, hooked and thrust with such effect that they confused each other. Glinnes swung to Way 3, which was open to the pedestal, but the guards recovered; one ran to cover the mouth of Way 3. The center guards meanwhile swung behind Glinnes. He tanked one; Savat tanked the other; both turned to race for the Gannet pedestal, with only two guards left to halt them. The light changed to green; Lord Gensifer bawled desperate orders. A gong! Glinnes looked back to see a Gannet forward on the pedestal with Zuranie's gold ring in his hand. Play halted; Lord Gensifer grudgingly paid ransom to Denzel Warhound.

The teams returned to their respective territories. Lord Gensifer spoke in irritation: "Execution: that's the word! We're falling over our own feet. They're actually no match for us; they caught us by a fluke."

Glinnes restrained the old maxim: *In hussade no flukes*. He said, "Let's advance at them across the field, station by station; don't let them get back to the guards!" For the Gannets had gained the pedestal by a simple feint and whirl past the inept Ramos.

Lord Gensifer ignored Glinnes. "The Jet Stream again, and this time let's do it right! Rovers, guard the side alleys; wings, blast up the center behind the strikes. We won't let these ninny-boys tank us again!"

The team deployed; the gong sounded and the green light gave the offensive to the Gorgons. "Thirteen-thirty, *ki-yik!*" cried Lord Gensifer. "Right at 'em all the way to the belly-ring."

Again the Gannet forwards slid aside to allow Savat and Glinnes across the moat. This time, however, they swung behind Glinnes and, to his intense annoyance, tripped him. He might still have held his own except for the rover swinging in upon the trapeze to hurl him into the tank.

Glinnes above all else hated to be tanked; the process was cold and wet and injured his self-esteem. Disconsolately he waded back under the ways and squelched up the ladder to the Gorgons' base area. He surfaced at an appropriate time, engaging a Gannet wing who already had worked his way almost to the pedestal. In a wet fury, Glinnes dazed him with thrusts and feints and toppled him head over heels into the tank.

Green light on. "Forty-five-twelve," cried Lord Gensifer. Glinnes groaned—Lord Gensifer's most complicated play, the Grenade, or double diagonal. No choice but to run the play; he would do his best. The forwards came together at the moat, and finding no opposition at the center bridge, sprang across in different directions, followed by the rovers. The single faint hope of success, thought Glinnes, was to drive upon the Gannet sheirl before the startled Gannets could reach Sheirl Zuranie. The Gannet guards shifted to hold the end of the way; two rovers were tanked, a Gannet and a Gorgon; and now Lord Gensifer ordered two guards across the moat, just as the light turned red.

Denzel Warhound stood by his hange, inviolate, grinning in total composure. He called his signals. Both Gorgon guards were intercepted and tanked. Glinnes, Savat, and the wings, recognizing disaster, raced back to guard the pedestal. Glinnes reached base area just in time to drive a Gannet forward back from the pedestal and into the tank; Lucho did the same to another, but almost the whole Gannet team was storming the base area. The tanked guards surfaced, wet and angry, and by dint of fury and superior weight bore the Gannets back.

Green light. Lord Gensifer's call: "Forty-five-twelve. We've got 'em now, lads; the way is clear! Go! go!"

Glinnes, furious over the call, disengaged and ran Lord Gensifer's pattern along with the other forwards. The light but agile Gannet guards broke back and kept pace with them . . . A gong. By some miracle of stealth and agility (more likely by someone's sheer ineptitude, thought Glinnes) one of the Gannet rovers had gained the pedestal and seized the gold ring at Zuranie's waist.

With trembling fingers Lord Gensifer paid another ransom. In conference his voice was hoarse with emotion. "You men aren't executing. We can't win if everyone walks around like sleepwalkers! We've got to take the game to these fellows! Why, they're hardly more than boys! This time let's make the play go. Double diagonal again, and everyone do his duty!"

The gong, the green light, Lord Gensifer's encouraging "Ki-yik," and the Gorgons deployed in Lord Gensifer's double diagonal.

A double gong, signifying a foul. Lord Gensifer himself had clutched the buff of a Gannet rover and was consigned to the foul tank up at the back of the Gannet base, where he hunched in sullen fury. Glinnes, the right forward, became acting captain.

The gong sounded, and the light was still green. Glinnes had no need to call a play. He gestured left and right; the wings and forwards advanced to the moat. The light went red. The Gannets, elated by their two-ring score, feinted at the left and sent two forwards across at the right side-way, with a rover leaping the moat. The rover and one of the forwards were tanked; the other forward retreated, and Denzel Warhound called back his attack until the tanked man returned to action. Green light. Lord Gensifer, in the foul tank, made urgent gestures appealing for rescue; Glinnes studiously looked the other way. He pointed the rovers to the side-ways, summoned the two middle guards forward. Red light. The Gannets massed on the left but forebore to cross the moat; the crafty Denzel Warhound preferred to bide his time until he could catch the Gorgons in disequilibrium.

Green light. Glinnes sent the Gorgon forward across the moat and brought the middle guards up to the center bridge—a slow exertion of mass and pressure upon a faster but lighter team. Two Gorgon wings were tanked, and two Gannet strikes. The Gorgons had established a solid line on the Gannet side of the field, and all the while Lord Gensifer beckoned frantically for rescue. The Gorgons pressed slowly up the ways, using their weight and experience to advantage, compressing the Gannets into their base area. Three Gannets were tanked, one after the other, then two more. Then the gong sounded. Tyran Lucho had gained the pedestal, his hand on the gold ring. Grim and disapproving, Lord Gensifer came up from the foul tank and took ransom from the Gannet captain.

The teams returned to base deployment. Lord Gensifer, angry from his long confinement in the foul tank, declared, "Rash, too rash tactics! When a team is two rings down, the guards should never move so far past the moat—that's one of Kalenshenko's first dictums!"

"We took their ring," said Lucho, the most outspoken man on the team. "That's the important matter."

"Regardless," said Lord Gensifer in a steely voice, "we will continue to play a sound basic game. They have the light; we'll use the Number 4 Feint."

Lucho was not to be silenced. "Let's simply mass on the moat. We don't need traps or feints or fancy tactics—simply basic play!"

"This is a hussade game," declared Lord Gensifer, "not a gang-fight. We'll show 'em tactics to make their heads swim."

The Gannets charged the moat with reckless verve; Denzel Warhound clearly intended to forestall the Gorgon tactics of the previous period. Gannets leaped the moat all across the field, while Denzel Warhound planted his hange on the center bridge, from which he could be dislodged only by Lord Gensifer. Right wing Cherst tanked the Gannet rover and was tanked in turn; Glinnes was forced to guard the right side-way.

Green light. "Forty-five-twelve!" cried Lord Gensifer. "This time, lads! Show them class!"

"I think we'll be showing them something else," Glinnes told Wilmer Guff. "Namely, Zuranie."

"He's the captain."

"So then—here we go."

Denzel Warhound might have been anticipating this exact play. His forwards returned to trap Glinnes, and again he was tanked by a swinging rover; Lucho met a similar fate on the opposite side. Together they made the best possible haste to the ladder, only to hear the Trevanyi orchestra break into the *Ode to Beauty Jubilant.*

"And there we have it," said Glinnes.

They surfaced in time to see Denzel Warhound on the pedestal, his hand on the gold ring. Zuranie looked up into the sky with a dazed expression. "Where is your money? Five hundred ozols will save your sheirl; five hundred ozols for her pride—is this so dear?"

"I'd pay it," Glinnes remarked to Wilmer Guff, "except that it would be money thrown away. Lord Gensifer would run me back and forth through his double-diagonal till I drowned."

The music surged loud—stately cadences which tickled the hair at the nape of the neck and brought a dryness to the mouth. From the crowd came a soft sound, a fluting of exaltation. Zuranie's face was frozen in a white mask—impossible to guess her emotions. The music halted. A low-voiced gong sounded—once, twice, three times—and the captain pulled the ring. Zuranie's gown came away; her shrinking flesh was exposed on the pedestal.

At the opposite end of the field Sheirl Baroba Felice performed an impromptu jig of delight and jumped down into the arms of the Gannets, who now departed the field.

Lord Gensifer silently brought a black velvet cloak to cover Zuranie; the Gorgons also departed the field.

In the dressing room Lord Gensifer bravely broke the silence.

"Well, men, this wasn't our day—so much is clear. The Gannets are a far better team than is supposed; their speed was a bit too much for us. Everybody out to Gensifer Manor. We won't call it a victory celebration, but we'll test the color of some good Sokal wine . . ."

At Gensifer Manor, Lord Gensifer regained his composure. He circulated affably among those of his aristocratic friends who had visited the Saurkash Stadium to watch him at his latest fad. Around the loaded buffets, under the glitter of the antique chandeliers, beside the magnificent collection of Rol Star gonfalons, the banter played back and forth.

"Never expected such speed from you, Thammas, till you went to denude that bouncy little Gannet sheirl!"

"Ha ha! Yes, I'm a real pacer where the ladies are concerned!"

"We've long known Thammas to be a great sportsman, but why oh why did the Gorgons take their only ring while he sat in the tank?"

"Resting, Jones, only resting. Why work when you can sit in nice cool water?"

"Good group, Thammas, good group. Your lads do you credit. Keep them up to snuff."

"Oh I will, sir, I will. No fear of that."

The Gorgons themselves stood somewhat stiffly to the side, or perched on the delicate jadewood furniture, sipping wines they had never before tasted, giving monosyllabic answers to the questions put by Lord Gensifer's friends. Lord Gensifer finally came up and spoke to them, by now in a benign mood. "Well then—no recriminations, no reproaches. I'll state only the obvious: I see room for improvement, and by the stars"—here Lord Gensifer raised his arms to the ceiling in the posture of an outraged Zeus— "we'll achieve it. From the forwards, I'll have more snap and dash. From the rovers, decisive buffing, quicker reactions! Did your feet hurt today, rovers? So it seemed. From the guards, more ferocity, more dependability. When the enemy confronts our guards, I want them to think only of home and mother. Any remarks?"

Glinnes looked off and up into the air and thoughtfully sipped pale-green Sokal wine from his goblet.

Lord Gensifer continued. "Our next opponents are the Tanchinaros; we meet them in two weeks at Saurkash Stadium. I'm sure that events will go differently. I've watched them; they're slow as Dido's one-legged grandmother. We'll simply stroll around them to the pedestal. We'll take their money and bare their sheirl, and be off and gone like Welshmen."

"Speaking of money," drawled Candolf, "how much is our treasure after today's fiasco? Also, who is our sheirl?"

"The treasure will be two thousand ozols," said Lord Gensifer coldly. "The sheirl might be any of several delightful creatures anxious to share our ascendancy."

Lucho said, "The Tanchinaros are slow up front, but with guards like Gilweg, Etzing, Barreu, and Shamoran, the forwards could play in wheelchairs."

Lord Gensifer waved the remark aside. "A good team plays its own game and forces the enemy to react. The Tanchinaro guards are only flesh and bone. We'll tank them so often they'll think they're tanchinaros* in sheer reality!"

"A toast to this!" called out Chaim, Lord Shadrak. "To eleven dripping-wet Tanchinaros and their bare-bottomed sheirl!"

CHAPTER I I

After Lord Gensifer's party, Glinnes went to spend the night with Tyran Lucho, who lived on Altramar Island, a few miles east of Five Islands, with the South Ocean a quarter mile south across a lagoon and a line of sand spits. A white beach was the Lucho front yard. Glinnes and Tyran arrived to find a star-watch in progress. Over a pair of soft red fires crabs, crayfish, sea-bulbs, pentabrachs, sourweed and a mix of smaller sea-stuffs grilled and sizzled. Kegs of beer had been broached; a table supported coarse crusty loaves, fruits and conserves. Thirty folk of all ages ate, drank, sang, played guitars and mouth-calliopes, romped in the sand, addressed themselves to someone they intended to lure up the beach later in the evening. Glinnes felt instantly at ease, in contrast to the restraint he had felt at Lord Gensifer's party, where the jocularity had been on a more formal level. Here were those Trills despised by Fanscherade—undisciplined, frivolous, gluttonous, amorous, some unkempt and dirty, others merely unkempt. Children played erotic games, and adults as well; Glinnes observed several noticeably under the influence of cauch. Each person wore those garments he deemed appropriate; a stranger might have thought himself at a fancy-dress charade. Tyran Lucho, conditioned and disciplined by hussade, used garments and manners less flamboyant; still, like Glinnes, he relaxed gratefully upon the sand with a mug of beer and a chino-leaf of grilled sea-meats. The party was nominally a "star-watch"; the air was soft and the stars hung close like great paper lanterns. But a mood of revelry was on the group and there would be small pondering of the stars this night.

Tyran Lucho had played with teams of reputation. On the field he

*tanchinaro: a black and silver fish of the Far South Ocean.

was regarded as a taciturn man of great skill and almost alone in his ability to break down the field through an apparently impervious front of opponents—dodging, feinting, swinging from way to way, or swinging out and snapping himself back, a trick which sometimes persuaded opponents to the ludicrous act of tanking themselves. Along with Wild Man Wilmer Guff, Lucho had been represented on Lord Gensifer's original dream-team. Glinnes settled himself beside Lucho and the two discussed the day's game. "Essentially," said Glinnes, "we're sound forward—with the exception of Clubfoot Chust—and pitifully weak back-field."

"True. Savat has excellent potential. Unfortunately, Tammi confuses him and he doesn't know whether to run forward or back."

"Tammi" was the team's jocular term for Thammas, Lord Gensifer.

"Agreed," said Glinnes. "Even Sarkado is at least adequate, though he's really too indecisive to make a good team."

"To win," said Lucho, "we need a back-field, but even more urgently we need a captain. Tammi doesn't know which direction he's going."

"Unfortunately it's his team."

"But it's our time and our profit!" declared Lucho with a vehemence that surprised Glinnes. "Also our reputation. It does a man no good to play with a set of buffoons."

"First of all," said Glinnes, "a man tends to relax his own standards of play."

"I've been thinking the matter over. I left the Poldan Avengers so that I could live at home, and I thought perhaps Lord Gensifer could field a team. But he'll never do so if he insists on running the team as if it were his private toy."

"Still, he's captain; who'd play his position? What about you?"

Lucho shook his head. "I don't have the patience. What about you?"

"I prefer to play strike. Candolf is pretty sound."

"He's possible, in a pinch. But I've got a better man in mind—Denzel Warhound."

Glinnes considered. "He's smart and he's quick, and he doesn't mind contact. He'd be a good one. How strong a Gannet is he?"

"He wants to play. The Gannets don't have a home stadium; theirs is a very makeshift operation. Warhound would switch if a good opportunity came up."

Glinnes emptied his mug of beer. "Tammi would lay an egg if he knew what we're talking about . . . Who is the pretty girl in the white smock? I ache to see her so lonely."

"She's second cousin to my brother's wife. Her name is Thaio and she's very sympathetic."

"I'll just go ask her if she wants to be a sheirl."
"She'll say that up till the age of nine this was her dearest ambition."

The game between the Gorgons and Tanchinaros occurred on the afternoon of a beautiful warm day, with the sky a hemisphere of milkglass. The
Tanchinaros were immensely popular in Saurkash, and the stadium was
crowded far beyond capacity. Out of idle curiosity Glinnes looked along the
line of boxes; there as before sat Lute Casagave, again with his camera. Odd,
thought Glinnes.

The teams formed in ranks for the parade and the sheirls came forth:
for the Tanchinaros, Filene Sadjo, a fresh-faced fisherman's daughter from
Far Spinney; for the Gorgons, Karue Liriant, a tall dark-haired girl with a
ripe and sumptuous figure, evident even under the classic folds of her white
gown. Lord Gensifer had kept her identity a mystery until a team meeting
three days before the game. Karue Liriant had not tried to make herself popular—a bad omen in itself. Still, Karue Liriant was only the least factor disruptive of morale. The left side guard Ramos, annoyed by Lord Gensifer's
criticisms, had quit the team. "It's not that I'm so expert," he told Lord
Gensifer, "it's just that you're so much worse. I should be *ki-yik-yik-yikking* at
you rather than you *ki-yikking* at me."

"Off the field with you!" barked Lord Gensifer. "If you hadn't quit I
would send you down in any case."

"Bah," said Ramos. "If you sent down all those complaining you'd be
playing by yourself."

The question of replacement arose during post-practice refreshment.
"Here's an idea to help the team," Lucho told Lord Gensifer. "Suppose you
were to play guard, as you're well able to do; you're big enough and obstinate enough. Then I know a man who'd make us a very able captain
indeed."

"Oh?" said Lord Gensifer frostily. "And who is this paragon?"

"Denzel Warhound, now with the Gannets."

Lord Gensifer took pains to control his voice. "It might be simpler and
less disruptive merely to recruit a new guard."

Lucho had no more to say. The new guard appeared at the next practice
session, a man even less capable than Ramos.

The Gorgons, therefore, came to play the Tanchinaros in less than an
optimum frame of mind.

After circling the field, the two teams pulled down their helmets to
accomplish that always startling metamorphosis of men into heroic demi-
urges, each assuming in some degree the quality of the mask. For the first
time Glinnes saw the Tanchinaro masks; they were striking affairs of silver
and black, with red and violet plumes—the Tanchinaros made a fine display as they took the field. As expected, the Tanchinaros were strong and

massive. "A team of ten guards and a fat old man," as Carbo Gilweg had expressed it. The "fat old man" was Captain Nilo Neronavy, who never left the protective radius of his hange, and whose plays were as forthright as Lord Gensifer's were intricate and confusing. Glinnes anticipated no diffi-culties in defense; the Tanchinaro forwards were inept on the trapeze, and the swift Gorgon front line could play them one at a time. Offense was a different matter. Glinnes, had he been captain, would have drawn them in and out—to one side, then another—until a path flickered open for a light-ning lunge by one of the forwards. He doubted if Lord Gensifer would use this strategy, or even if he could control the team well enough to orches-trate the quick feints and ploys.

The Gorgons won the green light. The gong sounded; the light flashed green; the game was on. "Twelve-ten, *ki-yik!*" cried Lord Gensifer, thrusting the forwards and rovers to the moat with the guards advancing two stations. "Thirteen-eight!"—a thrust at the side passages by wings and rovers, with strikes ready to jump the moat. So far, so good. The next call almost on the instant should be, "Eight-thirteen," signifying rovers across and forwards in a feint to the left. The rovers crossed the moat; the Tanchinaro forwards hesitated, and now there was time for a swift attack on the Tanchinaro right wing. But Lord Gensifer vacillated; the forwards recovered, the rovers recrossed the moat, and the light shone red.

So the game went for fifteen minutes. Two Tanchinaro forwards were tanked on offense but were able to return to the field before the Gorgons could exploit the advantage. Lord Gensifer became impatient and tried a new tactic—precisely that play which Glinnes had used to score against the Gannets, and which was quite inappropriate against the Tanchinaros. As a result, all four forwards, a rover, and Lord Gensifer himself were tanked, and the Tanchinaros marched down the field to an easy ring. Lord Gensifer paid over a thousand ozols ransom.

The teams regrouped. "I know one way to win the game," Lucho told Glinnes. "Keep Tammi in the foul tank."

"Very well," said Glinnes. "The 'Sheer Stupidity' play. Tell Savat; I'll tell Chust."

Green light; Lord Gensifer set his team into motion. Two seconds before the light changed the entire Gorgon front line moved out in an apparently senseless direction. In astounded reaction Lord Gensifer bel-lowed counter-plays well after the light had flashed red. The game halted while Lord Gensifer, not entirely unaware of what had happened, hunched himself down in the foul tank.

Glinnes, as right strike, assumed control. During red light the Tanchi-naros tried to storm the moat. By dint of precise timing, the Gorgon for-wards tanked both Tanchinaro strikes and the wings retreated. Green light. Glinnes put his ideas into effect. He called plays in a series. The front surged back and forth; then the Gorgon forwards and rovers were across. The Tanchinaro rovers were tanked, but the Tanchinaro guards remained—an inexorable bulwark. Glinnes called up his own two center guards; eight men drove down the center; the Tanchinaro guards were forced to mass. Glinnes crossed behind, thrust Carbo Gilweg into the tank as a friendly gesture, and seized the gold ring.

Lord Gensifer came sulkily forth from the tank, speaking no word to anyone, and collected a thousand ozols from Nilo Neronavy.

The teams took positions. Red light. The Tanchinaros massed on their own left side, hoping to tempt some reckless Gorgon across the moat. Glinnes caught Lucho's eyes; both knew the other's intent and both crossed, both raced up the center lanes at a speed to confound a team ostensibly on offense. Behind came the wings and the rovers. A flurry of feints and swings and the Gorgons were in the back court engaging the guards. Wild Man Wilmer Guff, the rover, slid past and grabbed the ring.

"That's another way to win," Lucho crowed to Glinnes. "We attack during off-light, when Tammi can't argue."

The teams regrouped. Red light again. Nilo Neronavy employed the strategy best suited to the Tanchinaro abilities: a grinding advance up the field. Both Lucho and Chust were tanked; Savat and Glinnes were driven back. The Tanchinaros brought all guards to the moat. Green light. Lord Gensifer called, "Twenty-two!", a simple play as good as any, sending the forwards pell-mell toward the Tanchinaro backcourt. The Tanchinaro guards retreated; the Gorgons could not win past. Carbo Gilweg engaged Glinnes; the two struggled with their buffs—up, back, hook, parry. Gilweg lowered his head, drove forward; Glinnes tried to dodge but could not avoid Gilweg's buff. Into the tank. Gilweg looked down at him. "How's the water?"

Glinnes made no reply. The gong had sounded. One or another of the Tanchinaros had taken a ring.

The teams took a five-minute rest period. Lord Gensifer moved austerely off to the side; Lucho nevertheless went to offer him counsel. "They'll be playing Big Push again for certain. In fact they won't wait; during green light they'll push. We've got to break down their center before they get their line across."

Lord Gensifer made no reply.

The teams once more took the field. Green light. Lord Gensifer brought his men up to the moat. The Tanchinaros had assumed a hedgehog formation, daring the Gorgons to attack, a situation where the agile Gorgon forwards, swinging the trapeze, might well tank isolated Tanchinaros—or might be tanked. Lord Gensifer refused to attack. Red light. The Tanchinaros remained in defensive formation. Green light. Lord Gensifer still restrained his men, a policy unwise only in that it indicated uncertainty. Glinnes called to him, "Let's go over; we can always come back!"

Lord Gensifer stood stonily silent.

Red light. The Tanchinaros came forward, all eleven men—"the sheirl guarding the pedestal," as the saying went. As before, they thrust past the moat, with only the guards on Tanchinaro territory.

Green light. Lord Gensifer called for a feint to right and an attack on the Tanchinaros who had gained a foothold on the left. In the scrimmage two men from each team were tanked, but meanwhile the Tanchinaros had thrust far down the Gorgon right wall, and the ineffectual new guard was tanked.

The light went red. The Tanchinaros, foot by foot, thrust toward the Gorgon pedestal, where Karue Liriant waited, showing no apparent distress.

Green light. Lord Gensifer was faced with a dire situation. His forwards held the center but Tanchinaro guards and rovers coming down the center lanes cramped and constrained them. Glinnes attacked the Tanchinaro strike; from the corner of his eye he thought to see a free course downfield, if he could only feint one of the guards out of position.

Red light. Glinnes swung away from the Tanchinaro strike. He raced to the moat and across. He was free; he was clear! Carbo Gilweg, making a desperate effort, dove out to hook Glinnes with his buff; both fell into the moat.

Gong—three times. The game was won.

The field judge summoned Lord Gensifer and called for ransom, which was denied. The music became exalted and sad, a music golden as sunset, with rhythm like a beating heart and chords sweet with human passion. For the third time the field judge called for ransom; for the third time Lord Gensifer ignored the call. The Tanchinaro strike pulled the ring; the gown fell away from Karue Liriant. Naked and unconcerned, she faced the audience; in fact, she showed a slight smile. Casually she preened herself, tilting up on one toe, looking over first one shoulder, then the other, while the crowd blinked in wonder at this unfamiliar demonstration.

An odd speculation came to Glinnes' mind. He peered at her. Karue Liriant was pregnant? The possibility occurred to others as well; a murmur rose in the stands. Lord Gensifer hurriedly brought up a cloak and escorted his still-smiling sheirl from the pedestal. Then he turned to the team. "There will be no party tonight. I now have the unpleasant duty of punishing insubordination. Tyran Lucho, you may regard yourself as at liberty. Glinnes Hulden, your conduct—"

Glinnes said, "Lord Gensifer, spare me your criticism. I resign from the team. Playing conditions are impossible."

Ervil Savat, the left strike, said, "I resign as well."

"And I," said Wilmer Guff, the right rover, one of the strong players who had carried the brunt of the load. The remainder of the team hesitated. If they all resigned they might find no other organized team on which to play. They held their tongues in a troubled silence.

"So be it," said Lord Gensifer. "We are well rid of you. All have been headstrong—and you, Glinnes Hulden, and you, Tyran Lucho, have sedulously sought to undermine my authority."

"Only that we might score a ring or two," said Lucho. "But no matter—good luck to you and your Gorgons." He removed his mask and handed it over to Lord Gensifer. Glinnes did likewise, then Ervil Savat and Wilmer Guff. Bump Candolf, the single effective guard, could see no future playing on the team as it was presently constituted, and he also gave his mask to Lord Gensifer.

Outside the dressing room, Glinnes told his four comrades, "Tonight, all to my house, for what in effect will be our victory party. We're free of that mooncalf Tammi."

"Basically a sound notion," said Lucho. "I'm in the mood for a jug or two, but there'll be more merriment along Altramar Beach, and we'll find a sympathetic audience."

"As you wish. My verandah is quiet of late. No one sits there but myself, and maybe a merling or two during my absence."

Along the way to the dock the five met Carbo Gilweg with two other Tanchinaro guards, all in high spirits. "Well played, Gorgons, but today you encountered the desperate Tanchinaros."

"Thank you for the consolation," said Glinnes, "but don't call us Gorgons. We no longer enjoy this distinction."

"What's all this? Did Lord Gensifer give up his wild scheme of directing a hussade team?"

"He gave up on us, and we gave up on him. The Gorgons still exist, or so I suppose. All Tammi needs is a new front line."

"By an odd coincidence," said Garbo Gilweg, "that's all the Tanchinaros need too . . . Where are you bound?"

"Out to Lucho's in Altramar, for our private victory party."

"Better yet, visit the Gilwegs for a more authentic version."

"I think not," said Glinnes. "You won't want our long faces at the feast."

"On the contrary! I have a special reason for inviting you. In fact, let's stop into The Magic Tench for a mug of beer."

The eight men seated themselves around a round table, and the serving girl brought forth eight ample goblets.

Gilweg frowned into his foam. "Let me develop an idea—an obvious and excellent idea. The Tanchinaros, like Lord Gensifer, need a front line. It's no secret; everybody admits the fact. We're a team of ten guards and a beer keg."

"That's all very well and I see your point," said Glinnes, "but your forwards, whether they're really guards or not, are sure to object."

"They have no right to object. The Tanchinaros are an open club; anyone can join, and if he cuts the mustard he plays. Think of it! For the first time in memory, the miserable Saurkash Tanchinaros a real team!"

"The idea has appeal." Glinnes looked at his fellows. "How do you others feel?"

"I want to play hussade," said Wilmer Guff. "I like to win. I am in favor of the scheme."

"Count me in," said Lucho. "Perhaps we'll have a chance to play the Gorgons."

Savat agreed to the proposal, but Candolf was dubious. "I'm a guard. There's no place for me on the Tanchinaros."

"Don't be too sure," said Gilweg. "Our left wing guard is Pedro Shamoran, and he's got a bad leg. There'll be a shuffle of places, and maybe you can even play left rover; you're certainly quick enough. Why not try?"

"Very well; why not?"

Gilweg drained his mug. "Good then. It's settled. And now we can all celebrate the Tanchinaro victory!"

CHAPTER 12

W hen Glinnes arrived home late the following morning he found a strange boat tied to his dock. No one sat on the verandah, and the house was empty. Glinnes went outside to look around and saw three men sauntering across the meadow: Glay, Akadie, and Junius Farfan. All three wore neat garments of black and gray, the uniform of Fanscherade. Glay and Farfan spoke earnestly together; Akadie walked somewhat apart.

Glinnes went forward to meet them. Akadie put on a half-sheepish smile in the face of Glinnes' scornful amazement. "I never thought you'd involve yourself in this rubbish," snorted Glinnes.

"One must move with the times," said Akadie. "Indeed, I find the garments a source of amusement." Glay turned him a cool glance; Junius Farfan merely laughed.

Glinnes waved his hand to the verandah. "Seat yourselves. Will you drink wine?"

Farfan and Akadie took a goblet of wine; Glay gave a curt refusal. He followed Glinnes into the house where he had spent his childhood and stood looking about the room with the eyes of a stranger. He turned and preceded Glinnes from the house.

"I have a proposition for you," said Glay. "You want Ambal Isle." He looked toward Junius Farfan, who laid an envelope on the table. "You shall have Ambal Island. There is the money to dislodge Casagave."

Glinnes reached for the envelope; Glay pushed it away. "Not so fast.

When Ambal is again your property you can go to live there if you choose. And I get the use of Rabendary."

Glinnes looked at him in astonishment. "Now you want Rabendary! Why can't we both live here as brothers, and work the land together?"

Glay shook his head. "Unless you changed your attitudes, there would only be dissension. I don't have energy to waste. You take Ambal; I'll take Rabendary."

"This is the most marvelous proposition I have ever heard," said Glinnes, "when both belong to me."

Glay shook his head. "Not if Shira is alive."

"Shira is dead." Glinnes went out to his hiding place, uncovered the pot, and removed the golden fob, which he brought back to the verandah. He tossed it on the table. "Remember this? I took it from your friends the Drossets. They killed and robbed Shira and threw him to the merlings."

Glay glanced at the fob. "Did they admit it?"

"No."

"Can you prove you took it from the Drossets?"

"You have heard me tell you."

"That's not enough," said Glay curtly.

Glinnes slowly turned his head and stared into Glay's face. Slowly he rose to his feet. Glay sat rigid as a steel post. Akadie said hurriedly, "Of course your word is sufficient, Glinnes. Sit down."

"Glay can withdraw his remark and then withdraw himself."

Akadie said, "Glay meant only that your word is legally insufficient. Am I right, Glay?"

"Yes, yes," said Glay in a bored voice. "Your word is sufficient, as far as I am concerned. The proposal remains the same."

"Why the sudden yearning to return home to Rabendary?" asked Glinnes. "Are you giving up your fancy-dress party?"

"To the contrary. On Rabendary we will found a Fanscherade community, a college of dynamic formulations."

"By the stars," marveled Glinnes. "Formulations. To what purpose?"

Junius Farfan said in a soft voice, "We intend to found an academy of achievement."

Glinnes looked out over Ambal Broad in bemusement. "I admit to perplexity. Alastor Cluster is thousands of years old; men by the trillions fill the galaxy. Great mentors here, there, everywhere across the whole pageant of existence, have propounded problems and solved them. Everything conceivable has been achieved and all goals attained—not once, but thousands of times over. It is well known that we live in the golden afternoon of the human race. Hence, in the name of the Thirty Thousand Stars, where will you find a fresh area of knowledge that must urgently be advanced from Rabendary meadow?"

Glay made an impatient motion, as if at Glinnes' embarrassing stupidity. Junius Farfan, however, responded politely. "These concepts are naturally familiar to us. It can easily be demonstrated, however, that the scope of knowledge, and hence achievement, is unlimited. A boundary between the known and the unknown always exists. In such a situation, opportunity is also unlimited for any number of folk whatever. We do not pretend or even hope to extend knowledge across new borders. Our academy is only precursory: before we explore new fields we must delineate the old, and define the areas where achievement is possible. This is a tremendous work in itself. I expect to work my life out only as a precursor. Even so, I will have given this life meaning. I invite you, Glinnes Hulden, to join Fanscherade and share our great aim."

"And wear a gray uniform and give up hussade and star-watching? By no means. I don't care whether I achieve anything or not. As for your college, if you laid it down on the meadow you'd spoil my view. Look at the light on the water yonder; look at the color in the trees! Suddenly it seems as if your talk of 'achievement' and 'meaning' is sheer vanity—the pompous talk of small boys."

Junius Farfan laughed. "I'll agree to 'vanity,' along with arrogance, egocentricity, elitism, whatever you wish. No one has claimed otherwise, any more than Jan Dublays claimed mortification of the flesh when he wrote *The Rose in the Gargoyle's Teeth.*"

"In other words," said Akadie gently, "Fanscherade deftly turns the force inherent in human vice to presumably useful ends."

"Abstract discussions are entertaining," remarked Junius Farfan, "but we must keep ourselves focused upon dynamic, rather than static, processes. Do you agree to Glay's proposal?"

"That Rabendary be turned into a Fanscherade madhouse? Of course not! Have you people no soul? Look out over this landscape! There's ample human achievement in the universe, but not nearly enough beauty. Establish your academy somewhere out on the lava beds, or back of the Broken Hills. Not here."

Junius Farfan rose to his feet. "We'll bid you good-day." He picked up the envelope. Glinnes reached forward; Glay's hand clamped his wrist. Farfan placidly tucked the envelope in his pocket.

Glay drew back with a wolfish grin. Glinnes leaned forward, muscles tense. Junius Farfan watched him soberly. Glinnes relaxed. Farfan's gaze was steady and sure, and disconcerting.

Akadie said, "I'll stay here with Glinnes; he'll ferry me home after a bit."

"As you will," said Farfan. He and Glay went to their boat, and after a last appraisal of Rabendary Meadow, the two departed.

"There's something downright insolent about that proposal," said

Glinnes through gritted teeth. "Do they take me for a dunderhead, to be fleeced so easily?"

"They are absolutely sure in their purpose," said Akadie. "Perhaps you mistake assurance for insolence . . . Agreed, the qualities sometimes converge. Still, neither Glay nor Junius Farfan is an insolent man. Farfan indeed is extraordinarily bland. Glay would appear somewhat remote, but still, all in all, a true-hearted fellow."

Glinnes could hardly control his indignation. "When they cheat me from eight directions and steal my property? Your concepts need reexamination."

Akadie signified that the matter lacked consequence. "I looked in at the hussade game yesterday. I must say that I was greatly diverted, though the play was not altogether precise. Hussade is intensely an interaction between personalities; no one game is ever like another. I might even believe that the masks are unconsciously recognized as a necessity, to prevent personalities from dominating the game."

"In hussade anything might be true. I know that I can't abide Lord Gensifer's personality, to such effect that I'll be playing with the Tanchinaros."

Akadie nodded sagely. "I chanced to meet Lord Gensifer this morning, in Voulash of all places, at the Placid Valley Inn. Over a cup of tea he mentioned that he had released several players for insubordination."

"Insubordination?" Glinnes snorted. "More accurately, for outright disgust. What did he want in Voulash? Mind you, the question is casual. I don't care to pay a fee."

Akadie spoke with dignity. "Lord Gensifer was discussing hussade with some of the Voulash Gannets. I believe that he induced several of them to join the Gorgons."

"Well indeed! So Lord Gensifer refuses to quit?"

"On the contrary. He seethes with dedication. He claims that he has been beaten only by flukes and sluggishness, and never by the opposition."

Glinnes laughed scornfully. "Whenever Lord Gensifer sat in the foul tank we were able to score. When he called plays, we were chased all over the field."

"Will you fare better with old Neronavy? He's not noted for imaginative play."

"Quite true. I think we could do better." Glinnes ruminated a moment. "Would you care to ride over to Voulash again?"

"I have nothing better to do," said Akadie.

Denzel Warhound lived in a cabin between two vast myrsile trees, at the head of Placid Valley. He had not yet been apprised of Lord Gensifer's visit to Voulash, but he displayed neither surprise nor rancor. "The Gannets were a part-time proposition; I'm surprised the team held together as well as it did. Just a moment." He went to the telephone and spoke several minutes with someone whose face Glinnes could not see, then returned to the porch. "Both strikes, both wings and a rover—all Gorgons now. The Gannets have flown for the last time this year, I assure you."

"As a matter of possible interest," said Glinnes, "the Tanchinaros could make good use of an aggressive captain. Neronavy is not as alert as he might be. With a clever captain, the Tanchinaros might well win considerable money."

Denzel Warhound pulled at his chin. "The Tanchinaros are an open club, I believe?"

"As open as the air."

"The idea has appeal, quite decidedly."

CHAPTER *I*3

The transition of the Tanchinaros from "ten guards and a fat old man" to a balanced and versatile team was not achieved without disgruntlement. The irascible Nilo Neronavy refused to concede the superior skills of Denzel Warhound. When the reverse was demonstrated he stormed from the field, accompanied by the displaced forwards and the sheirl, his niece. An hour later, in the arbor of The Magic Tench, Neronavy and his group declared themselves the nucleus of a new team, to be known as the Saurkash Fishkillers, and went so far as to challenge Lord Gensifer, who chanced to be passing by, to a match with his Gorgons. Lord Gensifer agreed to consider the offer.

The Tanchinaros, suddenly awake to their potentialities, drilled with care, developing precision, coordination, and a repertory of basic plays. Their first opponents would be the Raparees from Galgade in the East Fens. The Raparees would play for no more than fifteen hundred ozols, which in any event was about the capability of the Tanchinaro treasury. And who for sheirl? Perinda, the club manager, introduced several lackluster candidates, whom the team found unsuitable.

"We're a Class A team," declared Denzel Warhound. "Maybe better—so get us a Class A sheirl. We won't settle for any old slab of merling bait."

"I have a girl in mind," said Perinda. "She is absolutely first class—*sashei*, beauty, enthusiasm—except for one or two small points."

"Ah indeed? She is the mother of nine children?"

"No. I'm sure she's virgin. After all, she's Trevanyi, which is one of the small flaws I mentioned."

"Aha," said Glinnes. "And her other flaws?"

"Well—she seems rather emotional. Her tongue has a life of its own. All in all, she is a very spirited person—an ideal sheirl."

"Aha! And her name—conceivably Duissane Drosset?"

"Quite correct. Do you have objection?"

Glinnes pursed his lips, trying to define his precise attitude toward Duissane Drosset. No question as to her verve and *sashei*—she would certainly provide impetus for the team. He said, "I have no objection."

If Duissane was abashed to find Glinnes on the team, she gave no signal of the fact. She came alone to the practice field—independent conduct indeed for a Trevanyi girl. She wore a dark brown cloak, which the south wind pressed against her slight figure, and seemed very appealing, almost innocent. She had little to say but watched the Tanchinaros at their exercises with apparently intelligent attention, and the team performed with a considerable increment of energy.

Duissane accompanied the team to the arbor of The Magic Tench, where they usually took after-practice refreshment. Perinda seemed distrait, and when he introduced Duissane formally he somewhat pointedly described her as "one of our candidates."

Savat cried out, "So far as I'm concerned, she's our sheirl. Let's have no more of this 'candidate' talk."

Perinda cleared his throat. "Yes, yes, of course. But one or two matters have come up, and we traditionally choose our sheirls after full discussion."

"What remains to be discussed?" demanded the guard Etzing. He asked Duissane, "Are you prepared to serve us loyally as our sheirl, and take the bad with the good and the good with the bad?"

Duissane's luminous gaze, wandering over the group, seemed to rest an instant upon Glinnes. But she said, "Yes, certainly."

"Well then!" cried Etzing. "Shall we acclaim her?"

"A moment, just a moment!" said Perinda, slightly flushed. "As I say, one or two small points remain to be discussed."

"Such as what?" bawled Etzing. "Let's hear them!"

Perinda puffed out his cheeks, pink with embarrassment. "We can discuss the matter another time."

Duissane asked, "What are these small points? Discuss them now, for all of us. Perhaps I can explain whatever needs explaining. Go on," she commanded, as Perinda still hesitated. "If allegations have been made I want to hear them." And again it seemed as if her gaze rested a long instant upon Glinnes.

" 'Allegations' is too strong a word," stammered Perinda. "Just hints and rumors in regard to—well, your virginity. The condition seems to be doubtful, even though you are Trevanyi."

Duissane's eyes flashed. "How could anyone dare say such a thing about me? It is all so unjust and cowardly! Luckily I know my enemy, and I will never forget his antagonism!"

"No, no!" cried Perinda. "I won't say from where the rumor came to me. It's only that—"

"You wait here!" Duissane told them. "Do not depart until I return. If I must be distrusted and humiliated, allow me at least a contravention." She swept furiously from the arbor, almost colliding with Lord Gensifer and one of his cronies, Lord Alandrix, on their way into the bower.

"Stars!" exclaimed Lord Gensifer. "And who might she be? And at whom is she so enraged?"

Perinda spoke in a subdued voice. "My lord, she is a candidate for Tanchinaro sheirl."

Lord Gensifer laughed in great satisfaction. "She's made the wisest move of her life, fleeing the engagement. Truth to tell, she's a delicious little thing. I wouldn't mind pulling her ring myself."

"Almost certainly the opportunity will never arise," said Glinnes.

"Don't be too sure! The Gorgons are a different team now that changes have been made."

"I imagine that you can get a game with us, if the booty is adequate."

"Indeed. How much do you consider adequate?"

"Three thousand, five thousand, ten thousand—as much as you like."

"Bah. The Tanchinaros can't raise two thousand ozols, let alone ten thousand."

"Whatever booty the Gorgons put up, we'll match it."

Lord Gensifer nodded judiciously. "Something just might come of this. Ten thousand ozols, you say."

"Why not?" Glinnes looked around the arbor. All the Tanchinaros present knew as well as he did that the treasury contained three thousand ozols at the most, but only Perinda betrayed uneasiness.

"Very good," said Lord Gensifer briskly. "The Gorgons accept the challenge, and in due course we'll make the necessary arrangements." He turned to go, just as Duissane Drosset marched back into the arbor. Her golden-red curls were somewhat disarranged; her eyes glowed with equal parts of triumph and rage. She glared towards Glinnes and thrust a document at Perinda. "There! I must suffer inconvenience merely to quiet the spiteful tongues of vipers. Read! Are you satisfied?"

Perinda scrutinized the document. "This appears to be a document asserting the purity of Duissane Drosset, and the attestor is none other than Doctor Niameth. Well then, the unfortunate matter is settled."

"Not so fast," called Glinnes. "What is the date on the document?"

"What a degraded creature you are!" stormed Duissane. "The document is dated today!"

Perinda concurred, and added dryly, "Doctor Niameth did not note the precise hour and minute of his examination, but I suppose this is carrying exactitude too far."

Lord Gensifer said, "My dear young lady, don't you think you might fare better with the Gorgons? We are a courteous group, the exact opposite of these rude Tanchinaros."

"Courtesy wins no hussade games," said Perinda. "If you want to be snatched naked at your first game, go with the Gorgons."

Duissane flicked Lord Gensifer an appraising glance. Half-regretfully she shook her head. "I've only permission for the Tanchinaros. You'd have to supplicate my father."

Lord Gensifer raised his eyes to the ceiling, as if imploring one or another of the deities to witness the graceless demands put upon him. He bowed low. "My best regards." With another salute to the Tanchinaros he left the arbor.

Perinda looked at Glinnes. "Your badinage is all very well, but where will we find ten thousand ozols?"

"Where will Lord Gensifer find ten thousand ozols? He tried to borrow money from me. Who knows what a month or two will bring? Ten thousand ozols may seem a trivial sum."

"Who knows, who knows?" muttered Perinda. "Well then, back to Duissane Drosset. Is she our sheirl or is she not?"

No one protested; perhaps, with Duissane looking from face to face, no one dared. And so it was arranged.

The game with the Galgade Raparees went with almost embarrassing ease. The Tanchinaros were surprised to find their tactics so effective. Either they were six times more powerful than they had assumed, or the Raparees were the weakest team of Jolany Prefecture. Three times the Tanchinaros thrust the length of the field, their formations supple and decisive, the Raparees always seeming to find two Tanchinaros upon them, their sheirl in constant travail, while Duissane stood composed and cold, even somewhat stern, the white robe enhancing her frail charm. The Raparees, dejected and outclassed, paid three ransoms and resigned the field with their sheirl not denuded, to the displeasure of the crowd.

After the game the Tanchinaros assembled at The Magic Tench. Duissane held somewhat aloof from the conviviality, and Glinnes, chancing to look to the side, struck full into the lowering gaze of Vang Drosset. Almost immediately he conducted Duissane from the premises.

A week later the Tanchinaros fared up the Scurge River to Erch on Little Vole Island to play the Erch Elements, with almost the same results. Lucho had been shifted to left strike, the better to work in tandem with Glinnes Hulden, and Savat played right wing with adequate accuracy. Still, there were relatively weak areas in the deployment, which a skillful team would exploit. Gajowan, the left wing, was light and somewhat diffident, and Rolo, the left rover, was rather too slow. During the game with the Elements, Glinnes noticed Lord Gensifer in one of the middle boxes. He also noted Lord Gensifer's eyes turned often toward Duissane, though in this regard he was not alone, for Duissane projected an irresistible fascination. In the white gown, her Trevanyi background was forgotten; she seemed an entrancing confection—wistful, tart, gay, tragic, reckless, cautious, wise, foolish. Glinnes thought to see other attributes as well; he could never look at her without hearing a tinkle of laughter through the starlit darkness.

The next game, with the Hansard Dragons, pointed up the soft spot in the Tanchinaros' left wall, when the Dragons twice drove deep along the Tanchinaro left flank. In each case they were halted by the guards, then defeated by a thrust against the sheirl from the right, and the Tanchinaros won the game in three successive skirmishes. Again Lord Gensifer sat in one of the middle boxes, with several men strange to Glinnes, and after the game he appeared at The Magic Tench, where he renewed his challenge to the Tanchinaros. Each side would offer a treasury of ten thousand ozols, so Lord Gensifer stipulated, and the game must take place four weeks from the present date.

Somewhat dubiously, Perinda accepted the challenge. As soon as Lord Gensifer had departed, the Tanchinaros began to speculate as to what devious scheme Lord Gensifer had in mind. As Gilweg put it, "Not even Tammi could hope to win with his present team."

"He thinks he'll storm our left side," said Etzing dourly. "They almost got away with it today."

"He wouldn't speculate ten thousand ozols on that theory," said Glinnes. "I smell a whole set of startling antics, such as an entire new team—the Vertrice Karpouns, the Port Angel Scorpions—wearing Gorgon uniforms for the day."

"That must be what he's got in mind," Lucho agreed. "Tammi would think it a fine joke to beat us with such a team."

"The ten thousand ozols wouldn't hurt his feelings either."

"Such a team would rip open our left side as if it were a melon," predicted Etzing, and he glanced across the arbor to where Gajowan and Rolo listened with glum expressions. For these two, the conversation could have only a single implication: by the inexorable logic of competition, two-thousand-ozol players had no place on a ten-thousand-ozol team.

Two days later a pair of new men joined the Tanchinaros. The first, Yalden Wirp, had been represented on Lord Gensifer's original dream-team; the second, Dion Sladine, while playing with an obscure team from the Far Hills, had attracted Denzel Warhound's respectful attention. The vulnerable left flank of the Tanchinaros had been not only strengthened but converted into a source of dynamic potential.

R olo and Gajowan were persuaded to remain with the club in the capacity of substitutes and utility players, and in a game with the Wigtown Devisers, two weeks before the challenge match with the Gorgons, they played their old positions. The Devisers, a team of good reputation, lost a hard-fought ransom before they discovered the soft left side. They began to hurl probes and thrusts at the vulnerable area, and several times gained the back-court, only to fail before the mobile and massive Tanchinaro guards. For almost ten minutes the Tanchinaros defended their territory, apparently lacking offensive force, while Lord Gensifer watched from his box, occasionally leaning to mutter a comment to his friends.

The Tanchinaros finally won, if sluggishly, by the usual three successive takes. Duissane as yet had never known a hand on her ring.

The Tanchinaro treasury was now well in excess of ten thousand ozols. The players speculated upon the possibilities of wealth. Several options were open. They could regard themselves as a two-thousand-ozol team and try to play teams of such quality. For this they would find scheduling difficult, if not impossible. They might rate themselves a five-thousand-ozol team and play in this category, risking not too much, gaining moderately. Or they might rank themselves a team of the first quality, and play ten-thousand-ozol teams—to gain both wealth and that ineffable quality known as *isthoune*. If the *isthoune** became sufficiently intense, they might declare themselves a team of championship quality and engage to prove themselves against any team of Trullion or elsewhere, for any treasure within their capabilities.

The day of the challenge match began with a thunderstorm. Lavender lightning spurted from cloud to cloud and occasionally struck down at the hills, shivering one or another of the tall menas with incandescent electric ague. At noon the storm drifted over the hills and hung there muttering and grumbling.

The Tanchinaros were first on the field and were announced to a pulsing crowd of sixteen thousand folk: "The dynamic and inexorable Tanchinaros of the Saurkash Hussade Club, in their usual uniforms of silver, blue

---

isthoune: exalted pride and confidence; *mana*: the emotion which compels heroes to reckless feats. A word essentially untranslatable.

and black, who vow to defend forever the honor of their precious and exalted sheirl Duissane! The personnel includes the captain: Denzel Warhound; the strikes: Tyran Lucho and Glinnes Hulden; the wings: Yalden Wirp and Ervil Savat; the guards . . ." So down the roster. "And now appearing on the field, in their striking uniforms of maroon and black, the new and utterly determined Gorgons, under the wise captaincy of Thammas, Lord Gensifer, who champion the indescribable charm of their sheirl Arelmra. Strikes . . ."

Precisely as Glinnes had expected, Lord Gensifer brought on the field a team totally different from that which the Tanchinaros had previously defeated. These present Gorgons carried themselves with competence and purpose; they were clearly no strangers to victory. Only one man did Glinnes recognize as a local: the captain, Lord Gensifer. His scheme was, of course, immediately transparent, and would seem to have for its purpose the winning of a quick ten thousand ozols. Hussade sportsmanship was loose and chancy; the game depended much upon feints, tricks, intimidation, any sort of deception. Hence, Lord Gensifer's stratagem did him neither credit nor shame, though it made for a game in which certain niceties might be overlooked.

From the orchestra came music—the traditional *Marvels of Grace and Glory*—as the sheirls were escorted to their pedestals. The Gorgon sheirl, Arelmra, a stately dark-haired girl, evinced no great surge of that warm propulsive immediacy known as *emblance*. Lord Gensifer, so Glinnes noted, seemed placid and bland. His aplomb dwindled a trifle when he noticed the changes at wing and rover; then he shrugged and smiled to himself.

The teams took their places. The music of horns, drums, and flutes sounded—the poignant *Sheirls Softly Hopeful for Glory*.

The captains met at the center bridge with the field judge. Denzel Warhound took occasion to comment, "Lord Gensifer, your team is rife with strange faces. Are they all local folk?"

"We are all citizens of Alastor. We are local folk, all five trillion of us," said Lord Gensifer largely. "And your own team? All inhabit Saurkash?"

"Saurkash or the environs."

The field judge tossed up the rod. The Gorgons were awarded green and the game began. Lord Gensifer called his formation and the Gorgons moved forward—intent, keen, assured. The Tanchinaros instantly sensed a team of high quality.

The Gorgons feinted to the Tanchinaro right, then hurled a brutal assault at the left. Strong shapes in maroon and black, the masks leering in mindless glee, thrust against the silver and black. The Tanchinaro left side gave only enough to encapsulate a group of Gorgons and press them against the moat. The light went red. Warhound tried to close a trap around a pair of advanced Gorgons, but the Gorgon rovers came forward and opened an escape route. Patterns shifted; formations thrust and pulled, testing first one individual, then another. After about ten minutes of indecisive play, Lord Gensifer incautiously strayed from his hange. Glinnes leapt the moat, engaged Lord Gensifer, and toppled him into the tank.

Lord Gensifer emerged wet and furious, which had been Glinnes' intent; the Gorgons were now hindered by the fervor of his play-calling. The Tanchinaros made a sudden center lunge of classic simplicity: Ervil Savat leapt up on the pedestal and seized Arelmra's ring. Her patrician features drooped in annoyance; clearly she had expected no such invasion of her citadel.

Lord Gensifer stonily paid over five thousand ozols, and the field judge called a five-minute rest period.

The Tanchinaros conferred. "Tammi seethes with blue fury," said Lucho. "This isn't at all what he had in mind."

"Let's tank him again," Warhound suggested.

"My idea precisely. This is a good team, but we can get at them through Tammi."

"But stealth!" Glinnes warned. "So that they don't guess what we're up to! Tank Tammi by all means, but as if it were a casual by-blow."

Play resumed. Lord Gensifer came forth ominous in his wrath and the Gorgons themselves seemed to share his fury. Play moved up and down the field, fluid and fast. During red light, Warhound thrust out his left wing, which abruptly veered to come at Lord Gensifer, who raced back for the protection of his hange, but vainly—he was intercepted and tanked. For an instant an avenue lay open for the Tanchinaros forwards, and Warhound sent them pell-mell down the field. Lord Gensifer came mad-eyed up the ladder, just in time to pay a second ransom, and his ten thousand ozols were gone.

The Gorgons thoughtfully took counsel together. Warhound called over to the referee, "What does that other team call itself on ordinary occasions?"

"Didn't you know? They're the Stilettos from Rufous Planet, on exhibition tour. You're playing a good team today. They've already beaten Port Angel Scorpions and the Jonus Infidels—with their own captain, needless to say."

"Well then," said Lucho generously, "let's give them all a fine bath, to keep them humble. Why victimize poor Tammi alone?"

"Bravo! We'll send them back to Rufous clean and tidy!"

Red light. The Tanchinaros vaulted the moat to find the Gorgons in a Stern Redoubt formation. With two scores to the good, the Tanchinaro guards were able to play somewhat more loosely than usual. They advanced to the moat, then crossed—a procedure which showed an almost insulting disregard for the enemy's offensive capability. A sudden flurry of action, a melee; into the tank splashed Gorgons and Tanchinaros. On the ways, maroon and black strove with silver, blue and black; metal fangs glinted into ghoulish black grins. Figures swayed, toppled; captains uttered hoarse calls, almost unheard over the sounds of the crowd and the skirling music. Arelmra stood with hands clenched against her chest. Her detachment had vanished; she seemed to cry and groan, though her voice could not be heard through the din. The Tanchinaro guards burst into the ranked Gorgons, and Warhound, ignoring his hange, sprang past to snatch the golden ring.

The white gown fluttered away; Arelmra stood nude while passionate music celebrated the defeat of the Gorgons and the tragedy of the sheirl's humiliation. Lord Gensifer brought her a robe and conducted her from the field, followed by the despondent Gorgons. Duissane was lifted by exultant Tanchinaros and carried to the Gorgon pedestal, while the orchestra played the traditional *Scintillating Glorifications*. Overcome with emotion, Duissane threw up her arms and cried out in joy. Laughing and crying, she kissed the Tanchinaros, until she confronted Glinnes, and then she drew back and marched off the field.

The Tanchinaros presently assembled at The Magic Tench, to hear the congratulations of their well-wishers.

"Never a team with such decision, such impact, such finesse!"

"The Tanchinaros will make Saurkash famous! Think of it!"

"Now what will Lord Gensifer do with his Gorgons?"

"Maybe he'll try the Tanchinaros with the Solelamut Select, or the Green Star Falifonics."

"I'd put my ozols on the Tanchinaros."

"Tanchinaros!" cried Perinda. "I've just come from the telephone. There's a fifteen-thousand-ozol game for us in two weeks—if we want it."

"Naturally we want it! Who with?"

"The Vertrice Karpouns."

The arbor became silent. The Karpouns were reckoned one of the five best teams of Trullion.

Perinda said, "They know nothing of the Tanchinaros, except that we've won a few games. I think they expect an easy fifteen thousand ozols."

"Avaricious animals!"

"We're as avaricious as they—perhaps worse."

Perinda continued. "We would play at Welgen. In addition to the treasure—should we win—we would take a fifth of the gate. We might well share out a treasure of close to forty thousand ozols—close to three thousand apiece."

"Not bad for an afternoon's work!"

"That's only if we win."

"For three thousand ozols I'll play alone and win."

"The Karpouns," said Perinda, "are an absolutely proficient team.

They've won twenty-eight straight games and their sheirl has never been touched. As for the Tanchinaros—I don't think anybody knows how good we are. The Gorgons today were an excellent team, handicapped by an indecisive captain. The Karpouns are as good or better, and we might well lose our money. So—what's the vote? Shall we play them?"

"For a chance at three thousand ozols I'd play a team of real karpouns."*

CHAPTER 15

Welgen Stadium, largest of Jolany Prefecture, was occupied to its fullest capacity. The aristocracy of Jolany, Minch, Straveny, and Gulkin Prefectures filled the four pavilions. Thirty thousand common folk hunched on benches in the ordinary sections. A large contingent had arrived from Vertrice, three hundred miles west; they occupied a section decorated with orange and green, the Karpoun colors. Overhead hung twenty-eight orange and green gonfalons, signifying the twenty-eight successive Karpoun victories.

For an hour the orchestra had been playing hussade music: victory paeans of a dozen famous teams, traditional laments and exaltations; the *War Song of the Miraksian Players*, which chilled the nerves and constricted the viscera; the haunting sad-sweet *Moods of Sheirl Hralce*; then, five minutes before game time, the *Glory of Forgotten Heroes*.

The Tanchinaros came on the field and stood by the east pedestal, their silver masks tilted up and back. A moment later the Karpouns appeared beside the west pedestal. They wore dark green jerkins and trousers of striped dark green and orange; like the Tanchinaros, they wore their masks tilted back. The teams somberly examined each other across the length of the field. Jehan Aud, the Karpoun captain, veteran of a thousand games, was known to be a tactical genius; no detail escaped his eye; for every permutation of the action he instinctively brought to bear an optimum response. Denzel Warhound was young, innovative, lightning-swift. Aud knew the sureness of experience; Warhound seethed with a multiplicity of schemes. Both men were confident. The Karpouns had the advantage of long association. The Tanchinaros put against them a raw surge of vitality and élan, in a game where these qualities carried great weight. The Karpouns knew that they would win. The Tanchinaros knew that the Karpouns would lose.

*karpoun: a feral tiger-like beast of the Shamshin Volcanoes.

The teams waited while the orchestra played *Thresildama*, a traditional salute to the competing teams.

The captains appeared with the sheirls; the orchestra played *Marvels of Grace and Glory*. The Karpoun sheirl was a marvelous creature named Farero, a flashing-eyed blond girl, radiant with *sashei*. In accordance with some mystical process, when she stepped upon the pedestal she transcended herself, to become her own archetype. Duissane, likewise, became an intensified version of herself: frail, wistful, indomitably courageous, suffused with gallant derring-do and her own distinctive *sashei*, as compelling as that of the sublime Farero.

The players drew down their masks; the flashing silver Tanchinaros looked across at the cruel Karpouns.

The Karpouns won the green light and the first offensive deployment. The teams took their positions on the field. The music altered, each instrument performing a dozen modulations to create a final golden chord. Dead silence. The forty thousand spectators held their breath.

Green light. The Karpouns struck forward in their celebrated "Tidal Wave," intending to envelop and smother the Tanchinaros out of hand. Across the moat leapt the forwards; behind came the rovers and, close behind, the guards, ferociously seeking contact.

The Tanchinaros were prepared for the tactic. Instead of falling back, the four guards charged forward and the teams collided like a pair of stampeding herds, and the melee was indecisive. Some minutes later Glinnes won free and gained the pedestal. He looked Farero the Karpoun sheirl full in the face, and seized her ring. She was pale with excitement and disconcerted; never before had an enemy laid hands on her ring.

The gong sounded; Jehan Aud somewhat glumly paid over eight thousand-ozol certificates. The teams took a rest period. Five Tanchinaros had been tanked and five Karpouns; the honors were even. Warhound was jubilant. "They're a great team, no question! But our guards are unmovable and our forwards are faster! Only in the rovers do they show superiority, and not much there!"

"What will they try next time?" asked Gilweg.

"I suppose more of the same," said Warhound, "but more methodically. They want to pin our forwards and bring their strength to bear."

Play resumed. Aud now used his men conservatively, thrusting and probing, hoping to trap and tank a forward. The crafty Warhound, seeing how the land lay, purposely restrained his forces, and finally out-waited Aud. The Karpouns tried a sudden slash down the center; the Tanchinaros forwards slid to the side and let them pass, then jumped the moat. Lucho climbed the pedestal and seized Farero's ring.

Seven thousand ozols were paid as ransom.

.

Warhound told the team, "Don't relax! They'll be at their most dangerous! And they haven't won twenty-eight games by luck. I expect a Tidal Wave."

Warhound was correct. The Karpouns stormed the Tanchinaro citadel with all their forces. Glinnes was tanked; Sladine and Wilmer Guff were tanked. Glinnes returned up the ladder in time to tank a Karpoun wing only ten feet from the pedestal; then he was tanked a second time, and before he could return to the field the gong sounded.

For the first time Duissane had felt a hand at her gold ring. Warhound furiously paid back eight thousand ozols.

Glinnes had never played a more grueling game. The Karpouns seemed tireless; they bounded across the field, vaulting and swinging as if the game had only commenced. He could not know that to the Karpouns the Tanchinaro forwards seemed unpredictable flickers of silver and black, wild as devils, so unnaturally agile that they seemed to run on air, while the Tanchinaro guards loomed over the field like four inexorable Dooms.

Up and down the field moved the battle; step by step the Tanchinaros thrust against the Karpoun pedestal, the forwards wicked and remorseless, driving, bumping, swinging, thrusting. The roar of the crowd faded to the back of consciousness; all reality was compressed into the field, the runs and ways, the waters glinting in the sunlight. A heavy cloud passed briefly over the sun. Almost at this instant Glinnes saw a path open through the orange and green. A trap? With the last energy of his legs he darted forward, around, over, and through. Orange and green yelled hoarsely; the Karpoun masks, once so sage and austere, seemed contorted in pain. Glinnes gained the pedestal, seizing the gold ring at Farero's waist, and now he must pull the ring and lay the blue-eyed maiden bare before forty thousand exalted eyes. The music soared, stately and tragic; Glinnes' hand twitched and hesitated; he did not dare to shame this golden creature . . .

The dark cloud was not a cloud. Three black hulls settled upon the field, blotting out the light of afternoon. The music stopped short; from the public-address came a poignant cry: "Starmenters! Take—" The voice broke off in a gabble of words, and a new harsh voice spoke: "Keep your seats. Do not move or stir about."

Glinnes took Farero's arm, jerked her from the pedestal, down the ladder to the tank under the field. "What are you doing?" she gasped, pulling back in horror.

"I'm trying to save your life," said Glinnes. "The starmenters would never leave you behind, and you'd never see your home again."

The girl's voice quavered. "Are we safe under here?"

"I wouldn't think so. We'll leave by the outlet sump. Hurry—it's at the far end."

They splashed through the water at best speed, under the ways, past the center moat. And now down the other ladder came Duissane, her face pinched and white with fear. Glinnes called to her, "Come along—we'll leave by the sump; perhaps they'll neglect to guard it."

At the corner of the tank the water flowed out and down a flume into a narrow little waterway. Glinnes slid down the flume and jumped to a ledge of ill-smelling black mud. Next came Duissane, clutching the white gown about herself. Glinnes pulled her over to the mud bank; she lost her footing and sat back into the muck. Glinnes could not restrain a grin. "You did that on purpose!" she cried in a throbbing voice.

"I did not!"

"You did!"

"Whatever you say."

Farero came down the flume; Glinnes caught her and pulled her over to the ledge. Duissane struggled to her feet. The three looked dubiously along the channel, which meandered out of sight under arching hushberries and pipwillows. The water seemed dark and deep; a faint scent of merling hung in the air. The prospect of swimming or even wading was unthinkable. Moored across the way was a crude little canoe, evidently the property of a couple of boys who had gained illicit entry to the field through the sump.

Glinnes clambered over the flume to the canoe, which was half-full of water and wallowed precariously under his weight. He bailed out a few gallons of water, then dared delay no longer. He pushed the boat across the water. Duissane stepped in, then Farero, and the water rose almost to the gunwales. Glinnes handed the bailing bucket to Duissane, who went scowling to work. Glinnes paddled cautiously out into the waterway. Behind them, from the stadium, came the rasp of the announcement system: "Those folk in Pavilions A, B, C, and D will file to the south exits. Not all will be taken; we have an exact list of those we want. Be brisk and make no trouble; we'll kill anyone who hinders us."

Unreal! thought Glinnes. An outrageous avalanche of events: excitement, color, passion, music, and victory—now fear and flight, with two sheirls. One hated him. The other, Farero, examined him from the side of her magnificent sea blue eyes. Now she took the bucket from Duissane, who sulkily scraped the mud from her gown. What a contrast, thought Glinnes: Farero was rueful but resigned—indeed, she probably preferred flight through the sump to nudity on the pedestal; Duissane obviously resented every instant of discomfort and seemed to hold Glinnes personally responsible.

The waterway curved. A hundred yards ahead gleamed Welgen Sound, with South Ocean beyond. Glinnes paddled more confidently; they had escaped the starmenters. A massive raid! And no doubt long planned for a time when all the wealthy folk of the prefecture came together. There would be captives taken for ransom, and girls taken for solace. The captives would return crestfallen and impoverished; the girls would never be seen again. The stadium vaults would yield at least a hundred thousand ozols and the treasures of the two teams would supply another thirty thousand, and even the Welgen banks might be plundered.

The waterway widened and meandered away from the shore across a wide mud flat pimpled with gas craters. To the east ran Welgen Spit, on the other side of which lay the harbor; to the west the shore extended into the late afternoon haze. Under the open sky Glinnes felt exposed—unreasonably so, he told himself; the starmenters could not now afford the time to pursue them, even should they deign to note the wallowing canoe. Farero had never ceased to bail. Water entered through several leaks, and Glinnes wondered how long the boat would stay afloat. The shuddering black slime of the mud flats was uninviting. Glinnes made for the nearest of the wooded islets which rose from the sound, a hummock of land fifty yards across.

The boat rocked upon an ocean swell and shipped water. Farero bailed as fast as possible, Duissane scooped with her hands, and they reached the islet just as the canoe sank under them. With enormous relief Glinnes pulled the canoe up the little apron of beach. Even as he stepped ashore, the three starmenter ships rose into view. They slanted up into the southern sky and were gone, with all their precious cargo.

Farero heaved a sigh. "Except for you," she told Glinnes, "I'd be aboard one of those ships."

"I would also be up there, except for myself," snapped Duissane.

Aha, thought Glinnes, here is a source for her annoyance: she feels neglected.

Duissane jumped ashore. "And what will we do out here?"

"Somebody will be along sooner or later. In the meantime, we wait."

"I don't care to wait," said Duissane. "Once the boat is bailed out, we can row back to shore. Must we sit shivering on this miserable little spot of land?"

"What else do you suggest? The boat leaks and the water swarms with merling. Still, I might be able to mend the leaks."

Duissane went to sit on a chunk of driftwood. Whelm ships streaked in from the west, circled the area, and one dropped down into Welgen. "Too late, much too late," said Glinnes. He bailed the canoe dry and wadded moss into such cracks as he could find. Farero came to watch him. She said, "You were kind to me."

Glinnes looked up at her.

"When you might have pulled the ring, you hesitated. You didn't want to shame me."

Glinnes nodded and went back to work on the boat.

"This may be why your sheirl is angry."

Glinnes looked sideways toward Duissane, who sat scowling across the water. "She is seldom in a good humor."

Farero said thoughtfully, "To be sheirl is a very strange experience; one feels the most extraordinary impulses . . . Today I lost, but the starmenters saved me. Perhaps she feels cheated."

"She's lucky to be here, and not aboard one of the ships."

"I think that she is in love with you and jealous of me."

Glinnes looked up in astonishment. "In love with me?" He turned another covert glance toward Duissane. "You must be wrong. She hates me. I've ample evidence of this."

"It may well be. I am no expert in these affairs."

Glinnes rose from his work, studied the canoe with gloomy dissatisfaction. "I don't trust that moss—especially with the avness wind coming from the land."

"Now that we're dry it's not unpleasant. Though my people must be worried, and I'm hungry."

"We can find shore food," said Glinnes. "We'll have a fine supper— except that we lack fire. Still—a plantain tree grows yonder."

Glinnes climbed the tree and tossed fruit down to Farero. When they returned to the beach, Duissane and the canoe were gone. She was already fifty yards distant, paddling for that waterway by which they had left the stadium. Glinnes gave a bark of sardonic laughter. "She is so in love with me and so jealous of you that she leaves us marooned together."

Farero, flushing pink, said, "It is not impossible."

For a period they watched the canoe. The offshore breeze gave Duissane difficulty. She stopped paddling and bailed for a moment or two; the moss evidently had failed to stanch the leaks. When again she began to paddle she rocked the canoe, and while clutching at the gunwale, lost the paddle. The offshore breeze blew her back, past the isle where Glinnes and Farero stood watching. Duissane ignored them.

Glinnes and Farero climbed upon the central hummock and watched the receding canoe, wondering whether Duissane might be swept out to sea. She drifted among the islets and the canoe was lost to sight.

The two returned to the beach. Glinnes said, "If we had a fire we could be quite comfortable, at least for a day or so . . . I don't care for raw sea-stuff."

"Nor I," said Farero.

Glinnes found a pair of dry sticks and attempted to rub up a fire, without success. He threw the sticks away in disgust. "The nights are warm, but a fire is pleasant."

Farero looked here, there, everywhere but directly at Glinnes. "Do you think that we'll be here so long?"

"We can't leave till a boat comes past. It might be an hour; it might be a week."

Farero spoke in something of a stammer. "And will you want to make love to me?"

Glinnes studied her for a moment, and reaching out, touched her golden hair, "You are beautiful beyond words. I would take joy in becoming your first lover."

Farero looked away. "We are alone . . . My team today was defeated, and I won't be sheirl again. Still—" She stopped speaking, then pointed and said in a soft flat voice, "Yonder passes a boat."

Glinnes hesitated. Farero made no urgent movements. Glinnes said reluctantly. "We must do something about silly Duissane and the canoe." He went to the water's edge and shouted. The boat, a power skiff driven by a lone fisherman, altered course, and presently Glinnes and Farero were aboard. The fisherman had come in from the open sea and had noticed no drifting canoe; quite possibly Duissane had gone ashore on one of the islets.

The fisherman took his boat around the end of the spit and into Welgen dock. Farero and Glinnes rode in a cab to the stadium. The driver had much to say regarding the starmenter raid. "—never an exploit to match it! They took the three hundred richest folk of the region and at least a hundred maidens, poor things, who'll never be put up for ransom. The Whelm came too late. The starmenters knew precisely who to take and who to ignore. And they timed their operation to the second and were gone. They'll earn fortunes in ransom!"

At the stadium Glinnes bade Sheirl Farero a muted farewell. He ran to the dressing room, slipped off his Tanchinaro uniform, and resumed his ordinary clothes.

The cab carried him back to the dock, where Glinnes hired a small runabout. He drove around the spit, out into Welgen Sound. The flat light of avness painted sea, sky, islets and shore in pallid and subtle colors to which no name could be applied. The silence seemed surreal; the gurgle of water under the keel was almost an intrusion.

He passed the islet where he had originally landed with Farero and Duissane, and went beyond, out into the area where the canoe had drifted. He circled the first of the islets but saw no sign either of canoe or Duissane. The next three islets were also vacant. The sea spread vast and calm beyond the three little islets yet to be investigated. On the second of these he spied a slender figure in a white gown, waving frantically.

When Duissane recognized the man who drove the boat, she abruptly stopped waving. Glinnes leapt ashore and pulled the boat up the beach. He secured the bowline to a crooked root, then turned and looked about. The flat low line of the mainland was dim in the inconclusive light. The sea heaved slow and supple, as if constricted under a film of silk. Glinnes looked at Duissane, who had maintained a cold silence. "What a quiet place. I doubt if even the merlings swim out this far."

Duissane looked at the boat. "If you came out to get me, I am now ready to leave."

"There's no hurry," said Glinnes. "None whatever. I brought bread and meat and wine. We can bake plantains and quorls* and maybe a curset.† We'll have a picnic while the stars come out."

Duissane compressed her lips petulantly and looked off toward the shore. Glinnes stepped forward. He stood only a foot away from her—as close as he had ever been. She looked up at him without warmth, her tawny-gray eyes shifting, or so it seemed to Glinnes, through a dozen moods and emotions. Glinnes bent his head, and putting an arm around her shoulders, kissed her lips, which were cold and unresponsive. She pushed him away with a thrust of her hands, and seemed suddenly to recover her voice. "You're all alike, you Trills! You reek with cauch; your brain is a single lecherous gland. Do you aspire only to turpitude? Have you no dignity, no self-respect?"

Glinnes laughed. "Are you hungry?"

"No. I have a dinner engagement and I will be late unless we leave at once."

"Indeed. Is that why you stole the canoe?"

"I stole nothing. The canoe was as much mine as yours. You seemed content to ogle that insipid Karpoun girl. I wonder that you're not still at it."

"She feared that you would be offended."

Duissane raised her eyebrows high. "Why should I think twice, or even once, about your conduct? Her concern embarrasses me."

"It is no great matter," said Glinnes. "I wonder if you would gather firewood while I fetch plantains?"

Duissane opened her mouth to refuse, then decided that such an act was self-defeating. She found a few dry twigs, which she tossed haughtily down upon the beach. She scrutinized the boat, which was pulled far up on the beach, and beyond her strength to float. The starting key had been removed from the lock.

Glinnes brought plantains, kindled a fire, dug up four fine quorls, which he cleaned, rinsed in the sea and set to baking with the plantains. He brought bread and meat from the boat, and spread a cloth on the sand. Duissane watched from a distance.

Glinnes opened the flask of wine and offered it to Duissane.

"I prefer to drink no wine."

"Do you intend to eat?"

Duissane touched the tip of her tongue to her lips. "And then what do you plan?"

---

*quorls: a type of mollusk living in beach sand.
†curset: a crablike sea insect.

"We will relax on the beach and star-watch, and who knows what else?"

"Oh you are a despicable person; I want nothing to do with you. Untidy and gluttonous, like all the Trills."

"Well, at least I'm not worse. Settle yourself; we'll eat and watch the sunset."

"I'm hungry, so I'll eat," said Duissane. "Then we must go back. You know how Trevanyi feel about indiscriminate amorousness. Also, never forget—I am the Tanchinaro sheirl, and a virgin!"

Glinnes made a sign to indicate that these considerations were of no great cogency. "Changes occur in all our lives."

Duissane stiffened in outrage. "Is this how you plan to soil the team's sheirl? What a scoundrel you are, who so sanctimoniously insisted upon purity and then told such vicious lies about me."

"I told no lies," declared Glinnes. "I never even told the truth—how you and your family robbed me and left me for the merlings, and how you laughed to see me lying for dead."

Duissane said somewhat feebly, "You got only what you deserved."

"I still owe your father and your brothers a knock or two," said Glinnes. "As for you, I am of two minds. Eat, drink wine, fortify yourself."

"I have no appetite. None whatever. I do not think it just that a person should be so ill-treated."

Glinnes gave no answer and began to eat.

Presently Duissane joined him. "You must remember," she told him, "that if you carry out your threat, you will have betrayed not only me but all your Tanchinaros, and befouled yourself as well. Then, you will be faced with an accounting of another sort, from my family. They will dog you to the end of time; never will you know a moment's peace. Thirdly, you will gain all my contempt. And for what? The relief of your gland. How can you use the word 'love' when you really plan revenge? And this of a most paltry kind. As if I were an animal, or something without emotion. Certainly—use me, if you wish, or kill me, but bear in mind my utter contempt for all your disgusting habits. Furthermore—"

"Woman," roared Glinnes, "be kind enough to shut your mouth. You have blighted the day and the evening as well. Eat your meal in silence and we will return to Welgen." Scowling, Glinnes hunched down upon the sand. He ate plantains, quorls, meat, and bread; he drank two flasks of wine, while Duissane watched from the corner of her eye, a peculiar expression on her face, half-sneer, half-smirk.

When he had eaten, Glinnes leaned back against a hummock and mused for a time upon the sunset. With absolute fidelity the colors were reflected in the sea, except for an occasional languid black cusp in the lee of a swell.

Duissane sat in silence, arms clasped around her knees.

Glinnes lurched to his feet and thrust the boat into the water. He signaled Duissane. "Get in." She obeyed. The boat returned across the sound, around the point of the spit, and up to the Welgen dock.

A large white yacht floated beside the jetty, which Glinnes recognized to be the property of Lord Gensifer. Lights glowed from the portholes, signifying activity aboard.

Glinnes looked askance at the yacht. Would Lord Gensifer be hosting a party tonight, after the starmenter raid? Strange. But then, the ways of the aristocrats always had been beyond his comprehension. Duissane, to his amazement, jumped from the boat and ran to the yacht. She climbed the gangplank and vanished into the salon. Glinnes heard Lord Gensifer's voice: "Duissane, my dear young lady, whatever—" The remainder of his sentence was muffled.

Glinnes shrugged and returned the boat to the rental depot. As he walked back down the dock, Lord Gensifer hailed him from the yacht. "Glinnes! Come aboard for a moment, there's a good fellow!"

Glinnes sauntered indifferently up the gangway. Lord Gensifer clapped him on the back and conducted him into the salon. Glinnes saw a dozen folk in fashionable garments, apparently aristocratic friends of Lord Gensifer, and also Akadie, Marucha, and Duissane, who now wore over her sheet white gown a red cloak, evidently borrowed from one of the ladies present. "Here then is our hero!" declared Lord Gensifer. "With cool resource he saved two lovely sheirls from the starmenters. In our great grief we at least can be thankful for this boon."

Glinnes looked in wonder about the salon. He felt as if he were living a particularly absurd dream. Akadie, Lord Gensifer, Marucha, Duissane, himself—what a strange mix of people!

"I hardly know what happened today," said Glinnes, "beyond the bare fact of the raid."

"The bare fact is about all anyone knows," said Akadie. He seemed unusually subdued and neutral, and careful in his choice of words. "The starmenters knew exactly who they wanted. They took exactly three hundred folk of substance, and about two hundred girls as well. The three hundred are to be ransomed for a minimum of a hundred thousand ozols apiece. No ransom prices have been set on the girls, but we will do our best to buy them back."

"Then they've already been in communication?"

"Indeed, indeed. The plans were carefully made, and each person's financial capacity was carefully gauged."

Lord Gensifer said with facetious self-deprecation, "Those left behind have suffered a loss of prestige, which we keenly resent."

Akadie went on. "For reasons apparently good and sufficient, I have been appointed collector of the ransom, for which effort I am to receive a fee. No great amount, I assure you—in fact, five thousand ozols will requite my work."

Glinnes listened, dumbfounded. "So the total ransom will be three hundred times a hundred thousand, which is—"

"Thirty million ozols—a good day's work."

"Unless they end up on the prutanshyr."

Akadie made a sour face. "A barbaric relict. What benefit do we derive from torture? The starmenters come back regardless."

"The public is edified," said Lord Gensifer. "Think of the kidnaped maidens—one of whom might have been my good friend Duissane!" He placed his arm around Duissane's shoulders and gave her a mock-fraternal squeeze. "Is, then, the revenge too severe? Not to my way of thinking."

Glinnes blinked and gaped back and forth between Lord Gensifer and Duissane, who seemed to be smiling at a secret joke. Had the world gone mad? Or was he in truth living a preposterous dream?

Akadie formed a quizzical arch with his eyebrows. "The starmenters' sins are real enough; let them suffer."

One of Lord Gensifer's friends asked, "By the way, which particular band of starmenters is responsible?"

"There has been no attempt at anonymity," said Akadie. "We have attracted the personal attention of Sagmondo Bandolio—Sagmondo the Stern—who is as wicked as any."

Glinnes knew the name well; Sagmondo Bandolio had long been the quarry of the Whelm. "Bandolio is a terrible man," said Glinnes. "He extends no mercy."

"Some say he is a starmenter only for sport," Akadie remarked. "They say he has a dozen identities about the Cluster and that he could live forever on the fortunes he has gained."

The group mused in silence. Here was evil on a scale so vast that it became awesome.

Glinnes said, "Somewhere in the prefecture is a spy, someone intimate with all the aristocrats, someone who knows the exact level of every fortune."

"That statement must be reckoned accurate," said Akadie.

"Who could it be?" pondered Lord Gensifer. "Who could it be?"

And all persons present considered the matter, and each formed his private speculation.

· ·

The Tanchinaros, by defeating the Karpouns, had done themselves a disservice. Since Sagmondo Bandolio and his starmenters had taken their treasure, the team was without resources, and because of their demonstrated abilities, Perinda could schedule no thousand-ozol or two-thousand-ozol games. And now they lacked the treasure to challenge any teams in the ten-thousand-ozol class.

A week after the Karpoun game the Tanchinaros met at Rabendary Island, and Perinda explained the sorry state of affairs. "I've found only three teams willing to play us, and not one will risk their sheirl for less than ten thousand ozols. Another matter: we lack a sheirl. Duissane seems to have caught the interest of a certain lord, which naturally was her ambition. Now neither she nor Tammi choose to risk the exposure of her precious hide."

"Bah!" said Lucho. "Duissane never loved hussade in the first place."

"Naturally not," said Warhound. "She's Trevanyi. Have you ever seen a Trevanyi play hussade? She's the first Trevanyi sheirl I've ever known."

"Trevanyi play their own games," said Gilweg.

"Like 'Knives and Gullets,' " said Glinnes.

"And 'Trills and Robbers.' "

"And 'Merling, Merling, Who's Got the Cadaver?' "

"And 'Hide and Sneak.' "

Perinda said, "We can always recruit a sheirl. Our problem is money."

Glinnes said grudgingly, "I'd put up my five thousand ozols if I thought I'd get it back."

Warhound said, "I could scrape up a thousand, one way or another."

"That's six thousand," said Perinda. "I'll put in a thousand—or rather, I can borrow a thousand from my father . . . Who else? Who else? Come then, you miserly mud-thumpers, bring out your wealth."

Two weeks later the Tanchinaros played the Ocean Island Kanchedos, at the great Ocean Island Stadium, for a twenty-five-thousand-ozol purse, with fifteen thousand hazarded by each team and ten thousand by the stadium. The new Tanchinaro sheirl was Sacharissa Simone, a girl from Fal Lal Mountain—pleasant, naïve, and pretty, but lacking in that imponderable quality, *sashei*. There was likewise general doubt as to her virginity, but no one wanted to make an issue of the matter. "Let's all of us have a night with her," grumbled Warhound, "and resolve the question to everybody's satisfaction."

Whatever the reason, the Tanchinaros played sluggishly and committed a number of startling errors. The Kanchedos won an easy three-ring victory. Sacharissa's possibly innocent body was displayed in every detail to thirty-five thousand spectators, and Glinnes found himself with only three or four hundred ozols in his purse. In a state of stupefied depression he returned to Rabendary Island, and flinging himself down in one of the old string chairs, he spent the evening staring across the broad at Ambal Isle. What a chaotic mess he had made of his life! The Tanchinaros—impoverished, humiliated, on the verge of fragmentation. Ambal Isle—now farther from his grasp than ever. Duissane, a girl who had worked a curious enthrallment upon him, had now fixed her ambitions upon the aristocracy, and Glinnes, previously only lukewarm, now roiled at the thought of Duissane in another man's bed.

Two days after the catastrophic game with the Kanchedos, Glinnes rode the ferry into Welgen to find a buyer for twenty sacks of his excellent Rabendary musk-apples, a matter soon arranged. With an hour to wait for the return trip, Glinnes stopped for a bite of lunch at a small restaurant half indoors, half out under the shade of a fulgeria arbor. He drank a pot of beer and gnawed at bread and cheese, and watched the folk of Welgen move about their affairs . . . Here passed a group of true Fanschers—sober young folk, erect and alert, frowning into the distance as if absorbed in concepts of great portent . . . And here came Akadie, walking quickly, with his head lowered, his Fanscher-style jacket flapping out to the sides. Glinnes called out as he passed, "Akadie! Drop yourself in a chair; take a pot of beer!"

Akadie halted as if he had struck an invisible obstruction. He peered into the shade to isolate the source of the voice, glanced over his shoulder, and ducked hastily into a chair beside Glinnes. His face was pinched; his voice when he spoke was sharp and nervous. "I think I've put them aside, or at least I hope so."

"Oh?" Glinnes looked along the way Akadie had come. "Who have you put aside?"

Akadie's response was typically oblique. "I should have refused the commission; it has brought me only anxiety. Five thousand ozols! When I am dogged by avaricious Trevanyi, awaiting only a moment of carelessness. What a farce. They can take their thirty million ozols, together with my paltry five thousand, and fabricate the most expensive bumstopper in the marveling memory of the human universe."

"In other words," said Glinnes, "you have collected the thirty million ozols ransom?"

Akadie gave a peevish nod. "I assure you, it is not real money; that is to say, the five thousand ozols which becomes my fee represents five thousand spendable ozols. I carry thirty million ozols in this case"—here he nudged a small black case with a silver clasp—"but it seems like so much wadded paper."

"To you."

"Precisely." Akadie peered over his shoulder once again. "Other folk are less adept in abstract symbology, or more accurately, they use different symbols. These tokens to me are fire and smoke, pain and fear. Others perceive an entirely different set of referrents: palaces, space-yachts, perfumes and pleasures."

"In short, you fear that the money will be stolen from you?"

Akadie's nimble mind had far outdistanced a categorical response. "Can you imagine the vicissitudes liable to the man who withheld thirty million ozols from Sagmondo Bandolio? The conversation might go in this fashion: Bandolio: 'I now require of you, Janno Akadie, the thirty million ozols entrusted to your care.' Akadie: 'You must be brave and forebearing, since I no longer have the money.' Bandolio: '. . . Alas. My imagination falters. I can conceive no further.' Would he be cold? Would he rave? Would he utter a negligent laugh?"

"If indeed you are robbed," said Glinnes, "one small benefit will be the gratification of your curiosity."

Akadie acknowledged the remark with only a sour side glance. "If I could surely identify someone, or something; if I knew precisely whom or what to avoid . . ." He left the sentence unfinished.

"Have you noticed any specific threat? Or are you just nervous?"

"I am nervous, to be sure, but this is my usual state. I loathe discomfort, I dread pain, I refuse even to acknowledge the possibility of death. All these circumstances now seem to hover close."

"Thirty million ozols is an impressive sum," said Glinnes wistfully. "Personally, I need only twelve thousand of them."

Akadie pushed the case toward Glinnes. "Here you are; take whatever you require and explain the lack to Bandolio . . . But no." He jerked the case back once more. "I am not allowed this option."

"I am puzzled on one account," said Glinnes. "Since you are so anxious, why do you not simply place the money in a bank? Yonder, for instance, is the Bank of Welgen, twenty seconds from where we sit."

Akadie sighed. "If only it were that easy . . . My instructions are to keep the money ready at hand, for delivery to Bandolio's messenger."

"And when does he come?"

Akadie rolled his eyes up toward the fulgeria. "Five minutes? Five days? Five weeks? I wish I knew."

"It seems somewhat unreasonable," said Glinnes. "Still, the starmenters work by the systems they find most useful. And think! A year from today the episode will provide you many a merry anecdote."

"I can think only of this moment," grumbled Akadie. "This case sits in my lap like a red-hot anvil."

"Who exactly do you fear?"

Even at his most fretful, Akadie could not resist a didactic analysis. "Three groups hotly yearn for ozols: the Fanschers, that they may buy land, tools, information and energy; the noble folk, in order to refurbish their flaccid fortunes; and the Trevanyi, who are naturally avaricious. Only moments ago I discovered two Trevanyi walking unobtrusively behind me."

"This may or may not be significant," said Glinnes.

"All very well to deprecate." Akadie rose to his feet. "Are you returning to Rabendary? Why not ride out with me?"

They walked to the dock and in Akadie's white runabout set off eastward along the Inner Broad. Between the Lace Islands, across Ripil Broad they sped, past Saurkash, then along narrow Athenry Water and out upon Fleharish Broad, where they observed a rakish black and purple craft darting back and forth at great speed.

"Speaking of Trevanyi," said Glinnes, "notice who joyrides with Lord Gensifer."

"I noticed her." Akadie thoughtfully stowed his black case under the stern seat.

Lord Gensifer drove his boat through a sportive caracole, projecting a long feather of spume into the air, then rushed hissing forward to overtake Akadie and Glinnes. Akadie, murmuring an objurgation, allowed his boat to coast to a standstill; Lord Gensifer drew up alongside. Duissane, wearing a charming pale-blue gown, glanced sidewise with an expression of sulky boredom but made no other acknowledgment. Lord Gensifer was in one of his most expansive moods. "And where are you bound this lovely afternoon, with such a pair of hangdog looks about you? Off to rob Lord Milfred's duck preserve, or so I'd wager." Lord Gensifer here made waggish allusion to an ancient joke of the district. "What a pair of rogues, to be sure."

Akadie replied in his most polished voice. "I fear we have more important concerns, beautiful day or not."

Lord Gensifer made an easy gesture to signify that the course of his little joke was run. "How does your collection progress?"

"I took in the last monies this morning," said Akadie stiffly. The subject was clearly one he did not care to pursue, but Lord Gensifer tactlessly continued. "Just hand me over a million or two of those ozols. Bandolio would hardly feel the difference."

"I'd be pleased to hand you over the whole thirty million," said Akadie, "and you could settle accounts with Sagmondo Bandolio."

"Thank you," said Lord Gensifer, "but I think not." He peered into Akadie's boat. "You really carry the money about with you, then? Ah, there in the bilge, as casual as you please. Do you realize that boats sometimes sink? What would you say then to Sagmondo the Stern?"

Akadie's voice cracked under the strain of his displeasure. "The contingency is most remote."

"Undoubtedly true. But we're boring Duissane, who cares nothing for such matters. She refuses to visit me at Gensifer Manor—think of it! I've tempted her with luxury and elegance; she'll have none of it. Trevanyi through and through. Wild as a bird! You're sure you can't spare even a million ozols? What about half a million? A paltry hundred thousand?"

Akadie smiled with steely patience and shook his head. With a wave of his hand Lord Gensifer pulled back the throttle; the purple and silver boat lunged forward, swept around in a slashing arc, and drove north toward the Prefecture Commons, the heel of which closed off the tip of Fleharish Broad.

Akadie and Glinnes proceeded more sedately. At Rabendary Island, Akadie chose to stop ashore for a cup of tea, but sat on the edge of his chair peering first up Ilfish Way, then across Ambal Broad, then through the row of pomanders which screened Farwan Water. These, with their tall waving blades, created a sense of furtive motion which made Akadie more nervous than ever.

Glinnes brought forth a flask of old wine to soothe Akadie's apprehension, with such good effect that the afternoon waned into pale avness. At last Akadie felt obliged to go home. "If you like you can accompany me. Truth to tell, I'm a trifle on edge."

Glinnes agreed to follow Akadie in his own boat, but Akadie stood rubbing his chin as if reluctant to depart. "Perhaps you should telephone Marucha and let her know that we are on the way. Inquire also if she has noticed unusual circumstances of any sort whatever."

"Just as you like." Glinnes went to make the call. Marucha was indeed relieved to learn that Akadie was on his way home. Unusual circumstances? None of consequence. Perhaps a few more boats in the vicinity, or it might have been the same boat passing back and forth. She had barely noticed.

Glinnes found Akadie on the end of the dock, frowning up Farwan Water. He set off in his white runabout and Glinnes followed close behind, all the way to Clinkhammer Broad, clear, calm and empty in the mauve-gray light of evening. Glinnes saw Akadie safely to the dock, then swung about and returned to Rabendary.

Hardly had he arrived home before the telephone gong sounded. Akadie's face appeared on the screen with an expression of lugubrious triumph. "It went exactly as I had expected," said Akadie. "There they were, waiting for me behind the boat-house—four of them, and I'm sure Trevanyi, though they all wore masks."

"What happened?" Glinnes demanded, for Akadie seemed intent on arranging his tale to the best dramatic effect.

"Just what I expected; that's what happened," snapped Akadie. "They overpowered me and took the black case; then they fled in their boats."

"So. Thirty million ozols down the chute."

"Ha hah! Nothing of the sort. Only a locked black case packed with grass and dirt. There will be some sorry Drossets when they force the lock. I say Drossets advisedly, for I recognized the peculiar stance of the older son, and Vang Drosset's posture is also characteristic."

"You mentioned—*four?*"

Akadie managed a grim smile. "One of the thugs was somewhat frail. This person stood aside and kept a lookout."

"Indeed. Then where is the money?"

"This is why I called. I left it in the bait-box on your dock, and my fore-thought was amply justified. What I want you to do is this. Go out on your dock and make sure there are no observers. Take the foil-wrapped packet from the box and carry it inside your house, and I will call for it tomorrow."

Glinnes scowled at Akadie's image. "So now I'm in charge of your con-founded money. I don't want my throat cut any more than you. I fear I must charge you a professional fee."

Akadie instantly emerged from his preoccupation. "How absurd! You incur no risks. No one knows where the money is—"

"Someone might make a thirty-million-ozol guess. Don't forget who saw us together earlier today."

Akadie laughed somewhat shakily. "Your agitation is excessive. Still, if it gives you comfort, station yourself with your hand-gun where you can watch for trespassers. In fact, this is perhaps the judicious course. We'll both feel better for the vigilance."

Glinnes stuttered in indignation. Before he could speak, Akadie made a reassuring gesture and dimmed the screen.

Glinnes jumped to his feet and strode back and forth across the room. Then he brought forth his hand-gun, as Akadie had suggested, and went out on the dock. The waterways were empty. He made a circuit of his house, walking wide around the prickleberry bushes. So far as he could determine, there was no one on Rabendary Island but himself.

The bait-box exerted an intolerable fascination. He went back out on the dock and flipped up the lid. There indeed—a packet wrapped in metal foil. Glinnes took it forth and after a moment of indecision carried it into the house. What did thirty million ozols look like? No harm in soothing his curiosity. He unfolded the covering to find a wad of folded periodicals. Glinnes stared down aghast. He started for the telephone, then stopped short. If Akadie knew of the situation, his manner would be intolerably dry and jocular. If, on the other hand, Akadie were ignorant of the substitu-tion, the news would shatter him, and might well be postponed until the morning.

Glinnes rewrapped the packet and replaced it in the bait-box. Then he brewed himself a cup of tea and took it out on the verandah, where he sat brooding across the water. Night now fully encompassed the Fens; the sky was paved with stars. Glinnes decided that Akadie himself had transferred the money, leaving the foil-wrapped parcel as a decoy. A typically subtle joke . . .

Glinnes turned his head at the gurgle of water. A merling? No—a boat approaching slowly and softly from the direction of Ilfish Water. He jumped down from the verandah and went to stand in the deep shade under the sombarilla tree.

The air was absolutely quiet. The water lay like polished moonstone. Glinnes squinted through the starlight and presently perceived a nondescript skiff with a single, rather frail person aboard. Akadie returning for his ozols? No. Glinnes' heart gave a queer quick throb. He started to step forward from the shade, then halted and drew back.

The boat drifted to the dock. The person aboard stepped ashore and dropped the mooring line over a bollard. Quietly through the starlight she came, and halted in front of the verandah. "Glinnes! Glinnes!" Her voice was hushed and secretive, like the call of a night bird.

Glinnes watched. Duissane stood indecisive, shoulders drooping. Then she went up on the verandah and looked into the dark house. "Glinnes!"

Glinnes came slowly forward. "I'm over here."

Duissane walked while he crossed the verandah. "Did you expect me?"

"No," said Glinnes. "Not really."

"Do you know why I came?"

Glinnes slowly shook his head. "But I am frightened."

Duissane laughed quietly. "Why should you be frightened?"

"Because once you gave me to the merlings."

"Are you afraid of death?" Duissane moved a step closer. "What is there to fear? I have no fear. A soft-winged black bird carries our ghosts to the Vale of Xian, and there we wander, at peace."

"The folk eaten by merlings leave no ghosts. And in this connection, where are your father and your brothers? Arriving by way of the forest?"

"No. They would grind their teeth if they knew I was here."

Glinnes said, "Walk around the house with me."

Without protest she came with him. To the best effort of Glinnes' senses, Rabendary Island was deserted except for themselves.

"Listen," said Duissane. "Hear the tree-croakers . . ."

Glinnes nodded shortly. "I heard them. There's no one in the forest."

"Then do you believe me?"

"You've told me only that your father and brothers aren't here. I believe that, because I can't see them."

"Let's go into the house."

Inside the house Glinnes turned up the light. Duissane dropped her cape. She wore only sandals and a thin frock. She carried no weapon.

"Today," she said, "I rode in a boat with Lord Gensifer, and I saw you. I decided that tonight I would come here."

"Why?" asked Glinnes, not altogether puzzled but not altogether certain.

Duissane put her hands on his shoulders. "Do you remember on the little island, how I jeered at you?"

"Very well indeed."

"You were too vulnerable. I longed for your harshness. I wanted you to laugh at my words, to take me and hold me close. I would have melted on that instant."

"You dissembled very well," said Glinnes. "As I remember, you called me 'despicable, untidy and gluttonous.' I was convinced that you hated me."

Duissane made a sad grimace. "I have never hated you—never. But you must know that I am solitary and wayward, and I am slow to love. Look at me now." She tilted up her face. "Do you think I am beautiful?"

"Oh indeed. I've never thought otherwise."

"Hold me close, then, and kiss me."

Glinnes turned his head and listened. From Rabendary Forest the susurration of the tree-croakers had never ceased. He looked back at the face close under his own. It swam with unusual emotions, which he could not define and which therefore troubled him; he had never seen such a look in any other eyes. He sighed; how difficult to love a person so intensely distrusted! How far more difficult not to do so! He bent his head and kissed Duissane. It was as if he had never kissed anyone before. She smelled of a fragrant herb, of lemon, and, vaguely, of woodsmoke. With his pulses racing, he knew he now could never turn back. If she had set out to enthrall him, she had succeeded; he felt he could never get enough of her. But what of Duissane? From around her neck she drew a heart-shaped tablet. Glinnes recognized it as a lovers' cauch. With nervous fingers Duissane broke the tablet and gave Glinnes half. "I have never touched cauch before," she said. "I have never wanted to love anyone before. Pour us a goblet of wine."

Glinnes brought a flask of green wine from the cupboard and poured full a goblet. He went to the verandah and looked up and down the water. It lay calm and dreaming, broken only by the ripple of a merling who somewhere had surfaced.

"What did you expect to see?" asked Duissane softly.

"Half a dozen Drossets," said Glinnes, "with eyes spurting fire and knives in their mouths."

"Glinnes," said Duissane earnestly, "I swear to you that no one knows I am here but you and me. Are you not aware of how my people regard virginity? They would spare me no more than you."

Glinnes brought the goblet of wine across the room. Duissane opened her mouth. "Do as a lover would."

Glinnes placed the cauch on the tip of her tongue; she washed it down with the wine. "Now you."

Glinnes opened his mouth. She put her half of the lovers' tablet upon his tongue. It might be cauch, thought Glinnes, or she might have substituted a soporific, or a poison drug. He held the tablet in front of his teeth, and taking the goblet, drank the wine, and then made shift to eject the tablet into the goblet. He took the goblet to the sideboard, then turned to face Duissane. She had slipped off her gown; she stood nude and graceful before him, and Glinnes never had seen so delightful a sight. And he was finally convinced that the male Drossets were not quietly approaching through the dark. He went to Duissane and kissed her; she loosened the fastenings of his shirt. He slipped from his clothes and, taking her to the couch, would have proceeded, but she rose to her knees and held his head to her breast. He could hear her heart thumping; he felt sure her emotion was genuine. She whispered, "I have been cruel, but this is all past. Henceforth, I live only to exalt you, to make you the happiest of men, and you shall never regret it."

"You intend to live here with me on Rabendary?" inquired Glinnes, both cautious and puzzled.

"My father would kill me first," sighed Duissane. "You cannot imagine his hate . . . We must fly to a far world and there live as aristocrats. Perhaps we shall buy a space-yacht and wander among the colored stars."

Glinnes laughed. "All very well, but all this requires money."

"No problem there; we will use the thirty million ozols."

Glinnes somberly shook his head. "I am sure Akadie would object to this."

"How can Akadie deny us? My father and my brothers robbed him tonight. His case contained trash. He had the money today in the boat and he has been nowhere but here. He left the money here, did he not?" And Duissane peered into Glinnes' face.

Glinnes smiled. "Akadie left a parcel in my bait-box, for a fact." And now he would wait no longer and drew her down to the couch.

They lay engaged, and Duissane, her face rapt, looked up at Glinnes. "You will take me from Trullion, and off and away? I so want to live in wealth."

Glinnes kissed her nose. "Sh!" he whispered. "Be happy with what we have now and here . . ."

But she said, "Tell me, tell me that you'll do as I ask."

"I can't," said Glinnes. "All I can give you is myself and Rabendary."

Duissane's voice became anxious. "But what of the parcel in the bait-box?"

"That's trash too. Akadie has fooled us all. Or someone else swindled him before he left Welgen."

Duissane stiffened. "You mean that there is no money here?"

"So far as I know, not an ozol."

Duissane moaned, and the sound rose in her throat to become a wail of grief for her lost virginity. She tore herself free from the embrace and ran across the dim room, out on the dock. She opened the bait-box, and pulled out the foil-wrapped package, tore it open. At the sight of the wastepaper she cried out in agony. Glinnes watched from the doorway, rueful, grim and sad, but by no means bewildered. Duissane had loved him well enough, as well as she could. Heedless of her nakedness she ran blindly down the dock and jumped into her boat, but missed her footing and toppled screaming into the water. A splash, and her voice became a gurgle.

Glinnes raced down the dock and jumped into her boat. Her pale form floundered six feet beyond his reach. In the starlight he saw her terrified face—she could not swim. Ten feet behind her appeared the oily black dome of a merling head, with eye-disks glowing silver. Glinnes gave a hoarse call of desperation and reached for Duissane. The merling wallowed close and seized her ankle. Glinnes jumped at its head and managed to strike it between the eyes with his fist, which damaged his knuckles and perhaps surprised the merling. Duissane seized Glinnes in a frantic drowner's grip, and wrapped her legs around his neck. Glinnes swallowed water. He wrenched the girl loose and, gaining the surface, thrust her toward the boat. A merling's palp seized his ankle, and this was the nightmare that haunted every mind of Trullion—to be dragged alive down to the merlings' dinner table. Glinnes kicked like a maniac; his heel ground into the merling's maw. He twisted and broke loose. Duissane clung whimpering to the dock piling. Glinnes floundered to the ladder; he clambered into the boat and pulled her over the gunwales and aboard. They lay limp and gasping like netted fish.

Something bumped the bottom of the boat—a disappointed merling. It might try to tip the boat in its hunger. Glinnes staggered onto the dock, pulled Duissane up after him, and took her back along the starlit path to the house.

She stood, withdrawn and miserable, in the middle of the room, while Glinnes poured two goblets of Olanche rum. Duissane drank apathetically, thinking her own dreary thoughts. Glinnes rubbed her dry with a towel, and himself as well, then took her to the couch, where she began to cry. He stroked her and kissed her cheeks and forehead. Gradually she became warm and relaxed. Cauch worked in her blood; the thought of dark still water thrilled her mind; she became responsive and again they embraced.

Early in the morning Duissane rose from the couch and without words donned her gown and her sandals. Glinnes watched, dispassionate and lethargic, as if seeing her through a telescope. When she drew the cape around her shoulders, he sat up. "Where are you going?"

Duissane threw him the briefest of side-glances; her expression stilled the words in his mouth. He rose from the couch, wrapped a paray around his waist. Duissane was already out the door. Glinnes followed her down the path and out upon the dock, trying to think of something to say that would sound neither hollow nor petulant.

Duissane stepped into her boat. She turned him a flat glance and then departed. Glinnes stood looking after her, his mind whirling and confined. Why did she act so? She had come to him; he had solicited nothing, offered nothing . . . He discerned his error. It was necessary, he told himself, to see the situation from the Trevanyi point of view. He had seared her extravagant Trevanyi pride. He had accepted from her something of immeasurable value; he had returned nothing, let alone that which she had hoped to receive. He was callous, shallow, unfeeling; he had made a fool of her.

There were further, darker implications deriving from the Trevanyi world-view. He was not just Glinnes Hulden, not just a lecherous Trill; he represented dark Fate, the hostile Cosmic Soul against which the Trevanyi felt themselves in heroic opposition. For the Trills, life flowed with mindless ease—that which was not here today would arrive tomorrow; in the meantime it was negligible. Life itself was pleasure. For the Trevanyi, each event was a portent to be examined in all aspects and tested for consequences and aftermath. He shaped his universe piece by piece. Any advantage or stroke of luck was a personal victory to be celebrated and gloated over; any misfortune or setback, no matter how slight, was a defeat and an insult to his self-esteem. Duissane had therefore suffered psychological disaster, and by his instrumentality, even though from the Trill point of view, he had only accepted what had been freely offered.

Heavy at heart, Glinnes turned back to the house. His eye fell on the bait-box. A curious idea entered his mind. He raised the lid and looked within. There—the foil-wrapped parcel of wastepaper, which he took forth. He raked his fingers into the bottom layer of chaff and sawdust and encountered an object which proved to be a packet wrapped in transparent film. Glinnes saw pink and black Bank of Alastor certificates. Akadie had employed a sly trick to hide the money. Glinnes mused a moment, then took the foil-wrapped packet, discarded the wastepaper. He used the foil to wrap the money, which he replaced in the bait-box. Scarcely had he finished when he heard the sound of an approaching boat.

Down Farwan Water came Akadie's white boat, with two passengers: Akadie and Glay. The boat coasted up to the dock; Glinnes took the line and dropped the loop over the bollard.

Akadie and Glay jumped up on the dock. "Good-morning," said Akadie in a voice of subdued cheer. He examined Glinnes with a clinical eye. "You are pale."

"I slept poorly," said Glinnes, "what with worrying over your money."

"It is safe, I hope?" asked Akadie brightly.

"Duissane Drosset looked at it," said Glinnes ingenuously. "For some reason she let it lie."

"Duissane! How did she know it was there?"

"She asked where it was; I told her that you had left a packet in the bait-box. She claims that it contains only wastepaper."

Akadie laughed. "My little joke. I concealed the money rather cunningly, I do believe." Akadie went to the bait-box, removed the foil-wrapped package, which he dropped to the dock, and reached through the layer of chaff. His face froze. "The money is gone!"

"Imagine that!" said Glinnes. "It is hard to believe Duissane Drosset a thief."

Akadie scarcely heard him. In a voice strained with fear he cried, "Tell me, where is the money? Bandolio will not be kind; he'll send men to tear me apart . . . Where, oh where? Did Duissane take the money?"

Glinnes could torment Akadie no further. He nudged the foil-wrapped packet with his toe. "What's this?"

Akadie swooped at the packet and tore it open. He looked up at Glinnes in gratitude and exasperation. "How wicked, to bait a man already on tenterhooks!"

Glinnes grinned. "What now will you do with the money?"

"As before, I wait for instructions."

Glinnes looked at Glay. "And what of you? Still a Fanscher, it seems."

"Naturally."

"What of your headquarters, or central institute—whatever you call it?"

"We have claimed a tract of open land not too far from here, at the head of the Karbashe Valley."

"At the head of the Karbashe? Is that not the Vale of Xian?"

"The Vale of Xian is close at hand."

"A strange choice of location," said Glinnes.

"How strange?" retorted Glay. "The land is free and unoccupied."

"Except for the Trevanyi death-bird and uncounted Trevanyi souls."

"We will not disturb their occupancy, and I doubt if they will trouble ours. The land will be used in joint tenancy, so to speak."

"What then of my twelve thousand ozols, if your land is coming so cheap?"

"Never mind the twelve thousand ozols. We have sufficiently discussed the matter."

Akadie had already stepped into his boat. "Come along then; let us return to Rorquin before thieves appear on the river."

G linnes watched the white boat until it disappeared. He examined the sky. Heavy clouds hung over the mountains and loomed against the sun. The water of Ambal Broad seemed heavy and listless. Ambal Isle was a charcoal sketch on mauve-gray broad. Glinnes went up to the verandah and eased himself into one of the old string chairs. The events of last night, so rich and dramatic, now seemed stuff built of dream-vapor. Glinnes took no pleasure in the recollection. Duissane's motives, however ingenuous, had not been altogether false; he might have mocked her and sent her home in anger, but not in shame. How different everything seemed in the ashen light of day! . . . He jumped to his feet, annoyed at the uncomfortable trend of his thoughts. He would work. There was much to be done. He could pick musk-apples. He could go to the forest and gather pepperwort for drying. He could spade up the garden plot. He could repair the shed, which was about to collapse. The prospect of so much effort made him drowsy; he took himself inside to his couch and slept.

About midday he awoke to the sound of light rain on the roof. Glinnes drew a cloak over himself and lay pondering. Somewhere at the back of his mind hung a dark urgency, a matter requiring attention. Hussade practice? Lute Casagave? Akadie? Glay? Duissane? What about Duissane? She had come, she had gone, and would no longer wear a yellow flower in her hair. She might do so anyway, to hide the facts from Vang Drosset. On the other hand, she might risk his fury and tell him all. More likely, she might present an altered version of her nocturnal adventures. This possibility, already recognized by his subconscious, now caused Glinnes overt uneasiness. He rose to his feet and went to the door. A silver drizzle obscured much of Ambal Broad, but so far as Glinnes could detect, no boats were abroad. The Trevanyi, nomads by nature, considered rain an unlucky portent; not even to wreak vengeance would a Trevanyi set forth in the rain.

Glinnes rummaged through the larder and found a dish of cold boiled mudworm, which he ate without appetite. Then the rain came to a sudden halt; sunlight spread across Ambal Broad. Glinnes went out on the verandah. All the world was fresh and wet, the colors clarified, the water glistening, the sky pure. Glinnes felt a lift of the spirits.

There was work to be done. He lowered himself into the string chair to consider the matter. A boat entered Ambal Broad from Ilfish Water. Glinnes jumped to his feet, tense and wary. But the boat was only one of

Harrad's rental craft. The occupant, a young man in a semi-official uniform, had lost his way. He steered up to Rabendary dock and rose to stand on the seat. "Halloo there," he called to Glinnes. "I'm more than half lost. I want Clinkhammer Broad, near Sarpassante Island."

"You're far south. Who are you looking for?"

The young man consulted a paper. "A certain Janno Akadie."

"Up Farwan Water into the Saur, take the second channel to the left, and continue all the way into Clinkhammer Broad. Akadie's manse stands on a jut."

"Very good; the route is clear in my mind. Aren't you Glinnes Hulden, the Tanchinaro?"

"I'm Glinnes Hulden, true enough."

"I saw you play the Elements. It wasn't much of a contest, as I recall."

"They're a young team, and reckless, but I'd consider them basically sound."

"Yes, that's my opinion as well. So then—good luck to the Tanchinaros, and thank you for your help."

The boat moved up Farwan Water past the silver and russet pomanders and out of sight, and Glinnes was left thinking about the Tanchinaros. They had not practiced since the game with the Kanchedos; they had no money; they had no sheirl . . . Glinnes' thoughts veered to Duissane, who never again could be sheirl, and then to Vang Drosset, who might or might not be aware of the events of last night. Glinnes looked across Ambal Broad. No boats could be seen. He went to the telephone and called Akadie.

The screen glowed: Akadie's face was unwontedly peevish, and his voice was fretful. "Gong, gong, gong is all I hear. The telephone is a dubious convenience. I'm expecting a distinguished visitor and I don't care to be annoyed."

"Indeed!" said Glinnes. "Is he a young man in a pale-blue uniform and a messenger's cap?"

"Naturally not!" declared Akadie. His voice caught abruptly. "Why do you ask?"

"A few minutes ago such a man inquired the way to your house."

"I'll watch for him. Is that all you wanted?"

"I thought I might come by later today and borrow twenty thousand ozols."

"Puh! Where would I find twenty thousand ozols?"

"I know one place."

Akadie gave a sour chuckle. "You must borrow from someone more intent on suicide than myself." The screen went dead.

Glinnes ruminated a moment but could contrive no further excuses for idleness. He took crates out into the orchard and picked apples, working with the irritable energy of a Trill caught up in an activity which he considers a barely necessary evil. Twice he heard the gong of his telephone, but he ignored it, and thus knew nothing of a fateful event which had occurred earlier that day. He picked a dozen crates of apples, loaded them on a barrow which he trundled to a shed, then returned to the orchard to pick more and finish the job.

Afternoon waned; the dismal light of avness altered to the gunmetal, old rose and eggplant of evening. Stubbornly Glinnes worked on. A cold wind blew down from the mountains and struck through his shirt. Was more rain on the way? No. The stars already were showing—no rain tonight. He loaded the last of his apples on the barrow and started for the storage shed.

Glinnes halted. The door to the shed was half-ajar. Only half-ajar. Odd, when he purposely had left it open. Glinnes set down the barrow and returned into the orchard to think. He was not wholly surprised; in fact, he had gone to the unusual precaution of carrying his gun in his pocket. From the corner of his eye he looked back toward the shed. There would be one within, one behind, and a third lurking at the corner of the house, or so he suspected. In the orchard he had been beyond the range of a thrown knife, and in any event they would hardly want to kill him outright. First there would be words, then cutting and twisting and burning, to ensure that he derived no advantage whatsoever from his offense. Glinnes licked his lips. His stomach felt hollow and odd . . . What to do? He could not stand much longer in the twilight pretending to admire his apple crop.

He walked without haste around the side of the house; then, picking up a stave, he ran back and waited at the corner. There were running footsteps, a mutter of rapid words. Around the corner bounded a dark shape. Glinnes swung the stick; the man threw up his arm and took the blow on his wrist; he uttered a yell of distress. Glinnes swung the stick again; the man caught the stick under his arm. Glinnes tugged; the two swung and reeled together. Then someone else was on him, a man heavy, smelling of sweat, roaring in rage—Vang Drosset. Glinnes jumped back and fired his gun. He missed Vang Drosset but struck Harving, the first man, who groaned and tottered away. A third dark shape loomed from nowhere and grappled Glinnes; the two struggled while Vang Drosset danced close, his throaty rageful roar never ceasing. Glinnes fired his gun, but he could not aim and burnt the ground at Vang Drosset's feet; Vang Drosset leapt clumsily into the air. Glinnes kicked and stamped and broke the grip of Ashmor, but not before Vang Drosset had dealt him a blow to knock his head askew and daze him. In return Glinnes managed to kick Ashmor in the groin, sending him staggering against the wall of the house. Harving, on the ground, made a convulsive motion; a metallic flicker stung Glinnes' shoulder. Glinnes fired his gun; Harving slumped and was limp.

"Merling food," gasped Glinnes. "Who else? You, Vang Drosset? You? Don't move; don't even stir, or I'll burn a hole through your gut."

Vang Drosset froze; Ashmor leaned against the side wall. "Walk ahead of me," said Glinnes. "Out on the dock." When Vang Drosset hesitated, Glinnes picked up the stave and struck him over the head. "I'll teach you to come murdering me, my fine Trevanyi bullies. You'll regret this night, I assure you . . . Move! Out on the dock. Go ahead, run off if you dare. I might miss you in the dark." Glinnes plied the stave. "Move!"

The two Drossets lurched out on the dock, numbed by the failure of their mission. Glinnes beat them until they lay down, and beat them further until they seemed dazed; then he tied them with odd bits of cordage.

"So there you are, my fine lummoxes. Now then, which of you killed my brother Shira? . . . Oh, you don't feel like talking? Well, I won't beat you further, though I well recall another time when you left me for the merlings. Now I must explain to you—Vang do you hear me? Speak, Vang Drosset, answer me."

"I hear you well enough."

"Listen then. Did you kill my brother Shira?"

"What if I did? It was my right. He gave cauch to my young girl; it was my right to kill him. And my right to kill you."

"So Shira gave cauch to your daughter."

"That he did, the varmous* Trill horn."

"So now, what happens to you?"

Vang Drosset was silent a moment, then he blurted, "You can kill me or cut me apart, but that's the good it'll do you."

"Here is my bargain," said Glinnes. "Write out a notification that you killed Shira—"

"I know no characters. I'll write you nothing."

"Then before witnesses you must declare that you killed Shira—"

"And then the prutanshyr? Aha!"

"Provide your own reasons; at this time I don't care. Assert that he struck you with a club or molested your daughter or called your wife a varmous old crow—no matter. Declare the affidavit and I'll let you go free, and you must swear by your father's soul to leave me in peace. Otherwise I'll roll both you and yonder murderous Ashmor into the mud and leave you for the merlings."

Vang Drosset moaned and strained at his bonds. His son raved: "Swear as you will; it won't include me! I'll kill him if it takes forever!"

"Hold your tongue," said Vang Drosset in a weary croak. "We are beaten; we must slink for our lives." To Glinnes: "Once more—what do you want?"

*varmous: dirty, infamous, scurrilous; an adjective often applied to the Trills.

Glinnes restated his terms.

"And you won't prefer a legal charge? I tell you the great sweating horn thrust cauch at her and would have rolled her in the meadow yonder . . ."

"I'll prefer no legal charge."

The son sneered. "What about gelding or nose-cutting? Will you leave us our members?"

"I have no need for your filthy members," said Glinnes. "Keep them for yourself."

Vang Drosset gave a sudden furious groan. "And what of my daughter whom you ravished, whom you fed cauch, whose value has now decreased? Will you pay the loss? Instead you kill my son and utter threats against me."

"Your daughter made her own way here. I asked nothing of her. She brought cauch. She seduced me."

Vang Drosset chattered in rage. His son cried out a set of obscene threats. Vang Drosset at last became tired and commanded his son to silence. To Glinnes he said, "I agree to the bargain."

Glinnes freed the son. "Take your corpse and be off with you."

"Go," droned Vang Drosset.

Glinnes pulled his own boat close beside the dock and rolled Vang Drosset into the bilges. Then he went into the house and called Akadie, but could make no connection; Akadie had turned off his telephone. Glinnes returned to his boat and drove up Farwan Water at full speed, pale foam veering to either side.

"Where are you taking me?" groaned Vang Drosset.

"To see Akadie the mentor."

Vang Drosset groaned again, but made no comment.

The boat nosed up to the dock under Akadie's eccentric house. Glinnes cut Vang Drosset's legs loose and hoisted him up to the dock. Tripping and stumbling, they proceeded up the path. Lights blazed from the towers, glaring into Glinnes' face. Akadie's voice came sharp, from a loudspeaker. "Who arrives? Announce yourself, if you please."

"Glinnes Hulden and Vang Drosset, on the path!" bawled Glinnes.

"An unlikely pair of chums," sneered the voice. "I believe I mentioned that I was occupied this evening?"

"I require your professional services!"

"Come forward then."

When they reached the house the door stood ajar, with light streaming forth. Glinnes shoved Vang Drosset forward and into the house.

Akadie appeared. "And what business is this?"

"Vang Drosset has decided to clarify the matter of Shira's death," said Glinnes.

"Very well," said Akadie. "I have a guest, and I hope that you will be brief."

"The affair is important," Glinnes declared gruffly. "It must be conducted correctly."

Akadie merely motioned toward the study. Glinnes cut Vang Drosset's arms free and thrust him forward.

The study was dim and peaceful. A pink-orange fire of driftwood blazed in the fireplace. A man arose from one of the fireside chairs and performed a polite inclination of the head. Glinnes, his attention fixed on Vang Drosset, spared him only a glance and received an impression of medium stature, neutral garments, a face without notable or distinctive characteristics.

Akadie, perhaps recalling the events of the previous day, recovered something of his graciousness. He addressed his guest. "May I present Glinnes Hulden, my good neighbor, and also"—Akadie made an urbane gesture—"Vang Drosset, a member of that peregrine race, the Trevanyi. Glinnes and Vang Drosset, I wish to present a man of wide intellectual scope and considerable erudition, who interests himself in our small corner of the Cluster. He is Ryl Shermatz. From the evidence of his jade locket, I believe his home world to be Balmath. Am I correct in this?"

"As correct as needful," said Shermatz. "I am indeed familiar with Balmath. But otherwise you flatter me. I am a wandering journalist, no more. Please ignore me, and proceed with your business. If you require privacy I will remove myself."

"No reason why that should be necessary," said Glinnes. "Please resume your seat." He turned to Akadie. "Vang Drosset wishes to utter a sworn information before you, a legally accredited witness, which in effect will clarify the title of Rabendary and Ambal Isle." He nodded to Vang Drosset. "Proceed, if you will."

Vang Drosset licked his lips. "Shira Hulden, a dastardly horn, assaulted my daughter. He offered her cauch and attempted to force her. I came on the scene, and in the protection of my property accidentally killed him. He is dead and there you have it." The last was a growl toward Glinnes.

Glinnes inquired of Akadie, "Does this constitute a valid proof of Shira's death?"

Akadie spoke to Vang Drosset. "Do you swear by your father's soul that you have spoken the truth?"

"Yes," grumbled Vang Drosset. "Mind you, it was self-defense."

"Very good," said Akadie. "The confession was freely made before a mentor and public counselor and other witnesses. The confession holds legal weight."

"Be good enough, in this case, to telephone Lute Casagave and order him off my property."

Akadie pulled at his chin. "Do you propose to refund his money?"

"Let him collect from the man to whom he paid it—Glay Hulden."

Akadie shrugged. "I naturally must regard this as professional work, and I must charge you a fee."

"I expected nothing less."

Akadie went off to his telephone. Vang Drosset said in a surly voice, "Are you done? At my camp there'll be great grief tonight, and all due to the Huldens."

"The grief is due to your own murderousness," said Glinnes. "Need I go into details? Never forget how you left me for dead in the mud."

Vang Drosset marched sullenly to the door, where he turned and blurted, "No matter what, it's fair exchange for the shame you put on us, you and all the other Trills, with your gluttony and lust. Horns all of you! Guts and groins, so much for the Trills. And you, Glinnes Hulden, stay out of my way; you won't have it so easy next time." He turned and stamped from the house.

Akadie, returning to the study, watched him go with nostrils fastidiously pinched. "You had best guard your boat," he told Glinnes. "Otherwise he'll drive away and leave you to swim."

Glinnes stood in the doorway and watched Vang Drosset's burly form recede along the road. "He carries grief too heavy for the boat, or any other mischief. He'll find his way home by Verleth Bridge. What of Lute Casagave?"

"He refuses to answer his telephone," said Akadie. "You must postpone your triumph."

"Then you must postpone your fee," said Glinnes. "Did the messenger find his way here?"

"Yes indeed," said Akadie. "I can justly say that he carried away a great load of my responsibilities. I am gratified to be done with the business."

"In that case, perhaps you have a cup of tea to offer me? Or is your business with Ryl Shermatz absolutely private?"

"You may have tea," said Akadie ungraciously. "The conversation is general. Ryl Shermatz is interested in the Fanscherade. He wonders how a world so generous and easy could breed so austere a sect."

"I suppose we must consider Junius Farfan as a catalyst," remarked Shermatz. "Or perhaps, for better comparison, let us think in terms of a supersaturated solution. It seems placid and stable, but in a single microscopic crystal produces disequilibrium."

"A striking image!" declared Akadie. "Allow me to pour out a drop of something more energetic than tea."

"Why not indeed?" Shermatz stretched out his legs to the fire. "You have a most comfortable home."

"Yes, it is pleasant!" Akadie went to fetch a bottle.

Glinnes asked Shermatz, "I hope that you find Trullion entertaining?"

"I do indeed. Each world of the Cluster projects a mood of its own, and the sensitive traveler quickly learns to identify and savor this individuality. Trullion, for instance, is calm and gentle; its waters reflect the stars. The light is mild; the landscapes and waterscapes are entrancing."

"This gentle aspect is what strikes the eye," agreed Akadie, "but sometimes I wonder as to its reality. For instance, under these placid waters swim merlings, creatures as unpleasant as any, and these calm Trill faces conceal terrible forces."

"Come now," said Glinnes. "You exaggerate."

"By no means! Have you ever heard a hussade crowd cry out to spare the conquered sheirl? Never! She must be denuded to the music of—of what? The emotion has no name, but it is as rich as blood."

"Bah," said Glinnes. "Hussade is played everywhere."

Akadie ignored him. "Then there is the prutanshyr. Amazing to watch the rapt faces as some wretched criminal demonstrates how dreadful the process of dying can be."

"The prutanshyr may serve a useful purpose," said Shermatz. "The effects of such affairs are difficult to judge."

"Not from the standpoint of the miscreant," said Akadie. "Is this not a bitter way to die, to look out upon the fascinated throng, to know that your spasms are providing a repast of entertainment?"

"It is not a private or sedate occasion," said Shermatz with a sad smile. "Still, the folk of Trullion seem to consider the prutanshyr a necessary institution, and so it persists."

"It is a disgrace, to Trullion and to Alastor Cluster," said Akadie coldly. "The Connatic should ban all such barbarity."

Shermatz rubbed his chin. "There is something in what you say. Still, the Connatic hesitates to interfere with local customs."

"A double-edged virtue! We rely upon him for wise decisions. Whether or not you love the Fanschers, at least they despise the prutanshyr and would obliterate the institution. If they ever come to power they will do so."

"No doubt they would expunge hussade as well," said Glinnes.

"By no means," said Akadie. "The Fanschers are indifferent to the game; it has no meaning for them, one way or the other."

"What a grim fastidious lot!" said Glinnes.

"They seem even more so by contrast with their varmous parents," said Akadie.

"No doubt true," said Ryl Shermatz. "Still, one must note that an extreme philosophy often provokes its antithesis."

"That is the case here on Trullion," said Akadie. "I warned you that the idyllic atmosphere is delusive."

A glare of light flooded the study, persisting only a moment. Akadie uttered an ejaculation and went to the window, followed by Glinnes. They saw a great white cruiser coming slowly across Clinkhammer Broad; the masthead searchlight playing along the shore, briefly touching Akadie's manse, had illuminated the study.

Akadie said in a wondering voice, "I believe it's the *Scopoeia*, Lord Rianle's yacht. Why should it be here in Clinkhammer Broad, of all places?"

A boat left the yacht and made for Akadie's dock; simultaneously the horn sounded three peremptory blasts. Akadie muttered under his breath and ran from the house. Ryl Shermatz wandered here and there about the room inspecting Akadie's clutter of mementos, bric-à-brac, curios. A cabinet displayed Akadie's collection of small busts, each one or another of the personages who had shaped the history of Alastor—scholars, scientists, warriors, philosophers, poets, musicians, and on the bottom shelf, a formidable array of anti-heroes. "Interesting," said Ryl Shermatz. "Our history has been rich, and the histories before ours as well."

Glinnes pointed out a particular bust. "There you see Akadie himself, who fancies himself one with the immortals."

Shermatz chuckled. "Since Akadie has assembled the group, he must be allowed the right to include whom he pleases."

Glinnes went to the window in time to see the boat returning to the yacht. A moment later, Akadie entered the room, face ash-gray and hair hanging in lank strings.

"What's wrong with you?" demanded Glinnes. "You look like a ghost."

"That was Lord Rianle," croaked Akadie. "The father of Lord Erzan-Rianle, who was kidnaped. He wants his hundred thousand ozols back."

Glinnes stared in amazement. "Will he leave his son to rot?"

Akadie went to the alcove where he kept his telephone and switched the set back into operation. Turning back to Shermatz and Glinnes, he said, "The Whelm raided Bandolio's haven. They captured Bandolio, all his men and ships; they liberated the captives Bandolio took at Welgen, and many more besides."

"Excellent news!" said Glinnes. "So why walk around like a dead man?"

"This afternoon I sent away the money. The thirty million ozols are gone."

CHAPTER 18

Glinnes led Akadie to a chair. "Sit down, drink this wine." He turned a glance toward Ryl Shermatz, who stood looking into the fire. "Tell me, how did you send the money off?"

"By the messenger you directed here. He carried the correct symbol. I gave him the parcel; he went away, and that is all there is to it."

"You don't know the messenger?"

"I have never seen him before." Akadie's wits seemed to snap back in place. He glared at Glinnes. "You seem very concerned!"

"Should I be uninterested in thirty million ozols?"

"How is it that you did not hear the news? It's been current since noon! Everyone has been trying to telephone me."

"I was working in my orchard. I paid no heed to the telephone."

"The money belongs to the people who paid the ransoms," declared Akadie in a stern voice.

"Indisputably. But whoever retrieves it might legitimately claim a good fee."

"Bah," muttered Akadie. "Have you no shame?"

The gong sounded. Akadie gave a nervous start and stumbled to the telephone. After a moment he returned. "Lord Gygax also wants his hundred thousand ozols. He won't believe that I sent off the money. He became insistent, even somewhat insulting."

The gong sounded again. "You are in for a busy evening," said Glinnes, rising to his feet.

"Are you going?" asked Akadie in a pitiful voice.

"Yes. If I were you I'd turn the telephone off again." He bowed to Ryl Shermatz. "A pleasure to have met you."

Glinnes drove his boat at full speed west across Clinkhammer Broad, under the Verleth Bridge, down Mellish Water. Ahead shone a dozen dim lights: Saurkash. Glinnes drifted into the dock, moored his boat and jumped ashore. Saurkash was quiet except for a few muffled voices and a laugh or two from the nearby Magic Tench. Glinnes walked along the dock to Harrad's boat agency. An overhead light shone down on the rental boats. He went to the shop and looked in through the door. Young Harrad was nowhere to be seen, though a light glowed in the office. One of the men at the tavern rose to his feet and ambled down to the dock. It was Young Harrad. "Yes, sir, what might you be wanting? If it's boat repair, nothing till tomorrow . . . Ah, Squire Hulden, I didn't recognize you under the light."

"No matter," said Glinnes. "Today I saw a young man in one of your boats, a hussade player I'm anxious to locate. Do you recall his name?"

"Today? About mid-afternoon, or a trifle earlier?"

"That would be about the time."

"I've got it written down inside. A hussade player, you say. He didn't look the type. Still, you never know. What's next for the Tanchinaros?"

"We'll be back in action soon. Whenever we can collect ten thousand ozols for a treasury. The weak teams won't play us."

"For good reason! Well, let's look at the register . . . This might well be his name." Young Harrad turned the ledger first one way, then the other. "Schill Sodergang, or so I make it out. No address."

"No address? And you don't know where he can be found?"

"Perhaps I should be more careful," Young Harrad apologized. "I've never yet lost a boat, except when old Zax went blind on soursap."

"Did Sodergang have anything to say to you? Anything whatever?"

"Nothing much, except to ask the way to Akadie's house."

"And when he came back—what then?"

"He asked what time the Port Maheul boat came past. He had to wait an hour."

"He had a black case with him?"

"Why yes, he did."

"Did he talk to anyone?"

"He just sat dozing on the beach yonder."

"It's no great matter," said Glinnes. "I'll see him another time."

Glinnes drove pell-mell down the dark waterways, past the groves of silent trees, black stencils fringed with star-silver. At midnight he arrived in Welgen. He slept at a dockside inn and early in the morning boarded the eastbound ferry.

Port Maheul, named for its busy space-field rather than its site on the shores of the South Ocean, was the largest town of Jolany Prefecture and perhaps the oldest city of Trullion. The principal structures were built to archaic standards of solidity with glazed russet brick, timbers of ageless black salpoon, and steep roofs sheathed with blue glass shingles. The square was reckoned as picturesque as any in Merlank, with its perimeter of ancient buildings, black sulpicella trees, and herringbone pavement of russet-brown bricks and cobbles of mountain hornblende. At the center stood the prutanshyr, with its glass caldron, through the sides of which a criminal being boiled and the rapt crowd might inspect each other. Off the square sprawled an untidy market, then a clutter of ramshackle little houses, then the gaunt glass and iron space depot. The field extended east to the Genglin Marshes, where, so it was said, the merlings crept up through the mud and reeds to marvel at the spaceships coming and going.

Glinnes spent a toilsome three days in Port Maheul searching for Schill Sodergang. The steward of the ferry that plied between the Fens and Port Maheul vaguely remembered Sodergang as a passenger, but could recall nothing else, not even Sodergang's point of debarkation. The town roster listed no Sodergangs, nor was the name known to the constabulary.

Glinnes visited the spaceport. A ship of the Andrujukha Line had departed Port Maheul on the day following Sodergang's visit to the Fens, but the name Sodergang failed to appear on the manifest.

On the afternoon of the third day Glinnes returned to Welgen, and then by his own boat to Saurkash. Here he encountered Young Harrad, whom he found bursting with sensational information, and Glinnes had to delay his own questions to listen to Young Harrad's gossip—which was absorbing enough in itself. It seemed that an act of boldest villainy had been effected almost under Young Harrad's nose, so to speak. Akadie, whom Young Harrad never had wholly trusted, was the cool culprit who had decided to seize opportunity by the forelock and sequester to himself thirty million ozols.

Glinnes gave an incredulous laugh. "Sheer absurdity!"

"Absurdity?" Young Harrad looked to see if Glinnes was serious. "The lords all hold this opinion; can so many be wrong? They refuse to believe that Akadie closed off his telephone on the precise day that news of Bandolio's capture arrived."

Glinnes snorted in disparagement. "I did exactly the same thing. Am I a criminal on that account?"

Young Harrad shrugged. "Someone is thirty million ozols the richer. Who? The proof is not yet explicit, but Akadie has helped himself not at all by his actions."

"Come now! What else has he done?"

"He has joined Fanscherade! He's now a Fanscher. It's the common belief that they took him in because of the money."

Glinnes clutched his spinning head. "Akadie a Fanscher? I can't believe it. He's too clever to join a group of freaks!"

Young Harrad stuck to his guns. "Why did he depart in the dark of the night and travel up to the Vale of Green Ghosts? And remember, for ever so long he has worn Fanscher clothes and aped the Fanscher style."

"Akadie is merely somewhat silly. He enjoys a fad."

Young Harrad sniffed. "He can enjoy what he likes now, that's certain. In a way, I respect such audacity, but when thirty million ozols are at stake a switched-off telephone sounds pretty thin."

"What else could he say except the truth? I saw the switched-off telephone myself."

"Well, I'm sure the truth will be made clear. Did you ever find that hussade player, Jorcom, Jarcom, whatever his name?"

"Jorcom? Jarcom?" Glinnes stared in wonder. "Sodergang, you mean?"

Young Harrad grinned sheepishly. "That was somebody else, a fisherman down Isley Broad. I wrote the name in the wrong place."

Glinnes controlled his voice with an effort. "The man's name is Jorcom, then? Or Jarcom?"

"Let's take a look," said Young Harrad. He brought out his register. "Here's Sodergang, and here is the other name; it looks like Jarcom to me. He wrote it himself."

"It looks like Jarcom," said Glinnes. "Or is it Jarcony?"

"Jarcony! You're right! That's the name he used. What position does he play?"

"Position? Rover. I'll have to look him up sometime. Except that I don't know where he lives." Glinnes looked at Young Harrad's clock. If he drove at breakneck speed back to Welgen he could just barely connect with the Port Maheul ferry. He made a gesticulation of fury and frustration, then jumped in his boat and hurtled back east toward Welgen.

In Port Maheul, Glinnes found the name "Jarcony" as unknown as "Sodergang." Tired and bored beyond caring, he took himself to the arbor in front of The Stranger's Rest and ordered a flask of wine. Someone had discarded a journal; Glinnes picked it up and scanned the page. His eye was caught by an article:

AN ILL-FATED HOSTILITY AGAINST THE FANSCHERS

Yesterday news reached Port Maheul of an improper act committed by a Trevanyi gang against the Fanscher camp in the Vale of Green Ghosts, or, as the Trevanyi know it, the Vale of Xian. The Trevanyi motives are in doubt. It is known that they resent the Fanscher presence in their sacred vale. But also it will be remembered that the mentor Janno Akadie, for many years resident in the Saurkash region, has declared himself a Fanscher and now resides at the Fanscher camp. Speculation links Akadie with a sum of thirty million ozols, which Akadie claims to have paid to the starmenter Sagmondo Bandolio, but which Bandolio denies having received. It is possible that the leader of the Trevanyi gang, a certain Vang Drosset, apparently decided that Akadie had taken the money with him into the Vale of Green Ghosts, and so organized the raid. The facts are these: seven Trevanyi entered Akadie's tent during the night, but failed to stifle his outcries. A number of Fanschers responded to the call and in the ensuing fight two Trevanyi were killed and several others wounded. Those who escaped took refuge at a Trevanyi conclave nearby, where sacred rites are in progress. Needless to say, the Trevanyi failed to possess themselves of the thirty million ozols, which evidently has been hidden securely. The Fanschers are outraged by the attack, which they deem an act of persecution.

"We fought like karpouns," declared a Fanscher spokesman. "We attack no one, but will fiercely protect our rights. The future is for Fanscherade! We summon the youth of Merlank, and all those opposed to the varmous old life-ways: join Fanscherade! Lend us your strength and comradeship!"

Chief Constable Filidice declares himself perturbed by the circumstance and has launched an investigation. "No further disruptions of the public peace will be tolerated," he stated.

Glinnes threw the journal across the table. Slumping into his chair he poured half a goblet of wine down his throat. The world he knew and loved seemed in fragments. Fanschers and Fanscherade! Lute Casagave, Lord Ambal! Jorcom, Jarcom, Jarcony, Sodergang! He despised each of the names!

He finished the wine, then went down to the dock to wait for the boat back to Welgen.

CHAPTER 19

Rabendary Island seemed unnaturally still and lonesome. An hour after Glinnes' return the gong sounded; he discovered his mother's face on the telephone screen.

"I thought you'd gone to join the Fanschers," said Glinnes in a voice of hollow jocularity.

"No, no, not I." Marucha's voice was fretful and worried. "Janno went to avoid the confusion. You can't conceive the browbeating, the bluster, the accusations which have come our way! We had no respite and poor Janno finally felt obliged to leave."

"So he isn't a Fanscher after all."

"Of course not! You've always been such a literal-minded child! Can't you understand how a person might be interested in an idea without becoming its staunchest advocate?"

Glinnes accepted the deficiencies imputed to him. "How long will Akadie stay in the Vale?"

"I feel that he should return at once. How can he live a normal life? It's quite literally dangerous! Did you hear how the Trevanyi set upon him?"

"I heard that they tried to rob him of his money."

Marucha's voice raised in pitch. "You shouldn't say such a thing, even as a joke. Poor Janno! What he hasn't gone through! And he's always been such a good friend to you."

"I've done nothing against him."

"Now you must do something for him. I want you to go to the Vale and bring him home."

"What? I see no point in such an expedition. If he wants to come home, he'll do so."

"That's not true! You can't imagine his mood; he is limp with passivity! I've never seen him so before!"

"Perhaps he's just resting—taking a vacation, so to speak."

"A vacation? With his life in danger? It's common knowledge that the Trevanyi plan a massacre."

"Hmmf. I hardly think that is the case."

"Very well. If you won't help me, then I must go myself."

"Go where? Do what?"

"Go to the Fanscher camp and insist that Janno return home."

"Confound it. Very well. Suppose he won't come?"

"You must do your best."

Glinnes rode the air-bus to the mountain town Circanie, then hired an ancient surface-car to convey him to the Vale of Xian. A garrulous old man with a blue scarf tied around his head was included in the rental price; he manipulated the antique device as if he were directing a recalcitrant animal. The car at times scraped the ground; at other times it bounded thirty feet into the air, providing Glinnes with startling perspectives over the countryside. Two energy guns on the seat beside the driver attracted his attention and he inquired as to their purpose.

"Dangerous territory," said the driver. "Whoever thought we'd see such a day?"

Glinnes considered the landscape, which seemed as placid as Rabendary Island. Mountain pomanders stood here and there—clouds of pink mist clutched in silver fingers. Blue-green fials marched along the ridge. Whenever the car rose into the air the horizons widened; the land to the south fell away in receding striations of pallid colors.

Glinnes said, "I see no great cause for alarm."

"So long as you're not a Fanscher, your chances are tolerable," said the driver. "Not good, mind you, because the Trevanyi conclave is only a mile or two yonder, and they are as suspicious as wasps. They drink *racq*, which influences the nerves and makes them none the kindlier."

The valley grew narrow; the mountains rose steep on either side. A quiet river flowed along the flat floor; on each side stood groves of sombarilla, pomander, deodar.

Glinnes asked, "Is this the Vale of Green Ghosts?"

"Some call it so. The Trevanyi bury lesser dead among the trees. The true and sacred Vale lies ahead, behind the Fanschers. There—you can see the Fanscher camp. They are an industrious group, no question as to that . . . I wonder what they are trying to do? Do they know themselves?"

The car slid into the camp—a scene of confusion. Hundreds of tents had been erected along the riverbank; on the meadow, buildings of concrete foam were under construction.

Glinnes found Akadie without difficulty. He sat at a desk in the shade of a glyptus tree performing clerical work. He greeted Glinnes with neither surprise nor affability.

"I am here to bring you to your senses," said Glinnes. "Marucha wants you back at Rorquin's Tooth."

"I will return when the mood strikes me," said Akadie in a measured voice. "Until you arrived life was peaceful . . . Though for a fact my wisdom has been in no great demand. I expected to be greeted as a noble sage; instead I sit here doing footling sums." He made a deprecatory gesture at his desk. "I was told that I must earn my keep and this is a job no one cares to undertake." He cast a sour glance toward a nearby cluster of tents. "Everyone wants to participate in the grandiose schemes. Directives and announcements flow like chaff."

"I should think" said Glinnes, "that with thirty million ozols you could easily pay your way."

Akadie gave him a glance of weary reproach. "Do you realize that this episode has blasted my life? My integrity has been questioned and I can never again serve as mentor."

"You have ample wealth even without the thirty million," said Glinnes. "What shall I tell my mother?"

"Say that I am bored and overworked, but at least the accusations have not followed me here. Do you plan to see Glay?"

"No. What are all these concrete structures?"

"I have made it my business to know nothing," said Akadie.

"Have you seen the ghosts?"

"No, but on the other hand I have not looked for them. You'll find Trevanyi graves across the river, but the sacred home of the death-bird is a mile up the valley, beyond that copse of deodars. I made a casual exploration and was exalted. An enchanting place, beyond all question—too good for the Trevanyi."

"How is the food?" asked Glinnes ingenuously.

Akadie made a sour grimace. "The Fanschers intend to learn the secrets of the universe, but now they cannot so much as toast bread properly. Each meal is the same: gruel and a salad of coarse greens. There is not a flask of wine for miles . . ." Akadie spoke on for several minutes. He remarked upon Fanscher dedication and Fanscher innocence, but mostly of Fanscher austerity, which he found inexcusable. He trembled with rage at the mention of the thirty million ozols, yet he showed a pathetic anxiety for reassurance. "You yourself saw the messenger; you directed him to my house. Does the fact carry no weight?"

"No one has required my evidence. What of your friend Ryl Shermatz? Where was he?"

"He saw nothing of the transaction. A strange man, that Shermatz! His soul is quicksilver."

Glinnes rose to his feet. "Come along then. You achieve nothing here. If you dislike notoriety, stay quietly at Rabendary for a week or so."

Akadie pulled at his chin. "Well, then, why not?" He gave the papers a contemptuous flick. "What do the Fanschers know of style, urbanity, discernment? They have me doing sums." He rose to his feet. "I will leave this place. Fanscherade grows tiresome; these folk will never conquer the universe after all."

"Come along then," said Glinnes. "Have you anything to bring? Thirty million ozols, for instance?"

"The joke has lost its savor," said Akadie. "I will go as I am, and to lend flair to my departure, I will perform an unfamiliar equation." He scrawled a few flamboyant flourishes on the paper, then slung his cloak over his shoulder. "I am ready."

The ground-car slid down the Vale of Green Ghosts and toward avness arrived at Circanie. Akadie and Glinnes put up for the night at a little country inn.

At midnight Glinnes awoke to hear excited voices, and a few minutes later detected the sound of running footsteps. He looked out the window, but the street lay quiet in the starlight. Drunken revelry, thought Glinnes, and returned to his couch.

In the morning they heard the news that explained the occasion. During the night the Trevanyi had waxed passionate at their conclave; they had walked through fires; they had performed their bounding mood-dances; their "Grotesques," as they called their seers, had breathed the smoke of baicha roots and had belched forth the destiny of the Trevanyi race. The warriors responded with mad screams and ululations; running and leaping over the starlit hills, they had attacked the Fanscher camp.

The Fanschers were by no means unprepared. They employed their energy-guns with dire effect; the bounding Trevanyi became startled statues limned in blue sparks. Action became confused. The first zestful onslaught became a mournful writhing of bodies up and down the Vale, and presently there was no more fighting; the Trevanyi were either dead or had fled in a horror as full and wild as their attack. The Fanschers watched them go in dismal silence. They had won but they had lost. Fanscherade would never be the same; its verve and vivacity was gone, and in the morning there would be dreary work to do.

Akadie and Glinnes returned to Rabendary without incident, but Glinnes' slipshod housekeeping made Akadie irritable, and before the day was out he decided to return to Rorquin's Tooth.

Glinnes telephoned Marucha, who had undergone a change of mood; now she fretted at the prospect of Akadie's return. "There has been such turmoil and all unnecessary; my head is splitting. Lord Gensifer demands that Janno make instant contact with him. He is most persistent and not at all sympathetic."

Akadie's pent emotions burst forth in outrage. "Does he dare to hector me? I'll set him straight, and quickly too. Get him on the telephone!"

Glinnes made the connection. Lord Gensifer's face appeared on the screen. "I understand that you wish a word or two with Janno Akadie," said Glinnes.

"Quite true," stated Lord Gensifer. "Where is he?"

Akadie stepped forward. "I am here, and why not? I recall no pressing business with you; still, you have been incessantly telephoning my house."

"Come then," said Lord Gensifer, thrusting forth his lower lip. "There is still a matter of thirty million ozols to be discussed."

"Why should I discuss them with you, in any event?" demanded Akadie. "You have nothing at stake. You were not kidnaped; you paid no ransom."

"I am secretary to the Council of Lords, and I am empowered to look into the matter."

"I still do not take kindly to your tone of voice," said Akadie. "My position has been made clear. I will discuss the matter no further."

Lord Gensifer was silent a moment. "You may have no choice," he said at last.

"I really don't understand you," replied Akadie in an icy voice.

"The situation is quite simple. The Whelm is delivering Sagmondo Bandolio to Chief Constable Filidice in Welgen. Undoubtedly he will be forced to identify his accomplices."

"This means nothing to me. He can identify as he will."

Lord Gensifer cocked his head to the side. "Someone with intimate local knowledge furnished information to Bandolio. This person will share Bandolio's fate."

"Deservedly so."

"Let me say only that if you remember any helpful information, no matter how trifling, you may communicate with me at any hour of the day or night—excepting of course this day week"—Lord Gensifer chuckled benignly—"which is when I espouse to myself Lady Gensifer."

Akadie's professional interest was stirred. "Who is to be the new Lady Gensifer?"

Lord Gensifer half closed his eyes in beatific reflection. "She is gracious, beautiful, and virtuous beyond compare, far too fine for a person like myself. I refer to the former Tanchinaro sheirl Duissane Drosset. Her father was killed in the recent battle and she has turned to me for comfort."

Akadie added drily, "The day has then brought us at least one delightful surprise."

The screen dimmed on Lord Gensifer's countenance.

In the Vale a strange quiet prevailed. Never had the fabled landscape seemed so beautiful. The weather was exceptionally clear; the air, a crystal lens, intensified, deepened the colors. Sounds were clarified but somehow muted, or perhaps the folk in the Vale spoke in somber voices and avoided sudden sounds. At night the lights were few and dim, and conversations were murmurs in the dark. The Trevanyi raid had corroborated what many had suspected—that Fanscherade, if it were to succeed, must defeat a broad array of negative forces. Now was a time for resolution and a hardening of the spirit! A few persons abruptly left the Vale and were seen no more.

At the Trevanyi conclave fury had broadened and deepened. If any voices urged moderation, they no longer could be heard for the strident music of drums, horns, and that coiled full-throated instrument known as the *narwoun*. At night the men leapt through fires and cut themselves with knives to yield blood for their rites. Clans from far Bassway and the Eastlands arrived, and many carried energy-guns. Kegs of an ardent distillation known as *racq* were broached and consumed, and the warriors sang great oaths to the skirling music of the *narwoun*, drums and oboes.

On the third morning after the night raid a squad of constables appeared at the conclave, including Chief Constable Filidice. He advised the Trevanyi to reasonable conduct and announced his resolve to maintain order.

Trevanyi voices cried out in protest. The Fanschers encroached upon sacred soil, the Vale where ghosts walked!

Chief Constable Filidice raised his voice. "You have cause for concern. I intend to represent your case to the Fanschers. Nonetheless, whatever the outcome, you must abide by my decision. Do you agree?"

The Trevanyi remained silent.

Chief Constable Filidice repeated his demand for cooperation and again received no commitment. "If you refuse to accede to my judgment," he said, "obedience will be forced upon you. So be warned!"

The constables returned to their aircraft and flew over the hill into the Vale of Green Ghosts.

Junius Farfan conferred with Chief Constable Filidice. Farfan had lost weight; the garments hung loosely about his figure, and harsh lines marked his face. He listened to the Chief Constable in silence. His response was cold. "We have worked here for several months, without inconvenience to anyone. We respect the Trevanyi graves; there has been no irreverence; they are never denied freedom of passage into their Vale of Xian. The Trevanyi are irrational; we respectfully must refuse to leave our land."

Chief Constable Filidice, a bulky pallid man with ice-blue eyes, ponderous with the majesty of his office, had never taken kindly to recalcitrance. "Just so," he said. "I have enjoined restraint upon the Trevanyi; I now do the same to you."

Junius Farfan bowed his head. "We will never attack the Trevanyi. But we are ready to defend ourselves."

Chief Constable Filidice uttered a sarcastic snort. "The Trevanyi are warriors, every man of them. They would cut your throats with a flourish,

144 / JACK VANCE

should we allow them to do so. I strongly advise you to make other arrangements. Why need you build your headquarters in such a place?"

"The land was free and open. Will you provide us land elsewhere?"

"Naturally not. In fact, I see no reason why you need a great headquarters in the first place. Why not simply retire to your homes and avoid all
this contention?"

Junius Farfan smiled. "I perceive your ideological bias."

"It is not bias to favor the tried and true ways of the past; it is ordinary
common sense."

Junius Farfan shrugged and attempted no refutation of an irrefutable
point of view. The constables established a patrol across the ridge.

The day passed. Avness brought a lightning storm. For an hour lavender
strands of fire stroked the dark flanks of the hills. Fanschers came forth to
marvel at the spectacle. Trevanyi shuddered at the portent; in their world-
view, Urmank the Ghost-Killer stood on the clouds, spitting the souls of
Trevanyi and Trill alike. Nonetheless they arrayed themselves, drank *racq*,
exchanged embraces, and at midnight set forth upon their mission in order
that they might attack during the gray hour before dawn. They deployed
under the deodars and along the ridges, avoiding the constables and their
detection apparatus. In spite of their stealth they encountered a Fanscher
ambush. Shouts and screams ruptured the predawn silence. Energy-guns
flashed; struggling shapes created grotesque silhouettes against the sky. The
Trevanyi fought with hissing curses, guttural cries of pain; the Fanschers
strove in dire silence. The constabulary blew horns; waving the black and
gray flag of government authority, they advanced upon the conflict. The
Trevanyi, suddenly aware that they confronted an insensate foe, gave
ground; the Fanschers pursued like Fates. The constables blew their horns
and issued orders; they were handled roughly; the black and gray flag was
torn from their grasp. The constables radioed Circanie; Chief Constable
Filidice, aroused from his sleep and already out of sorts with Fanscherade,
ordered out the militia.

Halfway into morning the militia arrived in the Vale—a company of
Trill country-folk. They despised Trevanyi, but knew them and accepted
their existence. The freakish Fanschers were outside their experience, and
hence alien. The Trevanyi, recovered from their panic, followed the militia
into the valley, with musicians loping along at the flank playing screes and
warwhoops.

The Fanschers had retreated to the shelter of the deodar forest; only
Junius Farfan and a few others awaited the militia. They no longer hoped
for victory; the power of the state was now ranged against them. The captain of the militia came forward and issued orders: the Fanschers must leave
the Vale.

"On what grounds?" asked Farfan.

"Your presence provokes a disturbance."

"Our presence is legal."

"Nevertheless, it creates a tension which previously did not exist. Legality must encompass practicality, and your continued occupation of the Vale of Green Ghosts is impractical. I must insist that you depart."

Junius Farfan consulted with his comrades. Then, tears streaming down his cheeks for the destruction of his dream, he turned away to instruct those Fanschers who watched from the shade of the deodars. Addled by *racq*, the Trevanyi could not contain themselves. They sprang at the hated Farfan; a thrown knife struck squarely into the back of Farfan's neck. The Fanschers raised a weird moan. Eyes wide in horror, they fell upon militia and Trevanyi alike. The militia, uninterested in the quarrel, broke ranks and fled. Trevanyi and Fanschers tumbled about on the ground, each eager to destroy the other.

Eventually, through some mysterious process of mutual accord, the survivors crawled apart. The Trevanyi returned over the hills to the keening conclave. The Fanschers paused only a few moments in their camp, then wandered off down the valley. Fanscherade was finished. The great adventure was done.

Months later the Connatic, in conversation with one of his ministers, mentioned the battle in the Vale of Green Ghosts. "I was in the neighborhood and was kept apprised of events. It was a tragic set of circumstances."

"Could you not have halted the confrontation?"

The Connatic shrugged. "I might have brought down the Whelm. I tried this in a case not dissimilar—the affair of the Tamarchô on Rhamnotis—and there was no resolution. A troubled society is like a man with a stomach-ache. When he purges himself, he improves."

"Still—many folk must pay with their lives."

The Connatic made a wry gesture. "I enjoy the comradeship of the public house, the country inn, the dockside tavern. I travel the worlds of Alastor and everywhere I find people whom I find subtle and fascinating, people whom I love. Each individual of the five trillion is a cosmos in himself; each is irreplaceable, unique . . . Sometimes I find a man or a woman to hate. I look into their faces and I see malice, cruelty, corruption. Then I think, these folk are equally useful in the total scheme of things; they act as exemplars against which virtue can measure itself. Life without contrast is food without salt . . . As Connatic I must think in terms of policy; then I see only the aggregate man, whose face is a blur of five trillion faces. Toward this man I feel no emotion. So it was in the Vale of Green Ghosts. Fanscherade was doomed from its inception—was ever a man so fey as Junius

146 / JACK VANCE

Farfan? There are survivors, but there are no more Fanschers. Some will move on to other worlds. A few may become starmenters. A stubborn few may persist as Fanschers in their personal lives. And all who participated will remember the great dream and will feel as men apart from those who did not share the glory and the tragedy."

· ·

CHAPTER 20

To Rabendary Island came Glay, his clothes stained and rent, his arm in a sling. "I have to live somewhere," he said glumly. "It might as well be here."

"It's as good as any," said Glinnes. "I suppose you didn't bother to bring along the money."

"Money? What money?"

"The twelve thousand ozols."

"No."

"A pity. Casagave now calls himself Lord Ambal."

Glay was uninterested. He had no emotions left; his world was gray and flat. "Suppose he were Lord Ambal; does that give him the isle?"

"He seems to think so."

The gong summoned Glinnes to the telephone. The screen displayed Akadie's face. "Ah, Glinnes! I'm happy to have found you at home. I need your assistance. Can you come at once to Rorquin's Tooth?"

"Certainly, if you'll pay my usual fee."

Akadie made a petulant gesture. "I have no time for facetiousness. Can you come at once?"

"Very well. What is your difficulty?"

"I'll explain when you arrive."

Akadie met Glinnes at the door and led him almost at a trot into the study. "I wish to introduce two officials of the prefecture misguided enough to suspect my poor tired person of wrong-doing. On the right is our esteemed Chief Constable Benko Filidice; on the left is Inspector Lucian Daul, investigator, jailer, and sergeant of the prutanshyr. This, gentlemen, is my friend and neighbor Glinnes Hulden, whom you know better perhaps as the redoubtable right strike for the Tanchinaros."

The three men exchanged salutes; both Filidice and Daul spoke politely of Glinnes' play on the hussade field. Filidice, a large heavy-chested man with pale melancholy features and cold blue eyes, wore a suit of buff gabardine trimmed with black braid. Daul was thin and spare, with long thin arms, long hands, long fingers. Under a clot of dead black ringlets, his face was as pale as that of his superior, with bony over-emphatic features. Daul's manner was polite and delicate in the extreme, as if he could not bear the thought of giving offense.

Akadie addressed Glinnes in his most pedantic voice. "These two gentlemen, both able and dispassionate public servants, tell me that I have connived with the starmenter Sagmondo Bandolio. They have explained that the ransom money paid to me remains in my custody. I find myself doubting my own innocence. Can you reassure me?"

"In my opinion," said Glinnes, "you'd do anything to gain an ozol except take a chance."

"That's not quite what I meant. Did you not direct a messenger to my house? Did you not arrive to find me in conference with a certain Ryl Shermatz and my telephone switched off?"

"Precisely true," said Glinnes.

Chief Constable Filidice spoke in a mild voice. "I assure you, Janno Akadie, that we come to you principally because there is nowhere else to go. The money reached you, then disappeared. It was not received by Bandolio. We have explored his mind, and he is not deceiving us; in fact, he has been most frank and cordial."

Glinnes asked. "What were the arrangements, according to Bandolio?"

"The situation is most curious. Bandolio worked with a person fanatically cautious, a person who—to quote you—'would do anything to gain an ozol except take a chance.' This person initiated the project. He sent Bandolio a message through channels known only to starmenters, which suggests that this person—let us call him X—was either a starmenter himself or had such an accomplice."

"It is well known that I am no starmenter," declared Akadie.

Filidice nodded ponderously. "Still—speaking hypothetically—you have many acquaintances among whom might be a starmenter or an ex-starmenter."

Akadie looked somewhat blank. "I suppose that this is possible."

Filidice went on. "Upon receipt of the message Bandolio made arrangements to meet X. These arrangements were complicated; both men were wary. They met at a place near Welgen, in the dark. X wore a hussade mask. His plan was most simple. At a hussade game he would arrange that the wealthiest folk of the prefecture all sat in a single section; he would ensure this by sending out free tickets. X would receive two million ozols. Bandolio would take the rest . . .

"The scheme seemed sound; Bandolio agreed to the plan and events proceeded as we know. Bandolio sent a trusted lieutenant, a certain Lempel, here to receive the money from the collecting agency—which is to say, yourself."

Akadie frowned dubiously. "The messenger was Lempel?"

"No. Lempel arrived at the Port Maheul spaceport a week after the raid. He never departed; in fact he was poisoned, presumably by X. He died in his sleep at the Travelers Inn in Welgen the day before the news of Bandolio's capture arrived."

"That would be the day before I gave up the money."

Chief Constable Filidice merely smiled. "The ransom money was certainly not among his effects. So: I lay the facts before you. You had the money. Lempel did not have it. Where did it go?"

"He probably made arrangements with the messenger before he was poisoned. The messenger must have the money."

"But who is this mysterious messenger? Certain of the lords regard him as sheer fabrication."

Akadie said in a clear careful voice, "I now make this formal statement. I delivered the money to a messenger in accordance with instructions. A certain Ryl Shermatz was present at the time, and so much as witnessed the transfer."

Daul spoke for the first time. "He actually saw the money change hands?"

"He very probably saw me give the messenger a black case."

Daul fluttered one of his long-fingered hands. "A suspicious man might wonder if the case contained the money."

Akadie responded coldly. "A sensible man would realize that I would dare steal not so much as an ozol from Sagmondo Bandolio, let alone thirty million."

"But by this time Bandolio was captured."

"I knew nothing of this. You can verify the fact through Ryl Shermatz."

"Ah, the mysterious Ryl Shermatz. Who is he?"

"An itinerant journalist."

"Indeed! And where is he now?"

"I saw him two days ago. He said that he was soon to be leaving Trullion. Perhaps he is gone—where I don't know."

"But he is your single corroboratory witness."

"By no means. The messenger took a wrong turning and asked Glinnes Hulden for directions. True?"

"True," said Glinnes.

"Janno Akadie's description of this 'messenger' "—Daul gave the word a dry emphasis—"is unfortunately too general to assist us."

"What can I say?" demanded Akadie. "He was a young man of average size and ordinary appearance. He had no distinguishing features."

Filidice turned to Glinnes. "You agree to this?"

"Absolutely."

"And he provided no identification when he spoke to you?"

Glinnes cast his mind back across the weeks. "As I recall, he asked directions to Akadie's manse, no more." Glinnes broke off somewhat abruptly. Daul, instantly suspicious, thrust his face forward. "And nothing else?"

Glinnes shook his head and spoke decisively. "Nothing else."

Daul drew back. There was a moment of silence. Then Filidice said ponderously, "A pity that none of these persons you mention are available to confirm your remarks."

Akadie at last made a show of indignation. "I see no need for corroboration! I refuse to acknowledge that I need do more than enunciate the facts!"

"Under ordinary circumstances, yes," said Filidice. "With thirty million ozols missing, no."

"You now know as much as I," declared Akadie. "Hopefully you will pursue a fruitful investigation."

Chief Constable Filidice gave a disconsolate grunt. "We are grasping at straws. The money exists—somewhere."

"Not here, I assure you," said Akadie.

Glinnes could no longer restrain himself. He went to the door. "Fair weather for all. I must see to my affairs."

The constables gave him courteous farewell; Akadie spared only a peevish glance.

Glinnes almost ran to his boat. He drove east along Vernice Water, then instead of swinging south he turned north along Sarpent Channel, then out upon Junctuary Broad, where the Scurge River mingled its waters with the Saur. Glinnes turned up the Scurge. He proceeded back and forth up the meanders, every hundred yards cursing himself for his own stupidity. At the confluence of the Scurge with the Karbashe was Erch, a sleepy village almost hidden in the shade of enormous candlenut trees, where long ago the Tanchinaros had defeated the Elements.

Glinnes tied his boat to the dock and spoke to a man sitting outside the ramshackle wine-shop. "Where can I find a certain Jarcony? Or perhaps it's Jarcom?"

"Jarcony? Which one do you seek? Father? Son? Or the cavout dealer?"

"I want the young man who works in a blue uniform."

"That should be Remo. He's a steward on the Port Maheul ferry. You'll find him at home. Yonder, up the lane and under the thrackleberries."

Glinnes went up the path to where a great shrub almost engulfed a cabin of poles and fronds. He pulled a cord which swung the clapper of a little bell. A drowsy face peered from the window. "Who is it? And what for?"

"Resting after your labor, I see," said Glinnes. "Do you remember me?"

"Why, yes indeed. It's Glinnes Hulden. Well, well, think of that! Just a moment then."

Jarcony wrapped himself in his paray and swung back the creaking door. He pointed to a bower cut back into the thrackleberry thicket. "Sit down, if you will. Perhaps you'll take a cup of cool wine?"

"A good idea," said Glinnes.

Remo Jarcony brought forth a stoneware crock and a pair of mugs. "What conceivably brings you here to visit me?"

"A rather curious matter," said Glinnes. "As you recall, I met you while you were seeking the manse of Janno Akadie."

"Quite true. I'd contracted a small errand for a gentleman of Port Maheul. Surely there's been no difficulty?"

"I believe you were to deliver a parcel, or something similar?"

"Quite true. Will you take another cup of wine?"

"With great pleasure. And you delivered the parcel?"

"I did as I was instructed. The gentleman evidently was satisfied, as I haven't seen him since."

"May I ask the nature of those instructions?"

"Certainly. The gentleman required that I convey the parcel to the space depot at Port Maheul and place it in Locker 42, the key to which he gave me. I did as he required, thereby earning twenty ozols—money for nothing."

"Do you recall the gentleman who hired you?"

Jarcony squinted up into the foliage. "Not well. An off-worlder, or so I believe—a man short and stocky, with quick movements. He has a bald head as I recall, and a fine emerald in his ear, which I admired. Now, perhaps you'll enlighten me. Why do you ask such questions?"

"It's very simple," said Glinnes. "The gentleman is a publisher from Gethryn; Akadie wants to add an appendix to the treatise which he put into the gentleman's custody."

"Ah! I understand."

"There's nothing much to it. I'll notify Akadie that his work must already be in Gethryn." Glinnes rose to his feet. "Thank you for the wine, and I must now return to Saurkash . . . Out of sheer curiosity, what did you do with the key to the locker?"

"I did as I was instructed and left it at the accommodation desk."

Glinnes pushed westward at top speed, his wake bubbling the width of the narrow Jade Canal. He swept into Barabas River, hurling a white wave into the banked jerdine trees along the shore, and slid hissing westward, slowing only when he approached Port Maheul. He tied up at the main dock with a few deft twists of the mooring line, then half-walked, half-trotted the mile to the transport terminal, a tall structure of black iron and glass crusted pale green and violet with age. The field beyond was empty both of spaceships and local air transport.

Glinnes entered the depot and looked across the submarine gloom. Travelers sat on benches awaiting one or another of the scheduled air-buses. A bank of lockers stood along the wall beside the baggage office, where a clerk sat behind a low counter.

Glinnes crossed the room and inspected the lockers. Those available for use stood open, with magnetic keys in the lock holes. The door to Locker 42 was closed. Glinnes glanced toward the baggage clerk, then tested the door to find it immovable.

The locker was constructed of sound sheet-metal; the doors fit snugly. Glinnes seated himself on a nearby bench.

Various possibilities suggested themselves. Few of the lockers were in use. Among the fifty lockers, Glinnes counted only four closed doors. Was it too much to hope that Locker 42 still contained the black case? Not at all, thought Glinnes. It would seem that Lempel and the bald stocky off-worlder who had hired Jarcony were the same. Lempel had died before he had been able to claim the case in Locker 42 . . . So it would seem.

And now: how to get into Locker 42?

Glinnes examined the baggage clerk, a small man with wispy gray-russet hair, a long tremulous nose, and an expression of foolish obstinacy. Hopeless to seek either direct or indirect cooperation here; the man seemed a living definition of pettifoggery.

Glinnes cogitated for five minutes. Then he rose to his feet and walked to the bank of lockers. Into the coin slot on the face of Locker 30 he deposited a coin. Closing the door, he withdrew the key.

He approached the baggage desk and placed the key upon the counter. The clerk came forward. "Yes, sir."

"Be good enough to hold this key for me," said Glinnes. "I don't care to carry it around."

The clerk took the key with a twitch of mouth. "How long will you be gone, sir? Some folk leave their keys a remorseless time."

"I'll be no more than a day or so." Glinnes placed a coin upon the counter. "For your trouble."

"Thank you." The clerk opened a drawer and dropped the key into a compartment.

Glinnes walked away and seated himself on a bench where he could watch the clerk.

An hour passed. An air-bus from Cape Flory dropped down upon the field, discharging passengers, engulfing others. At the baggage desk there was a flurry of activity; the clerk scrambled here and there among his racks and shelves. Glinnes watched him carefully. It would seem that after his exertions he might feel the need for a rest or a visit to the lavatory, but instead, when the last patron had departed the clerk poured himself a mug of cold tea, which he drank in a gulp, and then a second mug, over which he ruminated a few minutes. Then he returned to his duties, and Glinnes resigned himself to patience.

Glinnes began to feel torpid. He watched folk come and go and amused himself for a while speculating upon their occupations and secret lives, but presently he became bored. What did he care for these commercial travelers, these grandfathers and grandmothers fresh home from visits, these functionaries and underlings? What of the clerk? And his bladder? Even as Glinnes watched the clerk sipped more tea. In what organ of his meager body was all this liquid stored? The idea provoked Glinnes himself to discomfort. He glanced across the depot to the lavatory. If he stepped within even for a moment the clerk might choose the same instant and his vigil would go for naught . . . Glinnes shifted his position. No doubt he could wait as long as the clerk. Fortitude had stood him in good stead on the hussade field; in a competition with the baggage clerk, fortitude once again would be the decisive factor.

People came and went—a man wearing a hat with a ridiculous yellow cockade, an old woman trailing an overpowering waft of musk, a pair of young men flaunting Fanscher costume and glancing from side to side to see who noticed their proud defiance . . . Glinnes crossed his legs, then uncrossed them. The baggage clerk went to a stool and began to make entries in a daybook. In order to slake his thirst he poured another mug of tea from the jug. Glinnes rose to his feet and walked back and forth. The baggage clerk now stood at the counter, looking out across the depot. He seemed to be gnawing his lower lip. He turned and reached—no! thought Glinnes, not for the jug of tea! The man could not be human! But the clerk merely tapped in the stopper to the jug. He rubbed his chin and seemed to consider, while Glinnes stood by the wall, swaying back and forth.

The clerk came to a decision. He stepped out from behind the counter and walked toward the men's lavatory.

Groaning in mingled relief and anxiety, Glinnes edged forward. No one seemed to heed him. He ducked behind the counter, opened the drawer, and looked into the compartment. Two keys. He took them both, closed the drawer, and returned to the waiting area. No one, so far as he could perceive, had noticed his conduct.

Glinnes went directly to Locker 42. The first key in his hand carried a brown tag stamped with the black numerals 30. The tag of the second key displayed the number 42. Glinnes opened the locker. He drew out the black case and closed the door once more. Was there time to replace the keys? Glinnes thought not. He walked from the depot into the smoky light of avness and headed back toward the dock. Along the way he stepped behind an old wall to relieve himself.

He found his boat as he had left it, and casting off the line, set forth to the east.

Steering with his knee, he attempted to open the case. The lock resisted the grip of his fingers; he applied a metal bar and snapped back the latch. The cover slid aside. Glinnes touched the money within: neat bundles of Alastor certificates. Thirty million ozols.

CHAPTER 21

Glinnes coasted into the Rabendary dock half an hour before midnight. The house was dark; Glay was not home. Glinnes put the case on the table and considered it a few minutes. He opened the lid and took forth certificates to a value of thirty thousand ozols, which he tucked into a jar and buried in the soil beside the verandah. Returning into the house, he telephoned Akadie, but elicted only expanding red circles, indicating that the telephone had been placed in a "non-receptive" condition. Glinnes sat on the couch, feeling fatigue but no lassitude. Once more he telephoned Akadie's manse without response; then he took the black case to his boat and set forth to the north.

From the water, Akadie's manse seemed dark. Yet it was not likely that Akadie, a man who enjoyed nocturnal activity, would be asleep . . .

On the dock Glinnes spied a man standing still and quiet. He sheered away and stood offshore. The dark figure made no move. Glinnes called out, "Who's that on the dock?"

After a pause a voice, throaty and muffled, came quietly across the water. "Constable of the Prefecture, on guard duty."

"Is Janno Akadie at home?"

Again the pause, and the low voice. "No."

"Where is he?"

The pause, the muffled disinterested voice. "He is in Welgen."

Glinnes jerked his boat around and sent it foaming back across Clinkhammer Broad, down the Saur, back down Farwan Water. When he arrived at Rabendary the house was still dark; Glay was elsewhere. Glinnes moored his boat and carried the black case inside. He telephoned the Gilweg house; the screen brightened to show the face of Varella, one of the younger girls. Only children were home; everyone else had gone visiting, to watch stars or drink wine, or perhaps to Welgen for the executions—she was not quite sure.

Glinnes darkened the telephone. He tucked the black case out of sight in the thatch, then, flinging himself on his couch, almost instantly fell asleep.

The morning was gay and crystalline. A warm breeze blew flurries of cat's paws across Ambal Broad; the sky showed a lilac clarity not often observed.

Glinnes ate a few bites of breakfast, then tried to call Akadie. A few minutes later a boat pulled up to the dock and Glay jumped ashore. Glinnes came out to meet him. Glay stopped short and looked Glinnes carefully up and down. "You seem excited."

"I've got enough money to pay off Casagave. We'll do it before the hour is out."

Glay looked across the broad at Ambal Isle, which in the fresh light of morning had never looked lovlier. "Just as you say. But you had better telephone him first."

"Why?"

"To give him warning."

"I don't want to give him anything," said Glinnes. Nevertheless he went to the telephone. Lute Casagave's face appeared on the screen. He spoke in a metallic voice. "What is your business?"

"I have twelve thousand ozols for you," said Glinnes. "I now wish to void the contract of sale. I'll bring the money over at this moment, if it's convenient."

"Send the money over with the owner," said Casagave.

"I am the owner."

"Shira Hulden is the owner. I suppose he can void that contract if he chooses."

"Today I'll bring over an affadavit certifying the death of Shira."

"Indeed. And where will you get it?"

"From Janno Akadie, an official mentor of the prefecture, who witnessed the confession of his murderer."

"Indeed," said Casagave with a chuckle. The screen went blank. Glinnes spoke to Glay in a voice of puzzlement. "That isn't quite the reaction I anticipated. He showed no concern whatever."

Glay shrugged. "Why should he? Akadie is in jail. They'll put him on the prutanshyr if the lords have their way. Any certification of Akadie's is meaningless."

Glinnes rolled his eyes back and drew his arms high in the air. "Was anyone ever so dogged by frustration?" he cried.

Glay turned away without comment. Presently he went to his couch and fell asleep.

Glinnes strode back and forth along the verandah, deep in thought.

Then, venting an inarticulate curse, he jumped into his boat and set forth to the west.

An hour later he arrived in Welgen, and only with difficulty found a mooring along the crowded dock. An unusual number of folk had chosen this day to visit Welgen. The square was the scene of intense activity. Folk of town and fen moved restlessly here and there, always with one eye turned upon the prutanshyr, where workmen adjusted the cogs of a ponderous mechanism, the functioning of which Glinnes found perplexing. He paused to make inquiry of an old man who stood leaning on a staff. "What goes on at the prutanshyr?"

"Another of Filidice's follies." The old man spat contemptuously upon the cobbles. "He insists on these novel devices, which can hardly be coaxed to perform their function. Sixty-two pirates to be killed, and yesterday the thing managed to grind asunder only a single man. Today it must be repaired! Have you ever heard the like? In my day we were content with simpler devices."

Glinnes went on to the Office of the Constabulary, only to learn that Chief Constable Filidice was not on hand. Glinnes then requested five minutes with Janno Akadie, but was denied the privilege; today the jail might not be visited.

Glinnes returned to the square and took a seat under the arbor of The Noble Saint Gambrinus, where so long ago (so it seemed) he had spoken with Junius Farfan. He ordered a half-gill of aquavit, which he drank at a gulp. How the fates conspired to thwart him! He had proved the fact of Shira's death and then had lost his money. He had gained new funds, but now he could no longer prove Shira's death. His witness Akadie was invalidated and his principal, Vang Drosset, was dead!

So now: what to do? The thirty million ozols? A joke. He would throw the money to the merlings before turning it over the Chief Constable Filidice. Glinnes signaled the waiter for another half-gill of aquavit, then turned a lambent glance toward the abominable prutanshyr. To save Akadie it might be necessary to surrender the money—though for a fact the case against Akadie seemed extraordinarily thin . . .

A shape darkened the entrance. Squinting up against the glare, Glinnes saw a person of middle height and unobtrusive demeanor, whom he might recognize. He looked more closely, then jumped to his feet with sudden energy. At his gesture the man approached. "If I am not mistaken," said Glinnes, "you are Ryl Shermatz. I am Glinnes Hulden, a friend of the mentor Janno Akadie."

"Of course! I remember you well," said Shermatz. "And how does our friend Akadie?"

· The waiter brought aquavit, which Glinnes placed in front of Shermatz.

"You will require this before long . . . I take it you have not heard the news?"

"I have only just returned from Morilla. Why do you ask?"

Stimulated by circumstances and by the aquavit, Glinnes spoke with a measure of hyperbole. "Akadie has been flung into a dungeon. He is accused of grand larceny, and if the lords have their way, Akadie may well be inserted into the cogs of yonder mincing machine."

"Sad news indeed!" said Shermatz. With a wry salute he raised the goblet to his mouth. "Akadie should never have aspired to chicanery; he lacks the cold decisiveness that distinguishes the successful criminal."

"You miss my point," said Glinnes somewhat testily. "The charge is absolutely absurd."

"I am surprised to hear you speak so definitely," said Shermatz.

"If necessary, Akadie's innocence could be demonstrated in a manner to convince anyone. But this is not the point. I wonder why Filidice, apparently from sheer suspicion, has imprisoned Akadie, while the guilty man goes free."

"An interesting speculation. Can you name the guilty man?"

Glinnes shook his head. "I wish I could—especially if a certain man is the guilty party."

"And why do you confide in me?"

"You observed Akadie transfer the money to the messenger. Your testimony will free him."

"I saw a black case change hands. It might have held almost anything."

Glinnes chose his words with care. "You probably wonder why I am so confident of Akadie's innocence. The reason is simple. I know for a fact that he disposed of the money as he claimed. Bandolio was captured; his aide Lempel was murdered. The money was never claimed. In my opinion, the importunate lords deserve the money no more than Bandolio. I am disinclined to assist either side."

Shermatz made a grave sign of comprehension. "A nod is as good as a wink. If Akadie is in fact innocent, who is Bandolio's real accomplice?"

"I am surprised that Bandolio has not provided definite information, but Chief Constable Filidice won't allow me a word with Akadie, much less Bandolio."

"I'm not so sure of that." Shermatz rose to his feet. "A few words with Chief Constable Filidice might be worthwhile."

"Return to your seat," said Glinnes. "He won't see us."

"I think he will. I am something more than a roving journalist, as I hold the commission of Over-inspector in the Whelm. Chief Constable Filidice will see us with pleasure. Let us go at once to make the inquiry. Where is he to be found?"

"Yonder is his headquarters," said Glinnes. "The structure is dilipidated, but here in Welgen it represents the majesty of Trill law."

Glinnes and Ryl Shermatz waited in a foyer only briefly before Chief Constable Filidice came forth, his face expressing concern. "What is this again? Who are you, sir?"

Shermatz placed a metal plate upon the counter. "Please assure yourself of my credentials."

Filidice glumly studied the plate. "I am of course at your service."

"I am here in connection with the starmenter Bandolio," said Shermatz. "You have questioned him?"

"To some extent. There was no reason to undertake any exhaustive inquiry."

"Have you discovered his local accomplice?"

Filidice gave a curt nod. "He was assisted by a certain Janno Akadie, whom we have taken into custody."

"You are assured, then, of Akadie's guilt?"

"The evidence very clearly suggests as much."

"Has he confessed?"

"No."

"Have you placed him under psychohallation?"

"We lack such equipment here at Welgen."

"I would like to examine both Bandolio and Akadie; Akadie first, if you please."

Filidice turned to an under-constable and gave the necessary orders. To Shermatz and Glinnes: "Will you be good enough to step into my office?"

Five minutes later Akadie was thrust complaining and expostulating into the office. At the sight of Glinnes and Shermatz he fell abruptly silent.

Shermatz said courteously, "Good morning, Janno Akadie; it is a pleasure to see you again."

"Not under these circumstances! Would you believe it? They have me pent in a cell, like a criminal! I thought they were taking me to the prutanshyr! Have you ever heard the like?"

"I hope that we will be able to clarify the matter." Shermatz turned to Filidice. "What precisely are the charges against Akadie?"

"That he conspired with Sagmondo Bandolio and that he has sequestered thirty million ozols which are not his property."

"Both charges are false!" cried Akadie. "Someone is plotting against me!"

"We will certainly arrive at the truth of the matter," said Shermatz. "Suppose we now hear what the starmenter Bandolio has to say?"

Filidice spoke to his underling and presently Sagmondo Bandolio entered the room—a tall black-bearded man, bald, with a black tonsure, lucent blue eyes, and a placid expression. Here was a man who had commanded five dire ships and four hundred men, who had dispensed tragedy ten thousand times for purposes he alone could define.

Shermatz signaled him forward. "Sagmondo Bandolio, out of sheer curiosity, do you regret the life you have lived?"

Bandolio smiled politely. "I regret the last two weeks, certainly. As to the period prior, the subject is complex, and in any event I would not know how to answer your question accurately; hindsight is the least useful of our intellectual capabilities."

"We are making an inquiry into the foray upon Welgen. Can you identify your local accomplice more definitely?"

Bandolio pulled at his beard. "I have not identified him at all, unless my recollection is at fault."

Chief Constable Filidice said, "He was subjected to mind-searching. He has retained no clandestine information."

"What information has he given to you?"

"The initiative came from Trullion. Bandolio received a proposal through secret starmenter channels; he sent down a subaltern by the name of Lempel to make a preliminary inspection. Lempel rendered an optimistic report and Bandolio himself came down to Trullion. On a beach near Welgen, he met the Trill who became his accomplice. The meeting occurred at midnight. The Trill wore a hussade mask and spoke in a cultivated voice Bandolio says he could not identify. They made their arrangements, and Bandolio never saw the man again. He assigned Lempel to the project; Lempel is now dead. Bandolio professes no other information and psychohallation corroborates his claim."

Shermatz turned to Bandolio. "Is this an accurate summation?"

"It is indeed, except for a suspicion that my local confederate persuaded Lempel to give information to the Whelm, so that the two might divide the whole of the ransom. After the Whelm was notified, Lempel's life came to an end."

"So then you have no reason to conceal the identity of your accomplice?"

"To the contrary. My dearest wish is to see him dance to music of the prutanshyr."

"Before you stands Janno Akadie. Is he known to you?"

"No."

"Is it possible that Akadie was your confederate?"

"No. The man was as tall as myself."

Shermatz looked at Filidice. "And there you have it: a grievous error which luckily was not consummated upon the prutanshyr."

Filidice's pale countenance showed a few drops of perspiration. "I assure you, I was exposed to intolerable pressure! The Order of Aristocrats insisted that I act; they authorized Lord Gensifer, the secretary, to demand definite activity. I could not locate the money, so then . . ." Filidice paused and licked his lips.

"To appease the Order of Aristocrats you imprisoned Janno Akadie."

"It seemed an obvious course of action."

Glinnes asked Bandolio, "You met your confederate by starlight?"

"So I did." Bandolio seemed almost jovial.

"What were his garments?"

"The Trill paray and the Trill cape, with wide padding, or epaulettes, or wings; only a Trill would know their function. His silhouette, as he stood on the shore in his hussade mask, was that of a great black bird."

"So you came to stand close to him."

"A distance of six feet separated us."

"What mask did he wear?"

Bandolio laughed. "How should I know your local masks? Horns protruded at the temple; the mouth showed fangs and a tongue lolled loose. Indeed, I felt I faced a monster there on the beach."

"What of his voice?"

"A hoarse mutter; he wanted no recognition."

"His gestures, mannerisms, quirks of stance?"

"None. He made no movement."

"His boat?"

"An ordinary runabout."

"And what was the date of this occasion?"

"The fourth day of Lyssum."

Glinnes considered a moment. "You received all further signals from Lempel?"

"True."

"You had no other contact with the man in the hussade mask?"

"None."

"What was his precise function?"

"He undertook to seat the three hundred richest men of the prefecture in section D of the stadium, and so he did to perfection."

Filidice interposed a remark. "The seats were bought anonymously and sent out by messenger. They offer no clue."

Ryl Shermatz considered Filidice for a long thoughtful moment, upon which Filidice became uneasy. Shermatz said, "I am puzzled as to why you imprisoned Janno Akadie on evidence which even at first glance seems ambiguous."

Filidice spoke with dignity. "I received confidential information from an irreproachable source. Under the conditions of emergency and public agitation, I decided to act with decision."

"The information is confidential, you say?"

"Well, yes."

"And who is the irreproachable source?"

Filidice hesitated, then made a weary gesture. "The secretary of the Order of Lords convinced me that Akadie knew the whereabouts of the ransom money. He recommended that Akadie be imprisoned and threatened with the prutanshyr until he agreed to relinquish the money."

"The secretary of the Order of Lords . . . That would be Lord Gensifer."

"Precisely so," said Filidice.

"That ingrate!" hissed Akadie. "I will have a word with him."

"It might be interesting to learn the rationale behind his accusation," mused Shermatz. "I suggest that we undertake a visit to Lord Gensifer."

Filidice held up his hand. "Today would be most inopportune for Lord Gensifer. The gentry of the region are at Gensifer Manse to celebrate Lord Gensifer's wedding."

"I am concerned for Lord Gensifer's convenience," declared Akadie, "to the exact extent that he is concerned with mine. We will visit him at this moment."

"I quite agree with Janno Akadie," said Glinnes. "Especially as we will be able to identify the true criminal and take him into custody."

Ryl Shermatz spoke in a quizzical voice. "You speak with peculiar assurance."

"Conceivably I am mistaken," said Glinnes. "For this reason I feel that we should take Sagmondo Bandolio with us."

Filidice, with affairs slipping beyond his control, became correspondingly assertive. "This is not a sensible idea. In the first place, Bandolio is most supple and elusive; he must not cheat the prutanshyr. Secondly, he has declared himself unable to render any identification; the criminal's features were concealed by a mask. Thirdly, I find questionable, to say the least, the theory that we will find the guilty person at Lord Gensifer's wedding ceremony. I do not wish to create a tomfoolery and make myself a laughingstock."

Shermatz said, "A conscientious man is never diminished by doing his duty. I suggest that we pursue our investigation without regard for side issues."

Filidice gave a despondent acquiescence. "Very well, let us proceed to Gensifer Manse. Constable, confine the prisoner! Let the shackles be doubly locked and a trip-wire fastened around his neck."

The black and gray official boat drove across Fleharish Broad toward the Five Islands. Half a hundred boats clustered against the dock, and the walk was decorated with festoons of silk ribbon, scarlet, yellow and pink. Through the gardens strolled lords and ladies in the splendid archaic garments worn only at the most formal occasions, and which ordinary folk were never privileged to glimpse.

The official party walked up the path, aware of their own incongruity. Chief Constable Filidice in particular struggled between pent fury and embarrassment, Ryl Shermatz was placid enough, and Sagmondo Bandolio seemed actively to enjoy the situation; he held his head high and turned his gaze cheerfully this way and that. An old steward saw them and hastened forward in consternation. Filidice gave a muttered explanation; the steward's face drooped in displeasure. "Certainly you cannot intrude upon the ceremonies; the rites are shortly to take place. This is a most outrageous proceeding!"

Chief Constable Filidice's self-control quivered. He spoke in a vibrant voice. "Silence! This is official business! Be off with you—no, wait! We may have instructions for you." He looked sourly at Shermatz. "What are your wishes?"

Shermatz turned to Glinnes. "What is your suggestion?"

"One moment," said Glinnes. He looked across the garden, seeking among the two hundred folk present. Never had he seen such a gorgeous array of costumes—the velvet capes of the lords, with heraldic blazons on the back; the gowns of the ladies, belted and fringed with black coral beads, or crystalized merling scales, or rectangular tourmalines, with tiaras to match. Glinnes looked from face to face. Lute Casagave—Lord Ambal, as he chose to call himself—would necessarily be on hand. He saw Duissane, in a simple white gown and a wisp of a white turban. Feeling his gaze, she turned and saw him. Glinnes felt an emotion to which he could put no name—the sense of something precious departing, something leaving, to be lost forever. Lord Gensifer stood nearby. He became aware of the new arrivals and frowned in surprise and displeasure.

Someone nearby turned on his heel and began to walk away. The motion caught Glinnes' attention; he jumped forward, caught the man's arm, swung him around. "Lute Casagave."

Casagave's face was pale and austere. "I am Lord Ambal. How dare you touch me?"

"Be so good as to step this way," said Glinnes. "The matter is important."

"I choose to do nothing of the kind."

"Then stand here." Glinnes signaled the members of his group. Casagave once again sought to walk away; Glinnes pulled him back. Casagave's face was now white and dangerous. "What do you want of me?"

"Observe," said Glinnes. "This is Ryl Shermatz, Over-inspector of the Whelm. This is Janno Akadie, a formerly accredited mentor of Jolany Prefecture. Both witnessed Vang Drosset's confession that he had murdered Shira Hulden. I am Squire of Rabendary and I now demand that you depart Ambal Isle at once."

Lute Casagave made no response. Filidice asked peevishly, "Is this why you brought us here, merely to confront Lord Ambal?"

Sagmondo Bandolio's merry laugh interrupted him. "Lord Ambal, now! Not so in the old days. Not so indeed!"

Casagave turned to depart, but Shermatz's easy voice checked him. "Just a moment if you please. This is an official inquiry, and the question of your identity becomes important."

"I am Lord Ambal; that is sufficient."

Ryl Shermatz swung his mild gaze to Bandolio. "You know him by another name?"

"By another name and by many another deed, some of which have caused me pain. He has done what I should have done ten years ago—retired with his loot. Here you see Alonzo Dirrig, sometimes known as the Ice Devil and Dirrig the Skull-maker, one-time master of four ships, as adept among the starmenters as any you might find."

"You are mistaken, whoever you may be." Casagave bowed and made as if to turn away.

"Not so fast!" said Filidice. "Perhaps we have made an important discovery. If this is the case, then Janno Akadie is vindicated. Lord Ambal, do you deny the charge of Sagmondo Bandolio?"

"There is nothing to deny. The man is mistaken."

Bandolio gave a mocking caw of laughter. "Look across the palm of his left hand; you'll see a scar I put there myself."

Filidice went on. "Do you deny that you are the person Alonzo Dirrig; that you conspired to kidnap three hundred lords of prefecture; that subsequently you killed a certain Lempel?"

Casagave's lips curled. "Of course I deny it. Prove it, if you can!"

Filidice turned to Glinnes. "Where is your proof?"

"One moment," said Shermatz in a voice of perplexity. He spoke to Bandolio. "Is this the man with whom you conversed on the beach near Welgen?"

"Alonzo Dirrig calling on me to implement his schemes? Never, never, never—not Alonzo Dirrig."

Filidice looked dubiously at Glinnes. "So then, you are wrong, after all."

Glinnes said, "Not so fast! I never accused Casagave, or Dirrig—whatever his name—of anything. I merely brought him here to clear up an incidental bit of business."

Casagave turned and strode away. Ryl Shermatz made a gesture; Filidice instructed his two constables; "After him! Take him into custody." The constables ran off. Casagave looked over his shoulder, and observing pursuit, bounded out upon the dock and into his boat. With a surge and thrash of foam he sped away across Fleharish Broad.

Filidice roared to the constables, "Follow in the launch; keep him in sight! Radio for reinforcements; take him into custody!"

Lord Gensifer confronted them, face clenched in displeasure. "Why do you cause this disturbance? Can you not observe that we celebrate a solemn occasion?"

Chief Constable Filidice spoke with what dignity he could muster. "We are naturally distressed by our intrusion. We had reason to suspect that Lord Ambal was the accomplice of Sagmondo Bandolio. Apparently this is not the case."

Lord Gensifer's face became pink. He glanced at Akadie, then back to Filidice. "Of course this is not the case! Have we not discussed the matter at length? We know Bandolio's accomplice!"

"Indeed," said Akadie in a voice like a saw cutting a nail. "And who is this person?"

"It is the faithless mentor who so craftily collected and then secreted thirty million ozols!" declared Lord Gensifer. "His name is Janno Akadie!"

Ryl Shermatz said silkily, "Sagmondo Bandolio disputes this theory. He says Akadie is not the man."

Lord Gensifer threw his arms up in the air. "Very well then; Akadie is innocent! Who cares? I am sick of the whole matter! Please depart; you are intruding upon my property and upon a solemn ritual."

"Accept my apologies," said Chief Constable Filidice. "I assure you that this was not my scheme. Come then, gentlemen, we will—"

"Just a moment," said Glinnes. "We haven't yet touched the nub of the matter. Sagmondo Bandolio cannot positively identify the man he faced on the beach, but he quite definitely can identify the mask. Lord Gensifer, will you bring forth one of the Fleharish Gorgon helmets?"

Lord Gensifer drew himself up. "I most certainly will not. What sort of farce is this? Once more I require that you depart!"

Glinnes ignored him and spoke to Filidice. "When Bandolio described horns and the lolling tongue of the mask I instantly thought of the Fleharish Gorgons. On the fourth day of Lyssum, when the meeting took place, the Gorgons had not yet been issued their uniforms. Only Lord Gensifer could have used a Gorgon helmet. Therefore, Lord Gensifer is the guilty man!"

"What are you saying?" gasped Filidice, eyes bulging in astonishment.

"Aha!" screamed Akadie and flung himself upon Lord Gensifer. Glinnes caught him and pulled him back.

"What insane libel are you setting forth?" roared Lord Gensifer, his face suddenly mottled. "Have you taken leave of your senses?"

"It is ridiculous," declared Filidice. "I will hear no more."

"Gently, gently," said Ryl Shermatz, smiling faintly. "Surely Glinnes

Hulden's theory deserves consideration. In my opinion it appears to be definite, particular, exclusive, and sufficient."

Filidice spoke in a subdued voice. "Lord Gensifer is a most important man; he is secretary of the Order—"

"And as such, he forced you to imprison Akadie," said Glinnes.

Lord Gensifer furiously waved his finger at Glinnes, but could bring forth no words.

Chief Constable Filidice, in a plaintive grumble, asked Lord Gensifer, "Can you refute the accusation? Did someone perhaps steal a helmet?"

Lord Gensifer nodded vehemently. "It goes without saying! Someone—Akadie, no doubt—stole a Gorgon helmet from my storeroom."

"In that case," said Glinnes, "one will now be missing. Let us go to count the helmets."

Lord Gensifer aimed a wild blow at Glinnes, who ducked back out of the way. Shermatz signaled Filidice. "Arrest this gentleman; take him to the jail. We will put him through psychohallation, and the truth will be known."

"By no means," belched Lord Gensifer in a guttural voice. "I'll never stand to the prutanshyr." Like Casagave, he turned and ran along the dock, while his guests watched in fascinated wonder; never had they known such a wedding.

"After him," said Shermatz curtly. Chief Constable Filidice lurched off in pursuit and pounded down the dock to where Lord Gensifer had jumped into his runabout. Dismissing caution, Filidice leapt after him. Lord Gensifer tried to buffet him aside; Filidice, falling upon Lord Gensifer, drove him backward, over the gunwale and into the water.

Lord Gensifer swam under the dock. Filidice called after him, "It's no use, Lord Gensifer; justice must be served. Come forth, if you will!"

Only a swirl of water indicated Lord Gensifer's presence. Filidice called again. "Lord Gensifer! Why make needless difficulty for us all? Come forth—you cannot escape!"

From under the dock came a hoarse ejaculation, then a moment of frantic splashing, then silence. Filidice slowly straightened from his crouching position. He stood staring down at the water, his face ashen. He climbed to the dock and rejoined Ryl Shermatz, Glinnes, and Akadie. "We may now declare the case closed," he said. "The thirty million ozols—they remain a mystery. Perhaps we will never learn the truth."

Ryl Shermatz looked toward Glinnes, who licked his lips and frowned. "Well, I suppose it makes little difference one way or the other," said Shermatz. "But where is our captive Bandolio? Is it possible that the rascal has taken advantage of the confusion?"

"So it would seem," said Filidice disconsolately. "He is gone! What an unhappy day we have had!"

"On the contrary," said Akadie. "It has been the most rewarding of my life."

Glinnes said, "Casagave has been evicted; for this I am most grateful. It's an excellent day for me as well."

Filidice rubbed his forehead. "I am still bewildered. Lord Gensifer seemed the very apotheosis of rectitude!"

"Lord Gensifer acted at precisely the wrong time," said Glinnes. "He killed Lempel after Lempel had instructed the messenger but before the money had been delivered. He probably believed Akadie to be as unprincipled as himself."

"A sad case," said Akadie. "And the thirty million ozols—who knows where? Perhaps on some distant world the messenger is now enjoying his astonishing new affluence."

"That is probably the size of it," said Filidice. "Well, I suppose I must make some sort of statement to the guests."

"Excuse me," said Glinnes. "There is someone I must see." He crossed the garden to where he had seen Duissane. She was gone. He looked this way and that, but saw no Duissane. Might she have gone into the house? He thought not—the house no longer had meaning for Duissane . . .

A path led around the house to the beach, which fronted on the ocean. Glinnes ran down the path and saw Duissane standing on the sand looking across the water, toward that blank area where the horizon met the ocean.

Glinnes joined her. She stopped and looked at him, as if never had she seen him before. She turned away and went slowly eastward along the water. Glinnes moved after her, and in the hazy light of middle afternoon they walked together down the beach.

MARUNE

ALASTOR 933

....

A lastor Cluster, a node of thirty thousand live stars, uncounted dead hulks and vast quantities of interstellar detritus, clung to the inner rim of the galaxy with the Unfortunate Waste before, the Nonestic Gulf beyond and the Gaean Reach a sparkling haze to the side. For the space traveler, no matter which his angle of approach, a remarkable spectacle was presented: constellations blazing white, blue, and red; curtains of luminous stuff, broken here, obscured there, by black storms of dust; star-streams wandering in and out; whorls and spatters of phosphorescent gas.

Should Alastor Cluster be considered a segment of the Gaean Reach? The folk of the Cluster, some four or five trillion of them on more than three thousand worlds, seldom reflected upon the matter, and indeed considered themselves neither Gaean nor Alastrid. The typical inhabitant, when asked as to his origin, might perhaps cite his native world or, more usually, his local district, as if this place were so extraordinary, so special and widely famed that its reputation hung on every tongue of the galaxy.

Parochialism dissolved before the glory of the Connatic, who ruled Alastor Cluster from his palace Lusz on the world Numenes. The current Connatic, Oman Ursht, sixteenth of the Idite dynasty, often pondered the quirk of fate which had appointed him to his singular condition, only to smile at his own irrationality: no matter who occupied the position, that person would frame for himself the same marveling question.

The inhabited planets of the Cluster had little in common except their lack of uniformity. They were large and small, dank and dry, benign and perilous, populous and empty: no two alike. Some manifested tall mountains, blue seas, bright skies; on others clouds hung forever above the moors, and no variety existed except the alternation of night and day. Such a world, in fact, was Bruse-Tansel, Alastor 1102, with a population of two hundred thousand, settled for the most part in the neighborhood of Lake Vain, where they worked principally at the dyeing of fabrics. Four space-ports served Bruse-Tansel, the most important being that facility located at Carfaunge.

CHAPTER I

The Respectable Mergan had achieved his post, Super-intendent at the Carfaunge spaceport, largely because the position demanded a tolerance for unalterable routine. Mergan not only tolerated routine; he depended upon it. He would have opposed the cessa-tion of such nuisances as the morning rains, the glass lizards with their squeaks and clicks, the walking slimes which daily invaded the area, because then he would have been required to change established procedure.

On the morning of a day he would later identify as tenth Mariel Gaean* he arrived as usual at his office. Almost before he had settled behind his desk, the night porter appeared with a blank-faced young man in a nonde-script gray suit. Mergan uttered a wordless grumble; he had no taste for problems at any time, least of all before he had composed himself for the day. The situation at the very least promised a disruption of routine. At last he muttered: "Well, Dinster, what do you have here?"

Dinster, in a piping over-loud voice, called out, "Sorry to bother you, sir, but what shall we do with this gentleman? He seems to be ill."

"Find him a doctor," growled Mergan. "Don't bring him here. I can't help him."

"It's not that kind of illness, sir. More mental, if you get my meaning."

"Your meaning escapes me," said Mergan. "Why not just tell me what's wrong?"

Dinster politely indicated his charge. "When I came on duty he was sit-ting in the waiting room and he's been there since. He hardly speaks; he doesn't know his name, nor anything about himself."

Mergan inspected the young man with some faint awakening of interest. "Hello, sir," he barked. "What's the trouble?"

The young man shifted his gaze from the window to Mergan, but offered no response. Mergan gradually allowed himself to become perplexed. Why

---

*Numerous systems of chronometry create confusion across Alastor Cluster and the Gaean Reach, despite attempts at reform. In any given locality, at least three systems of reckoning are in daily use: scientific chronometry, based upon the orbital frequency of the K-state hydrogen electron; astronomic time—Gaean Standard Time—which provides synchronism across the human universe; and local time.

had the young man's gold-brown hair been hacked short, as if by swift savage strokes of a scissors? And the garments: clearly a size too large for the spare frame!

"Speak!" commanded Mergan. "Can you hear? Tell me your name!"

The young man put on a thoughtful expression but remained silent.

"A vagabond of some sort," Mergan declared. "He probably wandered up from the dye-works. Send him off again down the road."

Dinster shook his head. "This lad's no vagabond. Look at his hands."

Mergan reluctantly followed Dinster's suggestion. The hands were strong and well kept and showed evidence neither of toil nor submersion in dye. The man's features were firm and even; the poise of his head suggested status. Mergan, who preferred to ignore the circumstances of his own birth, felt an uncomfortable tingle of deference and corresponding resentment. Again he barked at the young man: "Who are you? What is your name?"

"I don't know." The voice was slow and labored, and colored with an accent Mergan failed to recognize.

"Where is your home?"

"I don't know."

Mergan became unreasonably sarcastic. "Do you know anything?"

Dinster ventured an opinion. "Looks to me, sir, as if he came aboard one of yesterday's ships."

Mergan asked the young man: "What ship did you arrive on? Do you have friends here?"

The young man fixed him with a brooding dark-gray gaze, and Mergan became uncomfortable. He turned to Dinster. "Does he carry papers? Or money?"

Dinster muttered to the young man: "Excuse me, sir." Gingerly he groped through the pockets of the rumpled gray suit. "I can't find anything here, sir."

"What about ticket stubs, or vouchers, or tokens?"

"Nothing at all, sir."

"It's what they call amnesia," said Mergan. He picked up a pamphlet and glanced down a list. "Six ships in yesterday. He might have arrived on any of them." Mergan touched a button. A voice said: "Prosidine, arrival gate."

Mergan described the amnesiac. "Do you know anything about him? He arrived sometime yesterday."

"Yesterday was more than busy; I didn't take time to notice anything."

"Make inquiries of your people and notify me."

Mergan thought a moment, then called the Carfaunge hospital. He was connected to the Director of Admissions, who listened patiently enough, but made no constructive proposals. "We have no facilities here for such cases. He has no money, you say? Definitely not, then."

"What shall I do with him? He can't stay here!"

"Consult the police; they'll know what to do."

Mergan called the police, and presently an official arrived in a police van, and the amnesiac was led away.

At the Hall of Inquiry, Detective Squil attempted interrogation, without success. The police doctor experimented with hypnotism, and finally threw up his hands. "A most stubborn condition; I have seen three previous cases, but nothing like this."

"What causes it?"

"Autosuggestion, occasioned by emotional stress. This is most usual. But here"—he waved toward the uncomprehending amnesiac—"my instruments show no psychic charge of any kind. He has no emotions, and I have no leverage."

Detective Squil, a reasonable man, asked: "What can he do to help himself? He is obviously no ruffian."

"He should take himself to the Connatic's Hospital on Numenes."

Detective Squil laughed. "All very well. Who pays his fare?"

"The superintendent at the spaceport should be able to arrange passage, or so I should think."

Squil made a dubious sound but turned to his telephone. As he expected, the Respectable Mergan, having transferred responsibility to the police, wanted no further part of the situation. "The regulations are most explicit," said Mergan. "I certainly cannot do as you suggest."

"We can't keep him here at the station."

"He appears able-bodied; let him earn his fare, which after all is not exorbitant."

"Easier said than done, what with his disability."

"What generally happens to indigents?"

"You know as well as I do; they're sent out to Gaswin. But this man is mentally ill; he's not an indigent."

"I can't argue that, because I don't know. At least I've pointed out a course of action."

"What is the fare to Numenes?"

"Third class by Prydania Line: two hundred and twelve ozols."

Squil terminated the call. He swung about to face the amnesiac. "Do you understand what I say to you?"

The answer came in a clear voice. "Yes."

"You are ill. You have lost your memory. Do you realize this?"

There was a pause of ten seconds. Squil wondered if any response was forthcoming. Then, haltingly: "You have told me so."

"We will send you to a place where you can work and earn money. Do you know how to work?"

"No."

"Well, anyway, you need money: two hundred and twelve ozols. On Gaswin Moor you will earn three and a half ozols a day. In two or three months you will have earned enough money to take you to the Connatic's Hospital on Numenes, where you will be cured of your illness. Do you understand all this?"

The amnesiac reflected a moment, but made no response.

Squil rose to his feet. "Gaswin will be a good place for you, and perhaps your memory will return." He dubiously considered the amnesiac's blond-brown hair, which for mysterious reasons, someone had rudely cut short. "Do you have an enemy? Is there someone who does not like you?"

"I don't know. I can't remember any such person."

"What is your name?" shouted Squil, hoping to surprise that part of the brain which was withholding information.

The amnesiac's gray eyes narrowed slightly. "I don't know."

"Well, we have to find a name for you. Do you play hussade?"

"No."

"Think of that! A strong agile fellow like yourself! Still, we'll call you Pardero, after the great strike forward of the Schaide Thunderstones. So now, when someone calls out 'Pardero' you must respond. Is this understood?"

"Yes."

"Very well, and now you'll be on your way to Gaswin. The sooner you begin your work, the sooner you'll arrive on Numenes. I'll speak with the director; he's a good chap and he'll see to your welfare."

Pardero, as his name now would be, sat uncertainly. Squil took pity on him. "It won't be so bad. Agreed, there are tough nuts at the work camp, but do you know how to handle them? You must be just a bit tougher than they are. Still, don't attract the attention of the disciplinary officer. You seem a decent fellow; I'll put in a word for you, and keep an eye on your progress. One bit of advice—no, two. First: never try to cheat on your work quota. The officials know all the tricks; they can smell out the sluggards as a kribbat smells out carrion. Second, do not gamble! Do you know what the word 'gamble' means?"

"No."

"It means to risk your money on games or wagers. Never be tempted or inveigled! Leave your money in the camp account! I advise you to form no friendships! Aside from yourself, there is only riff-raff at the camp. I wish you well. If you find trouble, call for Detective Squil. Can you remember that name?"

"Detective Squil."

"Good." Squil led the amnesiac out to a dock and put him aboard the daily transport to Gaswin. "A final word of advice! Confide in no one! Your name is Pardero; aside from this, keep your problems to yourself. Do you understand?"

"Yes."

"Good luck!"

The transport flew low under the overcast, close above the mottled black and purple moors, and presently landed beside a cluster of concrete buildings: the Gaswin Work Camp.

At the personnel office Pardero underwent entry formalities, facilitated by Squil's notification to the camp director. He was assigned a cubicle in a dormitory block, fitted with work boots and gloves, and issued a copy of camp regulations, which he studied without comprehension. On the next morning, he was detailed into a work party and sent out to harvest pods from colucoid creeper, the source of a peculiarly rich red dye.

Pardero gathered his quota without difficulty. Among the taciturn group of indigents his deficiency went unnoticed.

He ate his evening meal in silence, ignoring the presence of his fellows, who at last had begun to sense that all was not well with Pardero.

The sun sank behind the clouds; a dismal twilight fell across the moors. Pardero sat to the side of the recreation hall, watching a comic melodrama on the holovision screen. He listened intently to the dialogue; each word seemed to find an instantly receptive niche inside his brain with a semantic concept ready at hand. His vocabulary grew and the range of his mental processes expanded. When the program was over he sat brooding, at last aware of his condition. He went to look into the mirror over the washbasin; the face which looked back at him was at once strange and familiar: a somber face with a good expanse of forehead, prominent cheekbones, hollow cheeks, dark-gray eyes, a ragged thatch of dark-gold hair.

A certain burly rogue named Woane attempted a jocularity. "Look yonder at Pardero! He stands like a man admiring a beautiful work of art!"

Pardero studied the mirror. Who was the man whose eyes stared so intently into his own?

Woane's hoarse murmur came from across the room. "Now he admires his haircut."

The remark amused Woane's friends. Pardero turned his head this way and that, wondering as to the motive behind the assault on his hair. Somewhere, it would seem, he had enemies. He turned slowly away from the mirror and resumed his seat at the side of the room.

The last traces of light left the sky; night had come to Gaswin camp.

Something jerked deep at the bottom of Pardero's consciousness: a compulsion totally beyond his comprehension. He jumped to his feet. Woane looked around half-truculently, but Pardero's glance slid past him. Woane nevertheless saw or felt something sufficiently eery that his jaw dropped a trifle, and he muttered to his friends. All watched as Pardero crossed to the door and went out into the night.

Pardero stood on the porch. Floodlights cast a wan glow across the compound, now empty and desolate, inhabited only by the wind from the moors. Pardero stepped off the porch into the shadows. With no purpose he walked around the edge of the compound and out upon the moor; the camp became an illuminated island behind him.

Under the overcast, darkness was complete. Pardero felt an enlargement of the soul, an intoxication of power, as if he were an elemental born of the darkness, knowing no fear . . . He stopped short. His legs felt hard and strong; his hands tingled with competence. Gaswin camp lay a half-mile behind him, the single visible object. Pardero took a deep throbbing breath, and again examined his consciousness, half-hoping, half-fearful of what he might find.

Nothing. Recollection extended to the Carfaunge spaceport. Events before were like voices remembered from a dream. Why was he here at Gaswin? To earn money. How long must he remain? He had forgotten, or perhaps the words had not registered. Pardero began to feel a suffocating agitation, a claustrophobia of the intellect. He lay down on the moor, beat his forehead, cried out in frustration.

Time passed. Pardero rose to his knees, gained his feet, and slowly returned to camp.

A week later Pardero learned of the camp doctor and his function. The next morning, during sick call, he presented himself to the dispensary. A dozen men sat on the benches while the doctor, a young man fresh from medical school, summoned them forward, one at a time. The complaints, real, imaginary, or contrived, were usually related to the work: backache, allergic reaction, congestion of the lungs, an infected lychbug sting. The doctor, young in years but already old in guile, sorted out the real from the fictitious, prescribing remedies for the first and irritant salves or vile-flavored medicines for the second.

Pardero was signaled to the desk and the doctor looked him up and down. "What's wrong with you?"

"I can't remember anything."

"Indeed." The doctor leaned back in his chair. "What is your name?"

"I don't know. Here at the camp they call me Pardero. Can you help me?"

"Probably not. Go back to the bench and let me finish up the sick call; it'll be just a few minutes."

The doctor dealt with his remaining patients and returned to Pardero. "Tell me how far back you remember."

"I arrived at Carfaunge. I remember a spaceship. I remember the depot—but nothing before."

"Nothing whatever?"

"Nothing."

"Do you remember things you like, or dislike? Are you afraid of anything?"

"No."

"Amnesia typically derives from a subconscious intent to block out intolerable memories."

Pardero gave his head a dubious shake. "I don't think this is likely."

The doctor, both intrigued and bemused, uttered an uneasy half-embarrassed laugh. "Since you can't remember the circumstances, you aren't in a position to judge."

"I suppose that's true . . . Could something be wrong with my brain?"

"You mean physical damage? Do you have headaches or head pains? Any sensation of numbness or pressure?"

"No."

"Well, it's hardly likely a tumor would cause general amnesia in any event . . . Let me check my references . . ." He read for a few moments. "I could try hypnotherapy or shock. Candidly, I don't think I'd do you any good. Amnesia generally cures itself if left alone."

"I don't think I can cure myself. Something lies on my brain like a blanket. It suffocates me. I can't tear it loose. Can't you help me?"

There was a simplicity to Pardero's manner which appealed to the doctor. He also sensed strangeness: tragedy and drama beyond his conjecture.

"I would help you if I could," said the doctor. "With all my soul I would help you. But I wouldn't know what I should be doing. I'm not qualified to experiment on you."

"The police officer told me to go to the Connatic's Hospital on Numenes."

"Yes, of course. This is best for you; I was about to suggest it myself."

"Where is Numenes? How do I go there?"

"You must go by starship. The fare is a little over two hundred ozols. That is what I have been told. You earn three and a half ozols a day—more if you exceed your quota. When you have two hundred and fifty ozols, go to Numenes. That is my best advice."

CHAPTER 2

....

Pardero worked with single-minded energy. Without fail he collected a half measure over his quota, and sometimes a total of two measures, which first excited jocular comment among his fellow workers, then sardonic sneers, and finally a cold, if covert, hostility. To compound his offenses Pardero refused to participate in the social activities of the camp, except to sit staring into the holovision screen, and thereby was credited with assumptions of superiority, which was indeed the case. He spent nothing at the commissary; despite all persuasions he refused to gamble, although occasionally he watched the games with a grim smile, which made certain of the players uneasy. Twice his locker was ransacked by someone who hoped to avail himself of Pardero's earnings, but Pardero had drawn no money from his account. Woane made one or two half-hearted attempts at intimidation, then decided to chastise the haughty Pardero, but he encountered such ferocious retaliation that he was glad to regain the sanctuary of the mess hall; and thereafter Pardero was strictly ignored.

At no time could Pardero detect any seepage through the barrier between his memory and his conscious mind. Always as he worked he wondered: "What kind of man am I? Where is my home? What do I know? Who are my friends? Who has committed this wrong upon me?" He expended his frustration on the colucoid creeper and became known as a man possessed by an inner demon, to be avoided as carefully as possible.

For his part Pardero banished Gaswin to the most remote corner of his mind; he would take away as few memories as possible. The work he found tolerable; but he resented the name Pardero. To use a stranger's name was like wearing a stranger's clothes—not a fastidious act. Still the name served as well as any other; it was a minor annoyance.

More urgently unpleasant was the lack of privacy. He found detestable the close intimacy of three hundred other men, most especially at mealtimes, when he sat with his eyes fixed on his plate, to avoid the open maws, the mounds of food, the mastication. Impossible to ignore, however, were the belches, grunts, hisses, and sighs of satiety. Surely this was not the life he had known in the past! What then had been his life?

The question produced only blankness, a void without information. Somewhere lived a person who had launched him across the Cluster with his hair hacked short and as denuded of identification as an egg. Sometimes

when he pondered this enemy he seemed to hear wisps of possibly imaginary sound—echoes of what might have been laughter, but when he poised
his head to listen, the pulsations ceased.

The onset of darkness continued to trouble him. Often he felt urges
to go forth into the dark—an impulse which he resisted, partly from fatigue,
partly from a dread of abnormality. He reported his nocturnal restlessness
to the camp doctor, who agreed that the tendency should be discouraged,
at least until the source was known. The doctor commended Pardero
for his industry, and advised the accumulation of at least two hundred and seventy-five ozols before departure, to allow for incidental
expenses.

When Pardero's account reached two hundred and seventy-five ozols,
he claimed his money from the bursar, and now, no longer an indigent, he
was free to pursue his own destiny. He took a rather mournful leave of the
doctor, whom he had come to like and respect, and boarded the transport
for Carfaunge. He left Gaswin with a twinge of regret. He had known little
pleasure here; still the place had given him refuge. He barely remembered
Carfaunge, and the spaceport was no more than the recollection of a
dream.

He saw nothing of Superintendent Mergan, but was recognized by Dinster the night porter, just coming on duty.

The *Ectobant* of the Prydania Line took Pardero to Baruilla, on Deulle,
Alastor 2121, where he transferred to the *Lusimar* of the Gaean Trunk Line,
and so was conveyed to Calypso Junction on Imber, and thence by the *Wispen Argent* to Numenes.

Pardero enjoyed the voyage: the multifarious sensations, incidents, and
vistas amazed him. He had not imagined the variety of the Cluster: the
comings and goings, the flux of faces, the gowns, robes, hats, ornaments,
and bijouterie; the colors and lights and strains of strange music; the babble
of voices; haunting glimpses of beautiful girls; drama, excitement, pathos;
objects, faces, sounds, surprises. Could he have known all this and forgotten?

So far Pardero had not indulged in self-pity and his enemy had seemed
a baleful abstraction. But how great and how callous the crime which had
been performed upon him! He had been isolated from home, friends, sympathy, security; he had been rendered a neuter; his personality had been
murdered.

Murder!

The word chilled his blood; he squirmed and winced. And from somewhere, from far distant, came the ghost of a sound: gusts of mocking laughter.

Approaching Numenes, the *Wispen Argent* first passed by Blazon, the
next world out in orbit, to be cleared for landing by the Whelm—a precau-

tion to minimize the danger of an attack from space upon the Connatic's Palace. Having secured clearance, the *Wispen Argent* proceeded; Numenes slowly expanded.

At a distance of about three thousand miles that peculiar referential displacement occurred; instead of hanging off to the side, a destination across the void, Numenes became the world below, upon which the *Wispen Argent* descended—a brilliant panorama of white clouds, blue air, sparkling seas.

The Central spaceport at Commarice occupied an area three miles in diameter, surrounded by a fringe of the tall jacinth palms and the usual spaceport offices, built in that low airy style also typical of Numenes.

Alighting from the *Wispen Argent*, Pardero rode a slideway to the terminal, where he sought information regarding the Connatic's Hospital. He was referred first to the Traveler's Aid station, then to an office at the side of the terminal, where he was presented to a tall spare woman of indeterminate age in a white and blue uniform. She gave Pardero a laconic greeting. "I am Matron Gundal. I understand that you wish to be admitted to the Connatic's Hospital?"

"Yes."

Matron Gundal touched buttons, evidently to activate a recording mechanism. "Your name?"

"I am called Pardero. I do not know my true name."

Matron Gundal made no comment. "Place of origin?"

"I don't know."

"Your complaint?"

"Amnesia."

Matron Gundal gave him a noncommittal inspection, which perhaps indicated interest. "What about your physical health?"

"It seems to be good."

"An orderly will conduct you to the hospital." Matron Gundal raised her voice. "Ariel."

A blond young woman entered the room, her uniform somewhat at discord with her sunny good looks. Matron Gundal gave her directions: "Please conduct this gentleman to the Connatic's Hospital." To Pardero: "Have you luggage?"

"No."

"I wish you a quick recovery."

The orderly smiled politely at Pardero. "This way, please."

An air-cab slid them northward across the blue and green landscape of Flor Solana, with Ariel maintaining an easy flow of conversation. "Have you visited Numenes before?"

"I don't know; I don't remember anything earlier than the last two or three months."

"Oh, I'm sorry to hear this!" said Ariel in confusion. "Well, in case you don't know, there are no real continents here on Numenes, just islands. Everybody who lives here owns a boat."

"That seems very pleasant."

Ariel gingerly touched upon Pardero's disability, watching sidelong to see if he evinced sensitivity or discomfort. "What a strange sensation not to know yourself! How does it feel?"

Pardero considered a moment. "Well, it doesn't hurt."

"I'm relieved to hear that! Think: you might be almost anyone—perhaps rich and important!"

"More likely I'm someone very ordinary: a roadmender, or a wandering dog-barber."

"I'm sure not!" declared Ariel. "You seem—well . . ." she hesitated, then continued with a half-embarrassed laugh "—a very confident and intelligent person."

"I hope you are right." Pardero looked at her and sighed, wistful that her fresh blond charm must so soon pass from his life. "What will they do with me?"

"Nothing alarming. Your case will be studied by very clever persons using the most elaborate mechanisms. Almost certainly you will be cured."

Pardero felt a pang of uneasiness. "It's quite a gamble. I might easily be someone I don't want to be."

Ariel could not restrain a grin. "As I understand it, this is the reason persons become amnesiac in the first place."

Pardero made a glum sound. "Aren't you alarmed, riding with a man who likely is a shameful criminal?"

"I'm paid to be brave. I escort persons much more alarming than you."

Pardero looked out across Flor Solana Island. Ahead he saw a pavilion constructed of pale ribs and translucent panels, whose complexity was obscured behind jacinth palms and cinniborines.

As the air-cab approached, six domes became evident, with wings radiating in six directions. Pardero asked: "Is this the hospital?"

"The hospital is everything you see. The Hexad is the computative center. The smaller buildings are laboratories and surgeries. Patients are housed in the wings. That will be your home until you are restored to health."

Pardero asked diffidently: "And what of you? Will I see you again?"

Ariel's dimples deepened. "Do you want to?"

Pardero soberly considered the range of his inclinations. "Yes."

Ariel said half-teasingly: "You'll be so preoccupied that you'll forget all about me."

"I never want to forget anything again."

Ariel chewed her lip thoughtfully. "You remember nothing of your past life?"

"Nothing."

"Maybe you have a family: someone who loves you, and children."

"I suppose this is possible . . . Somehow I suspect otherwise."

"Most men seem to suspect otherwise . . . Well, I'll have to think about it."

The air-cab landed; the two alighted and walked along a tree-shaded avenue toward the Hexad. Ariel glanced at him sidewise, and perhaps his obvious foreboding excited her compassion. She said in a voice that she intended to be cheerful but impersonal: "I'm out here often and as soon as you've started your treatments I'll come and see you."

Pardero smiled wanly. "I'll look forward to the occasion."

She conducted him to the reception area, and spoke a few words to an official, then took her leave. "Don't forget!" she called over her shoulder, and the impersonality, intentionally or not, was gone from her voice. "I'll see you soon!"

"I am O.T. Kolodin," said a large rather rumpled man with an oversize nose and sparse untidy dark hair. " 'O.T.' means 'Ordinary Technician'; just call me Kolodin. You're on my list, so we'll be seeing something of each other. Come along; I'll get you settled."

Pardero bathed, submitted to a physical examination, and was issued a pale-blue lightweight suit. Kolodin showed him to his chamber along one of the wings, and the two took a meal on a nearby terrace. Kolodin, not too much older than Pardero but incalculably more sophisticated, took a lively interest in Pardero's condition. "I've never come in contact with such a case before. Fascinating! It's almost a shame to cure you!"

Pardero managed a wry smile. "I have doubts of my own. I'm told that I can't remember because of something I want to forget. I might not like being cured."

"It is a difficult position," Kolodin agreed. "Still, affairs may not be so bad after all." He glanced at his thumbnail, which responded with a set of glowing numbers. "In fifteen minutes we'll meet with M.T. Rady, who will decide upon your therapy."

The two returned to the Hexad. Kolodin ushered Pardero into the office of Master Technician Rady, and a moment later Rady himself appeared: a thin, sharp-eyed man of middle age who already seemed to know the data relevant to Pardero's case. He asked: "The spaceship which brought you to Bruse-Tansel: how was it named?"

"I can't remember much about it."

Rady nodded and touched a square of coarse sponge to each of Pardero's shoulders. "This is an inoculation to facilitate a relaxed mind-state . . . Relax back into your chair. Can you fix your mind upon something pleasant?"

The room dimmed; Pardero thought of Ariel. Rady said: "On the wall you will see a pair of designs. I want you to examine them, or if you prefer, you may close your eyes and rest . . . In fact, relax completely, and listen only to my voice; and when I tell you to sleep, then you may sleep."

The designs on the wall pulsed and swam; a soft sound, waxing and waning, seemed to absorb and obliterate all other sounds of the universe. The shapes on the wall had expanded to surround him, and the only reality was himself and his inner mind.

"I don't know." The voice sounded as if it were coming from a distant room, although it was his own voice. Odd. He heard a mumble whose significance he only half-heeded: "What was your father's name?"

"I don't know."

"What was your mother's name?"

"I don't know."

More questions, sometimes casual, sometimes urgent, and always the same response, and finally the cessation of sound.

Pardero awoke in an empty office. Almost immediately Rady returned, to stand looking down at Pardero with a faint smile.

Pardero asked: "What did you learn?"

"Nothing to speak of. How do you feel?"

"Tired."

"Quite normal. For the rest of the day, rest. Don't worry about your condition; somehow we'll get to the bottom of your case."

"Suppose there's nothing there? Suppose I have no memory?"

Rady refused to take the idea seriously. "Every cell in your body has a memory. Your mind stores facts on many levels. For instance you have not forgotten how to speak."

Pardero said dubiously: "When I arrived at Carfaunge, I knew very little. I could not talk. As soon as I heard a word I remembered its meaning and I could use it."

Rady gave a curt nod. "This is the basis of a therapy we might well try."

Pardero hesitated. "I might find my memory and discover myself to be a criminal."

Rady's eyes gleamed. "That is a chance you must take. The Connatic, after restoring your memory, might then decide to put you to death."

Pardero grimaced. "Does the Connatic ever visit the hospital?"

"Undoubtedly. He goes everywhere."

"What does he look like?"

Rady shrugged. "In his official photographs he seems an important and imposing nobleman, because of his dress and accoutrements. But when he walks abroad, he goes quietly and is never recognized, and this is what he likes best. Five trillion folk inhabit Alastor Cluster, and it is said that the Connatic knows what each of them eats for breakfast."

"In that case," said Pardero, "perhaps I should simply go to ask the Connatic for the facts of my life."

"It might come to that."

The days passed, and then a week, and then two weeks. Rady attempted a dozen stratagems to loosen the blocked linkages in Pardero's mind. He recorded responses to a gamut of stimulations: colors, sounds, odors, tastes, textures; heights and depths; lights and degrees of darkness. On a more complex level he charted Pardero's reactions, overt, physiological, and cephalic, to absurdities and festivals, erotic conditions, cruelties and horrors, the faces of men, women, and children. A computational mechanism assimilated the results of the tests, compared them to known parameters, and synthesized an analog of Pardero's psyche.

Rady, when he finally assessed the results of his tests, found little enlightenment. "Your basic reflexes are ordinary enough; one anomaly is your reaction to darkness, by which you seem to be curiously stimulated. Your social perceptivity seems underdeveloped, for which the amnesia may be to blame. You appear to be assertive rather than retiring; your response to music is minimal and color symbology has little meaning for you—possibly by reason of your amnesia. Odors stimulate you rather more than I might expect—but to no significant degree." Rady leaned back in his chair. "These tests might easily provoke some sort of conscious response. Have you noticed anything whatever?"

"Nothing."

Rady nodded. "Very well. We will try a new tack. The theoretical basis is this: if your amnesia has resulted from circumstances which you are determined to forget, we can dissolve the amnesia by bringing these events to your conscious attention again. In order to do this, we must learn the nature of the traumatic circumstances. In short we must learn your identity and home environment."

Pardero frowned and looked out the window. Rady watched intently. "You don't care to learn your identity?"

Pardero gave him a crooked smile. "I did not say so."

Rady shrugged. "The choice is yours. You can walk out of here at any time. The Social Service will find you employment and you can start a new life."

Pardero shook his head. "I never could evade the pressure. Perhaps there are people who need me, who now grieve for me."

Rady said only: "Tomorrow we'll start the detective work."

An hour after twilight Pardero met Ariel at a café and reported the events of the day. "Rady admitted bafflement," said Pardero, with something like gloomy satisfaction. "Not in so many words of course. He also said that the only way to learn where I came from was to find out where I lived. In short, he wants to send me home. First we must find home. The detective work starts tomorrow."

Ariel nodded thoughtfully. Tonight she was not her usual self; in fact, thought Pardero, she seemed strained and preoccupied. He reached out to touch her soft blond hair, but she drew back.

"And then?" she asked.

"Nothing much. He told me that if I were reluctant to proceed, now was the time to make a decision."

"And what did you say?"

"I told him that I had to go on, that perhaps somewhere people searched for me."

Ariel's blue eyes darkened sorrowfully. "I cannot see you any more, Pardero."

"Oh? Why not?"

"For just the reasons you cited. Amnesiacs always wander away from their homes and then—well, form new attachments. Then their memory returns and the situation ends in tragedy." Ariel rose to her feet. "I'll say good-bye now, before I change my mind." She touched his hand, then walked away from the table. Pardero watched her diminish down the avenue. He made no move to stop her.

Instead of one day, three days passed before O.T. Kolodin sought out Pardero. "Today we visit the Connatic's Palace and explore the Ring of Worlds."

"I'll enjoy the excursion. But why?"

"I've been looking into your past, and it turns out to be a hopeless tangle; or, more properly, a blur of uncertainties."

"I could have told you that myself."

"No doubt, but one must never take anything for granted. The facts, duly certified, are these. Sometime on tenth Mariel Gaean you appeared at Carfaunge Spaceport. This was an unusually busy day and you might have arrived aboard any of six ships of four different transport lines. The previous routes of these ships took them to a total of twenty-eight worlds, any of which might be your place of origin. Nine of these worlds are important junctions and it is possible that you made your voyage by two or even three stages. Amnesia would not be an insuperable objection. Stewards and depot personnel, taking you for a lackwit, would consult your ticket and shift you from ship to ship. In any case the number of worlds, depots, ships, and possible linkages becomes unmanageable. Or at least an inquiry of last resort. First we will visit the Connatic! Though I doubt if he will receive us personally."

"Too bad! I would like to pay my respects."

They rode by air-cab across Flor Solana to Moniscq, a town beside the sea, thence under the Ocean of Equatorial Storms by submarine tunnel to Tremone Island. An air-bus flew them south, and presently the Connatic's so-called "palace" became visible, appearing first as a fragile shine, an unsubstantial glimmer in the air, which solidified into a tower of stupendous dimensions, standing upon five pylons, footed upon five islands. A thousand feet above the sea the pylons joined and flared, creating a dome of five groins, the underside of the first deck. Above rose the tower, up through the lower air, up through the sunny upper air, through a wisp of cirrus to terminate in the high sunlight. Kolodin asked casually: "Have you such towers on your home world?"*

Pardero glanced at him skeptically. "Are you trying to trick me? If I knew this, I wouldn't be here." He returned to contemplation of the tower. "And where does the Connatic live?"

"He has apartments at the pinnacle. Perhaps he stands up there now, by one of his windows. Again, perhaps not. It is never certain; after all, dissidents, rogues, and rebels are not unknown to Alastor, and precautions are in order. Suppose, for example, that an assassin were sent to Numenes in the guise of an amnesiac, or perhaps as an amnesiac with horrid instructions latent in his mind."

"I have no weapons," said Pardero. "I am no assassin. The very thought causes me to shudder."

"I must make a note of this. I believe that your psychometry also showed an aversion to murder. Well, if you are an assassin, the plan will not succeed, as I doubt if we shall see the Connatic today."

"Who then will we be seeing?"

"A certain demosophist named Ollave, who has access to the data banks and the collating machinery. Quite possibly we will today learn the name of your home world."

Pardero gave the matter his usual careful consideration. "And then what will happen to me?"

"Well," said Kolodin cautiously, "three options at least are open. You can continue therapy at the hospital, although I fear that Rady is discouraged. You can accept your condition and attempt a new life. You can return to your home world."

---

*A drab translation of the word *geisling*, which carries warmer and dearer connotations.

Pardero made no comment, and Kolodin delicately forebore to put any further questions.

A slideway conveyed them to the base of the near pylon, from which perspective the tower's proportions could no longer be sensibly discerned, and only the sensation of overwhelming mass and transcendent engineering remained.

The two ascended in an elevator bubble; the sea, the shore, and Tremone Island dropped below.

"The first three decks and the six lower promenades are reserved for the use and pleasure of tourists. Here they may wander for days enjoying simple relaxation or, at choice, exotic entertainments. They may sleep without charge in simple chambers, although luxurious apartments are available at nominal expense. They may dine upon familiar staples or they may test every reputable cuisine of the Cluster and elsewhere, again at minimal cost. Travelers come and go by the millions; such is the Connatic's wish. Now we pass the administrative decks, which house the government agencies and the offices of the Twenty-Four Agents . . . Now we pass the Ring of Worlds, and up to the College of Anthropological Sciences, and here is our destination. Ollave is a man most knowledgeable and if anything can be learned he will learn it."

They stepped forth into a lobby tiled in blue and white. Kolodin spoke the name Ollave toward a black disk, and presently Ollave appeared. He was a man of undistinguished appearance, his face sallow and pensive, with a long thin nose and black hair receding from a narrow forehead. He greeted Kolodin and Pardero in a voice unexpectedly heavy and took them into a sparsely furnished office. Pardero and Kolodin sat in chairs and Ollave settled behind his desk. Ollave addressed Pardero: "As I understand the situation, you remember nothing of your early life."

"This is true."

"I cannot give you your memory," said Ollave, "but if you are native to Alastor Cluster, I should be able to determine your world of origin, perhaps the precise locality of your home district."

"How will you do that?"

Ollave indicated his desk. "I have on record your anthropometry, physiological indices, details as to your somatic chemistry, psychic profile—in fact, all the information Technicians Rady and Kolodin have been able to adduce. Perhaps you are aware that residence upon any particular world in any specific society, and participation in any way of life, leaves traces, mental and physical. These traces unfortunately are not absolutely specific, and some are too subtle to be reliably measured. For instance, if you are characterized by blood type RC3, it is then unlikely that your home world is Azulias. Your intestinal bacteria furnish clues, as does the musculature of your legs, the chemical composition of your hair, the presence and nature of any body fungus or internal parasite, the pigments of your skin. If you make use of gestures these may be typified. Other social reflexes such as areas and degrees of personal modesty are also indicative, but these require long and patient observation and again may be obscured by the amnesia. Dentition and dental repairs sometimes offer a clue, as does hairstyling. So now: do you understand the process? Those parameters to which we can assign numerical weights are processed in a computer, which will then present us a list of places in descending order of probability.

"We will prepare two other such lists. To those worlds most convenient to Carfaunge Spaceport we will assign probability factors, and we will try to codify your cultural reflexes: a complex undertaking, as the amnesia no doubt has muted much of this data, and you have in the meantime acquired a set of new habits. Still, if you will step into the laboratory, we will try to make a reading."

In the laboratory Ollave sat Pardero in a massive chair, fitted receptors to various parts of his body, and adjusted a battery of contacts to his head. Over Pardero's eyes he placed optical hemispheres and clamped earphones to his ears.

"First we establish your sensitivity to archetypal concepts. Amnesia may well dampen or distort the responses, and according to M.T. Rady yours is an extraordinary case. Still, if the cerebellum only is occluded other areas of the nervous system will provide information. If we get any signals whatever, we will assume that their relative strength has remained constant. The recent overlay we will try to screen out. You are to do nothing, merely sit quiet; attempt neither to feel nor not to feel; your internal faculties will provide us all we want to know." He closed the hemispheres over Pardero's eyes. "First, a set of elemental concepts."

To Pardero's eyes and ears were presented scenes and sounds: a sunlit forest, surf breaking upon a beach, a meadow sprinkled with flowers, a mountain valley roaring to a winter storm; a sunset, a starry night, a view over a calm ocean, a city street, a road winding over placid hills, a spaceship.

"Now another series," came Ollave's voice. Pardero saw a campfire surrounded by shadowy figures, a beautiful nude maiden, a corpse dangling from a gibbet, a warrior in black steel armor galloping on a horse, a parade of harlequins and clowns, a sailboat plunging through the waves, three old ladies sitting on a bench.

"Next, music."

A series of musical sounds entered Pardero's ears: a pair of chords, several orchestral essays, a fanfare, the music of a harp, a jig, and a merrydown.

"Now faces."

A stern and grizzled man stared at Pardero, a child, a middle-aged woman, a girl, a face twisted into a sneer, a boy laughing, a man in pain, a woman weeping.

"Vehicles."

Pardero saw boats, chariots, land vehicles, aircraft, spaceships.

"The body."

Pardero saw a hand, a face, a tongue, a nose, an abdomen, male and female genital organs, an eye, an open mouth, buttocks, a foot.

"Places."

A cabin beside a lake, a palace of a dozen domes and cupolas in a garden, a wooden hut, an urban tenement, a houseboat, a temple, a laboratory, the mouth of a cave.

"Objects."

A sword, a tree, a coil of rope, a mountain crag, an energy gun, a plow with a shovel and hoe, an official proclamation with a red seal, flowers in a vase, books on a shelf, an open book on a lectern, carpenter's tools, a selection of musical instruments, mathematical adjuncts, a retort, a whip, an engine, an embroidered pillow, a set of maps and charts, drafting instruments and blank paper.

"Abstract symbols."

Patterns appeared before Pardero's vision: combinations of lines, geometrical shapes, numbers, linguistic characters, a clenched fist, a pointing finger, a foot with small wings growing from the ankles.

"And finally . . ." Pardero saw himself—from a distance, then close at hand. He looked into his own face.

Ollave removed the apparatus. "The signals were extremely faint but perceptible. We have recorded your psychometrics and now can establish your so-called 'cultural index.' "

"What have you learned?"

Ollave gave Pardero a rather queer look. "You reactions are inconsistent, to use an understatement. You would seem to derive from a most remarkable society. You fear the dark, yet it challenges and exalts you. You fear women; you are made uneasy by the female body—still the concept of femininity tantalizes you. You respond positively to martial tactics, heroic encounters, weapons and uniforms; on the other hand you abhor violence and pain. Your other reactions are equally contradictory. The question becomes, do all these strange responses form a pattern, or do they indicate derangement? I will not speculate. The data have been fed into an integrator together with the other material I mentioned. No doubt the report is ready for us."

"I am almost afraid to examine it," murmured Pardero. "I would seem to be unique."

Ollave made no further comment; they returned to the office, where O.T. Kolodin waited patiently. From a register Ollave drew forth a square of white paper. "Here is our report." In a manner perhaps unconsciously dramatic he studied the printout. "A pattern has appeared." He read the sheet again. "Ah, yes . . . Eighteen localities on five worlds are identified. The probabilities for four of these worlds, with seventeen of the localities, aggregate three percent. The probability for the single locality on the fifth world is rated at eighty-nine percent, which under the circumstances is equivalent to near-certainty. In my opinion, Master Pardero, or whatever your name, you are a Rhune from the Rhune Realms, east of Port Mar on the North Continent of Marune, Alastor 933."

CHAPTER 3

I n the blue- and white-tiled lobby Kolodin asked Pardero: "Well—so you are a Rhune. What then? Do you recognize the word?"

"Not at all."

"I suspected not."

Ollave joined them. "Let's go acquaint ourselves with this world of yours. The Ring is directly below; Chamber 933 will be on Level Five. To the descensor!"

As the bubble dropped them down the levels, Kolodin discoursed upon the Ring of Worlds. "—one of the few areas controlled by entrance permit. Not so in the early days. Anyone might visit his world's chamber and there perform whatever nuisance entered his head, such as writing his name on the wall, or inserting a pin into the globe at the site of his home, or altering the lineage of local nobility, or placing scurrilous reports into the records. As a result we must now declare ourselves."

"Luckily my credentials will facilitate the matter," said Ollave drily.

The formalities accomplished, an attendant took them to that portal numbered 933 and allowed them admittance.

In the center of the chamber a globe ten feet in diameter floated close above the floor, rotating easily to the touch. "And there you see Marune," said Kolodin. "Does it appear familiar? . . . As I expected."

Ollave touched the globe. "A small dense world of no great population. The color gradients represent relief; Marune is a most rugged world. Notice these peaks and chasms! The olive green areas are polar tundra; the smooth blue metal is open water: not a great deal, relatively speaking. Note too these vast equatorial bogs! Certainly there is little habitable land." He touched a button; the globe sparkled with small pink light-points. "There you see the population distribution: Port Mar seems to be the largest city. But feel free to look around the chamber; perhaps you will see something to stimulate your memory."

Pardero moved here and there, studying the exhibits, charts, and cases with only tentative interest. Presently he asked in a rather hollow voice: "How far away is this planet?"

Kolodin took him to a three-dimensional representation of Alastor Cluster. "Here we are on Numenes, beside this yellow star." He touched a button, a red indicator blinked, near the side of the display. "There is Marune, almost at the Cold Edge, in the Fontinella Wisp. Bruse-Tansel is somewhere about there, where those grid lines come together." He moved to another display. "This represents the local environment: a four-star group. Marune is"—he touched a button—"at the end of the red arrow, orbiting close around the orange dwarf Furad. The green star is Cirse, the blue dwarf is Osmo, the red dwarf is Maddar. A spectacular location for a planet, among such a frolic of stars! Maddar and Cirse swing close around each other; Furad, with Marune keeping its monthly orbit, curves around Osmo; the four stars dance a fine saraband down the Fontinella Wisp."

Then Kolodin read from a placard on the wall. " 'On Marune, day and night do not alternate as is the case with most planets. Instead, there are varying conditions of light, depending upon which sun or suns rule the sky; and these periods are designated by a specific nomenclature. Aud, isp, red rowan, green rowan, and umber are the ordinary gradations. Night occurs at intervals regulated by a complex pattern, on the average about once every thirty days.

" 'Most of Marune is poorly adapted to human habitation and the population is small, divided about equally between agriculturists of the lowland slopes and residents of the several cities, of which Port Mar is by far the most important. East of Port Mar are the Mountain Realms, inhabited by those aloof and eccentric warrior-scholars known as Rhunes, whose numbers are not accurately known. The native fauna includes a quasi-intelligent biped of placid disposition: the Fwai-chi. These creatures inhabit highland forests and are protected from molestation both by statute and by local custom. For more detailed information, consult the catalogue.' "

Pardero went to the globe and presently discovered Port Mar. To the east rose a succession of enormous mountain ranges, the high crags rising past the timber line, up past snow and glaciers, into regions where rain and snowfall no longer existed. A multitude of small rivers drained the region, wandering along narrow upland valleys, expanding to become lakes, pouring over precipices to reconstitute themselves in new lakes or new streams below. Certain of the valleys were named: Haun, Gorgetto, Zangloreis, Eccord, Wintaree, Disbague, Morluke, Tuillin, Scharrode, Ronduce, a dozen others, all sounding of an odd or archaic dialect. Some of the names lay easy on his tongue, as if he well knew their proper pronunciation; and when Kolodin, peering over his shoulder, read them off, he noticed the faulty inflections, though he told Kolodin nothing of this.

Ollave called him and indicated a tall glass case. "What do you think of this?"

"Who are they?"

"An eiodarkal trismet."

"Those words mean nothing to me."

"They are Rhune terms, of course; I thought you might recognize them. An 'eiodark' is a high-ranking baron; 'trisme' is an institution analogous to marriage. 'Trismet' designates the people involved."

Pardero inspected the two figures. Both were represented to be tall, spare, dark-haired, and fair of complexion. The man wore a complicated costume of dark-red cloth, a vest of black metal strips, a ceremonial helmet contrived of black metal and black fabric. The woman wore garments somewhat simpler: a long shapeless gown of gray gauze, white slippers, a loose black cap which framed the white starkly modeled features.

"Typical Rhunes," said Ollave. "They totally reject cosmopolitan standards and styles. Notice them as they stand there. Observe the cool and dispassionate expressions. Notice also, their garments have no elements in common, a clear signal that in the Rhune society male and female roles differ. Each is a mystery to the other; they might be members of different races!" He glanced sharply at Pardero. "Do they suggest anything to you?"

"They are not strange, no more than the language was strange at Carfaunge."

"Just so." Crossing the chamber to a projection screen, Ollave touched buttons. "Here is Port Mar, on the edge of the highlands."

A voice from the screen supplied a commentary to the scene. "You view the city Port Mar as you might from an air-car approaching from the south. The time is aud, which is to say, full daylight, with Furad, Maddar, Osmo, and Cirse in the sky."

The screen displayed a panorama of small residences half-concealed by foliage: structures built of dark timber and pink-tan stucco. The roofs rose at steep pitches, joining in all manner of irregular angles and eccentric gables: a style quaint and unusual. In many cases the houses had been extended and enlarged, the additions growing casually from the old structures like crystals growing from crystals. Other structures, abandoned, had fallen into ruins. "These houses were built by Majars, the original inhabitants of Marune. Very few pure-blooded Majars remain; the race is almost extinct, and Majar town is falling into disuse. The Majars, with the Rhunes, named the planet, which originally was known as 'Majar-Rhune.' The Rhunes, arriving upon Marune, decimated the Majars, but were expelled by the Whelm into the eastern mountains, where to this day they are allowed no weapons of energy or attack."

The angle of view shifted to a hostelry of stately proportions. The commentator spoke: "Here you see the Royal Rhune Hotel, invariably patronized by those Rhunes who must visit Port Mar. The management is attentive to the special and particular Rhune needs."

The view shifted across a river to a district somewhat more modern. "You now observe the New Town," said the commentator. "The Port Mar College of Arts and Technics, situated nearby, claims a distinguished faculty and almost ten thousand students, deriving both from Port Mar and from the agricultural tracts to the south and west. There are no Rhunes in attendance at the college."

Pardero asked Ollave, "And why is that?"

"The Rhunes prefer their own educational processes."

"They seem an unusual people."

"In many respects."

"So it would seem. Let us look into the Mountain Realms." Ollave consulted an index. "First I'll show you one of the autochthones: the Fwai-chi, as they are called." He touched a button, to reveal a high mountainside patched with snow and sparsely forested with gnarled black trees. The view expanded toward one of these trees, to center upon the rugose brown-black trunk, which stirred and moved. Away from the tree shambled a bulky brown-black biped with a loose pelt, all shags and tatters. The commentator spoke: "Here you see a Fwai-chi. These creatures, after their own fashion, are intelligent, and as such they are protected by the Connatic. The shags of their skin are not merely camouflage against the snow bears; they are organs for the production of hormones and the reproductive stimule. Occasionally the Fwai-chi will be seen nibbling each other; they are ingesting a stuff which reacts with a bud on the wall of their stomachs. The bud develops into an infant, which in due course is vomited into the world. Along the trailing fringes of other shags other semi-vital stimules are produced.

"The Fwai-chi are placid, but not helpless if provoked too far; indeed they are said to possess important parapsychic competence, and no one dares molest them."

The view shifted, down the mountainside to the valley floor. A village of fifty stone houses occupied a meadow beside the river; from a bluff a tall mansion, or castle, overlooked the valley. To Kolodin's eye, the mansion, or castle, evinced an archaic overelaboration of shape and detail; additionally the proportions appeared cramped, the construction disproportionately heavy, the windows too few, too tall and narrow. He put to Pardero a question: "What do you think of this?"

"I don't remember it." Pardero raised his hands to his temples, pressed and rubbed. "I feel pressure; I want to see no more."

"Certainly not," declared Ollave jauntily. "We'll go at once." And he added: "Come up to my office; I'll pour you a sedative, and you'll feel less perturbation."

Returning to the Connatic's Hospital, Pardero sat silently for most of the trip. At last he asked Kolodin: "How soon can I go to Marune?"

"Whenever you like," said Kolodin, and then added, in the tentative voice of a person hoping to persuade a captious child: "But why hurry? Is the hospital so dreary? Take a few weeks to study and learn, and to make some careful plans."

"I want to learn two names: my own and that of my enemy."

Kolodin blinked. He had miscalculated the intensity of Pardero's emotions. "Perhaps no enemy exists," stated Kolodin somewhat ponderously. "He is not absolutely necessary to your condition."

Pardero managed a small sour smile. "When I arrived at the Carfaunge spaceport, my hair had been hacked short. I considered it a mystery until I saw the simulated Rhune eiodark. Did you notice his hair?"

"It was combed straight over the scalp and down across the neck."

"And this is a distinctive style?"

"Well—it's hardly common, though not bizarre or unique. It is distinctive enough to facilitate identification."

Pardero nodded gloomily. "My enemy intended that no one should identify me as a Rhune. He cut my hair, dressed me in a clown's suit, then put me on a spaceship and sent me across the Cluster, hoping I would never return."

"So it would seem. Still, why did he not simply kill you and roll you into a ditch? How much more decisive!"

"Rhunes fear killing, except in war: this I have learned from Ollave."

Kolodin surreptitiously studied Pardero, who sat brooding across the landscape. Remarkable the alteration! In a few hours, from a person uninformed, vague, and confused, Pardero had become a man purposeful and integrated; a man, so Kolodin would guess, of strong passions under stern control, and after all was not this the way of the Rhunes? "For the sake of argument, let us assume that this enemy exists," said Kolodin laboriously. "He knows you; you do not know him. You will arrive at Port Mar at a disadvantage, and perhaps at considerable risk."

Pardero seemed almost amused. "So then, must I avoid Port Mar? I reckon on this risk; I intend to prepare against it."

"And how will you so prepare?"

"First I want to learn as much as possible about the Rhunes."

"Simple enough," said Kolodin. "The knowledge is in Chamber 933. What next?"

"I have not yet decided."

Sensing evasion, Kolodin pursed his lips. "The Connatic's law is exact: Rhunes are allowed neither energy weapons nor air vehicles."

Pardero grinned. "I am no Rhune until I learn my identity."

"In a technical sense, this is true," said Kolodin cautiously.

Something over a month later Kolodin accompanied Pardero to the Central spaceport at Commarice, and out across the field to the *Dylas Extranuator*. The two said good-bye at the embarkation ramp. "I probably will never see you again," said Kolodin, "and much as I would like to know the outcome of your quest, I probably will never learn."

Pardero responded in a flat voice: "I thank you for your help and for your personal kindness."

From a Rhune, thought Kolodin, even an occluded Rhune, this was almost effusiveness. He spoke in a guarded voice: "A month ago you hinted of your need for a weapon. Have you obtained such an item?"

"No," said Pardero. "I thought to wait until I was beyond the range of the Connatic's immediate attention, so to speak."

With furtive glances to left and right Kolodin tucked a small carton into Pardero's pocket. "You now carry a Dys Model G Skull-splitter. Instructions are included in the package. Don't flourish it about; the laws are explicit. Good-bye, good luck, and communicate with me if possible."

"Again, thank you." Pardero clasped Kolodin's shoulders, then turned away and boarded the ship.

Kolodin returned to the terminal and ascended to the observation deck. Half an hour later he watched the black, red, and gold spaceship loft into the air, slide off and away from Numenes.

CHAPTER 4

During the month previous to his departure, Pardero spent many hours in Chamber 933 along the Ring of Worlds. Kolodin occasionally kept him company; Oswen Ollave, as often, came down from his offices to discuss the perplexing habits of the Rhunes.

Ollave prepared a chart which he insisted that Pardero memorize.

·	FURAD	OSMO	MADDAR	CIRCE
AUD	✖	✖	✖ EITHER	✖ OR BOTH
ISP		✖	✖	WITH OR
CHILL ISP		✖		✖ WITHOUT
UMBER	✖			
LORN UMBER	✖			
ROWAN			✖	✖
RED ROWAN			✖	
GREEN ROWAN				✖
MIRK				

"The chart indicates Marune's ordinary conditions of daylight,* during which the character of the landscape changes profoundly. The population is naturally affected, and most especially the Rhunes." Ollave's voice had

---

*These are the modes recognized by the folk of Port Mar. Both the Majars and the Rhunes make more elaborate distinctions.

The progression of the modes is rendered complex by reason of the diurnal rotation of Marune, the revolution of Marune around Furad, the motion of Furad and Osmo around each other, the orbital motions of Maddar and Cirse, around each other and jointly around the Furad-Osmo system. The planes of no two orbiting systems are alike.

The Fwai-chi, who lack all knowledge of astronomy, can reliably predict the modes for as far in the future as anyone cares to inquire.

Among the low mountains south of Port Mar live a "lost" community of about ten thousand Majars, decadent, inbred, and gradually diminishing in numbers. These folks are slavishly affected by the modes of day. They regulate their moods, diet, attire, and activities by the changes. During mirk, the Majars lock themselves in their huts, and by the light of oil lamps chant imprecations against Galula the Goblin who mauls and eviscerates anyone unlucky enough to be abroad after dark. Some such entity as Galula indeed exists, but has never been satisfactorily identified.

The Rhunes, as proud and competent as the Majars are demoralized, are also strongly affected by the changing modes. Behavior proper during one mode may be considered absurd or in poor taste during another. Persons advance their erudition and hone their special skills during aud, isp, and umber. Formal ceremonies tend to take place during isp, as well as during the remarkable Ceremony of Odors. It may be noted that music is considered hyperemotional and inducive to vulgar conduct; it is never heard in the Rhune Realms. Aud is the appropriate time to go forth to battle, to conduct litigation, fight a duel, collect rent. Green rowan is a time for poetry and sentimental musing; red rowan allows the Rhune slightly to relax his etiquette. A man may condescend to take a glass of wine in company with other men, all using etiquette screens; women similarly may sip cordials or brandy. Chill isp inspires the Rhune with a thrilling

taken on a pedantic suavity, and he enunciated his words with precision. "Port Mar is hardly notable for sophistication. The Rhunes, however, consider Port Mar a most worldly place, characterized by shameless alimentation, slackness, laxity, and a kind of bestial lasciviousness to which they apply the term 'sebalism.'

"In the Old Town at Port Mar a handful of exiles live—young Rhunes who have rebelled against their society, or who have been ejected for lapses of conduct. They are a demoralized, miserable, and bitter group; all criticize their parents, who, so they claim, have withheld counsel and guidance. To a certain extent this is true; Rhunes feel that their precepts are self-evident even to the understanding of a child—which of course they are not; nowhere in the Cluster are conventions more arbitrary. For instance, the process of ingesting food is considered as deplorable as the final outcome of digestion, and eating is done as privately as possible. The child is supposed to arrive at this viewpoint as well as other Rhune conventions automatically. He is expected to excel in arcane and impractical skills; he must quell his sebalism."

Pardero stirred restlessly. "You have used this word before; I do not understand it."

"It is the special Rhune concept for sexuality, which the Rhunes find disgusting. How then do they procreate? It is cause for wonder. But they have solved the problem with elegance and ingenuity. During mirk, in the dark of the suns, they undergo a remarkable transformation. Do you wish to hear about it? If so, you must allow me a measure of discursiveness, as the subject is most wonderful!

"About once a month, the land grows dark, and the Rhunes become restless. Some lock themselves into their homes; others array themselves in odd costumes and go forth into the night where they perform the most astonishing deeds. The baron whose rectitude is unquestioned robs and beats one of his tenants. A staid matron commits daring acts of unmentionable depravity. No one who allows himself to be accessible is safe. What a mystery then! How to reconcile such conduct with the decorum of daylight? No one tries to do so; night-deeds are considered hardships for which no one is held responsible, like nightmares. Mirk is a time of unreality. Events during mirk are unreal, and guilt has no basis.

"During mirk, sebalism is rampant. Indeed, sexual activity occurs as a night-deed, only in the guise of rape. Marriage—'trisme,' as it is called—is never considered a sexual pairing, but rather an alliance—a joining of economic or political forces. Sexual acts, if they occur, will be night-deeds—

---

ascetic exultation, which completely supersedes lesser emotions of love, hate, jealousy, greed. Conversation occurs in a hushed archaic dialect; brave ventures are planned; gallant resolves sworn; schemes of glory proposed and ratified, and many of these projects become fact, and go into the Book of Deeds.

acts of purported rape. The male participant wears a black garment over his shoulders, arms, and upper chest, and boots of black cloth. Over his head he wears a man-mask. His torso is naked. He is purposely grotesque, an abstraction of male sexuality. His costume depersonalizes him and maximizes the fantasy or unreal element. The man enters the chamber where the woman sleeps, or pretends to sleep; and in utter silence copulation occurs. Neither virginity nor its absence is significant, nor are either so much as a subject for speculation. The Rhune dialect contains no such word.

"So there you have the state of 'trisme.' Between trismetics friendships may exist, but the two address each other formally. Intimacy between any two people is rare. Rooms are large, so that folk need not huddle together, nor even approach. No person purposely touches another; in fact the occupations which require physical contact, such as barbering, doctoring, clothesfitting, are considered pariah trades. For such services the Rhunes journey into Port Mar. A parent neither strikes nor caresses his child; a warrior attempts to kill his enemy at a distance, and weapons such as swords and daggers have only ceremonial function.

"Now allow me to describe the act of eating. On those rare occasions when a Rhune is forced to dine in the company of others he ingests his food behind a napkin, or at the back of a device unique to Marune: a screen on a metal pedestal, placed before the diner's face. At formal banquets no food is served—only wafts of varied and complicated odors, the selection and presentation being considered a creative skill.

"The Rhunes lack humor. They are highly sensitive to insult; a Rhune will never submit to ridicule. Lifelong friends must reckon with each other's sensibilities and then rely upon a complicated etiquette to lubricate social occasions. In short, it seems as if the Rhunes deny themselves all the usual human pleasures. What do they substitute?

"In the first place, the Rhune is exquisitely sensitive to his landscapes of mountain, meadow, forest, and sky—all changing with the changing modes of day. He reckons his land by its aesthetic appeal; he will connive a lifetime to gain a few choice areas. He enjoys pomp, protocol, heraldic minutiae; his niceties and graces are judged as carefully as the figures of a ballet. He prides himself on his collection of sherliken scales; or the emeralds which he has mined, cut, and polished with his own hands; or his Arah magic wheels, imported from halfway across the Gaean Reach. He will perfect himself in special mathematics, or an ancient language, or the lore of fanfares, or all three, or three other abstrusities. His calligraphy and draftsmanship are taken for granted; his life work is his Book of Deeds, which he executes and illustrates and decorates with fervor and exactitude. A few of these books have reached the market; in the Reach they command enormous prices as curios.

"The Rhune is not a likeable man. He is so sensitive as to be truculent;

he is contemptuous of all other races than the Rhune. He is self-centered, arrogant, unsympathetic in his judgments.

"Naturally I allude to the typical Rhune, from whom an individual may deviate, and everything I have said applies no less to the women as the men.

"The Rhunes display correspondingly large virtues: dignity, courage, honor, intellects of incomprehensible complexity—though here again individuals may differ from the norm.

"Anyone who owns land considers himself an aristocrat, and the hierarchy descends from kaiark, through kang, eiodark, baronet, baron, knight, and squire. The Fwai-chi have retreated from the Realms, but still make their pilgrimages through the upper forests and along the high places. There is no interaction between the two races.

"Needless to say, among a people so passionate, proud, and reckless, and so anxious to expand their landholdings, conflict is not unknown. The force of the Connatic's Second Edict and, more effectively, an embargo upon energy weapons, has eliminated formal war. But raids and forays are common, and enmities last forever. The rules of warfare are based upon two principles. First, no man may attack a person of higher rank than himself; second, since blood violence is a mirk-deed, killing is achieved at a distance with blast-bolts; aristocrats however use swords and so demonstrate fortitude. Ordinary warriors will not look at a man in the face and kill him; such an act haunts a man forever—unless the act is done by mirk, when it becomes no more than a nightmare. But only if unplanned. Premeditated murder by mirk is vile murder."

Pardero said, "Now I know why my enemy sent me off to Bruse-Tansel instead of leaving me dead in a ditch."

"There is a second argument against murder: it cannot be concealed. The Fwai-chi detect crimes, and no one escapes; it is said that they can taste a dead man's blood and cite all the circumstances of his death."

On this evening Pardero and Kolodin chose to spend the night in the tourist chambers on the lower decks of the tower. Kolodin made a videophone call and returned with a slip of paper, which he handed to Pardero. "The results of my inquiries. I asked myself, what ship leaving Port Mar would land you at Carfaunge Spaceport on tenth Mariel Gaean? Traffic Central's computer provided a name and a date. On 2 Ferario Gaean, the *Berenicia* of the Black and Red Line departed Port Mar. More than likely you were aboard."

Pardero tucked the paper into his pocket. "Another matter which concerns me: how do I pay my passage to Marune? I have no money."

Kolodin made an expansive gesture. "No difficulties there. Your rehabilitation includes an extra thousand ozols for just this purpose. Any more worries?"

Pardero grinned. "Lots of them."

"You'll have an interesting time of it," said Kolodin.

The *Dylas Extranuator* drove out past the Pentagram, circled the diadem in the horn of the Unicorn, and coasted into Tsambara, Alastor 1317. Here Pardero made connection with a ship of the Black and Red Line which, after touching into a number of remote little places, veered off along the Fontinella Wisp and presently approached an isolated system of four dwarfs, respectively orange, blue, green, and red.

Marune, Alastor 933, expanded below, to show a surface somewhat dark and heavy-textured below its fleets and shoals of clouds. The ship descended and settled upon the Port Mar spaceport. Pardero and a dozen other passengers alighted, surrendered their last ticket coupon, passed through the lobby and out upon the soil of Marune.

The time was isp. Osmo glared blue halfway up the southern sky; Maddar rode at the zenith; Cirse peered over the northeast horizon. The light was a trifle cold, but rich with those overtones provided by Maddar and Cirse, so that objects cast a three-phase shadow.

Pardero halted before the terminal, looked around the landscape, across the sky, inhaled a deep breath, exhaled. The air tasted fresh, cool, and tart, unlike both the dank air of Bruse-Tansel and the warm sweet air of Numenes. The suns sliding in different directions across the sky, the subtle lights, the taste of the air, soothed an ache in his mind he had not heretofore noticed. A mile to the west the structures of Port Mar stood clear and crisp: beyond the land fell away. The view seemed not at all strange. Whence came the familiarity? From research in Chamber 933? Or from his own experience? To the east the land swelled and rose in receding masses of ever higher mountains, reaching up to awesome heights. The peaks gleamed white with snow and gray with granite scree; below, bands of dark forest muffled the slopes. Mass collided with light to create shape and shadow; the clarity of the air as it swept through the spaces was almost palpable.

The waiting bus sounded an impatient chime; Pardero slowly climbed aboard, and the bus moved off along the Avenue of Strangers toward Port Mar.

The attendant made an announcement: "First stop, the Traveler's Inn. Second, the Outworld Inn. Then the Royal Rhune Hotel. Then over the bridge into New Town for the Cassander Inn and the University Inn."

Pardero chose the Outworld Inn which seemed sufficiently large and impersonal. Imminence hung in the air, so heavy that his enemy must also be oppressed.

Pardero cautiously surveyed the lobby of the Outworld Inn, but saw only off-world folk who paid him no heed. The hotel personnel ignored him. So far, so good.

He took a lunch of soup, cold meat, and bread in the dining room, as much to compose himself as to appease his appetite. He lingered at the table reviewing his plans. To broadcast the fewest ripples of disturbance he must move softly, delicately, working from the periphery inward.

He left the hotel and sauntered back up the Avenue of Strangers toward the green-glass dome of the spaceport terminal. As he walked, Osmo dipped low and sank behind the western edge of Port Mar. Isp became rowan, with Cirse and Maddar yet in the sky, to produce a warm soft light that hung in the air like haze.

Arriving at the terminal, Pardero entered and went to the reception desk. The clerk came forward—a small, portly man with the cinnamon skin and golden eyes of an upper-caste Majar, one of those who lived in the timber and stucco houses on the slopes at the back of Old Town.

"How may I serve you, sir?"

Clearly Pardero aroused in his mind no quiver of recognition.

"Perhaps you can provide me some information," said Pardero. "On or about 2 Ferario, I took passage aboard the *Berenicia* of the Black and Red Line. One of the other passengers asked me to perform a small errand, which I was unable to achieve. Now I must notify him but I have forgotten his name, and I would like to glance at the relevant passenger list."

"No difficulties here, sir; the ledger is easily consulted." A display screen lit up; the clerk turned a knob; figures and listings flicked past. "Here we are at 2 Ferario. Quite correct, sir. The *Berenicia* arrived, took aboard eight passengers, and departed."

Pardero studied the passenger list. "Why are the names in different columns?"

"By order of the Demographical Institute, so that they may gauge traffic between the worlds. Here are transients upon Marune taking departure. These names—only two, as you see—represent folk of Marune bound for other worlds."

"My man would be one of these. Which ones took passage to Bruse-Tansel?"

The clerk, somewhat puzzled, consulted the list. "Neither. Baron Shimrod's destination was Xampias. The Noble Serle Glaize boarded the ship on an 'open' ticket."

"What sort of ticket is this?"

"It is often purchased by a tourist who lacks a fixed destination. The ticket provides a stipulated number of travel-units; when these are exhausted the tourist purchases further units to fit his particular needs."

"This 'open ticket' used by Serle Glaize, how far might it have taken him? To Bruse-Tansel, for instance?"

"The *Berenicia* does not put into Bruse-Tansel, but let me see. One hundred and forty-eight ozols to Dadarnisse Junction; to Bruse-Tansel one hundred and two ozols . . . Yes, indeed. You will notice that the Noble Serle Glaize bought an open ticket to the value of two hundred and fifty ozols; to Bruse-Tansel exactly."

"So: Serle Glaize. This is my man." Pardero reflected upon the name. It lacked all resonance, all familiar flavor. He passed two ozols across the counter to the clerk, who took them with grave courtesy.

Pardero asked: "Who sold the ticket to Serle Glaize?"

"The initial is 'Y'; that would be Yanek, on the next shift."

"Perhaps you could telephone Yanek and ask if he recalls the circumstances. I will pay five ozols for significant information."

The clerk eyed Pardero sidelong. "What sort of information do you consider significant?"

"Who bought the ticket? I doubt if Serle Glaize did so himself. He must have come with a companion whose identity I wish to learn."

The clerk went to a telephone and spoke in a guarded manner, from time to time glancing over his shoulder toward Pardero. At last he returned, his manner somewhat subdued. "Yanek barely recalls the matter. He believes that the ticket was bought by a person in a black Rhune cape, who also wore a gray casque with a visor and malar flaps, so that his features made no impression upon Yanek. The time was busy; Yanek was preoccupied and noticed no more."

"This is not the information I require," Pardero grumbled. "Is there anyone who can tell me more?"

"I can think of no one, sir."

"Very well." Pardero counted down another two ozols. "This is for your kind cooperation."

"Thank you, sir. Allow me to make a suggestion. The Rhunes who visit Port Mar without exception use the Royal Rhune Hotel. Information, however, may be hard to come by."

"Thank you for the suggestion."

"Are you not a Rhune yourself, sir?"

"After a fashion, yes."

The clerk nodded and uttered a soft chuckle. "A Majar will mistake a Rhune never indeed, oh never . . ."

In a pensive mood Pardero returned along the Avenue of Strangers. The learned computations of M.T. Rady, the sociopsychic deductions of Oswen Ollave had been validated. Still, by what obscure means had the Majar recognized him? His features were not at all peculiar; his pigmentation was hardly distinctive; his clothes and hairstyle were, by cosmopolitan standards, ordinary enough; in short, he differed little from any other guest at the Outworld Inn. No doubt he betrayed himself by unconscious gestures or attitudes; perhaps he was more of a Rhune than he felt himself to be.

The Avenue of Strangers ended at the river; as Pardero reached the bridge Maddar slanted behind the western lowlands; Cirse moved slowly up the sky: green rowan. Green ripples flickered across the water; the white walls of New Town shone pale apple green. Along the riverfront festoons of lights appeared, indicating places of entertainment: beer-gardens, dance pavilions, restaurants. Pardero scowled at the brashness of the scene, then gave a soft rueful snort. Had he surprised a set of Rhune attitudes surfacing through his amnesia?

Pardero turned into the narrow Street of Brass Boxes, which curved gradually up-slope, between ancient structures of age-blackened wood. The shops facing out upon the street uniformly showed a pair of high windows, a brass-bound door, and only the most unobtrusive indication as to their wares, as if each strove to exceed his neighbor in reserve.

The Street of Brass Boxes ended in a dim shadowed square, surrounded by curio shops, bookstores, specialty houses of many varieties. Pardero saw his first Rhunes, moving from shop to shop, pondering the merchandise, indicating their needs to the Majar shopkeepers with indifferent flicks of the finger. None of them so much as glanced toward Pardero, which caused him irrationally mixed feelings.

He crossed the square and turned up the Avenue of Black Jangkars to an arched portal in a stone wall. He passed beneath and approached the Royal Rhune Hotel. He halted before the vestibule. Once inside the Royal Rhune there could be no turning back; he must accept the consequences of his return to Marune.

Through the tall doors stepped two men and a woman—the men wearing costumes of beige and black with dark red sashes, so similar as to suggest military uniforms; the woman, almost as tall as either of the men, wore a tight blue-gray suit, with an indigo cape draping from black epaulettes: a mode considered suitable for visits to Port Mar, where the formal gauze gowns of the Realms were inappropriate. The three marched past Pardero, each allowing him a single glance. Pardero sensed no flicker of recognition. Small cause for surprise since the Rhunes numbered well over a hundred thousand.

Pardero pushed aside the tall gaunt doors which seemed a part of the Rhune architectural environment. The lobby was an enormous high-ceilinged room with sounds echoing across a bare russet and black tile floor. The chairs were upholstered in leather. The central table displayed a variety of technical magazines, and at the far end of the room a rack held brochures advertising tools, chemicals, craft supplies, papers and inks, rare woods and stone. A tall narrow arch flanked by columns of fluted green stone communicated with the office. Pardero looked briefly around the lobby and passed through the arch.

A clerk of advanced age rose to his feet and approached the counter;

despite age, a bald head, and unctuous wattles, his manner was alert and punctilious. In an instant he assessed Pardero, his garments and manner-isms, and performed a bow of precisely calibrated courtesy. "How can we oblige you, sir?" As he spoke a trace of uncertainty seemed to enter his manner.

"Several months ago," said Pardero, "about the first of Ferario to be more precise, I was a guest at this hotel, and I wish to refresh my recollec-tions. Will you be so good as to show me the records for this date?"

"As you require, Your Dignity."* The clerk turned Pardero a second half-surreptitious side-glance, and his manner altered even further, becoming tinged with doubt, or uneasiness, or even anxiety. He bent with an almost audible creaking of vertebrae and elevated a leather-bound ledger to the counter. With a reverential flourish he parted the covers, and one by one turned the pages, each of which displayed a schematic chart of the hotel's accommodations, with notations in inks of various colors. "Here, Dignity, is the date you mention. If you choose to advise me, I will assist you."

Pardero inspected the ledger, but could not decipher the archaic callig-raphy.

In a voice meant to convey an exquisite and comprehensive discretion the clerk spoke on. "On this phase our facilities were not overextended. In our 'Sincere Courtesy' wing, we housed the trismets† of various gentlefolk. You will notice the chambers so indicated. In our 'Approbation' accommo-dations we served the Eiodark Torde and the Wirwove Ippolita, with their respective trismets. The 'Altitude' suite was occupied by the Kairak Rianlle of Eccord, the Kraike Dervas, the Lissolet Maerio. In the 'Hyperion' suite we entertained the late Kaiark Jochaim of Scharrode, may his ghost be quickly appeased, with the Kraike Singhalissa, the Kangs Efraim and Des-tian and the Lissolet Sthelany." The clerk turned his trembling and dubious smile upon Pardero. "Do I not now have the honor of addressing His Force the new Kaiark of Scharrode?"

Pardero said somewhat ponderously: "You recognize me, then?"

"Yes, Your Force, now that I have spoken with you. I admit to confu-sion; your presence has altered in a way which I hardly know how to explain. You seem, shall we say, more mature, more controlled, and of course your foreign garments enhance these differences. But I am certain that I am right." The clerk peered in sudden doubt. "Am I not, Your Force?"

---

*The all-purpose honorific, somewhat more respectful than a simple "sir," to be applied to Rhunes of inde-terminate status.

†Trismet: The group of persons resulting from a "trisme," the Rhune analog of marriage. These persons might be a man and his trismetic female partner; or a man, the female partner, one or more of her children (of which the man may or may not be the sire). "Family" approximates the meaning of "trismet" but carries a package of inaccurate and inapplicable connotations. Paternity is often an uncertain determination; rank and status, therefore, are derived from the mother.

Pardero smiled coolly. "How could you demonstrate the fact one way or the other without my assurance?"

The clerk muffled an exclamation. Muttering under his breath he brought to the counter a second leather-bound volume, twice the size of the ledger. He glanced peevishly toward Pardero, then turned thick pages of pale-brown parchment.

Pardero asked: "What book is that?"

The clerk looked up from the pages, and now his gray old lips sagged incredulously. "I have here the *Great Rhune Almanac*. Are you not familiar with it?"

Pardero managed a curt nod. "Show me the folk who occupied the Hyperion suite."

"Inexorable Force, I was about to do so." The clerk turned pages. On the left were genealogical charts, ladders, linkages, and trees, indited in rich inks of various colors; on the right photographs were arranged in patterns relative to the charts: thousands upon thousands of names, an equal number of likenesses. The clerk turned pages with maddening deliberation. At last he halted, pondered a moment, then tapped the page with his finger. "The lineage of Scharrode."

Pardero could restrain himself no longer. He turned the volume about and studied the photographs.

Halfway down the page a pale-haired man of middle maturity looked forth. His face, angular and bleak, suggested an interesting complexity of character. The forehead might have been that of a scholar, the wide mouth seemed composed against some unwelcome or unfashionable emotion, such as humor. The superscription read: *Jochaim, House of Benbuphar, Seventy-ninth Kaiark.*

A green linkage led to the still face of a woman, her expression unfathomable. The caption read: *Alferica, House of Jent.* Below, a heavy maroon line led to the countenance of an unsmiling young man: a face which Pardero recognized as his own. The caption read: *Efraim, House of Benbuphar, Kang of the Realm.*

At least I now know my name, thought Pardero. I am Efraim, and I was Kang, and now I am Kaiark. I am a man of high rank! He looked up at the clerk, surprising a shrewd and intent scrutiny. "You are curious," said Efraim. "There is no mystery. I have been off-planet and have just returned. I know nothing of what has happened in my absence. The Kaiark Jochaim is dead?"

"Yes, Your Force. There has been uncertainty and confusion, so I understand. You have been the subject of concern, since now, of course, you are the Eightieth Kaiark, and the allowable lapse has almost transpired."

Efraim nodded slowly. "So now I am Kaiark of Scharrode." He returned to the almanac, conscious of the clerk's gaze.

The other faces on the page were three. From Jochaim a second green line descended to the face of a handsome dark-haired woman with a pale high forehead, blazing black eyes, a keen high-bridged nose. The caption identified her as *Kraike Singhalissa*. From Singhalissa vermilion lines led first to a dark-haired young man with the aquiline features of his mother: Kang Destian, and a girl, dark-haired and pale, with pensive features and a mouth drooping at the corners, a girl in fact of rather remarkable beauty. The caption identified her as the *Lissolet Sthelany*.

Efraim spoke in a voice he tried to keep matter-of-fact: "What do you recall of our visit here to Port Mar?"

The clerk reflected. "The two trismets, of Scharrode and Eccord, arrived in concert, and in general conducted themselves as a single party. The younger persons visited New Town, while their elders transacted business. Certain tensions became evident. There followed a discussion of the visit to New Town, of which several of the older persons disapproved. Most exercised were the Kraike Singhalissa and the Kaiark Rianlle, who thought that the expedition lacked dignity. When you failed to appear by isp 25 of the Third Cycle, everyone felt concern; evidently you had failed to apprise anyone of your departure."

"Evidently," said Efraim. "Did mirk occur during our visit?"

"No; there was no mirk."

"You heard no remarks, you recall no circumstances which might explain my departure?"

The clerk looked puzzled. "A most curious question, Your Force! I remember nothing of consequence, though I was surprised to hear that you had acquainted yourself with that off-world vagabond." He sniffed. "No doubt he took advantage of your condescension; he is known as a persuasive rogue."

"Which off-world vagabond is this?"

"What? Do you not remember exploring New Town with the fellow Lorcas?"

"I had forgotten his name. Lorcas, you say?"

"Matho Lorcas. He consorts with New Town trash; he is fugleman for all these sebal cretins at the university."

"And when did Kaiark Jochaim die?"

"Soon after his return to Scharrode, in battle against Gosso, Kaiark of Gorgetto. You have returned opportunely. In another several days you would no longer be Kaiark, and I have heard that Kaiark Rianlle has proposed a trisme to unite the realms of Eccord and Scharrode. Now that you are returned, conditions may be altered." The clerk turned pages in the almanac. "Kaiark Rianlle is an intense and determined man." The clerk tapped a photograph. Efraim saw a handsome distinguished face, framed by a casque of shining silver ringlets. The Kraike Dervas looked forth blankly;

her face seemed to lack distinctive character. The same was true of the Lissolet Maerio, who stared forth expressionlessly, but who nonetheless displayed a youthful if rather vacuous prettiness.

The clerk asked cautiously: "Do you plan to stay with us, Force?"

"I think not. And I wish you to say nothing whatever of my return to Marune. I must clarify certain circumstances."

"I quite understand, Force. Thank you very much indeed!"—this last for the ten ozols which Efraim had placed on the counter.

Efraim emerged from the hotel into a melancholy umber. He walked slowly back down the Avenue of Black Jangkars, and coming once more to the square he now took time to walk around, and with awe and wonder investigated the shops. Could there exist anywhere in all Alastor Cluster a richer concentration of the arcane, the esoteric, the special? And Efraim wondered what had been his own fields of erudition, his own unique virtuosities. Whatever they were, he retained none of them; his mind was a blank.

Somewhat mournfully he proceeded down the Street of Brass Boxes to the river. New Town appeared quiet. Festoons of lights still glowed along the riverfront, but the beer-gardens and cafés lacked animation. Efraim turned away, walked up the Avenue of Strangers to the Outworld Inn. He went to his chamber and slept.

He dreamt a series of vivid dreams and awoke in a flush of excitement. After a moment he tried to reform the shattered images into focus so that he might grasp the meanings which had marched across his sleeping mind. To no avail. Composing himself, he slept once more until a gong announced the hour of breakfast.

CHAPTER 5

Efraim emerged from the hotel into that phase sometimes known as half-aud. Furad and Osmo ruled the sky, to produce a warm yellow light, which connoisseurs of such matters considered fresh, effervescent, and gay, but lacking the richness and suavity of full aud. He stood for a moment breathing the cool air. His melancholy had diminished; better to be Kaiark Efraim of Scharrode than Efraim the butcher, or Efraim the cook, or Efraim the garbage collector.

He set along the Avenue of Strangers. Arriving at the bridge, instead of veering left into the Street of Brass Boxes he crossed into New Town, and discovered an environment totally different from that of Old Town.

The geography of New Town, so Efraim would discover, was simple. Four thoroughfares paralleled the river: the Estrada, which terminated at the university; the Avenue of the Agency; then the Avenue of Haune and the Avenue of Douaune, after Osmo's two small dead planets.

Efraim walked westward along the Estrada, examining the cafés and beer-gardens with wistful interest. To his present perspective they seemed almost flagrantly innocent. He stepped into one of the beer-gardens and glanced toward the young man and girl who sat huddled so closely together. Could he ever feel so easily licentious in full view of everyone? Perhaps even now he had not escaped the strictures of his past, which after all was less than six months gone.

He approached a portly man in a white apron who seemed to be the manager. "Sir, are you acquainted with a certain Matho Lorcas?"

"Matho Lorcas? I do not know the gentleman."

Efraim continued west along the Estrada and presently at a booth devoted to the sale of off-world periodicals the name "Mathos Lorcas" sparked recognition. The girl attendant pointed along the avenue: "Ask there, in the Satyr's Cave. You might find him at work. If not, they know his dwelling."

Mathos Lorcas was indeed at work, serving mugs of beer along the bar. He was a tall young man with a keen vivacious face. His dark hair was cut short in a casual and unassuming style. When he spoke his thin crooked mouth worked dozens of changes across his face. Efraim watched him a moment before approaching. Matho Lorcas was a person whose humor, intelligence, and easy flamboyance might well excite the antagonism of less favored individuals. Hard to suspect malice, or even guile, in Matho Lorcas. The fact remained that soon after making Lorcas' acquaintance Efraim had been rendered mindless and shipped off across the Cluster.

Efraim approached the bar and took a seat; Lorcas approached. Efraim asked. "You are Matho Lorcas?"

"Yes indeed!"

"Do you recognize me?"

Lorcas gave Efraim a frowning scrutiny. His face cleared. "You are the Rhune! I forget your name."

"Efraim, of Scharrode."

"I remember you well, and the two girls you escorted. How grave and proper their behavior! You have changed! In fact you seem a different person. How goes life in your mountain realm?"

"As usual, or so I suppose. I am most anxious to have a few words with you. When will you be free?"

"At any time. Right now, if you like; I am bored with the work. Ramono! Take charge of affairs!" He ducked under the bar and asked of Efraim: "Will you take a mug of beer? Or perhaps a glass of Del wine?"

"No thank you." Efraim had decided upon a policy of caution and reserve. "It is early in the day for me."

"Just as you like. Come, let us sit over here where we can watch the river flow by. So. Do you know, I have often wondered about you, and how you eventually—well, shall we say, accommodated yourself to your dilemma, pleasant though it might have been."

"How do you mean?"

"The two beautiful girls you escorted—though I realize in the Mountain Realms things aren't done quite so easily."

Aware that he must seem dense and dull, Efraim asked: "What do you recall of the occasion?"

Lorcas held up his hands in protest. "So long ago? After so many other occasions? Let me think . . ." He grinned. "I deceive you. In truth, I've thought long and often of those two girls, so alike, so different, and oh, how wasted in those ineffable Mountain Realms! They walk and talk like enchanted blocks of ice—though I suspect that one or the other, or both, under the proper circumstances might easily melt; and I for one would rejoice to arrange such circumstances. You consider me sebal? I'm far worse; I'm positively chorastic!"* He glanced sidelong toward Efraim. "You don't seem appalled, or even shocked. For a fact you *are* a person different from the earnest young Kang of six months ago."

"This may well be true," said Efraim without impatience. "Returning to that occasion, what happened?"

Lorcas turned Efraim another quizzical side glance. "You don't remember?"

"Not well."

"Odd. You seemed quite alert. You recall how we met?"

"Not too well."

Lorcas gave a half-incredulous shrug. "I had just stepped out of the Caduceus Book Shop. You approached and asked directions to the Fairy Gardens, where at the time Galligade's Puppets were entertaining. The mode as I recall was low aud, going into umber, which always seems to me to be a rather festive time. I noted that you and the Kang Destian—so I recall his name—escorted not one but two pretty girls, and I'd never had the opportunity to meet a Rhune before, so I volunteered to conduct you in person. At the Fairy Gardens we found that Galligade had just finished his show and the disappointment of the girls prompted me to a spasm of insane altruism. I insisted on acting as your host—not my usual conduct, I assure you. I ordered a bottle of wine and etiquette screens for those who considered them necessary, and so there we were: the Lissolet Sthelany, observing me with aristocratic detachment, the other girl—I forget the name—"

"The Lissolet Maerio."

*Chorasm: sebalism carried to a remarkable extreme.

"Correct. She was only a trifle more cordial, though, mind you, I'm making no complaints. Then there was the Kang Destian, who was sardonic and surly, and yourself, who behaved with elegant formality. You were the first Rhunes I'd met, and when I found you to be of royal blood, I thought my efforts and ozols well spent.

"So we sat and drank the wine and listened to the music. More accurately, I drank wine. You and the Lissolet Maerio, thoroughly daring, sipped behind your etiquette screens. The other two declared themselves uninterested. The girls watched the students and marveled at the crassness and sebalism. I fell in love with the Lissolet Sthelany, who of course was oblivious. I used all my charm; she studied me with fascinated revulsion and presently she and Destian returned to the hotel.

"You and the Lissolet Maerio remained until Destian came back with orders that Maerio return to the hotel. You and I were left alone. I was due at The Three Lanterns; you walked up Jibberee Hill with me. I went to work; and you returned to the hotel. That's all there is to it."

Efraim heaved a deep sigh. "You did not accompany me to the hotel?"

"No. You went off by yourself, in a most unsettled mood. If I may make bold to ask—why are you so concerned about this evening?"

Efraim saw no reason to hold back the truth. "On that evening I lost my memory. I remember arriving at Carfaunge, on Bruse-Tansel, and I finally made my way to Numenes and the Connatic's Hospital. The experts declared me a Rhune. I returned to Port Mar; I arrived yesterday. At the Royal Rhune Hotel I learned my name, and I find that I am now the Kaiark of Scharrode. Other than this I know nothing. I recognize no one and nothing; my past is a blank. How can I conduct my own affairs responsibly, much less those of the Realm? I must set things right. Where do I start? How do I proceed? Why was my memory taken from me? Who took me to the spaceport and put me aboard the spaceship? How shall I explain myself to my people? If the past is empty, the future seems full, of concern and doubt and confusion. And I suspect that I will find little sympathy at home."

Lorcas gave a soft ejaculation, and sat back, his eyes glistening. "Do you know, I envy you. How lucky you are, with the mystery of your own past to solve!"

"I lack all such enthusiasm," said Efraim. "The past looms over me; I feel stifled. My enemies know me; I can only grope for them. I go out to Scharrode blind and helpless."

"The situation is not without compensations," murmured Lorcas. "Most people would gladly rule a mountain realm, or any realm whatever. Not a few would be pleased to inhabit the same castle with the Lissolet Sthelany."

"These compensations are all very well, but they do not expose my enemy."

"Assuming that the enemy exists."

"He exists. He put me aboard the *Berenicia* and paid my fare to Bruse-Tansel."

"Bruse-Tansel is not close. Your enemy would seem not to lack funds."

Efraim grunted. "Who knows how much money of my own I carried? Perhaps I paid my own fare out to the limit of my pocketbook."

"This would be a fine sardonic touch," Lorcas agreed. "If true, your enemy has style."

"Another possibility exists," mused Efraim. "I may be looking at the matter backwards."

"An interesting thought. In what exact regard?"

"Perhaps I committed some horrid deed which I could not bear to contemplate, thus inducing amnesia, and some person—my friend rather than my enemy—sent me away from Marune so that I might escape the penalty for my acts."

Lorcas uttered an incredulous laugh. "Your conduct in my presence was quite genteel."

"So how then, immediately after parting from you, did I lose my memory?"

Lorcas considered a moment. "This might not be so mysterious after all."

"The savants on Numenes were baffled. But you have gained an insight into my problems?"

Lorcas grinned. "I know someone who isn't a savant." He jumped to his feet. "Come along, let's visit this man."

Efraim dubiously arose. "Is it safe? You might be the guilty person. I don't want to end up on Bruse-Tansel a second time."

Lorcas chuckled. "You are a Rhune no longer. The Rhunes lack all humor; their lives are so strange that the absurd seems merely another phase of normality. I am not your secret enemy, I assure you. In the first place I lack the two or three hundred ozols to send you to Bruse-Tansel."

Efraim followed Lorcas out upon the avenue. Lorcas said: "We are bound for a rather peculiar establishment. The proprietor is an eccentric. Unkind folk consider him disreputable. At the moment he is out of vogue, owing to the efforts of the Benkenists, who are currently all the rage around the college. They affect a stoic imperturbability to everything except their inner norms, and Skogel's numbered mixtures seriously interfere with normality. As for me, I reject all fads except those of my own devising. Can you imagine what now preoccupies me?"

"No."

"The Mountain Realms. The genealogies, the waxing and waning of fortunes, the poetry and declamations, the ceremonial fumes, the gallantries and romantic postures, the eruditions, and scholarship. Do you realize that

Rhune monographs circulate throughout the Cluster and the Gaean Reach as well? Do you realize that sport is unknown among the Realms? There are neither games nor frivolous recreations, not even among the children?"

"The thought never occurred to me. Where are we going?"

"Yonder, up the Street of the Clever Flea . . . Naturally you would not know how the street got its name." As they walked, Lorcas recounted the ribald legend. Efraim listened with only half an ear. They turned the corner into a street of marginal enterprises: a booth selling fried clams, a gambling arcade, a cabaret decorated with red and green lights, a bordello, a novelty shop, a travel agency, a store which displayed in the show window a stylized Tree of Life, the golden fruit labeled in a flowing unreadable script. Here Lorcas paused. "Let me do the talking, unless Skogel asks you a direct question. He has a queer manner which antagonizes everyone, but which I happen to know is spurious. Or at least I strongly suspect as much. In any event, be surprised at nothing; also, if he quotes a price, agree, no matter what your reservations. Nothing puts him off like haggling. Come along then; let's try our luck." He entered the shop with Efraim following slowly behind.

From the dimness at the back of the shop Skogel appeared: a man of medium stature, thin as a post, with long arms and a round waxen face, above which rose spikes of dust-brown hair. "Pleasant modes," said Lorcas. "Have you collected yet from our friend Boodles?"

"Nothing. But I expected nothing and dealt with him accordingly."

"How so?"

"You know his requirements. He received only tincture of cacodyl in water, which may or may not have served his purposes."

"He made no complaints to me, though in truth he has seemed somewhat subdued of late."

"If he chooses, he may come to me for consolation. And who is this gentleman? Something about him seems Rhune, something else says outworld."

"You are right in both directions. He is a Rhune who has spent an appreciable time on Numenes, and Bruse-Tansel as well. You instantly wonder why. The answer is simple—he has lost his memory. I told him that if anyone could help him it would be you."

"Bah. I don't stock memories in boxes, neatly labeled like so many cathartics. He'll have to contrive his own memories. Isn't this easy enough?"

Lorcas looked at Efraim with an expression of rueful amusement. "Contrary fellow that he is, he wants his own memories back."

"He won't find them here. Where did he lose them? That's the place to look."

"An enemy stole his memory and put him on a ship to Bruse-Tansel. My friend is anxious to punish this thief, hence his set chin and gleaming eyes."

Skogel, throwing back his head, laughed and slapped the counter. "That's more like it! Too many wrong-doers escape with whole skins and profit! Revenge! There's the word! I wish you luck! Good modes, sir." And Skogel, turning his back, stalked stiff-legged back into the dimness of his shop. Efraim stared after him in wonder, but Lorcas signaled him to patience. Presently Skogel stalked forward. "And what do you require on this occasion?"

Lorcas said: "Do you recall your remarks of a week ago?"

"In regard to what?"

"Psychomorphosis."

"A large word," grumbled Skogel. "I spoke it at random."

"Would any of this apply to my friend?"

"Certainly. Why not?"

"And the source of this psychomorphosis?"

Skogel put his hands on the counter and leaning forward scrutinized Efraim with owlish intensity. "You are a Rhune?"

"Yes."

"What is your name?"

"I seem to be Efraim, Kaiark of Scharrode."

"Then you must be wealthy."

"I don't know whether I am or not."

"And you want the return of your memory?"

"Naturally."

"You have come to the wrong place. I deal in commodities of other sorts." Skogel slapped the counter and made as if to turn away again.

Lorcas said smoothly: "My friend insists that you at least accept a fee, or honorarium, for your advice."

"Fee? For words? For guesses and hypotheses? Do you take me for a man without shame?"

"Of course not!" declared Lorcas. "He only wants to learn where his memory went."

"Then this is my guess, and he may have it free of cost. He has eaten Fwai-chi shag." Skogel indicated the shelves, cases, and cabinets of his shop, which were stocked with bottles of every size and shape, crystalized herbs, stoneware jugs, metal oddments, tins, phials, jars, and an unclassifiable miscellaneity of confusing scope. "I will reveal a truth," declared Skogel portentously. "Much of my merchandise, on a functional level, is totally ineffective. Psychically, symbolically, subliminally, the story is different! Each item exerts its own sullen strength, and sometimes I feel myself in the presence of elementals. With an infusion of spider grass, mixed perhaps with pulverized devil's eye, I achieve astounding results. The Benkenists, idiots and witlings as they are, aver that only the credulous are affected; they are wrong! Our organisms swim in a paracosmic fluid, which no one can comprehend; none of our senses find scope or purchase, so to speak. Only by operative procedures, which the Benkenists deride, can we manipulate this ineffable medium; and by so stating, am I therefore a charlatan?" Skogel slapped the counter with a split-faced grin of triumph.

With delicate emphasis Lorcas inquired: "And what of the Fwai-chi?"

"Patience!" snapped Skogel. "Allow me my brief moment of vanity. After all, I do not veer too far astray."

"By all means," said Lorcas hastily. "Declaim to your heart's content."

Not altogether mollified, Skogel took up the thread of his remarks. "I have long speculated that the Fwai-chi interact with the paracosmos somewhat more readily than men, although they are a taciturn race and never explain their feats, or perhaps they take their multiplex environment for granted. In any event, they are a most peculiar and versatile race, which the Majar, at least, appreciate. I refer of course to that final poor fragment of the race who live over the hill." Skogel looked truculently from Lorcas to Efraim, but neither challenged his opinion.

Skogel continued. "A certain shaman of the Majars fancies to consider himself in my debt, and not too long ago he invited me to Atabus to witness an execution. My friend explained an innovation in Majar justice: the suspect, or the adjudged—among the Majars the distinction is slight—is dosed with Fwai-chi shag, and his reactions, which range from torpor through hallucination, antics, convulsions, frantic feats of agility, to instant death, are noted. The Majar are nothing but a pragmatic folk; they take a lively interest in the capabilities of the human organism, and consider themselves great scientists. In my presence they administered a golden-brown gum from dorsal Fwai-chi shags, and the suspect at once fancied himself four different persons who conducted a vivacious conversation among themselves and the onlookers, employing a single tongue and larynx to produce two and sometimes three voices simultaneously. My host described some of the other effects he had witnessed, and mentioned a certain shag whose exudation blotted away human memory. I therefore suggest that your friend has been dosed with Fwai-chi shag." He peered from one to the other, showing a small trembling smile of triumph. "And that, in short, is my opinion."

"All very well," said Lorcas, "but how is my friend to be cured?"

Skogel made a careless gesture. "No cure is known, for the reason that none exists. What is gone, is gone."

Lorcas looked ruefully at Efraim. "So there you have it. Someone dosed you with Fwai-chi shag."

"I wonder who," said Efraim. "I wonder who."

Lorcas turned to speak to Skogel, but the shopkeeper had disappeared into the dim chamber at the rear of his establishment.

Lorcas and Efraim returned along the Street of the Clever Flea to the Estrada, Efraim pensive and grim. Lorcas, after darting half a dozen glances toward his companion, could no longer contain his curiosity. "So now what will you do?"

"What must be done."

Ten paces later Lorcas said: "You evidently have no fear of death."

Efraim shrugged.

Lorcas asked: "How will you achieve this business?"

"I must return to Scharrode," said Efraim. "Is there any other way? My enemy is someone I know well; would I drink with a stranger? In Port Mar were the following persons: Kaiark Jochaim, who is dead, the Kraike Singhalissa, the Kang Destian, the Lissolet Sthelany. Then, from Eccord, the Kaiark Rianlle, the Kraike Dervas, and the Lissolet Maerio. And, conceivably, Matho Lorcas, except in this case, why would you take me to Skogel?"

"Precisely so," said Lorcas. "On that distant occasion I dosed you only with good wine from which you took no harm."

"And you saw nothing significant, nothing suspicious, nothing dire?"

Lorcas reflected. "I noticed nothing overt. I felt stifled passion and flows of emotion, but where they led I could not divine. To be candid, I expected strange personalities among the Rhunes, and I made no attempt to understand what I saw. Without a memory you will also be handicapped."

"Very likely. But now I am Kaiark and everyone must go at my pace. I can recover my memory at leisure. What is the best transportation to Scharrode?"

"There's no choice," said Lorcas. "You hire an air-car and fly out." He looked casually up into the sky, which Cirse was about to depart. "If you permit, I will accompany you."

"What is your interest in the affair?" asked Efraim suspiciously.

Lorcas responded with an airy gesture. "I have long wished to visit the Realms. The Rhunes are a fascinating people and I am anxious to learn more about them. And, if the truth be known, I am anxious to pursue one or two acquaintances."

"You might not enjoy your visit. I am Kaiark, but I have enemies and they might not distinguish between us."

"I rely upon the notorious Rhune revulsion against violent conduct, which they abandon only during their incessant wars. And who knows? You might find a companion useful."

"Perhaps. Who is this acquaintance whom you are anxious to cultivate? The Lissolet Sthelany?"

Lorcas nodded glumly. "She is an intriguing young woman; in fact, I will go so far as to say that she represents a challenge. As a rule, pretty ladies find me sympathetic, but the Lissolet Sthelany barely notices my existence."

Efraim gave a sour chuckle. "In Scharrode the situation will be worse rather than better."

"I expect no true triumphs; still, if I can persuade her to alter her expression from time to time, I will consider the journey a success."

"I doubt if all will go so easily. The Rhunes find outland manners coarse and vulgar."

"You are Kaiark; your orders must be obeyed. If you decree tolerance, then the Lissolet Sthelany must instantly bend to your will."

"It will be an interesting experiment," said Efraim. "Well, then, make yourself ready; we leave at once!"

CHAPTER 6

During early isp Efraim arrived at the office of the local air transport service, to find that Lorcas had already hired an air-car of no great elegance—its metalwork stained by long exposure to the elements, the glass of the dome clouded, the flanges around the pods cratered and corroded. Lorcas said apologetically: "It's the best available, and quite dependable; in a hundred and two years the engine has never failed, or so I'm told."

With a skeptical eye Efraim surveyed the vehicle. "If it flies us to Scharrode, I don't care what it looks like."

"Sooner or later the craft will collapse, most likely in mid-air. Still— the alternative is shank's mare along the Fwai-chi trails. The terrain is most impressive, nor would you make so dignified an arrival."

"There is something in what you say," Efraim admitted. "Are you ready to leave?"

"At any time. But let me make a suggestion. Why not send a message ahead to prepare them for your coming?"

"So that someone can fly out and shoot us down?"

Lorcas shook his head. "Air-cars are banned to the Rhunes, for just this reason. The present issue is one of dignity, and if I may presume to advise you, a Kaiark announces his arrival so that a formal reception may be arranged. I will speak for you, as your aide, which will lend dignity to the occasion."

"Very well, do as you like."

"The Kraike Singhalissa is now the head of the household?"

"So I would suppose."

At a videophone as antiquated as the air-car, Lorcas put through a call.

A footman in a black and scarlet uniform responded. "I speak for Benbuphar Strang. Please state your business."

"I want a few words with the Kraike Singhalissa," said Lorcas. "I have important information to transmit."

"You must call at some other time. The Kraike is in consultation regarding the investiture."

"Investiture? Of whom?"

"Of the new Kaiark."

"And who will this be?"

"The present Kang Destian, who is next in order of succession."

"And when does the investiture occur?"

"In one week's time, when the present Kaiark is to be declared derelict."

Lorcas laughed. "Please inform the Kraike that the investiture may be canceled, since Kaiark Efraim is immediately returning to Scharrode."

The footman stared into the screen. "I cannot take responsibility for such an announcement."

Efraim stepped forward. "Do you recognize me?"

"Ah, Force,* indeed I do!"

"Deliver the message as you heard it from the Noble Matho Lorcas."

"Instantly, Force!" The footman inclined himself in a stiff bow, and faded in a dazzle of halations.

The two returned to the air-car and clambered aboard. Without ceremony the pilot clamped the ports, opened the throttle and the ancient aircraft, creaking and vibrating, lurched up and away to the east.

With the pilot, who identified himself as Tiber Flaussig, talking over his shoulder and ignoring both altimeter and the terrain below, the aircraft cleared the ridges of the First Scarp with a hundred yards to spare. As if by afterthought the pilot lifted the craft somewhat higher, although the land at once fell away a thousand feet to become an upland plain. A hundred sprawling lakes reflected the clouds; scaur and deep-willow grew in isolated copses, with a gnarled catafalque tree here and there. Thirty miles east the Second Scarp thrust crags of naked rock up past the clouds. Flaussig, discussing certain outcrops below, declared them rich sources of such gems as tourmaline, peridot, topaz, and spinel—all protected from human exploitation by reason of Fwai-chi prejudice. "They claim this as one of their holy places, and so reads the treaty. They care no more for the jewels than for common stones; but they can smell a man from fifty miles away and lay on him their curse of a thousand itches, or a fiery bladder, or piebald skin. The area is now avoided."

Efraim pointed ahead to the looming scarp. "In a single minute we will all be crushed to pulp, unless you quickly raise this craft at least two thousand feet."

"Ah yes," said Flaussig. "The scarp approaches, and we will give it due

---

*The term *tsernifer*, here translated as "Force," refers to that pervasion of psychological power surrounding the person of a kaiark. The word is more accurately rendered as *irresistible compulsion, elemental wisdom, depersonalized force*. The appellative "Force" is an insipid dilution.

respect." The air-car rose at a stomach-gripping rate, and from the engine box came a stuttering wheeze which caused Efraim to twist about in alarm. "Is this vehicle finally disintegrating?"

Flaussig listened with a puzzled frown. "A mysterious sound certainly, one which I have not heard before. Still, were you as old as this vehicle, your viscera would also produce odd noises. Let us be tolerant of the aged."

As soon as the craft once more flew a level course the disturbing sounds dwindled into silence. Lorcas pointed ahead toward the Third Scarp, still fifty miles ahead. "Start now to ascend, in a gradual manner. The air-car is more likely to survive such treatment."

Flaussig acceded to the request, and the vehicle rose at a gradual angle to meet the prodigious bulk of the Third Scarp. Below passed a desolation of ridges, cols, chasms, and, rarely, a small forested valley. Flaussig waved his hand around the fearsome landscape. "Within the range of vision, around the whole of the cataclysmic tumble, live perhaps twenty fugitives: desperadoes, condemned criminals, and the like. Commit no crimes in Port Mar or here is where you will wind up."

Neither Lorcas nor Efraim saw fit to comment.

A cleft appeared; the air-car glided through with rock walls close to right and left and great buffets of wind thrusting the craft from side to side; then the cleft fell away and the air-car flew over a landscape of peaks, cliffs, and river valleys. Flaussig waved his hand in another inclusive arc. "The Realms, the glorious Realms! Beneath us now Waierd, guarded by the Soldiers of Silence . . . And now we fly across the realm Sherras. Notice the castle in the lake . . ."

"How far to Scharrode?"

"Yonder, over the crags. That is the answer given to all such questions. Why do you visit a place so dour?"

"Curiosity, perhaps."

"You'll learn nothing from them; they're as tight as stones, like all Rhunes. Below now and behind those great trees is the town Tangwill, home to no more than two or three thousand. The Kaiark Tangissel is said to be insane for women, so he keeps captives in deep dungeons where they don't know whether or not it is mirk, and he visits them during all the periods of the month, except during mirk when he's off on his prowling."

"Nonsense," muttered Efraim, but the pilot paid no heed.

"The great spire to the left is called Ferkus—"

"Up, man, up!" screamed Lorcas. "You're running us into the ridge!"

With a petulant gesture Flaussig jerked the aircraft high, to skim that crag to which Lorcas had made reference; for a period he flew in sullen silence. Below the ground rose and fell, and Flaussig, disdaining further altitude, veered back and forth among crystalline crags, grazed precipices, skirted glaciers and mounds of scree, the better to display his insouciant control over aircraft, landscape, and passengers. Lorcas made frequent expostulations, which Flaussig ignored, and at last guided the air-car down into an irregular valley three to four miles wide and fifteen miles long. At the eastern end a cascade fell two thousand feet into a lake, with nearby the town Esch. Away from the lake flowed a slow river, curving across a meadow and under Benbuphar Strang, then back and forth from pool to pool to the far western end of the valley, where it departed through a narrow gorge.

Near Esch the valley had been tamed to cultivation; the fields were enclosed by dense hedges of brambleberry, as if to hide them from view. In other such fields grazed cattle, while the slopes to either side of the valley were planted as orchards. Elsewhere meadows alternated with forests of banice, white oak, shrack, interstellar yew; through the clear air the foliages—dark green, crimson, sooty ocher, pale green—glowed like colors painted on black velvet. Efraim half-smiled to the fleeting brush with a sudden poignant emotion. Perhaps an exhalation from his occluded memory? Such twinges had been occurring with increasing frequency. He glanced at Lorcas to find him also staring about in wistful wonder. "I have heard how the Rhunes cherish each stone of the landscape," said Lorcas. "The reason is clear. The Realms are small segments of Paradise."

Flaussig, having unloaded the scanty luggage, now stood in an expectant attitude. Lorcas spoke with slow and careful diction. "The fee was prepaid in Port Mar. The management wished to make sure of their money, no matter what else happened."

Flaussig smiled politely. "In circumstances like the present, a gratuity is usually extended."

"Gratuity?" exclaimed Efraim in a passion. "You are lucky to escape a penalty for criminal ineptitude!"

"Further," said Lorcas, "remain here until his Force the Kaiark permits you to leave. Otherwise he will order his secret agent in Port Mar to meet you and break every bone in your body."

Flaussig bowed in a state of injured dignity. "It shall be as you wish. Our firm has built its reputation upon service. Had I known I was transporting grandees of Scharrode, I would have used more formality, since appropriate behavior is also a watchword at our firm."

Lorcas and Efraim had already turned toward Benbuphar Strang, a castle of black stone, umber tile, timber, and stucco, built to the dictates of that peculiar gaunt style typical of the Rhunes. The chambers of the first floor were enclosed by walls thirty feet high, with tall narrow windows, elaborating above into a complicated system of towers, turrets, promenades, bays, balconies, and eyries. This was home, mused Efraim, and this was terrain over which he had walked a thousand times. He looked westward along the valley, across the pools and meadows, past the successive silhouettes of the forests, the colors muted by the haze, until they became purple-gray shadow under the far crags: he had looked across this vista ten thousand times . . . He felt no recollection.

He had been recognized from the town. Several dozen men in black jackets and buff pantaloons hurried forth, with half as many women in gray gauze gowns.

The men, approaching, performed complicated gestures of respect, then came forward, halting at a distance precisely reckoned by protocol.

Efraim asked, "How have things gone during my absence?"

The most venerable of the men responded: "Tragically, Force. Our Kaiark Jochaim was pierced by a Gorget bolt. Otherwise not badly, but not well. There have been doubts and misgivings. From Torre a band of warriors invaded our land. The Kang Destian ordered out a force, but there was little correspondence in rank*; and no great combat ensued. Our blood boils for revenge upon Gosso of Gorgetto. The Kang Destian has delayed retaliation; when will he order forth our power? Remember, from the crest of Haujefolge our sails command his castle. We can invade them while Gosso sweats and wheezes, we can drop down a force and take Gorgance Strang."

"First things first," said Efraim. "I now go to Benbuphar Strang to discover what irregularities, if any, exist. Have you information, or even suspicions, in this regard?"

The sage performed another gesticulation of a ritual effacement. "I would never reflect upon Benbuphar irregularities, let alone give them voice."

"Do so now," said Efraim. "You will be doing your Kaiark a service."

"As you will, Force, but remember, by the nature of things, we of the town know nothing. Uncharitable persons blink askance at the Kraike Singhalissa's projected trisme with Kaiark Rianlle of Eccord."

"What?" exclaimed Efraim. "And how is it to be with the Kraike Dervas?"

"She is to be rusticated, or so goes the rumor. Such is Singhalissa's price for the Dwan Jar, where Rianlle yearns to build a pavilion. This at least is common knowledge. We learn also of trisme between the Kang Destian and the Lissolet Maerio. If these trismes were to take place, what then? Does it not seem that Rianlle would sit high in the counsels of Scharrode?

---

*Rhune warfare is controlled by rigid convention. Several types of engagement are recognized. In formal combat, fighting occurs between persons of equal rank. If a person of high caste attacks one of low caste, the low-caste person may protect, retreat, or retaliate. If a low-caste person attacks a person of high caste, he is reprimanded by everyone. The weapons employed are swords, used only for thrusting, and lances.

On occasion the raiders come masked; they are then known as "mirk-men" and treated as bandits. All weapons may be legitimately used against mirk-men, including the so-called "bore," which propels a short arrow or bolt by means of an explosive charge.

Occasionally large-scale battles occur, when the total manpower of one Realm is mobilized against that of another.

Warriors trained to the use of sky-sails command special prestige. The rules of sky-fighting are even more complex than those governing warfare afoot.

Still, now that you are at hand, and Kaiark by right, the question is moot."

"I am pleased with your candor," said Efraim. "What else has occurred during my absence?"

"Nothing of consequence, although, in my opinion, the mood of the Realm has become slack. Loons and villains wander by mirk, instead of remaining at home to guard their households; and then when light returns, we are reluctant to unbolt our doors, for fear of finding a corpse on the porch. Again, now that you are home, the evil influences must subside."

He bowed and withdrew; Efraim and Lorcas proceeded across the commons toward the castle, after first dismissing the sullen Flaussig and sending him back to Port Mar.

As they approached, a pair of heralds appeared on the twin bartizans over the portal; lifting coiled bronze sad-horns they blew a set of agitated fanfares. The portals swung wide; a platoon of guards stood at attention, and out marched four heralds playing further fanfares: wild excited progressions of sounds, just perceptibly contrapuntal.

Efraim and Lorcas passed through a vaulted tunnel into a courtyard. In a tall-backed chair sat the Kraike Singhalissa; beside her stood the Kang Destian, dark eyebrows lowering.

The Kraike rose to her feet, to stand almost as tall as Destian; she was a woman of obvious force, with lustrous eyes and angular features. A gray turban contained her dark hair; her gray gauze gown seemed dull and characterless until the eye took note of the subtle play of light, the shadow of the half-concealed figure.

Singhalissa spoke in a high sweet voice: "We give you a ritual welcome, although you have returned at an inconvenient time; why should we deny it? In less than a week the legitimacy of your tenure would have dissolved, as certainly you have instructed yourself. It seems far from civil that you have neglected to notify us of your plans, inasmuch as we have providently taken steps to transfer the succession."

"Your points are well-taken," said Efraim. "I could not dispute them if they were not founded upon incorrect premises. I assure you that my difficulties have far exceeded yours. Nevertheless, I am sorry that you have been inconvenienced and I sympathize with Destian's disappointment."

"No doubt," said Destian. "May we inquire the circumstances of your long absence?"

"Certainly; you are entitled to an explanation. At Port Mar I was drugged, placed aboard a spaceship, and sent far off across the Cluster. I encountered many difficulties and succeeded in returning to Port Mar only yesterday. As soon as possible I hired an air-car and was conveyed to Scharrode."

Destian's mouth compressed even deeper at the corners. He shrugged and turned away.

"Most curious," said Singhalissa, in her high clear voice. "Who worked this malignant deed?"

"I will discuss the matter with you in detail, at some future time."

"As you please." She inclined her head toward Lorcas. "And who is this gentleman?"

"I wish to present my friend, the Noble Matho Lorcas. He has given me invaluable assistance and will be our guest. I believe that he and the Kang Destian became casually acquainted at Port Mar."

Destian scrutinized Lorcas a brief three seconds. Then, muttering something under his breath, he turned away. Lorcas said gravely, "I recall the occasion perfectly; it is a pleasure to renew the acquaintance."

At the back of the colonnade, in the shadow of one of the tall portals, the form of a young woman seemed gradually to materialize. Efraim saw her to be the Lissolet Sthelany, slight and supple in her nimbus of translucent gray gauze. Her eyes, like those of the Kraike, were somber and lustrous, but her features were pensive rather than minatory, delicate rather than crisp, and only remotely similar to those of either Singhalissa or Destian. She was further differentiated by her expression of detachment and indifference. Efraim and Lorcas both might have been strangers for all the animation of her greeting. Lorcas had found Sthelany fascinating at Port Mar, and his interest, so Efraim noticed, had not diminished—almost too obviously, although no one troubled to take note.

Singhalissa, sensing Sthelany's presence, spoke over her shoulder. "As you see, the Kaiark Efraim is again with us. He has suffered outrageous indignities; some unknown person has played him a series of malicious tricks."

"I am dismayed to hear this. Still, one cannot expect to roam the back alleys of Port Mar and evade the consequences. As I recall, he was in the most questionable company."

"We are all disturbed by the situation," said Singhalissa. "The Kaiark of course has our sympathy. He has brought as his guest the Noble Matho Lorcas, or so I believe his name to be: his friend from Port Mar."

The Lissolet's acknowledgment of the introduction, if any less emphatic, would have been undetectable. She spoke to Efraim in a voice as clear and sweet as that of Singhalissa, "Who performed these heartless acts upon you?"

Singhalissa answered for Efraim. "The Kaiark prefers not to enlarge upon the matter at this time."

"But we are most interested! These indignities offend us all!"

"That is true enough," said the Kraike.

Efraim had been listening with a sour grin. "I can tell you very little. I am as puzzled as you are—perhaps more so."

"More so? I know nothing."

The Kraike said abruptly, "The Kaiark and his friend have had a fatiguing journey and will wish to refresh themselves." She addressed herself to Efraim. "I assume that you will now occupy the Grand Chambers?"

"It would seem appropriate that I do so."

Singhalissa turned and beckoned to a grizzled heavy-shouldered man who wore, over the black and scarlet Benbuphar livery, a black velvet mantle embroidered in silver and a black velvet tricorn cap. "Agnois, bring a selection of the Kaiark's effects down from the North Tower."

"At once, Your Presence." Agnois the First Chamberlain departed.

The Kraike Singhalissa ushered Efraim along a dim hall hung with portraits of all the dead kaiarks, each, by the urgency of his gaze and the poise of his upraised hand, straining to communicate his wisdom across the ages.

A pair of tall iron-bound doors barred the way, with a gorgon's head of oiled black iron at the center of each; perhaps contrived by a kaiark's cogence.* Singhalissa halted by the doors; Efraim stepped forward to fling them wide but could not discover the mechanism that controlled the latch. Singhalissa said drily, "Allow me," then pressed a boss. The doors swung open.

They entered a long antechamber, or trophy room. Cases lined the walls, displaying curios, collections, artifacts; objects of stone, wood, fired clay, glass; insects preserved in transparent cubes; sketches, paintings, calligraphy; Books of Life, a thousand other volumes and portfolios, monographs unnumbered. A long table occupied the center of the room, on which glowed a pair of lamps in green glass shades. Above the cases portraits of kaiarks and kraikes stared down at those who passed below.

The trophy room opened on a vast high-ceilinged room paneled in wood almost black with age. Rugs patterned in maroon, blue, and black covered the floor; tall narrow windows overlooked the valley.

The Kraike indicated a dozen cases along the wall. "These are Destian's belongings; he assumed that he would be occupying these chambers; he is naturally annoyed by the turn of events." She stepped to the wall and touched a button; almost at once Agnois the First Chamberlain appeared. "Yes, Your Presence?"

"Remove the Kang Destian's belongings."

"At once, Presence." He departed.

"How, may I ask, did the Kaiark meet his death?"

The Kraike looked sharply at Efraim. "You have heard nothing of this?"

"Only that he was killed by the Gorgets."

"We know little more. They came as mirk-men and one of them shot a

---

*The word *cogence* is used to express that fervent erudition and virtuosity of the Rhunes.

bolt at Jochaim's back. Destian planned a foray of vengeance immediately after his investiture."

"Destian can order a foray whenever he chooses. I will put no hindrance in his way."

"You intend not to participate?" The Kraike's clear voice tinkled with a cool emotion.

"I would be foolish to do so, while there are mysteries to be clarified. Who knows but what I also might die of a Gorget bolt?"

"You must act as your wisdom directs. When you are rested you will find us in the hall. With your permission I will now leave you."

Efraim bowed his head. "I am grateful for your solicitude."

The Kraike departed. Efraim stood alone in the ancient parlor. In the air hung a redolence of leather bookbindings, waxed wood, old fabric, and also a faint mustiness of disuse. Efraim went to look out one of the tall windows, each protected by an iron shutter. The time was green rowan; the light lay wan across the landscape.

He turned away and gingerly began to explore the chambers of the Kaiark. The parlor was furnished with massive pieces, well-worn and not uncomfortable, if somewhat stately and ponderous. At one end of the room cases ten feet tall displayed books of every description. Efraim wondered what had been Jochaim's special virtuosities. For that matter, what had been his own?

In a sideboard he found various flasks of liquor, for the Kaiark's private ingestion. A rack displayed a dozen swords, evidently weapons of fame and glory.

A portal nine feet tall and three feet wide opened into an octagonal sitting room. A segmented glass dome high above flooded the chamber with light. A green rug covered the floor; the wall panels were painted to represent views over Scharrode from several high vantages; the work, no doubt, of some long-dead kaiark who had professed the rendering of painted landscapes. A spiral stairs led aloft to a balcony, which led to an exterior promenade. Across the sitting room a short hall led into the Kaiark's wardrobe. Uniforms and formal dress hung in closets; chests contained shirts and underlinen; on shelves were ranged dozens of boots, shoes, sandals, slippers: all glossy with polish, brushed and burnished. Kaiark Jochaim had been a punctilious man. The personal belongings, the garments and uniforms communicated nothing. Efraim felt uneasy and resentful; why had not these garments long ago been discarded?

A tall door opened on the Kaiark's bedchamber: a relatively small room plainly furnished; the bed was little more than a cot, with a hard thin mattress. Efraim saw room for change here; he had no present taste for asceticism. A short hall opened first upon a bathroom and watercloset, then upon a small chamber furnished with a table and chair: the Kaiark's refectory.

Even as Efraim examined the room a dumbwaiter rumbled up from the cellar kitchens, bringing a tureen of soup, a loaf of bread, a plate of leeks in oil, a quantity of black-brown cheese, and a tankard of beer. The service, as Efraim would learn, was automatic; every hour the collation would be renewed, and the Kaiark never need suffer the embarrassment of calling for food.

Efraim discovered himself to be hungry and ate with good appetite. Returning into the hall, he noted that it continued to a flight of dark winding stairs. A noise from the bedroom attracted his attention. He returned to find a pair of valets removing the garments of the dead Kaiark and arranging in their stead a wardrobe conspicuously less ample: presumably the clothes he had left in his old quarters.

"I go now to bathe," Efraim told one of the valets. "Lay out something suitable for me to wear."

"With haste, Force!"

"Also, remove this bed, and bring in something larger and more comfortable."

"Immediately, Force!"

Half an hour later Efraim inspected himself in the mirror. He wore a gray coat over a white shirt, black breeches, black stockings, and black velvet shoes—garments suitable for informal occasions within the castle. The clothes hung loosely on his body; he had lost weight since the episode at Port Mar.

The stairs at the back of the hall had not yet been explored. He climbed twenty feet to a landing, where he opened a door and looked out into a hall.

He stepped through. The door seemed to be a section of the paneling, invisible when closed. As he stood examining the door and speculating upon its purpose, the Lissolet Sthelany emerged from a chamber at the end of the hall. At the sight of Efraim, she hesitated, then approached slowly, her face averted. The green rays of Cirse, shining from the window at the end of the hall, backlighted her figure; Efraim wondered how he had ever considered the gauze gowns drab. He watched her as she approached, and it seemed that her cheeks became suffused with a faint flush. Modesty? Annoyance? Excitement? Her expression gave no indication as to her feelings.

Efraim stood watching as she drew nearer. Evidently she intended to continue past, without acknowledging his presence. He leaned forward, half of a mind to put his arm around her waist. Sensing his intent, she stopped short and turned him an alarmed glance. No question as to her beauty, thought Efraim; she was enchanting, perhaps the more so for the peculiar Rhune predispositions.

She spoke in a light colorless voice: "Why do you bolt so precipitously from the mirk-hole? Do you intend to startle me?"

"Mirk-hole?" Efraim looked blankly over his shoulder at the passage. "Yes, of course. I had not considered . . ." Meeting her wondering gaze he stopped short. "No matter. Come down to the Grand Chamber, if you will. I would like to talk with you." He held open the door but Sthelany recoiled in amazement.

"Through the mirk-way?" She stared from Efraim to the passage, then gave a cool trill of laughter. "Do you care so little for my dignity?"

"Of course not," Efraim declared hastily: "I am absentminded of late. Let us go by the ordinary route."

"At your convenience, Force." She waited.

Efraim, recalling nothing of the castle's internal plan, reflected a moment, then set off down the corridor in the direction which seemed most logically to lead to the Kaiark's chambers.

Sthelany's cool voice came from behind him. "Does Your Awesome Presence first intend to inspect the tapestry collection?"

Efraim halted and reversed his direction. He walked past the Lissolet without comment and continued to a bend in the hall, which gave upon a foyer. Before him wide stone stairs flanked by heavy balustrades and archaic lamps of wrought iron led down to the main floor. Efraim descended, with the Lissolet coming demurely behind him. With only a second or two of hesitation he headed for the Kaiark's chambers.

He opened the tall doors with the gorgon's heads without difficulty, and ushered Sthelany into the trophy room. He closed the door and pulled a chair away from the table for her use. Giving him her now familiar glance of sardonic perplexity she asked: "Why do you do that?"

"So that you may sit, and hopefully relax, and so that we may talk at our ease."

"But I may not sit in your presence, under the eyes of your ancestors!" She spoke in a mild and reasonable voice. "Do you wish me to suffer a ghost-blight?"

"Naturally not. Let us go into the parlor, where the portraits will not trouble you."

"Again this is most unconventional."

Efraim lost patience. "If you don't care to talk with me, you certainly have my permission to go."

Sthelany leaned gracefully back against the table. "If you order me to talk, I must obey."

"Naturally I will not give such an order."

"What do you wish to talk about?"

"I don't really know. Truth to tell, I am puzzled. I have undergone a hundred strange experiences; I have seen thousands of new faces; I have visited the Connatic's Palace on Numenes . . . Now that I have returned, the customs of Scharrode seem strange."

226 / JACK VANCE

Sthelany considered the matter. "For a fact you seem a different person. The old Efraim was rigorously correct."

"I wonder . . . I wonder . . ." mused Efraim. He looked up to find Sthelany watching him intently. "So you notice a difference in me?"

"Of course. If I did not know you so well I would think you a different man—especially in view of your peculiar absentmindedness."

After a moment Efraim said, "I confess to confusion. Remember, I did not realize I was Kaiark until yesterday. And arriving here, I discover an atmosphere of resentment, which is not at all pleasant."

Sthelany showed surprise at Efraim's ingenuousness. "What would you expect? Singhalissa may no longer call herself Kraike; she lacks all legitimate place here at Benbuphar Strang. No less do I and Destian; we all must make plans for dreary old Disbague. We live here at your sufferance. It is a sad turn of events for us."

"I am not anxious that you leave, unless you wish to go."

Sthelany gave an indifferent shrug. "My feelings are of interest only to myself."

"Incorrect. I am interested in your feelings."

Again Sthelany shrugged. "Naturally I prefer Scharrode to Disbague."

"I see. Tell me, what is your recollection of events in Port Mar during those hours before I disappeared?"

Sthelany grimaced. "They were neither edifying nor entertaining. As you will recall, we stayed at the hotel, which was quite decent and proper. You, Destian, Maerio, and I decided to walk through the town to a place called the Fairy Gardens, where we were to watch puppets. All warned us against the vulgarity we were sure to encounter. But we considered ourselves indomitably callous and crossed the bridge, some of us not altogether enthusiastically. You asked directions of a typical young man of the place, capricious and hedonistic—in fact, I believe him to be the same person who accompanied you here. He led us to the Fairy Gardens, but the puppets were gone. Your friend, Lorca, or Lortha, whatever his name, insisted on pouring a bottle of wine, so that we should guzzle and gurgle and swell out our intestinal tracts in full view of all. Forgive my language; I can only report the truth. Your acquaintance showed no shame, and ridiculed matters of which he knew nothing. While you conversed, quite enthusiastically, as I recall, with the Lissolet Maerio, this Lorca became remarkably familiar with me, and indeed made some utterly witless proposals. Destian and I left the Fairy Gardens. Maerio, however, remained with you. She is really much too tolerant. We returned to the hotel, where the Kaiark Rianlle became quite perturbed. He sent Destian to escort Maerio back to the hotel, which he did, leaving you in the company of your friend."

"And shortly after," said Efraim, "I was drugged and sent off across space!"

"I should ask your friend what he knows of the matter."

"Bah," said Efraim shortly. "Why would he play me such a trick? Somewhere I have gained an enemy, but I cannot suspect Lorcas."

"You have gained many enemies," said Sthelany in her soft sweet voice. "There are Gosso of Gorgetto and Sansevery of Torre, both of whom owe you blood, and both expect your reprisals. The Kraike Singhalissa and the Kang Destian are much disadvantaged by your presence. The Lissolet Maerio suffered from your ebullience at Port Mar; neither she nor the Kaiark Rianlle will readily forgive you. As for the Lissolet Sthelany"—she paused and looked sidelong at Efraim; in someone else he might have suspected coquetry—"I reserve my thoughts for myself alone. But I wonder if I can any longer contemplate trisme with you."

"I hardly know what to say," Efraim muttered.

Sthelany's eyes glowed. "You seem distrait and not at all concerned. Of course, you have dismissed the compact as trivial, or even forgotten it."

Efraim made a lame gesture. "I have become absentminded . . ."

Sthelany's voice trembled. "For reasons beyond my imagination, you seek to wound me."

"No, no! So much has happened; I am truly confused!"

Sthelany inspected him with skeptically raised eyebrows. "Do you remember anything whatever?"

Efraim rose to his feet and started into the parlor, then imagining Sthelany's emotion should he offer her a cordial, returned slowly to the table.

Sthelany watched his every move. "Why have you returned to Scharrode?"

Efraim laughed hollowly. "Where else could I rule a realm and command the obedience of a person as beautiful as yourself?"

Sthelany abruptly stood back, her face pale save for spots of color in her cheeks. She turned to leave the trophy room.

"Wait!" Efraim stepped forward, but the Lissolet shrank back with a slack jaw, suddenly helpless and frightened. Efraim said: "If you were of a mind to trisme, you must have thought well of me."

Sthelany regained her composure. "This does not necessarily follow; and now I must leave."

Swiftly she departed the chamber. Like a wraith she fled down the corridor, across the Great Hall, in and out of a shaft of green light from the star Cirse, and then she was gone.

Efraim signaled Agnois the First Chamberlain. "Take me to the chambers of the Noble Matho Lorcas."

Lorcas had been lodged on the second level of Minot Tower, in rooms of grotesque and exaggerated amplitude. Hoary beams supported a ceiling almost invisible by reason of height and dimness; the walls, which were

faced with carved stone plaques—again the product of someone's cogence—showed a thickness of five feet where the four tall windows opened
to a view of the northern mountains. Lorcas stood with his back to a fireplace ten feet wide and eight feet high, in which a disproportionately small
fire was burning. He looked at Efraim with a rueful grin. "I am not at all
cramped, and there is much to be learned in the documents yonder." He
indicated a massive case thirty feet long and ten feet high. "I discover dissertations, contradictions, and reconsideration of these same dissertations:
and reconsiderations of the contradictions and contradictions of the reconsiderations—all indexed and cross-indexed in the red and blue volumes
yonder. I plan to use some of the more discursive reconsiderations for fuel,
unless I am furnished a few more sticks for my fire."

The Kraike Singhalissa hoped to awe and quell this flippant Port Mar
upstart, so Efraim suspected. "If you are uncomfortable, a change is easily
made."

"By no means!" declared Lorcas. "I enjoy the grandeur; I am accumulating memories to last a lifetime. Come join me by this miserable fire.
What have you learned?"

"Nothing of consequence. My return has pleased no one."

"And what of your recollections?"

"I am a stranger."

Lorcas ruminated a moment. "It might be wise to visit your old chambers, and examine your belongings."

Efraim shook his head. "I don't care to do so." He dropped into one of
the massive chairs and slumped back, legs out-thrust across the flags. "The
idea oppresses me." He glanced about the walls. "Two or three sets of ears
no doubt are listening to our conversation. The walls are shot with mirk-
ways." He jumped to his feet. "We had best look into the matter."

They returned to the Kaiark's chambers; Destian's effects had been
removed. Efraim touched the button to summon Agnois, who, upon entering, performed a stiff bow, which almost imperceptibly seemed to lack
respect. Efraim smiled. "Agnois, I plan many changes at Benbuphar Strang,
possibly including new staff. You may let it be known that I am carefully
evaluating the conduct of everyone, from top to bottom."

"Very good, Your Force." Agnois, bowing again, displayed considerably
more verve.

"In this regard, why have you denied the Noble Lorcas suitable fires? I
consider this an incredible failure of hospitality."

Agnois grew pink in the face; his lumpy nose twitched. "I was given to
understand, Force—or better to say—in actuality I must plead guilty of
oversight. The matter will be repaired at once."

"A moment, I wish to discuss another matter. I presume that you are
acquainted with the affairs of the house?"

"Only to the extent which might be considered discreet and proper, Your Force."

"Very well. As you may know I have been victimized in a most mysterious manner, and I intend to get to the bottom of the business. May I, or may I not, rely upon you for total cooperation?"

Agnois hesitated only an instant, then seemed to heave a doleful sigh. "I am at your service, Force, as ever."

"Very good. Now, let me ask you, is anyone overhearing our present conversation?"

"Not to my knowledge, Force." He went on reluctantly: "I suppose that such a possibility might be said to exist."

"Kaiark Jochaim kept an exact chart of the castle, with all its passages and mirk-holes." Efraim spoke at sheer hazard, on the assumption that among so many records and so much careful lore, a detailed chart of the castle's mirk-ways must inevitably be included. "Bring this article to the table; I wish to examine it."

"Very well, Force, if you will furnish a key to the Privy Case."

"Certainly. Where is Kaiark Jochaim's key?"

Agnois blinked. "Perhaps it bides with the Kraike."

"Where might I find the Kraike at this moment?"

"She refreshes herself* in her chambers."

Efraim made an impatient gesture. "Take me there. I wish a word or two with her."

"Force, do you order me to precede you?"

"Yes, lead the way."

Agnois bowed. He swung smartly around, conducted Efraim out into the Great Hall, up the stairs, along a corridor into the Jaher Tower, and halted before a tall door studded with garnets. At Efraim's signal he thrust the central garnet and the door swung wide. Agnois stood aside, and Efraim marched into the foyer of the Kraike's private chambers. A maid appeared, and performed a quick, supple curtsey. "Your orders, Force?"

"I wish an immediate word with Her Presence."

The maid hesitated, then taking fright at Efraim's expression disappeared the way she had come. A minute passed, two minutes. Then Efraim pushed through the door despite a muffled exclamation from Agnois.

He stood in a long sitting room hung with red and green tapestry, furnished with gilt wood settees and tables. Through an opening to the side he sensed movement; he went on swift strides to the portal and so discovered the Kraike Singhalissa at a small cabinet built into the wall, into which at the sight of Efraim she thrust a small object and slammed the door shut.

---

*The dialect of the Rhunes is rife with delicate ambiguities. The term "to refresh oneself" is susceptible to several interpretations. In this case it may be supposed that the Kraike indulges herself in a nap.

230 / JACK VANCE

Swinging about she faced Efraim, eyes glowing in fury. "Your Force has forgotten the niceties of conduct."

"All this to the side," said Efraim, "I desire that you open the cabinet."

Singhalissa's face became hard and gaunt. "The cabinet contains only personal treasures."

Efraim turned to Agnois. "Bring an axe, at once."

Agnois bowed. Singhalissa made an inarticulate sound. Turning to the wall she tapped a concealed button. The door to the cabinet opened. Efraim spoke to Agnois. "Bring what you find to the table."

Agnois gingerly brought forth the contents of the cabinet: several leather portfolios and on top an ornate key of iron and silver, which Efraim took up. "What is this?"

"The key to the Privy Case."

"And this other matter?"

"These are my private papers," declared Singhalissa in a voice of metal. "My contracts of trisme, the birth documents of the Kang and the Lissolet."

Efraim glanced through the portfolios. The first showed an intricate architectural plan. He glanced at Singhalissa, who stared back coldly. Efraim signaled to Agnois. "Look through these documents; return to Her Presence the effects she describes. All others, set aside."

Singhalissa settled herself into a chair and sat stiffly. Agnois leaned his heavy back over the table, peering diffidently into the documents. He finished and pushed one group of papers aside. "These concern the personal affairs of the Kraike. The others more properly belong in the Privy Case."

"Bring them along." With the coldest of nods to Singhalissa, Efraim departed the chamber.

He found Matho Lorcas where he had left him, lounging in a massive leather-backed chair, examining a history of the wars between Scharrode and that realm known as Slaunt, fifty miles south. Lorcas put aside the volume and rose to his feet. "What did you learn?"

"About what I expected. The Kraike has no intention of accepting defeat—not quite so easily." Efraim went to the Privy Case, applied the key, and threw wide the heavy doors. For a moment he regarded the contents: sheaves of documents, tallies, certificates, handwritten chronicles. Efraim turned away. "One time or another I must examine these. But for now"—he looked across the room to where Agnois stood, stiff and silent as a piece of furniture. "Agnois."

"Yes, Your Force."

"If you feel that you can serve me with single-minded loyalty, you may continue in your present post. If not, you may resign at this moment, without prejudice."

Agnois spoke in a soft voice: "I served Kaiark Jochaim many years; he discovered no fault with me. I will continue to serve the rightful Kaiark."

"Very good. Find suitable materials and prepare a sketch of Benbuphar Strang, indicating the chambers used by the various members of the household."

"At once, Force."

Efraim went to the massive central table, seated himself, and began to examine the documents he had taken from Singhalissa. He found what appeared to be a ceremonial protocol, certifying the lineage of the House of Benbuphar, beginning in ancient times and terminating with his own name. In crabbed Old Rhune typescript, Kaiark Jochaim acknowledged Efraim, son of the Kraike Alferica, from Cloudscape Castle,* as his successor. A second portfolio contained correspondence between Kaiark Jochaim and Kaiark Rianlle of Eccord. The most recent file dealt with Rianlle's proposal that Jochaim cede a tract of land known as Dwan Jar, the Whispering Ridge, to Eccord, in consideration of which Rianlle would offer the Lissolet Maerio in trisme to the Kang Efraim. Jochaim politely refused to consider the proposal, stating that trisme between Efraim and Sthelany was under consideration; Dwan Jar could never be relinquished for reasons of which the Kaiark Rianlle was well aware.

Efraim spoke across the table to Agnois. "Why does Rianlle want the Dwan Jar?"

Agnois looked up wonderingly. "For the same reason as always, Force. He would build his mountain eyrie on Point Sasheen, where the way is convenient to and from Belrod Strang. The Kaiark Jochaim, you will remember, refused to indulge the Kaiark Rianlle in his urgent caprice, citing an ancient compact with the Fwai-chi."

"The Fwai-chi? Why should the matter concern them?"

"The Whispering Ridge harbors one of their sanctuaries,† Force." Agnois spoke tonelessly, as if he had decided never again to display surprise at Efraim's vagueness.

"Yes, of course." Efraim opened the third folder and discovered a set of architectural sketches depicting various aspects of Benbuphar Strang. He noticed Agnois averting his gaze in conspicuous disinterest. Here, thought Efraim, were the secret ways of the castle.

The drawings were elaborate and not readily comprehensible. The Kraike might or might not have made copies of this document. At the very least she had pored over the plans in grim fascination; she undoubtedly knew the secret ways as well as she knew the open corridors.

"That will be all for the moment," Efraim told Agnois. "Under no circumstances discuss our affairs with anyone! If you are questioned, declare

---

*Rhune lineage is reckoned through the mother owing to the unregulated circumstances of procreation, although in many cases father and son are mutually aware of their relationship.

†Inexact translation. More accurately: place of spiritual regeneration, stage of pilgrimage, phase of the life-road.

that the Kaiark has explicitly forbidden discussion, hints, or intimations of any sort!"

"As you command, Force." Agnois raised his faded blue eyes to the ceiling. "Allow me, Force, if you will, a personal remark. Since the dysfunction of the Kaiark Jochaim, affairs at Benbuphar Strang have not gone altogether well, although the Kraike Singhalissa is, of course, a positive force." He hesitated, then spoke as if the words were forced from his throat by an irresistible inner pressure. "Your return naturally interferes with the plans of the Kaiark Rianlle, and his amicability cannot be taken for granted."

Efraim attempted to seem puzzled and sagacious at the same time. "I have done nothing to antagonize Rianlle—nothing purposeful certainly."

"Perhaps not, but purpose means nothing if Rianlle discovers himself to be thwarted. Effectively, you have annulled the trisme between the Kang Destian and the Lissolet Maerio, and Rianlle will no longer derive profit from a trisme between himself and the Kraike Singhalissa."

"He values the Dwan Jar that highly?"

"Evidently so, Force."

Efraim hardly troubled to dissemble his ignorance. "Might he then attack by force?"

"Nothing can be considered impossible."

Efraim made a sign of dismissal; Agnois bowed and departed.

Isp became umber. Efraim and Lorcas traced, retraced, simplified, coded, and rendered comprehensible the plans to Benbuphar Strang. The passage leading up from the back of the refectory seemed no more than a simple shortcut to the second floor of Jaher Tower. The true mirk-ways radiated from a chamber to the side of the Grand Parlor; passages threaded every wall of the castle, intersecting, opening into nodes, ascending, descending, each coded with horizontal stripes of color, each overlooking chambers, corridors and halls through an assortment of peepholes, periscopes, gratings, and image-amplifiers.

From the chambers of the former Kang Efraim and the current Kang Destian radiated less extensive passages, which could be entered by secret means from the Kaiark's mirk-ways. With a gloomy shiver, Efraim pictured himself in his grotesque man-mask purposefully striding these secret corridors, and he wondered into whose chambers he had thrust wide the door. He pictured the face of the Lissolet Sthelany: pale and taut, her eyes blazing, her mouth half-parted in an emotion she herself would not know how to interpret . . . He returned his attention to the red portfolio, and for the tenth time inspected the index which accompanied it, where the locks and springs controlling each exit were described in detail, together with the alarms intended to thwart illicit passage along the Kaiark's mirk-ways. Exit from the terminal chamber—the so-called "Sacarlatto"—was barred by an iron door, thus protecting the Kaiark from intrusion, and other such doors blocked the passages at strategic nodes.

Efraim and Lorcas, having achieved at least a superficial acquaintance with the maze, rose to their feet and considered the wall of the Grand Parlor. Silence was heavy in the chamber.

"I wonder," mused Lorcas, "I wonder . . . Might someone intend us unpleasantness? A pitfall, or a poison web? Perhaps I am oppressed by the atmosphere. Rhunes, after all, are not allowed to murder—except by mirk."

Efraim made an impatient gesture; Lorcas had accurately verbalized his own mood. He went to the wall, touched a succession of bosses. A panel slid aside; they climbed a flight of stone steps and entered the Sacarlatto. They walked upon a dark crimson carpet, under a chandelier of twenty scintillas. Upon each panel of the black- and red-enameled wainscoting hung a carved marble representation of a man-mask in low relief, so that the object lay near-flat against the panel. Each mask depicted a different distortion; each bore a legend in cryptic symbols. At six stations, mirrors and screens provided views across the Grand Parlor. Lorcas spoke in a hushed voice, which was further attenuated by a quality of the chamber. "Do you smell anything?"

"The carpet. Dust."

"I have a most sensitive nose. I detect a fragrance, an herbal essence."

Standing stiff and white-faced in the gloom, the two men seemed a pair of antique mannequins.

Lorcas spoke again. "The same essence hangs in the air after Singhalissa has passed."

"You believe then that she was here?"

"Very recently—watching us and listening as we worked. Notice, the iron door is ajar."

"We will close it; and now I will sleep. Later we will lock off the other doors and there will be no more prowling and spying."

"Leave this in my hands! I am fascinated by such matters and I am not at all tired."

"As you like. Remember, the Kraike may have set out alarms of her own."

"I will be careful."

CHAPTER 7

In the Kaiark's sleeping chamber, Efraim awoke and lay in the dimness.

On the mantelpiece a clock showed the mode to be aud, with Furad and Maddar about to set and abandon the sky to chill isp. A second dial reported Port Mar Local Time, and Efraim saw that he had slept seven hours—rather longer than he had intended.

He looked up toward the high ceiling, contemplating the condition in which he found himself. His advantages were easily enumerated. He ruled a beautiful mountain realm from a castle of archaic glamour. He had at least partially thwarted his enemy, or enemies; at this moment he, or she, or they, would be brooding long slow thoughts. Benbuphar Strang harbored antagonists, but to what purpose? These persons were at hand when his memory was smothered . . . The thought caused Efraim to shiver with rage and raise up from his couch.

He bathed and took a dismal breakfast of cold meat, bread, and fruit in the refectory. Had he not known the quality of Rhune custom he might have regarded the food as a purposeful affront . . . He speculated as to the advisability of innovation: why should the Rhunes conduct themselves with such exaggerated daintiness when trillions of other folk feasted in public, with never a concern for their alimentary processes? His own single example would only arouse revulsion and censure; he must think further on the matter.

On the racks and shelves of his dressing room he discovered what he took to be his wardrobe of six months before—a somewhat scanty wardrobe, he reflected. He pulled out a mustard-colored tunic with black frogging and dark-red lining, and looked it over: a jaunty garment which no doubt on some informal occasion had set off young Kang Efraim to advantage.

Efraim made a soft sound and examined the other garments. He tried to remember the Kaiark Jochaim's wardrobe, at which he had barely glanced, and could only summon an impression of understated elegance, kaiarkal restraint.

Efraim went thoughtfully into the Grand Parlor and summoned Agnois, who seemed uneasy. He shifted his pale-blue gaze aside, and as he bowed the fingers of his big white hands kneaded and twisted.

Before Efraim could speak, Agnois said: "Your Force, the eiodarks of Scharrode wish an audience, as soon as convenient. They will meet you in two hours if that suits Your Force."

"The audience can wait," growled Efraim. "Come along with me." He led Agnois to the dressing room, where he paused and turned a cold stare upon Agnois, causing the chamberlain to blink. "As you know, I have been away from Scharrode a matter of six months."

"Yes, Force."

"I have had many experiences, including an accident which has unfortunately obscured portions of my memory. I tell you this in absolute confidence."

"I will naturally respect this confidence, Your Force," stammered Agnois.

"I have forgotten many small niceties of Rhune custom, and I must rely upon your assistance. For instance, these garments: can this be the whole of my former wardrobe?"

Agnois licked his lips. "No, Your Force. The Kraike made a selection of certain garments; these were then brought here."

"These of course are garments I wore as Kang?"

"Yes, Force."

"They seem somewhat jaunty and extravagant in cut. Do you consider them suitable for a person of my present status?"

Agnois pulled at his pale pendulous nose. "Not altogether, Your Force."

"If I wore these before the eiodarks they would consider me frivolous and irresponsible—a callow young fool, in fact."

"I would suspect as much."

"What precisely were Singhalissa's instructions?"

"She ordered me to transfer these garments; she further suggested that any interference in Your Force's preferences might be considered insolence, both by Your Force and by the Noble Singhalissa herself."

"She told you, in effect, to help me make a fool of myself. Then she summoned the eiodarks to an audience."

Agnois spoke hurriedly: "This is accurate, Force, but—"

Efraim cut him short. "Postpone the audience with the eiodarks. Explain that I must study the events of the last six months. Then remove these garments. Instruct the tailors to prepare me a suitable wardrobe. In the meantime bring here whatever can be salvaged from my old wardrobe."

"Yes, Force."

"Further, inform the staff that the Noble Singhalissa will no longer exert authority. I am bored with these petty intrigues. She is to be known not as the 'Kraike' but as the Wirwove of Disbague."

"Yes, Your Force."

"Finally, Agnois, I am astounded that you failed to notify me of Singhalissa's intentions."

Agnois cried out in frustration: "Force, I intended to obey the Noble Singhalissa's instructions to the letter; but nonetheless, by one means or another, I planned to protect Your Force's dignity. Indeed, you divined the ploy before I had opportunity to alter the situation!"

Efraim gave a curt nod. "Lay out garments at least temporarily appropriate."

Efraim dressed and went out into the Grand Parlor, half-expecting to find Matho Lorcas awaiting him. The room was empty. Efraim stood irresolute a moment, then turned as Agnois entered the chamber. Efraim seated himself in a chair.

"Tell me how the Kaiark Jochaim died."

"Nothing, Force, is surely known. Semaphores warned of mirk-men riding down over the Tassenberg from Gorgetto. The Kaiark sent two troops to attack their flank and led a third force to punish the foreriders. The mirkmen raced for Suban Forest, then retreated up the defiles toward Horsuke. Suddenly the slopes swarmed with Gorget boremen—the Schardes had been lured into an ambush. Jochaim ordered retreat, and the Scharde warriors fought their way back down the gorge. Somewhere along the way Jochaim took a bolt in his back, and died."

"In the back? Had Jochaim taken flight? This is hard to believe!"

"It is my understanding that he had stationed himself on a knoll where he commanded the disposition of his forces. Evidently a mirk-man had slipped around through the rocks and discharged his bore from the rear."

"Who was he? What was his rank?"

"He was never killed, nor captured, Force. Indeed he was never seen. The Kang Destian assumed command of the troops and brought them safely back into Scharrode; and the folk of both Scharrode and Gorgetto expect that an awful retaliation must take place. Gorgetto is said to be an armed camp."

Efraim, suddenly stifled by his ignorance, pounded his fists upon the arms of his chair. "I feel like the fool in a game of blindman's bluff. I must inform myself; I must learn more of the Realm."

"This, Force, may be accomplished without delay; you need merely consult the archives, or if you prefer, the Kaiarkal Pandects along the wall yonder—the volumes in the green and red bindings." Agnois spoke eagerly, relieved that Efraim should be distracted from the episode of the wardrobe.

For three hours Efraim explored the history of Scharrode. Between Gorgetto and Scharrode had existed centuries of strife. Each had dealt the other cruel blows. Eccord had been sometimes an ally, sometimes a foe, but recently had gained greatly in power and now outmatched Scharrode. Disbague occupied a small shadowed valley high in the Gartfang Rakes, and was considered of small consequence, though the Disbs were credited with a dark deviousness, and many of the women were witches.

Efraim reviewed the noble lineages of Scharrode and learned something of trismes which united them with other realms. He read about himself: of his participation in arrays, exercises, and campaigns; he learned that he was considered bold, persistent, and somewhat assertive. In pressing for innovation he seemed often to have been at odds with Joachim, who insisted upon tradition.

He read of his mother, the Kraike Alferica, who had drowned in a boating accident on Lake Zule during a visit to Eccord. A list of those present at the obsequies included the then Lissolet Singhalissa of Urrue Strang in Disbague. Very shortly thereafter, Jochaim contracted a new trisme and Singhalissa came to live at Benbuphar Strang, along with her children Destian and Sthelany, who were both conceived out of trisme, a circumstance neither unusual nor consequential.

Bloated with facts, Efraim put aside the Pandects and rising to his feet he stretched and slowly paced the Grand Parlor. At a sound he looked up, expecting Matho Lorcas, but found only Agnois. Efraim continued his deliberations. He must reach a decision in connection with the Noble Singhalissa. She had attempted to conceal a number of important documents, then had tried to embarrass and demean him. If he simply adopted a manner of lofty disdain, she would certainly attempt new intrigues. Nonetheless—because of the revulsion which Singhalissa aroused in him—he felt an unconquerable reluctance toward dealing harshly with her; such acts created an intimacy of their own, like that hateful empathy between the torturer and his victim. Still, he must make some sort of response, lest she consider him futile and indecisive.

"Agnois, I have come to a decision. The Noble Singhalissa is to be transferred from her present suite into that now occupied by friend Matho Lorcas. Bring the Noble Lorcas to more congenial quarters in the Jaher Tower. Attend to this at once. I want no delay."

"Your orders shall be carried out! May I venture a comment?"

"Certainly."

"Why not send her back to Disbague? At Urrue Strang she would seem to be at a safe distance."

"The suggestion is sensible. However, she might not remain at Disbague, but set about organizing troubles from all directions. Here, at least, she is under my eye. Again, I do not know that person who dealt me harm six months ago. Why expel Singhalissa until I learn the truth? Also"—Efraim hesitated. If Singhalissa departed, Sthelany almost certainly would depart too, but he did not care to explain as much to Agnois.

He walked up and down the parlor wondering how much Agnois knew of mirk-deeds about the castle, and how much Agnois could tell him in regard to Sthelany. What was her usual conduct during mirk? Did she bolt her door and bar her windows, as fearful maidens were wont to do? Where was Sthelany now? In fact: "Where is Matho Lorcas?"

"He accompanies the Lissolet Sthelany; they walk in the Garden of Bitter Odors."

Efraim grunted and continued his pacing. As he might have expected. He gave Agnois a brusque gesture. "See that the Noble Singhalissa is moved to her new quarters at once. You need supply no explanations; your orders are simple and explicit. No, wait! You may say that I am angry with you for bringing useless old clothes to my wardrobe."

"Very well, Force." Agnois hurried from the chamber. After a moment Efraim followed. Passing through the silent Reception Hall, he went out upon the terrace. Before him spread the distant landscape, placid in the halcyon light of umber. Matho Lorcas came running up the steps.

"So ho!" cried Lorcas, in what Efraim considered unnatural cheer, or perhaps he was nervously gay. "I wondered how long you intended to sleep."

"I've been awake for hours. What have you been doing?"

"A great deal. I explored passages out of the Sacarlatto. For your information the passges leading to the chambers of both the Noble Singhalissa and the Lissolet Sthelany are obstructed—sealed off with walls of masonry. When mirk arrives, you must turn your attention elsewhere."

"Singhalissa has been busy."

"She overrates the magnetism of her precious body," said Lorcas. "Sthelany is a different matter."

"It appears that you must seduce her by more conventional means," said Efraim in a morose voice.

"Ha hah! I would expect more success chiseling through the masonry. Still, either method is a challenge, and I am stimulated by challenges. What a triumph for the liberal philosophy should I succeed!"

"True. If you want to see how the land lays, why not invite her to take lunch with you?"

"Oh, I know how the land lays. I learned the entire map six months ago in Port Mar. In a certain sense we're old friends."

Agnois stepped forth from the Reception Hall, his lined gray face limp and loose under the velvet tricorn emblematic of his office. He saluted Efraim. "The Noble Singhalissa states that she is most distressed by your orders, and that she finds them incomprehensible."

"You offered her my remark in regard to the wardrobe?"

"I did, Force, and she professed bewilderment. She urges that you condescend to receive her at an inhalation,* in order to discuss the matter."

"Certainly," said Efraim. "In, let us say, two hours, when umber becomes green rowan, if yonder phase-dial is faithful."

"Two hours, Force? She used an urgent form of speech, and evidently wishes the benefit of your wisdom at once."

"I am suspicious of Singhalissa's immediacies," said Efraim. "Two hours will enable you to provide exactly proper garments for me, and for the Noble Matho Lorcas. Additionally, I have certain arrangements to make."

Agnois departed, puzzled and resentful. For the tenth time Efraim wondered as to the advisability of replacing him. With his special knowledge, Agnois was almost indispensable; but Agnois also was given to vacillation

---

*The word *sherdas*, an inexact translation. Those attending a *sherdas* are seated around a table. From properly disposed orifices a succession of aromatic odors and perfumes is released. To praise the fumes too highly, or to inhale too deeply, is considered low behavior and leaves the guilty person open to suspicions of gourmandizing.

and was at the mercy of the last personality with whom he had come into contact.

Efraim said to Lorcas: "You would like to attend an inhalation, I take it?"

"Of course. It will be an unforgettable experience—one among many, if I may say so."

"Then meet me in the Grand Parlor in two hours. Your quarters have been changed to the Jaher Tower, incidentally. I am transferring Singhalissa to those you now occupy." Efraim grinned. "I hope to teach her not to play tricks on the Kaiark."

"I doubt if you'll succeed," said Lorcas. "She knows tricks you've never thought of. If I were you I'd look in my bed for snakes before jumping under the covers."

"Yes," said Efraim. "No doubt you are right." He entered the castle, crossed the Reception Hall, passed along the Corridor of Ancestors, but instead of entering the trophy room, turned aside into a corridor paved with brown and white tiles, and so came to a chamber which served as office, bursary, and domestic headquarters. A bench by the side wall supported an ancient communicator.

Efraim closed and locked the door. He addressed himself to the communicator code-book, then pressed a set of discolored old buttons. The screen glowed with pale light, showing sudden jagged disks of carmine red as the summons sounded at the opposite end of the connection.

Three or four minutes passed. Efraim sat patiently. To expect a crisp response would have been unrealistic.

The screen glowed green, powdered into fugitive dots which re-formed to display the visage of a pale old man with locks of lank white hair dangling past his ears. He peered at Efraim with a half-challenging, half-myopic glare and spoke in a rattling croak. "Who calls Gorgance Strang, and for what purpose?"

"I am Efraim, Kaiark of Scharrode. I wish to speak with your master the Kaiark."

"I will announce that Your Force awaits him."

Another five minutes passed, then upon the screen appeared a massive copper-colored face from which hung a great beak of a nose and a deep pendulum of a chin. "Kaiark Efraim, you have returned to Scharrode. Why do you call me, when no such communication has occurred for a hundred years."

"I call you, Kaiark Gosso, for knowledge. While I was absent, mirk-men from Gorgetto entered Scharrode. During this raid the Kaiark Jochaim suffered death from a Gorget bolt, which burst open his back."

Gosso's eyes contracted to ice-blue slits. "So much may be fact. What then? We await your onslaught. Send over your mirk-men; we will impale them on ridgeline saplings. Marshal your noblemen, advance upon us with open faces. We will face you rank for rank and slaughter the best of Scharrode."

"I did not call to inquire the state of your emotions, Gosso. I am not interested in rhodomontade."

Gosso's voice became profoundly deep. 'Why, then, have you called?'"

"I find the circumstances of Kaiark Jochaim's death peculiar. In the melee of mirk-men and Scharde troops, he commanded from the rear. Did he turn his back to the flight? Unlikely. So then, who among your mirk-men killed the Scharde Kaiark?"

"No one has asserted such a triumph," rumbled Gosso. "I made careful inquiry, to no avail."

"A provocative situation."

"From your point of view, indeed." Gosso's eyelids relaxed slightly; he moved back into his chair. "Where were you during the raid?"

"I was far away—at Numenes and the Connatic's Palace. I have learned many new things, and one of them is this—the raids and onslaughts between Gorgetto and Scharrode amount to mutual catastrophe. I propose a truce."

Gosso's ropy mouth drew back to display his teeth, not a grin, Efraim presently realized, but a grimace of reflection.

"What you say is true enough," said Gosso at last. "There are few old men either in Gorgetto or Scharrode. Still, everyone must die sooner or later, and if the warriors of Gorgetto are denied the raiding of Scharrode, how will I keep them occupied?"

"I have troubles of my own. No doubt you can find a way."

Gosso cocked his head to the side. "My warriors may protest such an insipid existence. The raids drain their energies, and life is easier for me."

Efraim said shortly: "You can notify those who question your authority that I am resolved to end the raids. I can offer honorable peace; or I can assemble all my forces and totally destroy Gorgetto. As I study the Pandects I see that this is within my capabilities, if at the cost of many lives. Most of these many lives will be Gorget, inasmuch as we command the heights with our sails. It appears to me that the first choice makes the fewest demands upon everybody."

Gosso gave a sardonic caw of laughter. "So it might appear. But never forget we have rejoiced in the slaughter of Schardes for a thousand years. In Gorgetto a boy does not become a man until he kills his Scharde. Still, you seem to be serious and I will consider the matter."

The Salon of Sherdas and Private Receptions occupied the third level of the squat Arjer Skyrd Tower. Instead of the modestly proportioned chamber Efraim had expected, he found a hall seventy feet long and forty feet wide, with a floor of black and white marble blocks. Six tall windows admitted floods of that curious olive-green light characteristic of umber passing into green rowan. Marble pilasters broke the wall into a series of bays, color-washed a pale russet. In each stood a massive urn three feet tall carved from black-brown porphyry; the product of a cogence. The urns contained white sand and plumes of dry grass, without odor. A table ten feet wide and twenty feet long supported four etiquette screens. At each side of the table a chair had been placed.

Agnois hurried forward. "Your Force has arrived a trifle early; our arrangements, I fear to say, are incomplete."

"I came early intentionally." Efraim inspected the chamber, then the table. He asked in a soft voice: "The Kaiark Jochaim frequented this salon?"

"Indeed, Force, when the company was not numerous."

"Which place was reserved for him?"

"Yonder, Force, is the Kaiark's place." Agnois indicated the far side of the table.

Efraim, now accustomed to the unconscious signals which indicated Agnois' moods, eyed him attentively. "That is the chair used by Kaiark Jochaim? It is precisely like the others; they are identical."

Agnois hesitated. "These are the chairs ordered out by the Noble Singhalissa."

Efraim controlled his voice with an effort. "Did I not instruct you to disregard Singhalissa's orders?"

"I recall something of the sort, Force," said Agnois lamely, "but I tend to obey her by reflex, especially in small matters such as this."

"Do you consider this a small matter?"

Agnois grimaced and licked his lips. "I had not analyzed it along such lines."

"But the chair is not that chair customarily used by the Kaiark?"

"No, Your Force."

"In fact, it is a chair quite unsuitable to the dignity of a Kaiark—especially under the present conditions."

"I suppose that I must agree with you, Force."

"So again, Agnois, you have at worst conspired, at best cooperated, with Singhalissa in her attempts to make me a buffoon and so diminish my authority."

Agnois uttered a cry of anguish. "By no means, Force! I acted in all innocence!"

"Set the table to rights, instantly!"

Agnois turned a side-look toward Lorcas. "Shall I seat five, Your Force?"

"Leave it at four."

The offending chair was removed; another more massive, inlaid with carnelians and turquoises, was brought in. "Notice, Force," said Agnois effusively, "the small mesh here by your ear, by which the Kaiark can receive messages and advice."

"Very good," said Efraim. "I will expect you to stand in concealment and advise me as to etiquette and custom."

"With pleasure, Your Force!"

Efraim seated himself and placed Lorcas at the end of the table to his right.

Lorcas said reflectively: "These tricks are really rather petty—not what one might expect of Singhalissa."

"I don't know what to expect from Singhalissa. I imagine that her aim is to demonstrate me a fool as well as an amnesiac, so that the eiodarks will eject me in favor of Destian."

"You'd do well to pack her off."

"I suppose so. Still—"

Singhalissa, Sthelany, and Destian entered the chamber; Efraim and Lorcas politely rose to their feet. Singhalissa came a few steps forward, then halted, regarding the two remaining chairs with pinched nostrils. She then spared a quick glance for the stately chair which Efraim occupied. "I am somewhat baffled," she said. "I envisioned an informal discussion, in which all opinions might most expeditiously be aired."

Efraim replied in an even voice: "I could not conceive a conference on a basis other than propriety. But I am surprised to see the Squire Destian; from the arrangements I understood that only you and the Noble Sthelany planned to attend our conference. Agnois, be so good as to arrange another place there, to the left of Her Dignity the Wirwove. Sthelany, be so good as to seat yourself in this chair to my left."

Smiling a faint vague smile, Sthelany took her seat. Singhalissa and Destian stood aside with dour faces as Agnois rearranged the table. Efraim watched Sthelany surreptitiously, as always wondering what went on in her brain. At this moment she seemed indolent, careless, and totally introverted.

Singhalissa and Destian at last were seated; Efraim and Lorcas gravely returned to their own places. Singhalissa made a small movement, but Lorcas gave a peremptory rap on the table with his knuckles, causing Singhalissa and Destian to look at him questioningly. Sthelany was studying Efraim with an interest almost embarrassingly intent.

Efraim spoke. "The present circumstances are strained, and certain of you have been forced to accept an attenuation of prospects. In reference to the events of the last six months, I remind you that I have been the chief victim. Excepting, of course, the Kaiark Jochaim, who was robbed of his life. Nevertheless, the inconveniences I personally have suffered have made me callous of lesser complaints, and it is on this basis that we hold our discussion."

Sthelany's smile became even more vague; Destian's sneer was almost audible. Singhalissa gripped the arms of her chair with long fingers, so tightly that bones shone luminous through the skin. Singhalissa replied: "Needless to say, we all must adapt to changing circumstances; it is sheer futility to do otherwise. I have conferred long and earnestly with the Noble Destian and the Lissolet Sthelany; we all are perplexed by your misfortunes. You have been a victim of unconventional violence,* which I understand is not uncommon at Port Mar." Singhalissa's flick of a glance toward Lorcas was almost too swift to be sensed. "You were doubtless waylaid by some off-worlder, for reasons beyond my comprehension."

Efraim grimly shook his head. "This theory commands low probability, especially in view of certain other facts. I was almost certainly beset by a Rhune enemy, for whom our standards of decency have lost all meaning."

Singhalissa's high sweet voice became a trifle strident. "We cannot evaluate undisclosed facts, but in any event your enemy is unknown to us. I only wonder if, after all, there has not been a mistake."

For the first time Lorcas spoke. "To clarify matters once and for all, are you giving His Force to understand that in the first place, none of you have knowledge of the event at Port Mar, and secondly, that none of you have received information regarding this event, and thirdly, that none of you can guess who might be responsible?"

No one answered. Efraim said gently: "The Noble Matho Lorcas is my friend and counselor; his question is a fair one. What of you, Squire Destian?"

Destian responded in a surly baritone: "I know nothing."

"Lissolet Sthelany?"

"I know nothing of anything."

"Your Dignity the Wirwove?"

"The affair is incomprehensible."

Through the mesh at the back of Efraim's chair sounded Agnois' hoarse whisper. "It would be politic to ask Singhalissa if she might care to refresh herself and the company with a medley of vapors."

Efraim said: "I naturally accept your explicit assurances. If anyone chances to recall some forgotten fact which may be relevant, I will be grateful to hear it. Perhaps we should now entreat Her Dignity to refresh us with vapors."

Singhalissa leaned stiffly forward and drew out a panel in front of her, displaying knobs, toggles, bulbs and other mechanisms, then drawers to right and left containing hundreds of small vials. Her long fingers worked with intricacy and deftness. Vials were lifted; drops of liquid poured into a silver orifice were followed by powders and a gout of seething green liquor. Then she pushed a button and a pump blew the fumes along tubes under

---

*An act of molestation or violence—a mirk-deed, so to speak—committed during the daylight hours, a depravity unimaginable among persons of dignity.

the table and up behind the etiquette screens. Meanwhile, with her left hand, Singhalissa was altering her first vapor so that it might modulate into a second which she was busy preparing with her right hand.

The fumes followed each other like musical tones, and ended, as with a coda, upon an artfully bitter nose-wrenching whiff.

Agnois' whisper sounded in Efraim's ear. "Call for more; this is etiquette!"

Efraim said: "Your Dignity has only stimulated our expectations; why must you stop now?"

"I am flattered that you honor my efforts." But Singhalissa sat back from the vials.

After a pause Destian spoke, a saturine half-smile trembling on his lips. "I am curious to learn as to how you intend to punish Gosso and his jackals."

"I will take counsel upon the matter."

Singhalissa, as if impelled by an irresistible creative urge, once more bent over the vials; again she poured and vapors issued from behind the etiquette screens. In Efraim's ear sounded Agnois' husky whisper: "She is discharging raw essences at random, concocting a set of stinks. She understands your distrait condition and hopes to draw forth fulsome compliments."

Efraim leaned back from the etiquette screen. He glanced at Destian, who could scarcely control his merriment. Sthelany sat with a wry expression. Efraim said: "Her Dignity the Wirwove suddenly seems to have lost her sure instincts. Some of these vapors are absolutely amazing, even for the entertainment of a group as informal as this. Perhaps Her Dignity attempts a set of new combinations imported from Port Mar?"

Singhalissa wordlessly desisted from her manipulations. Efraim sat erect in his chair. "The subject we had not yet touched upon was my order to move Your Dignity to Minot Tower. In view of the chairs and the fumes, I will not reconsider my decision. There has been altogether too much interference and meddling. I hope that we have seen the last of it, inasmuch as I would not care to inconvenience Your Dignity to an even greater extent."

"Your Force is most considerate," said Singhalissa, without so much as a quiver in her voice.

Through the tall windows the light had changed, as umber fully gave way to green rowan, with Cirse barely grazing the horizons.

Sthelany said: "Mirk approaches; dark hideous mirk when the gharks and hoos come forth and all the world is dead."

Lorcas asked in a cheerful voice: "What is a ghark and who is a hoo?"

"Evil beings."

"In human form?"

"I know nothing of such things," said Sthelany. "I take refuge behind a door triple-bolted and strong iron shutters at my windows. You must ask elsewhere for your information."

Matho Lorcas gave his head a shake of whimsical wonder. "I have traveled far and wide," he said, "and never cease to be amazed by the diversities of Alastor Cluster."

The Lissolet Sthelany half-yawned, then spoke in easy voice: "Does the Noble Lorcas include the Rhunes among those peoples who excite his amazement?"

Lorcas grinned and leaned forward. Here was the milieu he loved: conversation! Supple sentences, with first and second meanings and overtones beyond, outrageous challenges with cleverly planned slip-points, rebuttals of elegant brevity; deceptions and guiles, patient explanations of the obvious, fleeting allusions to the unthinkable. As a preliminary, the conversationalist must gauge the mood, the intelligence, and the verbal facility of the company. To this end a few words of pedantic exposition often proved invaluable. "By an axiom of cultural anthropology, the more isolated a community, the more idiosyncratic become its customs and conventions. This of course is not necessarily disadvantageous.

"On the other hand, consider a person such as myself: a rootless wanderer, a cosmopolitan. Such a person tends to flexibility; he adapts himself to his surroundings without qualms or misgivings. His baggage of conventions is simple and natural, the lowest common denominator of his experience. He evinces a kind of universal culture which will serve him almost anywhere across Alastor Cluster, throughout the Gaean Reach. I make no virtue of this flexibility, except to suggest that it is more comfortable to travel with than a set of conventions, which, if jostled, work emotional strains upon those who espouse them."

Singhalissa joined the conversation, speaking in a voice as dry as the rustle of dead leaves. "The Noble Lorcas with earnest conviction proposes a view which I fear we Rhunes regard as banal. As he knows, we never travel, except rarely to Port Mar. Even were we disposed to travel, I doubt if we would school ourselves in habits which we find not only vulgar but repellent. This is an informal gathering; I will venture upon an unpleasant topic. The ordinary citizen of the Cluster shows a lack of self-consciousness regarding his bowel which is typically animal. Without shame he displays his victual, salivates, wads it into his orifice, grinds it with his teeth, massages it with his tongue, impels the pulp along his intestinal tract. With only little more modesty he excretes the digested mess, occasionally making jokes as if he were proud of his alimentary facility. Naturally we obey the same biological compulsions, but we are more considerate of our fellows and perform these acts in privacy." As she spoke Singhalissa never abandoned her mordant monotone.

Destian uttered a soft chuckle endorsing her views.

Lorcas however would not be daunted. He nodded sagely. "Everything depends upon the quality of one's conventions. Agreed! But we must examine this so-called "quality" for its usefulness. Overcomplicated, overstrict conventions limit a person's life-options. They confine his mind and stunt his perceptions. Why, in the name of the Connatic's pet owl, should we even consider a limit to the possibilities of this, our one and single life?"

"You will confuse us all if you talk in ultimates and eschatologies," said Singhalissa with a cold smile. "They are not germane in any case. One may exemplify any point of view, no matter how absurd, by carefully citing an appropriate, or even an artificial, theory. The traveler and cosmopolitan whom you have chosen as your paladin above all else should realize the difference between abstractions and living human beings, between sociological concepts and durable communities. As I listen to you I hear only ingenuousness and didactic theory."

Lorcas compressed his lips. "Perhaps because you are hearing views which contradict your emotions. But I stray from the mark. The durable communities you mention are beside the point. Societies are amazingly tolerant of abuse, even those burdened with dozens of obsolete or unnatural or even baneful conventions."

Singhalissa allowed herself to show open amusement. "I suspect that you take an extreme position. Only children are intolerant of conventions. They are indispensable to an organized civilization, like discipline to an army, or foundations to a building, or landmarks to a traveler. Without conventions civilization is a handful of water. An army without discipline is a mob. A building without foundations is rubble. A traveler without landmarks is lost."

Lorcas stated that he opposed not all convention, but only those which he found irksome and pointless.

Singhalissa refused to let him off so easily. "I suspect that you refer to the Rhunes, and here, as a stranger, you are particularly handicapped in your judgments. I find my way of life orderly and reasonable, which should certainly satisfy you. Unless, of course, you consider me undiscriminating and stupid?"

Lorcas saw that he had caught a Tartar. He shook his head. "By no means! Quite the contrary. Without hesitation I agree that, at the very least, your outlook upon life is different from mine."

Singhalissa had already lost interest in the conversation. She turned to Efraim. "With your permission, Force, I take my leave."

"As you wish, Your Dignity."

Singhalissa stalked from the room in a flutter of gray gauze, followed by Destian, stiff and erect, and then, Sthelany. Behind marched Efraim and Matho Lorcas, somewhat subdued. They found themselves on the arcade which connected the third level of Arjer Skyrd to the high parlors of the North Tower, then gave upon the upper balcony of the herbarium.

Descending the North Tower staircase, they were arrested by a sudden clanging of gongs, followed by a wild braying of horns in an agitated fanfare.

Singhalissa glanced back over her shoulder; her thin cheeks were compressed into an unmistakable smile.

CHAPTER 8

E fraim continued down the staircase to the frenzy of the fanfare produced by six men with convolved bronze sad-horns. Six horns, wondered Efraim? He himself, the returning Kaiark, had only been greeted with four! A slight which he had failed to notice.

The front portals had been flung ajar, and here stood Agnois, wearing a long white cloak crusted over with blue and silver embroidery and a complicated turban-like headdress: garments reserved for the most profoundly serious occasions. Efraim compressed his lips. What to do with the wretched Agnois, who had assisted him during the reception, but who had failed to warn him of whatever now was about to ensue?

The fanfare became a hysteria of yelling horns, to halt abruptly as a man in splendid black garments, picked out with pink and silver stripes, strode through the portal. Behind him marched four eiodarks. All wore headgear of pink and black cloth, wound up on pronged fillets of silver.

Efraim halted a moment on the landing, then descended slowly. Agnois cried out: "His Majestic Force, the Kaiark Rianlle of Eccord!"

Rianlle halted, scrutinizing Efraim with pale hazel eyes under dark golden eyebrows. He stood stiffly erect, aware of the splendid spectacle he made: a man in the fullest vigor of his life, not yet middle-aged, square-faced, with curling dark golden hair; a man of pride and passion, perhaps lacking in humor, but certainly not a person to be taken lightly.

Efraim stood waiting until Rianlle advanced another two steps. Efraim said: "Welcome to Benbuphar Strang. I am pleased, if surprised, to see you."

"Thank you." Rianlle turned abruptly away from Efraim and performed a formal bow. Down the stairs came Singhalissa, Destian, and Sthelany.

Efraim said: "You are of course well-acquainted with Her Dignity the Wirwove, the Squire Destian, and the Lissolet Sthelany. This is the Noble Matho Lorcas, of Port Mar."

Rianlle acknowledged the introduction by no more than a cold glance. Matho Lorcas bowed courteously. "At your service, Force."

Efraim stepped aside and signaled to Agnois. "Conduct these noble gentlemen to appropriate chambers where they may refresh themselves, then come to the Grand Parlor."

Agnois presently appeared in the Grand Parlor. "Yes, Your Force?"

"Why did you not notify me that Rianlle was to arrive?"

Agnois spoke in an injured voice: "I did not know myself, until Her Dignity upon leaving the salon ordered me to prepare a reception. I barely had time to accomplish the task."

Efraim said, "I see. He wears his headgear in the castle; is this customary and polite?"

"It is formal usage, Force. The headdress signifies authority and autonomy. In a formal colloquy of equals both parties will dress similarly."

"Bring me suitable garments and headgear, if any are available."

Efraim dressed. "Conduct Rianlle here whenever he is so minded. If his retinue starts to come, explain that I prefer a private discussion with Rianlle."

"As you wish, Force." Agnois hesitated. "I might point out that Eccord is a powerful realm with victorious traditions. Rianlle is a vain man but not stupid. He esteems himself and his prestige at an exalted level."

"Thank you, Agnois. Bring in Rianlle; I will deal with him as carefully as possible."

Half an hour later Agnois ushered Rianlle into the Parlor. Efraim rose to greet him. "Will you sit? Those chairs are quite comfortable."

"Thank you." Rianlle settled himself.

"Your visit is of course most welcome," said Efraim. "You will forgive me if I seem disorganized; I have hardly had time to collect my wits."

"You returned at a most opportune moment," observed Rianlle, his hazel eyes wide and luminous. "At least for yourself."

Efraim sat back in his chair and inspected Rianlle a full five seconds. Then he said in a cool unaccented voice: "I did not time my return on this basis; I was unaware that Jochaim had been murdered until my arrival in Port Mar."

"Allow me to offer my personal condolences and those of all Eccord upon this untimely death. Did you use the word murder?"

"The evidence indicates something of the sort."

Rianlle nodded slowly and looked thoughtfully across the room. "I came both to express my sympathy and to consolidate the friendly relations between our realms."

"You may take for granted my desire that they continue."

·"Excellent. I assume that you intend a smooth continuity between the policies of Jochaim and your own?"

Efraim began to sense a pressure behind Rianlle's suave remarks. He said cautiously: "In many cases, no doubt this will be true. In others, the simple mutability of life and circumstance dictates changes."

"A prudent and flexible point of view! Allow me to offer my commendation. In the relations between Eccord and Scharrode there will be no mutability; I would like to assure you that I intend to honor to the letter every commitment made by me to Jochaim; I would like to hear that the converse holds true."

Efraim made an affable gesture. "Let us not talk of all the facts as anything I could now say would be tentative. But since our two realms are so closely knit in amity, what benefits one benefits the other, and you may be assured that I intend to do my best for Scharrode."

Rianlle glanced sharply at Efraim, then stared toward the ceiling. "Agreed; large matters may wait. There is one rather inconsequential issue which we can easily resolve now without prejudice to your program. I refer to that trifle of territory along Whispering Ridge where I wish to build a pavilion for our mutual enjoyment. Jochaim was on the point of signing the parcel over to me when he met his death."

"I wonder if there was any connection between the two events," mused Efraim.

"Of course not! How could there be?"

"My imagination is overactive. In regard to Whispering Ridge I must admit an aversion toward yielding so much as a square inch of our sacred Scharrode soil; still, I will study the matter."

"Not satisfactory!" Rianlle's voice had taken on an edge, and sang like a vibrating wire. "I am thwarted in my wishes!"

"Is anyone ever continually and completely gratified? Let us talk no more of the subject. Perhaps I can induce the Lissolet to contrive a series of stimulating atmospheres . . ."

At the great twenty-sided table in the Formal Reception Chamber, Rianlle sat stiff and glum. Sthelany formulated a series of fumes, somehow suggesting a walk over the hills—soil and sunlit vegetation, water and wet rocks, the perfume of anthion and wood violet, mold, rotten wood, and camphor. She worked without Singhalissa's deftness, rather seeming to amuse herself among the vials as a child might play with colored chalks. Sthelany's fingers began to move faster; she had become interested in her contrivances as a musician suddenly perceives meanings in his music which he is forced to explicate. Gone was the hillside, away the forest; the vapors were at first gay, tart, and light; gradually they lost character, only to become sweetly melancholic, like heliotrope in a forgotten garden. And this odor in turn became pervaded with a bitter exudation, then a salt pungency, then a final despairing black reek. Sthelany looked up with a twisted smile and closed the drawers.

Rianlle uttered an ejaculation: "You have performed with enormous artistry; you have shaken us all with cataclysmic visions!"

Efraim looked around the table. Destian sat toying with a silver bracelet; Singhalissa sat stiff and staring; the eiodarks of Eccord muttered together. Lorcas stared in wonder toward Sthelany. Efraim thought: he is totally fascinated, but he had better make his emotion less overt, or he will be accused of sebalism.

Rianlle turned to Efraim. "When you said murder, you used an inglorious word to describe the death of the honored Jochaim. How then will you deal with that dog Gosso?"

Efraim held his face immobile against a surge of annoyance. He had used the word murder perhaps indiscreetly; but need Rianlle blurt out the details of what Efraim had considered a confidential conversation? He felt the sudden interest of both Singhalissa and Destian.

"I have made no precise plans. I plan to end the war with Gorgetto on one basis or another; it is useless and it bleeds us white."

"If I understand you correctly, you intend to prosecute only useful wars?"

"If wars there must be, I intend to fight for only tangible and necessary goals. I do not regard war as entertainment and I shall not hesitate to use unusual tactics."

Rianlle's smile was almost openly contemptuous. "Scharrode is a small realm. Realistically, you are at the mercy of your neighbors, no matter how peculiar your campaigns."

"Your opinions of course carry great weight," said Efraim.

Rianlle went on in a measured voice. "I recall some previous discussion of a trisme, that the fortunes of Scharrode and Eccord might be joined. The subject at this moment is perhaps premature in view of the chaotic circumstances here in Scharrode."

From the corner of his eye Efraim noted a shifting of positions around the table, as tense muscles demanded relief. He met the dark gaze of Sthelany; her face seemed as pensive as ever, and—could it be true?—somehow wistful.

Rianlle once more was speaking, and everyone about the table fixed their gaze upon that unnaturally handsome face. "Nevertheless, all will no doubt sort itself out. Accommodation between our two realms must be achieved. An imbalance now exists, and I refer to the unfulfilled contract in regard to Dawn Jar, the Whispering Ridge. If a trisme will facilitate the hoped-for equilibrium, then I must give the matter serious consideration."

Efraim laughed and shook his head. "Trisme is a responsibility I do not care to assume at the moment, especially since Your Force displays such clear misgivings. Indeed, your perceptions are remarkable; you have correctly defined the situation here. Scharrode is a welter of mysteries which must be resolved before we can move onward."

Rianlle rose to his feet, as did his retinue of eiodarks. "Scharrode hospitality is as always correct, and induces us to prolong our visit, but we must take our leave. I trust that Your Force will make a realistic assessment of past, present, and putative future and act to the best interests of us all."

Efraim and Lorcas went out to the parapets of Deistary Tower and watched as Rianlle and his retinue climbed into the rented air-car,* which a moment later lifted high and flew north.

Lorcas had retired to his refectory to take a furtive meal; then he planned to sleep. Efraim remained on the parapets looking off over the valley, which in the light of half-aud presented so entrancing a vista that his heart missed a beat. From this land the substance of his body had been drawn; it was his own, to nurture and love and rule, for all foreseeable time; yet how useless! how forlorn! Scharrode was lost to him; he had broken the crust of tradition. Never again could he be a Rhune, nor could the damage be mended. He would never be a whole man in Scharrode, nor elsewhere; never would he be content.

He studied the landscape with the intensity of a man about to go blind. Light slanting down across Alode the Cliff illuminated a hundred forests; the irradiated foliage seemed to glow with internal light: bitter lime, intense gray-blue given pointillist fire by scarlet seedpods, dark umber, black-blue, black-green. Surrounding stood the great peaks, each named and known in ancient fable: aloof Shanajra bearded with snow, who, resenting the mockery of the Bird Crags, turned his face to the south to stand forever brooding; the Two Hags Kamr and Dimw, rancorous above Danquil, enchanted and sleeping under a blanket of murre trees; there, Whispering Ridge, coveted by Rianlle, where the Fwai-chi walked to their sacred places among the Lenglin Mountains. His land forever, his land never; and what was he to do? In all the Realm was but a single man he could trust, the Port Mar vagabond Matho Lorcas. Gosso might or might not interpret his offer as an admission of weakness. Rianlle's not too subtle threats might or might not be intended seriously. Singhalissa might yet intrigue with sufficient finesse to cause him woe. Efraim decided that he must, without further delay, call together the Scharde eiodarks, to assist him with his decisions.

The landscape dimmed, as Osmo dropped behind Alode the Cliff. Furad hung low in the sky over Shanajra.

A slow step sounded on the marble flags; turning, Efraim saw Sthelany. She hesitated, then came to join him. Together they leaned on the parapets. From the corner of his eye Efraim studied Sthelany's face. What transpired behind that clear pale brow; what prompted the half-wistful half-mocking twist of the lips?

---

*The Rhune Realms are allowed no air-cars because of their aggressive proclivities. When a Rhune wishes to make a journey, he must call into Port Mar and hire a suitable vehicle for the occasion.

"Mirk is near," said Sthelany. She glanced toward Efraim. "Your Force no doubt has thoroughly reconnoitered the passages which lead here and there about the castle?"

"Only in order to protect myself from the surveillance of your mother."

Sthelany shook her head smilingly. "Is she really interested in your activities?"

"Some female of the household has demonstrated that interest. Could it be you?"

"I have never set foot in a mirk-way."

Efraim took note of the equivocation. "To answer your question precisely, I have indeed explored the mirk-ways, and I am arranging that they be interrupted by heavy iron doors."

"Then it would seem that Your Force does not intend to exercise the prerogatives of rank?"

Efraim arched his eyebrows at the question. He responded in what he hoped to be dignified tones: "I certainly do not intend to violate the persons of anyone against their will. Additionally, as I'm sure you know, the passage to your chambers is blocked by masonry."

"Indeed! Then I am reassured once and once again! It has been my habit during mirk to sleep behind triply locked doors, but Your Force's assurances make such precautions unnecessary."

Efraim wondered: did she flaunt? Did she entice? Did she tease? He said: "I might change my mind. I have adopted certain off-planet attitudes and they prompt me to confess that I find you fascinating."

"*Psssh!* These are matters we must not discuss." Sthelany, however, showed no sign of outrage.

"And what of the three bolts?"

Sthelany laughed. "I cannot imagine Your Force engaging in such an outrageous and undignified escapade; the bolts are evidently unnecessary."

Even as they spoke Furad, slipping low to the horizon, dipped half-under, and the sky went dim. Sthelany, her mouth half-open in an expression of childlike wonder, exclaimed: "Is mirk upon us? I feel a strange emotion."

Her emotion, thought Efraim, seemed real enough. Color had come to her cheeks, her bosom heaved, her eyes glowed with dark light. Furad sank even lower, all but leaving the smoky orange sky. Was mirk upon them indeed? Sthelany gasped and seemed to sway toward Efraim; he sensed her fragrance but almost as he reached to touch her hand, she pointed. "Furad floats once more; mirk is averted, and all things live!"

With no more words Sthelany moved away across the terrace. She paused to touch a white flower growing in a pot, turned a fleeting glance back over her shoulder, and then she moved on.

Efraim presently went into the castle and descended to his office. In the corridor he came upon Destian, apparently bound for the same destination. Destian however gave a frigid nod and turned aside. Efraim closed the door, telephoned the rental agency at Port Mar and ordered out an air-car, requesting a pilot other than the redoubtable Flaussig. He left the office, hesitated, turned back, locked the door and took away the key.

CHAPTER 9

E fraim and Matho Lorcas climbed into the air-car and were carried high above the valley of the Esch River: up, up, until they hovered on a level with the surrounding peaks. Efraim called off their names: "Horsuke, Gleide Cliff, the Tassenberg; Alode the Cliff, Haujefolge, Scarlume and Devil Dragon, Bryn the Hero; Kamr, Dimw, and Danquil; Shanajra, the Bird Crags, Gossil the Traitor—notice the avalanches—Camanche, and there: Whispering Ridge. Driver: take us yonder to Whispering Ridge."

The peaks shifted across other farther peaks of other farther realms. Under the cloud-piercing claw of Camanche, Whispering Ridge came into full view—an upland meadow rather than a true ridge, to the south overlooking Scharrode and the valley of the Esch, to the north the multiple valleys of Eccord. The air-car landed; Efraim and Lorcas jumped out into ankle-deep grass.

The air was calm. Trees grew in copses; Whispering Ridge was like an island in the sky, a place of total peace. Efraim held up his hand. "Listen!"

From an indeterminate source came a low whisper, fluctuating musically, sometimes sighing into silence, sometimes almost singing.

"Wind?" Lorcas looked at the trees. "The leaves are still. The air is still."

"Strange in itself. Up here one would expect a wind."

They moved across the sward. In the shade of the forest Efraim noticed a group of Fwai-chi watching them impassively. Lorcas and Efraim halted. "There they stand," said Lorcas, "walking their 'Path through Life,' all shags and tatters, typical pilgrims in any language."

They continued across the meadow and looked over Eccord. Belrod Strang was lost among the folds of the forested hills. "The view is superb," said Lorcas. "Do you intend to deal generously with Rianlle?"

"No. The fact remains that he could send a thousand men up tomorrow to clear the site, and another thousand to start building his pavilion, and I could do very little to stop him."

"Peculiar," said Lorcas. "Peculiar indeed."

"How so?"

"This place is magnificent—superb, in fact. I'd like a pavilion here myself. But I have been studying the maps. The realms are thick with places like this. In Eccord alone there must be twenty sites as beautiful. Rianlle is capricious to insist on this particular spot."

"Odd, I agree."

They turned back across the meadow, to find four Fwai-chi awaiting them.

As Efraim and Lorcas approached they drew a few steps back, hissing and rumbling among themselves.

The two men halted. Efraim said: "You appear disturbed. We are bothering you?"

One spoke in a guttural version of Gaean: "We walk the Life Road. It is a serious work. We do not wish to watch men. Why do you come here?"

"For no particular purpose: to look about a bit."

"I see you plan no harm. This is our place, reserved to us by a very old treaty with the kaiarks. Do you not know? I see you do not know."

Efraim gave a bitter laugh. "I know nothing—of the treaty or anything else. A Fwai drug took my memory. Is there an antidote?"

"There is no antidote. The poison breaks the roads to the memory tablets. These roads will never mend. Still, you must remind your Kaiark—"

"I am the Kaiark."

"Then you must know the treaty is real."

"The treaty won't mean much if the land is transferred to Eccord."

"That may not be done. We repeated to each other the word 'forever.' "

"I would like to see this treaty myself," said Efraim. "I will carefully check my records."

"The treaty is not among your records," said the Fwai-chi, and the group shuffled back to the forest. Efraim and Lorcas stood looking after them.

"Now what did he mean by that?" demanded Efraim in wonder.

"He seems to feel that you won't find the treaty."

"We'll soon find out," said Efraim.

They continued across the meadow toward the air-car.

Lorcas paused and looked up toward Camanche. "I can explain the whisper. The wind pushes up over Camanche, and around. It splits and swirls and passes the meadow by. We hear innumerable small frictions: the sound of air against air."

"You may be right. Still I prefer other explanations."

"Such as?"

"The footsteps of a million dead pilgrims; cloud fairies; Camanche reckoning up the seconds."

"More convincing, I agree. Where to now?"

"Your idea of twenty equivalent sites in Eccord is interesting. I would like to look upon these sites."

They flew north, through the peaks, domes, and ridges of Eccord; and within an hour discovered a dozen high meadows with prospects at least as appealing as those of Whispering Ridge. "Rianlle is most arbitrary," said Lorcas. "The question is, why?"

"I cannot even speculate."

"Suppose he gains the meadow and proceeds with his plans. Then what of the Fwai-chi?"

"I doubt if Rianlle would enjoy Fwai-chi pilgrims trooping through his pavilion, resting on his terraces. But how could he stop them? They are protected by the Connatic."

The air-car spiraled down into Scharrode and landed at Benbuphar Strang. As the two alighted, Efraim said: "Would you not like to return to Port Mar? I value your companionship, but there is nothing to amuse you here; I foresee only unpleasantness."

"The temptation to leave is strong," Lorcas admitted. "The food here is abominable, and I don't like to eat in a closet. Singhalissa oppresses me with her cleverness. Destian is insufferable. As for Sthelany—ah, the magic Sthelany! I hope to persuade her to Port Mar for a visit. This may seem an impossible task but every journey begins with a single step."

"So then, you plan to stay at Benbuphar Strang?"

"With your permission, still a week or two."

Efraim dismissed the air-car; the two returned to the castle. "You have exercised your charm upon her?"

Lorcas nodded. "She is curiously ambiguous. To say that she blows first hot then cold is inaccurate; she blows first cold, then colder. But she could easily order me to keep my distance."

"Has she mentioned the horrors of mirk?"

"She assures me that she bolts her doors with three bars, clamps her windows, keeps vials of offensive odors at the ready, and generally is unavailable."

They halted and looked up at the balcony behind which were Sthelany's rooms.

"A pity the mirk-way is blocked," mused Lorcas. "When all else fails one can always pounce on a girl through the dark. Still she's hinted rather pointedly that I'm not to come around. In fact, after I tried to kiss her in the Garden of Bitter Odors she told me quite bluntly to keep my distance."

"Why not try Singhalissa? Or has she also warned you off?"

"What a thought! I suggest that we take a quiet bottle of wine together and search the archives for the Fwai-chi treaty."

The Index to the Archives mentioned no treaty with the Fwai-chi. Efraim summoned Agnois, who denied all knowledge of the document. "Such an understanding, Your Force, would hardly be expressed as a formal treaty in any case."

"Perhaps not. Why does Rianlle want Whispering Ridge?"

Agnois raised his eyes to a point above Efraim's head. "I suppose that he intends to build there a summer pavilion, Force."

"Surely Rianlle treated with the Kaiark Jochaim on this matter?"

"I cannot say, Your Force."

"Who maintains the archives?"

"The Kaiark himself, with such help as he requires."

At Efraim's nod, Agnois departed.

"So now, no treaty," said Efraim glumly. "Nothing whatever to show Rianlle."

"The Fwai-chi declared as much."

"How could they know? Our archives are nothing to them."

"The treaty probably was an oral understanding; they knew that no document existed."

In frustration Efraim jumped to his feet. "I must take counsel; the situation has become intolerable." Once again he summoned Agnois.

"Your Force requires?"

"Send messages to the eiodarks; I wish them to meet me here in twenty hours. The occasion is urgent; I will expect everyone."

"That hour, Your Force, will fall in the middle period of mirk."

"Oh . . . in thirty hours, then. One other matter—do not inform Singhalissa of this meeting, nor Destian, nor Sthelany, nor anyone who might transfer this news; further, do not give instructions within the hearing of these people, and do not make note of the occasion upon paper. Am I sufficiently explicit?"

"Perfectly so, Your Force."

Agnois departed the room.

"If he fails me this time," said Efraim, "he'll not find me lenient." He went to the window and presently observed the departure of six underchamberlains. "There they go with the message. The news will reach Singhalissa as soon as they return, but there is little she can do."

Lorcas said: "She's probably resigned herself to the inevitable by now. And yonder on the terrace, is that not Sthelany? With your permission, I will go out and enliven her life."

"As you like. But one word, while the thought is on my mind. The word is 'caution.' Mirk approaches. Unpleasant events occur. Lock yourself in your chambers, go to sleep, and don't stir till the light returns."

"Reasonable enough," said Lorcas slowly. "I wouldn't care to meet any gharks nor, for that matter, any hoos."

A fter six hours of aud, Furad and Osmo left the sky. Cirse and Maddar, instead of slanting toward the horizon, settled vertically with ponderous purpose. Maddar disappeared first, to leave the land momentarily in green rowan, then Cirse sank behind Whispering Ridge. The sky flared and dimmed; darkness fell. Mirk had come to Scharrode.

In the farmsteads lights flared and flickered, then were extinguished; in the town shutters clanged, doors slammed, bolts thudded home. Those secure or fearful or uninterested in adventure took themselves to bed. Others by candlelight denuded themselves, then donned black shoulder-pieces, black boots and hideous man-masks. Others removed gray gauze gowns, to don loose smocks of white muslin; then they loosened the shutters of their windows or the bolts of their doors, but never both; then, with a small taper in one corner of the room casting almost no light at all, they laid themselves on their couches in a tremulous mixture of hope and fear, or a peculiar emotion in which perhaps one component was muted horror. Some who had bolted both shutters and door, to huddle on their couches in a ferment of arching melancholy, presently arose to unbolt door or shutter.

Through the mirk moved the grotesque shapes, taking no heed of each other. When one found the window of his choice unshuttered, he hung a white flower on the hasp, that no one else should enter; then climbing through the window he displayed himself to the silent occupant of the room—an avatar of the demon Kro.

At Benbuphar Strang, lights were extinguished, doors bolted, windows shuttered and barred as everywhere else. In the servants' quarters, some made preparations; others composed themselves to uneasy slumber. In the towers, other folk performed their own arrangements. Efraim, armed with his small pistol, bolted shutters, barred and bolted doors, searched his quarters. He checked the security of the door blocking ingress from the Sacarlatto and also that passage to the second level of Jaher Tower.

He then returned to the parlor where he threw himself into a great scarlet leather chair, poured himself a goblet of wine, and sat in gloomy meditation.

He reviewed his time on Marune and tried to assess his progress. His memory was still gone, his enemy as yet unknown. Time passed. Faces floated before his eyes. One face returned and would not depart—a pale fragile face with lustrous eyes. She had as much as assured him that her door would not be bolted. He jumped to his feet and paced back and forth. A hundred yards away she waited. Efraim stopped short and considered. No harm could come by making a trial. He need only climb to the second level of Jaher Tower, inspect the corridor; then, if all were clear, stride fifty feet to her door. Should the door be locked, he could return the way he had come. Should the door be open, Sthelany expected him.

The mask? The boots? No, they were foreign to him; he would enter Sthelany's chamber as himself.

He climbed the steps of the shortcut and came to the exit panel. He slid aside the peephole, searched the corridor. Empty.

He opened the door and listened. Silence. A faint sound? He listened with even greater intensity. The sound might have been the blood rushing through his heart.

With stealth and care he opened the door a foot, two feet. He slipped out into the hall, feeling suddenly exposed and vulnerable. No one in sight; no sound. With racing pulse he ran to Sthelany's door. He listened. No sound. He inspected the door: six panels of heavy carved oak; three iron hinges, a heavy iron latch.

So now. He reached for the latch . . .

A sound within, a scraping as of metal. Efraim backed away and stood looking at the door. It seemed to look back at him.

Efraim moved further from the door, confused, uncertain. He retreated to the passage, closed and bolted the door, returned to his chambers.

He sank into the red leather chair and thought for five minutes. Once again he rose to his feet and, unbarring the main portal, went out into the foyer. In a storage closet he found a length of rope which he took back to his chamber, and again locked the door.

He brought out the chart of the mirk-ways and studied it for a few minutes. He then went up to the Sacarlatto, and so made his way to the unoccupied chamber directly above that of Sthelany.

He went out onto the balcony, made the rope fast, and tied a series of knots along its length, to serve as handholds and footrests. Cautiously he lowered the rope so that it hung down to Sthelany's balcony.

He descended with great care, and presently stood on the balcony. Shutters covered the glass, but a glow of light issued through a crack. Efraim pressed his eye close and peered into the room.

Sthelany sat beside a table in her usual garments. By the light of a candle she played with a toy puzzle. Beside the door stood two men in black pantaloons and man-masks. One carried a mace, the other a dagger. Behind the door, over the back of a chair, hung a large black sack. The man with the mace pressed his ear to the door. By his posture, by the stoop of his shoulders and long powerful arms, Efraim recognized Agnois the First

Chamberlain. The man with the dagger was Destian. Sthelany glanced at them, gave a slight shrug, and returned to her puzzle.

Efraim felt dizzy. He leaned on the balcony and looked off into the darkness. His stomach convulsed; he barely prevented himself from vomiting.

He did not look again into the room. With flaccid muscles he pulled himself back to the upper balcony. He hauled up the rope, coiled it, and returned to his chambers. Here he made everything secure, and placing his pistol on the table before him, poured out a goblet of wine and settled into the red leather chair.

CHAPTER I I

O smo rose in the east, followed by Cirse from the south and Maddar from the southwest to dispel the dark with the gay light of isp.

Matho Lorcas was missing from his chambers; nor was he to be found anywhere within Benbuphar Strang.

The mood in the castle was taut and sullen. Agnois brought word to Efraim that Singhalissa wished an audience with him.

"She must wait until I confer with the eiodarks," said Efraim. He could not bring himself to look at Agnois.

"I will so inform her, Your Force." Agnois' voice was gentle. "I must call to your attention a message from Kaiark Rianlle of Eccord to the members of the kaiarkal household. He invites you most urgently to a fête at Belrod Strang, during aud tomorrow."

"I will visit Belrod Strang with pleasure."

Hours of time moved past; Efraim went out into the meadow beside the castle, then wandered down beside the river. For half an hour he stood tossing stones into the water, then turned and looked back toward Benbuphar Strang—a silhouette of sinister significance.

Where was Matho Lorcas?

Efraim sauntered back to the castle. He climbed the flight of steps to the terrace and halted, reluctant to enter the oppressive dimness.

He forced himself to proceed. Sthelany, leaving the library, paused, as if wishing words with him. Efraim walked past without so much as a sideglance; in truth he dared not look at her, lest she read in his eyes the intensity of his emotion.

Sthelany stood looking after him, a forlorn and thoughtful figure.

At the time appointed, Efraim came forth from his chambers to greet the fourteen eiodarks of Scharrode, all wearing ceremonial black gowns and white vests. Their faces wore almost identical expressions of skepticism, even hostility.

Efraim ushered them into the Grand Parlor, where footmen and under-chamberlains had arranged a circular table. At the tail of the procession came Destian, dressed like the others. Efraim spoke crisply: "I do not recall summoning you to this meeting, Squire Destian, and in any event your presence will not be required."

Destian paused, glanced around the eiodarks. "What is the will of this company?"

Efraim signaled a footman: "Expel Squire Destian instantly from the chamber, by whatever means you find necessary."

Destian managed a mocking grin, turned on his heel, and departed. Efraim closed the door and joined his company. "This is an informal meeting. Feel at liberty to express yourself openly and candidly. I will respect you the more for it."

"Very good," responded one of the older eiodarks, a man solid and sturdy, brown as weathered wood. The man was Baron Haulk, as Efraim would presently learn. "I will take you at your word. Why have you expelled the Kang Destian from a colloquy of his peers?"

"There are several excellent reasons for my action, and you will learn some, if not all, of them presently. I will remind you that by protocols of rank, his title is only as good as that of his mother. As soon as I became Kaiark, she resumed her former status as the Wirwove of Urrue and Destian lapsed to Squire. A technicality perhaps, but by just such technicalities am I Kaiark and you Eiodark."

Efraim went to his place at the table. "Please be seated. I am sorry to have delayed so long with this meeting. Perhaps this apparent slight explains your lack of cordiality; am I correct?"

"Not entirely," said Baron Haulk in a dry voice.

"You have other grievances?"

"You have asked us to speak candidly. Historically, those foolish enough to accept such invitations usually suffer from their boldness. Nevertheless, I will take the risk upon myself.

"Our grievances are these. First, the indifference which you show the glorious tradition of your station, and I refer to the frivolous manner in which you return to claim your place only a few days before the deadline."

"I will consider this Item one," said Efraim. "Proceed."

"Item two. Since your return you have neglected to consult the eiodarks in regard to the urgent matters which confront the Realm; instead you hob-nob with a person of Port Mar, whose reputation, so I have upon good authority, does him no credit.

"Item three. In a most callous manner you have insulted and inconvenienced the Kraike Singhalissa, the Lissolet Sthelany, and the Kang Destian, depriving them of status and perquisites.

"Item four. You have wilfully antagonized our ally Kaiark Rianlle of Eccord, while ignoring the bandit Gosso, who slew Kaiark Jochaim.

"Item five. As I recite these grievances, you listen with a face of bored amusement and obduracy."

Efraim could not restrain a chuckle. "I thank you for your frankness. I shall respond in the same spirit. The amused boredom and obduracy of 'Item five' are far from my true emotions, I assure you. Before I reveal certain strange circumstances to you, may I ask whence came your information?"

"The Kang Destian has been good enough to keep us informed."

"I thought as much. Now, draw up your chairs and listen closely, and you will learn what has befallen me during these last months . . ."

Efraim spoke for an hour, withholding mention only of the events during mirk. "To summarize, I returned to Scharrode as soon as possible, but I delayed meeting the eiodarks because I wished to conceal my disability until I had in some measure repaired it. I proposed a truce to Gosso because war with Gorgetto is weary, hateful, and unproductive. Neither Gosso nor his Gorgets killed the Kaiark Jochaim; he was murdered by a Scharde traitor."

"*Murder!*" The word seemed to echo from wall to wall.

"As to Rianlle and his demands for Whispering Ridge, I acted as any responsible Scharde Kaiark must act: I temporized until I could search the archives and discover what, if any, had been his understanding with the Kaiark Jochaim. I found no such record. In company with Matho Lorcas, I inspected Whispering Ridge. Certainly a beautiful site for a summer pavilion, but no more so than a dozen similar sites within Eccord itself. I called you here to make an exposition of the facts, and to request your best advice."

Baron Faroz said: "The question immediately arises: why does Rianlle want Whispering Ridge?"

"The single distinguishing feature to Whispering Ridge, aside from the whisper itself, seems to be the Fwai-chi regard for the place. Whispering Ridge is their sanctuary, a station along their Path of Life. The Fwai-chi claim an accord with the Kaiarks of Scharrode in regard to Whispering Ridge, though I can find no mention of this accord in the archives. So then, gentlemen, what answer shall I take the Kaiark Rianlle when I visit Belrod Strang?"

Baron Haulk said: "I doubt if we need to vote. We refuse to cede Whispering Ridge. However, put this refusal in delicate language, in order that he may save face. It is not necessary to fling the refusal in his teeth."

Baron Alifer said: "We might declare that Whispering Ridge is prone to quakes and we will not permit our friend thus to risk himself."

Baron Barwatz suggested: "The pact with the Fwai-chi must carry weight. We can show reluctance on this basis."

"I will carefully consider all your suggestions," said Efraim. "In the meantime, I must trust no one now at Benbuphar Strang. I want a complete change of staff, with the exception of Agnois. He must not be allowed to leave. Who will see to this?"

Baron Denzil said: "I will do so, Your Force."

"A second matter. My friend and confidant Matho Lorcas disappeared during mirk."

"Many persons disappear during mirk, Your Force."

"This is a special case, which I must investigate. Baron Erthe, will you be good enough to initiate a search?"

"I will do so, Your Force."

The air-car conveyed Efraim, Singhalissa, Sthelany, and Destian high over the mountains. Conversation was limited to formal exchanges. Efraim for the most part sat silently looking across the landscape. From time to time he felt Sthelany's covert gaze, and once she essayed a wan secret smile, which Efraim looked blankly past. Sthelany's charm had completely evaporated; he could hardly bear her proximity. Singhalissa and Destian discussed their cogences, a common topic during Rhune conversations. Singhalissa, among her other competences, carved cameos upon carnelians, moonstones, chalcedony, and chrysoprase; Destian collected precious minerals, and these particular cogences complemented each other.

The air-car passed above Whispering Ridge. Destian explained the geology of the region: "Essentially a great hummock of diabase broken by pegmatite dikes. A few garnets can be found in the outcrops and occasionally a tourmaline of no great value. The Fwai-chi chip them out and keep them for souvenirs, so I'm told."

"The Dwan Jar, then, lacks mineral wealth?"

"For all practical purposes."

Singhalissa turned to Efraim: "What are your thoughts regarding this bit of hillside?"

"It is a delightful site for a pavilion. The fabled whisper is discernible as a pleasant half-heard sound."

"It would seem then that you have decided to implement the agreement between the Kaiarks Jochaim and Rianlle." Singhalissa spoke half-musingly, with the air of one reckoning imponderables.

"You state the matter too conclusively," said Efraim in a guarded voice. "Nothing is yet determined. I must verify the terms and in fact the very existence of this agreement."

Singhalissa raised her fine black eyebrows. "Surely you do not question Rianlle's word?"

"Decidedly not," said Efraim. "Still, he may have mistaken the force of the agreement. Remember, an ancient treaty with the Fwai-chi controls the region and may not honorably be ignored."

Singhalissa smiled her wintry smile. "Kaiark Rianlle might well concede the authority of this early treaty, if in fact it exists."

"We shall see. The subject probably will not arise; we have been invited to a fête, not a set of negotiations."

"We shall see."

The air-car dropped on a long slant toward Elde, Eccord's principal village. Nearby, four rivers had been diverted to create a circular waterway. At the middle of the central island stood Belrod Strang: a palace built of pale-gray stone and white enameled timber, with pink, black, and silver banderoles flying from eighteen minarets. By comparison Benbuphar Strang seemed dingy and grim.

The air-car landed before the main gates; the four alighted to be met by six youthful heralds carrying gonfalons and twenty musicians pumping forth a frantic fanfare on their bruehorns.

The new arrivals were conducted to private chambers, in order that they might refresh themselves. The chambers were luxurious past the scope of Efraim's experience. He bathed in a pool of scented water, then resumed his old garments rather than put on the flaring black gown lined with flame-colored silk which had been laid out for his use. An inconspicuous door led to a water closet and a refectory, where dishes of coarse bread, cheese, cold meat, and sour beer were laid out.

Kaiark Rianlle welcomed the four in his Grand Reception Hall. On hand also were the Kraike Dervas, a tall somber woman who spoke little, and the Lissolet Maerio, reportedly Dervas' daughter by Rianlle. The relationship could easily be credited; Maerio displayed Rianlle's topaz hair and clearly modeled features. She was a person of no great stature, slight and supple, and carried herself with barely restrained animation, like an active child on its best behavior. Her amber ringlets and clear tawny skin invested her with luminosity. From time to time Efraim noticed her watching him with mournful solemnity.

Belrod Strang far exceeded Benbuphar Strang in splendor, though it fell short in that quality expressed by the Rhune term which might be translated as tragic grandeur. Kaiark Rianlle conducted himself with great affability, showing Singhalissa a conspicuous consideration which Efraim thought somewhat tactless. The Kraike Dervas behaved with formal courtesy, speaking without expression, as if reciting phrases which had become automatic to persons among whom she could not differentiate. The Lissolet Maerio by contrast seemed self-conscious and somewhat awkward. Surreptitiously she studied Efraim; from time to time their eyes met and Efraim wondered how he could ever have been attracted to Sthelany, who during mirk had worked her toy puzzle. A young black wasp was Sthelany, in company with the old black wasp who was Singhalissa.

Rianlle presently took his guests into the Scarlet Rotunda; a twenty-sided chamber with a scarlet carpet under a multicrystalline dome, fashioned like a glittering twenty-sided snowflake. A chandelier of a hundred thousand scintillas hung over a table of pink marble, the centerpiece of which was a representation of Kaiark Rianlle's projected pavilion on Whispering Ridge. Rianlle indicated the model with a gesture and a quiet smile, then disposed his guests about the table. Into the chamber came a tall man in a gray robe embroidered with black and red cusps; he pushed before him a two-wheeled cart which he stationed near Rianlle, then folded back the top to reveal trays and racks containing hundreds of vials. Maerio, sitting next to Efraim, told him: "This is Berhalten, the Master Contriver; do you know of him?"

"No."

Maerio looked right and left, lowered her voice so that Efraim alone could hear. "They say you have lost your memory; is this true?"

"Unfortunately yes."

"And that is why you disappeared from Port Mar?"

"I suppose so. I'm not certain of all the facts."

Maerio spoke in a voice almost inaudible. "It is my fault."

Efraim was immediately interested. "How so?"

"Do you remember that we were all at Port Mar together?"

"I know this to be the case, but I don't remember."

"We spoke with an off-worlder named Lorcas. I did something he suggested. You were so stunned and shamed that your reason left you."

Efraim made a skeptical sound. "What did you do?"

"I could never tell you. I was giddy and wild; I acted on impulse."

"Did I lose my reason immediately?"

"Not immediately."

"I probably wasn't overwhelmed with horror. I doubt if you could shame me no matter how hard you tried." Efraim spoke with more fervor than he had intended. Maerio looked a bit confused.

"You must not talk like that."

"Do you find me so offensive?"

She turned him a quick side-look. "You know better than that! No. Of course not. You've forgotten all about me."

"As soon as I saw you I began to learn all over again."

Maerio whispered: "I'm afraid that you'll go mad again."

"I never went mad to begin with."

The Kaiark Rianlle spoke across the table. "I notice your admiration of the pavilion I hope to build on Whispering Ridge."

"I find the design most attractive," said Efraim. "It is interesting and well thought out, and could easily be adapted to an alternate site."

"I trust there will be no need for that?"

"I have conferred with my eiodarks. Like myself they are reluctant to cede Scharrode territory. There are difficulties in the way."

"All very well to talk of practicality," said Rianlle, still heavily jovial. "The fact remains that I have set my heart upon Whispering Ridge."

"The decision really lies beyond my discretion," said Efraim. "No matter how much I might wish to oblige you I am bound by our covenant with the Fwai-chi."

"I would like to see a copy of this convenant. Perhaps it was established for some fixed duration of time."

"I am not sure that a written version exists."

Rianlle leaned back in his chair in disbelief. "Then how can you so staunchly affirm its reality? Where have you learned its provisions? Through your own recollection?"

"The Fwai-chi have described the covenant; they are quite definite."

"The Fwai-chi are notoriously vague. On so tenuous a basis would you thwart the understanding between myself and the Kaiark Jochaim?"

"I would not wish to do so under any circumstances. Perhaps you will supply me with a copy of this agreement that I may show my eiodarks."

Rianlle stared at him coldly. "I would find undignified the necessity to document my clear recollections."

"Your recollections are not in question," Efraim assured him. "I only wonder how the Kaiark Jochaim could bring himself to ignore the Fwai-chi covenant. I must search my archives with great diligence."

"You are unwilling to cede Whispering Ridge on a basis of trust and cooperation?"

"I certainly cannot make important decisions precipitously."

Rianlle clamped shut his mouth and swung around in his chair. "I commend to your attention the artistry of Berhalten, who has a novel concept to introduce."

Berhalten, having completed his preparations, struck a rod with his knee, to sound a reverberant gong. From the passage seven pages in scarlet and white livery ran forth. Each carried on a silver tray a small ewer. Into each of these ewers Berhalten placed a cylinder of a solid substance, layered in eight colors, whereupon the pages took up tray and ewer and set it before each person at the table. Berhalten then inclined his head to Rianlle, closed up his cart, and stood waiting.

Rianlle said, "Berhalten has discovered an amusing new principle. Notice the golden button on top of the ewer. Press this button; it releases an agent to activate the odorifer. You will be charmed . . ."

Rianlle conducted the group to a balcony overlooking a large circular stage, constructed to represent a Rhune landscape. To right and left waterfalls cascaded from stone crags, forming streams which flowed into a central pool. A chime sounded, to initiate a wild clamor of gongs and florid brue-horns, controlled by a staccato brazen tone which varied in only three degrees.* From opposite directions advanced two bands of warriors in fanciful armor, grotesque metal masks, and helmets crested with spikes and barbs. They advanced with stylistic kicks and curious bent-legged strides, then attacked and fought in ritual attitudes to the wailing clatter of martial instruments. Rianlle and Singhalissa, at one side, spoke together briefly. Efraim sat at the far end with Sthelany beside him. Destian conversed with Maerio, his exact profile tilted to advantage. The Kraike Dervas sat staring at the ballet with eyes that seemed not to follow the movement. Sthelany turned a glance toward Efraim which in those uncertain days before mirk might have caused him inner palpitations. She spoke in a soft voice: "Do you enjoy this dance?"

"The performers are very skillful. I am not a good judge of such things."

"Why are you so distant? You have hardly spoken for days."

"You must forgive me; I find the effort of ruling Scharrode no easy matter."

"When you traveled off-planet, you must have known many interesting events."

"True."

"Are the folk of the outer worlds as gluttonous and sebal as we tend to believe?"

"Their habits certainly are different from those of the Realms."

"And how did you regard these folk? Were you appalled?"

"I was in no condition to worry about anything but my own troubles."

"Ah! Cannot you answer me without evasion?"

"In all honesty, I fear that my casual remarks, should they be reported to your mother, might well be distorted and used to discredit me."

Sthelany sat back. For several moments she watched the ballet, which now had reached a climax with the entry of the two legendary champions Hys and Zan-Immariot.

Sthelany again turned to Efraim. "You misjudge me. I do not tell everything to Singhalissa. Do you think that I do not feel stifled at Benbuphar Strang? I yearn for new experience! Perhaps you will think ill of me for my candor, but sometimes I constrain myself to prevent outbursts of emotion. Singhalissa glorifies rigid convention; I often feel that convention must apply to others but not me. Why should folk not decorously sip wine together as they do in Port Mar? You need not look at me with such wonder; I will show you that I too can transcend convention!"

*The Rhunes produce no true music and are incapable of thinking in musical terms. Their fanfares and clamors are controlled by mathematical progressions, and must achieve a mathematical symmetry. The exercise is intellectual rather than emotional.

"Such occasions might well relieve the tedium. However, Singhalissa would surely disapprove."

Sthelany smiled. "Need Singhalissa know everything?"

"Very definitely not. Still, she is an expert both at conducting intrigues and at sniffing them out."

"We shall see." Sthelany gave a breathless little laugh and sat back in her chair. On the stage Hys and Zan-Immariot had fought to mutual exhaustion. The lights dimmed; the instrumental tones descended in pitch and tempo, then became silent, save for a thrilling resonance of softly rubbed gongs. "Mirk!" whispered Sthelany.

Out upon the stage bounded three figures in costumes of black-horn and lacquered beetle-back, wearing demon-masks.

Sthelany leaned closer to Efraim. "The three avatars of Kro: Maiesse, Goun, and Sciaffrod. Notice how the champions strive! Ah! they are slain. The demons dance in triumph!" Sthelany turned toward Efraim; her shoulder touched his. "How it must be on the one-sun worlds where day and mirk alternate!"

Efraim glanced sidewise. Sthelany's face was close; her eyes shone in the stage glow. Efraim said: "Your mother looks this way. Peculiar! She seems neither surprised nor annoyed that we talk in an intimate manner."

Sthelany stiffened and leaning forward watched the demons stamping the corpses of the dead heroes into the dust, throwing their heads low, tossing them high, plunging arms low, thrusting them high.

Later, as the four guests took their leave, Efraim had a moment to pay his respects to Maerio. She said, somewhat wistfully, "I did not appreciate that you had become friendly with Sthelany. She is most fascinating."

Efraim managed a painful grin. "Appearances can be deceiving. Can you, will you, be discreet?"

"Of course."

"I believe that Singhalissa instructed Sthelany to pretend intimacy, to beguile me into a foolish act whereby she might discredit me with the Scharde eiodarks. In fact—"

Maerio asked breathlessly, "In fact, what?"

Efraim found that he could not express himself both with precision and delicacy. "I will tell you some other time. But it is you, not Sthelany, whom I find fascinating."

Maerio's eyes suddenly glistened. "Good-bye, Efraim."

As Efraim turned away he surprised Sthelany's gaze upon him, and it seemed that he saw there a hurt, wild, desperate expression. This was the same face, Efraim reminded himself, that had indifferently considered the workings of a toy puzzle while two men with mace, dagger, and sack waited by the door.

Efraim went to make his formal farewell to the Kaiark Rianlle. "Your hospitality is on a most magnificent scale. We could not think to duplicate it at Benbuphar Strang. Still, I am hoping that before long you will return our visit, in company with the Kraike and the Lissolet."

Rianlle's face showed no geniality. He said: "I accept the invitation, for myself and for the Kraike and Lissolet as well. Will you think me presumptuous if I set the occasion for three days hence? You will have had opportunity to search for the legendary covenant, and also to consult your eiodarks and to convince them that the accord between Kaiark Jochaim and myself must without fail be implemented."

Words pressed against Efraim's lips; he contained them with an effort.

"I will consult my eiodarks," he said at last. "We will reach a decision which may or may not please you, but which will be based upon how we regard our duty. In any event we shall look forward to entertaining you at Benbuphar Strang at the time you suggest."

CHAPTER 12

On their return to Benbuphar Strang the portals were thrown wide by footmen strange to Efraim.

Singhalissa stopped short. "Who are these people? Where is our old staff?"

"I have replaced them," said Efraim. "All except Agnois, whom you will still find in office."

Singhalissa turned him a curious glance. "Must all our arrangements be disrupted? Why have you done this?"

Efraim spoke in his most formal voice. "I wish to live among people who have no prior loyalties and on whom I can place reliance. I took steps to achieve this by the only possible means: a complete change."

"My life daily grows more hectic," cried Singhalissa. "I wonder where this turmoil will end! Do you also plan to take us to war for a miserable fragment of hillside?"

"I would like to know why Rianlle is so exercised over this 'miserable fragment of hillside.' Do you know?"

"I am not in the Kaiark Rianlle's confidence."

A footman approached. "Your Force, the Baron Erthe is at hand."

"Please introduce him."

The Baron Erthe came forward. He looked from Efraim to Singhalissa and back to Efraim. "Your Force, I have a report to render."

"Speak."

"In a rubbish heap near Howar Forest we discovered a corpse in a black sack. It has been identified as the remains of Matho Lorcas."

Efraim's stomach quivered. He looked at Singhalissa, who showed no emotion. But for a soft metallic scrape behind the door he would have been the corpse in the black sack, rather than Matho Lorcas.

"Bring the corpse to the terrace."

"Very well, Your Force."

Singhalissa said softly, "Why do you do that?"

"Can't you guess?"

Singhalissa turned slowly away. Efraim summoned Agnois. "Place a trestle or a bench on the terrace."

Agnois allowed an expression of puzzlement to cross his features. "At once, Your Force."

Four men carried a coffin across the terrace, and set it down upon the trestle. Efraim took a breath and lifted the lid. For a moment he looked down into the dead face, then he turned to Agnois. "Bring the mace."

"Yes, Force." Agnois started away, then halted and stared back aghast. "Which mace, Force? There are a dozen on the wall of the trophy room."

"The mace with which the Noble Lorcas was murdered."

Agnois turned and walked slowly into the castle. Efraim, gritting his teeth, examined the corpse. The head was crushed, and a wound in the back gave evidence of a dagger thrust.

"Close the lid," said Efraim. "There is no more to be learned. Where is Agnois? He loiters, he tarries!" He signaled a footman. "Find Agnois, ask him to make haste."

The footman presently returned on the run. "Agnois is dead, Force. He has taken poison."

Efraim clapped him on the back. "Return inside; make inquiries! Discover the circumstances!"

He turned sadly back to Baron Erthe. "One of the murderers has escaped me. Be so good as to bury this poor corpse."

In due course the footman reported his findings. Agnois, upon entering the castle, apparently had gone directly to his quarters and there swallowed a fatal draught.

Efraim bathed himself with unwonted zeal. He took a dismal meal in his refectory, then lay down on his couch. For six hours he dozed, tossed, twisted, dreamed evil dreams, then slept soundly from sheer exhaustion.

Efraim had not yet dismissed the air-car which had transported him to Belrod Strang. He now ordered the pilot to convey him to Whispering Ridge.

The air-car rose into the light of the colored suns and flew north around the flank of Camanche, then drifted down to settle on the grass. Efraim alighted, and walked out across the meadow. The serenity was that of lost Arcadia; except for the crag to the east, the view was of clouds and air; isolation from the anxieties, plots, and tragedies of Benbuphar Strang was complete.

At the center of the meadow he paused. The whisper was not perceptible. A moment passed. He heard a sigh, a mingling of a million soft tones, each no louder than a breath. The sigh became a murmur, faded tremulously, rose again, then dwindled toward silence—a sound of elemental melancholy . . . Efraim heaved a deep sigh of his own and turned toward the forest, to find, as before, a group of Fwai-chi watching from the shade. They shambled forward; he advanced to meet them.

"Before mirk I came here," said Efraim. "Perhaps I spoke to one of you?"

"We were all here."

"I am faced with problems, and they are your problems as well. The Kaiark of Eccord wants Whispering Ridge. He wants to build a pavilion here for his pleasure."

"That is not our problem. It is yours. The men of Scharrode have promised to defend our holy place forever."

"So you say. Do you possess a document attesting to this agreement?"

"We have no document. The promise was exchanged with the Kaiarks of old and transferred to each successive Kaiark."

"Kaiark Jochaim may so have informed me, but your drugs took my memory, and now I can assert nothing of my own knowledge."

"Still, you must enforce the covenant." The Fwai-chi returned into the forest.

Efraim despondently returned to Benbuphar Strang. He called a meeting of the eiodarks and reported Rianlle's demands. Certain of the eiodarks cried out for mobilization; others sat glum and silent.

"Rianlle is unpredictable," declared Efraim. "At least this is my opinion. Our preparation for war might dissuade him. On the other hand, he would not care to retreat before our defiance, when our resources are inferior to his. Perhaps he will send his troops to occupy the Dwan Jar and then ignore our protests."

"We should occupy the Dwan Jar first, and fortify it!" cried Baron Hectre. "Then we might ignore the protests of Rianlle!"

Baron Haulk said: "The concept is attractive, but the terrain hinders us. He can bring his troops around Camanche and up Duwail Slope; we can supply our forces only by the trail across the front of Lor Cliff, and Rianlle alone on the brink could interdict us. We would more profitably fortify Bazon Scape and the pass at the head of the Gryphon's Claw, but there we invade Eccord soil and prompt sure retaliation."

"Let us look at the physiograph," said Efraim.

The group filed into the octagonal Hall of Strategies. For an hour they studied the thirty-foot-long scale model of Scharrode and the adjoining lands, but only verified what they already knew: if Rianlle sent troops to occupy the Dwan Jar, then these troops would be vulnerable to attack along their supply routes and might well be marooned. "Rianlle may not be able to exercise his strength as effectively as he hopes," mused Baron Erthe. "We may force him into a stalemate."

"You are optimistic," said Baron Dasheil. "He can marshal three thousand sails. If he brings them here"—he pointed to a scarp overlooking the valley—"he can drop them down into Scharrode while our troops are occupied along Bazon Scape. We can either harass his position on the Dwan Jar, or we can guard the vale against his sails. I cannot define a system whereby we can do both."

Efraim asked: "How many sails can we ourselves muster?"

"We have fourteen hundred eagles and as many winglets."

"Perhaps we could send twenty-eight hundred sails against Belrod Strang."

"Suicide. The glide is too long; the air sweeps down the Groaning Crags."

The group returned to their places around the red syenite table.

Efraim said: "As I understand it, no one feels that we can effectively resist Eccord, if Rianlle decides to wage war in earnest. Am I right?"

No one contradicted him.

Efraim went on. "One point we have not discussed is why Rianlle is so anxious to obtain Dwan Jar. I cannot credit the pavilion theory. I have just returned from Whispering Ridge. The beauty and isolation are too poignant to be borne; I could think only of human transience and the vanity of hope. Rianlle is proud and stubborn, but is he insensitive? I find his plans for a pavilion far-fetched."

"Agreed, Rianlle is proud and stubborn," said Baron Szantho, "but this fails to explain his initial commitment to the project."

"There is nothing else on the Dwan Jar but the Fwai-chi sanctuary," Efraim remarked. "What profit could he gain from the Fwai-chi?"

The eiodarks considered the matter. Baron Alifer said tentatively: "I have heard a rumor that Rianlle's splendors exceed his income, that Eccord cannot support his fantasies. I could not discredit any theory that he hopes to exploit a hitherto untouched resource—the Fwai-chi. To guard their sanctuary they would be forced to pay him a toll of drugs, crystals, elixirs."

Baron Haulk said: "None of this bears upon our own problems. We must decide upon a policy."

Efraim looked around the table. "We have examined all our options except one: submission to Rianlle's demands. Does the council believe this to be our only feasible course of action, detestable though it is?"

"Realistically, we have no other choice," muttered Baron Haulk.

Baron Hectre pounded his fist on the table. "Can we not assume a defensive posture, even though it is only bluff? Rianlle may think better of forcing the issue!"

Efraim said: "Let us adjourn until next aud, and at that time we will reach a decision."

Again Efraim met with his eiodarks. There was little conversation; all sat with glum faces. Efraim said, "I have searched the archives. I find no sure reference to an agreement with the Fwai-chi. They must be betrayed, and we must submit. Who disagrees?"

"I disagree," growled Baron Hectre. "I am willing to fight."

"I am willing to fight," said Baron Faroz, "but I do not care to destroy myself and my folk to no purpose. We must submit."

"We must submit," said Baron Haulk.

Efraim said, "If the Kaiark Jochaim indeed acceded to Rianlle's demands, he must have been subjected to these same pressures. I hope that our humiliation serves a good purpose." He rose to his feet. "Rianlle arrives here tomorrow. I hope that all of you will be on hand, to lend the occasion dignity."

"We will be here."

CHAPTER 13

An hour before arrival of the Kaiark Rianlle, the eiodarks gathered on the terrace of Benbuphar Strang. Through psychological processes perhaps differing from case to case, many attitudes had hardened, and shameful misgivings had been converted into defiance. Where before all the eiodarks had resigned themselves to submission, now it seemed as if all had been inspired to obduracy.

"Rianlle challenged your memory?" cried out Baron Balthazar. "With reason, you admit. He cannot challenge mine. If the Fwai-chi declare the existence of this covenant and if the archives at least hint of its existence, then I distinctly recall the Kaiark Jochaim discussing this same covenant."

"I as well!" declared Baron Hectre. "He dare not challenge us."

Efraim laughed sadly. "He will dare; why not? You are powerless to damage him."

"This shall be our strategy," said Baron Balthazar. "We will deny his demands with fortitude. If he invests the Dwan Jar with his troops, we shall harass them and destroy his work. If Rianlle wafts his sails down into our vale, we shall plunge down from Alode the Cliff and rip their wings."

Baron Simic shook his fists into the air. "It shall not be so easy for Rianlle after all!"

"Very well," said Efraim. "If this is how you feel, I am with you. Remember, we shall be firm but not pugnacious; we shall mention self-defense only if he threatens. I am glad that, like myself, you find submission intolerable. And there, I believe, around Shanajra, comes Rianlle and his party."

The air-car landed; Rianlle alighted, followed by the Kraike Dervas, the Lissolet Maerio, and four Eccord eiodarks. The heralds quickstepped forth, producing ceremonial fanfares. Rianlle and his party marched to the steps leading up to the terrace; Efraim and the Scharde eiodarks descended to greet them.

Formalities were exchanged, then Rianlle, throwing back his handsome head, stated: "Today the Kaiarks of Scharrode and Eccord meet to certify an era of warm regard between their realms. It pleases me, therefore, to state that I will look favorably upon the possibility of trisme between yourself and the Lissolet Maerio."

Efraim bowed his head. "This is a most gracious offer, Force, and nothing could accord more to my own inclinations. But you are fatigued from the journey; I must allow you to refresh yourself. In two hours we shall meet in the Grand Parlor."

"Excellent. I may assume that you have found no further objections to my little scheme?"

"You may be sure, Your Force, that good relations between our two realms, on the basis of equity and cooperation, are the foundation of Scharde policy."

Rianlle's face darkened. "Can you not respond to the point? Do you or do you not intend to cede the Dwan Jar?"

"Your Force, let us not transact our important business upon the front steps. When you have rested an hour or two, I will clarify the Scharde point of view."

Rianlle bowed, swung about. Under-chamberlains conducted him and members of his party to the chambers which had been prepared for them.

Maerio stood by a tall arched window looking out across the valley. She rubbed her hand on the stone sill, thrilling at the coarse contact. How would it be to live here at Benbuphar Strang, among these tall shadowy chambers, surrounded by echoes? Many strange events had occurred here, some of which made dreary listening; nowhere in all the Realms, so it was said, could be found a castle so riddled with mirk-ways. Efraim had changed; as to this there was no denying. He seemed more mature, and he seemed to obey the Rhune conventions tentatively, without conviction. Perhaps this was all to the good. Her mother, Dervas, had once been as gay and as artless as herself, but Rianlle (whom she supposed to be her father) had insisted that the Kraike of Eccord must exemplify the Rhune Code, and Dervas was impelled to orthodoxy for the good of the realm. Maerio wondered about Efraim. He hardly seemed the sort to insist on orthodoxy. In fact, from her own experience she knew better!

A slight sound behind her; she whirled about. A panel in the wainscoting had slid aside and there stood Efraim.

He crossed the room and stood smiling down into her face. "Forgive me for startling you. I wanted to see you secretly and alone, and I knew no other way."

Maerio looked toward the door. "Let me shoot the bolt; we must not be discovered."

"True." Efraim bolted the door and returned to Maerio. "I have been thinking of you; I cannot get you out of my mind."

"I have been thinking of you too, especially since I learned that the Kaiark planned to join us in trisme."

"That is what I must tell you. As much as I long for such a trisme, it will never occur, because the eiodarks intend to fight rather than give up the Dwan Jar."

Maerio nodded slowly. "I knew this would happen . . . I don't want to go in trisme anywhere else. What shall I do?"

"For now nothing. I can only make plans for war."

"You might be killed!"

"I hope not. Give me time to think. Would you run away with me, away from the Realms?"

Maerio asked breathlessly, "Where would we go?"

"I don't know. We would not be privileged as we are now; we might be forced to toil."

"I will go with you."

Efraim took her hands. She shivered and closed her eyes. "Efraim, please! You will lose your memory again."

"I don't think so." He kissed her forehead. She gasped and drew back.

"I feel so strange! Everyone will recognize my agitation!"

"I must go now. When you have composed yourself, come down to the Grand Parlor."

Efraim returned through the mirk-way to his chambers, and arrayed himself in formal garments.

A knock at the door. Efraim looked at the clock. Rianlle so soon?

He opened the door to find Becharab, the new First Chamberlain. "Yes, Becharab?"

"Your Force, before the castle stand several natives. They wish to speak with Your Force. I told them you are resting, but they are insistent."

Efraim ran past Becharab, across the Reception Hall and foyer, to the haughty astonishment of Singhalissa who stood conversing with one of the eiodarks from Eccord.

Before the terrace stood four Fwai-chi—ancient brown-red bucks, all tatters and shags. A pair of footmen, making fastidious faces, attempted to shoo them away. The Fwai-chi, discouraged, were starting to sidle off when Efraim appeared.

He ran down the steps, motioned the footmen aside. "I am Kaiark Efraim. You wished to see me?"

"Yes," said one, and Efraim thought to recognize the old buck he had met up on Whispering Ridge. "You claim that you remember no covenant in regard to the Dwan Jar."

"That is true. The Kaiark of Eccord who wants the Dwan Jar is here now."

"He must not have it; he is a man who demands much. If he were to control the Dwan Jar, he would demand more, and we would be forced to glut his avarice." The Fwai-chi produced a dusty vial containing half a gill of dark liquid. "Your memory is locked and there are no keys to the locks. Drink this liquid."

Efraim took the vial and examined it curiously. "What will it do to me?"

"Your corporeal substance itself contains memory; it is called instinct. I give you a medicine. It will prompt all your cells to erupt memories—even those very cells which now block your memory. We cannot unlock the doors; but we can batter them open. Do you dare take this draught?"

"Will it kill me?"

"No."

"Will it make me insane?"

"Perhaps not."

"Will I know everything I knew before?"

"Yes. And when you have your memory, you must protect your sanctuary."

Efraim went thoughtfully up the steps.

By the balustrade Singhalissa and Destian stood waiting. Singhalissa asked sharply: "What is that vial?"

"It contains my memory. I need only drink it."

Singhalissa leaned forward, her hands quivered. Efraim moved back. She asked: "And will you drink it?"

"Naturally."

Singhalissa chewed at her lip. Efraim's vision suddenly seemed totally keen and clear; he noticed the lack of bloom on Singhalissa's skin, the minute wrinkles around her eyes and mouth, the birdlike thrust of her sternum.

"This may seem an odd point of view," said Singhalissa, "but consider. Events go well for you! You are Kaiark; you are about to make trisme with a powerful realm. What else do you need? The contents of the vial may well disturb these conditions!"

Destian spoke with an air of authority: "If I were in your position, I would let well enough alone!"

Singhalissa said: "You have best confer with Kaiark Rianlle; he is a wise man; he will advise you."

"The matter would seem only to concern myself," remarked Efraim. "I doubt if Rianlle's wisdom can apply in this case." He passed into the Reception Hall, to meet Rianlle coming down the grand staircase. Efraim paused. "I hope you enjoyed your rest."

Rianlle bowed politely. "Very much indeed."

Singhalissa came forward. "I have urged Efraim to solicit your advice in a very important matter. The Fwai-chi have provided him a liquid which they claim will restore his memory."

Rianlle reflected. "Excuse me a moment or two." He took Singhalissa aside; the two conversed in mutters. Rianlle nodded and thoughtfully returned to where Efraim waited.

"While I rested," said Rianlle, "I reviewed the situation which has caused a tension between our realms. I propose that we postpone further consideration of Dwan Jar. Why allow so paltry a matter to interfere with the trisme I have suggested? Am I not correct?"

"Entirely."

"However, I have no confidence in Fwai-chi drugs. Often they promote cerebral lesions. In view of our prospective relationship I must insist that you do not dose yourself with some vile Fwai-chi potion."

Very odd, thought Efraim. If the truncation of his memory were so advantageous to other folk, then the disadvantage to himself would seem correspondingly great. "Let us join the others who await us in the parlor."

Efraim seated himself at the red table and looked around the faces: fourteen Scharde and four Eccord eiodarks; Singhalissa, Destian, Sthelany; Rianlle, the Kraike Dervas, Maerio, and himself. He carefully placed the vial on the table before him.

"There is a new circumstance to be considered," said Efraim. "My memory. It is contained in this bottle. At Port Mar someone robbed me of my memory. I am intensely anxious to learn the identity of this person. Of the folk who were with me in Port Mar, two are dead—by coincidence, or perhaps not coincidentally after all, both were murdered.

"I have been advised not to drink this draught. I am told that it is best to let sleeping dogs lie. Needless to say, I reject this point of view. I want my memory back, no matter what the cost." He unstoppered the vial, raised it to his mouth and poured the contents down his throat. The flavor was soft and earthy, like pounded bark and mold mixed with stump water.

He looked around the circle of faces. "You must forgive this act of ingestion before your very eyes . . . I feel nothing yet. I would expect a delay while the material permeates my blood, courses around my body . . . I notice a shifting of lights and shadows—your faces flicker. I must shut my eyes . . . I see splashes of light: they shatter and burst . . . I see everywhere in my body . . . I see with my hands and inside my legs and down my back." Efraim's voice became hoarse. "The sounds—everywhere . . ." He could speak no more; he leaned back in his chair. He felt, he saw, he heard: a jumble of impressions: whirling suns and dancing stars, the froth of salt spume, the warmth of swamp mud, the dank flavor of waterweeds. The thrust of spears, the scorch of fire, and screaming women. Timelessness: visions swarmed past, then back, then away, like shoals of fish. Efraim became faint; his legs and arms went numb. He fought away the lethargy, and watched in fascination as the first furious explosion of images retreated and swirled away. The succession of sensations continued, but at a pace less blurred, as if to the control of chronology. He began to see faces and hear voices: strange faces, strange voices, of persons inexpressibly dear, and tears ran down his cheeks. He felt the extent of space; he knew the grief of departures, the exultation of conquest; he killed, he was killed; he loved and knew love; he nurtured a thousand families; he knew a thousand deaths, a thousand infancies.

More slowly came the images, as if the source were almost drained. He was the first man to arrive on Marune; he led the tribes east from Port Mar; he was all the Kaiarks of Scharrode and of many other realms as well; he was many of the ordinary folk; he lived all these lives in the course of five seconds.

Time began to decelerate. He watched the construction of Benbuphar Strang; he prowled by mirk; he scaled the Tassenberg and struck a blond warrior toppling down the face of the Khism. He began to see faces to which he could almost put names; he was a tall auburn-haired child who grew into a tall spare man with a bony face and short thick beard. With beating heart Efraim followed this man whose name was Jochaim through the chambers of Benbuphar Strang, by aud, isp, umber, and rowan. By mirk he wandered the mirk-ways, and he felt the intoxication of striding forth, clad only in shoulder-piece, man-mask, and boots into the chamber of his sometimes terrified elect. To Benbuphar Strang came the maiden Alferica from Cloudscape Castle, to be taken in trisme by Jochaim, and in due course a child was born who was named Efraim, and Jochaim faded from consciousness.

Efraim's youth passed. His mother, Alferica, drowned during a visit to Eccord; presently to Benbuphar Strang came a new Kraike, Singhalissa, with her two children. One of these was dark vicious Destian; the other, a pale big-eyed waif, was Sthelany.

Tutors educated the three children; they chose cogences and eruditions.

Sthelany professed the writing of poetry in an abstruse poetic language, the working of mothwing tapestry, and star-names, as well as the contriving of fumes and fragrances which all well-born ladies were expected to include among their skills. She also collected Glanzeln flower vases, glazed an ineffable transparent violet, and unicorn horns. Destian collected precious crystals, and replicas of medallions on the hilts of famous swords; he also professed heraldry and the intricate lore of fanfares. Efraim professed the architecture of castles, mineral identification, and the theory of alloys, although Singhalissa considered the choice insufficiently erudite.

Efraim politely acknowledged Singhalissa's remarks and put them to the back of his mind. He was First Kang of the Realm; Singhalissa's opinions need not concern him.

Singhalissa herself professed a dozen skills, didactics, and expertises; she was quite the most erudite person of Efraim's acquaintance. Perhaps once a year she visited Port Mar, that she might buy supplies and materials for the specialized needs of those at Benbuphar Strang. When Efraim learned that Kaiark Rianlle of Eccord, with the Kraike Dervas and the Lissolet Maerio, planned to accompany Jochaim and Singhalissa to Port Mar, he decided to join the party. After considerable discussion, Destian and Sthelany also decided to undertake the journey.

Efraim had been acquainted with Maerio for years, under the formal circumstances imposed upon all visits between kaiarkal households. At first he considered her frivolous and eccentric. She lacked all erudition, she was clumsy with the vials, and she seemed always to be restraining herself from some reckless spontaneity, which caused Singhalissa's eyebrows to twitch and Sthelany to look away in ostensible boredom. These very factors induced Efraim to cultivate Maerio. Gradually he noticed that her company was extraordinarily stimulating, and that she was remarkably pleasant to look at. Forbidden thoughts wandered into his mind; he ejected them from loyalty to Maerio, who would be shocked and horrified!

The Kaiark Rianlle, Kraike Dervas, and Maerio flew over the mountains to Benbuphar Strang; on the morrow all would journey to Port Mar. Rianlle, Jochaim, Efraim, and Destian gathered in the Grand Parlor for an informal talk; bobbing their heads behind etiquette screens they discreetly took small cups of arrack.

Rianlle was at his best. Always a remarkable speaker, on this occasion his conversation was brilliant. Like Singhalissa, Rianlle was most erudite; he knew the Fwai-chi signals and all the trails of their "Path through Life"; he knew the Pantechnic Metaphysic; he had collected and studied the insects of Eccord, and had indited three monographs upon the subject. Additionally Rianlle was a notable warrior, with remarkable exploits to his credit. Efraim listened to him with fascination. Rianlle was discussing Dwan Jar, the Whispering Ridge. "It has occurred to me," he told Jochaim, "that here is a site of sublime beauty. One of us should make use of it. Be generous, Jochaim; let me build myself a summer garden with a pavilion on the Dwan Jar. Think how I would rest and muse to the wild whispering sound!"

Jochaim had smiled. "Impossible! Have you no sense of fitness? My eiodarks would drive me forth for a madman if I agreed to your proposal. Additionally, I am bound by a covenant with the Fwai-chi. Certainly you are making a joke."

"No joke whatever. Truly I covet that bit, that trifle, that insignificant wisp of land!"

Jochaim shook his head. "When I am dead, I can no longer oppose; Efraim must then assume that responsibility. While I live, I must deny you your fancy."

Rianlle said: "It would seem that by the process of dying, you withdraw your opposition. I would not have you dead on that account, however. Let us talk along easier subjects . . ."

The group had flown into Port Mar, and as usual taken accommodation at the Royal Rhune Hotel, where the management knew and respected their customs . . .

Efraim raised his head from his hands and looked wildly around the table. Taut faces everywhere; eyes fixed upon him; silence. He closed his eyes. Recollections came soft and slow now, but with a wonderful luminous clarity. He felt himself leaving the hotel in company with Destian, Sthelany, and Maerio for a stroll through Port Mar, and perhaps a visit to the Fairy Gardens, where Galligade's Puppets provided entertainment.

They walked down the Street of Brass Boxes and across the bridge into New Town. For a few minutes they strolled along the Estrada, peering into the beer-gardens where the folk of Port Mar and students from the college drank beer and devoured food in full view of everyone.

Efraim at last asked direction from a young man emerging from a bookshop. Seeing the party to be Rhunes, he volunteered to serve as their escort to the Fairy Gardens. To everyone's disappointment the entertainment was at an end. Their guide introduced himself as Matho Lorcas and insisted upon ordering a bottle of wine, along with suitable etiquette screens. Sthelany raised her eyebrows in a fashion reminiscent of Singhalissa and turned away. Efraim, catching Maerio's eye, sipped the wine, protected by the propriety of the screen. Maerio, greatly daring, did likewise.

Matho Lorcas seemed a person of buoyant disposition and irrepressible wit; he refused to allow either Sthelany or Destian to sulk. "And how are you enjoying your visit?" he asked.

"Very much," said Maerio. "But surely there is more excitement than this? We always think of Port Mar as a place of wild abandon."

"Not quite accurate. Of course this is the respectable part of town. Doesn't it seem so to you?"

280 / JACK VANCE

"Our customs are rather different," said Destian frostily.

"So I understand, but here you are in Port Mar; why not attempt the Port Mar customs?"

"That logic does not quite follow," murmured Sthelany.

Lorcas laughed. "Of course not! I wondered if you'd agree. Still—don't you have any inclination to live, well, let us say, normal lives?"

Efraim asked: "You think we don't live normal lives?"

"Not from my point of view. You're smothered in convention. You're walking bundles of neuroses."

"Peculiar," said Maerio, "I feel quite well."

"I feel well," said Efraim. "You must be mistaken."

"Aha! Well, possibly. I'd like to visit one of the Realms and see how things go for myself. Do you like the wine? Perhaps you'd prefer punch."

Destian looked around the table. "I think we'd better return to the hotel. Haven't we seen enough of New Town?"

"Go, if you like," said Efraim. "I'm in no hurry."

"I'll wait with Efraim," said Maerio.

Matho Lorcas spoke to Sthelany. "I hope you'll wait too. Will you not?"

"Why?"

"I want to explain something which I believe you want to hear."

Sthelany languidly rose to her feet and without a word moved off. Destian, with a dubious look back at Efraim and Maerio, followed.

"A pity," said Lorcas. "I found her extremely attractive."

"Sthelany and Destian are both most stately," said Maerio.

Lorcas asked with a sly smile, "And what of you? Aren't you stately too?"

"When ceremony makes demands on me. Sometimes I find Rhune ways rather tiresome. If Efraim weren't here I'd try that punch. I'm not ashamed of my inner workings."

Efraim laughed. "Very well. If you will, I will too. But wait until Destian and Sthelany are out of sight."

Matho Lorcas ordered rum punch for all. Efraim and Maerio drank first behind the screens, then spluttering with embarrassed laughter, brought the goblets into the open and drank.

"Bravo!" declared Lorcas soberly. "You have taken a long step on the road to emancipation."

"It doesn't amount to all that much," said Efraim. "I'll buy another round. Lorcas, what about you?"

"With pleasure. Still, it wouldn't do for the two of you to stagger into the hotel drunk, would it?"

Maerio clasped her head. "My father would turn purple. Of all the folk alive he is the most rigid."

"My father would simply look the other way," said Efraim. "He seems rigid, and of course he is, but essentially he is quite reasonable."

"So, you two are not related?"

"Not at all."

"But you're fond of each other?"

Efraim and Maerio looked sidewise at each other. Efraim laughed uncomfortably. "I won't deny it." He looked again at Maerio, whose face was twisting. "Have I offended you?"

"No."

"Then why do you look so doleful?"

"Because we must come to Port Mar to tell each other such things."

"I suppose it is absurd," said Efraim. "But Port Mar is so much different from Eccord and Scharrode. Here I can touch you, and it is not mirk." He took her hand.

Matho Lorcas heaved a sigh. "Ah me. I should leave you two alone. Excuse me a moment; for a fact there is someone I wish to see."

Efraim and Maerio sat together. She leaned her head against his shoulder; he bent down, kissed her forehead. "Efraim! It is not even mirk!"

"Are you angry?"

"No."

Lorcas appeared beside the table. "Your friend Destian is here."

Efraim and Maerio drew apart. Destian approached and looked curiously from one to the other. He addressed Maerio. "The Kaiark Rianlle has asked me to conduct you back to the hotel."

Efraim stared up at Destian, who, so he knew, was not above misrepresenting facts. Maerio, sensing friction, jumped to her feet. "Yes. I'll welcome some rest, and look! with umber and the overcast and the shade from these enormous trees it is almost like mirk!"

Destian and Maerio departed. With a debonair gesture Lorcas settled into the seat beside Efraim. "And that is the way things go, my friend."

"I am embarrassed," said Efraim. "What will she think of me?"

"Get her alone somewhere and find out."

"That is impossible! Here in Port Mar perhaps we lost our equilibrium. In our realms we could never consider such display." He rested his chin on his hands and looked gloomily across the restaurant.

"Come along," said Lorcas. "Let's move down the avenue. I'm due at The Three Lanterns presently; first I'll show you a bit of the town."

Lorcas took Efraim to a cabaret frequented by students. They listened to music, drank light beer. Efraim explained to Lorcas how life went in the Realms. "A place like this by comparison seems a zoo of fecund animals. The Kraike Singhalissa, at least, would adopt this view."

"And you respect her judgment?"

"To the contrary; this is the principal reason I am here. I hope to discover benefits and redemptions in what I confess seems sickening behavior. Look at that couple yonder. Sweating, panting, shameless as dogs in rut. At the very least their activity is unhygienic."

"They are relaxed. Still, yonder other folk sit quite decorously, and none seem offended by the antics of the two reprobates."

"I am confused," admitted Efraim. "Trillions inhabit Alastor Cluster; not all can be deluded. Perhaps anything and everything is innocent."

"What you see here is relatively innocent," said Lorcas. "Come, I'll show you places less so. Unless you prefer your illusions, so to speak?"

"No. I will come with you, as long as I do not have to breathe too much fetid air."

"When you've seen enough, just say the word." He glanced at his watch. "I have just an hour to spare, then I must go to work at The Three Lanterns."

The two walked up the Street of Limping Children, then turned along the Avenue of Haune, Lorcas pointing out the more disreputable places of the town—an expensive bordello, bars frequented by sexual deviates, and a dim establishment, purportedly a tea shop which operated illegal nerve machines in the upper rooms; other sordid places offering even more questionable entertainment.

Efraim observed all with a stony face. He found himself not so much shocked as detached, as if what he saw were intended as a grotesque stage-setting. At last they reached The Three Lanterns, a rambling old structure from which issued the sound of fiddles with banjos playing merry jigs after the style of the Tinsdale Wayfarers.

Singhalissa was right, thought Efraim, when she declared music no more than symbolic sebalism—well, perhaps "sebalism" was not quite the right word. "Passion," perhaps, which encompassed sebalism and all the other strong emotions as well. At The Three Lanterns, Lorcas took his leave of Efraim. "Remember, I'd be enchanted for the opportunity to visit the Realms. Perhaps someday—who knows?"

Efraim, thinking of the frigid reception Lorcas would certainly receive at the hands of Singhalissa, restrained an invitation. "Perhaps someday. At the moment it might not be convenient."

"Good-bye then. Remember, directly back down the Avenue of Haune, turn south on any of the side streets to the Estrada, and along to the bridge. Then up the Street of Brass Boxes to your hotel."

"I am exactly oriented; I will not get lost."

Somewhat reluctantly Lorcas went into The Three Lanterns; at the entrance he waved farewell. Efraim turned back the way they had come.

Clouds hung heavy; the time was yet umber, though very dull. Furad hung low behind Jibberee Hill, and both Maddar and Cirse were obscured by overcast. Gloom almost as dense as mirk shrouded Port Mar, and colored lights invested the Avenue of Haune with a tipsy gaiety.

As Efraim walked, his thoughts returned to Maerio; how he wished she were with him now! But futile to counter the will of the Kaiark Rianlle, whose rectitude was matched only by that of Singhalissa.

Efraim at this moment was passing the expensive bordello, and even as he reflected upon the character of the Kaiark Rianlle, out the door of the bordello, his face blurred and clothes disheveled, stepped the Kaiark Rianlle himself.

Efraim stared, unbelievingly. He began to laugh first incredulously, then with the intoxication of total mirth.

Rianlle stood with his mouth first open, then closed; first swelling with purple wrath, then trying to achieve a comradely grin. Under the circumstances neither could be convincing or effective. Ridicule to a Rhune was insupportable; when Efraim told the story, as surely he must—the episode was too good to keep; even Rianlle realized this—the Kaiark Rianlle would thereafter be a figure of fun, and furtive snickers would accompany him through life.

Rianlle by dint of some desperate inner contortion composed himself. "What are you doing out along the avenue?"

"Nothing! Investigating weird antics!" And Efraim again began to chuckle. Rianlle managed a steely grin. "Ah, well, you must not judge me too harshly. Unfortunately for myself, I am expected to represent the apotheosis of Rhune gallantry. The pressure becomes overwhelming. Come along; we will take a hot drink together as the folk do without shame here at Port Mar. The drink is called coffee and is not considered intoxicating."

Rianlle led the way along the Street of the Clever Flea to an establishment called "The Great Alastor Coffee Emporium." He ordered the refreshment for both, then excused himself. "A moment; I have a small errand."

Efraim watched Rianlle cross the avenue and enter a dingy little shop whose windows were crowded with all manner of goods.

The coffee was served; Efraim tasted the brew and found it savory, aromatic, and to his liking. Rianlle returned; the two sipped coffee in cautious silence.

Rianlle lifted the lid to the silver ewer in which the coffee was served, peered within. His hand hovered a moment over the open mouth of the ewer, then the lid dropped with a clang. He poured a second cup for Efraim and a second cup for himself. He now became affable and expansive. Efraim drank more coffee, although Rianlle allowed his own portion to go cold. And Efraim's mind dimmed and lost itself in floating mists.

As if in a dream he felt himself walking with Rianlle along the Estrada, across the bridge, and by back alleys into the park at the Royal Rhune Hotel. Rianlle approached the hotel with great stealth; but as luck would have it, the path curved and Singhalissa stood before them.

She looked in disgust from Efraim to Rianlle. "You have found him in a state of intoxication! What shame! Jochaim will be furious!"

Rianlle considered a moment, then shook his head despondently. "Come with me, away from the path, and I will explain how things have gone."

On a secluded bench Rianlle and Singhalissa sat; Efraim stood watching a firefly. Rianlle cleared his throat. "Affairs are more serious than simple intoxication. Someone offered him a dangerous drug which he foolishly ingested; his memory has completely been destroyed."

"What a tragedy!" cried Singhalissa. "I must inform Jochaim; he will turn New Town topsy-turvy, and never stop until he learns the truth!"

"Wait!" said Rianlle in a low hoarse voice. "This may not be to our best interests."

Singhalissa fixed Rianlle with a cool stare which seemed to see everything. "*Our* best interests?"

"Yes. Consider. Jochaim must ultimately die—perhaps sooner than we might wish. When that unhappy event occurs, Efraim will become Kaiark."

"In his present condition?"

"Of course not. He will rapidly become whole and alert, and Jochaim will renew his memories. But—what if Efraim goes traveling?"

"And does not return?"

"On Jochaim's death, Destian than becomes Kaiark of Scharrode, and I will give him Maerio in trisme. Jochaim will never surrender Whispering Ridge; if I hold it I can levy a great toll upon the Fwai-chi. What, after all, are gems and elixirs to them? If Destian is Kaiark there will be no difficulty."

Singhalissa reflected. "Do not underrate Destian; he is obstinate at times! But he would never deny me were I Kraike of Eccord. In all candor, Belrod Strang is more to my taste than gloomy old Benbuphar."

Rianlle grimaced and uttered a soft involuntary moan. "What of Dervas?"

"You must dissolve the trisme; this is simple enough. If events proceed along these lines all will go well. If not, it is best that we forget the matter and I will take Efraim in to Jochaim. Never fear! Jochaim is both pertinacious and ruthless; he is fond of Efraim and will never stop until he learns all the circumstances!"

Rianlle sighed. "Destian shall be next Kaiark of Scharrode. We will then celebrate two trismes: between Destian and Maerio; between you and me."

"In that case, we will work together."

Though Efraim overheard much of their conversation, the subject matter made little impression on him.

Singhalissa went off, to return with a shabby gray suit and scissors. She cut Efraim's hair short, and the two dressed him in the gray suit. Then

Rianlle, stepping into his rooms, emerged wearing a black cape and a helmet which concealed his face.

Efraim's recollections blurred. He barely recalled walking to the spaceport, nor embarkation aboard the *Berenicia*, where money changed hands between Rianlle and the steward.

Events gradually merged into his conscious recollections. He opened his eyes to look into the face of the Kaiark Rianlle. Once again he saw that mixture of rage, shame, and desperate affability Efraim had noted on the Avenue of Haune.

"My memory is whole," said Efraim. "I know the name of my enemy and I know his reasons. Cogent reasons, they are. But these are personal matters and I will deal with them on a personal basis. Meanwhile, other more important affairs compel our attention.

"With the return of my memory I can now assert that the Kaiark Jochaim did indeed endorse the ancient covenant with the Fwai-chi, and that, also, he made to the Kaiark Rianlle the following remark: 'Only when I am dead will I abandon my opposition to your scheme,' which the Kaiark Rianlle interpreted as 'when I am dead, there shall be no further opposition to your scheme.' A most reasonable mistake, which the Kaiark Rianlle now appreciates. I suspect that he wishes to withdraw utterly and forever his claim to the Dwan Jar; am I right, Your Force?"

"Quite correct," stated the Kaiark Rianlle in a monotone. "I see where I misinterpreted the Kaiark Jochaim's jocularity."

"Three more matters should be considered," said Efraim. "Your Force, I apply to you for trisme between our houses and our realms."

"I am honored to accede to your proposal, if the Lissolet Maerio is like-minded."

"I agree," said Maerio.

"Temporarily I will abandon this happy subject," said Efraim, "to deal with the crime of murder."

"Murder!" The dreadful word rustled around the table.

"The Kaiark Jochaim," continued Efraim, "was murdered by a bolt in the back. The bolt was not discharged by a Gorget bore, hence the murderer is Scharde. Better to say, he accompanied the Scharde force.

"Another murder occurred during mirk. I am in a sense too close to this crime to avoid prejudice; hence you, the eiodarks of Scharrode, shall hear my evidence; you shall pass judgment, and I will not quarrel with your findings.

"I speak now as a witness.

"When I arrived at Benbuphar Strang in company with my friend Matho Lorcas, I encountered the coolest of welcomes, and in fact antagonism.

"A few days before mirk the Noble Sthelany surprised me by her cordiality and her assurances that for the first time she planned not to bolt her doors during mirk." Efraim described the events previous to, during, and after mirk.

"It is clear that an attempt was made to entice me into Sthelany's chambers; but poor Lorcas entered in my stead, or else he was recognized and murdered to prevent him from telling me of the trap.

"I well understand that strange deeds are done during mirk, but this murder falls into a different category. It was planned a week or more before mirk, and put into execution with cruel efficiency. It is not a mirk-deed. It is murder."

"The assertions are malicious fabrications," said Singhalissa. "They are too feeble to deserve refutal."

Efraim turned to Destian. "What is your comment?"

"I can only echo the Noble Singhalissa's remarks."

"And Sthelany?"

Silence. Then presently a low voice: "I will say nothing, except that I am sick of life."

At this point, in embarrassment, the party from Eccord departed from the Grand Parlor. The eiodarks went off to the far end of the room. For ten minutes they muttered together, then returned.

"The judgment is this," said Baron Haulk. "The three equally share guilt. They are guilty not of mirk-deed, but murder. They shall this moment be shaved bald and expelled from the Rhune Realms, carrying no property except the clothes on their backs. Forever they are exiled and no Rhune Realm will take them in. Murderers, at this moment divest yourselves of all jewels, ornaments, and valuables. Then go down to the kitchens where your heads will be shaved. You will then be escorted to the air-car and flown to Port Mar, where you must live as best you can."

CHAPTER 14

Maerio and Efraim stood on the parapets of Benbuphar Strang. "Suddenly," said Efraim, "we are at peace. Our difficulties have dissipated. Life lies before us."

"I fear that new difficulties are just beginning."

Efraim looked at her in surprise. "How can you say so?"

"It is clear you have known life outside the Realms; I have had the merest hint of a taste. Will we be content to live as Rhunes?"

"We can live in whatever fashion suits us," said Efraim. "I want nothing but happiness for both of us."

"Perhaps we will want to travel to far worlds. What then? How will the Schardes regard us on our return? They will consider us tainted—not true Rhunes."

Efraim looked away down the valley. "We are not Rhunes of the clearest water, for a fact. So then—what shall we do?"

"I don't know."

"I don't know either."

WYST

ALASTOR 1716

CHAPTER I

. . . .

A lastor Cluster, a node of thirty thousand live stars, uncounted dead hulks and vast quantities of interstellar detritus, clung to the inner rim of the galaxy with the Unfortunate Waste before, the Nonestic Gulf beyond and the Gaean Reach a sparkling haze to the side. For the space traveler, no matter which his angle of approach, a remarkable spectacle was presented: constellations blazing white, blue, and red; curtains of luminous stuff, broken here, obscured there by black storms of dust; star-streams wandering in and out; whorls and spatters of phosphorescent gas.

Should Alastor Cluster be considered a segment of the Gaean Reach? The folk of the Cluster seldom reflected upon the matter, and indeed considered themselves neither Gaean nor Alastrid. The typical inhabitant, when asked about his origin, might perhaps cite his native world or, more usually, his local district, as if this place were so extraordinary, so special and widely famed that its reputation hung on every tongue of the galaxy.

Parochialism dissolved before the glory of the Connatic, who ruled Alastor Cluster from his palace Lusz on the world Numenes: a structure famed across the human universe. Five pylons veered up from five islets to a groined arch a thousand feet above the ocean, supporting first a series of promenade decks; then a bank of administrative offices, ceremonial halls and the core of the Alastrid Communications System; then the Ring of Worlds; then further offices and residential suites for distinguished visitors; and finally, ten thousand feet above the ocean, the Connatic's private quarters. The highest pinnacle penetrated the clouds, sometimes piercing through to the upper sky. When sunlight glistened on its iridescent surfaces Lusz was a wonderful sight, and often considered the most inspiring artifact yet created by the human race.

Aloft in his eyrie, the Connatic lived without formality. For public appearances he arrayed himself in a severe black uniform and a black casque, in order to project an image of austerity, vigilance and inflexible authority: so he was known to his subjects. On more casual occasions—alone in his eyrie, as a high official on the Connatic's service, as an anonymous wanderer in the odd corners of the Cluster—he seemed a far easier man, of rather ordinary appearance, notable only for his manner of unobtrusive competence.

At Lusz, his workroom occupied the highest tip of the eyrie: a cupola with an outlook in all directions. The furnishings were constructed of massive dark wood: a pair of cushioned chairs, a work table, a sideboard supporting a clutter of souvenirs, photographs, curios, and oddments, including a globe of Old Earth. To one side of the work table a panel displayed a conventionalized chart of the Cluster with three thousand glittering lights of various colors* to represent the inhabited worlds.

The workroom served the Connatic as his most familiar and comfortable retreat. The time was now evening; plum-blue twilight suffused the room. The Connatic stood before the western window, watching the passing of the afterglow and the coming of the stars.

The quiet was broken by a brief clear sound: *tink!* Like a drop of water into a basin.

The Connatic spoke without turning: "Esclavade?"

A voice replied: "A deputation of four persons has arrived from Arrabus on Wyst. They announce themselves as 'the Whispers' and request a conference at your convenience."

The Connatic, still gazing out across the afterglow, reflected a moment, then said: "I will meet them in an hour. Take them to the Black Chamber, and provide suitable refreshment."

"As you say, sir."

Turning from the window, the Connatic went to his work table. He spoke a number: "1716." Three cards fell into a hopper. The first, dated two weeks previously at Waunisse, a city of Arrabus, read:

Sir:

My previous reports upon the subject at hand are identified by the codes appended below. In gist: Arrabus shortly celebrates a Centenary Festival, to mark a hundred years under the aegis of the so-called "Egal-

---

*The colors served as a code to local conditions. By adjusting a switch, the Connatic might select any of several categories of reference. With the switch in its ordinary position, at *General*, the Connatic at a glance could gauge the circumstances in aggregate of three trillion people. When the Connatic touched one of the lights, its name and number appeared on a pane. If he should increase the pressure, information cards detailing recent and significant local events dropped into a slot. Should he speak a number, the world so designated showed a brief burst of white light and again the cards were produced.

istic Manifold." If I may presume to refresh your memory, this document enjoins all men, and specifically all Arrabins, to a society based upon human equality in a condition of freedom from toil, want and coercion.

The realization of these ideals has not been without dislocation. I refer you to my previous reports.

The Whispers, an executive committee of four, have come to take a very serious view of the situation. Their projections convince them that certain fundamental changes are necessary. At the Centenary they will announce a program to revitalize the Arrabin economy, which may not be popular: the Arrabin folk, like any others, hope for and expect augmentation rather than constriction of their lives. The present work-week comprises thirteen hours of more or less uncomplicated routine, which the Arrabins nevertheless hope to reduce.

To dramatize the need for change, the Whispers will be coming to Lusz. They intend to consult with you on a realistic basis, and they hope that you will appear at the Centenary Festival, to identify yourself with the new program and perhaps provide economic assistance. I have been in consultation with the Whispers at Waunisse. Tomorrow they return to Uncibal, and will immediately depart for Numenes.

In my opinion they have made a realistic assessment of conditions, and I recommend that you listen to them with sympathetic attention.

Bonamico,
Connatic's Cursar at Uncibal, Arrabus.

The Connatic read the card with care, then turned to the second card, which had been dated at Waunisse on the day after the first message.

To the Connatic at Lusz:

Greetings from the Whispers of Arrabus.

We will presently arrive at Lusz, where we hope to confer with you upon matters of great scope and urgency. We will also convey to you an invitation to our Centenary Festival, which signalizes a hundred years of egalism. There is much to be said on this subject, and at our conference we will disclose our thoughts regarding the next hundred years, and the adjustments which must inevitably be made. At this time we will solicit your advice and constructive assistance.

In all respect, we are,

the Whispers of Arrabus.

The Connatic had studied the two messages previously and was familiar with their contents. The third message, arriving subsequent to the first two, was new to him.

The Connatic at Lusz:
From the Alastor Centrality at Uncibal, Arrabus.

It becomes my duty to report upon an odd and disturbing situation. A certain Jantiff Ravensroke has presented himself to the Centrality, with information which he declares to be of the most absolute urgency. Cursar Bonamico is unaccountably absent and I can think only to request that you immediately send an investigative officer, that he may learn the truth of what may be a serious matter.

Clode Morre, Clerk,
The Alastor Centrality, Uncibal.

Even as the Connatic brooded upon this third message, a fourth dropped into the hopper.

To the Connatic at Lusz:

Events are flying in all directions here, to my great distress and consternation. Specifically, I fear for poor Jantiff Ravensroke, who is in terrible danger; unless someone puts a stop, they'll have his blood or worse. He is accused of a vile crime but he is surely as innocent as a child. Clerk Morre has been murdered and Cursar Bonamico cannot be located; therefore I have ordered Jantiff south into the Weirdlands, despite the rigors of the way.

I send this off in agitation, and with the hope that help is on the way.

Aleida Gluster, Clerk,
The Alastor Centrality, Uncibal.

The Connatic stood motionless, frowning down at the card. After a moment he turned away and by a twisting wooden staircase descended to the level below. A door slid aside; he entered a car, dropped to the Ring of Worlds, and, by one of the radial slideways reserved to his private use, rode to Chamber 1716.

In the vestibule a placard provided basic data regarding Wyst—the single planet of the white star Dwan, was small, cool, dense, and populated by over three billion persons. He continued into the main chamber. At the center floated a seven-foot globe: a replica in miniature of Wyst, although physiographic relief had been exaggerated by a factor of ten in the interests of clarity. The Connatic touched the surface and the globe rotated under his hand. The opposed continents Trembal and Tremora appeared; the Connatic stopped the rotation. The continents together extended four thousand miles around the flank of Wyst, from the Northern Gulf to the Moaning Ocean in the south, to resemble a rather thick-waisted hourglass. At the equator, or the narrowest section of the hourglass, the continents were split apart by the Salaman Sea, a drowned rift averaging a hundred miles in width. That strip of littoral, never more than twenty miles wide, between sea and the flanking scarps to north and south, comprised the land of Arrabus. To the south were the cities Uncibal and Serce, to the north Propunce and Waunisse, each pair merging indistinguishably: in effect Arrabus was a single metropolitan area. Beyond the north and south extended the so-called "Weirdlands," one-time civilized domains, now a pair of wildernesses shrouded under dark forest.

The Connatic turned the globe a half-revolution and briefly inspected Zumer and Pombal, island continents opposed across the equator: each an uninviting terrain of mountain crags and half-frozen swamps, supporting a minimal population.

Moving away from the globe, the Connatic studied an array of effigies. Closest at hand stood a pair of Arrabins, dressed alike in gaily patterned smocks, short trousers and sandals of synthetic fiber. They wore their hair teased out into extravagant puffs and fringes, evidently to the prompting of individual whim. Their expressions were cheerful if rather distrait, like those of children contemplating a pleasant bit of mischief. Their complexions were pale to medium in tone, and their ethnic type seemed to be mixed. Nearby stood folk from Pombal and Zumer, men and women of a more distinctive character: tall, large-boned, with long beaked noses, bony jaws and chins. They wore padded garments studded with copper ornaments, boots and brimless hats of crumpled leather. On the wall behind a photograph depicted a Zur shunk-rider on his awesome mount* both caparisoned for the sport known as "shunkery." Somewhat apart from the other effigies crouched a middle-aged woman in a hooded gown striped vertically in yellow, orange and black; her fingernails gleamed as if gilded. *Weirdland Witch* read the identifying plaque.

Moving to the information register, the Connatic studied a synopsis of Arrabin history† with which he was familiar only in outline. As he read he nodded slowly, as if in validation of a private opinion. Turning from the register he went to examine three large photographs on the wall. The first, an aerial view of Uncibal, might have been a geometrical exercise in which rows of many-colored blocks dwindled to a point at the horizon. The second photograph depicted the interior of the 32nd District Stadium. Spectators encrusted the interior; a pair of shunk confronted each other across the field. The third photograph presented a view along one of the great Arrabin slideways: a moving strip something more than a hundred feet wide, choked with humanity, extending into the distance as far as lens could see.

---

*Shunk: monstrous creatures indigenous to the Pombal swamps, notably cantankerous and unpredictably vicious. They refuse to thrive on Zumer, though the Zur are considered the most adept riders. At the Arrabin stadia spectacles involving shunk are, along with the variety of hussade, the most popular of entertainments.

†See Glossary, i.

The Connatic studied the photographs with a trace of awe. The idea of human beings in vast numbers was familiar to him as an abstraction; in the photographs the abstraction was made real.

He glanced through a file of cursar's* reports; one of these, ten years old, read:

> Arrabus is the beating heart of Wyst. Despite rumor to the contrary, Arrabus functions; Arrabus is real; Arrabus, in fact, is an amazing experience. Whoever doubts can come to Wyst and learn for himself. Immigrants are no longer welcome additions to the overcrowded social facilities; still, anyone with a sufficiently thick skin can participate either temporarily or permanently in a fantastic social experiment, where food and shelter, like air, are considered the natural right of all men.
>
> The newcomer will find himself suddenly relieved of anxieties. He works two brief periods of "drudge" each week, with another two hours of "maintenance" at the block where he resides. He will find himself immediately caught up in a society dedicated to self-fulfillment, pleasure and frivolity. He will dance, sing, gossip, engage in countless love affairs, endlessly ride the "man-rivers" to no special destination, and waste hours in that obsessive occupation of the Arrabins, people-watching. He will make his breakfast, lunch and dinner upon wholesome "gruff" and nutritious "deedle," with a dish of "wobbly," as the expression goes, "to fill up the cracks." If he is wise he will learn to tolerate, and even enjoy, the diet, since there is nothing else to eat.
>
> "Bonter," or natural food, is almost unknown on Arrabus. The problems involved in growing, distributing, and preparing "bonter" for three billion persons are quite beyond the capacity of those who have resolutely eliminated toil from their lives. Occasionally "bonter" is a subject of wistful speculation but no one seems seriously troubled by its lack. A certain opprobrium attaches to the person who concerns himself overmuch with food. The casual visitor will refrain from grumbling unless he wishes to become known as a "guttrick." So much for the high cuisine of Arrabus; it fails to exist. A final note: intoxicants are not produced by any of the public agencies. Disselberg, who drank no wine, beer or spirit, declared against them as "social waste." Nevertheless, every day on every level of every block someone will be brewing a jug or two of "swill" from fragments of leftover gruff.

And another:

> Every visitor to Wyst expects shocks and surprises, but never can he prepare himself for the sheer bogglement inflicted upon him by real-

---

*Cursar: the Connatic's local representative, usually based in an enclave known as "Alastor Centrality."

ity. He observes the endless blocks dwindling in strict conformity to the laws of perspective until finally they disappear; he stands on an overpass watching the flow of a hundred-foot man-river, with its sensitive float of white faces; he visits Disjerferact on the Uncibal mud flats, a place of carnival, whose attractions include a death house where folk so inclined deliver eloquent orations, then die by suicide to the applause of casual passersby; he watches a parade of shunk lurch fatefully toward the stadium. He asks himself, is any of this truly real, or even possible? He blinks; all is as before. But the incredibility still persists!

Perhaps he may depart the confines of Arrabus, to wander the misty forests to north and south: the so-called "Weirdlands." As soon as he crosses the scarps, he finds himself in another world, which apparently exists only to reassure the Arrabins that their lot is truly a fortunate one. Hard to imagine that a thousand years ago these wastes were the provinces of dukes and princes. Trees conceal every trace of the former splendor. Wyst is a small world, only five thousand miles in diameter; a relatively few miles of travel takes one far around the horizons. If one travels south beyond the Weirdlands he comes at last to the shore of the Moaning Ocean, to find a land with a character all its own. Merely to watch the opal light of Dwan reflecting from the cold gray waves makes the journey well worth the effort.

The casual visitor to Wyst, however, seldom departs the cities of Arrabus, where he may presently feel an almost overpowering suffocation of numbers, a psychic claustrophobia. The subtle person becomes aware of a deeper darker presence, and he looks about him in fascination, with a crawling of the viscera, like a primeval man watching a cave mouth, certain that a horrid beast waits inside.

The Connatic smiled at the somewhat perfervid style of the report; he looked to see who had submitted it: Bonamico, the current cursar, a rather emotional man. Still—who could say? The Connatic himself had never visited Wyst; perhaps he might share Bonamico's comprehensions. He glanced at a final note, which was also signed by Bonamico:

> Zumer and Pombal, the small continents, are mountainous and half-frozen; they deserve mention only because they are home to the ill-natured shrunk and the no less irascible folk who manage them.

Time pressed: in a few minutes the Connatic must meet with the Whispers. He gave the globe a final glance and set it spinning; so it would turn for days, until air friction brought it to a halt.

Returning aloft, the Connatic went directly to his dressing room, where he created that version of himself which he saw fit to present to the people of the Cluster: first a few touches of skin toner to accentuate the bones of jaw and temple; then film which darkened his eyes and enhanced their intensity; then a clip of simulated cartilage to raise the bridge of his nose and produce a more incisive thrust to his profile. He donned an austere suit of black, relieved only by a silver button at each shoulder, and finally pulled a casque of black fabric over his close-cropped mat of hair.

He touched a button; across the room appeared the holographic image of himself: a spare saturnine man of indeterminate age, with an aspect suggesting force and authority. With neither approval nor dissatisfaction he considered the image; he was, so to speak, dressed for work, in the uniform of his calling.

Esclavade's quiet voice issued from an unseen source. "The Whispers have arrived in the Black Parlor."

"Thank you." The Connatic stepped into the adjoining chamber: a replica of the Black Parlor, exact to the images of the Whispers themselves: three men and a woman dressed in that informal, rather frivolous, style current in contemporary Arrabus. The Connatic examined the images with care: a reconnaissance he made of almost every deputation to offset, at least in part, the careful stratagems by which the visitors hoped to further their aims. Uneasiness, rigidity, anger, easy calm, desperation, fatalistic torpor: the Connatic had learned to recognize the indicators and to judge the mood in which the delegations came to meet him.

In the Connatic's estimation, this seemed a particularly disparate group, despite the uniformity of their garments. Each presented a different psychological aspect, which frequently signaled disunity, or perhaps mutual antagonism. In the case of the Whispers, who were selected by an almost random process, such lack of inner cohesion might be without significance, or so the Connatic reflected.

The oldest of the group, a gray-haired man of no great stature, at first glance appeared the least effectual of the four. He sat awry: neck twisted, head askew, legs splayed, elbows cocked at odd angles: a man sinewy and gaunt, with a long-nosed vulpine face. He spoke in a restless, peevish voice: "—heights give me to fret; even here between four walls I know that the soil lies far below; we should have requested a conference at low altitude."

"Water lies below, not soil," growled another of the Whispers, a massive man with a rather surly expression. His hair, hanging in lank black ringlets, made no concession to the fashionable Arrabin puff; of the group he seemed the most forceful and resolute.

The third man said: "If the Connatic trusts his skin to these floors, never fear! Your own far less valuable pelt is safe."

"I fear nothing!" declared the old man. "Did I not climb the Pedestal? Did I not fly in the *Sea Disk* and the spaceship?"

"True, true," said the third. "Your valor is famous." This was a man somewhat younger than the other two and notably well-favored, with a fine straight nose and a smiling debonair expression. He sat close beside the fourth Whisper, a round-faced woman with a pale, rather coarse complexion and a square assertive jaw.

Esclavade entered the room. "The Connatic will give you his attention shortly. He suggests that meanwhile you might care to take refreshment." He waved toward the back wall; a buffet slid into the parlor. "Please serve yourselves; you will find that we have taken your preferences into account." Only the Connatic noticed the twitch at the corner of Esclavade's mouth.

Esclavade departed the parlor. The crooked old Whisper at once jumped to his feet. "Let's see what we have here." He sidled toward the buffet. "Eh? Eh? What's this? Gruff and deedle! Can't the Connatic afford a trifle of bonter for our poor deprived jaws?"

The woman said in an even voice: "Surely he thinks it only courteous to serve familiar victuals to his guests."

The handsome man uttered a sardonic laugh. "The Connatic is hardly of egalistic persuasion. By definition he is the elite of the elite. There may be a message here."

The massive man went to the buffet and took a cake of gruff. "I eat it at home; I shall eat it here, and give the matter no thought."

The crooked man poured a cup of the viscous white liquid; he tasted, and made a wry grimace. "The deedle isn't all that good."

Smiling, the Connatic went to sit in a heavy wooden chair. He touched a button and his image appeared in the Black Parlor. The Whispers jerked around. The two men at the buffet slowly put down their food; the handsome man started to rise, then changed his mind and remained in his place.

Esclavade entered the Black Parlor and addressed the image.

"Sir, these are the Whispers of Arrabus Nation on Wyst. From Waunisse, the lady Fausgard." Then he indicated the massive man. "From Uncibal, the gentleman Orgold." The handsome man: "From Serce, the gentleman Lemiste." The crooked man: "From Propunce, the gentleman Delfin."

The Connatic said: "I welcome you to Lusz. You will notice that I appear before you in projection; this is my invariable precaution, and many uncertainties are circumvented."

Fausgard said somewhat tartly, "As a monomarch, and the elite of the elite, I suppose you go in constant fear of assassination."

"It is a very real risk. I see hundreds of folk, of every condition. Some, inevitably, prove to be madmen who fancy me a cruel and luxurious tyrant. I use an entire battery of techniques to avoid their murderous, if well-meant, assaults."

Fausgard gave her head a stubborn shake. The Connatic thought: Here is a woman of rock-hard conviction. Fausgard said: "Still, as absolute master of several trillion persons, you must recognize that yours is a position of unnatural privilege."

The Connatic thought: She is also of a somewhat contentious disposition. Aloud he said, "Naturally. The knowledge is never far from my mind, and is balanced, or neutralized, only by the fact of its total irrelevance."

"I fear that you leave me behind."

"The idea is complex, yet simple. I am I, who by reason of events beyond my control am Connatic. If I were someone else, I would not be Connatic; this is indisputable. The corollary is also clear: there would be a Connatic who was not I. He, like I, would ponder the singularity of his condition. So, you see, I as Connatic discover no more marvelous privilege to my life than you in your condition as Fausgard the Whisper."

Fausgard laughed uncertainly. She started to reply only to be preceded by the suave Lemiste. "Sir, we are here not to analyze your person, or your status, or the chances of Fate. In fact, as pragmatic egalists, we deny the existence of Fate, as a supernormal or ineffable entity. Our mission is more specific."

"I shall be interested to hear it."

"Arrabus has existed one hundred years as an egalistic nation. We are unique in the Cluster, perhaps across the Gaean universe. In a short time, at our Centenary Festival, we celebrate a century of achievement."

The Connatic reflected in some puzzlement: They take a tone rather different from what I had expected! Once more: take nothing, ever, for granted! He said: "I am of course aware of the Centenary, and I am considering your kind invitation to be on hand."

Lemiste continued, in a voice somewhat quick and staccato: "As you know we have constructed an enlightened society, dedicated to full egalism and individual fulfillment. We are naturally anxious to advertise our achievements, both for glory and for material benefit: hence our invitation. But let me explain. Ordinarily the Connatic's presence at an egalistic festival might be considered anomalous, even a compromise of principle. We hope, however, that should you choose to attend, you will put aside your elitist role and for a period become one with us: residing in our blocks, riding the man-ways, attending the public spectacles. You will thereby apprehend our institutions on a personal basis."

After a moment's thoughtful silence the Connatic said: "This is an interesting proposal. I must give it serious attention. You have taken refreshment? I could have offered you more elaborate fare, but in view of your principles I desisted."

Delfin, who had restlessly restrained his tongue, at last broke forth. "Our principles are real enough! That is why we are here: to advance them, but yet to protect them from their own success. Everywhere in the Cluster live jackals and interlopers, by the millions; they consider Arrabus a charitable hospice, where they flock by the myriads to batten upon the good things which we have earned through toil and sacrifice. It is done in the name of immigration, which we want to stop, but always we are thwarted by the Law of Free Movement. We have therefore certain demands that we feel—"

Fausgard quickly interrupted: "More properly: 'requests.' "

Delfin waved his arm in the air. "Demands, requests, it all comes out the same end! We want, first, a stop to immigration; second, Cluster funds to feed the hordes already on hand; third, new machinery to replace the equipment worn out nurturing the pests."

Delfin apparently was not popular with his fellow Whispers; each sought to suggest disassociation from Delfin's rather vulgar manners.

Fausgard spoke in a tone of brittle facetiousness: "Well then, Delfin; let's not bore the Connatic with a tirade."

Delfin slanted her a crooked grin. "Tirade, is it? When one talks of wolves, one does not describe mice. The Connatic values plain talk, so why sit here simpering with our fingers up our arses? Yes, yes, as you like. I'll hold my tongue." He squinted toward the Connatic. "I warn you, she'll use an hour to repeat what I gave you in twenty seconds."

Fausgard ignored the remark. "Sir, the Whisper Lemiste has spoken of our Centenary: this has been the primary purpose of our deputation. But other problems, to which Whisper Delfin has alluded, also exist, and perhaps we might also consider them at this time."

"By all means," said the Connatic. "It is my function to mitigate difficulties, if effectuation is fair, feasible and countenanced by Alastrid Basic Law."

Fausgard said earnestly, "Our problems can be expressed in very few words—"

Delfin could not restrain himself. "A single word is enough: immigrants! A thousand each week! Apes and lizards, airy aesthetes, languid ne'er-do-wells with nothing on their minds but girls and bonter. We are not allowed to halt them! Is it not absurd?"

Lemiste said smoothly: "Whisper Delfin is exuberant in his terms; many of the immigrants are worthy idealists. Still, many others are little better than parasites."

Delfin would not be denied. "Were they all saints, the flow must be halted! Would you believe it? An immigrant excluded me from my own apartment!"

Fausgard said wryly: "Here may be the source of Whisper Delfin's fervor."

Orgold spoke for the first time, in plangent disgust: "We sound like a gaggle of cackshaws."

The Connatic said reflectively: "A thousand a week in a population of three billion is not a large percentage."

Orgold replied in a business-like manner, which affected the Connatic more favorably than did Orgold's coarse and vaguely untidy appearance. "Our facilities already are overextended. At this moment we need eighteen new sturge plants—"

Lemiste helpfully inserted an annotation: " 'Sturge' is raw food-slurry."

"—a new deep layer of drains, tanks, and feeders, a thousand new blocks. The toil involved is tremendous. The Arrabins do not wish to devote whole lifetimes to toil. So steps must be taken. First, and perhaps least—if only to quiet Delfin—the influx of immigrants must be halted."

"Difficult," said the Connatic. "Basic Law guarantees freedom of movement."

Delfin cried out: "Egalism is envied across the Cluster! Since all Alastor cannot come to Arrabus, then egalism must be spread across the Cluster. This should be your immediate duty!"

The Connatic showed the trace of a somber smile. "I must study your ideas with care. At the moment their logic eludes me."

Delfin muttered under his breath, and swung sulkily sideways in his chair. He snapped across his shoulder: "The logic is the immigrants' feet; in their multitudes they march on Arrabus!"

"A thousand a week? Ten times as many Arrabins commit suicide."

"Nothing is thereby proved!"

The Connatic gave an indifferent shrug and turned a dispassionate inspection around the group. Odd, he reflected, that Orgold, Lemiste and Fausgard, while patently uninterested in Delfin's views, should allow him to act as spokesman, and to present absurd demands, thereby diminishing the dignity of them all. Lemiste's perceptions were perhaps the keenest of the group. He managed a deprecatory smile. "The Whispers are necessarily strong-minded, and we do not always agree on how best to solve our problems."

Fausgard said shortly: "Or even to identify them, for that matter."

Lemiste paid her no heed. "In essence, our machinery is obsolescent. We need new equipment, to produce more goods more efficiently."

"Are you then requesting a grant of money?"

"This certainly would help, on a continuing basis."

"Why not reclaim the lands to north and south? At one time they supported a population."

Lemiste gave his head a dubious shake. "Arrabins are an urban folk; we know nothing of agriculture."

The Connatic rose to his feet. "I will send expert investigators to Arrabus. They will analyze your situation and make recommendations."

Tension broke loose in Fausgard; she exclaimed sharply: "We don't want investigators or study commissions; they'll tell us: 'Do this! Do that!'—all contra-egalistic! We want no more competition and greed; we can't abandon our gains!"

"Be assured that I will personally study the matter," said the Connatic.

Orgold dropped his air of stolid detachment. "Then you will come to Wyst?"

"Remember," Lemiste called out cheerfully, "you are invited to participate at the Centenary!"

"I will consider the invitation most carefully. Now then, I noticed you showed only small interest in the collation I set forth; you might prefer a more adventurous cuisine, and I wish you to be my guests. Along the lower promenades are hundreds of excellent restaurants; please dine where you like and instruct the attendant to place all charges to the Connatic's account."

"Thank you," said Fausgard rather tersely. "That is most gracious."

The Connatic turned to go, then halted as if on sudden thought. "By the way, who is Jantiff Ravensroke?"

The Whispers stared at him in frozen attitudes of doubt and wonder. Lemiste said at last: "Jantiff Ravensroke? I do not recognize the name."

"Nor I!" cried Delfin, hoarse and truculent.

Fausgard numbly shook her head and Orgold merely gazed impassively at a point above the Connatic's head.

Lemiste asked: "Who is this 'Jantiff?'"

"A person who has corresponded with me; it is no great matter. If I visit Arrabus I will take the trouble to look him up. Good evening to you all."

His image moved into the shadows at the side of the room, and faded.

In the dressing room the Connatic removed his casque. "Esclavade?"

"Sir?"

"What do you think of the Whispers?"

"An odd group. I detect voice tremor in Fausgard and Lemiste. Orgold's assurance is impervious to tension. Delfin lacks all restraint. The name 'Jantiff Ravensroke' may not be unfamiliar to them."

"There is a mystery here," said the Connatic. "Certainly they did not travel all the way from Wyst to make a series of impossible proposals, quite at odds to their stated purposes."

"I agree. Something has altered their viewpoint."

"I wonder if there is a connection with Jantiff Ravensroke?"

CHAPTER 2

Jantiff Ravensroke had been born in comfortable circumstances at Frayness on Zeck, Alastor 503. His father, Lile Ravensroke, calibrated micrometers at the Institute of Molecular Design; his mother held a part-time job as technical analyst at Orion Instruments. Two sisters, Ferfan and Juille, specialized respectively in a sub-phase of condaptery* and the carving of mooring posts.†

At the junior academy Jantiff, a tall thin young man with a long bony face and lank black hair, trained first in graphic design, then, after a year, reoriented himself into chromatics and perceptual psychology. At senior school he threw himself into the history of creative imagery, despite the opinion of his family that he was spreading himself too thin. His father pointed out that he could not forever delay taking a specialty, that unrelated enthusiasms, while no doubt entertaining, would seem to merge into frivolity and even irresponsibility.

Jantiff listened with dutiful attention, but soon thereafter he chanced upon an old manual of landscape painting, which insisted that only natural pigments could adequately depict natural objects; and, further, that synthetic substances, being bogus and unnatural, subconsciously influenced the craftsman and inevitably falsified his work. Jantiff found the argument convincing and began to collect, grind and blend umbers and ochers, barks, roots, berries, the glands of fish and the secretions of nocturnal rodents, while his family looked on in amusement.

Lile Ravensroke again felt obliged to correct Jantiff's instability. He took an oblique approach to the topic. "I take it that you are not reconciled to a life of abject poverty?"

Jantiff, naturally mild and guileless, with occasional lapses into absent-mindedness, responded without hesitation: "Certainly not! I very much enjoy the good things of life!"

Lile Ravensroke went on, in a casual voice: "I expect that you intend to earn these good things not by crime or fraud but through your own good efforts?"

---

*From the Gaean *condaptriol*: the science of information management, which includes the more restricted field of cybernetics.

†Zeck is a world of a hundred thousand islands scattered across a hundred seas, inlets and channels; the single continent is mottled with lakes and waterways. Many families live aboard houseboats, and often own a sea-sailer as well. Mooring posts are ornate constructions, symbolic of status, profession, or special interests.

"Of course!" said Jantiff, now somewhat puzzled. "That goes without saying."

"Then how do you expect to profit from your training to date, which is to say, a smattering of this and an inkling of that? 'Expertise' is the word you must concentrate upon. Sure control over a special technique: this is how you put coin in your pocket!"

In a subdued voice Jantiff stated that he had not yet discovered a specialty which he felt would interest him across the entire span of his existence. Lile Ravensroke replied that to his almost certain knowledge no divine fiat had ever ordained that toil must be joyful or interesting. Aloud Jantiff acknowledged the rightness of his father's views, but privately clung to the hope that somehow he might turn his frivolity to profit.

Jantiff finished his term at senior school with no great distinction, and the summer recess lay before him. During these few brief months he must define the course of his future: specialized study at the lyceum, or perhaps apprenticeship as a technical draftsman. It seemed that youth, with all its joyful vagaries, lay definitely behind! In a morose mood Jantiff happened to pick up the old treatise on the depiction of landscapes, and there he encountered a tantalizing passage:

> For certain craftsmen, the depiction of landscapes becomes a life-long occupation. Many interesting examples of the craft exist. Remember: the depiction reflects not only the scene itself but the craftsman's private point of view!
>
> Another aspect to the craft must at least be mentioned: sunlight. The basic adjunct to the visual process varies from world to world, from a murky red glow to a crackling purple-white glare. Each of these lights makes necessary a different adjustment of the subjective-objective tension. Travel, especially trans-planetary travel, is a most valuable training for the depictive craftsman. He learns to look with a dispassionate eye; he clears away films of illusion and sees objects as they are.
>
> There is one world where sun and atmosphere cooperate to produce an absolutely glorious light, where every surface quivers with its true and just color. The sun is the white star Dwan and the fortunate world is Wyst, Alastor 1716.

Juille and Ferfan decided to cure Jantiff of his wayward moods. They diagnosed his problem as shyness, and introduced him to a succession of bold and sometimes boisterous girls, in the hope of enhancing his social life. The girls quickly became either bored, puzzled or uneasy. Jantiff was neither ill-favored, with his black hair, blue-green eyes, and almost aquiline profile, nor shy; nevertheless he lacked talent for small talk, and he suspected, justly

enough, that his unconventional yearnings would only excite derision were
he rash enough to discuss them.

To avoid a fashionable social function, Jantiff, without informing his
sisters, took himself off to the family houseboat, which was moored at a pier
on the Shard Sea. Fearful that either Juille or Ferfan or both might come
out to fetch him, Jantiff immediately cast off the mooring lines and drove
across Fallas Bay to the shallows, where he anchored his boat among the
reeds.

Solitude—peace at last, thought Jantiff. He boiled up a pot of tea, then
settled into a chair on the foredeck and watched the orange sun Mur settle
toward the horizon. A late-afternoon breeze rippled the water; a million
orange coruscations twinkled among the slender black reeds. Jantiff's mood
loosened; the quiet, wide sky, the play of sunlight on the water were balm
to his uncertain soul. If only he could capture the peace of this moment
and maintain it forever! Sadly he shook his head: life and time were inexorable; the moment must pass. A photograph was useless, and pigment
could never reproduce such space, such glitter and glow. Here in fact was
the very essence of his yearnings: he wanted to control that magic linkage
between the real and the unreal, the felt and the seen. He wanted to per-
vade himself with the secret meaning of things and use this lore as the
mood took him. These "secret meanings" were not necessarily profound or
subtle; they simply were what they were. Like the present circumstances
for instance: the mood of late afternoon, the boat among the reeds, with—
perhaps most important of all—the lonely figure on the deck. In his mind
Jantiff composed a depiction, and went so far as to select pigments . . . He
sighed and shook his head. An impractical idea. Even were he able to
achieve such a representation, what could he do with it? Hang it on a wall?
Absurd. Successive viewings would neutralize the effect as fast as repetition of a joke.

The sun sank; water moths fluttered among the reeds. From seaward came the sound of quiet voices in measured discussion. Jantiff listened intently, eery twinges coursing along his skin. No one could explain the sea-voices. If a person tried to drift stealthily near in a boat,
the sounds ceased. And the meaning, no matter how intently one listened, always just evaded intelligibility. The sea-voices had always
haunted Jantiff. Once, he had recorded the sounds, but when he played
them back, the sense was even more remote. Secret meanings, mused
Jantiff . . . He strained to listen. If he could comprehend, only a word so
as to pick up the gist, then he might understand everything. As if becoming aware of the eavesdropper, the voices fell silent, and night darkened
the sea.

Jantiff went into the cabin. He dined on bread, meat, and beer, then
returned to the deck. Stars blazed across the sky; Jantiff sat watching, his

mind adrift among the far places, naming those stars he recognized, speculating about others.* So much existed: so much to be felt and seen and
known! A single life was not enough . . . Across the water drifted a murmur
of voices, and Jantiff imagined pale shapes floating in the dark, watching
the stars . . . The voices dwindled and faded. Silence. Once more Jantiff
retreated into the cabin, where he boiled up another pot of tea.

Someone had left a copy of the *Transvoyer* on the table. Leafing
through the pages Jantiff's attention was caught by a heading:

THE ARRABIN CENTENARY:
A Remarkable Era of Social Innovation on
the Planet Wyst: Alastor 1716

Your Transvoyer correspondent visits Uncibal, the mighty city beside the sea. Here he discovers a dynamic society, propelled by novel philosophical energies. The Arrabin goal is human fulfillment, in a condition of leisure and amplitude. How has this miracle been accomplished? By a drastic revision of traditional priorities. To pretend that racks and stress do not exist would cheapen the Arrabin achievement, which shows no signs of flagging. The Arrabins are about to celebrate their first century. Our correspondent supplies the fascinating details.

Jantiff read the article with more than casual interest; Wyst rejoiced in the
remarkable light of the sun Dwan, where—how did the phrase go?—"every
surface quivers with its true and just color." He put the magazine aside, and
went once more out upon the deck. The stars had moved somewhat across
the sky; that constellation known locally as the "Shamizade" had risen in
the east and was reflected on the sea. Jantiff inspected the heavens, wondering which star was Dwan. Stepping back into the cabin, he consulted
the local edition of the *Alastor Almanac*, where Dwan was identified as a
dim white star in the Turtle constellation, along the edge of the carapace.†

Jantiff climbed to the top deck of the houseboat and scanned the sky.
There, to the north, under the Stator hung the Turtle, and there shone the
pale flicker of Dwan. Perhaps imagination played Jantiff tricks, but the star
indeed seemed charged with color.

---

*For the folk of Alastor Cluster, the stars are near and familiar, and "astronomy" (star-naming) is taught to all children. A knowledgeable person can name a thousand stars or more, with as many apposite anecdotes. Such star-namers in the olden times commanded great fame and prestige.
†It is no doubt unnecessary to point out that constellations as seen from one world of the Cluster differ from those of every other; accordingly, each world uses its local nomenclature. On the other hand, certain structural features of the Cluster—for instance, the Fiamifer, the Crystal Eel, Koon's Hole, the Good-bye Place—are terms in the common usage.

The information regarding Wyst might have been only of idle interest, had not Jantiff on the very next day noticed an advertisement sponsored by Central Space Transport Systems, announcing a promotional competition. For that depiction best illustrating the scenic charm of Zeck, the System would provide transportation to and from any world of the Cluster, with an additional three hundred ozols spending money. Jantiff instantly assembled panel and pigments and from memory rendered the shallows of the Shard Sea, with the houseboat at anchor among the reeds. Time was short; he worked in a fury of concentrated energy, and submitted the composition to the agency only minutes before the deadline.

Three days later he was notified, not altogether to his surprise, that he had won the grand prize.

Jantiff waited until evening to break the news to his family. They were astounded both that Jantiff's daubings could command value and that he yearned for far strange worlds. Jantiff tried earnestly to explain his motives. "Naturally I'm not unhappy at home; how could I be? I'm just at loose ends. I can't settle myself. I have the feeling that just out of sight, just past the corner of my eye, something new and shimmering and wonderful waits for me—if only I knew where to look!"

His mother sniffed. "Really, Jantiff, you're so fanciful."

Lile Ravensroke asked sadly: "Haven't you any ambition for a normal and ordinary life? No shimmering flapdoodle, just honest work and a happy home?"

"I don't know what my ambitions are! That's the entire difficulty. My best hope is to get away for a bit and see something of the Cluster. Then perhaps I'll be able to settle down."

His mother in distress cried, "You'll go far from here and make your career, and we'll never see you again!"

Jantiff gave an uneasy laugh. "Of course not. I plan nothing so stern! I'm restless and uneasy; I want to see how other people live so that I can decide how I want to live myself."

Lile Ravensroke said somberly: "When I was young I had similar notions. For better or worse, I put them aside and now I feel sure that I acted for the best. There's nothing out there that isn't better at home."

Ferfan said to Jantiff, "There'll never be sour-grass pie, or brunts, or shushings the way Mother cooks."

"I'm prepared to rough it for a bit. I might even like the exotic foods."

"Ugh," said Juille. "They all sound so odd and rank."

The group sat silent for a moment. Then: "If you feel you must go," said Lile Ravensroke, "our arguments won't dissuade you."

"It's really for the best," said Jantiff hollowly. "Then, when I come back, with the wander-dust off my heels, I'll hopefully be settled and definite, and you'll be proud of me."

"But Janty, we're proud of you now," said Ferfan without any great conviction.

Juille asked: "Where will you go, and what will you do?"

Jantiff spoke with spurious joviality: "Where will I go? Here, there, everywhere! And what will I do? Everything! Anything! All for the sake of experience. I'll try the carbuncle mines on Arcady; I'll visit the Connatic at Lusz; perhaps I'll drop at Arrabus and spend a few weeks with the emancipated folk."

"'Emancipated folk?'" growled Lile Ravensroke. "A twittering brook of dilly-bugs is more likely."

"Well, that's their claim. They only work thirteen hours a week, and it seems to agree with them."

Juille cried: "You'll settle in Arrabus and become emancipated and we'll never see you again!"

"My dear girl, there is not the slightest chance of such a thing."

"Then don't go to Wyst! The *Transvoyer* article said that people arrive from everywhere and never leave."

Ferfan, who also cherished secret dreams of travel, said wistfully: "If it's such a wonderful place, perhaps we'd all better go there."

Her father laughed humorlessly. "I can't spare the time from work."

CHAPTER 3

A rriving at Uncibal on a rainy night Jantiff was reminded of a paragraph in the *Alastrid Gazeteer*: "Across many years wise travelers have learned to discount their first impression of a new environment. Such judgments are derived from previous experience in previous places and are infallibly distorted." On this dismal evening Uncibal Spaceport lacked every quaint or charming quality, and Jantiff wondered why a system which for a century had gratified uncounted Arrabins could not better promote the comfort of a relatively few visitors.

Two hundred and fifty passengers, debarking from the spaceships, found themselves alone in the gloom, a quarter-mile from a line of low blue lights which presumably marked the terminal building. Muttering and grumbling, the passengers squelched off through the puddles.*

Jantiff walked to the side of the straggling troop, thrilling to contact with alien soil. From the direction of Uncibal drifted a waft of odor, oddly

*See Glossary, ii.

sour and heavy, yet half-familiar, which only served to emphasize the strangeness of the world Wyst.

At the terminal a droning voice addressed the newcomers: "Welcome to Arrabus. We distinguish three types of visitors: first, commercial representatives and tourists intending brief visits; second, persons planning sojourns of less than a year; third, immigrants. Please form orderly queues at the designated doorways. Attention: the import of foodstuffs is prohibited. All such items must be surrendered at the Contraband Property desk. Welcome to Arrabus. We distinguish three types of visitors . . ."

Jantiff pushed through the crowds; apparently several hundred arrivals from a previous ship still waited in the reception hall. Eventually he discovered the file marked 2, which snaked back and forth across the room in a most confusing manner, and took his place in the line. Most arriving persons, he noted, intended immigration, and the queue in File 3 stretched several times as far as that in File 2. The queue in File 1 was very short indeed.

Step by sidling step Jantiff crossed the room. At the far end an array of eight wickets controlled the movement of the new arrivals, but only two of these wickets were in operation. A corpulent man, immediately behind Jantiff, thought to hasten the motion of the line by standing close to Jantiff and pressing with his belly. When Jantiff, to avoid the contact, moved as close as convenient to the person ahead, the corpulent man promptly inched forward, to squeeze Jantiff even more closely. The man ahead at last looked around at Jantiff and said in a cold voice: "Really, sir, I am as anxious as you to negotiate this file; no matter how you press the line moves no faster."

Jantiff could offer no explanation which would not offend the corpulent man, who now stood so close that his breath warmed Jantiff's cheek. Finally, when the man ahead stepped forward, Jantiff resolutely held his ground, despite the fat man's breathing and jostling.

Ultimately Jantiff arrived at the wicket, where he presented his landing pass. The clerk, a young woman with extravagant puffs of blond hair over her ear, thrust it aside. "That's not correct! Where is your green clearance card?"

Jantiff fumbled through his pockets. "I don't seem to have any green card. They gave me no such document."

"Sir, you'll have to go back to the ship for your green clearance card."

Jantiff chanced to notice that the fat man carried a white card similar to his own. In desperation he said: "This man here has no green card either."

"That's a matter of no relevance. I can't allow you entry unless you present the proper documents."

"This was all they gave me; surely it's sufficient?"

"Sir, please, you're obstructing the line."

In numb dismay Jantiff stared at his white card. "It says here, 'Landing pass and clearance card.' "

The clerk looked at it sidelong, and made a clicking sound with her tongue. She went to the second booth and conferred with the clerk, who made a telephone call.

The blond girl returned to the wicket. "This is a new form; it was introduced only last month. I haven't drudged this office for a year and I've been sending everyone back to the ship. Your questionnaire, please—no, the blue sheet."

Jantiff produced the proper document: an intricate form which he had painstakingly completed.

"Hm . . . Jantiff Ravensroke . . . Frayness, on Zeck. Occupation: technical graphics expert. Reason for visit: curiosity." She glanced at him with raised eyebrows. "Curiosity? About what?"

Jantiff hurriedly said: "I want to study the Arrabin social system."

"Then you should have written 'study.' "

"I'll change it."

"No, you can't alter the document; you'll have to fill out a new form. Somewhere in the outer chambers you'll find blank forms and a desk; at least that's how it went a year ago."

"Wait!" cried Jantiff. "After 'curiosity' I'll write: 'about Arrabin social system.' There's plenty of room, and that's not alteration."

"Oh, very well. It's not regular, of course."

Jantiff quickly made the entry and the clerk reached for the validation stamp. A gong sounded; she dropped the stamp, rose to her feet and went to the back of the wicket where she tossed a cape around her shoulders. A young man entered the wicket: round-faced, boyish, his eyelids drooping as if from lack of sleep. "Here I am!" he told the blond girl. "A trifle late, but that's not too bad; I've only just returned from a swill at Serce and directly to drudge. Still, I might as well recover on drudge as off. Come to think, it's the best way."

"Lucky you. I'm low tomorrow. I'll probably draw sanitation or greasing the rollers."

"I drew a shoe machine last week; it's really rather amusing once you learn which handles to pull. Halfway through my stint the circuits went wrong and the shoes all came away with funny big toes. I sent them on anyway, in hopes of launching a new style. Think of it! Maybe I'll be famous!"

"Small chance. Who wants to wear funny shoes with big toes?"

"Somebody had better want to wear them; they've gone into boxes."

The fat man called over Jantiff's shoulder: "Can't we hurry things just a bit? Everyone's anxious to rest and have a bite of food."

The two clerks turned him identical stares of blank incomprehension. The girl picked up her handbag. "Off to bed for me. I'm too tired even to copulate."

"I know those days . . . Well, I suppose I'd better be earning my gruff." He stepped forward and picked up Jantiff's papers. "Now then, let's see . . . First, I'll need your green entry card."

"I don't have any green card."

"No green card? Then, my friend, you'd better get one. I know that much, at least. Just run back to the ship and locate the purser; he'll fix you up in a jiffy."

"This white card supersedes the green card."

"Oh, is that how they do it now? Good enough then. So now, what else? The blue questionnaire: I won't bother with that; it's boring for both of us. You'll want a housing assignment. Do you have any preferences?"

"Not really. Where would you suggest?"

"Uncibal, of course. Here's a decent location." He gave Jantiff a metal disk. "Go to Block 17-882 and show this disk to the floor clerk." He lifted the stamp and gave Jantiff's papers a resounding blow. "There you are, my friend! I wish you the enjoyment of your bed, the digestion of your gruff, and lucky draws from the drudge barrel."

"Thank you. Can I spend the night in the hotel? Or must I go to Block 17-whatever-it-is?"

"The Travelers Inn by all means, if you've got the ozols.* The man-ways are wet tonight. It's no time to be seeking out a block."

The Travelers Inn, an ancient bulk with a dozen wings and annexes, stood directly opposite the terminal exit. Jantiff entered the lobby and applied at the desk for a chamber. The clerk handed him a key: "That will be seven ozols, sir."

Jantiff leaned back aghast. "Seven ozols? For one room with one bed? For a single night?"

"Correct, sir."

Jantiff reluctantly paid over the money. When he saw the chamber he became more indignant than ever; in Frayness such a room would be considered minimal and rent for an ozol or less.

Returning downstairs to the restaurant, Jantiff seated himself at one of the enameled concrete counters. An attendant placed a covered tray in front of him.

"Not so fast," said Jantiff. "Let me look at the menu."

"No menu here, my friend. It's gruff and deedle, with a bit of wobbly to fill in the chinks. We all eat alike."

*Ozols: a monetary unit roughly equivalent to the Gaean SVU: the value of an adult's unskilled labor under standard conditions for the duration of an hour.

Jantiff lifted the cover from the tray; he found four cakes of baked brown dough, a mug of white liquid, and a bowl of yellow paste. Jantiff tasted the "gruff"; the flavor was mild and not unpleasant. The "deedle" was tart and faintly astringent, while the "wobbly" seemed a simple custard.

Jantiff finished his meal and the attendant gave him a slip of paper. "Please pay at the main desk."

Jantiff glanced at the slip in wonder. "Two ozols. Can this price be correct?"

"The price may not be 'correct,' " said the attendant. "Still it's the price we exact here at the Travelers Inn."

A cavernous bathroom was shared by both sexes, personal modesty having succumbed to egalism. Jantiff diffidently made use of the facilities, wondering what his mother would say, then thankfully retired to his chamber.

In the morning, after Wyst's short night, Jantiff rose from his bed to find Dwan already halfway up the sky. Jantiff looked out across the city in great interest, studying the play of light among the blocks and along the man-ways. Each of the blocks showed a different color, and, possibly because Jantiff was bringing to bear an expectant vision, the colors seemed peculiarly rich and clean, as if they had just been washed.

Jantiff dressed and, descending to the ground floor, took advice from the desk clerk as to the location of Block 17-882. Giving the restaurant and its two-ozol breakfast a wide berth, Jantiff set off along the man-way: a sliding surface thronged with Arrabins, rapid toward the center, slow at the edges.

Dwan-light illuminated the city-scape to either side in a manner Jantiff found entrancing, and his spirits rose.

The man-way curved westward; the blocks in lines to right and left marched away to the horizon, dwindling to points. Laterals poured human streams upon the man-way; Jantiff had never imagined such vast crowds: a marvelous spectacle in itself! The city Uncibal must be reckoned one of the wonders of the Gaean universe! Across his course at right angles slid another of the mighty Arrabin man-rivers: a pair of boulevards flowing in opposite directions. Jantiff glimpsed rank behind rank of men and women riding with faces curiously serene.

The man-way swerved and joined another, larger man-way. Jantiff began to watch the overhanging signs which gave warning of lead-offs. He diverted to a slow neighborhood feeder and presently stepped off in front of a weathered pink block, two hundred feet square and twenty-three stories high. Block 17-882, his designated home.

Jantiff paused to inspect the face of the structure. The surface paint, peeling off in areas, showed blotches of pink, old rose and pale pink which gave the block a raffish and restless air, in contrast to its neighbor, which was painted a supercilious blue. Jantiff found the color congenial and congratulated himself on the lucky chance of his allotment. Like all the other blocks, the walls showed no windows, nor any openings except for the entrance. Over the parapet surrounding the roof hung foliage from the roof garden. Constant traffic passed in and out of the portal: men, women and a few children, in identical garments, of colors somewhat too garish for Jantiff's taste, as if the folk were dressed for a carnival. Their faces likewise were gay; they laughed and chattered and walked jauntily; Jantiff's spirits rose to look at them, and his misgivings began to dwindle.

Jantiff passed into the lobby and approached the desk. He presented his requisition to the clerk, a short round-bodied man with gingery hair arranged in ear-puffs and elaborate love-locks. The round cheerful face instantly became petulant. "My aching bowels! Is it yet another immigrant?"

"No, indeed," said Jantiff with dignity. "I am a visitor."

"What's the odds? You're one more cup of water in the full bucket. Why don't you start an Egalism Society on your own world?"

Jantiff replied politely: "People aren't so inclined on Zeck."

"Neither Zeck nor the whole elitist covey! We can't absorb their ne'er-do-wells indefinitely. Our machines break down, so what happens when the sturge stops and there's no more wump? We'll all go hungry together."

Jantiff's jaw dropped. "Are there really that many immigrants?"

"Too true! A thousand each and every week!"

"But surely some of them leave?"

"Not enough! Only six hundred, or hopefully seven; still, hope won't mend machines." He handed Jantiff a key. "Your roommate will show you the wumper, and explain the rules. You'll receive a drudge schedule this afternoon."

Jantiff said tentatively: "I'd prefer a single apartment, if any are available."

"You've got a single apartment," said the clerk. "It comes with two beds. If the population rises another billion we'll put in hammocks. Floor 19, Apartment D 18. I'll call up and mention that you're coming."

The ascensor conveyed Jantiff to the nineteenth floor. He found Corridor D and presently arrived at Apartment 18. He hesitated, raised his hand to knock, then decided that under the circumstances he was entitled to effect his own entry; accordingly he touched his key to the latch plate. The door slid aside to reveal a sitting room furnished with a pair of low couches, a table, a set of cases and a wall screen. A patterned beige and black rug covered the floor; from the ceiling hung a dozen globes fashioned from wire and colored paper. On one of the couches sat a man and a woman, both considerably older than Jantiff.

Jantiff stepped forward, feeling a trifle sheepish. "I'm Jantiff Ravensroke, and I've been assigned to this apartment."

The man and the woman showed gracious smiles and jumped smartly to their feet. (Later, when Jantiff recalled his sojourn at Uncibal, he never failed to reflect upon the careful etiquette by which the Arrabins eased the circumstances of their lives.)

The man was tall and elegant, with a fine straight nose and flashing eyes. He wore his black hair in glossy ear-puffs, with artful cusps down the forehead; of the two he seemed the more forthright. He gave Jantiff a friendly salute which conveyed nothing of the desk clerk's disapproval. "Welcome to Arrabus, Jantiff! Welcome to Old Pink and to this excellent apartment!"

"Thank you very much," said Jantiff. This affable and intelligent man was evidently to be his roommate and Jantiff's misgivings dissolved.

"Allow me to perform the introductions. This lady is the miraculous Skorlet, a person of charm and capability, and I am Esteban."

Skorlet spoke in a quick husky voice: "You seem clean and quiet, and I'm sure that we'll have no difficulties. Please don't whistle in the apartment, or inquire the purpose of my work more than once, or belch loudly. I can't abide a belching man."

With an effort Jantiff maintained his sangfroid. Here was a situation which he had not anticipated. With desperate facility he said: "I'll keep your remarks very much in mind." He surveyed Skorlet from the corner of his eye. An introverted woman, he thought, perhaps a bit tense. She stood almost as tall as he was with rather heavy arms and legs. Her face was pale and round; her features were unremarkable except for the eyes glowing under strong black eyebrows. She wore her ear-puffs small, with black curls piled in a heap above: a woman neither comely nor yet repulsive. She might not be so easy a roommate as Esteban, however. He said: "I hope you won't find me too difficult."

"I'm sure not. You seem a nice lad. Esteban, borrow three mugs from the wumper; I'll pour out a taste of swill* to mark the occasion. You brought in a pack or two of bonter, or so I hope?"

"Sorry," said Jantiff. "The idea never occurred to me."

Esteban went off on his errand; Skorlet rummaged under the case and brought out a jug. "Please don't think me non-mutual.† I just can't believe that an occasional jug of swill will destroy Arrabus. You're sure there's not even a trace of bonter in your luggage?"

"I don't carry any luggage; only this handbag."

"Pity. There's nothing like pickles and pepper sausage to advance the swill. While we're waiting, I'll show you your bed."

---

*The illicit Arrabin intoxicant: a heavy beer prepared from salvaged gruff, industrial glucose and sometimes tar-pods from the roof garden.

†Mutuality: the Arrabin code of conduct, with force deriving not from abstraction, or tradition, but from mutuality of interest.

Jantiff followed her into a small square chamber, furnished with two wardrobes, two cases, a table, now cluttered with Skorlet's small belongings, and two cots separated by a flimsy curtain. Skorlet brushed the trinkets to one side of the table. "Your half," she said, "and your bed." She jerked her thumb. "During my drudge the apartment is at your disposal, should you wish to entertain a friend, and vice versa. Things work out well unless we draw the same stint, but that's not too often."

"Aha, yes, I see," said Jantiff.

Esteban returned with three blue glass mugs; Skorlet solemnly poured them full. "To the Centenary!" she called in a brassy voice. "May the Connatic do his duty!"

Jantiff drank down the murky liquid and controlled a grimace at the aftertaste, which he associated with mice and old mattresses.

"Very bold," said Esteban approvingly. "Very bold indeed. You have an active thumb for the swill!"

"Yes, very good," said Jantiff. "And when does the Centenary occur?"

"Shortly—a matter of a few months. There's to be a simply explosive festival, with free games and dancing along the ways, and probably no end of swill. I'll surely put down a good supply. Esteban, can't you scrounge me a dozen jugs?"

"My dear, I've drawn the vitamin stint only once, and the Mutual stood right on top of me, watching my every move. I was lucky to capture the two of them."

"Then we must do without swill."

"Can't you use a plastic bag?" Jantiff suggested. "After all, the container need not be rigid."

Esteban ruefully shook his head. "It's been tried many times; our plastic bags all leak."

Skorlet said: "Old Sarp has a jug which he's too parsimonious to use. I'll have Kedidah put the snerge on it. That's three jugs at least. Now where's the gruff?"

"I'll contribute from lunch," said Esteban.

"If it's needed," said Jantiff, "I will too."

Skorlet looked at him approvingly. "That's the spirit! Who said the immigrants are lampreys sucking our juices? Not the case with Jantiff!"

Esteban said meditatively: "I know a chap in Purple Vendetta who taps sturge from the pipe and he makes a very fierce swill indeed. I might just promote a bucket or two of raw sturge; it's worth the experiment."

Jantiff asked: "What is 'sturge'?"

"Simple food pulp. It's piped out from the central plant. In the kitchen it magically becomes gruff, deedle and wobbly. No reason why it shouldn't make good swill."

Skorlet carefully poured each of the three mugs half-full. "Well—once again to the Festival, and may the Connatic put all would-be immigrants to work making pickles and pepper sausage, for consignment to Uncibal!"

"And let the Propuncers gnaw last week's gruff!"

"Save some for the Connatic. He can be as egal as the rest of us."

"Oh, he'll dine on bonter at the Travelers Inn; no fear of that."

Jantiff asked: "Is the Connatic actually coming to the Festival?"

Skorlet shrugged. "The Whispers are going out to Lusz to invite him, but who knows what he'll say?"

"He won't come," said Esteban. "Total fool he'd feel at the ceremony, with everybody screaming 'Hurrah for egalism!' and 'Egalism for the Cluster!'"

"And 'Low drudge for the Connatic, just like the rest of us!'"

"Exactly. What could he say?"

"Oh, something like, 'My dear subjects, I'm disappointed that you haven't laid red velvet along Uncibal River for my delicate feet. Now it's not well known, and I'd never reveal it anywhere but here on Arrabus, but I'm actually a chwig.* I command that you fill me a tank with your best bonter."

Half-amused, half-scandalized, Jantiff protested: "Really, you do him injustice! He lives a most sedate life!"

Skorlet sneered. "That's all smarm from his Bureau of Acclamation. Who knows what the Connatic's really like?"

Esteban drained his blue glass mug and looked in calculation toward the jug.

"We all know that the Connatic often disappears from Lusz. Now I've heard—this is admittedly rumor, but where there's smoke there's fire—that during these exact intervals, and only during these intervals, Bosko Boskowitz† makes his depredations. This correspondence has been thoroughly researched, so I've heard, and there's no doubt about it."

"Interesting!" said Skorlet. "Doesn't Bosko Boskowitz maintain a secret palace among the starments staffed only with beautiful children, who must obey his every whim?"

"That's the case! And isn't it odd that the Whelm never interferes with Bosko Boskowitz?"

"More than odd! That's why I say: 'Egalism across the Cluster!'"

Jantiff said in disgust: "I don't believe a word of it."

Skorlet laughed her gloomy laugh. "You're young and naïve."

"As to that I can't say."

*Reference to a peculiar vice associated with food, encountered almost exclusively on Wyst.
†An almost fabulous starmenter, guilty of the most atrocious ravages. See Glossary, iii.

"No matter." Skorlet peered into the jug. "I suppose we might as well put a term to it."

"Excellent idea!" declared Esteban. "The strength is always at the bottom of the jug."

Skorlet raised her head. "No time now; there goes the gong. Let's go for wump. Then, afterwards, why not conduct our new friend around the city?"

"Certainly. I'm always ready for a promenade! It's a fine day after the rain. And what of Tanzel? We could pick her up along the way."

"Yes, of course. Poor little dear; I haven't seen her for days. I'll call her right now." She went to the screen, but pushed buttons in vain. "It still won't go! Idiotic thing! There's been maintenance on it twice!"

Jantiff went to the screen, touched the buttons, listened. He slipped up the retainer ring and lowered the screen upon its hinge.

Skorlet and Esteban came to look over his shoulder. "Do you understand these things?"

"Not really. As children, we're trained to elementary circuits, but I haven't gone much further. Still, this is very simple equipment; all plug-ins, and the telltale shows when they're bad . . . Hm. These are all in order. Look here; this filter bank isn't slotted accurately. Try now."

The screen glowed. Skorlet said bitterly: "The maintenance fellow studied his instruction book for two hours and still couldn't do the job."

"Oh well," said Esteban, "he was just someone like me on high drudge."

Skorlet merely gave a sour grunt. She touched buttons, and spoke to the woman whose face appeared. "Tanzel, please."

A girl nine or ten years old looked forth from the screen. "Hallo, Mother. Hallo, Father."

"We're dropping by in about an hour, and we'll go for a nice promenade. Will you be ready?"

"Oh, yes! I'll wait in front."

"Good! In just about an hour."

The three turned to go. Jantiff stopped short. "I'll just put my bag in the wardrobe; no harm starting out tidy at least."

Esteban clapped Jantiff on the shoulder. "I think you've got a jewel here, Skorlet."

"Oh, I suppose he'll do."

As they walked along the corridor Jantiff asked, "What happened to your last roommate?"

"I don't know," said Skorlet. "She went out one day and never came back."

"How strange!"

"I suppose so. No one ever knows what's in another person's mind. Here's the wumper."

The three entered a long wide room, lined with tables and benches, and already filled with chattering residents of Level 19. An attendant punched their apartment numbers into a register; the three took covered trays from a dispenser and went to a table. The tray contained exactly the same rations Jantiff had been served the previous evening at the Travelers Inn.

Skorlet put a cake of gruff to the side. "For our next swill."

Esteban with an expression of whimsical grief did likewise. "For swill, any sacrifice is worthy."

"Here's mine," said Jantiff. "I insist on contributing."

Skorlet gathered the three cakes together. "I'll take them back to the apartment, and we'll all just pretend that we've eaten them."

Esteban jumped to his feet. "A good idea, but let me! I'll be glad to run the errand."

"Don't be silly," said Skorlet. "It's only a step or two."

Esteban said, laughing, "We'll both go, if you're so stubborn."

Jantiff looked from one to the other, bemused, "Is it really such a point of courtesy? I'll come too, in that case."

Esteban sighed and shook his head. "Of course not. Skorlet is merely a wayward person . . . None of us will go."

Skorlet shrugged. "As you wish."

Jantiff said, "We can easily restrain our appetites. At least I can. And we'll drop off the gruff on our way out."

"Of course," said Esteban. "That's the fair way."

Jantiff wondered at the exquisite nicety of Esteban's politesse.

"Eat the wump and shut up," said Skorlet.

The meal was taken in silence. Jantiff inspected his fellow residents with interest. There was no reserve and anonymity; everyone seemed to know everyone else; cheerful greetings, banter, allusion to social events and mutual friends rang around the room. A slender girl with fine honey-colored hair paused beside Skorlet and whispered something in her ear, with an arch side-glance toward Jantiff. Skorlet gave a dreary laugh. "Go on with you! It's all nonsense, as well you know!"

The girl went on to a nearby table, where she joined friends. Jantiff thought her slender round body, her charming features and her saucy spontaneity all attractive, but made no comment.

Skorlet noticed the direction of his gaze. "That's Kedidah. The old sandpiper yonder is Sarp, her roommate. He tries to copulate a dozen times a day, which makes for an inconvenient roommate; after all, one's social life is usually elsewhere. She just offered to trade you for Sarp, but I wouldn't hear of it. Esteban is always handy when I'm in the mood, which perhaps isn't as often as it should be."

Jantiff, spooning up his wobbly, forbore comment.

Upon leaving the refectory, the three stopped by the apartment where Skorlet dropped off the three cakes of gruff. Skorlet turned to Jantiff. "Are you ready?"

"I'm just debating whether to bring my camera. My family wants photographs by the dozen."

"Better not this time," said Esteban. "Wait till you know the ropes. Then you can get some really dramatic photographs. And also you'll have learned to cope with the, alas, all too prevalent snergery."

"'Snergery'? What is that?"

"Theft, to put it bluntly. Arrabus abounds with snerges. Haven't you heard?"

Jantiff shook his head. "I can't understand why anyone should steal under egalism."

Esteban laughed. "Snerging ensures egalism. It's a very direct remedy against anyone accumulating goods. In Arrabus we share and share alike."

"I can't understand the logic in all this," said Jantiff, but neither Esteban nor Skorlet showed any interest in pursuing the topic.

The three proceeded to the man-way and rode half a mile to the district crèche, where Tanzel waited: a pretty wisp of a girl with Skorlet's round face, Esteban's fine features and a thoughtful intelligence all her own. She greeted Skorlet and Esteban with restrained affection, and Jantiff with quite obvious curiosity. After a few moments of covert inspection, she told him: "Really, you look much like the rest of us!"

"Of course! How did you expect me to look?"

"Like a cannibal, or an exploiter, or maybe one of their victims."

"What odd ideas!" said Jantiff. "On Zeck at least no one would care to be thought an exploiter, much less a victim."

"Then why did you come to Arrabus?"

"That's a hard question," said Jantiff somberly. "I'm not sure that I know the answer myself. At home too much pressed on me, while all the time I searched for something I couldn't find. I needed to get away and order my mind."

Esteban and Skorlet had been listening to the conversation with distant half-smiles. Esteban inquired in a light voice: "And then, when your mind has been ordered?"

"This is what I don't know. In essence I want to create something remarkable and beautiful, something that is my very own . . . I want to indicate the mysteries of life. I don't hope to explain them, mind you; I wouldn't, even if I could. I want to reveal their dimensions and their wonder, for people who are interested or even people who aren't . . . I'm afraid I don't explain myself very well."

Skorlet said in a rather cool voice, "You explain well enough, but no one quite understands."

Tanzel, listening with knitted eyebrows, said: "I understand a little of what he's saying, I wonder about these mysteries too. For instance, why am I me, and not somebody else?"

Skorlet said roughly: "You'll wear your brain out, thinking along those lines."

Esteban told her earnestly: "Remember, my dear, that Jantiff isn't an egalist like the rest of us; he wants to do something quite extraordinary and individualistic."

"Yes, partly that," said Jantiff, wishing that he had never ventured an opinion. "But it's more like this: here I am, born into life with certain capabilities. If I don't use these capabilities and achieve my utmost then I'm cheating myself, and living a soiled life."

"Hmm," said Tanzel sagely. "If everyone were like you, the world would be a very nervous place."

Jantiff gave an embarrassed laugh. "No cause for worry; there don't seem to be many people like me."

Tanzel gave her shoulders a jerk of somber disinterest, and Jantiff was pleased to drop the subject. A moment later her mood changed; she tugged at Jantiff's sleeve and pointed ahead. "There's Uncibal River! I do so love watching from the bridge! Oh, please come, everyone! Over to the deck!"

Tanzel ran out upon the prospect deck. The others followed more sedately, and all stood leaning on the rail as Uncibal River passed below; a pair of slideways, each a hundred feet wide, crowded close with the folk of Arrabus. Tanzel told Jantiff excitedly: "If you stand here long enough, you'll see everyone in the world!"

"That of course isn't true," said Skorlet crisply, as if she did not altogether approve of Tanzel's fancies.

Below passed the Arrabins: folk of all ages, faces serene and easy, as if they walked alone, rapt in contemplation. Occasionally someone might raise his eyes to look at the line of faces along the deck; for the most part the crowds passed below oblivious to those who watched from above.

Esteban began to show signs of restlessness. He straightened, slapped the rails and, with a thoughtful glance toward the sky, said: "Perhaps I'd better be moving along. My friend Hester will be expecting me."

Skorlet's black eyes glittered. "There is no need whatever for you to rush off."

"Well, in a way—"

"Which route do you go?"

"Oh—just along the river."

"We'll all go together and take you to Hester's block. She's at the Tesseract, I believe."

Dignity struggling with annoyance, Esteban said curtly, "Shall we move along then?"

A ramp curved down and around to the boarding platform; they stepped out into the crowd and were carried away to the west. As they moved across to the faster lanes, Jantiff discovered an odd effect. When he looked over his shoulder to the right, faces in his immediate vicinity receded and fell away into the blur. When he looked back to his left, the faces surged up from nowhere, drew abreast and passed ahead into an equally anonymous beyond. The effect was disturbing for reasons he could not precisely define; he began to feel vertigo and turned away to face forward, to watch the blocks move past, each a different color: pinks and browns and yellows; greens of every description: moss, mottled green-white, cadaverous blue-green, black-green; faded reds and orange-purples—all augmented to a state of clarity by the Dwan-light.

Jantiff became interested in the colors. Each no doubt exerted a symbolic influence upon those who lived with them. Peach, blotched with stump-water tan—who chose these colors? What canons were involved? Lavender-white, blue, acid green—on and on, each color no doubt dear to the folk who lived there . . . Tanzel tugged at his elbow. Jantiff looked around to see Esteban moving swiftly away to the right. Tanzel said somberly: "He just remembered an important engagement; he asked me to express his regrets to you."

Skorlet, her face flushed with annoyance, stepped smartly past. "Something I've got to do! I'll see you later!" She likewise was gone through the crowd, and Jantiff was left with Tanzel. He looked at her in bewilderment. "Where did they go so suddenly?"

"I don't know, but let's go on. I could ride Uncibal River forever!"

"I think we'd better go back. Do you know the way?"

"Of course! We just revert to Disselberg River, then cross to 112th Lateral."

"You show me the way. I've had enough promenading for the day. Strange that both Esteban and Skorlet decided to leave so suddenly!"

"I suppose so," said Tanzel. "But I've come to expect strange things . . . Well, if you want to go back, we'll take the next turnaround."

As they rode Jantiff gave his attention to Tanzel: an appealing little creature, so he decided. He asked if she enjoyed her school. Tanzel shrugged. "I'd have to drudge otherwise, so I learn counting, reading and ontology. Next year I'll be into personal dynamics, and that's more fun. We learn how to express ourselves and dramatize. Did you go to school?"

"Yes, indeed: sixteen long years."

"What did you learn?"

"An amazing variety of facts and topics."

"And then you went out to drudge?"

"No, not yet. I haven't found anything I really want to do."

"I don't suppose you live at all egalistically."

"Not as you do here. Everyone works much harder; but most everyone enjoys his work."

"But not you."

Jantiff gave an embarrassed laugh. "I'm willing to work very hard, but I don't quite know how. My sister Ferfan carves mooring posts. Perhaps I'll do something like that."

Tanzel nodded. "Someday let's talk again. There's the crèche; I'll turn off here. Your block is straight along; it's Old Pink, on the left. Goodbye."

Jantiff proceeded along the man-way and presently saw ahead that block which he now must consider "home": Old Pink.

He entered, ascended to Level 19 and sauntered around the corridor to his apartment. He opened the door and tactfully called out: "I'm home. It's Jantiff!"

No response. The apartment was empty. Jantiff entered and slid the door shut. He stood for a moment wondering what to do with himself. Still two hours until dinner. Another ration of gruff, deedle, and wobbly. Jantiff grimaced. The globes of paper and wire caught his eye; he went to examine them. Their function was not at all clear. The paper was green flimsy, the wire had been salvaged from another operation. Perhaps Skorlet intended to decorate the apartment with gay green bubbles. If so, thought Jantiff, her achievement was remarkably slipshod.* Well, so long as they pleased Skorlet, it was none of his affair. He looked into the bedroom, to appraise the two cots and the not-too-adequate curtain. Jantiff wondered what his mother would say. Certainly nothing congratulatory. Well, this was why he had come traveling, to explore other ways and other customs. Though for a fact, since matters were so casual he would definitely have preferred the young woman—what was her name? Kedidah?—whom he had noticed in the refectory.

He decided to unpack his satchel and went to the wardrobe where he had left it. He looked down in consternation. The lock was broken; the lid was askew. Opening the case, Jantiff examined the contents. His few clothes apparently had not been molested, except for his spare shoes, of fine gray lantile. These were missing, as well as his pigments and pad, his camera and recorder, a dozen other small implements. Jantiff went slowly into the sitting room and sank into a chair.

*Jantiff would later learn that many folk furnished their apartments in unique, or even bizarre, styles, scrounging and pilfering materials over a period of years, and spending immense effort to achieve some special effect. Such apartments were generally considered unegalistic, and those who lived there often incurred derision.

A brief few minutes later Skorlet entered the apartment. Jantiff thought that she looked in a very bad mood, with her black eyes glittering and her mouth set in a hard line. Her voice crackled as she spoke: "How long have you been here?"

"Five or ten minutes."

"Kindergoff Lateral was down to the contractors," she said bitterly. "I had to walk an entire mile."

"While we were gone someone broke into my case and stole most of my things."

The news seemed to drive Skorlet close to the limits of self-control. "And what do you expect?" she snapped in an unpleasantly harsh voice. "This is an egalistic country; why should you have more than anyone else?"

"I have been over-egalized," said Jantiff drily. "To the effect that I now have less than anyone else."

"Those are problems you must learn to cope with," said Skorlet and marched into the bedroom.

A few days later Jantiff wrote a letter to his family:

My dearest mother, father and sisters:
   I am now established in what must be the most remarkable nation of Alastor Cluster: Arrabus of Wyst. I inhabit a two-room apartment in close contiguity to a handsome woman with strong views on egalism. She doesn't approve of me particularly. However, she is civil and on occasion helpful. Her name is Skorlet. You may wonder at this unconventional arrangement; it is really quite simple. Egalism refuses to recognize sexual differences. One person is considered equal to every other, in all respects. To emphasize sexual differences is called "sexivation." For a girl to primp or show her figure to best advantage is "sexivation" and it is considered a serious offense.
   The apartments were originally intended to house male or female couples, or mated couples, but the philosophy was denounced as "sexivationist," and apartment assignments are now made at random, though often persons will trade about. Anyone coming to Arrabus must leave his prejudices behind! Already I have learned that, no matter what the apparent similarities of a new place to one's home, the stranger must not be misled! *Things are never what they seem!* Think of this! And think of all the Cluster worlds and all the Gaean Reach, and the Erdic Realms, and the Primarchic! Think of these trillions of folk, each with his singular face! A frightening thought, really. Still I am much impressed by Arrabus. The system works; there is no desire for change. The Arrabins seem happy and content, or at the very least, passive. They place their highest value upon leisure, at the expense of personal

possessions, good food, and a certain degree of freedom. They are far from well educated, and no one has expertise in any specific field. Maintenance and repairs are done by whomever is assigned the job, or in serious cases, to contracting firms from the Weirdlands. (These are the provinces to north and south. They are not nations; I doubt if they have any formal government whatever, but I don't know much about them.)

I have not been able to do any serious work because my apparatus has been stolen. Skorlet considers this quite normal and cannot understand my distress. She jeers at my "anti-egalism." Well, so be it. As I say, the Arrabins are a strange folk, who become excited only by food—not their usual "wump" but good natural food; in fact an acquaintance by the name of Esteban has mentioned one or two vices so odd and repellent as to be unspeakable, and I will say no more.

The block where I live is known as "Old Pink" because of its eczematous color. Each block, ostensibly identical to all others, is vividly distinctive, at least in the minds of the folk who live there, and they will characterize the blocks as "dreary," "frivolous," "teeming with sly snerges," "serves good wump," "serves bad wump," "too many pranksters," "sexivationist." Each block has its own legends, songs and special jargon. "Old Pink" is considered easygoing and faintly raffish, which of course describes me very well, too.

You ask, What is a "snerge"? A thief. I have already suffered the attentions of a snerge, and my camera is missing so I can't send photographs. Luckily I was carrying my ozols with me. Please send me by return mail new pigments, vehicle, applicators and a big pad of matrix. Ferfan will tell you what I need. Send them insured; if they came by ordinary delivery, they might be egalized.

Later: I have done my first stint of drudge, at an export factory, for which I receive what is called "drivet": ten tokens for each hour worked. My weekly drivet is a hundred and thirty tokens, of which eighty-two must immediately be paid to the block, for food and lodging. The remainder is not too useful, since there is not much to buy: garments, shoes, stadium tickets, toasted seaweed at Disjerferact. I now dress like an Arrabin, so as not to be conspicuous. Certain shops at the space-port sell imported goods—tools, toys, occasional trifles of "bonter," at the most astonishing prices! In tokens, of course, which have almost no exchange value against the ozol—something like five hundred tokens to the ozol. Absurd, of course. On second thought, not so absurd. Who wants tokens? There is nothing to buy.

Still, this way of life, peculiar as it seems, is not necessarily a bad system. I suspect that every style of life works out to be a trade-off between various kinds of freedoms. There are naturally many different freedoms, and sometimes one freedom implies the absence of another.

In any event I've been getting ideas for depictions, which I know you don't take seriously. The light here is absolutely ravishing: a deceptively pale light, which seems to diffract everywhere into colored fringes.

I have much more to tell you, but I'll reserve something for my next. I won't ask you to send in "bonter"; I'd be—well, to tell the truth, I don't know what would happen, but I don't want to learn.

Immigrants and visitors are not well liked, yet I find that my fame as a "fixer" has already spread far and wide. Isn't this a joke? I know only what we were taught at school and what I learned at home. Still, everyone who has a bad screen insists that I fix it for him. Sometimes utter strangers! And when I do these favors, do they thank me? Verbally, yes, but there is a most peculiar expression on their faces: I can't describe it. Contempt, distaste, antipathy? Because I so easily command this (to them) recondite skill. I have on this instant come to a decision. No longer will I perform favors free. I will demand tokens or hours of drudge. They will sneer and make remarks, but they will respect me more.

Here are some of my ideas for depictions:

The blocks of Uncibal, in the colors which hold so much meaning for the Arrabins.

The view along Uncibal River from a prospect deck, with the oncoming sea of faces, all blank and serene.

The games, the shunk battles, the Arrabin version of hussade.*

Disjerferact, the carnival along the mud flats. More of this later.

Just a word or two about the local version of hussade, and I hope no one in the family will be shocked or dismayed. The game is played to standard rules; the defeated sheirl, however, must undergo a most distressing experience. She is disrobed and placed upon a cart with a repulsive wooden effigy, which is so controlled as to commit an unnatural act upon the sheirl; meanwhile, the losing team must pull this cart around the stadium. The wonder never leaves me: how are sheirls recruited? Each must realize that sooner or later her team must lose, yet none ever seems to consider this contingency.

They are either very brave or very foolish, or perhaps they are impelled by some dark human inclination which rejoices at public degradation.

*Hussade: See Glossary, iv.

Well, enough on this subject. I think I mentioned that my camera has been stolen: hence no photographs. In fact, I'm not sure that there is any agency at Uncibal to make prints from my matrix.

I will report further in my next letter.

From your loving,
Jantiff

CHAPTER 4

One morning Esteban came by Jantiff's apartment with a friend. "Attention, please, Janty Ravensroke! This is Olin, a dear good fellow, for all his portly abdomen. It signifies sound sleep and a peaceful conscience, or so Olin assures me; he owns no magic bonter cabinet."

Jantiff politely acknowledged the introduction, and offered a pleasantry of his own: "Please don't consider me guilt-ridden because I am thin!"

Olin and Esteban were provoked to hearty laughs. Esteban said: "Olin's screen has developed a most curious ailment; it spits up plumes of red fire, even at amusing messages. He naturally suffers agonies of distress. I told him: Be of good cheer! My friend Jantiff is a Zeck technician who likes nothing better than setting such things right."

Jantiff attempted a bright tone. "I have rather a good idea along these lines. Suppose I conduct a seminar on small repairs, at a charge per session, say, of fifty tokens a student. Everyone—you and Olin included—can learn all I know, and then you can do your own repairs and also oblige those of your friends who lack the skills."

Olin's smile trembled uncertainly; Esteban's handsome eyebrows peaked emphatically. "My dear fellow!" exclaimed Esteban. "Are you really in earnest?"

"Of course! Everyone gains. I earn extra tokens and also avoid the nuisance of running about performing favors. You in turn augment your capabilities."

For a moment Esteban stood speechless. Then, half-laughing, he said: "But Jantiff, dear naïve Jantiff! I don't want to augment my capabilities! This implies a predisposition for work. For civilized men work is an unnatural occupation!"

"I suppose there is no inherent virtue in work," Jantiff conceded. "Unless, of course, it is performed by someone else."

"Work is the useful function of machines," said Esteban. "Let the machines augment their capabilities! Let the automatons ponder and drudge! The span of existence is oh! so brief; why should a single second be wasted?"

"Yes, yes, of course," said Jantiff. "An ideal concept and all very well. In practice however both you and Olin already have wasted two or three hours inspecting Olin's screen, exclaiming at the flaw, formulating plans and coming here. Assume that I agree to look into the matter, then you and Olin must return to Olin's apartment to watch me make the repair. Let us say a total of four hours apiece. Eight man-hours as a grand total, not even counting my time, when Olin probably could have set the matter to rights in ten minutes. Isn't this a case where capabilities saves time?"

Esteban gave his head a grave shake. "Jantiff, above all you are a master of casuistry. This 'capability' implies a point of view quite at odds with the beatific* life."

"I feel that I must agree to this," said Olin.

"You'd rather lose the use of your screen than fix it yourself?"

Esteban's versatile eyebrows performed another feat, this time indicating quizzical distaste. "It goes without saying! This practicality of yours is a backward step. I also might mention that your proposed class is exploitative, and would surely excite the Monitors."

"I hadn't thought in those terms," said Jantiff. "Well, in all candor, I find that these little favors are taking too much of my time and destroying the beatitude of my life. If Olin wants to work my next drudge, I'll fix his screen."

Olin and Esteban exchanged amused glances. Both shrugged, turned away, and departed the apartment.

From Zeck came a parcel for Jantiff, containing pigments, applicators, papers and mats. Jantiff immediately set to work making real the images which haunted his imagination. Skorlet occasionally watched him, making no comments and asking no questions; Jantiff did not trouble to ask her opinion.

In the refectory one day, the girl whom Jantiff previously had admired plumped herself down opposite him. With her lips twitching against a grin of sheer exuberance, she pointed a finger toward Jantiff. "Explain something: do! Every time I come to the wumper you stare at me first from one side of your face and them the other. Why should this be? Am I so outrageously attractive and extraordinarily beautiful?"

---

*An arbitrary rendering of a word in the Arrabin dialect, expressing the quality of leisurely, luxurious and well-arranged existence.

Jantiff grinned sheepishly. "I find you outrageously attractive and extraordinarily beautiful."

"Sh!" The girl glanced mischievously right and left. "Already I'm considered a sexivationist. You'll absolutely confirm the general suspicion!"

"Well, be that as it may, I can't keep my eyes off of you, and that's the truth of it."

"And all you do is look? How odd! But then, you're an immigrant."

"Just a visitor. I hope that my coarse behavior hasn't disturbed you."

"Not in the slightest. I've always thought you rather pleasant. We'll copulate if you like; you can show me some new and amusing antics. No, not now; low drudge awaits me, curse all of it. Another time, if you're of a mind."

"Well, yes," said Jantiff. "I suppose it boils down to that. Your name, I believe, is Kedidah."

"How did you know?"

"Skorlet told me."

Kedidah made a wry face. "Skorlet doesn't like me. She says I'm flippant, and an arrant sexivator, as I mentioned."

"I'm bewildered. Why?"

"Oh—I don't really know. I like to tease and play. I arrange my hair to suit my mood. I like men to like me and I'm not concerned about women."*

"These aren't flagrant crimes."

"Aha! Ask Skorlet!"

"I'm not concerned for Skorlet's opinions. In fact, I find her overly intense. My name, incidentally, is Jantiff Ravensroke."

"What an odd name! No doubt you're an ingrained elitist. How are you adapting to egalism?"

"Quite well. Although I'm still perplexed by certain of the Arrabin customs."

"Understandably. We're a most complicated people, maybe to compensate for our egalism."

"I suppose that's possible. Would you like to visit other worlds?"

"Of course, unless I had to toil constantly, in which case I'll stay here where life is gay. I have friends and clubs and games; I never gloom because I think only of pleasure. In fact, some of us are going out on forage in a day or so; you're welcome to come along if you like."

---

*A more or less accurate paraphrase. The Arrabin dialect avoids distinction of gender. Masculine and feminine pronouns are suppressed in favor of the neutral pronoun. "Parent" replaces "mother" and "father"; "sibling" serves for both "brother" and "sister." When distinctions must be made, as in the conversation transcribed above, colloquialisms are used, almost brutally offensive in literal translation, reference being made to the genital organs.

"What's a 'forage'?"

"An expedition into the primitive! We ride up into the hills, then maraud south into the Weirdlands. This time it's to be Pamatra Valley, where we know secret places. We'll hope to find some very good bonter; but even if not, it's always a lark."

"I'd like to go, if I'm not a drudge."

"We'll start Twisday morning, right after wump and return Fyrday night, or even Dwanday morning."

"That suits me very well."

"Good. We'll meet here. Bring some sort of robe, since we'll probably sleep in the open. With luck we'll find all kinds of tasty things."

Early Twisday morning, as soon as the refectory opened its doors, Jantiff went to take his breakfast. On Skorlet's advice he carried a knapsack containing a blanket, a towel and two days' advance ration of gruff. Skorlet had spoken brusquely of the expedition, with something of a sneer: "You'll get wet in the fog and scratch yourself on brambles and run through the night until you're exhausted and if you're lucky you'll build a fire if someone thinks to bring along matches. Still, by all means, go out and flounder through the forest and dodge the man-traps and who knows? Maybe you'll find a berry or two or a bit of toasted meat. Where are you going?"

"Kedidah spoke of secret places in Pamatra Valley."

"Pah. What does she know of secret places, or anything else for that matter? Esteban is planning a real bonterfest before long; save your appetite for that."

"Well, I've already agreed to go with Kedidah's group."

Skorlet shrugged and sniffed. "Do as you like. Here, take these matches and be prepared, and don't eat toad-wort, otherwise you'll never return to Uncibal. As for Kedidah, she's never been right about anything, and I'm told she doesn't clean herself, when you copulate you never know what you're wading around in."

Jantiff mumbled something incoherent and busied himself with his painting. Skorlet came to look over his shoulder. "Who are those people?"

"They're the Whispers, receiving a committee of contractors in Serce."

Skorlet gave him a searching scrutiny. "You're never been to Serce."

"I used a photograph from the *Concept*. Didn't you see it?"

"No one sees anything in the *Concept* except hussade announcements." She studied another picture: a view along Uncibal River. She gave her head a shake of distaste. "All those faces, each so exact! It quite makes me uneasy!"

"Look carefully," Jantiff suggested. "Are there any you recognize?"

After a moment's silence Skorlet said: "To be sure! There's Esteban! And can this be me? Very clever; you have a remarkable knack!" She took up another sheet. "And what is this? the wumper? All these faces again; they seem so blank." She turned Jantiff another searching look. "What effect is this?"

Jantiff said hurriedly: "Arrabins seem, somehow, composed, let us say."

"Composed? What a thought! We're fervent, idealistic, reckless—when we have the opportunity—mutable, passionate. All these, yes. Composed? No."

"No doubt you're right," said Jantiff. "Somehow I haven't captured this quality."

Skorlet turned away, then spoke over her shoulder. "I wonder if you could spare some of that blue pigment? I'd like to paint symbols on my cult globes."

Jantiff looked first up at the constructions of paper and wire, each a foot in diameter, then to the wide coarse brush which Skorlet habitually employed, and finally with eyebrows ruefully raised, to the rather small capsule of blue pigment. "Really, Skorlet, I don't see how this is possible. Can't you use house paint or ink, or something similar?"

Skorlet went pink in the face. "And how or where can I get house paint? Or ink? I know nothing of these things; they aren't available to just anyone, and I've never been on a drudge where I could snerge any."

"I think I saw ink for sale on Counter 5 at the Area Store," Jantiff said cautiously. "Perhaps—"

Skorlet made a vehement gesture, expressing rejection and disgust. "At a hundred tokens the dram? You foreigners are all alike, so pampered by your wealth, yet heartless and selfish beneath it all!"

"Oh, very well," said Jantiff despondently. "Take the pigment if you really need it. I'll use another color."

But Skorlet, flouncing away, went to the mirror and began to change the decoration of her ears. Jantiff heaved a sigh and continued with his painting.

The foragers gathered in the lobby of Old Pink; eight men and five women. Jantiff's knapsack instantly aroused jocular attention. "Ha, where does Jantiff think we're off to, the Far Edge?"

"Jantiff, dear fellow, we're only going on a bit of a forage, not a migration!"

"Jantiff is an optimist! He takes trays and bags and baskets to bring home his bonter!"

"Bah, I'll bring mine home, too, but on the inside!"

A young man named Garrace, portly and blond, asked: "Jantiff, tell us really and in truth: what are you carrying?"

Jantiff, grinning apologetically, said: "Actually, nothing of any consequence: a change of clothes, a few cakes of gruff, my sketch pad, and, if you must know the truth, some toilet paper."

"Good old Jantiff! He is at least candid!"

"Well then, let's be off, toilet paper and all!"

The group proceed to the man-way, rode to Uncibal River, moved west for an hour, changed to a lateral which took them south into the hills.

Jantiff had studied a map the previous day, and now tried to identify features of the landscape. He pointed to a great granite abutment looming over the way ahead. "That must be the Solitary Witness; am I right?"

"Exactly," said Thworn, an assertive young man with russet hair. "Over and beyond is the Near Wold and a spate of bonter if we're lucky. See that notch? That's Hebron Gap; it will take us into Pamatra Valley and that's where we're bound."

"I suspect we'd do better out on the Middle Wold, toward Fruberg," said a saturnine young man named Uwser. "Some people I know worked Pamatra Valley two or three months ago and came home hungry."

"Nonsense," scoffed Thworn. "I can smell the vat berries dripping from here! And don't forget the Frubergers: a stone-throwing gang of villains!"

"The Valley folk are no better," declared Sunover, a girl as tall as Jantiff and of far more impressive girth. "On the whole, they're fat and smelly, and I don't like to copulate with them."

"In that case, run," said Uwser. "Have you no imagination?"

"Eat, copulate, run," intoned Garrace. "The three dynamics of Sunover's existence."

Jantiff asked Sunover: "Why either copulate or run, if you're not of a mind to do so?"

Sunover merely made an impatient clucking sound. Kedidah gave Jantiff a pat on the cheek. "They're both good for the soul, dear boy, and sometimes they aid one's comfort as well."

Jantiff said in a worried voice: "I'd like to know what's expected of me. Do I copulate or do I run? What are the signals? And where do we find the bonter?"

"Everything happens at once," said Garrace with an impish grin.

"All in good time, Jantiff!" spoke the imperious Thworn. "Don't become anxious at this stage of the game!"

Jantiff shrugged and gave his attention to a set of industrial buildings toward which most of the traffic on the man-way seemed to be directed. In response to his question Garrace informed him that here those hormones which figured largely in Arrabin exports were extracted, refined and packaged. "You'll get your notice before long," Garrace told him. "It's our common fate. Into the plant like so many automatons, down on the pallet, along the operation line. They milk your glands, distill your blood, tap your spinal ducts, and in general have their way with all your most private parts. Don't worry; you'll have your turn."

Jantiff had not previously known of this aspect to life in Arrabus. He frowned over his shoulder toward the cluster of pale-brown buildings. "How long does all this take?"

"Two days, and for another two or three days you are totally addled. Still, export we must, to pay for maintenance, and what, after all, is two days a year in the interests of egalism?"

The man-way ended at a depot, where the group boarded an ancient omnibus. Swaying and wallowing perilously, the omnibus slid them up the road between slopes overgrown with blue canker-wort and black dendrons studded with poisonous scarlet seed balls.

After an hour's ride the bus arrived at the head of Hebron Gap. "End of the road, all out!" cried Thworn. "Now we must march off on foot, like the adventurers of old!"

The troop set off along a lane leading downhill through a stand of kirkash trees smelling strong and sweet of resin. Ahead the land flattened to become Pamatra Valley; beyond stretched the Weirdlands under a smoke-colored shroud of forest.

Garrace called over his shoulder: "Jantiff, shake a leg there; you'll have to keep up. What are you doing?"

"Just making a sketch of that tree. Look at the way the branches angle out! They're like dancing maenads!"

"No time for sketching!" Thworn called back. "We've still got five or ten miles to go."

Jantiff reluctantly put away his sketch pad and caught up with the others.

The lane swung out on a meadow and broke into a half-dozen trails leading off in various directions. Here the group encountered another set of foragers. "Hello there," called Uwser, "what's your house?"

"We're desperadoes from Bumbleville in Two-twenty."

"That's a long way from us. We're all Old Pinkers, from Seventeen— except Woble and Vich; they're denizens of the infamous White Palace. What luck are you having?"

"Nothing to speak of. We heard a rumor of a lovely bitternut tree, but we couldn't find it. We ate a few sweet-hops and looked into an orchard, but the locals warned us off and sent a boy to spy us clear of the premises. What are you for?"

"Bonter of all sorts, and we're a determined group. We'll probably push south five or ten miles before we start our forage."

"Good luck to you!"

Thworn led the Old Pinkers south along a trail which took them at once into a dense forest of black mace trees. The air in the shade was dank and chill and smelled strong of moldering vegetation. Thworn called out: "Everyone watch for bitternuts and remember there's a wild plum tree somewhere in the vicinity!"

A mill passed with no evidence either of nuts or plums, and the trail came to a fork. Thworn hesitated. "I don't recall this fork . . . I wonder if we set off along the wrong trail? Well, no matter; the bonter is out there somewhere! So then—the right-hand fork!"

Ernaly, a rather frail girl with a fastidious manner, said plaintively: "How far must we go? I'm really not all that keen on hiking, especially if you don't know the way."

Thworn said sternly: "My dear girl, naturally we've got to hike! We're in the middle of the forest with nothing to eat but skane bark."

"Please don't talk about eating," cried Rehilmus, a blond, kitten-faced girl with small feet and a ripe figure displayed almost to the point of sexivation, "I'm ravenous right now."

Thworn swung his arm in a gesture of command. "No complaints! Up and away and after the bonter!"

The group set out along the right-hand path, which presently dwindled to a trail winding this way and that under the lowering mace trees. Kedidah, walking at the rear with Jantiff, grumbled under her breath. "Thworn doesn't know where he's going any more than I do."

"What, exactly, are we looking for?" Jantiff asked.

"These Wold farms are the riches of Weirdland, because they fringe on the Pleasant Zone. The farmers are mad for copulation; they give baskets of bonter for a bit of fondling. You can't imagine the tales I've heard: roasted fowl, fried salt-side, pickled batracher, baskets of fruit! All for a brisk bit of copulation."

"It seems too good to be true."

Kedidah laughed. "Only if there's fair play. It's not unknown that while the girls are copulating the men are eating until there's nothing left, and the walk home is apt to be moody."

"So I would imagine," said Jantiff. "Sunover, for instance, would never accept such a situation without protest."

"I suspect not. Look, Thworn has discovered something!"

In response to Thworn's signals the group fell silent. They advanced cautiously, at last to peer through the foliage out upon a small farmstead. To one side a half-dozen cattle grazed the meadow; to the other grew rows of bantock and mealie-bush and tall racks of vat berries. At the center stood a rambling structure of timber and petrified soil.

Garrace pointed: "Look—yonder! Lyssum vines! Is anyone about?"

"The place seems deserted," Uwser muttered. "Notice the fowl roost to the side!"

"Well then, I'm for being bold," said Garrace. "They're all within, gulping down their noon bonter, and here stand we with our mouths open. I accept the unspoken invitation!"

He stepped out from the forest and advanced upon the lyssum vines, followed by Colcho, Hasken, Vich, Thworn and the others, with Jantiff thoughtfully keeping to the rear. Garrace uttered a startled cry as the ground gave way under his feet; he disappeared from view. The others paused uncertainly, then went forward to peer down at Garrace, where he floundered among sodden brambles. "Get me out of here," he roared. "Don't just stand there gaping!"

"No need to be offensive," said Thworn. "Here; give me your hand!" He pulled and Garrace was dragged up to solid ground.

"What a vile trick!" exclaimed Rehilmus. "You might have been seriously hurt!"

"I'm not at all comfortable," growled Garrace. "I'm full of thorns and they've poured a year's worth of slops down there. But I'm still for that lyssum, and now I'll have it for sure."

"Do be careful!" cried Maudel, another of the girls. "These folk are obviously unfriendly."

"And now I'm unfriendly too!" Garrace proceeded toward the vines, testing the ground ahead of him. After a moment's hesitation the others followed.

Twenty yards short of the vines he stumbled and almost fell. He looked down: "A trip-wire!"

From the farmhouse issued two men, a stout woman and a pair of striplings. They picked up cudgels and one of the boys raised a hatch in the side of the structure. Out rushed four black delps of that sort known as "mouthers." Baying and moaning, they charged the foragers, followed by the farm folk with their cudgels. With one accord the foragers turned and ran toward the forest, led by Jantiff who had not ventured any great distance into the meadow.

The slowest of the foragers was the amiable Colcho, who had the misfortune to fall. The delps were upon him, but the farm folk called them off and sent them after the other fugitives while they beat Colcho with their cudgels, until Colcho finally managed to break away, and running faster than ever, gained the relative security of the forest. The delps leapt upon Rehilmus and Ernaly and might have done them damage had not Thworn and Jantiff beaten them away with dead branches.

The group returned the way they had come. Reaching the fork they found that Colcho had evidently fled in a direction different from their own and was now missing. Everyone called, "Colcho! Colcho! Where are you?" But Colcho failed to reply, and no one felt in any mood to return along the trail looking for him. "He should have stayed with the group," said Uwser.

"He had no chance," Kedidah pointed out. "The farm folk were beating him and he was lucky to get away at all."

"Poor Colcho," sighed Maudel.

" 'Poor Colcho?' " cried Garrace in outrage. "What about me? I've been scratched and stabbed; I'm stinking with nameless muck! I've got to do something for myself!"

"There's a stream yonder; go bathe," Thworn suggested. "You'll feel much better."

"Not if I have to get back into these clothes; they're absolutely befouled."

"Well, Jantiff is carrying a spare outfit: you're about of a size and I'm sure he'll let you have them. Right, Jantiff? It's all for one and one for all among the jolly Old Pinkers!"

Jantiff reluctantly brought the garments from his knapsack, and Garrace went off to bathe.

Kedidah demanded of Thworn: "What now? Have you any notion of where we are?"

"Of course. We take the left fork instead of the right; I had a momentary lapse of memory; there's really no problem."

Rehilmus said crossly: "Except that it's time for wump, and I'm famished. In fact I can't go another step."

"We're all hungry," said Hasken. "You're not really alone."

"Yes, I am," declared Rehilmus. "No one becomes as hungry as I do, because I just can't function without food."

"Oh, the devil," said Thworn in disgust. "Jantiff, give her a bite or two of gruff, to keep her on her feet."

"I'm hungry too," said Ernaly peevishly.

"Oh, don't pout so," said Rehilmus. "I'll share with you."

Jantiff brought out his four cakes of gruff and placed them upon a stump. "This is all I have. Divide it as you like."

Rehilmus and Ernaly each took a cake; Thworn and Uwser shared the third; Kedidah and Sunover shared the fourth.

Garrace returned from washing in the stream. "Feeling better?" asked Rehilmus brightly.

"To some extent, although I wish Jantiff's clothes came a size larger. Still, far better than these befouled rags." He held them away from him with exaggerated disgust. "I won't carry them with me; I guess I'll just leave them here."

"Don't give up good clothes," Thworn advised. "There's room in Jantiff's knapsack, just drop them in."

"That would solve everything," said Garrace, and he turned to Jantiff. "You're sure you don't mind?"

"Quite sure," said Jantiff in a gloomy voice.

Thworn rose to his feet. "Everybody ready? Away we go!"

The foragers set off along the trail, Thworn again in the lead. Presently he made a clenched-fist sign of jubilation and swung around. "This is the trail; I recognized that knob of rock. There's bonter ahead; I smell it from here!"

"How much farther?" demanded Rehilmus. "Quite candidly, my feet hurt."

"Patience, patience! A few miles farther, over that far ridge. This is my secret place, so everyone must pledge absolute discretion!"

"Whatever you say. Just show us the bonter."

"Come along then; don't delay."

The group, enlivened, jogged forward and even sang jocular songs, of gluttony, legendary forages and chwig.

The countryside became more open as they climbed the slope. At the ridge a vast panorama extended to the south: dark forests, a line of river and a dramatic sky, leaden violet at the horizon, pearl white on high, mottled with shoals of white, gray and black clouds. Jantiff halted to absorb the scene and reached for his pad to make a rough sketch, but his hand encountered Garrace's dank garments and he gave up the idea.

The others had gone ahead; Jantiff hurried to catch up. As they descended the trees grew thickly over the trail.

Thworn called a halt. "From here on quiet and caution; let's not create any more fiascos."

Sunover, peering ahead, said: "I don't see anything whatever. Are you sure this is the right trail?"

"Dead sure. We're at the far edge of Pamatra Valley, where the best limequats grow, and the river flat-fish cook up sweet as nuts. That's further south, to be sure, but the first farms are just below us, so caution all. Jantiff, what in the world are you mooning at?"

"Nothing of consequence: just the lichens on this old log. Notice how the oranges contrast with the blacks and browns!"

"Charming and quaint, but we can't spare time for poetic ecstasies. Onward all, with caution!"

The foragers proceeded in utter silence: a half-mile, a mile. Once again Rehilmus became restive, but Thworn furiously signaled her to silence. A moment later he brought the group to a halt. "Look yonder now, but don't let yourselves be seen."

"Everyone be vigilant," Uwser cautioned. "Spy out the trip-wires, pit-falls, electric pounces and other such nuisances."

Peering through the trees Jantiff saw another farmstead not a great deal different from the first they had encountered.

Thworn, Garrace, Uwser and the others conferred, pointing here and there. Then all armed themselves with stout sticks, in the event delps should again be encountered.

Thworn told the group: "We'll go quietly yonder, where there don't seem to be any trip-wires, then make for the fowl-run at the rear of the house. So now, keep low to the ground. Good luck and good bonter!"

He hunched himself almost double and ran off at a curious wobbling shuffle; the others followed. As before Garrace was the boldest. He ventured into the vegetable garden, to pull up the root crops, cramming some in his mouth, some in his pockets. Doble, Vich and Sunover busied themselves at the vat-berry arbor, but the season was past and only a few husks remained. Thworn proceeded toward the fowl-run.

Someone blundered into a trip-wire. A dismal clanking sound issued from a belfry on top of the house. The door opened and out ran an old man, an old woman and a small boy. The old man picked up a stick and attacked Garrace, Maudel, and Hasken, who were among his radishes; they flung him to the ground and did the same for the old woman. The boy ran into the house and emerged with an axe; flaming-eyed he lunged for the for-agers. Thworn raised his voice in a shout: "Everybody off and away, on the double!"

Snatching up a few last radishes the foragers departed the way they had come, Thworn and Uwser exultant in the possession of a pair of rather thin old fowl, the necks of which they had already wrung.

The group halted, panting and triumphant in the lane. "We should have stayed longer," Rehilmus protested. "I saw a really choice melon."

"Not with that alarm going! We were away in good time; let's be gone before their reinforcements arrive. This way down the trail!"

In a clearing beside a small stream the group halted. Thworn and Uwser plucked and eviscerated the fowl while Garrace built a fire; the meat was skewered upon sharp sticks and toasted.

Kedidah looked this way and that. "Where is Jantiff?"

No one seemed interested.

"He seems to have gotten lost," said Rehilmus.

Garrace glanced down the path. "Nowhere in sight. He's back there somewhere gazing raptly at an old stump."

"Well, no great loss," said Thworn. "So much more for the rest of us."

The foragers began their feast.

"Ah! This is good stuff!" declared Garrace. "We should do this more often."

"Ah!" sighed Rehilmus. "Marvelous! Throw a few of those radishes this way; they're ideal!"

"The Connatic himself never ate better," declared Sunover.

"A pity there's not just a bit more," said Rehilmus. "I could eat on for hours and never stop; I love it so!"

Thworn reluctantly rose to his feet. "We'd better be starting back; it's a long march over the hills."

CHAPTER 5

On the following day Kedidah, entering the refectory, discovered Jantiff sitting unobtrusively alone in a far corner. She marched across the room and plumped herself down beside him. "What happened to you yesterday? You missed all the fun."

"Yes, I suppose so. I decided that I wasn't all that hungry."

"Oh, come now, Jantiff. I can see through you. You're annoyed and sulky."

"Not really. I just don't feel right stealing from other people."

"What nonsense!" declared Kedidah loftily. "They've got plenty; why can't they share a bit with us?"

"There wouldn't be much to share among three billion people."

"Perhaps not." She reached out and took his hand. "I must say that you acted very nicely yesterday. I was quite pleased with you."

Jantiff flushed. "Do you really mean that?"

"Of course!"

Jantiff said haltingly, "I've—been thinking."

"About what?"

"That old man in your apartment; what's his name?"

"Sarp."

"Yes. I wonder if he would trade apartments with me. Then we could be together constantly."

Kedidah laughed. "Old Sarp wouldn't dream of moving, and anyway, there's no fun when people live together and see each other at their worst. Isn't that really true?"

"Oh, I don't know. If you're fond of someone, you like to be with him or her as much as possible."

"Well, I'm fond of you and I see you as much as possible."

"But that isn't enough!"

"Besides, I've got lots of friends, and all of them make demands upon me."

Jantiff started to speak, then decided to hold his tongue. Kedidah picked up his portfolio. "What have you here? Pictures? Oh, please, may I look?"

"Of course."

Kedidah turned the sketches exclaiming in pleasure. "Jantiff, how exciting! I recognize this; it's our foraging group on the trail. This is Thworn, and here's Garrace, and—this is me! Jantiff! Do I look like that? All stiff and pale and staring, as if I'd seen a goblin? Don't answer me; I'll only be annoyed. If only you'd do a nice drawing of me that I could hang on the wall!" She returned to the sketch. "Sunover—Uwser—Rehilmus—everybody! And this glimpse of a person at the rear—that's you!"

Skorlet and Esteban came into the refectory, and with them that sprite of contradictory moods who was their daughter Tanzel. Kedidah called out: "Come look at Jantiff's wonderful pictures! Here's our forage party; we're on the trail! It's so real you can smell the kirkash balm!"

Esteban examined the sketch with an indulgent smile. "You don't seem overloaded with bonter."

"Naturally not! It's still morning and we're on our way south. And don't worry about bonter; we dined in style, all of us. Roast fowl, a salad of fresh herbs, buckets of fruit—all magnificent!"

"Oh!" exclaimed Tanzel. "I wish I'd been there!"

"Moderation, please," said Esteban, "I've gone foraging myself."

Kedidah said with dignity: "Next time come along with us and make certain how we fare."

"Which reminds me," mused Jantiff. "Did Colcho ever find his way home?"

No one troubled to answer. Esteban said: "I'm as keen for bonter as the next, but nowadays I pay the tokens and the gypsies provide the feast. Indeed, I have plans afoot at this very moment. Join the group, if you like. You'll have to pay your share, of course."

"How much? I just might go."

"Five hundred tokens, which includes air transport into the Weirdlands."

Kedidah clapped at her golden brown ear-puffs in shock. "Do you take me for a contractor? I can't fetch any such sum!"

Tanzel said sadly, "I don't have five hundred tokens either."

Skorlet turned a sharp glance towards Esteban, another at Jantiff. "Don't worry, dear. You'll be included."

Esteban, ignoring the remarks, continued to turn through Jantiff's sketches. "Very good . . . A bit over-ambitious, this one. Too many faces . . . Aha! I recognize someone here."

Kedidah looked. "That's myself and Sarp sitting in our chairs. Jantiff, when did you do this?"

"A few days ago. Skorlet, would you trade apartments with Kedidah?"

Skorlet gave an ejaculation of startled amusement. "Whatever for?"

"I'd like to share an apartment with her."

"And I'd share with that muttering old madman? Not on your life!"

Esteban offered advice: "Never share with someone you fancy; when the edge wears off, irritation wears on."

"It's not sensible to copulate too much with one person," said Kedidah.

"In fact, I don't like copulation," said Tanzel. "It's quite tiresome."

Esteban turned over the sketches. "Well, well! Whom do we have here?"

Tanzel pointed excitedly. "That's you and that's Skorlet, and that's old Sarp. I don't know that big man."

Esteban laughed. "Not quite. I see a resemblance, but only because Jantiff draws all his faces with the same expression."

"By no means," said Jantiff. "A face is the symbol—the graphic image— of a personality. Consider! Written characters represent spoken words. Depicted features represent personalities! I depict faces still and at rest so as not to confuse their meaning."

"Far, far beyond my reach," sighed Esteban.

"Not at all! Consider once more! I might depict two men laughing at a joke. One is really cantankerous, the other is good-natured. Since both are laughing, you might believe both to be good-natured. When the features are still, the personality is free to reveal itself."

Esteban held up his hands. "Enough! I submit! And I'll be the last to deny that you've a great knack for this sort of stuff."

"It's not a knack at all," said Jantiff. "I've had to practice for years."

Tanzel said brightly: "Isn't it elitism when someone tries to do something better than everyone else?"

"Theoretically, yes," said Skorlet, "but Jantiff is an Old Pinker and certainly not an elitist."

Esteban chuckled. "Any other crimes we can lay upon Jantiff's head?"

Tanzel thought a moment. "He's a monopolist who hoards his time and won't share with me, and I like him very much."

Skorlet snorted. "Jantiff's tit-willow mannerisms are actually arrant sexivation. He even affects poor little Tanzel."

"He's also an exploiter, because he wants to use up Kedidah."

Jantiff opened his mouth to roar an indignant rebuttal, but words failed him. Kedidah patted him on the shoulder. "Don't worry, Tanzel; I like him

342 / JACK VANCE

too and today he can monopolize me all he likes, because I want to go to the games and we'll go together."

"I'd like to go myself," said Esteban. "That great new Shkooner is fighting the piebald Wewark: both awesome beasts."

"Perhaps so, but I'm mad for Kizzo in the second event. He's mounted on the blue Jamouli, and he's so absolutely gallant I swoon to watch him."

Esteban pursed his lips. "He's really too exuberant in his flourishes, and I can't approve of his knee action. Still, he's reckless to a fault, and makes poor Lamar and Kelchaff seem a pair of fearful old ladies."

"Oh, dear," said Skorlet. "I've got drudge and can't go!"

"Save your tokens for the gypsies," said Esteban. "If you're planning to join the feast, that is to say."

"True. I must work on my globes. I wonder where I can find more pigment?" Her gaze rested speculatively on Jantiff, who said hurriedly, "I can't possibly spare any more. I'm very low on everything."

Esteban spoke to Jantiff: "What of you? Are you for this bonterfest?"

Jantiff hesitated. "I've just been foraging, and I'm not sure I enjoy it."

"My dear fellow, it's not the same thing at all! Do you have ozols?"

"Well, a few. Safely locked away, of course."

"Then you can afford the bonterfest. I'll mark you down for a place."

"Oh—very well. Where and when does the event take place?"

"When? As soon as I make proper arrangements. Everything must be right! Where? Out in the Weirdlands where we can enjoy the countryside. I have recently become acquainted with Contractor Shubart; he'll allow us use of an air-car."

Jantiff gave a hollow laugh. "Who now is the exploiter, monopolist, elitist tycoon and all the rest? What of egalism now?"

Esteban retorted in a debonair, if somewhat edgy, voice: "Egalism is all very well, and I subscribe to it! Still: why deny the obvious? Everyone wants to make the most of their life. If I were able, I'd be a contractor; perhaps I'll become one yet."

"You've picked the wrong time," said Kedidah. "Did you read the Concept? The Whispers insist that the contractors cost too much and that changes must be made. Perhaps there'll be no more contractors."

"Ridiculous!" snorted Skorlet. "Who'll do the work?"

"I've no idea," said Kedidah. "I'm neither a Whisper nor a contractor."

"I'll ask my friend Shubart," said Esteban. "He'll know all about it."

"I don't understand!" said Tanzel plaintively. "I thought contractors were all ignorant outsiders, vulgar and mean, who did our nasty work for us. Would you really want to be someone like that?"

Esteban gave a gay laugh. "I'd be a very nice contractor, as polite and clever as I am now!"

Kedidah jumped to her feet. "Come, Jantiff! Let's be off, if we're to get good seats. And bring along a few extra tokens; this week I'm totally bankrupt."

Late in the afternoon Jantiff returned home along Disselberg River. The shunk contests* had exceeded all his expectations; his mind seethed with sensations and images.

The crowds had early obtruded themselves, choking all man-ways leading to the stadium. Jantiff had noted the vivacity of their faces, the wet shine of their eyes, the tremulous flexibility of their mouths as they talked and laughed: these were not the folk, serene and bland, who promenaded along Uncibal River! The stadium itself was a gigantic place, rearing high in a succession of levels: bank on bank, buttress over buttress, balcony after balcony, closing off the sky, with the spectators a crusted blur. From everywhere came a pervasive whisper, hoarse as the sea, waxing and waning to the movement of events.

The preliminary ceremonies Jantiff found rather tedious: an hour of marching and counter-marching by musicians in purple and brown uniforms to music of horns, grumbling bass resonators and three-foot cymbals. At last eight portals slid aside; eight men rode forth, erect and somber on the pedestals of power-chariots. They circled the field, gazing straight ahead, as if oblivious to all but their own fateful thoughts. Staring directly ahead, the riders departed the field.

The stadium-sound rose and fell, reflecting the consonance of moods of half a million people in close proximity, and Jantiff wondered at the psychological laws governing such phenomena.

Abruptly, responding to an influence beyond Jantiff's perception, the sounds halted and the air became tense with silence.

The portals to east and west slid apart; out lurched a pair of shunk. They rumbled in rage, stamped the turf, reared thirty feet into the air as if to fling away those calm and indomitable riders who stood on their shoulders. So began the contests.

The hulks collided with awesome impacts; the poise of the riders transcended belief. Even though the fact occurred before Jantiff's eyes. Time and time again they evaded the great pads, to remount with calm authority as the shunk lurched to its feet. He communicated his wonder to Kedidah: "What a miracle they stay alive!"

"Sometimes two or even three are killed. Today—they're lucky." Jantiff turned her a curious side-glance; was the wistful note in her voice for the crushed riders or for those who managed to evade death?

---

*A pallid rendering of the Arrabin term, which translates into something like: "confrontations of fateful glory."

"They train for years and years," Kedidah told him as they left the stadium. "They live in the stink and noise and feel of the beasts; then they come to Arrabus and hope to ride at ten contests; then they can return to Zonder with their fortunes." Kedidah fell silent and seemed to become distrait. Where the lateral joined Disselberg River she said abruptly: "I'll leave you here, Janty; there's an appointment I simply must keep."

Jantiff's jaw sagged. "I thought we could spend the evening together; maybe at your apartment—"

Kedidah smilingly shook her head. "Impossible, Janty. Now excuse me, please; I've got to hurry."

"But I wanted to discuss moving in with you!"

"No, no, no! Janty, behave yourself! I'll see you in the wumper."

Jantiff returned to Old Pink with hurt feelings. He found Skorlet busy with her globes, daubing the last of his blue, black, dark green and umber pigments upon the paper contrivances.

Jantiff stared in shock. "Whatever are you up to? Really, Skorlet, that isn't a decent thing to do!"

Skorlet flung him a glance, and in her white face he saw a desperation he had never previously noticed. She turned back to her work, then after a moment found words and spoke through gritted teeth. "It's not fair that you should have everything and me nothing."

"But I don't have everything!" Jantiff bleated. "I have nothing! You've taken them all! Brown, black, green, blue! I have a few reds, true, and orange and ocher and yellow—no, now you've deprived me of my yellow as well—"

"Listen, Jantiff! I need tokens to take myself and Tanzel on the bonterfest. She's never been anywhere and seen nothing, much less tasted bonter. I don't care if I use all your pigments! You are so rich, you can get more, and I must make these cult-globes, dog defile them!"

"Why doesn't Esteban pay for Tanzel? He never seems to lack tokens."

Skorlet gave a bitter snort. "Esteban is too self-important to spare tokens for anyone. In all candor, he should have lived out in the Bad Worlds where he could be a tycoon. Or an exploiter. For certain he's no egalist. And you'd never imagine the wild schemes that throng his mind."

Surprised by Skorlet's vehemence, Jantiff went to his chair. Skorlet continued to daub grimly at her contrivances and Jantiff growled: "What good are those things that you're wasting my pigments on?"

"I don't know what good they are! I take them down to Disjerferact and people pay good tokens for them and that's all I care. Now I need just a bit of that orange—Jantiff, it's no use showing me that mulish expression!"

"Here, take it! This is the last time! From now on I'm locking everything up in my case!"

"Jantiff, you're a very small person."

"And you're very large—with other people's belongings!"

"Control your tongue, Jantiff! You have no right to hector me! Now turn on the screen. The Whispers are making an important speech and I want to hear it."

"Bah," muttered Jantiff. "Just more of the same." Nevertheless, upon meeting Skorlet's lambent gaze, he rose to his feet and did her bidding.

Jantiff wrote a letter home:

Dearest family:

First my inevitable requests. I don't want to be a nuisance, but circumstances are against me. Please send me another selection of pigments, of double size. They cannot be obtained here, like everything else. Still, life progresses. The food of course is deadly dull; everyone is obsessed with "bonter." Some friends are planning a "gypsy banquet," whatever that is. I've been invited, and I'll probably attend, if only to get away from gruff and deedle for a few hours.

I fear that I'm developing a fragmented personality. I wonder sometimes if I'm not living in a dreamland, where white is black and black is not white, which would be too simple, but something totally absurd like, say, ten dead dogfish or the smell of gilly-flowers. Mind you, Arrabus was at one time a very ordinary industrialized nation. Is this the inevitable sequence? The ideas succeed each other with a frightening logic. Life is short; why waste a second on thankless drudgery? Technology exists for this purpose! Therefore, technology must be augmented and extended, to dispel as much drudgery as possible. Let the machines toil! Leisure, the rich flavor of sheer existence, is the goal! Very good, if only the machines could do everything. But they won't repair themselves, and they won't perform human services, so even Arrabins must drudge: a sour thirteen hours a week. Next, the machines are unkind enough to break down. Contractors must be hired, from compounds in Blale and Froke and other places at the back of the Weirdlands. Needless to say, the contractors refuse to work on the cheap. In fact, or so I am told, they absorb almost the whole of the gross Arrabin product. The Arrabins could relieve the situation by training persons so inclined to be technicians and mechanics, but egalists assert that specialization is the first step toward elitism. No doubt they are right. It never occurs to anyone that the contractors are elitists of the very finest water, who grow rich exploiting the Arrabins—if exploiting is the proper word.

I wrote "never occurs to anyone," but perhaps this isn't quite accurate. The other night I heard a public address by the Whispers. I made some sketches as they appeared on the screen; I enclose one of them. The Whispers are chosen by a random process. On each level of every block someone, selected by lot, becomes a Monitor. The twenty-three monitors choose by lot a Block Warden. From the Block Wardens of each district a Delegate is selected, by lot of course. Each of the four great metropolitan divisions: Uncibal, Propunce, Waunisse and Serce, is represented by its Panel of Delegates. By lot one of these Delegates becomes a Whisper. The Whispers are expected to wield their authority, such as it is, in a subdued, egalistic manner: hence the title "Whispers" which developed, so I am told, from a jocular conversation many years ago.

In any event the Whispers appeared on the screen the other night. They spoke very guardedly, and made dutiful obeisance to the glories of egalism. Still, the effect was hardly optimistic. Even I apprehended the hints, and my ears are not as keen in this regard as those of the Arrabins. The woman Fausgard read out statistics making no comment, but everyone could hear that the equilibrium was failing, that capital deterioration exceeded repair and replacement, from which everyone could draw whatever conclusion they chose. The Whispers announced that they will shortly visit the Connatic at Lusz to discuss the situation. These ideas aren't popular; the Arrabins reject them automatically, and I have heard grumbling that the expedition to Numenes is just a junket in search of high living. Remember, the Whispers live in the same apartments and eat the same gruff, deedle and wobbly as anyone else; however, they do no drudge. At the Centenary they will make a further announcement, undoubtedly to the effect that the contractors must be phased out. This idea in itself hurts no Arrabin feelings. The contractors live baronial lives on their country estates, and the Arrabins know them (enviously?) for elitists.

Items of incidental intelligence: Blale, at the south edge of "Weirdland," is warmed by an equatorial current and is not as cold as its latitude suggests. Remember, Wyst is a very small world! The folk who live in Froke, to the west of Blale, are called Frooks. Nomads wander Weirdland forests; some are called "gypsies" and others "witches," for reasons past my comprehension. The gypsies range closer to Arrabus and provide feasts of bonter for a fee. The Arrabins lack all interest in music. None play musical instruments, presumably because of the drudgery involved. Indeed this is a strange place! Shocking, disturbing, uncomfortable, hungry, but fascinating! I never tire of watching the great crowds: everywhere people! There is sheer magnificence to these numbers; it is marvelous to stand above Uncibal River, gazing down at the faces. Invent a face: any face you like. Big nose, little ears, round eyes, long chin—sooner or later you'll see it in Uncibal River! And do these numbers create a drabness? or uniformity? To the contrary! Every Arrabin desperately asserts his individuality, with personal tricks and fads. A futile kind of life, no doubt, but isn't all life futile? The Arrabins enter life from nowhere and when they die no one remembers them. They produce nothing substantial; in fact—so it now occurs to me—the only commodity they produce is leisure!

Enough for now. I'll write soon again.

As usual all my affection,

Jantiff

Jantiff had locked away those pigments remaining to him. Skorlet perforce decided that her cult-globes were complete and began to tie them into clusters of six. Jantiff's restless activities at last attracted her notice. She looked up from her work and uttered a peevish complaint. "Why in the name of all perversity must you flutter here and there like a bird with a broken wing? Settle yourself, I beg you!"

Jantiff responded with quiet dignity. "I made certain sketches of the Whispers the other night. I wanted to send one or two to my family, but they have disappeared. I am beginning to suspect snergery."

Skorlet gave a bark of rude laughter. "If this is the case, you should be flattered!"

"I am merely annoyed."

"You make such an absurd fuss over nothing! Draw up another sketch, or send off others. The affair is quite inconsequential and you cannot imagine how you distract me."

"Excuse me," said Jantiff. "As you suggest, I will send another sketch, and please convey my compliments to the snerge."

Skorlet only shrugged and finished her work. "Now, Jantiff, please help me carry the globes down to Esteban's apartment; he knows the dealer who sells for the best price."

Jantiff started to protest but Skorlet cut him short: "Really, Jantiff, I'm dumbfounded! In your life you've enjoyed every known luxury, yet you won't help poor Tanzel to a single taste of bonter!"

"That's not true," cried Jantiff hotly. "I took her to Disjerferact the other day and bought her all the poggets* and water-puffs and eel-pies she could eat!"

---

*Shredded seaweed, wound around a twig and fried in hot oil.

"Never mind all that! Just bear a hand now; I'm not asking anything unreasonable of you."

Jantiff sullenly allowed himself to be loaded down with cult-globes. Skorlet gathered up the rest and they proceeded around the corridors to Esteban's apartment. In response to Skorlet's kick at the door, Esteban peered out into the corridor. He saw the globes without show of enthusiasm. "So many?"

"Yes, so many! I've made them and you can trade them, and please bring back whatever old wire you can salvage."

"It's really an enormous inconvenience—"

Skorlet tried to make a furious gesture but, impeded by the globes, managed only to flap her elbows. "You and Jantiff are both insufferable! I intend to go to the feast and Tanzel is coming as well. Unless you care to pay for her bonter, then you must help me with these globes!"

Esteban gave a groan of annoyance. "An abominable nuisance! Well, dog defile it, what must be, must be. Let's count them out."

While they worked Jantiff seated himself upon the couch, which Esteban had upholstered with a fine thick cloth, patterned in a dramatic orange, brown and black geometry. The other furnishings showed similar evidence of taste and discrimination. Upon an end table Jantiff noticed a camera of familiar aspect. He picked it up, looked at it closely and put it in his pocket.

Skorlet and Esteban finished the count. "Kibner is not the effusively generous person you take him for," said Esteban. "He'll want at least thirty percent of the gross."

Skorlet gave a poignant contralto cry of distress. "That's utterly exorbitant! Think of the scrounging, the work, the inconvenience I've suffered! Ten percent is surely enough!"

Esteban laughed dubiously. "I'll start with five and settle as low as I can."

"Be steadfast! Also you must carefully impress values upon Kibner! He seems to think we don't know the worth of money."

"Creeping elitism there!" Esteban warned her facetiously. "Curb that tendency!"

"Yes, of course," said Skorlet sarcastically. "Come along, Jantiff. It's almost time for evening wump."

Esteban's gaze brushed the end table, stopped short, veered around the room, returned briefly to the end table, then came to rest upon Jantiff. "Just a moment. There's snergery going on, and I don't care to be a party to it."

"What are you talking about?" snapped Skorlet. "You have nothing worth attention."

"What of my camera? Come now, Jantiff, disgorge. You were sitting on the couch, and I even saw you make the move."

"This is embarrassing," said Jantiff.

"No doubt. The camera is missing. Do you have it?"

"As a matter of fact I have my own camera with me, the one I brought from Zeck. I haven't so much as seen yours."

Esteban took a menacing step forward and extended his hand. "No snerging here, please. You took my camera; give it back."

"No, this is definitely my own camera."

"It's mine! It was on the table and I saw you take it."

"Can you identify it?"

"Naturally! Beyond all equivocation! I could even describe the pictures on the matrix." He hesitated and added: "If I chose to do so."

"Mine has the name Jantiff Ravensroke engraved beside the serial number in twisted reed Old Mish characters. Does yours?"

Esteban stared at Jantiff with hot round brown eyes. He spoke in a harsh voice: "I don't know what's engraved beside the serial number."

Jantiff wrote in elegant flourishes on a piece of paper. "This is Old Mish. Do you care to inspect my camera?"

Esteban made an incomprehensible sound and turned his back.

Jantiff and Skorlet left the apartment. As they walked the corridor Skorlet said: "That was both childish and unnecessary. What do you gain by antagonizing Esteban?"

Jantiff stopped short in shock and astonishment. Skorlet strode grimly forward without slackening her pace. Jantiff ran to catch up. "You can't be serious!"

"Naturally I'm serious!"

"But I only reclaimed the property he stole from me! Isn't that a reasonable act?"

"You should use the word 'snerge'; it's far more polite."

"I was quite polite to Esteban, under the circumstances."

"Not really. You know how fastidiously proud he is."

"Hmmf. I don't understand how any Arrabin can be proud."

Skorlet swung around and briskly slapped Jantiff's face. Jantiff stood back, then shrugged. In silence they returned to their apartment. Skorlet flung open the door and marched into the sitting room. Jantiff closed the door with exaggerated care.

Skorlet swung around to face him. Jantiff retreated, but Skorlet now was remorseful. In a throbbing voice she cried: "It was wrong to strike you; please forgive me."

"My fault, really," mumbled Jantiff. "I should not have mentioned the Arrabins."

"Let's not talk about it; we're both tired and troubled. In fact, let's go to bed and copulate, to restore our equanimity; I simply must relax."

"That's an odd notion but—oh, I suppose so, if you're of a mind."

Arriving at Kedidah's apartment, Jantiff found only Sarp on the premises. Sarp announced gruffly that Kedidah would be back shortly "—with noise and confusion and jerking about this way and that. Not an easy one to share with, I'll tell you!"

"A pity!" said Jantiff. "Why don't you trade apartments with someone?"

"Easier said than done! Who'd choose to burden their lives with such a hity-tity waloonch? And will she pick up behind herself? Never. She creates disorder out of the thin air!"

"As a matter of fact I find my own roommate just a bit too quietly self-contained," said Jantiff. "One hardly knows she is about, and she has an almost geometrical sense of tidiness. Perhaps I might be persuaded to trade with you."

Sarp cocked his head to the side, and squinted dubiously at Jantiff. "It's always a gamble. Who is this paragon of yours?"

"Her name is Skorlet."

Sarp emitted a wild hoot of derision. "Skorlet! Neat? With her incessant cult-globes? And 'quietly self-contained'? She is not only talkative but meddlesome and domineering! She hectored poor Wissilim so that he not only changed levels but moved clear out of Old Pink! What kind of fool do you take me for?"

"You misunderstand her; she is actually quite mild. Look here; I'll even include an inducement."

"Such as what?"

"Well, I'll paint your portrait, in several colors."

"Ha! Yonder hangs the mirror; what else do I need?"

"Well—here is a fine stylus I brought from Zeck: a scientific marvel. It draws carbon and water and nitrogen from the air to formulate a soft ink which it then burns permanently upon paper. It never fails and lasts a lifetime."

"I write very little. What else can you offer?"

"I don't have a great deal else. A jade and silver medallion for your cap?"

"I'm not a vain man; I'd only trade it out on the mud flats for a mouthful of bonter, so what's the odds? Good old gruff and deedle with wobbly to fill in the chinks: that'll do for me."

"I thought Kedidah was such a trial."

"Compared to Skorlet she's an angel of mercy. A bit noisy and over-gregarious; who could deny it? And now she's taken up with Garch Darskin of the Ephthalotes . . . In fact, here she comes now."

The door swung aside; into the apartment burst Kedidah with three muscular young men. "Good, kind Sarp!" cried Kedidah. "I knew I'd find him home! Bring out your jug of swill and pour us all a toddy! Garch has been at practice and I'm exhausted watching him."

"The swill is gone," growled Sarp. "You finished it yesterday." Kedidah took heed of Jantiff. "Here's an obliging fellow! Jantiff, fetch us in your jug of swill. Hussade is a taxing occupation and we're all in need of a toddy!"

"Sorry," said Jantiff rather stiffly. "I'm not able to oblige you."

"What a bore. Garch, Kirso, Rambleman; this is Janty Ravensroke, from Zeck. Janty, you are meeting the cutting edge of the Ephthalotes: the most efficient team on Wyst!"

"I am honored to make your acquaintance," said Jantiff in his most formal voice.

"Jantiff is very talented," said Kedidah. "He produces the most fascinating drawings! Jantiff, do us a picture!"

Jantiff shook his head in embarrassment. "Really, Kedidah, I just don't knock out these things on the spur of the moment. Furthermore, I don't have my equipment with me."

"You're just modest! Come now, Janty, produce something witty and amusing! Look, there's your stylus, and somewhere, somewhere, somewhere, a scrap of paper . . . Use the back of this registration form."

Jantiff reluctantly took the materials. "What shall I draw?"

"Whatever suits you. Me, Garch, or even old Sarp."

"Don't bother with me," said Sarp. "Anyway I'm going out to meet Esteban. He's got some mysterious proposal to communicate."

"It's probably just his bonterfest; I'd go instantly if I had the tokens. Jantiff, perform for us! Do Rambleman; he's the most picturesque! Notice his nose; it's like the fluke of an anchor: pure North Pombal for you!"

With stiff fingers Jantiff set to work. The others watched a moment or two then fell to talking and paid him no further heed. In disgust Jantiff rose to his feet and left the apartment. No one seemed so much as to notice his going.

Dear all of you:

Thanks forever for the pigments; I'll guard these with great care. Skorlet snerged my last set to paint designs upon her cult-globes. She hoped to sell them for a large sum, but now she thinks Kibner, the Disjerferact booth-tender, cheated her. She's dreadfully exasperated, so I walk very carefully around the apartment. She's become abstracted and distant; I can't understand why. Something is hanging in the air. The bonterfest? This is a big event both for herself and for Tanzel. I don't pretend to understand Skorlet; still I can't evade the impression that she's disturbed and unsettled. Tanzel is a pleasant little creature. I took her to Disjerferact and spent all of half an ozol buying her such delicacies as toasted seaweed and sour eel tarts. The Disjerferact traders are none of them Arrabins, and a more curious collection you never saw. Disjerferact covers a large area and there are thousands of them: folk from I don't know where. Montebanks, junk dealers, prestidigitators, gamblers, puppeteers and clown-masters, illusionists and marvel-makers, tricksters, grotesques, musicians, acrobats, clairvoyants, and of course the food sellers. Disjerferact is pathetic, sordid, pungent, fascinating and a tumult of color and noise. Most amazing of all are the Pavilions of Rest, which must be unique in the Gaean universe. To the Pavilions come Arrabins who wish to die. Proprietors of the various pavilions vie in making their services attractive. There are five currently in operation. The most economical operation is conducted upon a cylindrical podium ten feet high. The customer mounts the podium and there delivers a valedictory declamation, sometimes spontaneous, sometimes rehearsed over a period of months. These declamations are of great interest and there is always an attentive audience, cheering, applauding or uttering groans of sympathy. Sometimes the sentiments are unpopular, and the speech is greeted with catcalls. Meanwhile a snuff of black fur descends from above. Eventually it drops over the postulant and his explanations are heard no more. An enterprising Gaean from one of the Home Worlds has recorded a large number of these speeches and published them in a book entitled *Before I Forget*.

Nearby is Halcyon House. The person intent upon surcease, after paying his fee, enters a maze of prisms. He wanders here and there in a golden shimmer, while friends watch from the outside. His form becomes indistinct among the reflections and then is seen no more.

At the next pavilion, the Perfumed Boat floats in a channel. The voyager embarks and reclines upon a couch. A profusion of paper flowers is arranged over his body; he is tendered a goblet of cordial and sent floating away into a tunnel from which issues strains of ethereal music. The boat eventually floats back to the dock clean and empty. What occurs in the tunnel is not made clear.

The services provided by the Happy Way-Station are more convivial. The wayfarer arrives with all his boon companions. In a luxurious wood-paneled hall they are served whatever delicacies and tipple the wayfarer's purse can afford. All eat, drink, reminisce; exchange pleasantries, until the lights begin to dim, whereupon the friends take their leave and the room goes dark. Sometimes the wayfarer changes his mind at the last minute and departs with his friends. On other occasions (so I am told) the party becomes outrageously jolly and mistakes may be made. The wayfarer manages to crawl away on his hands and knees, his friends remaining in a drunken daze around the table while the room goes dark.

The fifth pavilion is a popular place of entertainment, and is conducted like a game of chance. Five participants each wager a stipulated sum and are seated in iron chairs numbered one through five. Spectators also pay an admission fee and are allowed to make wagers. An index spins into motion, slows, and stops upon a number. The person in the chair so designated wins five times his stake. The other four drop through trap doors and are seen no more. A tale—perhaps apocryphal—is told of a certain desperate man named Bastwick, who took Seat Two on a stake of only twenty tokens. He won and remained seated, his stake now a hundred tokens. Two won again, and again Bastwick remained seated, his stake now five hundred tokens. Again Two won, and Bastwick had gained twenty-five hundred tokens. In a nervous fit he fled the pavilion. Seat Two won twice more running. Had Bastwick remained seated, he would have won 62,500 tokens!

I visited the pavilions with Tanzel, who is very knowing; in fact my information is derived from her. I asked what happened to the cadavers, and I learned rather more than I wanted to know! The objects are macerated and flushed into a drain, along with all other wastes and slops. The slurry, known as "spent sturge," is piped to a central processing plant, along with "spent sturge" from everywhere in the city. Here it is processed, renewed and replenished and piped back to all the blocks of the city as "ordinary sturge." In the block kitchens the sturge becomes the familiar and nutritious gruff, deedle and wobbly.

While I am on the subject, let me recount a rather odd event which took place one morning last week. Skorlet and I chanced to be up on the roof garden when a corpse was discovered behind some thimble-pod bushes. Apparently he had been stabbed in the throat. People stood around muttering, Skorlet and I included, until eventually the Block Warden arrived. He dragged the body to the descensor, and that was that.

I was naturally perplexed by all this. I mentioned to Skorlet that no one on Zeck would touch the corpse until the police had investigated thoroughly.

Skorlet gave me her customary sneer. "This is an egalistic nation; we need no police, we have our Mutuals to advise us and to restrain crazy people."

"Evidently the Mutuals aren't enough!" I told her. "We've just seen a murdered man!"

Skorlet became annoyed. "That was Tango, a boisterous fellow and a cheat! He notoriously trades his drudge, then never finds time to work off the stint. He won't be missed by anyone."

"Do you mean to say that there won't be an investigation of any kind?"

"Not unless someone files a report with the Warden."

"Surely that's unnecessary! The Warden hauled the body away."

"Well, he can hardly write out a report to himself, can he? Be practical!"

"I am practical! There's a murderer among us, perhaps on our very own level!"

"Quite likely, but who wants to make the report? The Warden would then be obliged to interrogate everyone, and take endless depositions; we would hear no end of disgraceful disclosures and everyone would be upset, to what real end?"

"So poor Tango is murdered, and no one cares."

"He's not 'poor Tango'! He was a boor and a pest!"

I pursued the subject no further. I speculate that every society has a means of purging itself and ejecting offensive elements. This is how it is accomplished under egalism.

There's so much to tell you that I can't come to a stopping place. The public entertainments are prodigious. I have attended what they call a "shunkery," which is beyond belief. Hussade is also very popular here; in fact, a friend of mine is acquainted with certain of the Ephthalotes, a team from Port Cass on the north coast of Zumer. None of the Arrabins play hussade. All the players hail from other parts of Wyst or off-planet. I understand that the games are rather more intense here than—

A tap-tap-tap. Jantiff put aside his letter and went to the door. Kedidah stood in the corridor. "Hello, Jantiff. Can I come in?"

Jantiff moved aside; Kedidah sauntered into the room. She gave Jantiff a look of mock-severe accusation. "Where have you been? I haven't seen you for a week! You're never even in the wumper!"

"I've been going late," said Jantiff.

"Well, I've missed you. When one gets used to a person, he has no right to slink off into hiding."

"You seem preoccupied with your Ephthalotes," said Jantiff.

"Yes! Aren't they wonderful? I adore hussade! They play today as a matter of fact. I was supposed to have a pass but I've lost it. Wouldn't you like to go?"

"Not particularly. I'm rather busy—"

"Come, Janty, don't be harsh with me. I believe that you're jealous. How can you worry about a whole hussade team?"

"Very easily. There's exactly nine times the worry, not counting substitutes. Nor the sheirl."

"How silly! After all, a person can't be split or diminished merely because she's very busy."

"It depends upon what she's busy at," muttered Jantiff.

Kedidah only laughed. "Are you going with me to the hussade game? Please, Janty!"

Jantiff sighed in resignation. "When do you want to go?"

"Right now; in fact this very minute, or we'll be late. When I couldn't find my pass, I was frantic until I thought of you, dear good boy that you are. Incidentally, you'll have to pay my way in. I'm utterly bereft of tokens."

Jantiff turned to face her, mouth quivering in speechless indignation. At the sight of her smiling face he gave a sour shrug. "I simply don't understand you."

"And I don't understand you, Janty, so we're in balance. What if we did? How would we benefit? Better the way we are. Come along now or we'll be late."

Jantiff returned to his letter:

—elsewhere.

By the strangest coincidence, I have just escorted my friend to the hussade game. The Ephthalotes played a team known as the Dangsgot Bravens, from the Caradas Islands. I am still shaken. Hussade at Uncibal is not like hussade at Frayness. The stadium is absolutely vast, and engorged with unbelievable hordes. Nearby one sees human faces and can even hear individual voices, but in the distance the crowd becomes a palpitating crust.

The game itself is standard, with a few local modifications not at all to my liking. The initial ceremonies are stately, elaborate, and prolonged; after all, everyone has plenty of time. The players parade in splendid costumes, and are introduced one at a time. None, incidentally, are Arrabin. Each performs a number of ritual postures then retires. The two sheirls appear at each end of the field, and ascend into their temples while a pair of orchestras play *Glory to the Virgin Sheirls*. At the same time a great wooden effigy is brought out on the field: a twelve-foot representation of the karkoon* Claubus, which the sheirls pointedly ignore, for reasons you will presently understand. A third orchestra plays blatant braying "karkoon" music, in antiphony to the two *Glorys*. I took note of the folk nearby; all were uneasy and

---

*In the Alastrid myths karkoons are a tribe of quasi-demonic beings, characterized by hatred of mankind and insatiable lust.

restless, shuddering at the discords, yet earnest and intent and keyed taut for the drama to come. The sheirls at this point stand quietly in their temples, enveloped in Dwan-light and a wonderful psychic haze, each the embodiment of all the graces and beauties; yet, certainly, through the minds of each whirl the thrilling questions: Will I be glorified? Will I be given to Claubus?

The game proceeds, until one of the teams can pay no more ransom. Their sheirl thereupon is defiled by Claubus in a most revolting and unnatural manner; in this condition she and Claubus are trundled around the field in a cart pulled by the defeated team, to the accompaniment of the coarse braying music. The victors enjoy a splendid feast of bonter; the spectators undergo a catharsis and presumably are purged of their tensions. As for the humiliated sheirl, she has forever lost her beauty and dignity. She becomes an outcast and, in her desperation, may attempt almost anything. As you will perceive, hussade at Uncibal is not a merry pastime; it is a grim and poignant spectacle: an immensely popular public rite. Under the circumstances, it seems very odd that the teams never lack for beautiful sheirls, who are drawn to danger as a moth to flame. The Arrabins are indeed an odd people, who like to toy with the most morbid possibilities. For instance: at the shunk contests the barriers are quite low, and the shunk in their mad antics often charge over and into the spectators. Dozens are crushed. Are the barriers raised? Are those lower seats empty? Never! In such a way the Arrabins participate in these rituals of life and death. Needless to say, none *expects* to be torn to bits, just as no sheirl expects to be defiled. It is all sheer egocentricity: the myth of self triumphant over destiny! I believe that as folk become urbanized, just so intensely are they individuated, and not to the contrary. From this standpoint the crowds flowing along Uncibal River quite transcend the imagination. Try to think of it! Row after row, rank after rank of faces, each the node of a distinct and autonomous universe.

On this note I will close my letter. I wish I could inform you of definite plans, but for a fact I have none; I am torn between fascination and revulsion for this strange place.

Now I must go to drudge: I have traded stints with a certain Arsmer from an apartment along the hall. This week is unusually busy. Still, by Zeck standards, an idyll of leisure!

With my dearest love to all: your wayward

Jantiff

CHAPTER 6

∙∙

J antiff became ever more aware of Skorlet's strange new manner. Never had he thought her placid or stolid, but now she alternated between fits of smoldering silence and a peculiar nervous gaiety. Twice Jantiff discovered her in close colloquy with Esteban, and the discussions came to such an abrupt halt that Jantiff was made to feel an intruder. Another time he found her pacing the apartment, shaking her hands as if they were wet. This was a new manifestation which Jantiff felt impelled to notice. "What is bothering you now?"

Skorlet stopped short, turned Jantiff an opaque black glance, then blurted forth her troubles. "It's Esteban and his cursed bonterfest. Tanzel is sick with excitement, and Esteban wants full payment. I don't have the tokens."

"Why doesn't he pay for Tanzel himself?"

"Hah! You should know Esteban by this time! He's absolutely heartless when it comes to money."*

Jantiff began to sense a possible trend to the conversation. He gave his head a sympathetic shake and sidled away toward the bedroom. Skorlet caught his arm, and Jantiff's fears were quickly realized. Skorlet spoke in a throaty voice: "Jantiff, I have a hundred tokens; I need five hundred more for the bonterfest. Won't you lend me that much? I'll do something nice for you."

Jantiff winced and shifted his gaze around the room. "There's nothing nice I need just now."

"But Jantiff, it's only an ozol or two. You've got a whole sheaf."

"I'll need those ozols on the way home."

"You already have your ticket! You told me so!"

"Yes, yes! I have my ticket! But I might want to stop off along the way, and then there'll be no money because I squandered it at Esteban's bonterfest."

"But you're squandering money on your own place in the group."

"I also squandered my pigments on your cult-globes."

"Must you be so petty?" snarled Skorlet, suddenly furious. "You're too paltry to bother with! Give thanks that I convinced Esteban of this!"

---

*Among the Arrabins paternity is always in doubt, but even when an acknowledged fact, incurs no burden of obligation.

"I don't know what you're talking about," said Jantiff stiffly. "It's not Esteban's affair whether I'm paltry or petty or anything else."

Skorlet started to speak, then suppressed her remarks and said merely: "I'll say no more on that subject."

"Exactly so," said Jantiff frigidly. "In fact, nothing more need be said on any subject whatever."

Skorlet's face twisted askew in a darkling leer. "No? I thought you wanted to move in with that slang* Kedidah."

"I spoke along those lines," said Jantiff in a measured voice. "Evidently it can't be done, and that seems to be the end of it."

"But it can be done, and quite easily, if I choose to do it."

"Oh? How will you accomplish this miracle?"

"Please, Jantiff, don't analyze my every statement. What I undertake to do, I achieve, and never doubt it. Old Sarp will move here if Tanzel will copulate with him from time to time, and she's very anxious for the feast so everything works out nicely."

Jantiff turned away in disgust. "I don't want to be part of any such arrangement."

Skorlet stared at him, her brows two black bars of puzzlement. "And why not? Everyone gets what he wants; why should you object?"

Jantiff tried to formulate a lofty remark, but none of his sentiments seemed appropriate. He heaved a sigh. "First, I want to discuss the matter with Kedidah. After all—"

"No! Kedidah has no force in this affair. What's it to her? She's busy with her hussade team; she cares not a whit whether you're here or there!"

Jantiff, looking up at the ceiling, composed an incisive rejoinder, but at the end held his tongue. Skorlet's concepts and his own were incommensurable; why incite her into a new tirade?

Skorlet needed no stimulation. "Frankly, Jantiff, I'll be pleased to have you out of here. You and your precious posturings! Piddling little sketches hung up everywhere to remind us of your talents! You'll never forget your elitism, will you? This is Arrabus, Jantiff! You're here on sufferance, so never forget it!"

"Nothing of the sort!" stormed Jantiff. "I've paid all my fees and I do my own drudge."

Skorlet's round white face underwent a sly and cunning contortion. "Those sketches, they're very strange! It gives me to wonder, these endless faces! Why do you do it? What or whom are you looking for? I want the truth!"

---

*A hairless rodent, long and slender, capable of producing a variety of odors at will.

"I draw faces because it suits me to do so. And now, unless I'm to be late for drudge—"

"And now: bah! Give me the money and I'll make the arrangements."

"Absolutely not. You make the arrangements first. In any event, I don't have so many tokens; I'll have to change ozols at the spaceport."

Skorlet gave him a long grim look. "So long as I can make Esteban a definite answer, and I'm seeing him directly."

"Be as definite as you like."

Skorlet marched from the apartment. Jantiff changed into his work overalls and descended to the street where suddenly he recalled that today Arsmer had taken over his stint. Feeling foolish he returned up the ascensor to his apartment. Stepping into the bedroom he removed boots and coveralls, and took them to the cabinet. At this moment the outer door opened and several people entered. Heavy footsteps approached the bedroom; someone pushed aside the door and looked in, but failed to notice Jantiff by the cabinet. "He's not here," said a voice Jantiff recognized as that of Esteban.

"He's gone off to drudge," said Skorlet. "Sit, and I'll see if the swill is fit to drink."

"Don't bother so far as I'm concerned," said a husky-harsh voice which Jantiff failed to recognize. "I can't abide the stuff."

Sarp's plangent rasp sounded in reply: "Easy for you to say, with all your wines and fructifers!"

"Never fear, soon you'll say the same!" declared Esteban in a voice of reckless enthusiasm. "Just give us a couple months."

"You're either a genius or a lunatic," said the unknown voice.

"Use the word 'visionary,' " said Esteban. "Isn't this how great events have gone in the past? The visionary seizes upon an idle reverie; he constructs an irresistible scheme and topples an empire! From Jantiff's miserable little sketch comes this notion of a lifetime."

" 'Lifetime': that is apt usage," said the unknown man drily. "The word reverberates."

"Here and now we abandon negativity!" exclaimed Esteban. "It's only a hindrance. We succeed by our very boldness!"

"Still, let's not be rash. I can point out a hundred avenues into disaster."

"Very good! We'll consider each in turn and give them all wide berths. Skorlet, where is the swill? Pour with a loose hand."

"Don't neglect me," said Sarp.

Jantiff went to sit on the bed. He uttered a tentative cough, just as Esteban spoke out. "Success to our venture!"

"I'm still not altogether attuned to your frequency," grumbled the unknown man. "To me it sounds implausible, improbable, even unreal."

360 / JACK VANCE

"Not at all," declared Esteban gaily. "Break the affair into separate steps. Each is simplicity in itself. In your case especially; how can you choose to act otherwise?"

The unknown man gave a sour grunt. "There's something in what you say. Let me see that sketch again . . . Yes; it's really most extraordinary."

Skorlet spoke in a sardonic aside. "Perhaps we should drink our toast to Jantiff."

"Quite so," said Esteban. "We must think very carefully about Jantiff."

Jantiff stretched himself out on the bed and considered crawling underneath.

"He only typifies the basic problem," said the unknown voice. "In simple terms: how do we avoid recognition?"

"This is where you become indispensable," said Esteban.

Sarp gave a rasping chuckle. "By definition, we're all indispensable."

"True," said Esteban. "For one of us to succeed, all must succeed."

"One thing is certain," mused Skorlet. "Once we commit ourselves there's no turning back."

Jantiff could not help reflecting that Skorlet's voice, cool and steady, was far different from the voice she had used during their recent quarrel.

"Back to the basic problem," said the husky-harsh voice. "Your absence from Old Pink will certainly be noticed."

"We'll have transferred to other blocks!"

"Well and good, until someone looks at the screen and says: 'Why, there's Sarp! And dog defile us all, that's surely Skorlet! And Esteban!' "

"I've considered this at length," said Esteban. "The problem is surmountable. Our acquaintances, after all, are not innumerable."

Sarp asked: "Are you forgetting Loudest Bombah?* The Whispers are inviting him to the Centenary."

"He's invited, but I can't believe that he'll come."

"You never know," said the unknown voice. "Stranger things have happened. I insist that we leave nothing to chance."

"Agreed! In fact I've considered the matter. Think! If he's on hand he'll be sure to mount the monkey-pole.† Correct?"

"A possibility, but not a certainty."

"Well, he's either on hand or he isn't."

"That is definitely true."

"If someone gave you a bag of poggets and you knew one might be deadly poisonous, what would you do?"

---

*Bombah: Arrabin slang for a wealthy off-worlder: by extension a tourist.
Loud Bombah: an important and powerful off-worlder.
Loudest Bombah: the Connatic.
†Monkey-pole: the Pedestal overlooking the Field of Voices.

"Throw away the whole bag."

"That's certainly one possibility. A good number of poggets are wasted, of course."

"Hmmf . . . Well, we'll discuss it another time. Are you still planning your bonterfest?"

"Most definitely," said Skorlet. "I've promised Tanzel and there's no reason to disappoint her."

"It makes us all conspicuous, after a fashion."

"Not really. Bonterfests aren't uncommon."

"Still, why not cancel the affair? There'll be opportunities in the future."

"But I'm not confident of the future! It's a spinning top which can totter in any direction!"

"Whatever you like. It's not a critical matter."

Skorlet, for one reason or another, chose to enter the bedroom. She went to her cabinet, then, turning, saw Jantiff. She gave a croak of astonishment. "What are you doing here?"

Jantiff feigned the process of awakening. "Eh? What? Oh, hello, Skorlet. Is it time for wump?"

"I thought you were at drudge."

"Arsmer took my drudge today. Why? What's the problem? Are you having guests?" Jantiff sat up and swung his legs to the floor. From the sitting room came a mutter of voices, then the outer door slid open and shut. Esteban sauntered into the bedroom.

"Hello, Jantiff. Did we disturb you?"

"Not at all," said Jantiff. He looked up uneasily at Esteban's looming bulk. "I was sound asleep." He rose to his feet. Esteban stood aside as Jantiff went into the sitting room, which was now empty.

Esteban's voice came softly against his back. "Skorlet tells me that you are advancing her money for the bonterfest."

"Yes," said Jantiff shortly. "I agreed to this."

"When can I have the money? Sorry to be abrupt, but I've got to meet my commitments."

"Will tomorrow do?"

"Very well indeed. Until tomorrow, then."

Esteban turned a significant glance toward Skorlet and left the apartment. Skorlet followed him into the corridor.

Jantiff went to the wall where he had pinned up certain of his sketches. He studied each in turn; none, to Jantiff's eyes at least, seemed in the slightest degree inflammatory. A most peculiar situation!

Skorlet returned. Jantiff quickly moved away from the sketches. Skorlet went to the table and rearranged her few trifles of bric-à-brac. In an airy voice she said: "Esteban is such an extravagant man! I never take him seriously. Especially after a mug or two of swill, when he fantasizes most outrageously. I don't know if you heard him talking—" She paused and looked sideways, dense black eyebrows arched in question.

Jantiff said hurriedly, "I was dead asleep; I didn't even know he was there."

Skorlet gave a curt nod. "You can't imagine the intrigues and plots I've heard over the years! None ever amounted to anything, of course."

"Oh? What of the bonterfest? Is that a fantasy too?"

Skorlet laughed in brittle merriment. "Definitely not! That's quite real! In fact you'd better go change your money and I'll make arrangements with Sarp."

CHAPTER 7

Jantiff departed Old Pink and walked slowly to the manway. The day was cool, clear and crisp. Dawn hung in the sky, coruscating like a molten pearl, but for once Jantiff paid no heed to chromatic effects. He rode the lateral to Uncibal River, and diverted east toward the space-port. Odd, most decidedly odd, this affair. What could it all mean? Certainly nothing constructive.

A mile east of the space-port a lateral led north past the Alastor Centrality and on to the Field of Voices. Almost without conscious intent Jantiff diverted upon the lateral and rode to the Centrality: a structure of black stone, set to the back of a compound paved with slabs of lavender porphyry and planted with twin rows of lime trees.

Jantiff crossed the compound, passed through an air curtain into a foyer. Behind a counter sat a slender dark-haired young man, apparently no Arrabin by evidence both of his hairstyle and an indefinable off-world manner. He addressed Jantiff politely: "What are your needs, sir?"

"I wish a few moments with the cursar," said Jantiff. "May I inquire his name?"

"He is Bonamico, and I believe that he is presently disengaged. May I ask your name?"

"I am Jantiff Ravensroke, from Frayness on Zeck."

"This way, if you please."

The clerk touched a button and spoke: "The Respectable Jantiff Ravensroke of Zeck is here, sir."

A voice responded: "Very good, Clode; I'll see him at once."

Clode made a sign to Jantiff and conducted him across the foyer. A door slid aside; they entered a study paneled in white wood with a green rug upon the floor. A massive table at the center of the room supported a variety of objects: books, charts, photographs, cubes of polished wood, a small hologram stage, a six-inch sphere of rock crystal which seemed to function as a clock. Against the table leaned the cursar: a short sturdy man with pleasant blunt features and blond hair cropped close.

Clode performed a formal introduction: "Cursar Bonamico, this is the Respectable Jantiff Ravensroke."

"Thank you, Clode," said the cursar. He spoke to Jantiff: "Will you be pleased to take a cup of tea?"

"By all means," said Jantiff. "That is very kind of you."

"Clode, would you see to it? Be seated, sir, and tell me how I can be of service."

Jantiff lowered himself into a cushioned chair. The cursar remained by the table. "You are a recent arrival?"

"Quite true," said Jantiff. "But how did you know?"

"Your shoes tell the tale," said the cursar with a faint smile. "They are of better quality than one sees about the ways of Arrabus."

"Yes, of course." Jantiff gripped the arms of his chair and leaned forward. "What I have to tell you is so odd that I don't quite know where to begin. Perhaps I should mention that at Frayness on Zeck I trained in dimensional drafting and pictorial composition, so that I have some small skill at depiction. Since arriving here I've made dozens of sketches: folk along the man-ways and at my block, which is Old Pink, 17-882."

The cursar nodded. "Proceed, please."

"My roommate is a certain Skorlet. Today, one of her friends, Esteban, arrived at the apartment with a man named Sarp and a fourth man whom I don't know. They were not aware that I was in the bedroom and held a colloquy which I could not help but overhear." To the best of his ability Jantiff reproduced the conversation. "Eventually Skorlet found me in the bedroom and became very disturbed. Sarp and the fourth man left instantly. The episode impressed me very unfavorably. In fact, I regard it as rather sinister." He paused to sip the tea which Clode had brought in during his account.

The cursar considered a moment. "You have no inkling as to the identity of the fourth man?"

"None whatever. I glimpsed his back through the door as he left the apartment; he seemed large, with heavy shoulders and black hair. This is my impression, at least."

The cursar gave his head a dubious shake. "I don't quite know what to tell you. The tone of the conversation certainly suggests something more than idle mischief."

"That was my definite impression."

"Still, no overt acts have been committed. I can't exert the Connatic's authority on the basis of a conversation which, after all, might be only wild talk. The Arrabins, as you may have noticed, are prone to extravagance."

Jantiff frowned in dissatisfaction. "Can't you make inquiries, or perform an investigation?"

"How? The Centrality here is a very minor affair, to an extraordinary degree. We're like an enclave on foreign soil. I have a staff of two: Clode and Aleida. They're underworked, but neither qualifies as a secret operative; no more, in fact, do I. There's not even an Arrabin police agency to deal with."

"Still, something must be done!"

"I agree, but first let's assemble some facts. Try to discover the identity of the fourth man. Can you do this?"

Jantiff said reluctantly, "I suppose this is possible. Esteban has organized a bonterfest, and this man apparently intends to be on hand."

"Very good; learn his name, and watch what goes on. If their activities exceed simple talk then I can act."

Jantiff grumbled: "That's like waiting for the rain before you start to fix the roof."

The cursar chuckled. "The rain at least shows us where the leaks are. I'll do this much. Tomorrow I leave for Waunisse to confer with the Whispers. I'll report what you have told me and they can take what steps they think necessary. They're a sensible group and won't automatically dismiss the matter. For your part, try to assemble more facts."

Jantiff gave a glum assent. He finished his tea and departed the Centrality.

The man-way took him toward the space-port. Jantiff looked back at the Centrality with the uneasy sense of lost opportunity. But what more could he say or do? And, under the circumstances, what more could the cursar say or do?

At the space-port exchange office he converted five ozols into tokens, and returned toward Old Pink. His thoughts turned to Kedidah. She would certainly be pleased at the change; Sarp, after all, could not be the easiest person in the world to live with. Still, Jantiff reflected uneasily, she had expressed herself quite definitely on the subject. Probably not in all seriousness, Jantiff assured himself. In due course he arrived at Old Pink.

Skorlet was out. Jantiff packed his belongings. At last the tide of events was flowing in his favor! Kedidah! Marvelous feckless delightful Kedidah! How surprised she'd be! . . . Jantiff's mental processes became sluggish. A future without Kedidah seemed dark and lorn, but—and why deny it?—a future with her seemed impossible! Nonetheless, they'd work it out together. They'd naturally move out of Uncibal, but where? It was hard to imagine Kedidah and her flamboyant habits in the context of, say,

Frayness. A contrast indeed! Kedidah would simply have to restrain her-self . . . The absurdity caused Jantiff to wince. He paced back and forth across the sitting room, three steps this way, three steps that. He stopped short, looked at the door. The die was cast: Sarp was coming; he was going. Oh, well, it might turn out for the best. Kedidah thought well of him; he was certain of this. No doubt they'd work out a happy accommo-dation of some kind . . . The door opened; Skorlet entered the room. She stood just inside the doorway, glowering at him. "All right; it's done. Are you packed?"

"Well, yes. Actually, Skorlet, I've been thinking that maybe I might not move after all."

"What!" cried Skorlet. "You can't be serious!"

"I've been thinking that maybe—"

"I don't care what you've been thinking! I've made the arrangements and you're going. I don't want you here!"

"Please, Skorlet, be reasonable. Your 'wants' are not altogether relevant to the matter."

"Yes they are!" Jutting out her head, Skorlet took an abrupt step ahead; Jantiff moved a corresponding pace backward. "You're a trial, Jantiff, I won't conceal it! Always peering and lurking and listening."

Jantiff tried to protest, but Skorlet paid no heed. "Quite honestly, Jan-tiff, I've had it with you! I'm sick of your namby-pamby postures, your ridiculous paintings, your eccentricities! You can't even copulate without counting your fingers! By all means move in with that shrick*; that's two of you. If you're a voyeur you'll have plenty to see; she's quite tireless! Time and time again I've seen the Ephthalotes stagger away on limp legs. Per-haps she'll allow you a turn or two at the end—"

"Stop, stop!" cried Jantiff. "I'll move if only to get away from your tirades!"

"Then give me the money! Nine hundred and twenty tokens!"

"Nine hundred and twenty!" exclaimed Jantiff. "I thought you said five hundred!"

"I've had to take three places: for you, me, and Tanzel. At three hun-dred tokens apiece, plus twenty tokens for minor expenses."

"But you said you had a hundred tokens!"

"I'm not spending them! Come now, the money!" She lurched forward; Jantiff stared fascinated into the round face, congested with emotion like a bruise with blood. He shuddered: how could he ever have fondled this appalling woman?

"The money!"

*Untranslatable.

Jantiff numbly counted over nine hundred and twenty tokens; Skor-let thrust a yellow card at him. "There's your place; go or stay as you like."

The door slid aside; Sarp thrust his head into the room. "Is this home? Good enough; one crib is much like another. Show me my bed."

Jantiff quietly took his belongings and departed. Kedidah, arriving home an hour later, found him in her sitting room, arranging his painting equip-ment on one of the shelves. Kedidah, abstracted, failed to notice what he was doing. "Hallo, Janty, nice to see you, but you'll have to scamper; I've no time at all today."

"Kedidah! There's lots of time! I've succeeded."

"Magnificent. How?"

"I pawned old Sarp off on Skorlet! We're living together at last!"

Kedidah thrust her arms stiffly down, fingers outspread, thumbs to her hips, as if galvanized by an electric shock. "Jantiff, this is the most idiotic behavior; I don't know what to say!"

"Say: 'Jantiff, how wonderful!' "

"Not quite. How can it be wonderful when my teammates are here and you stand in the corner glowering?"

Jantiff's jaw dropped. "Did you say 'teammates'?"

"Yes, I did. I'm the new Ephthalote sheirl. It's absolutely marvelous and I love it! We're going to play in the tournament and we're going to win; I feel it in my bones, and there'll be nothing but gay times forever!"

Jantiff somberly seated himself. "Who was the last sheirl?"

"Don't mention her, the catrape*! She carried bad luck on her back; she infested everyone with despair! The Ephthalotes say so themselves! Don't sneer, Jantiff, you'll see!"

"Kedidah, my dear, listen to me. Seriously now!" Jantiff jumped to his feet, ran across the room and took her hand. "Please, don't be sheirl! What's to be gained? Just think, if you and I share life together, how happy we'll be! Give up the Ephthalotes! Say no to them! Then we'll start making plans for the future!"

Kedidah patted Jantiff's cheek, then gave him a grim little slap. "When do you drudge?"

"I'm done for the week."

"A pity. Because I'm entertaining friends tonight and you'll be in the way."

There was a brief silence. Jantiff rose to his feet. "You need only specify when you need the apartment and I'll leave you free to exert yourself as thoroughly as you like."

Kedidah said: "Sometimes I think that in my heart of hearts I despise

---

*Offensive epithet signifying bedragglement, offensive odor and vulgarity of manner.

you, Jantiff. Also don't ask me to change the door code to suit your convenience, because I won't."

Not trusting himself to speak, Jantiff stormed from the room, out of Old Pink and away into the late afternoon. Along Uncibal River he rode, as far as Marchoury Lateral, bowing his head to gusty winds, striding ahead through the crowds careless of whom he shouldered aside. The folk so treated moaned in outrage and hissed epithets, which Jantiff ignored. He collided with a fat woman wearing flamboyant orange and red; she tottered, lurched and fell with a great thrashing of limbs and a fluttering of garish garments. Raising her head she bawled a horrid curse at Jantiff's back: Jantiff hurried away, while the woman heaved herself to her feet. No one paused to help her; all passed by with preoccupied expressions, nor did anyone so much as glare at Jantiff, nor call out censure, of which in any event he had had a surfeit. Through Jantiff's mind passed the melancholy reflection: this is precisely the pattern of life! One moment a person rides Uncibal River, comfortable with his or her thoughts, serenely proud of his or her orange and red costume; the next instant an insensate force sends one head over heels, rolling and tumbling under the feet of the passersby.

Jantiff thoughtfully strode along Uncibal River. With the toppling of the fat woman his fury had waned, and he looked along the current of oncoming faces in a spirit of moody detachment.

What strange people these were, and also, for a fact, all other people of the Gaean universe! He studied the faces carefully, as if they were clues to the most profound secrets of existence. Each face alike and each face different, as one snowflake both simulates and differs from all others! Jantiff began to fancy that he knew each intimately, as if he had seen each a hundred times. That crooked old man yonder might well be Sarp! The tall thin woman with her head thrown back could as easily be Gougade, who lived on the Sixteenth level of Old Pink. And Jantiff amused himself with the fancy that along Uncibal River might come a simulacrum of himself, exact in every detail. What kind of person might be this pseudo-Jantiff, this local version of his own dreary self?

The idea presently lost whatever glimmer of interest it might have possessed, and Jantiff returned to his immediate circumstances. The options open to him were pitifully few however, and gratefully, they included immediate departure. No question about it; he'd had his fill of insults and tirades, not to mention gruff, deedle, and wobbly. He felt a new spasm of resentment, most of it directed against himself. Was he such a sorry creature then? Jantiff, shame on you! Let's have no self-pity! What of all those wonderful plans? They depend on no one but yourself! Must they be tossed aside like so many scraps of trash just because your feelings have been hurt? As if to point up the issue, the setting sun passed behind a wisp of cloud, which instantly showed fringes of glorious color, and Jantiff's heart turned over within him. The Arrabins might be dense, obscure and impenetrable, but Dwan shone as clear and pure as light across mythical Heaven.

Jantiff drew a deep regenerative breath. His work must now absorb him. He would prove himself as rigid as any Arrabin; he would show regard for no one. Courtesy, yes. Formal consideration, yes. Warmth, no. Affection, no. As for Kedidah, she could be sheirl to four teams at once, with his best wishes. Skorlet? Esteban? Whatever their sordid plot he could only hope that they should fall over backwards and break their heads. The yellow card and the bonterfest? The group might include a massive black-haired man with a husky-harsh voice; it would certainly be interesting to learn his identity and pass the information along to Bonamico. And why should he not attend the bonterfest? After all, he had paid for it, and Esteban certainly would refuse to refund his money. So be it! From now on the primary concern of Jantiff Ravensroke was Jantiff Ravensroke, and that was all there was to it! Perhaps he should once more change apartments, and make a clean break with his problems. And leave Kedidah? The thought gave him pause. Charming, foolish Kedidah. Fascinating Kedidah. No doubt about it, she had befuddled him. There was always the possibility that she might change her ways. Devil take her! Why should he inconvenience himself to any slightest degree? He would take up his rightful residency; she would notice his detachment and possibly, from sheer perversity, begin to take an interest in him. Such a pattern of events was not impossible, at the very least! Jantiff diverted to a lateral and was carried north to the mud flats. On the outskirts of Disjerferact he purchased a dozen water-puffs, and so fortified, returned to Old Pink.

With careless bravado he let himself into his new apartment. Kedidah was not at home. On the wall someone had scrawled a memorandum in chalk:

> GAME TOMORROW! EPHTHALOTES AGAINST
> THE SKORNISH BRAGANDERS! PRACTICE
> THIS AFTERNOON! VICTORY TOMORROW!
> EPHTHALOTES FOREVER!

Jantiff read the notice with a curled lip, then set about arranging his belongings in those few areas where Kedidah had not strewn her own gear.

Late the following afternoon Kedidah brought an exultant party of teammates, friends and well-wishers to the apartment. She ran across the sitting room and ruffled Jantiff's hair. "Janty, we won! So much for all your grizzling and croaking! On five straight power drives!"

"Yes," said Jantiff. "I know. I attended the game."

"Then why aren't you cheering with the rest of us? O hurrah everyone! The Ephthalotes are the best ever! Jantiff, you can come along to the party. There'll be swill by the crock and you'll quite get over your dudgeon."

"No dudgeon whatever," said Jantiff coldly. "Unfortunately I have work to do and I don't think I had better come."

"Don't be such an old crow! I want you to do a picture of the Ephthalotes with their glorious good-luck sheirl!"

"Some other time," said Jantiff. "At a party it would be totally impossible."

"You're right! In a day or so then. For now—pour out the swill! A lavish hand there, Scrive! Here's joy for the Ephthalotes!"

The hubbub became too much for Jantiff. He left the apartment and went up to the roof garden where he sat brooding under the foliage.

After an hour he returned to find the apartment empty but in a terrible state of disorder; chairs were overturned; crockery mugs lay broken on the floor and someone had spilled a cup of swill on his bed.

He was only vaguely aware of Kedidah's return to the apartment, and somehow ignored the subsequent sounds from her side of the curtain.

In the morning Kedidah was ill, and Jantiff lay stiffly on his cot while Kedidah uttered small plaintive moans of distress. At last she called out: "Jantiff, are you awake?"

"Naturally."

"I'm in the most fearful condition; I don't think I can stir."

"Oh?"

"Yes, really, Janty! I'm sore everywhere; I can't imagine what happened to me."

"I could guess."

"Jantiff, I've got drudge and I'm simply not up to going out. You'll trade off with me, won't you?"

"I'll do nothing of the sort."

"Jantiff, please don't say no! This is an emergency; I absolutely can't make it out of the apartment. Be kind to me, Janty!"

"Certainly I'll be kind to you. But I won't take your drudge. In the first place you'd never pay me back. Secondly, I've got my own drudge today."

"Dog defile all! Well I'll have to bestir myself; I don't know how I'll manage. My head feels like a big gong."

During the next two days Kedidah left the apartment early and returned late and Jantiff saw little of her. On the third day, Kedidah remained at home, but the Ephthalotes' forthcoming game against the well-regarded Vergaz Khaldraves had put her in a trembling state of nerves. When Jantiff suggested that she sever her connection with the team she stared at him in disbelief. "You can't be serious, Janty! We've only got to beat the Khaldraves and then we're into the semi-finals, and then the finals and then—"

"Those are many 'and thens.' "

"But we can't lose! Don't you realize, Janty, that I'm a lucky talisman? Everyone says so! After we win we're established forever! We can chwig it in the bonter, not to mention a total end to drudge!"

"Very nice, but wouldn't you like to visit other places on other worlds?"

"Where I'd have to kowtow to all the plutocrats, and drudge eight days a week forever? I can't envision such a life. It must be appalling!"

"Not altogether. Many folk around the Cluster live this way."

"I prefer egalism; it's much easier on everyone."

"But you really don't prefer egalism! You want to be triumphant so that you'll have bonter and never any drudge. That's elitism!"

"No, it's not! It's because I'm Kedidah and because we're going to win! Say what you like but it's not elitism!"

Jantiff gave a sad chuckle. "I'll never fathom the Arrabins!"

"It's you who are illogical! You don't understand the simplest little things! Instead you dabble all day in those ridiculous colors. Which reminds me: when will you do our picture, as you promised?"

"Well, I don't know. I'm not really sure—"

"It can't be today, we're practicing; nor tomorrow, that's game day; nor the next day, because we'll be recovering from the celebration. You'll just have to wait, Jantiff!"

Jantiff sighed, "Let's forget the whole thing."

"Yes; that will be best. Instead, you can make a fine bold poster for the wall: 'Ephthalotes Triumphant' with titans and cockaroons and darting thunderbolts—all in orange and red and smashing green. Please do, Janty; we'll all be thrilled to see such a thing!"

"Really, Kedidah—"

"You won't do it? Such a trifling favor?"

"Go arrange the pigments and paper. I refuse to waste my own on something so ridiculous."

Kedidah uttered a yelp of sick disgust. "Jantiff, you're really extreme! You niggle over such trivial things!"

"Those pigments were sent to me from Zeck."

"Please, Jantiff, I can't bear to bicker with you."

Summoning all his dignity, Jantiff vacated the apartment.

In the ground-level foyer he encountered Skorlet. She greeted him with unconvincing affability. "Well, Jantiff, are you honing your appetite? The bonterfest is all arranged." She turned him a sly sidelong glance. "I suppose you're surely coming?"

Jantiff did not care for her manner. "Certainly; why not? I paid for the ticket."

"Very good. We leave early the day after tomorrow."

Jantiff calculated days and dates. "That will suit me very well. How many are going?"

"An even dozen; that's all the air-car will take."

"An air-car! How did Esteban promote such a thing?"

"Never underestimate Esteban! He always lands on his feet!"

"Quite so!" said Jantiff coldly.

Skorlet suddenly became gay—again a patently spurious display. "Also very important: be sure to bring your camera! The gypsies are quaint; you'll want to record every incident!"

"It's just something more to carry."

"If you don't bring it you're sure to be sorry. And Tanzel wants a remembrance. You'll do it for her, won't you?"

"Oh, very well."

"Good. We'll meet here in the lobby directly after wump."

Jantiff watched her cross to the lift. Skorlet obviously wanted mementos of the great occasion and expected Jantiff to provide them. She could expect in vain.

He went out upon the loggia and sat on a bench. Presently Kedidah emerged from the foyer. She paused, stretched her arms luxuriously to the sunlight, then set off at a pace somewhere between a skip and a trot toward the man-way. Jantiff watched her disappear into the crowd, then rose to his feet and went up to the apartment. Kedidah as usual had left disorder in her wake. Jantiff cleaned up the worst of the mess, then went to lie on his bed. No doubt in his mind now: it was time to be leaving Uncibal . . . Skorlet's manner in regard to the camera had been most odd. She had never shown any interest in photographs before . . . He dozed and woke only when Kedidah returned with a group of swaggering Ephthalotes, who chaffed each other in raucous voices and discussed tactics for tomorrow's game. Jantiff turned on his side and tried to cover his ears. At last he rose, stumbled up to the roof garden where he sat until time for the evening meal.

Kedidah came into the refectory, still aglow with excitement; Jantiff averted his eyes.

Kedidah bolted her food and departed the refectory. When Jantiff returned to the apartment she was in bed and asleep, without having troubled to draw the curtain. How innocent and pure she looked, thought Jantiff. Turning sadly away, he undressed and went to bed. Tomorrow: the dangerous Khaldraves, in combat against the Ephthalotes and their glorious sheirl!

Late the next afternoon Jantiff returned to Old Pink. The day had been warm; the air even seemed heavy. Black thunderheads rolled across the city; the sky to westward glistened like fish skin. Jantiff grimaced: was his imagination far, far, too vivid, or did a sickly odor indeed hang in the air? He suppressed the thought with a shudder: what revolting tricks one's mind played on oneself! Sternly ordering his thoughts, he went up to the apartment. He halted outside the door, to stand rigidly in an odd posture: head down, right hand half-raised to the lock. He stirred, opened the door, entered the empty apartment. The lights were low; the room was dim and still. Jantiff closed the door, crossed to his chair and seated himself.

An hour passed. Out in the corridor sounded a soft footstep. The door slid aside; Kedidah entered the room. Jantiff silently watched her. She went to her chair and sat down: stiffly, laboriously, like an old woman. Jantiff dispassionately studied her face. The jawbones glimmered pale through her skin; her mouth drooped at the corners.

Kedidah appraised Jantiff with no more expression than his own. She said in a soft voice: "We lost."

"I know," said Jantiff. "I was at the game."

Kedidah's expression changed, if only by a twitch of her mouth. She asked in the same soft voice: "Did you see what they did to me?"

"Yes, indeed."

Kedidah, watching him with a queer twisted smile, made no comment.

Jantiff said tonelessly: "If you had to bear it, I could be brave enough to watch."

Kedidah turned away and looked at the wall. Minutes passed. A gong sounded along the corridor. "Ten minutes to wump," said Jantiff. "Take a shower and change your clothes; you'll feel better."

"I'm not hungry."

Jantiff could think of nothing to say. When the second gong sounded, he rose to his feet. "Are you coming?"

"No."

Jantiff went off to the refectory. Skorlet, arriving a moment later, brought her tray to the place opposite him. She pretended to look up and down the room. "Where's Kedidah? Isn't she here?"

"No."

"The Ephthalotes lost today." Skorlet surveyed Jantiff with a tart smile. "They took a terrible trouncing."

"I saw the game."

Skorlet gave a curt nod. "I'll never understand how anyone can put herself into such a position. It's unnatural display! Presently the team loses, and then it's the most grotesque display of all. No one can tell me that it's not purposeful! Criminal sexivation, really; I wonder that it's not banned."

"The stadiums are always full."

Skorlet gave a sour snort. "Be that as it may! The Ephthalotes and Khaldraves and all the other foreign teams mock us in our own stadium. Why won't they bring in their own sheirls? Never! They prefer to suborn antiegalism. At the core, that's what sexivation is; don't you agree?"

"I've never thought much about it," said Jantiff listlessly.

Skorlet was not satisfied with the response. "Because in your heart of hearts you're not truly egal!"

Jantiff had nothing to say. Skorlet became heavily jovial. "Still, cheer up! Think of tomorrow: the bonterfest! All day you can be as anti-egal as you like, and no one will deny you your fun."

Jantiff sought phrases to suggest that Skorlet's zest for the occasion was far greater than his own. He chose simple candor. "I'm not altogether sure that I'll be going."

Skorlet jerked up her black eyebrows and stared hard across the table. "What! After you've paid all those tokens? Of course you're going."

"Really, I'm not in the mood."

"But you promised!" Skorlet blurted. "Tanzel expects you to take photographs! So do I! So does Esteban! We're counting on you!"

Jantiff began a grumbling counter-argument, but Skorlet refused to listen. "You'll come then, in absolute certainty?"

"Well, I don't like—" Skorlet leaned balefully forward; Jantiff stopped short. He remembered his conversation with the cursar. "Well, if it makes all that much difference I'll come."

Skorlet relaxed back into her chair. "We leave directly after wump, so don't go mooning off in all directions. Remember: bring your camera!"

Jantiff could think of no dignified retort. He swallowed the last of his deedle, rose and marched from the refectory, with the weight of Skorlet's gaze against his back.

He returned to his apartment and quietly entered. The sitting room was empty. He looked into the bedroom. The curtain was drawn around Kedidah's couch.

Jantiff stood uncertainly a moment, then returned to the sitting room. He lowered himself into his chair and sat staring at the wall.

In the morning Jantiff awoke early. Behind the curtain Kedidah lay inert. Jantiff dressed quietly and went to the refectory. Skorlet arrived a moment later, to stand by the doorway in an almost swashbuckling posture: legs apart, head thrown back, eyes glittering. She searched up and down the tables, spied Jantiff and came marching across the room. In annoyance Jantiff raised his eyes to the ceiling. Why must Skorlet be so bumptious? Skorlet either ignored or failed to notice his attitude, and swung herself into the chair beside him. Jantiff glanced sourly at her from the corner of his eye. This morning Skorlet was not at her best. She had obviously dressed in haste, perhaps not troubling to wash. When she leaned over to pluck Jantiff's sleeve, a rank sebaceous waft followed her gesture, and Jantiff drew fastidiously away. Skorlet again failed to notice, either through callousness or inattention. "It's the great day! Don't eat your gruff; save it for swill; you'll be so much the hungrier at the feast!"

Jantiff looked dubiously at his tray. Skorlet, as if at a sudden recollection, reached over and scooped up Jantiff's gruff. "You've got no hand for swill; I'll take care of it."

Jantiff tried to recover his gruff, but Skorlet dropped it into her pouch. "I'm hungry now!" cried Jantiff.

"There's bonter ahead! Take my advice: don't wad your gut solid with gruff!"

Jantiff moved his deedle and wobbly out of Skorlet's reach. "All very well," he growled, "but maybe I won't like the bonter."

"No fear on that score! The gypsies are marvelous cooks; nowhere in the Cluster will you eat better. First, tidbits: pastels of spiced meat, chobchows, fish sausages, pepper pancakes, borlocks. Next course: a pie of diced morels, garlic, and titticombs. Next course: wild forest greens with musker sauce and toasted crumbs. Next course: meat grilled over coals with onions and turnips. Next course: cakes in flower syrup. And all washed down in Houlsbeima wine! Now then, what of that?"

"A most impressive menu; in fact I'm amazed—where do they get their materials?"

Skorlet made an airy gesture. "Here, there; who cares so long as it sits well on the tongue?"

"No doubt they rob the farm cattle for the meat."

Skorlet scowled sidewise. "Really, Jantiff, what is to be gained by all this careful analysis? If the meat is savory, don't concern yourself as to its source."

"Just as you say." Jantiff rose to his feet. Skorlet eyed him in speculation. "Where are you going?"

"To my apartment. I want a word with Kedidah."

"Hurry, because we leave at once. I'll meet you downstairs. And don't forget your camera."

With defiant deliberation Jantiff strolled around to his apartment. The curtains were still drawn around Kedidah's bed. She'll miss her breakfast, thought Jantiff, unless she moves very briskly indeed. "Time to get up!" he called out. "Kedidah, are you awake?"

No answer. Jantiff went to the bed and pulled back the curtains. Kedidah was not there.

Jantiff stared down at the empty bed. Had she passed him in the corridor? Might she be bathing? Why leave the curtain drawn? A horrid suspicion sprang full-blown into his mind. He turned to the cupboard. Her newest costume and sandals were gone. Jantiff opened the drawer where she kept her tokens. Empty.

He ran from the apartment, rode down to the lobby, raced out, ignoring Skorlet's hoarse call. Boarding the man-way, he thrust himself through the crowds, ignoring angry curses, searching right and left for the glint of golden brown hair.

Arriving at Disjerferact he ran dodging and sidling to the Pavilions of Rest, paid his token, and entered the area.

On the Pier of Departure a red-haired man read a valedictory ode to a small audience. Kedidah was nowhere to be seen; she would render no declamations in any event. The Perfumed Voyage? Jantiff peered into the floral atrium. Six folk silently waited for boats: he recognized none of them. Jantiff ran to Halcyon House and walked around the arcade, peering into the golden prisms. From time to time a reflection reached him: a flutter of garments, a groping hand, and suddenly the glimpse of a familiar and dear profile. Jantiff frantically rapped on the glass. "Kedidah!" The prisms moved; the face, just as it turned toward Jantiff, was lost in the golden shimmer.

Jantiff stared and called to no avail. "She's gone," said an annoyed voice. "Come along now; we're all waiting."

Looking over his shoulder Jantiff saw Skorlet. "I can't be sure," he muttered. "It looked like her, still . . ."

"We can easily find out," said Skorlet. "Come over to the booth." She took Jantiff by the elbow and led him to the wicket. She called through the aperture: "Anyone from Old Pink been through this morning? That's 17-882."

The clerk ran his finger down a list. "Here's a tag from Apartment D6 on the Nineteenth."

Skorlet said to Jantiff, "She's been here, but she's gone now."

"Poor Kedidah!"

"Yes, it's sad, but we haven't time to mope. Do you have your camera?"

"I left it at the apartment."

"Oh bother! Why can't you be more thoughtful? Everyone's hopping from one foot to the other on your account!"

Jantiff silently followed Skorlet to where Esteban stood waiting. "Kedidah went through the prisms," said Skorlet.

"A pity," said Esteban. "I'm sorry to hear that; she was always so gay. But we'd better get in motion. The day's not all that long. Where's Tanzel?"

"I left her at Old Pink. We've got to go for Jantiff's camera in any case."

"Well then, let's meet where Uncibal River crosses Tumb Flow, on the north deck."

"Very good. Give us twenty minutes and we'll be there. Come along, Jantiff."

Jantiff and Skorlet returned to Old Pink. Jantiff felt curiously light-headed. I'm almost happy! he told himself, marveling. How can it be when darling Kedidah is gone? . . . It's because she was never mine. I never could have her, and now I'm free. I'll go on this bonterfest; I'll identify the fourth man; then I'll leave Arrabus, most definitely . . . Peculiar, Skorlet's insistence on the camera! Quite odd, really. What can it mean?

In the lobby Skorlet said in a crisp voice, "I'll find Tanzel; you run up for your camera, and we'll meet here."

Jantiff spoke with dignity: "Please, Skorlet, try to be just a trifle less domineering."

"Yes; yes; just hurry; the others are waiting."

Jantiff rode the ascensor to the Nineteenth level, entered his apartment, opened the strongbox, brought out the camera. He weighed it on his hand, thought a moment; then, removing the matrix, he replaced it with a spare, and locked the first crystal into the strongbox.

Returning to the lobby he found Skorlet and Tanzel awaiting him. Skorlet's eyes went instantly to the camera. She gave a brisk nod. "Good; we're off at last."

"Hurry, hurry!" cried Tanzel, running ahead, then turning to run backward, the better to signal Jantiff and Skorlet to haste. "The flibbit will go and we'll be left behind!"

Skorlet gave a grim laugh. "No chance of that. Esteban will wait for us, never fear. We're all most important to the success of the bonterfest."

"Hurry anyway!"

The lateral took them to Uncibal River, where they diverted and rode east. Tanzel spoke in awe. "Think of all these people, millions and millions, and we're the only ones going out on a bonterfest! Isn't that marvelous?"

"It's a bit anti-egal to think of it so," Skorlet reproved her. "More properly, you should say: 'Today is our turn for the bonterfest.'"

Tanzel screwed up her face into a grimace of quaint frivolity. "Just as you like, so long as we are going, and not someone else."

Skorlet ignored the remark. Jantiff watched Tanzel's impish quirks with detached amusement. In some manner she reminded him of Kedidah, even though her hair was short, dark, and curling. Kedidah also had been silly and gay and artless . . . Jantiff blinked back tears and looked up into the sky, where shoal after shoal of herringbone cirrus floated in the blissful Dwan-light. Somewhere up there in the radiance Kedidah's spirit drifted:

such, at least, was the doctrine of the True Quincunx Sect accredited by his father and mother. Wonderful, if only he could believe as much! Jantiff scrutinized the clouds for even the most subtle sign, but saw only that ravishing interplay of nacreous color which was the special glory of Wyst. Skorlet's voice sounded in his ear: "What are you staring at?"

"The clouds," said Jantiff.

Skorlet inspected the sky, but apparently saw nothing out of the ordinary and made no comment.

Tanzel called back over her shoulder: "There's Tumb Flow Lateral. I see Esteban on the north deck and all the other people!"

Jantiff, suddenly mindful of his mission, became alert. He inspected Esteban's companions with the keenest interest. They numbered eight: four men and four women; Jantiff recognized only Sarp. None displayed the broad-shouldered bulk of the man Jantiff had glimpsed in the apartment.

Esteban wasted no time on introductions; the group continued westward along Uncibal River. Jantiff, having discovered no massive black-haired man among the party once again became apathetic and rode somewhat behind the others. For a moment or two he considered leaving the group, inconspicuously of course, and returning to Old Pink. But what then? Only the empty apartment awaited him. The idea lacked appeal. Skorlet and Esteban, so Jantiff noticed, had taken themselves somewhat apart from the others, and rode with their heads together in earnest conversation. From time to time they glanced back toward Jantiff, who became convinced that the two were talking about him. He felt a tremor of uneasiness: perhaps he was not, after all, among friends.

Jantiff stirred himself from his listlessness and examined the others of the party. None had given him any particular attention, save for Sarp, who periodically turned him glances of crooked amusement, no doubt inspired by the news of Kedidah's journey into the prisms.

Jantiff sighed and fatalistically decided to continue with the party; after all, the day had only begun and there still might be much to be learned.

At the Great Southern Adit the group diverted to the left, and rode away through District 92: finally through the fringes of the city and out upon a soggy wasteland, grown over with salt grass, tattersack and burdock. The land was utterly deserted save for a pair of small boys flying a kite who only served to emphasize the desolation of the area.

The adit climbed a long gradual slope; behind, Uncibal could be seen as a pattern of rectangular protuberances, the colors dulled by distance. The way swung into Outpost Valley and Uncibal was blotted from view. In the distance, under the first ledges of the scarp, Jantiff saw a cluster of long low buildings. Almost simultaneously he became aware of a grumbling, mumbling roar, which as the group approached became broken into a hundred components: pounding, grating, whistling screams, the trundling of iron wheels, low-pitched thuds and impacts, grinding vibrations, flutings and warbles. A tall prong-bar fence angled across the flat, then turned sharply to parallel the man-way. The message of the prongs was emphasized by bolts of blue-white energy snapping at random between the strands. Behind the fence gangs of men and women crouched over a pair of long slide belts burdened with rock. Jantiff took a step forward and put a question to Sarp: "What goes on yonder?"

Sarp inspected the activity with placid and almost benevolent contempt. "Alas, Jantiff, there you see our nursery for bad children: in short, the Uncibal Penal Camp, which both of us, so far, have fortuitously evaded. Still, never become complacent; never let the Mutuals prove you at your sexivation."

Jantiff stared in astonishment. "These folk are all sexivators?"

"By no means; they run the criminal gamut. You'll find shirkers there and shiftills, not to mention flamboyants, performers and violeers."

Jantiff watched the prisoners a moment and could not restrain a sneer. "The murderers go free but the flamboyants and sexivators are punished."

"Of course!" declared Sarp with relish. "We've got lots of folk to be murdered, but only one egalism to be suborned. So never waste your pity: they all befouled our great society and now they sort ore for the Metallurgical Syndicate."

Skorlet snapped over her shoulder: "There's Jantiff for you, full of pity, but always for the deviates. Well, Jantiff, that's how such persons fare in Arrabus: double-drudge, no swill and they're tapped three times a year besides. Hard lives, eh, Jantiff?"

"What's it to me?" Jantiff asked shortly. "I'm not an Arrabin."

"Oh?" inquired Skorlet in a voice of silken mockery. "I thought you had come to Wyst to enjoy our egalistic achievements."

Jantiff merely shrugged and turned back toward Sarp. "And what is this Metallurgical Syndicate?"

"It's the facility of the five High Contractors, so naturally it is here that the deviates learn egalism." Sarp gave a cackle of wild laughter. "Let me name these eminent teachers: Commors, Grand Knight of the Eastern Woods. Shubart, Grand Knight of Blale. Farus, Grand Knight of Lammerland. Dulak, Grand Knight of Froke. Malvesar, Grand Knight of the Luess. There're five good plutocrats for you despite subservience!* And Shubart, who contracts the Mutuals, is the most arrant of all."

*Subservience: In the Arrabin world-view, the contractors, their technicians and mechanics are a caste of interplanetary riff-raff, quite outside all considerations of egalistic dignity. The Arrabins like to think of the contractors as servile work masters, eager to oblige the noble egalists and at all times conscious of their inferior status. Hence the word "subservience" often appears in conversations concerning the contractors.

"Come now, if you please," said Esteban shortly. "Don't castigate Shubart, who is good enough to fly us out to Ao River Meadow; otherwise we'd all be for the bumbuster."*

A man named Dobbo called out jocularly: "What's wrong with the old bumbuster? How better to see the countryside?"

"And if you fall asleep you're carried all the way to Blale," snapped Esteban. "No, thanks. I'll ride the flibbit, and let's offer Contractor Shubart a soft lip."

Sarp, who seemed to take a positive delight in baiting Esteban, would not be daunted. "I'll fly Shubart's flibbit and hold never a grudge. He lives in manorial style at Balad; why shouldn't he call himself 'Grand Knight' and go forth in pomp?"

"I'd do the same," said Dobbo, "given opportunity, of course. I'm egal, certainly, because I hold no other weapon against drudgery. Still, give and I'll take."

Ailas said: "Dobbo takes even when no one gives. When he takes his title, it should properly go: 'The Grand Knight of Snergery.' "

"Oh, ho!" cried Dobbo, "you wield a most wicked tongue! Still I admit I'll use anything available, including that title!"

The man-way proceeded past the sorting belts, then curved toward the foundries and fabricating plants, glided beside slag dumps, hoppers where barges unloaded raw ore, and a pair of maintenance hangars. The man-way split; Esteban led the group to a terminus in front of the administration complex, then around to the side where a dozen vehicles rested on a landing plat . . . Esteban stepped into the dispatcher's office, reappeared a moment later and signaled the group toward a battered old carry-all. "All aboard for the bonterfest! Transportation courtesy of Contractor Shubart, whom I happen to know!"

"While you were scrounging, why didn't you promote a Kosmer Ace or a Dacy Scimitar?" called out Sarp.

"No complaints from the infantry!" Esteban retorted. "This is not absolutely deluxe, but isn't it better than traveling by bumbuster? And here comes our operator."

From the administration office came a heavily muscled man with black hair, a sagging portentous visage. Jantiff leaned forward: could this be the fourth party to the cabal? Not impossibly, although this man seemed burly, rather than massive.

Esteban addressed the group: "Bonterfesters, allow me to introduce the Respectable Buwechluter, factotum, and aide indispensable to Contractor Shubart, more commonly known as 'Booch.' He has kindly agreed to fly us to our destination."

*Omnibus.

Intoxicated with excitement, Tanzel cried out: "Three cheers for the Respectable Booch! Hurrah, hurrah, hurrah!"

Esteban threw up his hands in facetious admonition. "Not too much adulation! Booch is a very suggestible man and we don't want him to become vainglorious!"

Jantiff cocked his ears as Booch gave a not altogether amiable snort. Inconclusive. Jantiff studied Booch's features: narrow heavy-lidded eyes, ropy jowls, a heavy mouth pouting over a creased receding chin. Booch was not a prepossessing man, though he exuded a coarse animal vitality. He muttered inaudibly to Esteban and swung up to the operator's station. "Everybody aboard!" called Esteban. "Briskly, now! We're an hour late."

The bonterfesters climbed into the carry-all and took seats. Esteban bent over Booch and gave instructions. Jantiff studied the back of Booch's head. Almost definitely, Booch was not the fourth conspirator.

Esteban seated himself behind Booch, who with contemptuous familiarity flicked fingers across the controls: the carry-all rose into the air and flew south over the scarp. In the seat behind Jantiff Ailas and a woman named Cadra seemed to be discussing Esteban. Cadra said, "This carry-all enhances a bonterfest beyond description; suddenly all the tedium disappears! As a scrounger Esteban ranks supreme."

"Agreed," said Ailas sadly. "I wish I knew his technique."

"There's no mystery whatever," said Cadra. "Combine persistence, ingenuity, charm, an exact sense of timing, persuasiveness: you've created a scrounger."

"For best effect, include bravado and a quantum of sheer brashness!" noted a man named Descart, to which Rismo, a tall plain woman, replied rather sarcastically: "What about simple ordinary luck? Has that no meaning?"

Cadra chuckled. "Most significant of all: Esteban is acquainted with the Contractor Shubart!"

"Oh, give the devil his due!" Ailas said. "Esteban definitely has a flair. Out in the Bad Places he'd be a top-notch entrepreneur!"

"Or a tycoon."

"Or a starmenter," suggested Rismo. "I can just see him swaggering about in a white uniform and a gold helmet—great cudgers in his harness, bluskin at his hip."

"Esteban, come listen to this!" Descart called. "We're trying to establish your previous incarnations!"

Esteban came aft. "Indeed? What indignities are you putting me to now?"

"Nothing extreme, nothing outrageous," said Cadra. "We just consider you a monster of anti-egalism."

"So long as you don't accuse me of anything sordid," said Esteban with suave equanimity.

"Today we're all anti-egal!" Ailas declared grandly. "Let's wallow in our shortcomings!"

"I'll drink to that!" called a man named Peder. "Esteban! Where's the swill?"

"No swill aboard," said Esteban shortly. "Control your thirst till we put down at Galsma. The gypsies are providing an entire keg of Houlsbeima wine."

Cadra asked mischievously: "Does anyone know that song: 'Anti-Egalists Eat Roast Bird, While Arrabins Get Only Feathers in the Mouth'?"

"I know it but I don't intend to sing it," said Skorlet.

"Oh, come! Don't be stuffy, today of all days!"

"I know the song," said Tanzel. "We sing it at the crèche. It goes like this." In an earnest voice she sang the scurrilous ditty. One by one the others joined in—all except Jantiff, who had never heard the song and in any case was in no mood to sing.

The landscape slid past below: the long southern slopes of the scarp, forests and high moors, then valleys opening down upon a rolling plain. The Great Dasm River, smooth as an eel, coiled across the landscape. Near a bend where the river turned southeast appeared a village of a hundred small houses, and the carry-all started to descend. Jantiff at first assumed that the village was their destination, but the carry-all flew another twenty miles: over a marsh overgrown with reeds, then a forest of gray and russet spider-leg, then a sluggish tributary of the Great Dasm, then another forest and at last down into a clearing from which rose a wisp of smoke.

"We've arrived!" Esteban announced. "At this point a word or two of caution, no doubt unnecessary to so many veteran bonterfesters, but I'll say them anyway. Tanzel, take special note! The gypsies are a peculiar race, and all very well in their own way, no doubt, but they have callous habits and they are by no means egalists. As Arrabins, we mean no more to them than so many shadows! Don't drink too much wine, if for no other reason than you'll lose zest for your bonter. And naturally—it goes without saying!—don't stray off by yourself—for unknown reasons!"

"Unknown reasons?" An odd phrase, thought Jantiff. If "reason" were "unknown," why had everyone's face gone bland and blank? Jantiff decided that when opportunity offered, he would put a question to Sarp. Meanwhile, whether for reasons known or unknown, he would heed Esteban's warning.

The carry-all touched ground; the passengers, pushing rather rudely past Jantiff, alighted. He followed with ostentatious deliberation, which, however, no one noticed.

The gypsies waited across the meadow, beside a row of trestle tables. Jantiff first saw a flutter of rich costumes striped in ocher, maroon, blue and green. Upon closer inspection he noted four men in short loose pantaloons, and three women swathed in ankle-length gowns: slender dark-haired folk, quick of motion, fluid of gesture, sallow-olive of complexion, with straight narrow noses, eyes tilted mournfully down at the corners and shadowed under dark eyebrows. A handsome people, thought Jantiff, but in some inexplicable fashion rather repellent. And once again he was assailed by second thoughts in regard to his participation at the bonterfest, though again for no definable reason: perhaps because of the gypsies' expressions as they regarded the Arrabins: a coolness distinguished from contempt only by virtue of indifference. Jantiff wondered whether he cared to eat gypsy food: surely they would feed the Arrabins anything palatable, without regard to fastidiousness. Jantiff managed a wry grin for his own qualms; after all, he had eaten ration after ration of Arrabin wump, prepared from sturge, with hardly more than a grimace or two. He followed the other bonterfesters across the meadow.

Despite Esteban's warnings all hurried to the keg, where the youngest of the gypsy women dispensed wooden cups of wine. Jantiff approached the keg, then moved back because of the crush. Turning away he appraised the other arrangements. The tables supported pots, tureens and trenchers, all exuding odors which Jantiff despite his reservations found undeniably appetizing. To the side hard knots of timber burnt to coals under a metal rack.

Esteban and the oldest of the gypsy men went to the table. Esteban checked items off against his list, and apparently found all to his satisfaction. The two turned and surveyed the group at the wine keg and Esteban spoke with great earnestness.

Tanzel tugged at Jantiff's sleeve. "Please, Jantiff: get me a cup of wine! Every time I step forward someone reaches past me."

"I'll do my best," said Jantiff dubiously, "although I've had the same experience. This group of egalists seems unusually assertive."

Jantiff managed to obtain two cups of wine, one of which he brought to Tanzel. "Don't drink it too fast or your head will swim, and you won't want to eat."

"No fear of that!" Tanzel tasted the wine. "Delicious!"

Jantiff cautiously sipped from the mug, to find the wine tart and light, with a faintly musky redolence. "Quite decent, indeed."

Tanzel drank again. "Isn't this fun? Why can't bonterfests be for every day? Everything smells so good! And, no argument, I'm ravenous!"

"You'll probably overeat and get sick," said Jantiff morosely.

"I have no doubt!" Tanzel drained her wine cup. "Please—"

"Not just yet," said Jantiff. "Wait a few minutes; you might not want another."

"Oh, I'll want another, but I suppose there's no great hurry. I wonder what Esteban is talking about; he keeps looking over toward us."

Jantiff turned his head, but Esteban and the gypsy had completed their conversation.

Esteban came over to the group. "Appetizers will be served in five minutes. I've had an understanding with the hetman. Courtesy and freedom have been guaranteed; everyone is safe from molestation so long as he doesn't stray too far from the clearing. The wine is of prime quality, as I specified; you need fear neither agues nor gripes. Still, moderation, I beg of all of you!"

"But not too much of it!" Dobbo called out. "We'd be defeating only ourselves. Moderation must be practiced in moderation."

Esteban, now in the best of moods, made a gesture of concession. "Well, no matter. Enjoy yourself in your own fashion. That's the slogan for today!"

"Here's to Esteban and future bonterfests!" called out Cadra. "Damnation to all croakers!"

Esteban smilingly accepted the congratulations of his friends, then gestured toward the table. "We can now enjoy our appetizers. Don't overeat; the meat is just now going on the grill."

And again Jantiff stood back as the group surged toward the table.

Never, for so long as Jantiff lived, was the bonterfest far from his memory. The recollections came always in company with a peculiar throat-gripping emotion which Jantiff's mind reserved for this occasion alone, and always in swirling clots of sensation: the gypsy gowns and breeches, in striking contrast to the pallid faces; flames licking up at the spitted meat; the table loaded with pots and tureens; the bonterfesters themselves: in Jantiff's memory they became caricatures of gluttony while the gypsies moved in the background, silent as shadows. Ghost odors might drift through his mind: pungent pickles, pawpaws and sweetsops, roasting meat. Always the faces reasserted themselves: Skorlet, at one juncture transcending the imaginable limits of emotion; Tanzel, vulnerable to both pleasure and pain; Sarp with his slantwise leer, Booch, coarse, reeking, suffused with animal essence; Esteban . . .

Nowhere to be seen was the fourth man to the cabal, and Jantiff lost whatever zest he might have felt for the occasion. Tanzel brought her mug and a heaped platter of food to the bench where he sat. "Jantiff! Aren't you eating?"

"After a bit, when the elbowing subsides."

"Be sure to try the pickles. Here, take this one. Isn't it wonderful? The whole inside of my mouth tingles."

"Yes, it's very good."

"You'd better hurry or there'll be none left."

"I don't care much, one way or the other."

"Jantiff, you are a strange, strange person! Excuse me while I eat."

Jantiff at last went to the table. He served himself a plate of food and accepted a second mug of wine from the impassive woman at the keg. Returning to the bench, he found that Tanzel already had devoured the contents of her platter. "You have an excellent appetite," said Jantiff.

"Of course! I've been starving myself for two days. So now, more chob-chows? Or another portion of those delicious pepper pancakes? Or should I wait until the meat is served out?"

"If I were you I'd wait," said Jantiff. "Then you can go back for whatever you like the best."

"I believe you're right. Oh, Jantiff, isn't this exciting? I wish times like these would go on forever. Jantiff, are you listening?"

"Yes indeed." Jantiff had in fact been distracted by a rather odd inci-dent. Off to the side Esteban stood talking to the gypsy hetman. Esteban gestured with his mug, and both turned to look in Jantiff's direction. Jantiff feigned inattention, but a thrill ran along his nerves.

Someone had approached. Jantiff looked up to find Skorlet standing beside him. "Well, Jantiff? How goes the bonter?"

"Very well. I like these little sausages—although I can't help but wonder what goes into them."

Skorlet gave a bark of harsh laughter. "Never ask, never wonder! If it's savory, eat every morsel! Remember, it all flushes down the same drain in the end."

"Yes, no doubt you're right."

"Eat hearty, Jantiff!" Skorlet returned to the table and filled her platter for the third time. Jantiff watched from the corner of his eye, not altogether happy with her manner. Now he saw Esteban saunter across the clearing to where Skorlet stood devouring her food. Esteban spoke a question into her ear; Skorlet, her mouth full, shrugged, and managed to utter a reply. Esteban nodded and continued his circuit around the fringes of the group.

He halted beside Jantiff. "Well, how goes it? Is everything to your satis-faction?"

"Exactly so," said Jantiff guardedly.

"All I want to know," declared Tanzel, "is when we can come again!"

"Aha! We mustn't become guttricks, with thought for nothing but food!"

"Of course not; still—"

Esteban laughed and patted her head. "We'll make plans, never fear. So far, it's been a great success, eh?"

"It's all wonderful."

"Well, don't fill up too soon. There's more to come. Jantiff, have you taken photographs?"

"Not yet."

"My dear Jantiff! The banquet table: loaded, aromatic, inviting! You missed that?"

"I'm afraid so."

"And our picturesque hosts? Their magnificent faces, so placid and remote? Their boisterous breeches and pointed boots? Ah, then, allow me the use of your camera!"

Jantiff hesitated. "Well, I don't know. In fact I'd prefer not. You might somehow lose it."

"By no means! Put that other small escapade out of your mind; it was only a lark. The camera will be safe, I assure you."

Jantiff reluctantly brought out the instrument.

"Thank you," said Esteban. "I assume there's still ample scope to the matrix?"

"Take as many pictures as you like," said Jantiff. "It's a new matrix."

Esteban stiffened; his fingers clenched at the camera. "What of the other matrix?"

"It was almost full," said Jantiff. "I didn't want to risk losing it."

Esteban stood silent. "Where is this old matrix? Are you carrying it with you?"

Surprised by the blunt question, Jantiff raised his eyes to find Esteban glowering in obvious annoyance. Jantiff spoke with cold politeness: "Why do you ask? I can't account for your interest."

Esteban tried to throttle the fury in his own voice, without success. "Because there are pictures of mine on that matrix, as you're perhaps aware."

"You need not worry," said Jantiff. "The matrix is absolutely safe."

Esteban recovered his aplomb. "In that case I'm quite content. Aren't you drinking? This is Houlsbeima wine; they've done famously for us today."

"I'll have more presently."

"Do so, by all means!" Esteban sauntered away. A few minutes later Jantiff saw him conferring first with Skorlet, then Sarp.

Discussing me and the matrix, thought Jantiff. Here was surely the reason for Skorlet's urgency in connection with the camera. She and Esteban were interested in the matrix. But why? Enlightenment broke suddenly upon Jantiff: of course! Upon the matrix were imprinted images of the fourth man!

Jantiff shook his head in sad self-recrimination: after recovering his camera from Esteban he had never thought to examine the matrix. What a foolish oversight! Of course, at the time there had been no particular reason to do so; he lacked all interest in Esteban's activities. Now the situation was different. Lucky the matrix was locked securely in his strongbox! Which stimulated a new and chilling thought: Sarp still knew the code, since Jantiff had never thought to change it. Immediately upon his return to Uncibal he must rectify this oversight!

The gypsies ordered the table, then, taking the meat from the fire, arranged it upon long wooden platters. One of the women poured sauce over the meat; another set out crusty loaves; a third brought forth a great wooden bowl of salad. All then returned to the forest shadows.

Esteban called: "Everyone to the table! Eat as you've never eaten before! For once, we're all guttricks together!"

The bonterfesters surged forward, with Jantiff, as usual, bringing up the rear.

Half an hour later the group sprawled lethargic and sated around the meadow. Esteban roused himself to croak in a rich glottal voice: "Everyone remember: the sweet is still to come! White millicent cake in flower syrup! Don't give up now!"

From the group came groans of protest. "Show us mercy, Esteban!"

"What? Are there no more courses?"

"Bring my ration of gruff!"

"With wobbly to fill in the chinks!"

The gypsies passed among the group serving out portions of pastry with mugs of verbena tea. They then set about packing together their equipment.

Tanzel whispered to Jantiff, "I've got to go off in the woods."

"In that case, go, by all means."

Tanzel grimaced. "That person Booch has been making himself gallant. I don't want to go alone; he's sure to follow."

"Do you really think so?"

"Yes indeed! He watches my every move."

Jantiff, glancing around the clearing, saw that Booch's eyes were fixed upon Tanzel with more than casual interest. "Oh, very well; I'll come with you. Lead the way."

Tanzel rose to her feet and moved off toward the forest. Booch rather sluggishly bestirred himself, but Jantiff quickly went after Tanzel, and Booch glumly subsided into his position of rest.

Jantiff caught up with Tanzel in the shade of the sprawling elms. "Just this way a bit," said Tanzel, and presently: "You wait here; I won't be long."

She disappeared into the foliage. Jantiff sat upon a fallen tree and looked off through the forest. The sounds from the clearing already had muted to inaudibility. Bars of Dwan-light slanted down through the foliage, to shatter upon the forest floor. How far seemed the vast cities of Arrabus! Jantiff mused upon the circumstances of his life at Uncibal, and the folk he had come to know: for the most part Old Pinkers. Poor proud Kedidah, going dazed and humiliated to her death! And Tanzel: whatever might she hope to achieve? He looked over his shoulder, expecting to see Tanzel returning from her errand. But the glade was vacant. Jantiff composed himself to wait.

Three minutes passed. Jantiff became restless and jumped to his feet. Surely she should have returned by now! He called: "Tanzel!"

No response.

Odd.

Jantiff went off into the shrubbery, looking left and right. "Tanzel! Where are you?"

He saw a fresh mark on the turf which might have been a footprint, and nearby, in damp lichen, what might that series of parallel scratches signify? Jantiff came to a halt, in utter perplexity. He looked quickly over his shoulder, then licked his lips and called once more, but his voice was little more than a cautious croak: "Tanzel?" Either she was lost, or she had returned to the bonterfest by a different route.

Jantiff retraced his steps to the clearing. He looked here and there. The gypsies had departed with all their gear. Tanzel was nowhere to be seen.

Esteban saw Jantiff. His face sagged in blank dismay. Jantiff approached him: "Tanzel went off into the forest; I can't find her anywhere."

Skorlet came running forward, eyes distended, to show white rims around the glaring black. "What's this, what's this? Where's Tanzel?"

"She went off into the woods," stammered Jantiff, awed by Skorlet's face. "I've looked for her and called but she's gone!"

Skorlet emitted a horrid squeal. "The gypsies have taken her! Oh, they have taken her! This vile bonterfest, and now there'll be another!"

Esteban, jerking her elbow, spoke through clenched teeth: "Control yourself!"

"We have eaten Tanzel!" bawled Skorlet. "Where is the difference? Today? Tomorrow?" She lifted her face to the sky and yelled forth a howl so wild that Jantiff's knees went limp.

Esteban, his own face gray, shook Skorlet by the shoulders. "Come along! We can catch them at the river!" He turned and called to the others: "The gypsies have taken Tanzel! Everyone after them! To the river; we'll stop their boat!"

The erstwhile bonterfesters lurched off after Esteban and Skorlet. Jantiff followed a few steps, but could not control the spasmodic pumping of his stomach. He veered off the path, and, only half-conscious, fell to his knees, where he vomited, again and again.

Someone nearby was moaning a weird song of two alternating tones. Jantiff presently became aware that the sound proceeded from himself. He crawled a few yards across the dark mold and lay flat. The shuddering in his stomach became intermittent.

His mouth tasted sour and oily; and he remembered the sauce which had been poured over the meat. Again his organs twisted and squeezed, but he could bring up only a thin acrid gruel, which he spat to the ground. He rose to his feet, looked blearily here and there, then returned to the path. From the distance came shouts and calls, to which Jantiff paid no heed.

Through a gap in the foliage he glimpsed the river. He picked his way to the water's edge, rinsed his mouth, bathed his face, then slumped down upon a chunk of driftwood.

Along the trail returned the bonterfesters, mumbling disconsolately to each other. Jantiff hauled himself to his feet, but as he started back toward the trail he heard first Skorlet's voice, then Esteban's baritone mutter; they had turned off the trail and were coming toward him.

Jantiff halted, appalled at the prospect of meeting Skorlet and Esteban face to face in this isolated spot. He jerked himself behind a clump of polyptera and stood in concealment.

Esteban and Skorlet passed by and went to the water's edge, where they peered up and down the river.

"Nowhere in sight," croaked Esteban. "By now they're halfway to Aotho."

"I can't understand," cried Skorlet tremulously. "Why should they hoodwink you; why play you false?"

Esteban hesitated. "It can only be a misunderstanding, a terrible blunder. The two were sitting together. I spoke to the hetman and made my wishes known. He looked across and asked, as if in doubt: 'That young one yonder? The stripling?' Never thinking of Tanzel, I assured him: 'Exactly so!' The hetman took the younger of the two. Such are the bitter facts. I will now purge them from my mind and you must do the same."

For a space Skorlet said nothing. Then she spoke in a voice harsh with strain: "So what now—with him?"

"First the matrix. Then I'll do whatever needs to be done."

"You'll have to be quick," said Skorlet tonelessly.

"Events are under control. Three days remain."

Skorlet looked out across the river. "Poor little creature. So dear and gay. I can't bear to think of her. But the thoughts come."

"No help for it now," said Esteban, his own voice uncertain. "We can't become confused. Too much hangs in the balance."

"Yes. Too much. Sometimes I am staggered by the scope."

"Now then! Don't create bugbears! The affair is simplicity itself."

"The Connatic is a very real bugbear."

"The Connatic sits in his tower Lusz, brooding and dreaming. If he comes to Arrabus, we'll prove him as mortal as the next man."

"Esteban, don't speak the words aloud."

"The words must be spoken. The thoughts must be thought. The plans must be planned. The deeds must be done."

Skorlet stared out across the water. Esteban turned away. "Put her out of your mind. Come."

"The cursed stranger lives, and poor little Twit is gone."

"Come," said Esteban shortly.

The two went up the path. Jantiff presently followed, walking like a somnambulist.

CHAPTER 8

The bonterfesters returned to Uncibal in a mood greatly in contrast to that in which they had set out. Aside from one or two muttered conversations, the group rode in silence. Skorlet and Esteban sat grimly erect, looking neither right nor left; Jantiff watched them in covert fascination, his skin crawling at the thought of their conversation. They had meant him to be taken and dragged away by the mournful-eyed gypsies. At the contractor's depot Esteban went off with Booch to the dispatcher's office. Jantiff took advantage of the occasion to slip quietly away from the group. He jumped aboard the man-way and rode north, walking and trotting to increase his speed. Every few moments he looked back even though no one could possibly be so close on his heels. He gave a nervous laugh: in truth he was frightened, and no denying the fact. By sheer chance he had stumbled upon something awful, and now his very existence was threatened: Esteban had left him in no doubt of this.

The Great Southern Adit intercepted Uncibal River; Jantiff diverted eastward, and as before traveled at the best speed possible: pushing through the crowds, sidling and side-stepping, trotting when space opened before him. He diverted from Uncibal River along Lateral 26, and presently arrived at Old Pink.

Jantiff loped into the block, across the foyer, into the ascensor. Its familiar musty reek already seemed alien, and no longer part of his life. He alighted at the Nineteenth level, raced around the corridor to his apartment.

He entered, and stood stock-still an instant, to pant and organize his thoughts. He glanced around the room. Kedidah's belongings already appeared to show a thin film of dust. How remote she seemed! A week from now she would be gone from memory; that was the way of Uncibal. Jantiff quietly closed the door and made sure of the lock; then he went to his strongbox in the bedroom and opened the door. Into his pouch he packed ozols, family amulet, pigments, applicators and a pad of paper. Into one pocket he tucked his passage voucher, personal certificate and tokens; the matrix he hefted in his hand, glancing toward the door. Urgency struggled with curiosity. Surely he had a few moments; the bonterfesters rode Uncibal River far to the west. Time for a quick look. He slid the new matrix from the camera, inserted the old, turned the switch to "Project" and pointed the camera at the wall.

Images: the blocks of Uncibal, dwindling in perspective; the crowds of Uncibal River; the mud flats and Disjerferact. Old Pink: the facade, the foyer, the roof garden. More faces: the Whispers addressing an audience; Skorlet with Tanzel, with Esteban, Skorlet alone, Kedidah with Sarp, Kedidah in the refectory, Kedidah laughing, Kedidah pensive.

Then Esteban's photographs during his custody of the camera: persons known and unknown to Jantiff; copies of pictures from a red reference volume; a sequence of shots of a heavy-shouldered dark-haired man wearing a black blouse and breeches, ankle-boots and short-billed cap. This was the man of the secret meeting. Jantiff studied the face. The features were blunt and uncompromising; the eyes, narrow under black eyebrows, gleamed with shrewdness. Somewhere and recently, Jantiff had seen such a face, or one very similar. Frowning in concentration, Jantiff stared at the face. Could it be—

Jantiff jerked around as someone pushed at the door latch and then, failing to secure ingress, rapped sharply on the panel. Jantiff instantly turned off the projector. He removed the matrix, fingered it indecisively, then tucked it into his pocket.

Again a rap at the door, and a voice, muffled behind the panel: "Open up!" Esteban's voice, harsh and hostile. Jantiff's heart sank. How had Esteban arrived so soon?

"I know you're there," came the voice. "They told me below. Open up!"

Jantiff approached the door. "I'm tired," he called out. "Go away. I'll see you tomorrow."

"I want to see you now. It's important."

"Not to me."

"Oh, yes! Important indeed." The words carried sinister import, thought Jantiff. In a hollow voice Jantiff called: "What's so important?"

"Open up."

"Not just now. I'm going to bed."

A pause. Then, "As you like."

Silence from the hall. Jantiff put his ear to the door. Ten seconds passed, twenty seconds, then Jantiff sensed the diminishing pad of steps. He threw a slantwise glance over his shoulder in farewell to the room, with its

ghosts and dead voices. Picking up his pouch and camera he slid back the
door and peered out into the corridor.

Empty.

Jantiff emerged, closed the door, and set off toward the lift, uncomfortably aware that he must pass in front of Apartment D18, where now lived
Skorlet and Sarp.

The door to Apartment D18 was closed. Jantiff lengthened his stride
and ran past on springing tiptoe paces, like a dancer miming stealth.

The door to D18 slid back. Esteban and Sarp emerged.

Esteban, looking back into D18, made a final remark to Skorlet.

Jantiff tried to glide soundlessly up the corridor, but Sarp, peering past
Esteban's elbow, noticed him. Sarp tugged at Esteban's arm. Esteban swung
about. "Wait! Jantiff! Come back here!"

Jantiff paid no heed. He raced to the descensor, touched the button.
The door opened; Jantiff stepped aboard. The door closed almost upon Esteban's distorted face. In his hand shone the glint of metal.

With heart pounding Jantiff descended to the ground floor. He loped
across the foyer, out the portal, and away to the man-way.

Sarp and Esteban emerged from Old Pink. They paused, looked right
and left, saw Jantiff, and came in pursuit. Jantiff bounded recklessly across to
the crowded high-speed lane, where he thrust forward past other passengers, heedless of their annoyance, pouch and camera still gripped in his
hand. After came Esteban, with Sarp lagging behind. The blade in Esteban's hand was plainly visible. Jantiff lurched ahead, eyes starting from his
head in disbelief. Esteban meant to kill him! On the man-way, in full view
of the passengers? Impossible! It wouldn't be allowed! People would help
him; they would restrain Esteban! . . . Or would they? As Jantiff lunged forward he looked despairingly right and left but met only expressions of glazed
annoyance.

Esteban, shouldering ahead even more roughly than Jantiff, gained
ground. Jantiff could see his intent expression, the glitter of his eyes. Jantiff
stumbled and lurched to the side; Esteban was upon him, knife raised high.
Jantiff seized a tall sharp-featured woman and pushed her into Esteban. In a
rage she snatched out at Jantiff and tore away his pouch; Jantiff relinquished
pouch and camera and fled, heedful only of his own life. Behind came the
remorseless Esteban.

At the diversion upon Uncibal River the way was open and Jantiff
gained a few yards, only to lose it almost at once among the crowds. Sidling,
elbowing, shoving, buffeting, Jantiff thrust his way through the protesting
folk. Twice Esteban approached close enough to brandish his blade; the
folk nearby called out in fear and pushed pell-mell to escape. Jantiff on each
occasion managed to evade the attack, once through a spasmodic spurt of

agility, again by pushing a man into Esteban's path, so that both fell and Jantiff was able to gain ten yards' running room. Someone, either inadvertently or through malice, tripped Jantiff; he fell flat and once again Esteban was on him. As the riders of Uncibal River watched to observe the outcome, Jantiff kicked Esteban in the groin, rolled frantically aside. Clambering to his feet he swung a short square woman screaming into Esteban, who fell on top of the woman. The knife jarred free; Jantiff groped to pick it up, but the woman hit him in the face, and Esteban reached the knife first. Croaking in despair Jantiff sprang away and fled along the river.

Esteban was tiring. He called out: "Snerge! Snerge! Hold the snerge!" Folk turned to look back and observing Jantiff stood quickly aside. Esteban's calls therefore worked to Jantiff's benefit, and he lengthened his lead. Esteban presently stopped shouting.

Ahead Uncibal River intersected Lateral 16. Jantiff veered to the side as if intending to divert; instead, he crouched behind a knot of folk and let himself be carried along the river. Esteban, deceived, rushed out the diversion to the lateral and so lost his quarry.

At the next switch-over, Jantiff reversed direction and rode back to the east, keeping sharp lookout to all sides. He discovered no evidence of pursuit: only the faces of Uncibal, rank on rank, back along the river.

His pouch was gone with all his ozols, and likewise his camera. Jantiff gave a great shuddering groan of fury; he cursed Esteban with all the invective at his command and swore restitution for himself. What an abominable day! From now and into the future things would go differently!

Where Uncibal River made its great swerve toward the spaceport, Jantiff continued toward Alastor Centrality. With a sense of deliverance he passed under the black and gold portal, crossed the compound and entered the agency. The clerk, Clode, in the black and beige of the Connatic's Service, rose to his feet. Jantiff cried out: "I am Jantiff Ravensroke of Zeck! I must see the cursar at once!"

"I'm sorry, sir," said the clerk. "This is impossible at the moment."

Jantiff stared aghast. "Impossible? Why?"

"The cursar is not presently in Uncibal."

Jantiff barely restrained a cry of anguish. He looked over his shoulder. The compound was empty. "Where is he? When will he return?"

"He has gone to Waunisse; he counsels the Whispers before they leave for Numenes. He returns Aensday with the Whispers aboard the *Sea Disk*."

"Aensday? Three days from now! What will I do till then? I've discovered a dangerous plot against the Connatic!"

Clode looked dubiously sideways at Jantiff. "If such is the case, the cursar must be informed as soon as possible."

"If I survive until Aensday. I have no place to go."

"What of your apartment?"

"It's not safe for me. Why can't I stay here?"

"The chambers are locked. I can't let you in."

Jantiff darted another glance over his shoulder. "Where shall I go?"

"I can only suggest the Travelers Inn."

"But my money is gone; it's been taken from me!"

"You need not pay your bill until Aensday. The cursar will surely advance you funds."

Jantiff gave a glum nod. He thought carefully and brought the matrix from his pocket. "Please give me paper."

Clode tendered paper and stylus. Jantiff wrote:

This is the matrix from my camera. Certain of the pictures indicate a plot. The Connatic himself may be threatened. The people responsible live in Old Pink, Block 17-882. Their names are Esteban, Skorlet, and Sarp. There is another unknown person. I will return Aensday unless I am killed.

> Jantiff Ravensroke,
> Frayness, Zeck

Jantiff wrapped the message around the matrix and handed the parcel to Clode. "This must be kept safe and delivered to the cursar at the earliest opportunity! In the event that I—" here Jantiff's voice quavered a trifle— "that I am killed, will you do this?"

"Certainly, sir, I'll do my very best."

"Now I must go, before someone thinks to look for me here. Inform no one of my whereabouts!"

Clode managed a strained grin. "Naturally not."

Jantiff slowly turned away, reluctant to leave the relative security of the Centrality. But no help for it: he must immure himself in the Travelers Inn until Aensday, and all would be well.

In the shadows under the portal he halted and surveyed the territory beyond. He spied Esteban immediately, not fifty yards distant, striding purposefully toward the Centrality. Jantiff's jaw dropped in consternation. He shrank back into the compound and pressed himself to the inner surface of the portal. There, holding his breath, he waited.

Footsteps. Esteban marched past and away across the compound. As soon as Jantiff saw the retreating back he slipped through the portal and raced away on long fleet-footed strides toward the man-way.

"Hey! Jantiff!" Esteban's furious cry struck at his back. As Jantiff stepped aboard the man-way he looked over his shoulder, to find that Esteban had halted at the portal to stand swaying, as if in response to conflicting urgencies.

Jantiff wondered what might have ensued had the cursar been on hand.

Jantiff jumped across to the speed lane. He looked back to catch a last glimpse of Esteban, still under the portal, then was carried past the range of vision.

At the Travelers Inn Jantiff signed the register as Arlo Jorum of Pharis, Alastor 458. Without comment the clerk assigned him a chamber.

Jantiff bathed and stretched himself out on his couch, aware of aching muscles and comprehensive fatigue. He closed his eyes; the three days to Aensday would pass most rapidly in sleep.

Jantiff inhaled and exhaled several deep breaths. Circumstances at last were under control. The Travelers Inn at the very least provided security; if Esteban offered offense, Jantiff need merely notify the Mutuals* on duty at the inn.

Jantiff opened his eyes, blinked and grimaced, and closed them again. Images from across the terrible day passed before his eyes; Jantiff writhed on the couch.

His stomach began to gripe; Jantiff sat erect. He needed food. Dressing, he went down to the cafeteria where he made a meal of gruff, deedle, and a bowl of wobbly, which he charged to his account.

The public address system, which had been projecting a series of lethargic popular tunes, suddenly enunciated a bulletin:

"Attention all! Take note of a heinous murder, just reported to the Uncibal Mutuality. The assassin is one Jantiff Ravensroke, a probationary visitor, originally of Zeck. He is a man of early maturity, tall, slender, with dark hair worn nondescript. He has a thin face, a long nose, and eyes noticeably green in color. The Mutuals urgently require that he be held in detention, pending full investigation of his foul act. A search at the highest level of intensity is already being prosecuted. Egalists all, keep a vigilant watch for this dangerous alien!"

Jantiff jumped to his feet to stand quivering in consternation. He went on delicate steps to the arch giving on the lobby. At the registration desk two men in low-crowned black hats loomed over the clerk. Jantiff's heart rose into his throat: Mutuals! Responding with nervous volubility, the clerk waved a long pale finger toward the ascensor and Jantiff's room.

The two men turned from the desk and strode to the ascensor. As soon as they were gone, Jantiff stepped out into the lobby, sidled unobtrusively around the far wall to the door and departed into the night.

*Mutality: a contract police force of non-Arrabins, inconspicuous, small in number, efficient in practice, directed and controlled by the local Panel of Delegates.

Disjerferact, the carnival strip along the mud flats, had never failed to fascinate Jantiff with its contrasts and paradoxes. Disjerferact! Gaudy and gay, strident and makeshift, trading brummagem for equally valueless tokens, achieving no more than the dream of a dream! By the light of Dwan, and from a distant perspective, the dark-red paper pavilions, the tall blue tents, the numberless festoons, banners, and whirligigs conjured a brave and splendid fantasy. By night, uncounted flambeaux flared to the sea breeze; the consequent gleams and shadows, darting and jerking, suggested a barbaric frenzy—in the end as factitious as all else of Disjerferact. Still, the confusion and helter-skelter provided Jantiff an effective refuge: who at Disjerferact cared a whit for anything other than his own yearnings?

For three days Jantiff skulked through nooks and back passages, venturing never a step without seeking the low black hats of Mutuals or the dread shape of Esteban. During daylight hours he occupied a cranny between the booth of a pickle merchant and a public latrine. By night he ventured forth, disguised by a mustache fashioned from his own hair and a head rag in the fashion of the Carabbas Islanders. His tokens—those remaining to him after paying bonterfest fees—he grudgingly exchanged for poggets and cornucopias of fried kelp. He slept by day in fits and starts, disturbed by the calls of hawkers, the puffworm vendor's bugle, the screeching of child acrobats, and from a booth across the way, the thud of clog-dancing and simulated enthusiasm from shills.

Early Aensday morning, while Jantiff lay half-torpid, the public megaphones spoke loud across the mud flats.

"Attention, all! Today greet the Whispers as they embark on their mission to Numenes! As adumbrated in recent statements, they intend a daring and innovative program, and they have proclaimed a slogan for the next century: *Viable egalism must fulfill both needs and aspirations, and provide scope for human genius!* They go to Lusz Tower to urge the Connatic's sympathetic support for the new scheme, and they will draw strength from your advocacy. Therefore, come today to the Public Zone. The Whispers fly from Waunisse aboard the *Sea Disk*; their time of arrival is high noon and they will speak from the Pedestal."

Jantiff listened apathetically while the megaphones broadcast a second and yet a third repetition of the message. For an instant, while the echoes died, Disjerferact hung suspended in an unnatural silence; then the customary tumult returned.

Jantiff rose to a kneeling position, peered right and left from his cranny, then, finding nothing to foster his anxieties, he stepped out into the flow of pleasure-seekers. At a nearby refreshment booth he exchanged a token for a spill of fried kelp. Leaning against a wall he consumed the crisp, if insipid, strands, then for want of a better destination he wandered eastward toward the Public Zone, or the Field of Voices, as it was sometimes called. The cursar returned with the Whispers aboard the *Sea Disk*; he would not be likely to return to the Centrality before the Whispers departed for Numenes: so there was time enough for Jantiff to hear the remarks of the Whispers, perhaps at close range.

Jantiff sauntered eastward, across Disjerferact and the mud flats beyond, over the Whery Slough Bridge and out upon the Public Zone: an expanse a mile long and almost as wide. At regular intervals poles rose high to support quatrefoil megaphones, each pole likewise displaying a numerical code to assist in the arrangement of rendezvous. Almost against the eastern boundary a pylon held aloft a circular platform under a glass parasol: this was the so-called "Pedestal." Beyond spread the scarred grounds of the space-port.

By the time Jantiff crossed over the Whery Slough Bridge, folk by the thousands were migrating across the field, to pack into a vital sediment around the Pedestal. Jantiff was annoyed to find that he could approach no closer than a hundred yards to the Pedestal, which would hardly allow him an intimate inspection of the Whispers.

As Dwan rose toward the zenith, crowds debouched from Uncibal River in a solid mass, to disperse and sift across the Zone, until presently no further increment was possible: the Zone was occupied to its capacity and past. Those arriving on Uncibal River could not alight, but must continue into the round-about, and return the way they had come. On the Zone folk stood elbow to elbow, chin to shoulder. A sour-sweet odor arose from the crowd to drift away on airs from the sea. Jantiff recalled his first impressions of Arrabus, upon debarking from the spaceship: at last he could identify that odor which then had caused him puzzlement and perhaps a trace of revulsion.

Jantiff attempted to calculate the number of persons surrounding him, but became confused: the number was surely somewhere among the millions . . . He felt a pang of claustrophobic alarm: he was confined, he could not move! Suppose something prompted these millions of entities into a stampede? A horrifying thought! Jantiff pictured tides of people surging over one another, rising and climbing, at last to topple and break in churning glimpses of arms, faces, legs . . . The crowd produced a sudden mumble of sound, as out over the water appeared the *Sea Disk*, inbound from Waunisse. The vessel veered over the space-port, descended in a smart half-spiral and dropped to a landing near the Public Zone. The port opened; an attendant stepped out, followed by the four Whispers: three men and a woman wearing formal robes. Ignoring the crowd they disappeared into a subsurface walkway. Two minutes passed. Out on the Zone gazes lifted to the platform at the top of the Pedestal.

The Whispers appeared. For a moment they stood looking over the crowd: four small figures indistinct in the shade of the parasol. Jantiff tried to match them with the Whispers he had seen on the screen. The woman was Fausgard; the men were Orgold, Lemiste, and Delfin. One of the men spoke—which could not be discerned from below—and a thousand quatrefoil megaphones broadcast his words.

"The Whispers are revivified by this contact with the folk of Uncibal! We take nourishment from your benevolence; it flows in upon us like a mighty tide! We shall bring it forth when we confront the Connatic, and the sheer power of egalistic doctrine shall overcome every challenge!

"Great events are in the offing! At our noble Centenary we celebrate a hundred years of achievement! A new century lies before us, and succeeding centuries in grand succession, each to ratify anew our optimum style of life. Egalism shall sweep Alastor Cluster, and all the Gaean Reach! So much is foreordained, if it be your will! Is it so?"

The Whisper paused; a somewhat perfunctory and even uncertain mutter of approval arose from the crowd. Jantiff himself was puzzled. The tone of the address was not at all consonant with the announcement he had heard that morning in Disjerferact.

"So be it!" declared the Whisper, and a thousand quatrefoil megaphones magnified his words. "There shall be no turning back, or faltering! Egalism forever! Man's great enemies are tedium and drudgery! We have broken their ancient tyranny; let the contractors do the drudge for their lowly pittances. Egalism shall ensure the final emancipation of Man!

"So now: your Whispers go forth to Numenes, impelled by our composite will. We shall take our message to the Connatic and make our three important desires known.

"First: no more immigration! Let those who envy us impose egalism on their own worlds!

"Second: Arrabins are a peaceful folk. We fear no attack; we intend no aggression. Why then must we subsidize the Connatic's power? We require none of his advice, nor the force of his Whelm, nor the supervision of his bureaucrats. We will therefore require that our annual tax be reduced, or even abolished.

398 / JACK VANCE

"Third: our exports are sold at the cheap, yet the items we import come dear. Effectually, we subsidize those inefficient systems still in force elsewhere. Believe this: your Whispers shall press for a new schedule of exchange between the token and the ozol; in fact, they should go at par! Is not an hour of our toil equal to that hour worked by some whey-faced diddler of, let us say, Zeck?"

Jantiff jerked his head and frowned in displeasure. The remarks seemed both absurd and inappropriate.

The megaphones rang on.

"Our Centenary is at hand. At Lusz we shall invite the Connatic to visit Arrabus, to join our festival, and appraise for himself our great achievements. If he declines, the loss is his own. In any case, we shall make our report to you at a great rally of the Arrabin egalists. We now depart for Numenes; wish us well!" The Whispers raised arms in salute; the crowd responded with a polite roar. The Whispers stepped back and disappeared from view. Several minutes later they emerged from the ingress kiosk out upon the space-port. A car awaited them; they entered and were conveyed to the great hulk of the spaceship *Eldantro*.

The crowd began to depart the field, but without haste. Jantiff, now impatient, thrust, sidled and slid through the obstructive masses to no great effect, and a full two hours elapsed before he managed to squeeze aboard Uncibal River, sweating, tired, and temper at the quick.

He rode directly to Alastor Centrality. Entering the structure he found behind the counter, not Clode, but a woman tall and portly, with an imposing bust and austere features. She wore a severe gown of gray twill over a white blouse; her hair was drawn to the back of her head and held in a handsome silver clip. As in the case of Clode, her place of origin was clearly other than Arrabus. She spoke in a formal voice: "Sir, how may I assist you?"

"I must see the cursar at once," said Jantiff. Out of reflexive habit he darted a nervous glance over his shoulder. "The matter is most urgent."

The woman inspected Jantiff for a long five seconds, and Jantiff was made conscious of his disheveled appearance. She answered in a voice somewhat crisper than before. "The cursar is not in his office. He has not yet returned from Waunisse."

Jantiff stood rigid with disappointment. "I expected him today," he said fretfully. "He was to have returned with the Whispers. Is Clode here?"

The woman turned another searching inspection upon Jantiff, who became uneasy. She said: "Clode is not here. I am Aleida Gluster, clerk in the Connatic's service, and I can discharge any business which you might have had with Clode."

"I left a parcel with him, a photographic matrix, for delivery to the cursar. I merely wanted to assure myself of its safety."

"There is no such parcel in the office. Clode Morre, I regret to say, is dead."

Jantiff stared aghast, "Dead?" He collected his wits. "How did this happen? And when?"

"Three days ago. He was attacked by a ruffian and stabbed through the throat. It is tragic for us all."

Jantiff asked in a hollow voice: "Has the murderer been apprehended?"

"No. He has been identified as a certain Jantiff Ravensroke, of Zeck."

Jantiff managed to blurt a question: "And the parcel I left is gone?"

"There is definitely no such parcel in the office."

"Has the cursor been notified?"

"Naturally! I telephoned him immediately at the Waunisse Centrality."

"Then call Waunisse now! If the cursar is there I must speak to him. The matter is most important, I assure you."

"And what name shall I announce if he is there?"

Jantiff made a feeble attempt to wave the question aside. "It is really of no great consequence."

"Your name is of considerable consequence," said Aleida crisply. "Is it by any chance 'Jantiff Ravensroke'?"

Jantiff quailed before the searching inspection. He nodded meekly. "I am Jantiff Ravensroke. But I am no murderer!"

Aleida gave him a level glance of unreadable significance and turned to the telephone. She spoke: "This is Aleida, at Uncibal Centrality. Is Cursar Bonamico anywhere at hand?"

A voice responded: "Cursar Bonamico has returned to Uncibal. He departed this morning on the *Sea Disk*, in company with the Whispers."

"Odd. He has not yet looked into his office."

"Evidently there has been some delay."

"Yes, quite likely. Thank you." Aleida Gluster turned back to Jantiff. "If you are not the assassin, why do the Mutuals insist otherwise?"

"The Mutuals are mistaken! I know the murderer; he has influence with Contractor Shubart, who contracts the services of the Mutuals. I am anxious to lay all facts before the cursar."

"Doubtless." Aleida looked past Jantiff through the glass panels of the front wall. "Here are the Mutual now. You can place your information before them."

Jantiff turned a glance of startled terror over his shoulder, to see two men in low black hats marching in ponderous certitude across the compound. "No! They will take me away and kill me! I have urgent news for the cursar; they wish to stifle me!"

Aleida nodded grimly. "Step into the inner office: quickly now!"

Jantiff sped through the door into the cursar's chamber. The door closed; Jantiff pressed his ear to the panel to hear a measured thud of footsteps, then Aleida's voice: "Sirs, how may I be of service?"

A resonant baritone voice spoke: "We wish to apprehend a certain Jantiff Ravensroke. Is he on the premises?"

"You are the Mutuals," said Aleida curtly. "You must determine the facts for yourself."

"The facts are these! For three days we have kept close watch on this place, fearful that the assassin might attempt a second murder, perhaps on your own person. Now five minutes ago Jantiff Ravensroke was seen arriving at the Agency. Call him forth, if you please, and we will take him into protective custody."

Aleida Gluster spoke in her coldest tones. "Jantiff Ravensroke has been accused of murder: this is true. The victim was Clode Morre, clerk in the Connatic's service, and the deed occurred upon the extraterritorial grounds of Alastor Centrality. Responsibility for the detection and punishment of this crime, therefore, is beyond the legal competence of the Mutuals."

After a pause of ten seconds, the baritone voice spoke. "Our orders are definite. We must do our duty and search the premises."

"You shall do nothing of the sort," said Aleida Gluster. "At your first move I will touch two buttons. The first will destroy you, through robot sensors; the second will call down the Whelm."

The baritone voice made no response. Jantiff heard the measured thud of retreating footsteps. The door opened; Aleida looked in at him. "Quickly now, go after them; it is your only chance. They are confused and return for orders, and they will find that I waived extraterritoriality when I reported Clode's murder."

"But where shall I go? If I could get aboard a spaceship, I have my passage voucher—"

"The Mutuals will certainly guard the space-port. Go south! At Balad there is a space-port of sorts; go there and take passage for home."

Jantiff grimaced sadly. "Balad is thousands of miles away."

"That may well be. But if you stay in Uncibal, you will surely be taken. Leave now, by the rear exit. When you reach Balad telephone the Agency."

To the Connatic at Lusz:

Events are flying in all directions here, to my great distress and consternation. Specifically, I fear for poor Jantiff Ravensroke, who is in terrible danger; unless someone puts a stop, they'll have his blood or worse. He is accused of a vile crime but he is surely as innocent as a child. Clerk Morre has been murdered and Cursar Bonamico cannot be located; therefore I have ordered Jantiff south into the Weirdlands, despite the rigors of the way.

I send this off in agitation, and with the hope that help is on the way.

Aleida Gluster, Clerk,
The Alastor Centrality, Uncibal.

CHAPTER 10

W ith hunched shoulders and smoldering gaze, Jantiff rode Uncibal River west: away from the space-port, away from Alastor Centrality, away forever from the detestable Old Pink, where all his troubles had originated. Fragmented images whirled through his mind, churned by rage and by sick misgivings at the prospect of traversing the Weirdlands. How far to Balad? A thousand miles? Two thousand miles? An enormous distance, in any event, across a land of forests, moldering ruins, and great sluggish rivers gleaming like quicksilver in the Dwanlight . . . Something tickled Jantiff's mind: the mention of an omnibus, its terminus at the Metallurgical Syndicate. Someone had joked of riding all the way to Balad, so presumably a connection existed. Regrettably, transportation came dear on Wyst when bought with Arrabin tokens, of which Jantiff had but few in any case. Glumly he thought of his family amulet: a disk of carved rose quartz on a stelt armstrap. Perhaps this might buy his passage to Balad.

So Jantiff rode across the waning afternoon, through the twilight and into the night. Diverting to the Great Southern Adit he was carried along the route of the bonterfesters. How far now seemed that occasion, though only four days gone! Jantiff's stomach twisted at the recollection.

South through the fringes of the city he rode. Night had fallen in earnest: a damp dark night by reason of a low overcast. Strands of cold mist blew along the avenues of District 92, and the overhead lamps became eerie puffs of luminosity. Few folk were abroad at this time, and as the adit slanted away from the city their number dwindled even further, so that Jantiff rode almost alone.

The way climbed a long slope: Uncibal, behind and below, became a ribbon of hazy light, streaming far to the right and far to the left; then the way swung into Outpost Valley and Uncibal was blotted from sight.

Ahead appeared the lights of the Metallurgical Syndicate. The fence came to parallel the man-way, and the fat bolts of energy playing among the strands were more sinister than ever through the darkness.

Mounds of ore, slag and sinter loomed against the sky; a barge discharged ore into an underground hopper, to create a clattering roar. Jantiff watched in sudden interest. Presumably, after unloading the ore, the barge would return to the mines, somewhere in Blale, at the southern fringe of the Weirdlands . . . Here was transportation quick and cheap, if he could avail himself of it. Jantiff moved to the side of the way and stepped off. The barge slid off and stationed itself under another hopper; again came a clatter as material poured into the barge. Jantiff appraised the situation. The fence no longer barred the way, but between himself and the barge interposed an area illuminated by overhead lamps; he would surely be seen if he approached from the direction of the man-way.

Jantiff returned to the man-way and rode a hundred yards past the lighted area. Alighting once more, he set off across the dark field, which was dank with seepage from the slag piles; the mud released an acrid reek as Jantiff trudged through. Cursing under his breath, he approached the shadow side of the mound, where the ground became somewhat firmer. Cautiously Jantiff moved to where he could view the field: just in time to see the barge lift and sweep away through the night.

Jantiff looked forlornly after the receding side-lights: there went his transportation south. He hunched his shoulders against the chill. Standing in the shadows he felt more alone than ever before in his life: as isolated and remote as if he were already dead, or floating alone in the void.

He stirred himself. No point standing stupidly in the cold, though indeed he could see small scope for anything better.

Lights slid across the sky: another barge! It settled upon the discharge hopper, the operator leaning from his cab to perceive signals from the hopper attendant.

The compartments tilted; out poured the ore with a rush and a rattle. Jantiff poised himself at the ready. The barge slid to a hopper near the slag pile; slag roared down the chute into the barge. Jantiff bounded at best speed across the intervening area. He reached the barge and climbed upon a horizontal flange at the base of the cargo bins. Grasping for a secure handhold, he found only vertical flanges; he would lose his grip as soon as the barge lurched to a cross gust. Jantiff jumped, caught the upper lip of the ore compartment; kicking and straining he hauled himself up, slid over the lip into the compartment, which just at this moment received its charge from the hopper above. Jantiff danced and trod this way and that, and climbed sprawling across the slag and so managed to avoid burial. In the cab the operator turned his head; Jantiff threw himself flat. Had be been seen? . . . Evidently not. The loaded barge lurched aloft and slid away through the darkness. Jantiff heaved a great shuddering sigh. Arrabus lay behind him.

The barge flew a mile or two, then slowed and seemed to drift. Jantiff lifted his head in perplexity. What went on? A lamp on top of the control cab illuminated the cargo area; the operator stepped from his cab and walked astern along the central catwalk. He called harshly to Jantiff. "Well, then, fellow. What's your game?"

Jantiff crawled across the slag until, gaining his feet, he was able to look up at the menacing figure. He did not like what he saw. The operator was a notably ugly man. His face, round and pale, rested directly upon a great tun of a torso; his eyes were set far apart, almost riding the cheekbones. The nose, no more than a button of gristle, seemed vastly inadequate for the ventilation of so imposing a body. The operator repeated himself, in a voice as harsh as before: "Well, then: what's the game? Haven't you read the notices? We're sharp for restless custodees."

"I'm no custodee," cried Jantiff. "I'm trying to leave Uncibal; I only want to ride across Weirdland into Blale."

The operator looked down in sardonic disbelief. "What are you seeking in Blale? You'll find no free wump for certain; everyone earns his keep."

"I'm not Arrabin," Jantiff explained eagerly. "I'm not even an immigrant; I'm a visitor from Zeck. I thought I wanted to visit Wyst, but now I'm anxious only to leave."

"Well, I can believe you're no custodee; you'd know better than to ride the ore-barge. Can you guess how you might have fared, had I not taken pity on you?"

"No, not exactly," mumbled Jantiff. "I intended no harm."

The operator spoke in a lordly tone. "First, to clear Daffledaw Mountains, I raise to three miles, where the air is chill and the clouds are shreds of floating ice. So then, you freeze rigid and die. No, no, don't argue, I've seen it happen. Next. Where do you think I take this slag? To be set into a tiara for the contractor's lady? No indeed. I float over Lake Neman, where Contractor Shubart builds his ramp. I turn up the compartments; out pours the slag, and your frozen corpse as well, to fall a mile into the black water. And what do you think of that?"

"I was not aware of such things," said Jantiff mournfully. "Had I known, I would certainly have chosen some other transportation."

The operator rocked his head briskly back and forth. "You're no custodee; this is clear. They know well enough what happens to illicit vagabonds." The operator's voice became somewhat more lenient. "Well then, you're in luck. I'll fly you to Blale—if you pay a hundred ozols for the privilege. Otherwise you can take your chances with the chill and Lake Neman."

Jantiff winced. "The Arrabins robbed me of everything I own. I have nothing except a few tokens."

The operator stared down a long grim moment. "What do you carry in that sack at your belt?"

Jantiff displayed the contents. "Fifty tokens and some bits of kelp."

The operator gave a groan of disgust. "What good is such trash to me?" He wheeled and marched back along the catwalk toward the cab.

Jantiff stumbled and slid in the loose slag as he tried to keep pace. "I have nothing now, but my father will pay; I assure you of this!"

The operator turned and scrutinized the compartments with exaggerated care. "I discern no one else; where is your father? Let him come forth and pay."

"He is not here; he lives at Frayness on Zeck."

"Zeck? Why did you not say so?" The operator reached down and yanked Jantiff up to the catwalk. "I'm a Gatzwanger from Kandaspe, which is not all that far from Zeck. The Arrabins? Madmen all, and slovens, as well. Into the cab with you. I marvel to see a decent elitist in such a plight."

Jantiff gingerly followed the operator's great bulk into the cab.

"Sit on the bench yonder. I was about to take a bite of food. Do you care to join me, or would you prefer your kelp?"

"I will join you with pleasure," said Jantiff. "My kelp has become a bit stale."

The operator set out bread, meat, pickles, and a jug of wine, then signaled Jantiff to serve himself.

"You are a lucky man to have fallen in with me, Lemiel Swarkop, rather than certain others I could name. The truth is, I despise the Arrabins and I'll ferry away anyone who wants to leave, custodee or not. There is a certain Booch, now Contractor Shubart's personal chauffeur, but a one-time operator. He shows a kind face only to obliging girls, and even then is fickle—if one is to believe his tales."

Jantiff decided not to mention his acquaintance with Booch. "I am grateful both to you and to Cassadense."*

"Whatever the case," said Swarkop, "the Weirdlands are no place for a person like yourself. No one maintains order; it is every man for himself, and you must either fight, hide, or run, unless you have a submissive disposition."

"I only want to leave Wyst," said Jantiff. "I am going to the Balad spaceport for this purpose only."

"You may have a long wait."

Jantiff instantly became alarmed. "Why so?"

"Balad Spaceport is just a field beside the sea. Perhaps once a month a cargo ship drops down to discharge goods for Balad township and Contractor Shubart; you'd be in great luck if you found a ship to carry you toward Zeck."

Jantiff pondered the information in gloomy silence. At last he asked: "How then should I return to Zeck?"

*See Glossary, v.

Swarkop turned him a wondering gaze. "The obvious choice is Uncibal Spaceport, where ships depart each day."

"True," said Jantiff lamely. "There is always that possibility. I must give it some thought."

The barge slid south through the night. Overcome by fatigue, Jantiff drowsed. Swarkop sprawled out on a couch to the side of the cab and began to snore noisily. Jantiff went to look out the front windows, but found only darkness below and the stars of Alastor Cluster above. Down to the side a flickering light appeared and passed abeam. Who might be abroad in that dark wilderness? Why were they showing so late a light? Gypsies? Vagabonds? Someone lost in the woods? The light fell astern and was gone.

Jantiff stretched himself out on the bench and tried to sleep. Eventually he dozed, to be aroused some hours later by the thump of Swarkop's boots.

Jantiff blinked and groaned, and reluctantly hunched himself up into a sitting position. Swarkop washed his face at the basin, gurgling, blowing and snorting like a drowning animal. A bleary gray light gave substance to the interior of the cab. Jantiff rose to his feet and went to the forward window. Dwan had not yet appeared; the sky was a sullen mottled gray. Below spread the forest, marked only by an occasional glade, out to a line of hills in the south.

Swarkop thumped a mug of tea down in front of Jantiff. He peered down at the landscape. "A dreary morning! The clouds are dank as dead fish and the Sych is the most dismal of forests, fit only for wild men and witches!" He raised his hand and performed a curious set of signals. Jantiff eyed him askance but delicately forbore comment. Swarkop said heavily: "When a wise man lives in a strange place he uses the customs and believes the beliefs of that place, if only as sensible precaution. Each morning the wild men of the Sych make such signs and they are persuaded of the benefits; why should I dispute them, or despise what, after all, may be a very practical technique?"

"Quite true," said Jantiff. "This seems a sensible point of view."

Swarkop poured out more tea. "The Sych guards a thousand secrets. Ages ago this was a fruitful countryside; can you believe it? Now the palaces are covered with mold."

Jantiff shook his head in awe. "It seems impossible."

"Not to Contractor Shubart! He intends to break the forests and open up the land. He'll establish farms and homesteads, villages and counties, and then he'll make himself King of the Weirdlands. Oh, he has a taste for pomp, does Contractor Shubart; never think otherwise!"

"It seems an ambitious program, to say the least."

"Ambitious and expensive. Contractor Shubart milks a golden stream from the Arrabin teat, so there's no lack of ozols. Oh, I'll fly his barges and work to his orders, and someday I'll be Viscount Swarkop. Booch no doubt will ordain himself Duke, but that's nothing to me, so long as he keeps to his own domain. Ah well, that's all for the future." Swarkop pointed to the southeast. "There—Lake Neman, where Contractor Shubart builds his causeway, and where I must relinquish your company."

Jantiff had hoped for transportation all the way to his destination. He asked despondently, "And then how far to Balad?"

"A mere fifty miles; no great matter." Swarkop put a plate of bread and meat before him. "Eat; fortify yourself against the promenade, and please do not mention my name in Balad! The news of my altruism would soon reach the Contractor's manse and I might be deprived of my title."

"Naturally, I'll say nothing whatever!" Jantiff glumly addressed himself to the food; the next meal might be long in coming. He voiced a forlorn hope: "Perhaps I can somehow secure passage out of Balad on a cargo ship?"

"Most unlikely. Cargo ships reject all passengers. Otherwise starmenters dressed like tourists would take passage, destroy captain and crew and whisk their booty away across space. Anywhere in the Primarchic* a cargo ship sells for a million ozols and no questions asked. And you may be sure that the shipping lines are well aware of this. I suggest that you dismiss Balad Spaceport from your plans."

Jantiff looked out across the dour forest he must traverse afoot: all to no purpose if Swarkop were to be believed. At Balad he was further removed than ever from his passage home. Still, under the circumstances, what better options had been open to him? He said tentatively: "Perhaps I could persuade you to deliver a message to the cursar in Uncibal? The matter is of great importance."

Swarkop's eyes bulged in disbelief. "You suggest that I ride that vile man-way into Uncibal? My dear fellow, not for a hundred ozols! You must transmit your messages by telephone, like everyone else."

Jantiff hastened to agree. "Yes, that's the best idea, of course!" He stood aside as Swarkop manipulated controls; the barge slanted down upon Lake Neman: a great gash across the wilderness brimming with black water and never more than two or three miles wide. Swarkop brought the barge to a halt and thrust a lever: slag poured down upon the end of a dike already half across the lake.

"The plan is to strike a road from Balad across the Sych to Lake Neman, thence to the head of the Buglas River, then across the Dankwold; or perhaps Shubart intends to blast through the Daffledaws: yes, that must be the case, since I've carried six great cargoes of frack north to Uncibal

---

*The Primarchic is an aggregation of stars somewhat lesser than Alastor Cluster, at one time controlled by the Primarch, now in a chronic state of disorder, factionalism and war.

An important function of the Connatic's Whelm is protection against raids from the Primarchic.

Depot—enough to pulverize Zade Mountain and cut a new Dinklin River gorge."

"It seems a tremendous project."

"True, and quite beyond my understanding. But then I am Lemiel Swarkop, hireling, while Shubart is Grand Knight and Contractor, and there the matter rests."

Swarkop lowered the barge to the base of the causeway. Throwing open the cab door, he leaned out to inspect the countryside. The air was cold and still; Lake Neman lay flat as a black mirror. "The day will be fine," declared Swarkop with a heartiness Jantiff refused to find infectious. "Trudging the Sych in the rain is not good sport. Good luck to you, then! Fifty miles to Balad: two days' easy journey, unless you are delayed."

Jantiff's ear discovered alarming overtones in the remark. "Why should I be delayed?"

Swarkop shrugged. "I could lay forth a thousand ideas and still fall short of reality. Giampara* will dispose."

"Is there an inn along the way where I might rest the night?"

Swarkop pointed to the shore of the lake. "Notice that tumble of milk-stone; it marks a grand resort of the ancient times, when lords and ladies dallied up and down the lake in barges with carved silver screens and velvet sails. Then there were inns along the road to Balad. Now you'll find only a roadmender's hut just past Gant Gap; use it at your own risk."

" 'Risk'?" cried Jantiff. "Why should there be risk?"

"The roadmenders sometimes set out traps to startle the witches. The witches sometimes leave hallucinations to startle the roadmenders. Build four blazing fires against the gaunch; lie down in the middle and you'll be safe until morning. But keep the fires flaming high."

"What is a gaunch?" asked Jantiff, looking dubiously along the edge of the forest.

"That question is often asked but never answered. The witches know but they say nothing, not even to each other." Swarkop mused a moment. "I suggest that you put the matter out of your mind. You'll know the gaunch when you meet him face to face. If you do not do so the matter becomes moot. Fire is said to be a deterrent, if it blazes higher than the creature cares to step, and there is my best advice."

Swarkop bundled up what remained of his provisions and thrust the pack upon Jantiff. "You'll find plums, kakajous, and honeybuttons along the way. But don't steal so much as a turnip from the farmers: they'll take you for a witch and hunt you down with their wurgles. Once again: good luck."

---

*Swarkop's reference to Giampara is facetious. Were he in earnest he would no doubt have invoked Corè of the Four Bosoms, who controls his home world Kandaspe. Jantiff perceives this nuance of usage but is not altogether reassured.

Swarkop backed into the cab and closed the door. The barge lifted and slid off across the lake.

Jantiff watched until the barge disappeared into the distance. Swinging around, he scrutinized the edge of the forest but found only dark foliage and darker shadows. He squared his shoulders to the road and trudged off south toward Balad.

CHAPTER I I

Dawn, rising into the sky, projected Jantiff's shadow along the road ahead of him; as in Arrabus the light seemed to shimmer with an oversaturation of color. In these middle latitudes half around the curve of Wyst, the effect if anything seemed emphasized, and Jantiff fancied that if he were to examine one of the light spatters, where a ray struck down through the foliage, he would find innumerable points of color, as if from ten million microscopic dew drops . . . He recalled his first wonder at the light and the stimulation it had worked on him; small benefit had he derived! In fact, to the contrary: his sketches and depictions had set in motion those events which were the source of all his troubles! And the end not yet in sight! At least from Balad he could telephone the cursar, who would certainly provide him transportation back to Uncibal and safe access through Uncibal Spaceport. And Jantiff, marching south at a brisk stride, began to take an interest in the landscape. When eventually he returned to Zeck, what wonderful tales he would be able to tell!

The road led up a long slope through sprawling heavy-boled trees, then breasted a low ridge. Ahead lay forest and yet more forest: trees indigenous and exotic, some perhaps tracing a lineage back through the Gaean Reach, all the way to Old Earth itself! Jantiff's imagination was stirred; he imagined himself arriving at Alpha Gaea Spaceport on Earth, with fabulous cities and unimaginable antiquities awaiting his inspection! How much would it cost? Two or perhaps three thousand ozols. Where would he ever gain so much money? One way or another; nothing was impossible. First: a safe return to Zeck!

Beguiling himself with fancies and prospects, Jantiff put miles behind him, walking with long steady strides. When Dwan reached its zenith, little more than halfway up the sky to the north, Jantiff halted beside a rivulet and ate a portion of his provisions. For the moment, at least, the forest seemed placid and devoid of menace. How far had he come? Ten miles at least . . . Fifty yards along the road a group of eight folk emerged from the forest. Jantiff tensed, then decided to sit quietly.

Three of the folk were women in long gowns, and three were men, wearing black vests over pale green pantaloons; one was a child and another a stripling. All were blond; the child's hair was flaxen. Upon spying Jantiff, the group came to a wary halt, then, neither speaking nor making signals, they turned and went off along the road to the south, the stripling and the child bringing up the rear.

Jantiff watched them go. From time to time the child looked back, whether or not by reason of instruction, Jantiff could not determine, since the child made no comment to its elders. They rounded a bend and were lost to view.

Jantiff immediately jumped to his feet and went to that spot where the witches had emerged from the forest. A few yards off the road he saw a tree burdened with plump purple fruit. Jantiff restrained himself. The witches might or might not have been eating the fruit; perhaps it carried a venom which must be dispelled by cooking or other treatment . . . Jantiff proceeded on his way, and at his previous gait, unconcerned whether or not he might overtake the witches. They had shown no hint of hostility, and surely they could apprehend no threat from him. But when presently he commanded a view along the road the witches were nowhere to be seen.

Jantiff walked steadily onward, his strides becoming slower and his legs beginning to ache as the afternoon waned. As Dwan angled low into the northwest the land heaved up ahead in a line of stony juts and retreating gullies. On a promontory overlooking the road the ruins of a great palace lay tumbled among a dozen black tzung trees: a dolorous place, thought Jantiff, no doubt a rendezvous for melancholy ghosts. He hastened past with all the speed his legs could provide: up a gulch where a small river bounded back and forth between rocks—Gant Gap, Jantiff decided. It was a place dark and cold; he was pleased to emerge upon a meadow.

Dwan almost brushed the horizon. Jantiff looked in all directions for the shed Swarkop had mentioned, but no such structure could be seen. Lowering his head he set off once more along the road, as the last rays of Dwan-light played across the meadow. The road entered a new forest, and Jantiff hunched along in the gathering darkness, assured that he had passed the shed by.

A waft of smoke reached his nostrils: Jantiff stopped short, then walked slowly forward and presently saw a spark of firelight fifty yards ahead.

Jantiff approached with great caution and looked out upon a small meadow. Here, in fact, was the shed: a crude structure set thirty yards back from the road. Around the fire sat eight folk: three men of widely disparate age; three women, equally various; a boy of four or five and a girl somewhat past her adolescence. These were evidently the folk Jantiff had seen earlier in the day: how had they arrived so soon? Jantiff could not fathom their speed; they clearly had been at rest for at least an hour. He studied them from the shadows. They seemed neither uncouth nor horrid, after the reputed witchling style; indeed they seemed quite ordinary. Jantiff recalled that their far ancestors were the nobility whose palaces lay shattered across the Weirdlands. All were blond, their hair ranging from flaxen through pale brown to dusty umber. The girl in particular seemed almost comely. A trick of the firelight? Perhaps one of her hallucinations or glamours?

None spoke; all stared into the fire as if deep in meditation.

Jantiff stepped forward. He attempted a hearty greeting, but achieved only a rather reedy "Hallo!"

The small boy troubled to turn his head; the others paid no heed.

"Hallo there!" called Jantiff once more, and stepped forward. "May I join you at your fire?"

Certain of the folk gave him a brief inspection; none spoke.

Accepting the absence of active hostility as an invitation, Jantiff knelt down beside the blaze and warmed his hands. Once again he essayed conversation: "I'm on my way to Balad where hopefully I'll take passage off-planet. I'm a stranger to Wyst, actually; my home is Zeck, out along the Fiamifer. I spent a few months in Uncibal but had quite enough of it. Too many people, too much confusion . . . I don't know if you've ever visited there . . ." Jantiff's voice dwindled off to silence; no one seemed to be listening. Odd conduct, to be sure! Well, if they preferred silence to conversation they were well within their rights. If these were truly witches, they might know mysterious means to communicate without sound. Jantiff felt a tingle of awe; covertly he inspected the group, first left, then right. Their garments, woven from bast and dyed variously green, pink or pale brown, were serviceable forest wear; in the place of hats the men wore kerchiefs, the women's hair fell loosely over the ears. Each had gilded his or her fingernails so that they glinted in the firelight. Otherwise they displayed no ornaments, talismans or amulets. Whatever mysteries they controlled, their methods were not obtrusive. Apparently they had supped; a cooking pot rested upside down on a bench, and also a platter with fragments of skillet cake.

Emboldened by the acceptance of his presence, Jantiff put forward: "I am very hungry; I wonder if I might finish off the skillet cake?"

No one seemed to care one way or another. Jantiff took a modest portion of the cake and ate with good appetite.

The fire began to burn low; the girl rose to her feet and went to fetch logs. She was slender and graceful, so Jantiff noticed; he leapt to his feet and ran to assist her, and it seemed that her lips twitched in an almost imperceptible smile. None of the others paid any heed, save the small boy, who watched rather sternly.

Jantiff ate another piece of skillet cake, wondering meanwhile whether the group planned to sleep in the shed . . . The door was closed; perhaps they feared the roadmenders' tricks.

The fire glowed warm; the silence soothed; Jantiff's eyelids drooped. He fell asleep.

By slow and fitful degrees Jantiff awoke. He lay on the ground, cramped and cold; the fire had burnt down to embers. Jantiff peered through the darkness; no one was visible: the witches were gone.

Jantiff sat up and hunched over the coals. A spatter of cold rain fell against his face. Laboriously he rose to his feet and stood swaying in the darkness. Shelter would be most welcome. Dubiously he considered the shed; it should be in yonder direction.

Groping through the darkness, he found the plank walls, and sidled to the door. The latch moved under his hand; the door creaked ajar. Jantiff's heart jerked at the sound, but no one, or nothing, seemed to notice. He listened. From inside the hut: silence. Neither breathing, nor movement, nor any of the sounds of sleep. Jantiff tried to step forward, but found that he could not do so: his body thought better of the idea.

For a minute Jantiff stood wavering, every instant less disposed to enter the hut. There was something within, said a mid-region of his brain; it would seize him with a horrible babbling sound. So in his childhood had gone a remembered nightmare, perhaps an anticipation of this very moment. Jantiff backed away from the door. He stumbled off to where he and the girl had gathered firewood, and presently found dead branches which he brought to the embers. After great effort he blew up the fire and finally achieved a heartening blaze. Warm once more he sat down, resolved to remain awake. He turned to look at the hut, now visible in the firelight. Through the open door nothing could be seen. Jantiff quickly averted his gaze, to avoid giving offense . . . His mind wandered; his eyes closed . . . A creaking sound brought him sharply awake. Someone had closed the door to the shed.

Jantiff jerked up to his knees. Run! Take wild and instant flight! The hysterical animal within himself keened and raved . . . But run where? Off into the darkness? Jantiff fetched more wood and built up the fire, and no longer was he urged to sleep.

A dank light seeped into the sky. The meadow took on substance. Beside the guttering fire Jantiff was like a figure carved from wood. He stirred up the fire, feeling ancient as the world itself, then rose stiffly to his feet and ate the last of his bread and meat. He turned a single incurious glance toward the shed, then trudged somberly away toward the south.

Halfway through the morning the overcast lifted. Lambent Dwan-light burst down upon the landscape and Jantiff's spirits lifted. Already the events of the previous night were sliding from his mind, like the episodes of a dream.

The road crossed a river; Jantiff drank, bathed his face, and ate berries from a low-growing thicket. For ten minutes he rested, then once again went his way.

Gradually the land altered. The forest thinned and sheered back from stony meadows. At noon Jantiff encountered a lane leading away to the right, and thereafter similar lanes left the road every mile or so. Jantiff walked across a wild stony land, grown over with coarse shrubs and land corals. To his left the forest continued into the southeast dark and heavy as ever.

During the middle afternoon he came upon a farmstead of modestly prosperous appearance. A young man of his own age worked behind a fence whitewashing the trunks of young fruit trees. He stood erect at Jantiff's approach, and came to the fence to secure a better view: a sturdy fellow with a narrow long-nosed face and sleek black hair tied in three tufts. Jantiff gave him a courteous greeting, then, not caring for the farmer's expression of sardonic bewilderment, continued along his way.

The farmer's curiosity, however, was not to be denied. "Hola there! Hold up a minute!"

Jantiff paused. "Are you addressing me?"

"Naturally. Is anyone else present?"

"I believe not."

"Well, then! You're not of these parts certainly."

"True," said Jantiff coldly. "I am a visitor to Wyst. My home is Frayness on Zeck."

"I don't know the place. Still I daresay there are millions of chinks and burrows about the Cluster of which I know nothing."

"No doubt this is the case."

"Well then—why are you walking the Sych Road which leads nowhere but to Lake Neman?"

"A friend flew me out from Uncibal and put me down at Lake Neman," said Jantiff. "I walked the road from there."

"And what of the witches: did you see many? I am told a new tribe just moved over from the Haralumilet."

"I encountered a group of wandering folk, yes," said Jantiff. "They troubled me not at all; in fact, they seemed quite courteous."

"So long as they forbore to feed you their tainted* food you're in luck."

Jantiff managed a smile. "I am fastidious about such things, I assure you."

"And what will you do in these parts?"

Jantiff had prepared an answer to such a question: "I am a student trav-

*Inexact translation. *Uslak* is "devil's dross"; the adjective *uslakain* means unholy, unclean, profane, repulsive.

WYST:ALASTOR 1716 / 413

eling on a research fellowship. I wanted to visit Blale before returning home."

The farmer gave a skeptical grunt. "You'll find nothing here to study; we are quite ordinary folk. You might have studied to better effect at home."

"Possibly so." Jantiff bowed stiffly. "Excuse me; I must be on my way."

"As you like, so long as you don't wander into the orchard among my good damsons, whether to study or to meditate or just to stroll, because I'll believe you're there to pilfer, and I'll loose Stanket on you."

"I have no intention of stealing your produce," said Jantiff with dignity. "Good-day to you."

He continued south where the road skirted the damson orchard; he noted clusters of fruit dangling almost within reach. He marched resolutely past, even though he was apparently not under observation.

The land became settled. To the west spread cultivated lands: farmstead after farmstead, with orchards and fields of cereal. To the east the forest thrust obdurately south, as heavy, tall, and dense as ever. Jantiff presently saw ahead a cluster of ramshackle structures: the town Balad. To the right a group of warehouses and workshops indicated the site of the space-port. The field itself was barren of traffic.

Jantiff urged his weary legs to a final effort and moved at his best speed.

A slow full river swung in from the east; the road veered close to the Sych. Jantiff, chancing to look off into the forest, stopped short, on legs suddenly numb. Twenty yards away, camouflaged by the light and shadow, three men in black vests and pale-green pantaloons stood motionless and silent, like fabulous animals.

Jantiff stared, his pulse pounding from the startlement; the three gazed gravely back, or perhaps beyond.

Jantiff released his pent breath; then, thinking to recognize the men of the night before, he raised his hand in an uncertain salute. The three men, giving back no acknowledgment, continued to gaze at, or past, Jantiff, as before.

Jantiff trudged wearily onward, away from the forest, across the river by an ancient iron bridge, and finally arrived at the outskirts of Balad.

The road broadened to become an avenue fifty yards wide, running the length of the town. Here Jantiff halted, to look glumly this way and that. Balad was smaller and more primitive than he had anticipated: essentially nothing more than a wind-swept village on the dunes beside the Moaning Ocean. Small shops lined the south side of the main street. Opposite were a marketplace, a dilapidated hall, a clinic and dispensary, a great barn of a garage for the repair of farmers' vehicles, and a pair of taverns: the Old Groar and the Cimmery.

Lanes angled down to the river, where half a dozen fishing boats were moored. Cottages flanked the lanes and overlooked the river which, a half-mile after leaving Balad, became a shallow estuary and so entered the ocean. A few pale dark-haired children played in the lanes; half a dozen wheeled vehicles and a pair of ground-hoppers were parked beside the Old Groar and as many near the Cimmery.

The Old Groar was the closest: a two-story structure, sinter blocks below and timber painted black, red, and green above to produce an effect of rather ponderous frivolity.

Jantiff pushed through the door and entered a common room furnished with long tables and benches and illuminated by panes of dusty magenta glass set high in the side wall. At this slack hour of the day the room was vacant of all but seven or eight patrons, drinking ale from earthenware vessels and playing sanque.*

Jantiff looked into the kitchen, where a portly man, notable for a shining bald pate and a luxuriant black mustache, stood with a knife and brush, preparatory to cleaning a large fish. His attitude suggested peevishness, provoked by conditions not immediately evident. Upon looking up and seeing Jantiff he lowered knife and brush and spoke in a brusque voice: "Well, sir? How may I oblige you?"

Jantiff spoke in an embarrassed half-stammer: "Sir, I am a traveler from off-world. I need food and lodging, and since I have no money, I would be pleased to work for my keep."

The innkeeper threw down the knife and brush. His manner underwent a change, to become what was evidently a normal condition of pompous affability. "You are in luck! The maid is hard at it, giving birth, the pot-boy is likewise ill, perhaps in sympathy. I lack a hundred commodities but work is not one of them. There is much to be done and you may start at once. As your first task, be so good as to clean this fish."

CHAPTER 12

Fariske the innkeeper had not deceived Jantiff: there was indeed work to be accomplished. Fariske, himself inclined to ease and tolerance, nevertheless, through sheer force of circumstances, kept Jantiff constantly on the move: scouring, sweeping, cutting,

*A complicated game of assault and defense, played on a board three feet square, with pieces representing fortresses, estaphracts and lancers.

paring, serving food and drink; washing and cleaning pots, plates and uten-
sils; husking, shelling and cleaning percebs.*

Jantiff was allowed the use of a small chamber at the back of the second
floor, whatever he chose to eat and drink, and a daily wage of two ozols.
"This is generous pay!" declared Fariske grandly. "Still, after you perform
the toil that I require, you may think differently."

"At the moment," said Jantiff feelingly, "I am more than satisfied with
the arrangement."

"So be it!"

On the morning after his arrival in Balad, Jantiff took himself to
the local post and communications office and there telephoned Alastor
Centrality at Uncibal—a call for which, by Cluster law, no charge
could be levied. On the screen appeared the face of Aleida Gluster.
"Ah ha ha!" she exclaimed in excitement. "Jantiff Ravensroke! Where are
you?"

"As you suggested, I came to Balad; in fact I arrived yesterday afternoon."

"Excellent! And you will now take passage from the space-port?"

"I haven't applied yet," said Jantiff. "It may well be useless. Only cargo
ships put down here; and they take no passengers, or so I'm told."

Aleida Gluster's jaw dropped. "I had not considered this aspect of
affairs."

"In any event," said Jantiff, "I must speak to the cursar. Has he returned
to Uncibal?"

"No! Nor has he called into the office! It is most strange."

Jantiff clicked his tongue in disappointment. "When he arrives, will you
telephone me? I am at the Old Groar Tavern. My business is really important."

"I will give him your message, certainly."

"Thank you very much."

Jantiff left the post office and hurried back to the Old Groar, where
Fariske had already become petulant because of his absence.

The custom of the Old Groar comprised a cross-section of local society:
farmers and townspeople, servants from the manor of Grand Knight
Shubart (as he was locally known), warehousemen and mechanics from
the space-port and the port agent himself: a certain Eubanq. Jantiff found
most of these folk somewhat coarse and not altogether congenial, especially the farmers, each of whom seemed more positive, stubborn and curt

---

*Percebs: a small mollusk growing upon subsurface rocks along the shores of the Moaning Ocean. The
percebs must be gathered, husked, cleaned, fried in nut oil with *aiole*, whereupon they become a famous
local delicacy.

than the next. They drank Fariske's compound ale and smoky spirits with zeal and ate decisively. They derived neither expansion nor ease from their drinking, and when drunk became torpid. As a rule Jantiff paid little heed to their conversation; however, overhearing mention of the witches, he asked a question: "Why do they never speak? Can anyone tell me this?"

The farmers exchanged smiles at Jantiff's ignorance. "Certainly they can speak," declared the oldest and most amiable of the group, a person named Skorbo. "My brother trapped two of them in his barn. The first got away; the other he tied to the farrel-post and took the truth out of her; I won't say how. The witch agreed that she could talk as well as the next person, but that words carried too much magic for ordinary occasions; therefore they were never used unless magic was to be worked, as at that very moment, so said the witch. Then she sang out a rhyme, or whatever it might be, and Chabby—that's my brother—felt the blood rush to his ears in a burst and he ran from the barn. When he came back with his vyre* the creature was walking away. He took aim, and would you think it? The vyre exploded and tore open his hands!"

A farmer named Bodile jerked his head in scorn for the folly of Chab, the brother. "No one should use a vyre, nor any complex thing, against a witch. A cudgel cut from a nine-year-old hawber and soaked nine nights in water which has washed no living hand: that's the best fend against witches."

"I keep a besom of prickle-withe and it's never failed me yet," said one named Sansoro. "I've laid it out ready for use and I'm smarting up my wurgles; there's a new coven into Inkwood."

"I saw some yesterday," said Duade, a lanky young man with a great beak of a nose and crow-wing eyebrows. "They seemed on the move toward Wemish Water. I shouted my curse, but they showed no haste."

Skorbo drained his mug and set it down with a rap. "The Connatic should deal with them. We pay our yearly stiver† and what do we get in return? Felicitations and high prices. I'd as soon spend my tax on ale. Boy! Bring another pint!"

"Yes, sir."

Nearby sat a man in a suit of fawn-colored twill, to match his sparse sandy hair. His shoulders were heavy, but narrow and sloping above a pear-shaped torso. This was Eubanq, the port agent, an out-worlder appointed by Grand Knight Shubart. Eubanq, a regular of the Old Groar,

---

*A light weapon used for the control of rodents, the hunting of wild fowl, and like service.
†Colloquialism for the Connatic's head tax.

came every afternoon to sip ale, munch percebs and play sanque at a dinket* a game, with whomever chose to challenge him. His manner was equable, humorous, soft and sedate; his lips constantly pursed and twitched as if at a series of private amusements. Eubanq now called from a nearby table. "Never scurrilize the Connatic, friends! He might be standing among us at this very minute. That's his dearest habit, as we all know quite well!"

Duade uttered a jeering laugh. "Not likely. Unless he's this new serving boy. But somehow I don't see Janx in the part."

"Janx" was a garbled mishearing of "Jantiff," which had gained currency around the tavern.

"Janx is not our Connatic," Eubanq agreed, with humorous emphasis. "I've seen his picture and I can detect the difference. Still, never begrudge the Connatic's stiver. Have you ever looked up into the sky? You'll see the stars of Alastor Cluster, all protected by the Whelm."

Bodile grunted. "The stiver is wasted. Why should starmenters come to Blale? There's nothing for them to take; certainly not at my house."

"Grand Knight Shubart is the bait," said Skorbo. "He surrounds himself with richness, as is his right; but by the same token he now must fear the starmenters."

Duade grumbled: "We both pay the same stiver! Who does the Whelm protect? Shubart? Or me? Justice is remote."

Eubanq laughed. "Take comfort! The Whelm is not all-powerful! Perhaps they will fail to guard the Grand Knight, then your stivers are equally misspent, so there you have your justice after all. And who is for a quick go at the sanque board?"

"Not I," said Duade sourly. "The Connatic takes his stiver; you take our dinkets, Bahevah only knows by what set of artifices. I'll play no more with you."

"Nor I," said Bodile. "I know a better use for my dinkets. Boy! Are the percebs on order?"

"In just a few minutes, sir."

Eubanq, unable to promote a game, turned away from the farmers. A few minutes later, finding a lull in his work, Jantiff approached him. "I wonder, sir, if you'd be good enough to advise me."

"Certainly, within the limits of discretion," said Eubanq. "I should warn you, however, that free advice is usually not worth its cost."

Jantiff ignored the pleasantry. "I wish to take passage to Frayness on Zeck; this is Alastor 503, as no doubt you know. Is it possible to arrange this passage from the Balad spaceport?"

---

*A coin worth the tenth part of an ozol.

Eubanq shook his head. "Ships clearing Balad invariably make for Hilp and then Lambeter, to complete a circuit of the Gorgon's Tusk."

"Might I make connections from either Hilp or Lambeter to Zeck?"

"Certainly, except for the fact that the ships putting down here won't carry you; they're not licensed to do so. Go to Uncibal and take a Black Arrow packet direct."

"I am bored with Uncibal," Jantiff muttered. "I don't want to set foot there again."

"Then I fear that you must reconcile yourself to residence in Blale."

Jantiff considered a moment. "I hold a passage voucher to Zeck. Could you issue me a ticket from Balad directly through to Frayness, so that I could board the packet without going through Uncibal Terminal?"

Eubanq's glance became shrewd and inquisitive. "This is possible. But how would you travel from Balad to Uncibal?"

"Is there no connecting service?"

"No scheduled commercial flights."

"Well, suppose you were making the trip: how would you go?"

"I would hire someone with a flibbit to fly me. Naturally it wouldn't come cheap, as it's a far distance."

"Well then—how much?"

Eubanq pulled thoughtfully at his chin. "I could arrange it for a hundred ozols; that's my guess. It might come more. It won't come less."

"A hundred ozols!" cried Jantiff in shock. "That's a vast sum!"

Eubanq shrugged. "Not when you consider what's involved. A man with a sound flibbit won't care to work on the cheap. No more do I, for that matter."

A call came from the farmers: "Boy! Service!"

Jantiff turned away. A hundred ozols! Surely the figure was excessive! At two ozols a day and not a dinket wasted, a hundred ozols meant fifty days; the Arrabin Centenary would have come and gone!

No doubt the hundred ozols included a substantial fee for Eubanq, thought Jantiff glumly. Well, either Eubanq must reduce his fee or Jantiff must earn more money. The first proposition was far-fetched: Eubanq's parsimony was something of a joke around the Old Groar. According to Fariske, Eubanq had arrived at Balad wearing his fawn twill costume and never had worn anything else. So then: how to earn more money? No easy accomplishment in view of the demands Fariske made upon his time.

So Jantiff reflected as he cleared a vacated table. He glanced resentfully toward Eubanq, who was deep in colloquy with a person newly arrived at the Old Groar. Jantiff froze in his tracks. The new arrival, a person large and heavy, with coarse black hair, narrow eyes, a complexion charged with heavy reeking blood, commanded local importance, to judge from Eubanq's obsequious manner. His garments by Balad standards were rather grand: a pale-blue suit (somewhat soiled) cut in military style, black boots, a black harness and a cap of black bast set off with a fine panache of silver bristles. He now looked around the room, saw Jantiff, signaled. "Boy! Bring ale!"

"Yes, sir." With a beating heart Jantiff served the table. Booch glanced at him again without any trace of recognition. "Is this Fariske's old Dark Wort? Or the Nebranger?"

"It's the best Dark Wort, sir."

Booch dismissed Jantiff with a brusque nod. If he had so much as noticed Jantiff at the bonterfest, the recollection apparently had dissolved. More reason than ever to leave Balad, Jantiff told himself through gritted teeth. A hundred ozols might turn out to be a dramatic bargain!

Eubanq presently rose to his feet and took leave of Booch. Jantiff accosted him near the door. "I don't have a hundred ozols now, but I'll make up the amount as soon as possible."

"Good enough," said Eubanq. "I'll check the Black Arrow schedule, and we can set up definite arrangements."

Jantiff made a half-hearted proposal: "If you could get me away sooner, I'd pay you as soon as I arrived on Zeck."

Eubanq gave an indulgent chuckle. "Zeck is far from Balad; memories sometimes don't extend such distances."

"You could trust me! I've never cheated anyone in my life!"

Eubanq raised his hand in a laughing disclaimer. "Nevertheless and notwithstanding! I invariably do business in proper fashion, and that means ozols on the barrel head!"

Jantiff gave a morose shrug. "I'll see what I can do. Er—who is your friend yonder?"

Eubanq glanced back across the room. "That's the Respectable Buwechluter, usually known as Booch. He's factotum to Grand Knight Shubart, who happens to be off-planet at the moment, so Booch takes his ease at the manor and regales us all with his blood-curdling anecdotes. Step smartly when he calls his order and you'll find no difficulties."

"Boy!" called out Booch at this moment. "Bring a double order of percebs!"

"Sorry, sir! No percebs left; we've had a run on them today."

Booch uttered a curse of disgust. "Why doesn't Fariske plan more providentially? Well then, bring me a slice of good fat grump and a half-pound of haggot."

Jantiff hastened to do Booch's bidding, and so the evening progressed.

The patrons departed at last and went their ways through the misty

Blale night. Jantiff cleared the tables, set the room to rights, extinguished lights and gratefully retired to his room.

Taking all with all, Jantiff had no fault to find with the Old Groar. But for his anxiety and Fariske's importunities, he might have taken pleasure in Balad and its dim, strange surroundings. He was aroused early by Palinka, Fariske's robust daughter, who then served him a breakfast of groats, sausage, and blackmold tea. Immediately thereafter he swabbed out the common room, brought up supplies from the cellar and smartened up the bar in preparation for the day's business. After his third day a new task was required of Jantiff. In rain or shine, mist or storm, he was sent out with a pair of buckets to gather the day's supply of percebs from the offshore rocks. Jantiff came to enjoy this particular task above all others, in spite of the uncertain weather and the chill water of the Moaning Ocean. Once beyond the immediate precincts of Balad, solitude was absolute, and Jantiff had the shore to himself.

Jantiff's usual route was eastward along Dessimo Beach, where half-sunken platforms of rock alternated with pleasant little coves. Dunes along the shore-side supported a multitude of growths: purple gart, puzzle-bush, ginger-tufts, creeping jilberry, which squeaked when trod upon. Interspersed were patches of silicanthus: miniature five-pronged radiants of a stuff like frosted glass, stained apparently at random in any of a hundred colors. Here and there granat trees twisted and humped to the wind, with limbs wildly askew like harridans in flight. When Jantiff looked south across the ocean, the near horizon never failed to startle him with the illusion that he stood high in the air. The wet days were undeniably dreary; and when the wind blew strong, the ocean swells toppled ponderously over the rocks; and sometimes Jantiff slouched empty-bucketed back to the Old Groar.

On fine days the ocean sparked and scintillated to the Dwan-light; the gart glowed like purple glass; the sand beneath Jantiff's feet seemed as clean and fresh as at the beginning of time; and Jantiff, swinging his buckets and breathing the cool salt air, felt that life was well worth living, despite every conceivable tribulation.

Halfway along the Dessimo headland an arm of the Sych swung out and approached the ocean. Here Jantiff discovered a dilapidated shack, half-hidden in the shadows of the forest. The roof had dropped; one wall had collapsed; the floor was buried under the detritus of years. Jantiff prodded here and there with a stick, but found nothing of interest.

One day Jantiff walked to the end of the headland: a massive tongue of black rock protecting a dozen swirling pools of chilly water in its lee. Exploring these pools Jantiff found quantities of excellent percebs, including many of the prized coronel variety, and thereafter he visited the area daily. Passing the old hut, he occasionally troubled to fit a stone or two back into the wall, or clear an armload of litter from the interior. One sunny morning he circled the headland and returned to Balad along the shore of Lulace Sound, and so obtained a view of Lulace, Grand Knight Shubart's manor, at the back of an immaculate formal garden. Jantiff paused to admire the place, of which he had heard a dozen marvelous tales. Immediately he noticed Booch sunning himself on a garden bench, and as he watched, a young maid in black and red livery came out from the kitchen with a tray of refreshments. Booch seemed to make a facetious invitation, but the maid sidled nervously away. Booch reached out to haul her back and caught one of the red pompoms of her livery. The girl protested, pleaded and at last began to cry. Booch's gallantry instantly vanished. He gave the girl a buffet across the buttocks, to send her stumbling and weeping toward the manor. Jantiff took an impulsive step forward, ready to call out a reprimand, but thought twice and held his tongue. Booch, chancing to notice him, jumped to his feet in a fury; Jantiff was relieved that sixty yards of water lay between them. He took up his percebs and hurried away.

Halfway through the evening Booch appeared at the Old Groar. Jantiff went about his duties, trying to ignore Booch's glowering glances. At last Booch signaled and Jantiff approached. "Yes, sir?"

"You were spying on me today. I've half a mind to shove your head in the cesspool."

"I was not spying," said Jantiff. "I happened to be walking along the shore with percebs for today's custom."

"Don't walk that way again. The Grand Knight likes his privacy, and so do I."

"Did you wish to order?" asked Jantiff with what dignity he could muster.

"When I see fit!" growled Booch. "I have the feeling that I've seen your unwholesome face before. I did not like it then, nor do I like it now, so have a care."

Jantiff went stiffly off about his duties.

In the corner of the room sat Eubanq, who presently signaled to Jantiff. "What's your difficulty with Booch?"

Jantiff described the episode. "And now he's in a rage."

"No doubt, and the whole situation has curdled, since I intended Booch to fly you to Uncibal in one of the Grand Knight's flibbits."

Booch loomed over the table. "This is the person you want flown to Uncibal?" A grin spread over his face. "I'll be happy to take him aloft, at no payment whatever."

Neither Jantiff nor Eubanq made response. Booch chuckled and departed the tavern.

Jantiff said bleakly: "I certainly won't fly to Uncibal with Booch."

Eubanq made one of his easy gestures. "Don't take him seriously. Booch is bluff and bluster, for the most part. I've consulted the schedule and now I'll need your passage voucher. Do you have it with you?"

"Yes, but I don't care to let it out of my hands."

Eubanq smilingly shook his head. "There's no way to negotiate a firm reservation without it."

Jantiff reluctantly surrendered the certificate.

"Very good," said Eubanq. "You will depart Uncibal in three weeks aboard the *Jervasian*. How much money do you have now?"

"Twenty ozols."

Eubanq clicked his tongue in vexation. "Not enough! In three weeks you'll have at most eighty ozols! Well, I'll simply have to reschedule you for the *Serenaic*, in about six weeks."

"But that will be after the Arrabin Centenary Festival!"

"What of that?"

Jantiff was silent a moment. "I have business at Uncibal, but before the Centenary. Can't you trust me for twenty ozols? As soon as I'm home I'll send back whatever money is lacking. I swear it!"

"Of course!" said Eubanq wearily. "I believe you, never doubt it! You are deadly in earnest—now. But on Zeck there might be needs more urgent than mine here at this dismal little outpost. That is the way things go. I fear that I must have the money in hand. Which shall it be? The *Jervasian* or the *Serenaic*?"

"It will have to be the *Serenaic*," said Jantiff hollowly. "I simply won't have the money sooner. Remember: under no circumstances will I fly with Booch."

"Just as you say. I can hire Bulwan's flibbit and fly you myself. We'll plan on that basis."

Jantiff went off about his work. Six weeks seemed a very long time. What of the Arrabin Centenary? He must telephone Alastor Centrality again, and yet again, until finally he had unloaded all his burden of facts and suspicions upon the cursar . . . From the distance of Balad, his notions seemed strange and odd: incredible, really—even to Jantiff himself. Might he had suffered a set of vivid paranoid delusions? Jantiff's faith in himself wavered, but only for a moment or two. He had not imagined Esteban's murderous attempts, nor the overheard conversation, nor the camera matrix, nor the death of Clode Morre.

During the course of the evening Jantiff noticed a plump pink-faced young man in the kitchen, and just before closing time, Fariske called him aside. "Jantiff, conditions have more or less returned to normal, and I'm sorry to say that I must let you go."

Jantiff stared aghast. At last he managed to stammer: "What have I done wrong?"

"Nothing whatever. Your work has been in the main satisfactory. My nephew Voris, nevertheless, wants his position back. He is an idler; he drinks as much as he serves; still, I must oblige him or risk the rough edge of my sister's tongue. That is the way we do things in Balad. You may use your chamber tonight, but I must ask you to vacate tomorrow."

Jantiff turned away and finished the evening's duties in a fog of depression. Two hours before he had been disturbed by a delay of six weeks; now how blessedly fortunate seemed that prospect!

The patrons departed. Jantiff set the room to rights and went off to bed, where he lay awake into the small hours.

In the morning Palinka awoke him at the usual time. She had never been wholly cordial, and today even less so. "I have been ordered to feed you a final breakfast, so bestir yourself; I have much else to do."

Defiance trembled upon Jantiff's tongue, but second thoughts prevailed. He muttered a surly acknowledgment, and presented himself to the kitchen as usual.

Palinka put before him his usual gruel, tea, bread and conserve; Jantiff ate listlessly and so aroused Palinka's impatience. "Come, Jantiff, eat briskly, if you please! I am waiting to clear the table."

"And I am waiting for my wages!" declared Jantiff in sudden fury. "Where is Fariske? As soon as he pays me, I will leave!"

"Then you will be waiting the whole day long," Palinka retorted. "He has gone off to the country market."

"And where is my money? Did he not instruct you to pay me?"

Palinka uttered a coarse laugh. "It is too early for jokes. Fariske has made himself scarce hoping that you would forget your money."

"Small chance of that. I intend to claim every dinket!"

"Come back in the morning. For now, be off with you!"

Jantiff left the Old Groar in a sullen mood. For a moment he stood in the street, hands tucked into the flaps of his jacket, shoulders hunched against the wind. He looked east along the street, then west, where his eyes focused upon the Cimmery. Jantiff grimaced; he had lost all zest for the taverns of Balad. Nonetheless, he settled his jacket and sauntered down the street to the Cimmery, where he found Madame Tchaga, a short stout woman with an irascible manner, employed at a task Jantiff knew only too well: scrubbing out the common room. Jantiff addressed her as confidently as possible, but Madame Tchaga, pausing not a stroke of the push broom, uttered a bark of sour amusement. "The ozols I take in are not enough for me and mine; I've no need for you. Seek elsewhere for work; try the Grand Knight. He might want someone to pare his toenails."

Jantiff returned to the street, where he considered Madame Tchaga's suggestion.

From one of the side lanes came Eubanq on his way to his office at the space-port. At the sight of Jantiff he nodded and would have proceeded had not Jantiff eagerly stepped forward to accost him. Here, after all, was the obvious solution to his problems!

Eubanq greeted him politely enough. "What brings you out in this direction?"

"Fariske no longer needs me at the Old Groar," said Jantiff. "This may be a blessing in disguise, since you can surely put me to work at the space-port, hopefully at a much better wage."

Eubanq's expression became distant. "Unfortunately not. In truth, there's little enough work to keep my present crew busy."

Jantiff's voice rose in frustration. "Then how can I earn a hundred ozols?"

"I don't know. One way or another, you must discover the money. Your voucher has been sent to Uncibal and you are booked aboard the *Serenaic*."

Jantiff stared in consternation. "Can't the passage be postponed?"

"That's no longer possible."

"Can't you suggest something? What of the Grand Knight? Could you put a word in for me?"

Eubanq started to make small sidling moves, preparatory to moving on past Jantiff. "The Grand Knight is not in residence. Booch now rules the roost, when he's not wenching or witch-chasing or drinking dry the Old Groar vats, and he's not likely to assist you. But no doubt your dilemma will resolve itself: happily, I hope. Good day to you." Eubanq went his way.

Jantiff slouched eastward along the street: past the Old Groar to the edge of town and beyond. Arriving at the seashore, he sat upon a flat stone and looked out across the rolling gray water. Morning light from Dwan, collecting in the wave hollows, washed back and forth like quicksilver. Silver foam broke around the rocks. Jantiff stared morosely at the horizon and pondered his options. He might, of course, try to return to Uncibal and his refuge behind the Disjerferact privy—but how to cross the thousand miles of wilderness? Suppose he were to steal one of the Grand Knight's flibbits? And suppose Booch caught him in the act? Jantiff's shoulder blades twitched. His best hope, as always, lay with the cursar. To this end he must make daily telephone calls to Alastor Centrality. In the morning he would collect his wages from Fariske: a not too satisfactory sum which nonetheless would feed him for an appreciable period. Of more immediate concern was shelter. An idea crossed his mind. He rose to his feet and walked along the shore to the ruined fisherman's shanty, if such it were. Without enthusiasm he examined the structure, although he knew it well already, then set to work clearing the interior of trash, dead leaves, and dirt.

From the forest he brought saplings which he arranged over the walls in a mat which was strong and resilient but hardly waterproof. Jantiff considered the problem carefully. He had no money to spare for conventional roofing; a solution, therefore, must be improvised. The obvious first attempt must be thatch—and even thatch involved financial outlay.

Returning into Balad, Jantiff invested an ozol in cord, knife, and a disk of hard bread, then trudged back to the shack. The time was now afternoon; there was no time to rest. From the beach he brought armloads of seaweed, and laid it out into bundles. Some of the stalks were old and rotten, and smelled of fetid sea life; before Jantiff had fairly started he was cold and wet and covered with slime. Doggedly ignoring discomfort he tied up the bundles and fixed them to his roof in staggered layers.

Sunset found the job still short of completion. Jantiff built a fire, washed himself and his garments in the stream, and before the light had died, gathered a quart of percebs for his supper. He hung up his clothes to dry, then huddled naked in the firelight, trying to keep warm on all sides at once. Meanwhile the percebs baked in their shells, and Jantiff presently ate his supper of bread and percebs with a good appetite.

Night had come; darkness cloaked both land and sea. Jantiff lay back and studied the sky. Since he had never learned the constellations as seen from Wyst, he could name none of the stars, but surely some of these blazing lights above him were famous places, home to noble men and beautiful women. None could even remotely suspect that far below, on the beach of the Moaning Ocean, sat that entity known as Jantiff Ravensroke!

Letting his mind wander free, Jantiff thought of all manner of things, and presently decided that he had divined the soul of this odd little planet, Wyst. On Wyst nothing was as it seemed: everything was just a trifle askew or out of focus, or bathed in a mysterious quivering light. This quality, Jantiff reflected, was analogous to the personality of a man. Undoubtedly men tended to share the personality of that world to which they were born . . . Jantiff wondered about his own world, Zeck, which had always seemed so ordinary: did visitors find it odd and unusual? By analogy, did Jantiff himself seem odd and unusual? Quite conceivably this was the case, thought Jantiff.

The fire burned down to embers. Jantiff rose stiffly to his feet. His bed was only a heap of leaves, but for tonight, at least, it would have to serve. Jantiff made a final survey of the beach, then took shelter in his hut. Burrowing into the leaves, he contrived to make himself tolerably comfortable and presently fell asleep.

At sunrise Jantiff crawled out into the open air. He washed his face in the stream, and ate a few mouthfuls of bread and cold percebs, by no means a heartening breakfast. If he were to stay here even so long as a week he would need pot, pan, cup, cutlery, salt, flour, a few gills of oil, perhaps an ounce or two of tea—at considerable damage to his meager store of ozols. But where was any rational alternative? Sleep had clarified his thinking: he would make a temporary sojourn in the hut and telephone Alastor Centrality at regular intervals; sooner or later he must reach the cursar: perhaps today!

Jantiff rose to his feet, brushed the chaff and twigs from his clothes, and set out toward Balad. Arriving at the Old Groar, he went around to the back and knocked at the kitchen door.

Palinka looked forth. "Well, Jantiff, what do you want?"

"I came for my money; what else?"

Palinka threw back the door and motioned him within. "Go talk to Fariske; there he sits."

Jantiff approached the table. Fariske puffed out his cheeks and, raising his eyebrows, looked off to the side as if Jantiff thereby might be persuaded to go away. Jantiff seated himself in his old place and Fariske was obliged to notice him. "Good morning, Jantiff."

"Good-morning," said Jantiff. "I have come for my money."

Fariske heaved a weary sigh. "Come back in a few days. I bought various necessities at the market and now I am short of cash."

"I am even more short than you," cried Jantiff. "I intend to sit in this kitchen and take my meals free of charge until you pay me my wages."

"Now, then!" said Fariske. "There is no cause for acrimony. Palinka, pour Jantiff a cup of tea."

"I have not yet taken breakfast; I would be glad to accept some porridge, were you to offer it."

Fariske signaled Palinka. "Serve Jantiff a dish of the coarse porridge. He is a good fellow and deserves special treatment. What is the sum due you?"

"Twenty-four ozols."

"So much?" exclaimed Fariske. "What of the beer you took and the other extras?"

"I took no beer, and no extras, as you well know."

Fariske glumly brought out his wallet and paid over the money. "What must be must be."

"Thank you," said Jantiff. "Our relationship is now on an even balance. I assume that the situation is like that of yesterday? You still have no need for my services?"

"Unfortunately true. As a matter of fact, I have come to regret your departure. Voris suffers a distension of the leg veins, and is unable to collect percebs. The task therefore devolves upon Palinka."

"What!" cried Palinka in a passion. "Can I believe my ears? Am I suddenly so underworked that I can now while away my hours among the frigid waves? Think again!"

"It is only for today," said Fariske soothingly. "Tomorrow Voris will probably feel fit."

Palinka remained obdurate. "Voris does not lack ingenuity; when his leg veins heal, he will contrive new excuses: the counter needs waxing; ale has soured his stomach; the waves thrash too heavily on the rocks! Then once more the cry will ring out: 'Palinka, Palinka! Go out for percebs! Poor Voris is ill!' " Palinka struck a pan down upon the table in ringing emphasis. "For all Jantiff's oddities, at least he fetched the percebs. Voris must learn from the example."

Fariske attempted the cogency of pure logic. "What, after all, is the fetching of a few percebs? The day contains only so many minutes; it passes as well one way as another."

"In that case, go fetch them yourself!" Palinka took herself off to indicate that the subject was closed.

Fariske pulled at his chin, then turned toward Jantiff. "Might you oblige me, for today only, by bringing in a few percebs?"

Jantiff sipped his tea. "Let us explore the matter in full detail."

Fariske spoke pettishly: "My request is modest; is your response so hard to formulate?"

"Not at all," said Jantiff, "but perhaps we can proceed further. As you know, I am now unemployed. Nevertheless I am anxious to earn a few ozols."

Fariske grimaced and started to speak, but Jantiff held up his hand. "Let us consider a bucket of percebs. When shelled and fried a bucket yields twenty portions, which you sell for a dinket per portion. Thus, a bucket of percebs yields two ozols. Two buckets: four ozols, and so forth. Suppose every day I were to deliver to you the percebs you require, shelled and cleaned, at a cost to you of one ozol per bucket? You would thereby gain your profit with no inconvenience for Palinka, or yourself, or even Voris."

Fariske mulled over the proposal, pulling at his mustache. Palinka, who had been listening from across the kitchen, once again came forward. "Why are you debating? Voris will never fetch percebs! I also refuse to turn my legs blue in the swirling water!"

"Very well, Jantiff," said Fariske. "We will test the system for a few days. Take another cup of tea, to signalize the new relationship."

"With pleasure," said Jantiff. "Also, let us agree that payments will be made promptly upon delivery of the percebs."

"What do you take me for?" Fariske exclaimed indignantly. "A man is only as large as his reputation; would I risk so much for a few paltry mollusks?"

Jantiff made a noncommittal gesture. "If we settle accounts on a day-to-day basis, we thereby avoid confusion."

"The issue is inconsequential," said Fariske. "A further matter: since you evidently intend to pursue this business in earnest, I will command four buckets of percebs from you, rather than the usual two."

"I intended to suggest something of the sort myself," said Jantiff. "I am anxious to earn a good wage."

"You will of course provide your own equipment?"

"For the next few days, at least, I will use the buckets, pries and forceps which you keep in the shed. If there is any deterioration, I will naturally make good the loss."

Fariske was not inclined to let the matter rest on a basis so informal, but Palinka made an impatient exclamation. "The day is well advanced! Do you expect to serve percebs tonight? If so, let Jantiff go about his business." Fariske threw his hands into the air and stalked from the kitchen. Jantiff went to the shed, gathered buckets and tools, and went off down the beach.

The day before he had marked a ledge of rock twenty yards offshore which he had never previously explored, because of the intervening water. Today he contrived a raft from dead branches and bits of driftwood, upon which he supported the buckets. Immersing himself to the armpits, with a shuddering of the knees and a chattering of the teeth, Jantiff pushed the raft out to the ledge and tied it to a knob of rock.

His hopes were immediately realized: the ledge was thickly encrusted with percebs and Jantiff filled the buckets in short order.

Returning to the shore he built a fire, at which he warmed himself while he shelled and cleaned the percebs.

The sun had hardly reached the zenith when Jantiff made his delivery to the Old Groar. Fariske was somewhat puzzled by Jantiff's expedition. "When you worked for me, you used as much time to gather two buckets, and they were not even shelled."

"The conditions are not at all comparable," said Jantiff. "Incidentally, I notice that the shed is cluttered with broken furniture and rubbish. For three ozols I will order the confusion and carry the junk to the rubbish dump."

By dint of furious argument, Fariske reduced Jantiff's price to two ozols, and Jantiff set to work. From the discards Jantiff reserved two old chairs, a three-legged table, a pair of torn mattresses, a number of pots, canisters and dented pans. The ownership of these items, in fact, had been his prime goal, and he suspected that Fariske would have put an inordinate value upon the items had he requested them directly. With considerable satisfaction Jantiff calculated the yield of his day's employment: six ozols and the furnishing of his hut.

On the following day, Jantiff went early to work. He gathered, shelled and cleaned seven buckets of percebs. After delivering the stipulated quota to Fariske, he took the remaining percebs to the Cimmery, where he found no difficulty in selling them to Madame Tchaga for three ozols.

Madame Tchaga was notable for her verbosity. Lacking any better company, she served Jantiff a bowl of turnip soup and described the vexations inherent in trying to gratify the tastes of a fickle and unappreciative clientele.

Jantiff agreed that her frustrations verged upon the insupportable. He went on to remark that the prosperity of an inn often depended upon its cheerful ambience. Possibly a profusion of floral designs upon the Cimmery's façade and a depicted procession of jolly townsfolk on a long panel, perhaps to be hung over the door, might enhance the rather bleak atmosphere of the establishment.

Madame Tchaga dismissed the idea out of hand. "All very well to talk about designs and depictions, but who in Balad is capable of such cleverness?"

"As a matter of fact, I am gifted with such talent," said Jantiff. "Possibly I might find time to do certain work along these lines."

During the next hour and a half Jantiff discovered that Madame Tchaga, as a shrewd and relentless negotiator, far surpassed even Fariske. Jantiff, however, maintained a detached and casual attitude, and eventually won a contract on essentially his own terms, and Madame Tchaga even advanced five ozols for the purchase of supplies.

Jantiff went immediately to the general store where he bought paint of various colors and several brushes. Returning to the street he noticed a plump, heavy-faced man in fawn-colored garments approaching at a leisurely splay-footed gait. "Eubanq! Just the person I want to see!" called Jantiff in a jovial voice. "We now return to our original plan!"

Eubanq halted and stood in apparent perplexity. "What plan is this?"

"Don't you remember? For a hundred ozols—an exorbitant sum, incidentally—you are to convey me to Uncibal Spaceport in time for me to board the *Serenaic*."

Eubanq gave a slow thoughtful nod. "The hundred ozols naturally are to be paid in advance. You understand this?"

"I foresee no difficulty," said Jantiff confidently. "I have on hand something over thirty ozols. My arrangement with Madame Tchaga will net another twenty-two ozols, and I regularly earn six or seven ozols a day."

"I am pleased to hear of your prosperity," said Eubanq courteously. "What is your secret?"

"No secret whatever! You could have done the same! I simply wallow around the ocean until I have gathered seven buckets of percebs, which I clean and shell and deliver to the Cimmery and the Old Groar. Might you need a bucket or two for your own use?"

Eubanq laughed. "My taste is amply satisfied at the Old Groar. You might make your proposal to Grand Knight Shubart. He is back in residence with a houseful of guests. He'll certainly require a supply of percebs."

"A good idea! So then it's all clear for the *Serenaic*!"

Eubanq smiled his somewhat distant smile and went his way. Jantiff paused to consider a moment. The sooner he earned a hundred ozols the better. The Grand Knight's ozols were as good as any, so why not hazard a try?

Jantiff left off his paints in Fariske's shed, then set out along the northern shore of Lulace Sound to the Grand Knight's manor. Approaching Lulace he sensed bustle and activity where before there had been somnolence. Keeping a wary eye open for Booch, Jantiff went to the service entrance at the back of the building. A scullion fetched the chief cook, who made no difficulty about placing a continuing order for two buckets every third day, at two ozols the bucket; double Jantiff's usual price, for a period of twenty-four days. "The Grand Knight entertains important guests until the Centenary at Uncibal," explained the cook. "Thereafter, all will return to normal."

"You can rely upon me to satisfy your needs," said Jantiff.

In a mood almost buoyant, Jantiff returned up the road to Balad. The hundred ozols were well within his reach; he could confidently look forward to a comfortable passage home . . . He heard the whir of driven wheels and jumped to the side of the road. The vehicle, guided by Brooch, approached and passed. Booch's expression was rapt and glazed, his ropy lips drawn back in a foolish grin.

Jantiff returned to the road and watched the vehicle recede toward Balad. Where would Booch be going in such a fervor of anticipation? Jantiff proceeded thoughtfully into town. He went directly to the telephone and once again called the Alastor Centrality of Uncibal.

Upon the screen appeared the face of Aleida Gluster. Her cheeks, once plump and pink, sagged; Jantiff thought that she seemed worried and even unwell. He spoke apologetically. "Once again it's Jantiff Ravensroke, and I fear that I'm a great nuisance."

"Not at all," said Aleida Gluster. "It is my duty to serve you. Are you still at Balad?"

"Yes, and temporarily at least all seems to be going well. But I must speak to the cursar. Has he returned to Uncibal?"

"No," said Aleida in a tense voice. "He has not yet returned. It is most remarkable."

Jantiff could not restrain a peevish ejaculation. "My business is absolutely vital!"

"I understand as much from our previous encounters," said Aleida tartly. "I cannot produce him by sheer effort of will. I wish I could."

"I suppose that you've tried the Waunisse office again?"

"Of course. He has not been seen."

"Perhaps you should notify the Connatic."

"I have already done so."

"In that case there is nothing to do but wait," said Jantiff reluctantly. "A message to the Old Groar Tavern will reach me."

"This is understood."

Jantiff went out to stand in the wide main street. The weather had changed. Clouds hung heavy and full, like great black udders; huge rain-drops struck into the sandy dust. Jantiff hunched his shoulders and hurried to the Old Groar. With a confident step he entered the common room, seated himself at a table, and signaled Voris for a mug of ale.

Fariske, glancing through the kitchen door, saw Jantiff, and approached in a portentous manner. "Jantiff, I am vexed with you."

Jantiff looked up in wonder. "What have I done?"

"You are supplying percebs to the Cimmery. This is not conceivably a benefit to me."

"It is neither a benefit nor a hindrance. Her patrons eat percebs like your own. If I failed to supply them, someone else would do so."

"Using my buckets, my pry-bars, my forceps?"

Jantiff contrived a negligent laugh. "Really, a trivial matter. The equipment is not damaged. I reserve all the best coronels for the Old Groar. No matter what fault your patrons may find, they will always say: 'Fariske's percebs, at least, are superior to those at the Cimmery.' So why do you complain?"

"Because I had hoped for your loyalty."

"That you have, naturally."

"Then why do I hear that you are about to paint that ramshackle old place, so that it presents an impression of sanitary conditions?"

"I will do the same for the Old Groar, if you will pay my wage."

Fariske heaved a sigh. "So that is how the wind blows. How much does Madame pay?"

"The exact amount is confidential. I will make a general statement to the effect that forty ozols is quite a decent sum."

Fariske jerked around in astonishment. "Forty ozols? From old Tchaga, who carries every dinket she has ever owned strapped to the inside of her legs?"

"Remember," said Jantiff, "I am an expert at the craft!"

"How can I remember something you never told me?"

"You gave me hardly enough time to clear my throat, much less describe my talents to you."

"Bah!" muttered Fariske. "Forty ozols is an outrageous sum, just for a bit of daubing."

"How would you like a series of ten decorative plaques to hang on your walls, at five ozols each? Or for six ozols I will use silver-gilt accentuations. It will put the Cimmery to shame."

Fariske made a cautious counter-proposal and the discussion proceeded.

Meanwhile Booch came into the tavern with a number of burly young men: farmhands, fishermen, laborers, and the like. They seated themselves, commanded ale, and discussed their affairs in boisterous voices. Jantiff could not evade their conversation: "—with my four wurgles through the Sych—"

"—out to Wamish Water; thar's where the creatures collect!"

"Careful, Booch! Remember the yellows!"

"No fear: I'll get none in my mouth!"

At last Jantiff complained to Fariske. "What are those people shouting about?"

"They're off for a bit of witch-chasing. Booch is famously keen."

"Witch-chasing? To what end?"

Fariske considered the group over his shoulder. "Herchelman farms his acres like a priest growing haw; last year someone stole a bushel of wattle-dabs, and now he punishes the witches. Klaw ate witch-tainted food; he underwent the cure and now he carries a great club when he goes on a hunt. Sittle is bored; he'll do anything novel. Dusselbeck is proud of his wurgles and likes to put them to work. Booch specializes in witch-kits; he chases them down and forces his body upon them. Pargo's case is absolutely simple; he enjoys witch-killing."

Jantiff darted a lambent glance toward the witch-chasers, who had just commanded additional ale from the sweating Voris. "It seems a vulgar and brutal recreation."

"Quite so," said Fariske. "I never relished the sport. The witches were fleet; I continually blundered into bogs and thickets. The witches enjoy the game as much as the chasers."

"I find this hard to believe."

Fariske turned up the palms of his hands. "Why else do they frequent our woods? Why do they steal wattledabs? Why do they startle our nights with witchfires and apparitions?"

"Nevertheless, witch-chasing seems an ugly recreation."

Fariske gave a snort of rebuttal. "They are a perverse folk; I for one cannot understand their habits. Still, I agree that the chases should be conducted with decorum. Booch's conduct is vulgar; I am surprised that he has not come down with the yellows. You know how the disease is cured? Booch, for his risks, must be considered intrepid."

Jantiff, finding the topic oppressive, tilted his mug but found it dry. He signaled, but Voris was busy with the witch-chasers. "If we are entirely agreed upon the decorative panels and their cost—"

"I will pay twenty ozols, no more, for the ten compositions, and I insist upon a minimum of four colors, with small touches of silver-gilt."

Jantiff squared around as if to depart. "I can waste no more time. With works of aesthetic quality one does not niggle over an ozol or two."

"The concept works in a double direction, like an apothecary's tremblant. Remember: it is you, not I who will experience the joys of artistic creation. This is no small consideration, or so I am told."

Jantiff refuted the remark and eventually the two reached agreement. Fariske served Jantiff a pint of old Dark Wort and the two parted on good terms.

Jantiff returned to his hut with Dwan low in the west and the pale light slanting over his shoulder down Dessimo Beach. The clouds had scattered to blasts of wind from the south which had now abated to random gusts of no great force. The Moaning Ocean still churned in angry recollection, and pounded itself to spume on the offshore rocks; Jantiff was grateful that he need collect no more percebs this day. Passing the forest, he halted to listen to the far hooting of wurgles, a mournful throbbing sound which sent tingles of ancient dread along Jantiff's back. More faintly came whoops and ululations from the throats of men. Hateful sounds, thought Janiff. He walked more quickly along the beach, shoulders hunched, head low.

The outcry of the wurgles waxed and waned, then suddenly grew loud. Jantiff stopped short and stared in apprehension toward the Sych. He glimpsed movement under the trees, and a moment later discerned a pair of human figures scurrying through the shadows. Jantiff stirred his numb limbs and proceeded on his way. A frightful outcry sounded suddenly loud: the wailing of wurgles, gasps of human horror and pain. Jantiff stood frozen, his face wrenched into a contorted grimace. Then, crying out wordlessly, he ran toward the sound, pausing only to pick up a stout branch to serve as a cudgel.

A brook, issuing from the Sych, widened into a pond. The wurgles bounded back and forth across the brook and splashed into the pond, the better to tear at the woman who had mired herself in the mud. Jantiff ran screaming around the pond, to halt at the edge of the mire. Two wurgles hanging on the woman's shoulders had borne her down to press her head into the water. One gnawed at her scalp; the other rent the nape of her neck. Blood swirled out to darken the pond; the woman made spasmodic motion and died. Jantiff backed slowly away, sick with disgust and fury. He turned and lurched away toward the road. The wurgles keened again; Jantiff swung around with ready cudgel, hoping for attack, but the wurgles had flushed forth the second member of the pair. From the Sych ran a girl with contorted features and streaming brown-blond hair; Jantiff instantly recognized the witch-girl he had met at the roadmender's shed. Four wurgles bounded in pursuit, massive heads out-thrust to display gleaming fangs. The girl saw Jantiff and stopped short in dismay; the wurgles lunged and she fell to her knees. But Jantiff was already beside her. He swung his cudgel, to break the back of the foremost wurgle; it slumped and lay kinked on the trail, bending and unbending in agonized jerks. Jantiff struck the second wurgle on the head; it somersaulted and lay still. The two survivors, backing away, set up a desolate outcry. Jantiff chased them but they leapt smartly away.

Jantiff returned to the girl, who knelt gasping for breath. From the Sych came the calls of the witch-chasers, ever more distinct; already different voices and different cries could be detected.

Jantiff spoke to the witch-girl. "Listen carefully! Do you hear me?"

The girl lifted a face bloated with despair; she gave no other sign.

"Up! To your feet," cried Jantiff urgently. "The chasers are coming; you've got to hide." He seized her arm and hauled her erect. The third wurgle suddenly darted close; Jantiff was ready with his cudgel and struck hard. The animal ran screaming in a circle, snapping at its own mouse-colored hindquarters. Jantiff struck again and again in hysterical energy until the creature dropped. He stood panting a moment, listening. The chasers had become confused; Jantiff could hear them calling to each other. He thrust the dead wurgle into the brook, then did the same with the other two bodies. The current swung them away, and they drifted toward the sea.

Jantiff turned back to the witch-girl. "Come, quickly now! Remember me? We met in the forest. Now, this way, at a run!"

Jantiff tugged her into a trot; they ran beside the brook, across the road, over the shore stones to the water's edge. The girl stopped short; by main force Jantiff pulled her out into the surf and led her stumbling and tottering for fifty yards parallel to the shore. For a moment they rested, Jantiff anxiously watching the edge of the forest, the girl staring numbly down at the surging water. Jantiff lifted her into his arms and staggered up the beach to his hut. Kicking open his makeshift door he carried her to one of his rickety chairs. "Sit here until I come back," said Jantiff. "I think—I hope—you'll be safe. But don't show yourself, and don't make any noise!" This last, so Jantiff reflected, as he went back along the beach, was possibly an unnecessary warning; she had uttered no sound from the moment he had seen her.

Jantiff went back to where the brook crossed the path. From the Sych came three men, the first two led by leashed wurgles. The third man was Booch.

The wurgles, sniffing out the witch-girl's track, paused where she had fallen, then strained toward the sea.

Booch caught sight of Jantiff. "Hallo, you, whatever your name! Where are the witches we chased through the Sych?"

"I saw but one," said Jantiff, contriving a meek and eager voice. "I heard the wurgles as I came from town. She crossed the path and led them yonder." He pointed toward the sea, in which direction the wurgles already strained.

"What did she look like?" rasped Booch.

"I barely saw her, but she seemed young and agile: a witch-kit, for sure!"

"Quick then!" cried Booch. "She's the one I've ranged the forest to find!"

The wurgles followed the trail to the water's edge, where they halted and made fretful outcries. Booch looked up and down the beach, then out to sea. He pointed. "Look! There's something out there: a body!"

"It's a wurgle," one of his fellows said. "Damnation and vileness!* I believe it's my Dalbuska!"

"Then where's the kit?" bellowed Booch. "Did she drown herself? Hey, fellow!"—this to Jantiff—"What did you see?"

"The kit and the wurgles. She led them down to the water and when I came to look she was gone."

"And my good wurgles! Pastola put a curse on her; the witches swim underwater like smollocks!"

Booch shouldered Jantiff aside and returned to the road. The other two followed.

Jantiff watched as they marched to the pool and there observed the corpse of the witch-woman. After a few minutes' muttered conversation they called up their wurgles and tramped off toward Balad into the last lavender rays of the setting sun.

Jantiff returned to his hut. He found the witch-girl where he had left her, sitting wan and still.

"You're safe now," said Jantiff. "Don't be frightened; no one will harm you here. Are you hungry?"

The girl responded by not so much as quiver. *In a state of shock*, thought Jantiff. He built a good blaze in his fireplace and turned her chair toward the heat. "Now: warm yourself. I'll cook soup, and there'll be roast percebs as well, with scallions and oil!"

The girl stared into the fire. After a few moments she listlessly held out her hands to the blaze. Jantiff, preparing the meal, watched her from the corner of his eye. Her face, no longer contorted by terror, was pinched and pale; Jantiff wondered about her age. It was certainly less than his own, still he could not regard her as a child. Her breasts were small and round; her hips, while unmistakably feminine, were slender and unobtrusive. Perhaps, thought Jantiff, she was of a constitution naturally slight. He bustled here and there, and presently served up the best meal his resources allowed.

The girl showed no diffidence about eating, though she took no great quantity of food. Jantiff from time to time attempted conversation: "There, now! Are you feeling better?"

---

*The oath spoken in Blale idiom exerts considerably more impact: *Shauk chutt!*

No response.

"Would you like more soup? And here: a nice perceb."

Again no answer. When Jantiff tried to serve out more food, she pushed the plate away.

Her conduct was almost that of a deaf-mute, thought Jantiff. Nonetheless, something about her manner left him in doubt. Perhaps his language was strange to her? This consideration bore no weight: at the clearing in the woods there had likewise been no conversation.

"My name is Jantiff Ravensroke. What is your name?"

Silence.

"Very well then; I must supply a name for you. What about 'Pusskin' or 'Tickaboo' or 'Parsnip'? Even better, 'Jilliam';* that would do nicely. But I mustn't make jokes. I shall call you 'Glisten' because of your hair and your golden fingernails. 'Glisten' you shall be."

But "Glisten" would not acknowledge her new name, and sat leaning forward, arms on knees, staring into the fire. Presently Jantiff saw that she was weeping.

"Come, come, this won't do! You've had a miserable time, but . . ." Jantiff's voice trailed off. How could he console her for the loss of someone who might have been her mother? Indeed, her self-control was marvelous in itself. He knelt beside her and gingerly patted her head. She paid no heed, and Jantiff desisted.

The fire burnt low. Jantiff went outside, to fetch wood and look around the night. When he returned within, Glisten—so he had resolved to call her—had lain herself on the damp floor with her face to the ground. Jantiff surveyed her a moment, then bent over and with a bit of undignified stumbling, carried her to the bed. She lay limp and passive, eyes closed. Jantiff somberly banked the fire with three green logs and removed his boots. After a moment's hesitation he diffidently removed Glisten's sandals, noting that she had also gilded her toenails. A curious vanity! A symbol perhaps of caste, or status? Or an ornamental convention, no more? He lay down beside her and pulled up the ragged old coverlet—an item also rescued from Fariske's shed. For a long time he lay awake until finally the witch-girl's breathing indicated sleep.

---

*In the traditional fables of Zeck, Jilliam is a talkative girl who is captured by a starmenter and almost immediately set free because of her incessant prattle.

T he light of dawn entered Jantiff's makeshift window. He cautiously raised himself on his elbow. Glisten was awake, and lay with her eyes fixed on the ceiling.

"Good morning," said Jantiff. "Are you speaking to me today? . . . I thought not . . . Well, life goes on and I must gather my percebs. But first, breakfast!"

Jantiff blew up the fire, boiled tea, and toasted bread. For five minutes Glisten watched apathetically, then—abruptly, as if prodded—she sat up, swung her legs to the floor. She slipped on her sandals and with an inscrutable sidelong glance toward Jantiff, walked from the hut. Jantiff sighed and shrugged and turned his attention back to the food. Glisten doubtless longed for the company of her own kind. He could offer only temporary security, at best. She was better off in the Sych. Nevertheless he felt a pang of regret; Glisten had invested his hut with something heretofore lacking: companionship? Perhaps.

Jantiff prepared to eat a solitary breakfast . . . Footsteps. The door swung open. Glisten entered, her face washed, her hair ordered. She carried in her skirt a dozen brown pods which Jantiff recognized as the fruit of the turnover vine. Glisten deftly husked the pods, dropped them into a pan. Five minutes later, Jantiff gingerly tasting, found them a most savory adjunct to the toasted bread.

"I see that you are a wise girl, indeed," said Jantiff. "Do you like the name 'Glisten'? If you do, nod—or better, smile!" He watched her closely and Glisten, whether or not responding to his instruction, seemed to manage a twist of the lips.

Jantiff rose to his feet and gazed out over the dreary ocean. "Well, no avoiding it. The percebs must be harvested, and now I need nine bucketloads! Oh, my clammy skin; can it tolerate such abuse?"

Luckily for Jantiff his shoal of rocks had lain fallow for years and the outer face was heavily encrusted. Jantiff worked with an energy born of discomfort, and in record time gathered his nine buckets. Glisten meanwhile had wandered about, often looking toward the forest, as if listening for a summons or a call, which evidently she failed to hear. At last she came down to the shore, and seating herself primly on a rock, watched Jantiff at his work. When Jantiff began to shell and clean his catch, she helped him: listlessly at first, then with increasing deftness. Well before noon, Jantiff was ready to make his deliveries.

"I must leave you," he told Glisten. "If you decide to go away, then you must do so, without regrets. Of course if you care to stay, you are more than welcome. But above all remember: If you see anyone, hide, and quickly!"

Glisten listened soberly and Jantiff went off about his business.

The Old Groar was full of gossip about the witch-chasing, which by general consensus had gone well. "They're cleared from the Sych, this end at least," declared one man. "Cambres caught his two garden thieves and downed them on the spot."

"Ha! That will soothe his soul!"

"Booch is in an awful state; he missed his young kit. He swears she ran out on the water and led Dusselbeck's good Feigwel wurgles to their death."

"Ah, the thing!"

"Still the wurgles tore a witch-mother properly to bits!"

"Now they'll have to take the treatment!"

This last was evidently a jocularity; everyone laughed, and at this point Jantiff departed the tap room.

During the afternoon he started his decoration of the Cimmery; working with great intensity he completed perhaps a third of his job. He might have accomplished more had he not found himself fretting and anxious to return to his hut. Along the way he stopped by the general store and bought new bread, oil, a packet of dehydrated goulash and another of candied persimmon slices.

When he returned to the hut, Glisten was nowhere to be seen, but the fire was burning, the bed had been put in order and the hut seemed unaccountably tidy. Jantiff went out to look this way and that. "Better, far better, if she's gone," he muttered. "After all, she can't stay here after I've gone off to Uncibal." Even as he turned to enter the hut, Glisten came trotting across the meadow, looking back over her shoulder. Jantiff seized up his cudgel but whatever had alarmed her made no appearance.

At the sight of Jantiff, Glisten slowed her pace to a demure walk. She carried a cloth sling full of green finberries. Ignoring Jantiff as if he were invisible, she put down the berries, then stood looking pensively back toward the forest.

"I'm home," said Jantiff. "Glisten! Look at me!"

Somewhat to his surprise—by coincidence, so he suspected—the witch-girl turned her head and studied him somberly. Half in frustration, half in jest, Jantiff asked: "What goes on in your mind? Do you see me as a person? or a shadow? or a chattering mooncalf?" He took a step toward her, thinking to arouse some flicker of reaction: surprise, alarm, perplexity, anything. Glisten hardly seemed to notice, and Jantiff rather sheepishly contented himself with handing over the packet of sweetmeats. "This is for you," he said. "Can you understand? For Glisten. For dear little Glisten, who refuses to talk to Jantiff."

Glisten put the packet aside, and began to clean the berries. Jantiff watched in a warm suffusion. How pleasant this might have been under different circumstances! But in a month he would be gone and the hut would again fall into ruins, and Glisten must return to the forest.

Jantiff, contriving fanciful arabesques in red, gold, dark blue and lime green across the front of the dreary old Cimmery, looked around to find Eubanq shuffling quietly past. Jantiff jumped down from the trestle. "Eubanq, my good fellow!"

Eubanq halted somewhat reluctantly, shoving his hands into the pockets of his fawn-colored jacket. He cast an eye over the decorated timbers. "Ah, Jantiff. You're doing fine work, getting the old Cimmery ready for the fair. Well, you'll want to get along with your work, and I mustn't disturb your concentration."

"Not at all!" said Jantiff. "This is no more than improvisation; I can do it in my sleep. I have a question for you: a business matter, so to speak."

"Yes?"

"I'm paying a hundred ozols for transportation to Uncibal Spaceport, in time to catch the *Serenaic*; correct?"

"Well, yes," said Eubanq guardedly. "That was the proposal we discussed, I believe."

"A hundred ozols is a large sum of money and naturally pays all costs for the trip. I may want to bring a friend along; the hundred ozols will of course suffice. I mention this now to avoid any possible misunderstanding."

Eubanq's pale blue eyes flicked across Jantiff's face, then away. "What friend might this be?"

"No matter; it's really all hypothesis at the moment. But you agree that the hundred ozols will cover our costs?"

Eubanq considered, pursing his thick lips, and at last shook his head. "Well, Jantiff, I should hardly think so. In this business we've got to work to rules; otherwise everything goes topsy-turvy. One passage: one fare. Two passages: two fares. That's the universal rule."

"Another hundred ozols?"

"Correct."

"But that's an enormous amount of money! I'm renting the flibbit on a trip basis, not by fares."

"That's one way of looking at it. On the other hand, I've got a hundred expenses to consider: overhead, maintenance, depreciation, interest on the initial investment—"

"But you don't own the boat!"

"It's all to the same effect. And never forget, like anyone else I hope to gain a bit of profit from the transaction."

"A very generous profit," cried Jantiff. "Have you no human feelings or generosity?"

"Very little of either," Eubanq confessed with his easiest grin. "If you don't like my price, why not try elsewhere? Booch might be persuaded to borrow the Grand Knight's Dorphy for the afternoon."

"Hmf. I expect that you've received confirmation of my passage aboard the *Serenaic?*"

"Well, no," said Eubanq. "Not yet. Apparently there's been some sort of mix-up."

"But time is getting short!"

"I'll surely do my best." Eubanq waved his hand and went on his way.

Jantiff continued painting, using furious emphatic strokes which lent a remarkable brio to his work. He calculated his assets. A hundred ozols was well within his reach, but two hundred? Jantiff counted forward and backward, but in every case fell short by fifty or even sixty ozols.

Later in the day at the Old Groar, Jantiff cut and primed the panels he would paint for Fariske. There was still talk of the witch-chasing, to which Jantiff listened with a curled lip. Someone had noted remnants of the band straggling north toward the Wayness Mountains. All agreed that the Sych had been effectively cauterized, and talk turned to the forthcoming Market Fair. A certain portly fisherman went to watch Jantiff at his work. "What will you paint on these panels?"

"I haven't quite decided. Landscapes, perhaps."

"Bah, that's no entertainment! You should paint a humorous charade, with all the Old Groar regulars dressed in ridiculous costumes!"

Jantiff nodded politely. "An interesting idea, but some might object. Also, I'm not being paid to paint portraits."

"Still, put my picture somewhere in the scene; that's easy enough."

"Certainly," said Jantiff. "At a charge of, say, two ozols. Fariske, of course, must agree."

The fisherman drew back his head like a startled turtle. "Two ozols? Ridiculous!"

"Not at all. Your image will hang on this wall forever, depicting you in all your joviality. It is a kind of immortality."

"True. Two ozols it is."

"You may also paint my image," said another. "I'll pay the two ozols now."

Jantiff held up a restraining hand. "First Fariske must be consulted."

Fariske made no difficulties. "These fees will naturally reduce your payment from me."

"By not so much as a dinket!" Jantiff declared stoutly. "In fact, I want half of my fee now, so that I may buy proper pigments."

Fariske protested, but Jantiff held firm and finally had his way.

As he returned to the hut Jantiff once again totted up his expectations. "Ten panels . . . I can crowd five faces into each panel, if necessary. That's fifty faces at two ozols each: one hundred solid ringing ozols, and my difficulties vanish like smoke!" Jantiff arrived home in an unusually optimistic mood.

As usual, Glisten was nowhere to be seen; apparently she did not care to stay alone in the hut. But almost immediately upon Jantiff's return she came from the forest with a bundle of shaggy bark, which when scraped and washed yielded a nourishing porridge.

Jantiff ran to take her bundle. He put his arm around her waist and swung her up and around in a circle. Setting her down, he kissed her forehead. "Well, young Glisten, my lovely little sorceress: what do you think! Money pours in by the bucketful! Faces for Fariske's panels, at two ozols per face! So then: would you like to live at Frayness on Zeck? It's a long way and there's no wild forest like this, but we'll find what's wrong with your voice and have it fixed, and there'd be no witch-chasing, I assure you, except the kind of pursuit every pretty little creature enjoys. What about it? Do you understand me? Away from Wyst, off across space to Zeck? I don't quite know how I'll manage the fare, but no doubt the cursar will help. Ah, that elusive cursar! Tomorrow I must telephone Uncibal!"

At the moment he was more interested in Glisten. He sat on the bench and pulled her down upon his lap, so that he was looking directly into her face. "Now then," said Jantiff, "you must really concentrate. Listen closely! If you understand, nod your head. Is this understood?"

Glisten seemed to be amused by Jantiff's earnestness, though her lips twitched by no more than an iota.

"You wretched girl!" cried Jantiff. "You're absolutely frustrating! I want to take you to Zeck and you show not a flicker of interest. Won't you please say something or do something?"

Glisten comprehended that somehow she had distressed Jantiff. Her mouth drooped and she looked off across the sea. Jantiff groaned in exasperation. "Very well then; I'll take you willy-nilly and if you want to come back to your dank black forest you shall do so!"

Glisten turned back; Jantiff leaned forward and kissed her mouth. She gave no response, but neither did she draw away. "What a situation," sighed Jantiff. "If only you'd give me some little inkling, just a hint, that you understand me."

Glisten once again produced her wisp of a smile. "Aha!" said Jantiff. "Perhaps you understand me after all, and only too well!"

Glisten became restive; Jantiff reluctantly allowed her to leave his lap. He rose to his feet. "Zeck it is then, and please, at the last minute, don't cavort and hide like a wild thing."

During the night a storm blew in from the south; in the morning long combing breakers pounded the rocks and Jantiff despaired of gathering percebs. An hour later the wind moderated. A black rain sizzled upon the surface of the ocean, somewhat moderating the surf. Jantiff forced his shrinking flesh into the water, but was unmercifully swept back and forth, and finally retreated to the shore.

·Taking his buckets he set off eastward along the beach, hoping to find a sheltered pool. At the far end of Isbet Neck, with the ocean on the right hand and Lulace Sound on the left, he found a spot where the currents swung past two long fingers of rock, and created a still deep pool between. Here the percebs grew large and heavy, with a large proportion of the prized coronels, and Jantiff harvested a day's quota in short order. Glisten appeared from nowhere; together they shelled the catch and carried the yield back to the hut for cleaning. "Everything seems to work for the best," declared Jantiff. "A storm drives us from our rocks and we find the home of all percebs!"

And it seemed that Glisten gave a nod of endorsement for Jantiff's opinions.

"If only you could speak!" sighed Jantiff. "The local folk wouldn't dare to chase you, since you could go to the telephone and notify the cursar . . . Ah, that cursar! where can he be? He is duty bound to hear petitions, but he has become thin air!"

CHAPTER *14*

Jantiff finished the Cimmery decorations and even Madame Tchaga was pleased with the effect. At the Old Groar, Jantiff began to paint his panels. Not a few of Fariske's patrons paid two ozols each to gain Jantiff's version of immortality. Eubanq declined to lend his own visage to the decorations. "I'll spend my two ozols on ale and percebs. I have no desire to see myself as others see me."

Jantiff took him aside. "Another hypothetical question. Suppose one of my friends decided to visit Zeck: what might be the fare aboard the *Serenaic*?"

"Sixty or seventy ozols, or in that general area. Who is this friend?"

"Just one of the village girls; it's no great matter. But I'm surprised that the interstellar voyage to Zeck comes so much cheaper than the hop, skip and jump to Uncibal."

"Odd indeed, on the face of it," Eubanq agreed. "Still, what is money to you, prosperous perceb merchant that you are?"

"Ha! When, or if, I pay you your two hundred and seventy ozols, I will consider myself fortunate. By the way, I'm sure that passage aboard the *Serenaic* has now been confirmed?"

"Not quite yet. I must jostle them along."

"I would hope so! Perhaps I should call them myself!"

"Leave it to me. Do you seriously plan to take someone else to Zeck?"

"It's just a notion. But surely there would be no difficulty, if I were to pay over the ozols?"

"None that I can envision."

"I must give the matter serious thought." Jantiff returned to his panels.

As he worked he heard talk of the fair, an occasion which this year would occur only a week before the Arrabin Centenary. Jantiff suddenly saw how he might earn a goodly sum of money, perhaps enough to pay Eubanq his requirements.

That night, as he sat by the fire with Glisten, he explained his scheme. "Hundreds of folk come to the fair, agreed? All will be hungry; all want percebs, so why not satisfy this need? It will mean a great deal of work for both of us, but think! Perhaps we can pay your passage to Zeck. What do you think of that?" Jantiff searched Glisten's face as he was wont to do, and she responded with her glimmer of a smile.

"You're so pretty when you smile," said Jantiff with feeling. "If only I weren't afraid that I'd frighten you and drive you away . . ."

Toiling long hours Jantiff gathered twenty buckets of percebs and penned them into a quiet pool near his hut. On the day before the fair he set up a booth not far from the Old Groar and provided himself with a kettle, salt and cooking oil. Early on the morning of the fair he delivered his usual quota of percebs to the Cimmery and the Old Groar, then, starting his fire and warming the oil, he began to sell percebs to the farm folk arriving from the outer districts.

"Come buy, come buy!" called Jantiff. "Fresh percebs from the briny deep, cooked to a crisp and appetizing succulence! Come buy! A dinket for a portion, percebs to your taste!"

Jantiff became very busy, so that he found time to cry his wares only at odd intervals. Halfway through the morning Eubanq stopped by the booth. "Well, Jantiff, I see that you intend to prosper one way or another."

"I hope so! If business continues I'll be able to pay you off either today or tomorrow, as soon as I collect from Fariske. And then, mind you, I want the tickets, all confirmed, most definitely witha written guarantee of passage to Uncibal."

Eubanq put on his easy grin. "These are meticulous precautions. Don't you trust me?"

"Did you trust me to pay after I arrived home on Zeck? Am I less honorable than you?"

Eubanq laughed. "A good point! Well, we'll arrange the matter one way or another. In the meantime, give me a dinket's worth of those percebs. They look to be exquisite; where do you find such excellent quality?"

"Aha! That's my little secret!" To a farmer: "Yes, sir; three packets, three dinkets!" Back to Eubanq: "I'll say this, that we came upon, that is to say, I came upon a ledge that has obviously lain fallow for years. And here you are; one dinket, if you please."

Eubanq, taking the packet, chanced to notice Jantiff's hands. He became rigid, as if arrested by a startling thought. Slowly he raised his eyes to Jantiff's face. "One dinket," said Jantiff. "Hurry, please! Others are waiting."

"Yes, of course," said Eubanq in an odd choked voice. "And cheap at the price!" He paid over his coin and turned away, carrying the packet gingerly between forefinger and thumb. Jantiff watched him go with a puzzled frown. What had come over Eubanq?

Outside the Old Groar, Eubanq met Booch. They talked earnestly for a period. Jantiff watched them from the corner of his eye as he worked. Something, so his sensitive instincts assured him, was in the wind.

One of Eubanq's remarks startled Booch. He swung around and stared toward Jantiff. Eubanq quickly took his arm and the two men entered the Old Groar.

Business became even brisker. An hour later his stock of percebs ran out. He hired a boy to stand by the booth; then, chinking up his earnings and taking his sacks, he set off toward his hut for fresh stock.

Halfway along the beach he noticed Eubanq approaching at a rapid stride, his loose fawn shoes scuffing up little eruptions of sand. A parcel dangled from his right hand.

Eubanq swerved aside and vanished momentarily from sight behind a granat tree. When he reappeared he walked at his usual saunter and carried no parcel.

The two drew abreast. Jantiff asked in an edgy voice: "What are you doing out here? Just an hour ago I saw you go into the Old Groar."

"Occasionally I take a stroll to ease my lungs of the town air. Why aren't you tending business?"

"I sold out of percebs." Jantiff looked Eubanq up and down without cordiality. "Did you pass by my hut?"

"I went nowhere near so far . . . Well, I'll be getting along." Eubanq strolled back toward Balad.

Jantiff hastened along the beach, and presently broke into a trot. There ahead, his hut. Glisten was nowhere to be seen. Near the water's edge a pair of buckets indicated where she had been working; one of the buckets was half-full of cleaned percebs. But no Glisten.

Jantiff looked up and down the beach, then went to his hut. Glisten was not within, which caused him no surprise. In the corner of the hut stood the old pot where he kept his money. He crossed the room to unburden himself of the morning's take. The pot was quite empty.

Jantiff stared at the cracked old vessel with shoulders sagging and mouth agape.

Jantiff went outside to stand in the pale sunlight. Serene detachment blanketed his mood: a fact which puzzled and disturbed him. "Why am I not more shocked?" he asked himself. "Very odd! I would expect to be sick with anguish, yet I seem quite unmoved. Evidently I have transcended ordinary emotion. This, of course, is remarkable. A notable achievement, I should say. I have instantly seized upon the proper way to deal with catastrophe, which is to ignore it. And meanwhile, my customers wait for percebs. By all precepts of decency I ought not deny them their treat because of a personal matter, which in any event I have dealt with most efficiently. Yes, most curious. The worlds seems far away."

Jantiff loaded himself with percebs from the pool and marched stiff-legged back up the beach and to his booth. Once more he began to serve his customers.

"Percebs!" cried Jantiff to the passersby. "Choice morsels direct from the ocean! I guarantee quality! A dinket for a generous portion! Come buy these excellent percebs!"

From the Old Groar came Eubanq. He turned a smiling glance toward Jantiff and started up the street. Words burst up Jantiff's throat of their own volition; Jantiff was surprised to hear them. "Eubanq! I say, Eubanq! Step over here, if you please!"

Eubanq paused and looked back with an expression of polite inquiry. "You called to me, Jantiff?"

"Yes. Bring me my money at once. Otherwise I will notify the Grand Knight, and lay all particulars before him."

Eubanq turned his smiling glance around the circle of onlookers. He muttered a few quiet words to a strapping young farmer who, a moment before, had purchased a packet of Jantiff's percebs. The farmer gaped down at the half-empty packet, then shouldered through Jantiff's waiting customers to the booth. "Show me your hands!"

"What's wrong with my hands?" demanded Jantiff.

The farmer and the customers stared at Jantiff's fingernails. Jantiff looked also and saw a glint of that golden sheen which he had often noted upon Glisten's fingernails.

"The yellows!" roared the farmer. "He's given us all the yellows!"

"No, no!" cried Jantiff. "My fingernails are stained because of working in the cold water with the percebs . . . Or perhaps my gamboge pigment . . ."

"Not true," Eubanq explained. "You have eaten witches' food, and now we have eaten your food and all of us are infected, and all of us must undergo the treatment. I assure you that any money which might have changed hands is no compensation."

The farmer began to shout curses. He kicked over Jantiff's booth and tried to seize Jantiff, who backed away and then, turning, walked quickly off down the street. The farmer and others came in pursuit; Jantiff broke into a run and so proceeded from town, along the familiar beach road. The road forked; to avoid being trapped on the headland, Jantiff swung to the left, toward Lulace Sound and Lulace, the Grand Knight's manor. Behind came his pursuers, bawling threats and curses.

Jantiff pushed through the ornate front gate at Lulace, and ran at a failing lope through the garden. He staggered across the verandah, leaned against the front door. Along the road came his enemies.

Jantiff tugged at the massive latch. The door swung aside; Jantiff staggered into the mansion.

He stood in a tall reception room, paneled in pale wood and furnished a trifle too elaborately for Jantiff's taste, had he been in a mood to exercise his faculties.

To the left a pair of wide steps gave upon a salon carpeted in green and illuminated by high windows facing to the north. Jantiff went to the steps and looked into the salon. A dark-haired man with heavy shoulders conversed with two other men and a woman. Jantiff timidly stepped forward. The woman turned; Jantiff looked into her face. "Skorlet!" he cried in a voice of wonder.

Skorlet, sleek and well-fed, froze into an almost comical rigidity, mouth half-open, one hand aloft in a gesture. The others turned; Jantiff looked from Sarp to Esteban to Contractor Shubart, as he was known in Uncibal.

Skorlet spoke in a strangled voice, "It's Jantiff Ravensroke!"

Contractor Shubart marched forward and Jantiff retreated into the foyer.

The Contractor spoke in a heavy voice: "What do you want? Why weren't you announced? Can't you see I'm entertaining guests?"

Jantiff responded in a stammer: "Sir, I intend nothing wrong. My life is threatened by the folk in the road. They say that my percebs gave them a disease, but it's not true; at least not purposeful. Eubanq, the shipping agent, stole my money and incited them to attack me. I didn't mean to intrude upon your guests." Jantiff's voice faltered as he considered the identity of these guests. "I will return when you are less busy."

"Wait a minute. Booch! Where is Booch?"

A footman stepped forward and murmured a few quiet words.

Contractor Shubart growled: "Be damned to his wurgles and witch-kits! Why isn't he on hand when I need him? Take this fellow to the gardener's shed and keep him safe until Booch returns."

"Yes, sir. Come along, please." But Jantiff lurched backward to the door, groped for the latch, threw open the door and ran out into the garden.

The footman came running after, calling: "Here, fellow! Stop! By the Grand Knight's orders, halt!"

Jantiff ran around the manor and with a cunning born of desperation, waited at the corner. When the footman lunged past, Jantiff held out his foot. The footman sprawled; Jantiff struck him with a stake and the footman lay limp. Jantiff continued around to the back of Lulace, through the kitchen garden and out into the park. Behind a tree he caught his breath. No time now for crafty or complicated planning. "I shall go directly to Eubanq's house," Jantiff told himself. "I will kill and rob Eubanq, or perhaps force him to provide me an air-car. I will then fly him high over the Sych and throw him out; then I will continue on to Uncibal and demand protection from the cursar. If, of course, the cursar has returned. If not, I will hide once more in the Disjerferact."

Jantiff set off at once toward Balad. Unfortunately his exaltation caused him to ignore elementary caution; he was seen and identified as he came along the river road. Sullen folk surrounded him. The women began to call out invectives; the crowd pressed closer and Jantiff was backed up against a wall. He cried out in anguish: "I have done nothing! Leave me be!"

A dockworker named Sabrose, whom Jantiff had often served at the Old Groar, bellowed him down: "You have given us all the yellows, and we must now undergo the treatment, unless we want to be deaf and dumb witches. Do you call that nothing?"

"I don't know anything about it! Let me pass!"

Sabrose gave a ferocious laugh. "Since all Balad must be treated, you shall be the first!"

Jantiff was dragged up to the main street and across to the apothecary's shop. "Bring out the treatment!" bawled Sabrose. "Here's the first patient; we'll cure him on the cheap, without the headbangers."

The treatment device was wheeled from the shop. The apothecary, a mild old man who had frequented neither of the taverns nor Jantiff's booth, dropped two pills in a mug of water and held it to Jantiff's face. "Here; this will dull the pain."

Sabrose brushed away the mug. "Take away your headbangers! Let him know what he's done to us!"

Jantiff's hands were fixed into metal gloves, with loose joints over the fingernails. Sabrose wielded a mallet to crush Jantiff's fingertips. Jantiff croaked and groaned.

"Now then!" said Sabrose. "When the nails drop off, apply black niter of argent; maybe you'll be cured."

"He's getting off too easy!" screamed a woman. "Here: my frack sludge! Turn his face about; he'll never see his mischief."

Sabrose said: "Enough is enough; he's beyond knowing anything."

"Not yet! Let him pay to the full. There! Now! Right in the face!"

A thick acrid fluid was flung into Jantiff's face, scalding his skin and searing his vision. He gave a strangled cry and tore at his eyes with mutilated fingers.

The apothecary threw water into Jantiff's face and wiped his eyes with a rag. Then he turned in fury on the crowd. "You've punished him beyond all justice! He's only a poor sad lout."

"Not so!" cried a voice which Jantiff recognized as that of Eubanq. "He housed himself with a witch-woman; I saw her at his hut, and he poisoned us knowingly with witch food!"

Jantiff mumbled: "Eubanq is a thief; Eubanq is a liar." But none heard him. Jantiff opened his eyes a crack, but a granular fog obscured his vision. He moaned in shock and grief. "You've blinded me! I will never see the colors!"

One of the women cried out: "Where now the horrid witch? Do her like the others!"

"No fear," said Eubanq. "Booch has taken her in hand."

Jantiff gave a call of mindless woe. He struggled to his feet, flailed his arms to right and left, an act which the crowd considered ludicrous. They began to bait Jantiff, shoving him, prodding his ribs, hissing into his face. Jantiff at last threw up his hands and staggered off down the street.

"Catch him!" screamed the most vindictive. "Bring him back and deal with him properly!"

"Let him go," growled an old fisherman. "I've seen enough."

"What? After he has given us all the yellows?"

"And all must take the treatment?"

"He fed us witch food; never forget it!"

"Today let him go; tomorrow we will put him on a raft."

"Quite right! Jantiff! Can you hear? Tomorrow you float south across the ocean!"

Jantiff lurched heedlessly down the street. For a space children followed him, jeering and throwing stones; then they were called back and Jantiff went his way alone.

Out to the beach he stumbled, and along the familiar track. With his eyes wide and staring he could see only a vague luminosity; he walked a good distance but could not find his hut. Finally he dropped down upon the sand and turned his face to the sea. He sat a long time, confused and listless, his hands throbbing with a pain to which he gave no heed. The fog across his vision grew thick as Dwan set and night came to Dessimo Beach and the Moaning Ocean. Still Jantiff sat, while water sucked across the off-shore ledges.

A breeze drifted in from the ocean: at first a chilly breath which tingled Jantiff's skin, then gusts which penetrated his threadbare garments.

Jantiff saw himself as if in a clairvoyant vision: a gaunt creature crouched on the sand, all connections to the world of reality broken. He began to grow warm and comfortable; he realized that he was about to die. Images formed in his mind: Uncibal and Old Pink; the human tides along Uncibal River; the four Whispers on the Pedestal. He saw Skorlet and Tanzel, Kedidah and the Ephthalotes; Esteban and Booch and Contractor Shubart. Glisten appeared, facing him from a distance of no more than an arm's length, and gazed steadfastly into his eyes. Miracle of miracles. He heard her speak, in a soft quick voice: "Jantiff, don't sit in the dark! Jantiff, please lift yourself! Don't die!"

Jantiff shuddered and blinked, and tears ran from his eyes. He thought of his cheerful home at Frayness; he saw the faces of his father and mother and sisters. "I don't want to die," said Jantiff. "I want to go home."

With a prodigious effort he hauled himself to his feet and stumbled off along the beach. By chance he encountered an object he recognized: the branches of a misshapen old codmollow tree. His hut stood only fifty yards beyond; the ground was now familiar.

Jantiff groped his way to the hut, entered, carefully closed the door. He stood stock-still. Someone had only recently departed; his odor, rank and heavy, hung on the air. Jantiff listened, but heard no sound. He was alone. Tottering to his bed, he lay himself down and instantly fell asleep.

Jantiff awoke, jarred to consciousness by an awful imminence.

He lay quiet. His blinded eyes registered a watery gray blur: daylight had arrived. A rank harsh odor reached his nostrils. He knew that he was not alone.

Someone spoke. "So, Jantiff, here you are after all. I looked for you last night, but you were out." Jantiff recognized the voice of Booch. He made no response.

"I looked for your money," said Booch. "According to Eubanq, you control quite a tidy sum."

"Eubanq took my money yesterday."

Booch made an unpleasant nasal sound. "Are you serious?"

"I don't care about money now. Eubanq took it."

"That cursed Eubanq!" groaned Booch. "He'll make an accounting to me!"

"Where is Glisten?"

"The kit? Ha, don't worry about her, not a trifle. In five minutes you'll be past caring for anything. I've had my orders. I'm to put a wire around your neck, without fail. Then I'll settle with Eubanq. Then I'm off to Uncibal, where I can take any woman I see for a dish of tripes . . . Raise your head, Jantiff. This won't take long."

"I don't want to die."

"No use to whine. My orders are strict. Jantiff must definitely be dead. So then—now none of your kicking or flailing about! Hold now."

Jantiff scuttled sideways like a crab and through some mad accident, pushed Booch off balance and rolled out the door. From far up the beach came a jeering cry: "Mad Jantiff: there! You see him now!"

Jantiff heard Booch's heavy tread. Two steps, then an uncertain halt and a mutter of annoyance. "Now, in the name of Gasmus, who can that be? A stranger, an off-worlder. Does he plan to interfere? I'll stop him short."

Steps approached. A boy's voice cried out in glee: "That's Mad Jantiff on the ground, and there's Constable Booch, who'll give it to him properly; you'll see!"

"Good morning to you both," said a pleasant voice. "Jantiff, you seem to be in poor condition."

"Yes, I've been blinded, and my fingers are all broken."

The boy cried out in eager fury: "Never fear, there's more to come! Sir, he gave us all the yellows, and he consorted with a witch! May I strike him with this stick?"

"By no means!" said the newcomer. "You are far too ardent; calm yourself! Jantiff, I am here in response to your numerous messages. I am the Respectable Ryl Shermatz, a representative of the Connatic."

Jantiff sat dazed on the ground. "You are the cursar?"

"No. My authority considerably exceeds his."

"Then ask Booch what he did with Glisten. He may have killed her."

"Utter nonsense," said Booch in jovial, if uneasy, tones. "Jantiff, you have peculiar notions about me."

"You brought your wurgle and hunted her down! Where is she now?"

Ryl Shermatz said: "Constable Booch, I suggest that you respond to Jantiff's question, in all candor."

"Lacking facts, how can I answer? And why all the anxiety? She was just a witch-kit."

"You speak in the past tense," noted Ryl Shermatz. "Is this significant?"

"Of course not! I chanced to stroll past with my wurgle, admittedly, and she ran off, but what's that to me? Or to you, for that matter?"

"I am the Connatic's agent. I am required to adjust situations such as this."

"But there is no situation to adjust! Look yonder; even now she's coming out of the Sych!"

Jantiff struggled to his knees. "Where? Tell me where. But I can't see."

The boy gave a screech of panic. There came an odd sequence of sounds: a stamping of feet, a whisper as if of spurting gas, a thud, a gasp, a scuffling sound. Then, for a moment, silence.

The boy babbled: "He's dead! He tried to kill you! How did you know?"

Ryl Shermatz spoke without perturbation: "I am sensitive to danger, and well trained to deal with it."

"Who came from the forest?" cried Jantiff. "Was it Glisten?"

"No one came from the forest; Booch attempted a ruse."

"Then where can she be?"

"We shall do our best to find her. But now: tell me why you sent so many urgent messages."

"I will tell you," mumbled Jantiff. "I want only to talk; I must do hours and hours of talking—"

"Steady, Jantiff. Come, sit here on the bench. Boy, run to town; bring back new bread and a pot of good soup. Here, an ozol for your pains . . . Now, Jantiff, talk, if you are able."

CHAPTER 15

D wan, halfway up the sky, shone from behind films of shifting mist. Jantiff sat on the bench, leaning back against his ramshackle stone and seaweed hut. Ryl Shermatz, a person of medium stature, with well-formed features and short brown hair, stood beside him, one leg propped upon the bench. He had dragged the dead hulk around to the side; only Booch's black boots, extending past the edge of the hut, bore witness to his presence.

Jantiff spoke at length, in a voice which presently dwindled to a husky croak.

Ryl Shermatz said little, inserting only an occasional question. From time to time he nodded as if Jantiff's remarks reinforced opinions of his own.

Jantiff's account came to an end: "My only uncertainty is Glisten. Last night I dreamt of her, and in my dream she spoke; it was strange to hear her, and even in my sleep I felt as if I would weep."

Ryl Shermatz gazed south over the gray ocean. "Well, Jantiff," he said at last, "it is clear that you have endured hard times. Let me summarize your statement. You believe that Esteban, looking over your drawings of the four Whispers, noticed the resemblance between three of the Whispers, and himself, Skorlet and Sarp. You theorize that Esteban, with his devious and supple mind, inevitably recognized the potentiality of the situation, and began, idly at first, to consider methods for making the possible real. A fourth member of the cabal was needed; who better than a man of wealth, power and motivation; in short, a contractor? Esteban searched the reference book, and there, made for the part, he discovered Contractor Shubart.

"Esteban, Skorlet and Sarp were motivated by their lust for food and luxury. Shubart had long enjoyed the good things of life, but now was threatened by the Whispers who intended to free Arrabus from the contractors and already had informed the Connatic of their plans. Shubart needed funds to implement his grand plans for the Weirdlands; he readily joined Esteban, Skorlet and Sarp.

"They contrived a bold and very simple scheme. Here you assert that Skorlet, Esteban, Sarp and Shubart journeyed to Waunisse and there boarded the airship on which the Whispers would return to Uncibal. During the flight the Whispers were killed with all their entourage and dropped into the sea. When the *Sea Disk* landed, Esteban, Skorlet, Sarp and Shubart had become the Whispers. They showed themselves briefly on the Pedestal. No one inspected them closely; no one could have suspected their deed; except you, who were disturbed and perplexed.

"The new Whispers traveled to Numenes, where they consulted the Connatic at Lusz. He found them an unsympathetic group: insincere, evasive and tawdry. Their statements rang false, and failed to accord with their purported mission, as proposed by the original Whispers. The Connatic decided to look more closely into the matter, especially since he had received urgent messages concerning a certain Jantiff Ravensroke.

"I was assigned to the task and arrived at Uncibal two days ago. Immediately I tried to find Cursar Bonamico. I learned that he had flown to Waunisse, on business connected with the Whispers, that he had boarded the same aircraft on which the Whispers returned to Uncibal.

"He never alighted from this aircraft, and the inference is clear. He was murdered and thrust into the Salaman Sea. I naturally took note of the messages you had dispatched from Balad. Last night a final message arrived. The voice was that of a woman—a girl, according to the clerk Aleida Gluster. The woman, or girl, spoke in great agitation: 'Come quickly, come quickly to Balad; they're doing terrible things to Jantiff!' And that was all."

"A girl spoke?" muttered Jantiff. "Who could that have been? Glisten can't speak, except in dreams . . . Might the clerk have been asleep and dreaming?"

"An interesting conjecture," said Ryl Shermatz. "Aleida Gluster said nothing in this regard, one way or the other . . . Here we are at Balad. We shall go to the Old Groar Tavern and refresh ourselves. Then we shall try to subdue these obstreperous folk."

"Eubanq is more than obstreperous," Jantiff muttered. "He stole my money and told Booch about Glisten."

"I have not forgotten Eubanq," said Ryl Shermatz.

The two men entered the Old Groar. At the tables sat a considerable number of customers: double the usual for this hour of the day. Fariske came hurriedly forward, his round white forehead glistening with droplets of sweat. "This way, gentlemen," he cried in brave joviality. "Be seated! Will you drink ale? I recommend my old Dark Wort!"

Clearly the boy who had guided Ryl Shermatz to Jantiff's hut had returned to Balad bearing large tales. "You may bring us ale and something to eat," said Shermatz. "But first: is the person known as Eubanq present in the room?"

Fariske darted a series of nervous glances along the tables. "He is not here. You will probably find him at the depot, where he serves as general agent."

"Be good enough to select three reliable men from among your customers and bring them here."

" 'Reliable'? Well, let me consider. That is a hard question. I'll summon the best of the lot. Garfred, Sabrose, Osculot! Step over here, at once!"

The three men approached with varying degrees of truculence.

Ryl Shermatz appraised them with an impassive gaze. "I am Ryl Shermatz, the Connatic's agent. I appoint you my deputies for the period of one day. You are now, like myself, invested with the inviolable authority of the Connatic, under my orders. Is this clear?"

The three men shuffled their feet and signified their understanding: Garfred with a surly grunt; Sabrose making an amiable gesture; Osculot showing a grimace of misgiving.

Ryl Shermatz spoke on. "Proceed at once to the depot. Place Eubanq under the Connatic's arrest. Bring him here at once. Under no circumstances allow him freedom from your custody: not so much as a minute. Be on the guard for any weapons he may carry. Go in haste!"

The three men departed the tavern. Ryl Shermatz turned to Fariske, who stood anxiously to the side. "Send other men to summon all the folk of Balad to an immediate assembly in front of the Old Groar. Then you may serve us our refreshment."

Jantiff sat in the dark, listening to the mutter of voices, the clink of mugs, the scrape of feet. Warmth and relaxation eased his limbs; lassitude came upon him. Ryl Shermatz spoke quietly to someone who made no response: perhaps by means of a transceiver, thought Jantiff. A moment later Shermatz sent Voris to fetch the apothecary, who arrived within the minute.

Shermatz took the apothecary aside; the two conferred and the apothecary departed. Shermatz spoke to Jantiff: "I have specified a treatment to restore a certain fraction of your vision. Later, of course, we will arrange a thorough therapy."

"I will be grateful for any improvement."

The apothecary returned. Jantiff heard muted voices as his case was discussed; then the apothecary addressed him directly. "Now, Jantiff, here is the situation. The surfaces of your eyes have been frosted by the caustic, and are no longer transparent to light. I am about to attempt a rather novel treatment: I coat the surface of your eyes with an emulsion, which quickly dries to a transparent film. Perhaps you will feel discomfort, perhaps you will notice nothing whatever. With the irregularities smoothed out, light should once again reach your retina. I will mention that the film is microscopically porous to allow passage of oxygen. Please lean back, open your right eye wide, and do not move . . . Very good. Now the left. Do not blink, if you please."

Jantiff felt a cool sensation across the front of his eyes, then an odd not unpleasant constriction across the eyeballs. Simultaneously the blur before his vision began to dissipate as if a wind blew through the optic fog. Objects loomed, assumed density; for a time they wavered in a watery medium and presently stilled. Jantiff once more could see, with almost the old clarity.

He looked around the room. He saw the grave faces of Ryl Shermatz and the apothecary. Fariske stood by the counter, abdomen bulging out ahead. Palinka peered from the kitchen, annoyed by the disruption to her daily routine. Hunched over the tables, for the most part glowering and surly sat the regular Old Groar customers. Jantiff looked this way and that, entranced by the wonder of this miraculous faculty which he thought that he had previously exploited to the fullest. He studied the umber-black shadows at the back of the room, the sheen of pewter mugs, the sallow milkwood tables, the shafts of pale lavender light streaming down through the high windows. Jantiff thought: *In later years, when I look across my life, I will mark well this moment in the Old Groar Tavern at Balad on the planet Wyst* . . . A shuffle of activity distracted Jantiff from his musing. Ryl Shermatz sauntered to the door. Jantiff, hauling himself erect, threw back his shoulders and in unconscious imitation of Shermatz's confident stride, went to the door.

A crowd had gathered before the Old Groar: the entire population of Balad, except for Madame Tchaga, who stood peering from the Cimmery. Along the street came Sabrose and Garfred, with Eubanq between them and Osculot bringing up the rear. Eubanq wore his fawn-colored suit, and today a hat with a jaunty pointed bill. His expression, however, was not at all jaunty. His cheeks sagged, his mouth hung in a lugubrious droop. Before Jantiff's inner vision came a remembered illustration from a story-book, depicting a worried brown rat being brought before a tribunal of stately cats by a pair of bulldog sergeants.

After a single glance, Shermatz turned away from Eubanq and spoke to the crowd. "I am Ryl Shermatz, the Connatic's agent, and I am here at Balad in an official capacity.

"The Connatic's policy is to allow all possible independence of thought and action. He welcomes diversity and rules with restraint.

"Nonetheless, he cannot tolerate a disregard for basic law. Such occurs here at Balad. I refer to the persecution of certain forest wanderers, whom you miscall witches. It now must terminate by the Connatic's edict. The ailment known as 'the yellows' results from a fungus-like growth; it can be cured by a pill taken with water. The so-called 'witches' are deaf-mute not because of 'the yellows' but through a hysterical obsession. Organically they are quite normal, and sometimes, under stress of emergency, they can force themselves to speak. As for hearing, my advisers tell me that sound enters their brain at a subliminal level; they do not know they are hearing, but nevertheless are invested with information, much as telepathy affects the mind of an ordinary person.

"Conditions at Balad are unsatisfactory. The Grand Knight seems to act as an informal magistrate and dispenses such justice as he sees fit through his constable. On other occasions, as when unforgivable violence was done to the person of Jantiff Ravensroke, the community is guided by irresponsible fury.

"A cursar will presently arrive to arrange a more orderly system. He will right certain wrongs, and certain persons will regret his coming; especially those who have taken part in the recent witch-chasing. They may expect severe penalties. At the moment I intend to deal only with the assault performed upon Jantiff. Constable Sabrose, bring forward the woman who blinded Jantiff."

"It was Nellick, yonder."

"Your Lordship, I acted not from malice; indeed, I thought I held simple and wholesome water in my bucket. I am a laughing woman; I acted in fun and only to ease the situation for the general benefit."

"Jantiff, does this match your recollection?"

"No. She said, 'Here, turn his face about; he will never see the results of his mischief, even though I waste my frack.' "

"Well then: which version is correct? Constable?"

Sabrose grunted. "I don't like to say. I was holding Jantiff when she flung the stuff. It burnt my arms as well."

Jantiff grimaced. "Don't bother with any of them; there were twenty or thirty people, all doing me harm. Except Grandel the apothecary, who wiped my eyes."

"Very well. Grandel, I instruct you to make a careful list of those people who participated in the episode, and to fine them in proportion to their guilt. The sum collected must be paid over to Jantiff. I suggest a fine of five hundred ozols for the woman Nellick."

Grandel looked uncomfortably around the crowd. "I will do my best, though my popularity will not be enhanced."

Fariske called out: "Not so! I took no part in the assault, even though Jantiff sold percebs in competition with me. I believe that stern fines are necessary to redeem the honor of Balad! I will help Grandel discover each name and I will counsel him against leniency. If Grandel suffers unpopularity, I will join him!"

"Then I will entrust the matter to the two of you. Now, another matter. Your name is Eubanq?"

Eubanq nodded and smiled. "Sir, that is my name."

"It is your entire name?"

Eubanq hesitated only the fraction of an instant. "Eubanq is the name by which I am known."

"Where is your place of birth?"

"Sir, as to that I cannot be sure. I was orphaned as a child."

"That is a tragic circumstance. Where were you reared?"

"I have visited many worlds, sir. I call no place home."

"The Connatic's cursar, when he arrives, will examine your background with great care. At this moment I will only concern myself with events of the recent past. First, I believe that you cashed in Jantiff's passage voucher and pocketed the money."

Eubanq considered a moment, then, no doubt reflecting that the matter was susceptible to quick verification, one way or the other, he gave a slow polite nod. "I felt sure that Jantiff would never use the ticket, and I saw no need to waste the money."

"Then, when you learned that Jantiff indeed had earned the fare, you stole his money from him?"

"Do you assert this, sir, or is it the Connatic's justice that a man must incriminate himself from his own mouth?"

"That is a clever reply," said Shermatz graciously. "But the matter is not quite so intricate. Jantiff's information makes it clear that you are the robber beyond all reasonable doubt. My question gave you the opportunity for denial. Secondly, it is clear that you informed Booch in regard to the forest waif whom Jantiff had befriended, in full knowledge of what must occur, your motive being to destroy Jantiff. The cursar will undertake an investigation. If you deny the charges, you will undergo mind-search and the truth will be made known. In the meantime, your possessions are totally confiscated. You are now a pauper, lacking so much as a single dinket."

Eubanq's jaw dropped; his eyes became moist. In a voice musical in its poignancy he cried: "This is most unreasonable! Will you sequester all my poor savings?"

"I suspect that you will fare even worse. I believe that you provoked Booch to assault and murder. If this is so demonstrated the cursar will show you no leniency."

"Take me to Lulace! The Grand Knight will prove my good character!"

"The Grand Knight is no longer at Lulace. He and his guests departed last night. In any event, he is not a trustworthy guarantor; his troubles may exceed your own." Shermatz signaled Garfred and Osculot. "Take Eubanq to a place of security. Make certain that he cannot escape. If he does so, you will each be fined one thousand ozols."

"Smartly then, Eubanq," said Osculot. "We will take you to my root cellar, and if you escape, I will pay both fines."

"One moment!" Jantiff confronted Eubanq. "What happened to Glisten? Tell me if you know!"

Eubanq's expression was opaque. "Why ask me? Put your questions to Booch."

"Booch answers no questions; he is dead."

Eubanq turned away without comment. The two constables marched him up the street and out of sight.

Ryl Shermatz once more addressed the people of the town. "The new cursar will arrive within three days. Remember: he represents the Connatic and he must be obeyed! You may now go about your affairs. Jantiff, come along. We have no further need to remain at Balad."

"But what of Glisten? I can't leave until I know what has happened!"

"Jantiff, let us face the sad facts. Either she is dead or she has returned to the forest. In either case she is beyond our reach."

"Then who was the woman who notified you of my trouble?"

"This is another affair which the cursar must look into. But let us be off to Arrabus. There is nothing more to be accomplished here."

CHAPTER 16

In a black space-car the two men rode north from Balad: over the gloomy Sych, across Lake Neman and the Weirdlands beyond.

Jantiff sat brooding and made no effort at conversation. Ryl Shermatz finally said: "I suspect that you are still disturbed by recent events—understandably so. Unfortunately, by the very nature of my position I can achieve only an approximate justice. The witch-killing farmers, for instance: are they not murderers? Why are they not punished? Truthfully, I am less interested in punishment than setting things to rights. I make one or two dramatic examples, hoping to frighten all the others into regeneracy. The method works unevenly. Often the most iniquitous are the least inconvenienced. On the other hand an absolutely exact justice may well destroy the community; this might have been the case at Balad. By and large, I am satisfied."

Jantiff said nothing.

Ryl Shermatz continued: "In any event we must now turn our attention to Arrabus and the Whispers. Their conduct puzzles me. Do they intend to live in isolation? If they attend the Centenary fête, or speak before a television audience, their identity must instantly become evident to their old intimates: all those residents of Old Pink, for example."

"They probably rely upon the close similarity," said Jantiff. "When no one suspects, no one notices."

Ryl Shermatz remained dubious. "I can't believe that the similarities are that close. Perhaps they plan cosmetic devices or facial surgery: in fact this may already have occurred."

"At Lulace they were the same as ever."

"And this is the great puzzle! Clearly they are not fools. They must recognize obvious dangers, and they must have prepared for them. I am amazed and fascinated; there is grandeur to their scheme."

Jantiff put a diffident question: "How will you deal with them?"

"Two options, at least, are open. We can denounce them publicly and create an enormous sensation, or we can secretly dispose of the whole affair, and presently nominate a new set of Whispers. I am inclined to the first concept. The Arrabins will enjoy the drama—and why should we not give pleasure to these essentially decent, if indolent, folk?"

"And how will this drama be managed?"

"No difficulty whatever; in fact the event has already been arranged, and by the Whispers themselves. At a Grand Rally they intend to address a select group of notables, while all the rest of Arrabus watches by television. This is an appropriate time to set matters right."

Jantiff mulled over the situation. "They will speak as before from the Pedestal, remote and obscure so that no one can recognize them, and no cameras will be allowed close views."

"I expect that you are right," said Ryl Shermatz. "At the denouement they will be seen clearly enough."

The space-car crossed over the scarp, and Uncibal lay sprawled before them, with the Salaman Sea beyond, flat and listless, the color of moonstone. Ryl Shermatz veered toward the space-port and landed close beside the depot.

"Tonight we will rest at the Travelers Inn," said Shermatz. "As an elitist monument, it has suffered decay; still we can do no better, and you will no doubt prefer it to your lair behind the privy."

"I intend to revisit this lair, for old time's sake," said Jantiff. "My hut on the beach was actually not much better . . . Still, it felt like home. As I think back, I was happy there. I had food; I had Glisten to look at; I had goals, impractical though they might have been, and for a time I thought I was realizing them. Yes! I was truly alive!"

"And now?"

"I am old and dull and tired."

Shermatz laughed. "I have felt the same way many times. Life goes on, despite all."

"I find life to be a very peculiar affair."

At the Travelers Inn Shermatz bespoke a suite of six rooms, specifying a high standard of cuisine and service.

Jantiff grumbled that his expectations were not likely to be realized in view of the Arrabin attitude.

"We shall see," said Ryl Shermatz. "As a rule I make few demands, but here, at the Travelers Inn, for non-egalistic prices I insist upon non-egalistic value. Unlike the ordinary traveler, I can instantly avenge sloth, slights and poor service. It is a perquisite of my job. I think that you will notice a distinct improvement over your previous visit. Now I have a few trifles of business, and I will leave you to your own devices."

Jantiff went to his rooms, where, as Shermatz had predicted, he discovered remarkably better conditions. He reveled in a hot bath, donned fresh garments and dined upon the most elaborate repast available. Then, bone-weary but not yet ready for sleep, he wandered out into the city and rode the man-ways as he had done so often in the past. Perhaps by unconscious design he passed Old Pink. After a moment's indecision he stepped off the way, crossed the yard and entered the foyer. The air hung heavy with familiar old odors, compounded of gruff, deedle, wobbly and swill; the sourness of old concrete; the condensed exhalations of all those who across the years had called Old Pink home.

Recollections swept over Jantiff: events, adventures, emotions, faces. He went to the administration desk, where a man, strange to him, sat sorting slips of paper.

Jantiff asked: "Does Skorlet still occupy Apartment D18, on the Nineteenth level?"

The clerk spun an index, glanced at a name. "No longer. She's transferred out to Propunce."

Jantiff turned to the bulletin board. A large placard composed in an eye-catching yellow, white, blue and black read:

In regard to the
GRAND RALLY:
Hail, all, to our second century! May it exceed the grandeur of the first!

The Centenary celebrates our confident advocacy of egalism. From the ends of the Cluster pour congratulations, sometimes couched in candid admiration, sometimes through the tight teeth of bombahs biting back dismay.

On Onasday next: the Grand Rally! at the Field of Voices the Panel of Delegates and many other notables will gather to partake of a ceremonial banquet and to hear the Whispers propose startling new concepts for the future.

The Connatic of Alastor Cluster will definitely be on hand, to share the Pedestal with the Whispers, in comradeship and egality. He is at this moment consulting with the Whispers and hearing their wise counsel. At the Grand Rally he will reveal his program for an augmented interchange of goods and services. He believes that Arrabins should export ideas, artistic creations and imaginative concepts in exchange for goods, foodstuffs, and automatic processing devices. At the Grand Rally, Onasday, on the Field of Voices, he and the Whispers will make concrete the details of this proposal.

Only persons with entry permits will be admitted to the Field. All others will participate at this epochal occasion by television in the social halls on their apartment levels.

Jantiff reread the placard a second and a third time. Odd and wonderful! He stood pondering the garish type. At the back of his mind milled fragments of information, small disparate ideas, echoes of half-remembered conversations: all jumbled like the elements of a puzzle shaken in a box.

Jantiff turned away from the placard and departed Old Pink. He rode out Lateral 112 to Uncibal River and diverted into the human flood. For once, with nervous guesses and suspicious conjectures whirling through his head, Jantiff ignored the panorama of faces; as blank and withdrawn as any of the others, he returned to the Travelers Inn.

Back in his rooms, he discovered that a supper had been laid out on the parlor buffet. Jantiff poured out a goblet of wine and took it to a settee. The window overlooked a corner of the space-field and, beyond, the dancing lights of Disjerferact. Jantiff watched with a smile half-bitter, half-wistful. Would he ever be able to escape his recollections? Vividly now they passed before his inner mind: the House of Prisms; Kedidah's haunted countenance. The flavor of toasted kelp and poggets. The squeaking fifes, the tinkle of pilgrim bells, the calls and importunities, the whirling lights and park fountains . . . Ryl Shermatz emerged from his chambers.

"Aha, Jantiff, you have returned in good time. Have you noticed this array of bonter?"

"Yes. I am amazed. I had no idea that so many good things were available."

"Tonight we are bombahs for sure! I see wines from four different worlds, a noble assortment of meats, pastas, rissoles, salads, cheeses, and all manner of miscellaneous confections. A far more elaborate meal than is my usual habit, I assure you! But tonight let us revel in the ignobility of it all!"

Jantiff served himself such items as met his fancy, and joined Ryl Shermatz at the table. "An hour ago I visited Old Pink, the block where I once lived. In the lobby I saw an amazing placard. It advertised that the Connatic will definitely appear at the Grand Rally, to endorse the Whispers and all their programs."

"I saw a similar placard," said Ryl Shermatz. "I can assert even more definitely that the Connatic plans nothing of the sort."

"In that case I am relieved, but how can the Whispers make such promises? When the Connatic fails to appear, they will be left with lame excuses by the mouthful, and no one will be deceived."

"I have become fascinated by the Grand Rally," said Ryl Shermatz. "Half a dozen courtesy tickets were left at Alastor Centrality. I availed myself of two; we shall not fail to witness this remarkable occasion."

"I am absolutely bewildered," said Jantiff. "The Whispers must know that the Connatic will not appear; it follows, therefore, that they have contrived a plan to cope with this contingency."

"Admirably put, Jantiff! That is the situation in a nutshell, and I admit to curiosity. Might they go so far as to put forward a purported Connatic, to speak as they might wish the real Connatic to speak?"

"It is well within their audacity. But how could they hope to gain? When the news arrived at Lusz, the Connatic could not fail to be annoyed."

"Exactly so! The Connatic is always amused by verve and sometimes by brashness; still he would be forced to take harsh and definite action. Well, on Onasday the event will be revealed, and we will watch carefully before we put our own program into effect."

Jantiff made a cautious observation: "You persist in using the words 'we' and 'our,' but I must admit that I am confused as to the details of our program."

Ryl Shermatz chuckled. "Our plan is simple. The Whispers appear on the Pedestal. They make their address to the notables, and by television to all the other Arrabins. A purported Connatic may appear on the Pedestal; if not, the Whispers may repair the lack by methods yet unknown, and we will watch with interest. Then, at an appropriate moment, four Whelm corvettes of the *Amaraz* class drop from the sky. They maneuver close to the Pedestal and officers jump across. They place the Whispers under arrest. The cursar now appears. He explains to all Arrabus the crimes perpetrated by the Whispers. He reveals that Arrabus is bankrupt, and he makes a rather harsh announcement to the effect that the Arrabins must awake from their century-long trance and return to work. He announces that he is assuming authority as interim governor, until a proper set of local officials once more assume responsibility.

"The four corvettes then rise to an elevation of a thousand feet, each trailing a long line with a noose at the end. A noose is fitted about the neck of each Whisper; the corvettes rise once more until they and the suspended Whispers are out of sight in the upper atmosphere. The program is crisp, decisive, and sufficiently spectacular to command attention." Ryl Shermatz glanced sideways at Jantiff. "You take exception to the plan?"

"Not at all. I am uneasy, for a reason I find hard to define."

Shermatz rose to his feet and went to look out across Disjerferact. "The plan is too forthright, perhaps?"

"There is nothing wrong with the plan. I wonder only why the Whispers seem so confident. What do they know that we do not?"

"That is a provocative concept," said Shermatz. He mused a moment. "Short of asking the Whispers, I can't see how to arrive at an explanation."

"I will try to put my ideas in an orderly sequence," said Jantiff. "Perhaps something will occur to me."

"You have infected me with your uneasiness," Shermatz grumbled. "Well—there is tonight and tomorrow for conjecture. On the day after: the Grand Rally, and then we must act."

CHAPTER 17

The night passed by, and Dwan rose pale as a frozen tear into the sky. The day ran its course. Jantiff remained at the suite in the Travelers Inn. For a time he paced the parlor back and forth, trying to define his qualms, but the thoughts fled past before he could analyze them. He seated himself with paper and stylus and found no better success; his mind persisted in wandering. He thought of the early days at Old Pink, his dismal romance with Kedidah, the bonterfest, his subsequent flight to Balad . . . The flow of his thoughts suddenly became viscous and slowed to a halt. For a moment Jantiff thought of nothing whatever; then, with great caution, as if opening a door from behind which something awful might leap, he reconsidered his flight across the Weirdlands, and his association with Swarkop.

Jantiff presently relaxed, indecisively, into the settee. Swarkop's conversation had been suggestive but no more. He would mention the matter and Shermatz could make of it what he chose.

During the afternoon, bored and uneasy, he walked across the mud flats to Disjerferact, and as he had promised himself, made a pilgrimage to his old lair behind the privy, and for old time's sake bought a spill of fried kelp, which he ate dutifully but without enthusiasm. There had once been a time, he reflected sadly, when he could not get enough of this rather insipid delicacy.

At sundown Jantiff returned to the Travelers Inn. Ryl Shermatz had not returned. Jantiff ate a pensive supper, then went to his rooms.

In the morning he awoke to find that Ryl Shermatz had come and gone, leaving a note on the parlor table.

For the notice of Jantiff Ravensroke:
    A good morning to you, Jantiff! Today we resolve all mysteries and bring our drama to its climax and then its close. Details press upon me; I have gone off unavoidably early to brief the cursar, and so will be unable to take breakfast with you. Please allow me to issue instructions in regard to the Grand Rally. I have our two tickets and will meet you to the right of Hanwalter Gate, where the Fourteenth Lateral terminates, at half-morning, or as close thereafter as possible. This is not as early as I had hoped; still we shall no doubt find positions of advantage. Take breakfast with a good appetite! I will see you at half-morning.

                                                                    Shermatz

Jantiff frowned and put the note aside. He went to the window where he could see people already arriving upon the Field of Voices, hastening to take up places as close as possible to the Pedestal. Turning away, he went to the buffet, served himself breakfast, which he ate without appetite.

The time was still early; nevertheless he threw a cape over his shoulders and departed the inn. He walked to Uncibal River, rode a half-mile, diverted upon the Fourteenth Lateral, which discharged him directly before Hanwalter Gate: a three-wicket passage through a tall fence of supple louvres. Half-morning was yet an hour off; Jantiff was not surprised to find Shermatz nowhere on the scene. He stationed himself at the stipulated place to the right of the gate, and stood watching the arrival of the "notables" who had been invited to the Field to hear the Whispers and the Connatic at first hand, and to partake of the festive banquet. An odd assortment of "notables," thought Jantiff. They were persons of all ages and types. Presently he noticed a man whom he thought to recognize; their eyes met and the man halted to exchange greetings: "Aren't you Jantiff Ravensroke from Old Pink? With Skorlet?"

"Precisely right. And you are Olin, Esteban's friend. I forget your block exactly: wasn't it Fodswollow?"

Olin made a wry grimace. "Not for months. I transferred to Winkler's Hovel out along Lateral 560, and I must say I'm pleased with the change. Why don't you move out from Old Pink? We could use someone like you, clever with his hands!"

Jantiff said in a noncommittal voice: "I'll have to call on you one of these days."

"By all means! It's often been remarked how a block stamps its nature on those who live there. Old Pink, for instance, seems so intense, always seething with intrigue. At the Hovel we're a raffish hell-for-leather crew, I assure you! The garden simply vibrates! I've never seen such a flow of swill! It's a miracle that we survive starvation, with the wump all going into jugs."

"Old Pink is somber in comparison," said Jantiff. "And, as you say, the intrigues are extraordinary. Speaking of intrigues, have you seen Esteban lately?"

"Not for a month or more. He's involved in some scheme or other that takes up all his time. An energetic fellow, Esteban! He never fails the game."

"Yes, he's quite a chap!" Jantiff agreed. "But how is it that you're invited to the Field? Are you a notable?"

"Hardly! You know me better than that! The invitation came as quite a surprise! Not an unpleasant one, of course, if there's a banquet of bonter at the other end of it. Still, I can't help but wonder whose invitation I've been tendered by mistake. But what of you? Surely you're not a notable?"

"No more than you. We both know Esteban; that's the only notable thing about us."

Olin laughed. "If that's what brings us bonter, all glory to Esteban! I'll be going on in; I want to place myself as close to the tables as possible. Are you coming?"

"I must wait for a friend."

"A pleasure seeing you again! Come visit Winkler's Hovel!"

"Yes indeed," said Jantiff in a pensive voice. "As soon as possible."

Olin presented his ticket and was admitted to the field. In Jantiff's mind the pieces of the puzzle had dropped together to form a unit, of startling proportions. Surely a flaw marred the pattern? But where? Jantiff thought first one way, then another. The concept stood unchallenged, noble in its simplicity and grandeur.

Half-morning approached: where was Ryl Shermatz? The "notables" poured onto the field by the hundreds! Jantiff scanned their faces with furious intensity. Would Shermatz never arrive?

The time became half-morning. Jantiff glared into the oncoming faces, trying to evoke the presence of Shermatz by sheer force of will.

To no avail. Jantiff began to feel listless. Peering over his shoulder through the louvres, he saw that the Field had become crowded: there were "notables" from everywhere in Arrabus. "Notables" and persons like Olin! But no one from Old Pink! The idea froze his thoughts; they began again only sluggishly. Was this the flaw in the pattern? Perhaps. Again, perhaps not.

A fanfare sounded across the field, then the Arrabus anthem. The ceremonies had begun. A few hurrying latecomers jumped off the lateral to push through the gates. Still no Shermatz!

The field megaphones broadcast a great voice: "Notables of Arrabus! Egalists across all our nation! The Whispers give you greetings! They will shortly arrive on the Pedestal to communicate their remarkable plans, despite furious efforts by the forces of reaction! Hear this, folk of Arrabus, and remember! The Whispers are disputed by enemies to egalism, and events will demonstrate the evil scope of the opposition! But be of brave heart! Our path leads to—"

Jantiff ran forward, as Shermatz stepped from the man-way. Shermatz called out: "My apologies, Jantiff! I could not avoid the delay. But we are still in time. Come along; here is your ticket."

Jantiff's tongue felt numb; he could only stammer disconnected phrases. "No, no! Come back! No time remains!" He took Shermatz's arm to halt his motion toward the gate. Shermatz turned on him a look of surprise. Jantiff blurted: "We can't stay here; there's nothing we can do now. Come, we've got to leave!"

Shermatz hesitated only an instant. "Very well; where do you want to go?"

"Your space-car is yonder, by the depot. Take us up, away from Uncibal."

"Just as you say, but can't you explain?"

"Yes, as we go!" Jantiff set off at a run, throwing bits of sentences over his shoulder. Shermatz, jogging alongside became grim. "Yes; logical . . . Even probable . . . We can't take the chance that you're wrong . . . "

They boarded the space-car; Uncibal fell away below: row after row of many-colored blocks receding into the haze. To the side spread the Field, dark with the "notables" of Arrabus. Shermatz touched the telescreen controls; the voice spoke "—delay of only a few minutes; the Whispers are on their way. They will tell you how bitterly our enemies resent the success of egalism! They will name names and cite facts! . . . The Whispers are still delayed; they should be on the Pedestal now. Patience for another minute or two!"

"If the Whispers appear on the Pedestal I am wrong," said Jantiff.

"Intuitively I accept your conclusion," said Shermatz. "But I am still confused by your facts. You mentioned a certain Swarkop and his cargoes, and also a person named Olin. How do they interrelate? Where do you start your chain of logic?"

"With an idea we have discussed before. The authentic Whispers were known to many folk; the new Whispers as well. There is a strong similarity between the two groups, but not an identity. The new Whispers must minimize the risk of recognition and exposure.

"Olin came to the Field; someone sent him a ticket. Who? He is a friend of Esteban, but hardly a notable. There are legitimate notables present: the Delegates, for instance. They are well acquainted with the old Whispers. I imagine that all Esteban's acquaintances are at the Field, and all those of Skorlet and of Sarp: all received tickets, and all wondered why they were considered 'notable.' I saw no one from Old Pink, but they would arrive by a different lateral. Again, six tickets were sent to Alastor Agency. Assume that the Connatic was visiting Arrabus. His curiosity might well be piqued by the placards. He certainly would not have joined the Whispers on the Pedestal, but he very likely would have used one of the tickets."

Shermatz gave a curt nod. "I am happily able to assure you that the Connatic definitely did not use one of these tickets. So now, what of Swarkop?"

"He is a barge operator who carried six cargoes of frack . . ." Jantiff had the odd sensation that his words triggered the event. Below them the landscape erupted. The Field became an instant seethe of white flame, then disappeared under a roiling cloud of gray dust. Other blurts of white flame with subsequent billows of dust appeared elsewhere across Uncibal. The craters they left behind marked the sites of Old Pink and six other blocks, the Travelers Inn and Alastor Centrality. In the cities Waunisse, Serce, and Propunce, thirteen other blocks, each with its full complement of occupants, in like fashion became columns of dust and hot vapor.

"I was right," said Jantiff. "Very much too right."

Shermatz slowly reached out and touched a button. "Corchione."

"Here, sir."

"The program is canceled. Call down hospital ships."

"Very well, sir."

Jantiff spoke in a dreary voice: "I should have understood the facts sooner."

"You understood in time to save my life," said Shermatz. "I am pleased on this account." He looked down across Uncibal, where the dust was drifting slowly south. "The plan now becomes clear. Three classes of people were to be eliminated: persons who knew the old Whispers, persons who knew the new Whispers, and a rather smaller group, consisting either of the Connatic or the Connatic's representative, should either be on hand. But you survived and I survived and the plan has failed.

"The Whispers will not know of the failure. They will consider themselves secure, and they will be preparing the next stage of their plan. Can you guess how this will be implemented?"

Jantiff made a weary gesture. "No. I am numb."

"Scapegoats are needed: the enemies of egalism. Who on Wyst is still acquainted with one of the Whispers?"

"The Contractors. They know Shubart."

"Exactly. Within hours all contractors will be arrested. The Whispers will announce that the criminals have made abject confessions, and that justice has been done. All future contracting will be managed by a new egalistic organization, at improved efficiency; and the Whispers will share the wealth of Arrabus between them. Any moment now we can expect their first indignant outcries." Shermatz fell silent; the two sat looking across battered Uncibal. A chime sounded. On the screen appeared the four Whispers: Skorlet, Sarp, Esteban and Shubart, their images blurred as if seen through wavering water.

"They still are afraid to exhibit themselves in all clarity," Shermatz observed. "Not too many people survive who might recognize them but there are probably a few. In the next week or so they would no doubt disappear. Quietly, mysteriously: who would be troubled or wonder why?"

Esteban stepped forward a half-pace and spoke, his voice ringing with dull passion: "Folk of Arrabus! By the chance of a few minutes' delay, your Whispers have survived the cataclysm. The Connatic hopefully has also escaped; he never arrived at the stipulated place of rendezvous, and we as yet have no sure knowledge. Unless he went incognito out upon the Field, he escaped, and the assassins failed in double measure! We are not yet able to make a coherent statement; all of us are grief-stricken by the loss of so many cherished comrades. Be assured, however, the demons who planned this frightful deed will never survive—"

Shermatz touched a button. "Corchione."

"Here, sir."

"Trace the source of the message."

"I am so doing, sir."

"—a day of sorrow and shock! The Delegates are gone, all gone; by the caprice of Fate we ourselves escaped, but by sheerest accident! Our enemies will not be pleased: be sure that we will hunt them down! That is all for now; we must attend to acts of mercy." The screen went dead.

"Corchione?"

"The transmission originated from Uncibal Central. We could not fix upon the feed-in."

"Seal off the space-port. Allow no egress from the planet."

"Yes, sir."

"Send a team down to Uncibal Central; determine the source of the transmission. Notify me at once."

"Yes, sir."

"Monitor all air traffic. If anyone is moving, discover his destination."

"Yes, sir."

Shermatz leaned back in his seat. He spoke to Jantiff: "After today your life may seem pallid and uneventful."

"I won't complain as to that."

"I am alive only through your common sense, of which I myself showed a dismal lack."

"I wish this 'common sense' had come to life sooner."

"Be that as it may. The past is fixed, and the dead are dead. I am alive and thankful for the fact. In reference to the future, may I inquire your goals?"

"I want to repair my vision. It is starting to blur. Then I will go back to Balad and try to learn what happened to Glisten."

Shermatz gave his head a sad shake. "If she is dead, you'll search in vain. If she is alive, how will you find her in the Weirdland forests? I have facilities for such a search; leave the matter in my hands."

"Just as you say."

Shermatz turned back to his control panel. "Corchione."

"Sir?"

"Order the *Isirjir Ziaspraide* down to Uncibal Spaceport, and also a pair of patrol cruisers. The *Tressian* and the *Sheer* are both at hand."

"Very good, sir."

Shermatz said to Jantiff: "In times of uncertainty, it is wise to display symbols of security. The *Isirjir Ziaspraide* admirably suits this purpose."

"How will you deal with the Whispers?"

"I can't quite make up my mind. What would you suggest?"

Jantiff shook his head in perplexity. "They have committed awful deeds. No penalty seems appropriate. Merely to kill them is an anticlimax."

"Exactly! The drama of retribution should at least equal that of the crime: in this case an impossible undertaking. Still something must be contrived. Jantiff, put your fecund mind to work!"

"I am not skilled at inventing punishments."

"Nor are they to my taste. I enjoy creating conditions of justice. All too often, however, I must ordain harsh penalties. It is the disagreeable side to my work. The preferences of the criminal, of course, can't be considered; as often as not, he will opt for leniency or even no punishment whatever."

A chime sounded. Shermatz touched a button; Corchione spoke.

"The transmission originated at a lodge owned by Contractor Shubart, on the upper slopes of Mount Prospect, eighteen miles south of Uncibal."

"Send out an assault force; seize the Whispers and bring them to the *Ziaspraide*."

"At once, sir."

CHAPTER 18

The *Isirjir Ziaspraide*, flagship of the Thaiatic* Fleet, and a vessel of awesome magnitude, served less as a weapon of war than as an instrument of policy. Wherever the *Isirjir Ziaspraide* showed itself, the majesty of the Connatic and the force of the Whelm were manifest.

The great hull, with its various sponsons, catwalks and rotundas, had long been regarded as a masterpiece of the naaetic† art. The interior was no less splendid, with a main saloon a hundred feet long and thirty-seven feet wide. From the ceiling, which was enameled a warm lavender-mauve, hung five scintillants. The floor, of a dead-black substance, lacked all luster. Around the periphery white pilasters supported massive silver medallions; depictions of the twenty-three goddesses, clothed in vestments of purple, green and blue, occupied the spaces between. Jantiff, upon entering the saloon, studied the intricacy of these designs with wondering envy; here were subtle skills, of draftsmanship and understated color, beyond his present capacity. Sixty officers of the Whelm, wearing white, black and purple dress uniforms, followed him into the saloon. They ranged themselves along the walls to either side and stood in silence.

A far sound broke the silence: a drum roll, and another, and another, in fateful slow cadence. The sound grew loud. Into the hall marched the drummer, somberly costumed after the ancient tradition, with a black mask across the upper half of his face. Behind came the Whispers, each accom-

---

*From Thaia, one of the twenty-three goddesses.

†From *naae*: a set of aesthetic formulae peculiar to the Space Ages; that critique concerned with the awe, beauty, and grandeur associated with spaceships. Such terms are largely untranslatable into antecedent languages.

panied by a masked escort: first Esteban and Sarp, then Skorlet and Shubart. Their faces were bleak; their eyes glistened with emotion.

The drummer led the way to the end of the hall. He ceased drumming and stepped aside. The ensuing silence tingled with imminence.

The Commander of the *Isirjir Ziaspraide* stepped out upon a raised platform, and seated himself behind a table. He addressed the Whispers: "By the authority of the Connatic, I fix upon you the guilt of multiple murders, in yet unknown number."

Sarp clenched his fingers together; the others stood rigid. Esteban spoke out in a brassy voice: "One murder, many murders: what is the difference? The crime is not multiplied."

"The point is of no consequence. The Connatic admits himself in a quandary. He feels that in regard to your case, death is an almost trivial disposition. Nevertheless, after taking advice, he has issued the following decree. You shall immediately be housed in spheres of transparent glass twenty feet above the Field of Voices. The spheres shall be twenty feet in diameter, and furnished with a minimum of facilities. One week hence, after your crimes have been elucidated in full detail to all Arrabus, you shall be taken into a vehicle. At the hour of midnight this vehicle will rise to an altitude of seven hundred and seventy-seven miles and there explode with a spectacular effulgence of light. Arrabus will thereby be notified that your deeds have been expiated. That is to be your fate. Take your farewells of each other; you will meet again but only briefly, one week hence."

The Commander rose to his feet and departed the hall. The four stood stiffly, showing no desire to exchange sentiments of any sort whatever.

The drummer stepped forward, and ruffled his drums; again, again, at a portentous tempo. The escorts led the four back down the length of the hall. Esteban's eyes darted this way and that, as if he intended a desperate act; the escort at his elbow paid no heed. Esteban's gaze suddenly became fixed. His head thrust forward; he stopped short and pointed a finger. "There stands Jantiff! Our black demon! We have him to thank for our fate!"

Skorlet, Sarp and Shubart turned to look; their gazes struck into Jantiff's face. He stood coldly watching.

The escorts touched the arms of their charges; the group moved on, at the tempo of the drum roll.

Jantiff turned away, to find Shermatz at his side.

"Events have run their course, so far as you and I are concerned," said Shermatz. "Come; the Commander has assigned us comfortable quarters, and for a period we can relax without startlements or dismal duties."

An ascensor lifted them to a high rotunda. Entering, Jantiff stopped short, taken aback by opulence on a scale which exceeded all his previous concepts. Shermatz could not restrain a laugh; he took Jantiff's arm and led him forward. "The appointments are perhaps a trifle grand," said Shermatz, "but, adaptable as you are, you will quickly find them comfortable. The view, especially when the *Ziaspraide* coasts quietly among the stars, is superb."

The two seated themselves on couches upholstered in purple velvet. A mess boy, stepping from an alcove, proffered a tray from which Jantiff took a goblet carved from a single topaz crystal. He tasted the wine, looked deep into the swimming depths, tasted again. "This is very good wine indeed."

Shermatz took a goblet of the same vintage. "This is the Trille Aegis. As you see, we who labor in the Connatic's service enjoy perquisites as well as hardships. On the whole it is not a bad life; sometimes pleasant, sometimes frightening, but never monotonous."

"At the moment I would enjoy a certain level of monotony," said Jantiff. "I feel almost inanimate. There is still a single matter which gnaws at my mind: probably something which is futile to think about. Still . . ." He fell silent.

Shermatz reflected a moment. "I have made certain arrangements. Tomorrow your eyes will be repaired; you will see better than ever. In about a week's time the *Ziaspraide* leaves Wyst, and will cruise down the Fayarion. Zeck is not far to the side, and so you shall be delivered to your very doorstep. In fact, we will have the *Ziaspraide* hover over Frayness and send you down in the gig."

"That is hardly necessary," mumbled Jantiff.

"Perhaps not, but you are spared the inconvenience of finding your own way home from the space-port. So shall it be done. Along the way of course you will use these chambers."

"What of yourself? Why not come visit me at our house in Tanglewillow Glen? My family will make you most welcome and you would very much enjoy our houseboat, especially when we moor it among the reeds on the Shard Sea."

"The prospect is appealing," said Shermatz. "But to my vast distaste I must remain at Uncibal, and help put together a new Arrabin government. I expect that the cursars, in all discretion, will manage Arrabus perhaps for decades, until the Arrabins regain their morale. They are now confirmed city-dwellers, and generally indecisive. Each person is isolated; among the multitudes he is alone. Detached from reality he thinks in abstract terms; he thrills to vicarious emotions. To ease his primal urges he contrives a sad identification with his apartment block. He deserves better than this; so does anyone. The blocks of Arrabus will come down, and the folk will go north and south to reclaim the Weirdlands and again they will become competent individuals."

Jantiff drank from his goblet. "I remember the farmers of Blale: famous witch-chasers all."

Shermatz laughed. "Jantiff, you are unkind! You would have these poor folk moving from one extreme to the other! Are there no farmers on Zeck? Surely they are not witch-chasers!"

"That's true. Still, Wyst is quite a different world."

"Precisely so, and these concepts must be carefully weighed when one works in the service of the Connatic. Does such a career attract your interest? Don't tell me 'yes' or 'no' at this instant; take time to collect your thoughts. A message sent to my name in care of the Connatic at Lusz will always be delivered."

Jantiff found difficulty in expressing himself. "I very much appreciate your kind interest."

"Nothing of the sort, Jantiff; the thanks are on my side. Were it not for you, I would be part of the atmospheric dust."

"Were it not for you, I would be blind and dead on the beach beside the Moaning Ocean."

"Well then! We have traded good deeds, and this is the stuff of friendship. So now, your immediate future is arranged. Tomorrow the opthalmologists will repair your eyes. Shortly thereafter you depart for home. As for the other matter which preys on your mind, I have a dreary suspicion that all is finished, and that you must turn your mind away."

Jantiff said: "Quite candidly, I still feel impelled to go south and search the Sych. If Glisten is dead: well then, she is dead. If she escaped Booch and still lives, then she is wandering alone in the forest, a poor lost little waif."

"I half expected such an intention on your part," said Shermatz. "Now I see that I must reveal a plan which I kept secret for fear of arousing your hopes. Today I am sending a team of experienced trackers south. They will probe all circumstances and make a definite determination one way or another. Will this satisfy you?"

"Yes, of course. I am more than grateful."

CHAPTER 19

The *Isirjin Ziaspraide* hovered over Frayness, and while all came out to watch, a gig descended into Tanglewillow Glen and delivered Jantiff to his front door.

"Jantiff, what does all this mean?" gasped his father.

"Not a great deal," said Jantiff. "I may go into the Connatic's service, and on this account was accorded the courtesy of transportation to my home. But I will tell you all about it, and I assure you there is a great deal to tell!"

One morning two months later a set of chords announced the presence of a visitor. Jantiff went to the door and slid it aside. On the porch stood a slender blond girl. Jantiff's voice stuck in his throat. He could manage only a foolish grin.

"Hello, Jantiff," said the girl. "Don't you remember me? I'm Glisten."

GLOSSARY

Wyst is the single planet of Dwan, the Eye of the Crystal Eel, in Giampara's Realm,* low to the side of Alastor Cluster. Wyst is small, damp, cool, and unremarkable except for its history, which is as extravagant, desperate, and strange as any of the Cluster.

The four continents of Wyst: Zumer and Pombal, Trembal and Tremora, had been settled by different fluxes of peoples. Each evolved in isolation with little interaction until the Great Hemispheric War between Trembal and Tremora, which destroyed the social order of both continents and reduced the lands to wilderness.

Trembal and Tremora faced each other across the narrow Salaman Sea, a drowned rift valley. The littoral strip between palisades and water—mud flat and swamp for the most part—was the land of Arrabus, inhabited only by a few farmers, bird trappers and fishermen. To Arrabus now, for want of better destination, migrated refugees from both continents: for the most part members of the gentry. These folk, with neither training nor inclination for agriculture, organized small factories and technical shops, and within three generations were the privileged class of Arrabus, while the native Arrabins became a caste of laborers. With a great increase in population, food was imported for the new gentry and synthesized for the laboring classes.

The social contrasts necessarily created dissatisfactions, ever more

---

*Alastor Cluster is divided into twenty-three realms, each nominally ruled by one of the twenty-three mythical goddesses, and the Connatic is formally styled: "Consort to the Twenty-three." In early times each realm selected a maiden to personify its tutelary goddess, with whom the Connatic, during his ceremonial visits, was expected to cohabit.

acerb. A certain Ozzo Disselberg presently published a tract, *Protocols of Popular Justice*, in which he not only codified the general discontent, but went considerably further, into allegations which might or might not be accurate, and in any event were scarcely susceptible to proof. He asserted that the Arrabin industries were purposefully operated at low efficiency, that enormous toil was wasted upon archaic flourishes and unnecessary refinements, in order to restrict real production. By this callous policy, declared Disselberg, the carrot was suspended tantalizingly just beyond the nose of the worker, so that he would strive for rewards always to be denied him. He further asserted that the Arrabin industries could easily provide everyone with the goods and services now enjoyed only by the privileged few, at a cost of half as much human toil.

The gentry predictably denounced Disselberg as a demagogue, and refuted his arguments with statistics of their own. Nevertheless, the *Protocols* gained wide currency and, for better or worse, altered the attitudes of the working population.

One dismal morning, on a date later to be celebrated as the "Day of Infamy," Disselberg was discovered dead in his bed, apparently the victim of assassination. Ulric Caradas* immediately called for a massive demonstration, which escalated first into violence, then disintegration of the old government. Caradas organized the First Egalistic Manifold and proclaimed Disselberg's principles to be the law of the land; overnight Arrabus was transformed.

The erstwhile gentry responded variously to the new conditions. Some emigrated to worlds where they had providentially invested funds; others integrated themselves into the new order; still others took themselves north or south into the Weirdlands,† or districts beyond, such as Blale and Froke.

Thirty years later, Ozzo Disselberg might have considered himself vindicated. The labor force, striving under the exhortations of Caradas and the Egalistic Manifold, had performed prodigies of construction: a magnificent system of sliding roadways, that the folk might be freely transported; a complex of food synthesizers, to ensure everyone at least a minimum diet; row after row, sector after sector, of apartment blocks, each to house three thousand folk. The Arrabins, emancipated from toil and need at last, were free to exercise those prerogatives of leisure once solely at the disposal of the gentry.

*Historians (non-Arrabin) are generally of the opinion that Caradas strangled Disselberg during an ideological dispute.
†Weirdlands: those areas of Trembal and Tremora to the north and south of Arrabus, once civilized and cultivated, now wilderness inhabited only by nomads and a few isolated farmers.

ii.

From *Owl-thoughts of a Peripatetic Pedant*

Arrabus makes few if any concessions to the visitor, and the casual tourist is not likely to discover much comfort or convenience, let alone luxury. At Uncibal City a single hotel serves the needs of transients: the rambling old Travelers Inn at the space-port, where ordinary standards of hospitality are for the traveler no more than a pious hope. Immigrants encounter an even more desolate welcome; they are hustled into a great gray barracks where they wait, perforce with stoicism, until they are assigned to their blocks. After a few meals of "gruff" and "deedle" they are likely to ask themselves: "Is this why I came to Wyst?" and many hurry back the way they came. On the other hand, the visitor who has firmly established his departure date may well find Arrabus exhilarating. The Arrabins are gregarious, extroverted, and dedicated to pleasure; the visitor will make dozens of friends, who as often as not will dispose themselves for his erotic recreations. (As a possible irrelevance, it may be noted that in an absolutely egalistic society, the distinction between male and female tends to become indistinct.)

The visitor, despite the animation of his friends and the insistent gaiety of their company, will presently begin to notice a pervading shabbiness, only thinly disguised under coats of color-wash. The original "sturge" plants have never been replaced; it is still nothing but "gruff" and "deedle" "with wobbly to fill up the cracks," as the popular expression goes. The folk work thirteen hours a week at "drudge," high and low, but they hope to reduce the stint to ten hours and eventually six. "Low" toil—anything to do with machinery, assembly, repair, cleaning, or digging—is unpopular. "High" toil—records, calculation, decoration, teaching—is preferred. Essential maintenance and major construction are contracted out to companies based elsewhere. Foreign exchange is earned through the export of fabric, toys, and glandular extracts, but production is inefficient. Machinery falters; the labor force constantly shifts. Management ("high" drudge shared in turn by all), by the nature of things, lacks coercive power. Critical jobs are left to the contractors, whose fees absorb all the foreign exchange. Arrabin money, therefore, is worthless elsewhere.

How can such an economy survive? Miraculous to state, it does: unevenly, veering and jerking, with surprises and improvisations; meanwhile the Arrabins live their lives with zest and charming ingenuousness.

Public spectacles are popular. Hussade assumes an exotic and even grotesque semblance, where catharsis supersedes skill. "Shunkery" includes combats, trials, races and games involving enormous ill-smelling beasts from

Pombal. The shunk-riders have recently become disaffected and are demanding higher wages, which the Arrabins resist.

Naturally, despite general gaiety and good cheer, all is not positive in this remarkable land. Frustration, annoyance, inconvenience are endemic. Bizarre and incessant erotic activity, petty thievery, secret malice, stealthy nuisances: these are commonplaces of the Arrabin scene, and the Arrabins are certainly not a folk of strong psychological fiber. Each society, so it is said, generates its characteristic set of crimes and vices. Those of Arrabus exude the cloying stink of depravity.

iii.

Asteroids, stellar detritus, broken planets and the like afford bases to the pirates and raiders whom even the Whelm seems unable to expunge.

Andrei Simić, the Gaean philosopher, has theorized that primitive man, evolving across millions of years in chronic fear, pain, deprivation and emergency, must have adapted intimately to these excitations. In consequence, civilized men will of necessity require occasional frights and horrors, to stimulate their glands and maintain their health. Simić has jocularly proposed a corps of dedicated public servants, the Ferocifers, or Public Terrifiers, who severely frighten each citizen several times a week, as his health requires.

Uncharitable critics of the Connatic have speculated that he practices a version of the Simić principle, never eradicating the starmenters once and for all, to ensure against the population becoming bland and stolid. "He runs the Cluster as if it were a game preserve," declares one of these critics. "He stipulates so many beasts of prey to so many ruminants, and so many scavengers to devour the carrion. By this means he keeps all his animals in tone."

A correspondent of the *Transvoyer* once asked the Connatic point-blank if he subscribed to such a doctrine. The Connatic replied only that he was acquainted with the theory.

iv.

For a detailed discussion of hussade, see *Trullion: Alastor 2262*. Like most, if not all, games, hussade is symbolic war. Unlike most games, hussade is played at a level of intensity transcending simple competitive zeal. At hussade, the penalties of defeat are extremely poignant, comparable to the penalties of defeat at war. A team, when defeated at a ploy, or play series, pays a financial indemnity to ransom the honor of its sheirl. The game proceeds until a team is defeated in so many successive ploys that its game fund is exhausted, whereupon the sheirl of the defeated team undergoes a more or less explicit ravishment at the hands of the victors, depending upon local custom. The losers suffer the humiliation of submission. Hussade is never played in lackadaisical style. Spectators, victors, and vanquished alike experience a total emotional discharge: hence the universal popularity of the game.

Hussade puts a premium not only on strength, but on skill, agility, fortitude, and careful strategy. Withal, hussade is not a violent game; personal injury, aside from incidental scrapes and bruises, is almost unknown.

v.

According to the canons of Alastrid mythology, twenty-three goddesses rule the twenty-three segments of the Cluster. Each goddess is a highly individual entity; each expresses a different set of attributes. Discord often results from the disparities. None of the goddesses is content to confine herself to her own realm; all constantly meddle in the affairs of other realms. When a man encounters an extraordinary circumstance, he more or less jocularly cites the influence of a goddess. Jantiff hence gives thanks to Cassadense, whose realm includes Zeck. For this reason she is presumably concerned with Jantiff's welfare, especially since he travels the realm of her great rival Giampara.

Printed in Great Britain
by Amazon